Grid Down

Reality Bites

By Bruce Buckshot Hemming and Sara Freeman

Grid Down tells a series of chilling scenarios about how things may very well "go down" when it's TEOTWAWKI. The authors are captivating story tellers, and they spin an often shocking tale of post EMP America. This narrative is so realistic and detailed, and it's all too likely this won't turn out to be a story after all, but our reality.

V Stevens, MD

Grid Down is a very informative book project that I am happy to know is going to print. It was hard to wait for each chapter to come out because of the impact and activity in the book effort. Story flow is very good and kept me very interested from the beginning.

Good Luck Bruce and Sara! Congrats, William Guinn, OK

Grid Down is a great training manual written in the form of a fictional novel about what could very possibly be our future. Bruce and Sara not only tell you what you need, they also tell you why you need it.

GM Holland, MI

Grid Down is an Edge of your seat nail biter that you can't put down! Bruce and Sara have brought a dramatic in depth look into a fierce reality we may all face, in this TEOTWAWKI scenario. This book is not only suspenseful, gripping, but eye opening informative on ways to prepare for a very possible future!!! A+

Jeffrey Crawford, South Carolina

Grid Down Reality Bites is not only a spectacular learning experience of everyday needs for survival but it is also a magnificent suspense thriller. At the end of each chapter I was held breathless and wanting more. I became one with each set of characters and felt their joy and sorrow. Now I wait with bated breath for the sequel.

Best of luck with the publishing. Don Biscardi, Kenosha, Wisconsin

Grid Down is a post-EMP disaster novel, carefully researched and entertaining. However, its true value is as a manual for would-be survivors. The well-developed characters in the story are each at different stages of life and of personal disaster preparation, and the author does a superb job of presenting solid advice and concrete actions that readers can follow to increase the likelihood of their own personal survival. This book is an excellent addition to any survival library, and a fine book to loan a friend or family member not yet convinced of the necessity for disaster preparations.

Name withheld by request

Grid Down is a remarkable masterpiece that will become a classic in the survival category. So much is going on that every single person out there will be able to identify with at least one of the characters. Keeps you on the edge of your seat, great information, great story line. What more could you want? I highly recommend this book.

Name withheld by request

Contents

Chapter 1

Strange Times

"If God is watching us, we might as well be interesting."

Solomon Short

Working as a nurse in a hospital took a special kind of person. Jane Goodwin was this special type of person. She met the challenges she faced daily in her job with compassion and caring. It was hard, rewarding work that took a person from the highs of saving someone's life to the lows of watching a child die unable to save them. In those intense moments when someone's life hung in the balance was what it was all about. Meeting those challenges with skill and calmness was second nature to her. It was easy sometimes to forget they were people you were working on and not just bodies that required your services. She had made a conscious decision to never forget they were people with feelings and loved ones waiting and praying for them to recover. It showed in all she did. She was respected by both doctors and colleagues. Her patients loved her. She usually had a kind word for almost anyone.

She always thought of everyone's needs and the little details that brightened even the most horrendous day for her charges and coworkers. Everyone said she was much too giving, much too kind. They seemed to forget those quick stinging rebukes she could deal out if she caught you in a mistake.

Jane understood the stress everyone was under. Especially lately with all the new biological training they were doing. Since the anthrax scare of 2001-2002, this new training was mandatory at most hospitals. They were taught the guidelines and procedures that had been set up to help lessen the impact of contamination. Containment, isolation and biological sterile procedures were for the protection of health care workers. They were being taught that using these strict guidelines it would stop the spread of a biological contaminate. Or so they said. It was all just a theory. It had not been proven yet. Still, it was better than nothing, Jane thought.

How little people truly understood was about to become painfully clear. The U. S. and the world were not ready for the devastating effects and the speed of infection a highly contagious virus would cause. Nor were they ready for the deadly results that would follow.

When people would say how good she was she always laughed and said, "You have it all wrong. I am very selfish. I do it because it makes me feel good." They would laugh and shake their heads at her, not quite understanding her meaning. They just didn't get it at all, she thought. The running joke on her floor was "And who takes care of you?" She would always smile and say, "Joe does." Joe was her husband.

Jane's husband, Joe Goodwin was a retired Army Sergeant. Joe and Jane had a small twenty acre farmstead in southern Minnesota with chickens and they raised a pig for butchering every summer. It was a good life. He was a hard working man and very good at his job. He was very down to earth and practical. Just like most folks, he had always concentrated on his job and daily living concerns. At home it seemed that there just never were enough hours in the day to complete all that needed to be done that day. Running a farmstead was not an easy thing to do and organize when the two caretakers also had full time jobs. You could make lists of what you planned on accomplishing in a day and were happy if you really had the time to do half on the list. It seemed every job that should take x amount of time ended up taking twice to three times as long as it should. He thought, 'Just like contact with the enemy. That is how long any plan really lasts. You do the best you could.'

They loved the life they had even if at times it was pretty frustrating trying to get everything done when you wanted. The running joke between them was how long and what jobs were on the "List." Things were running a lot smoother since Joe had retired.

In 2009, Joe went on a survivalist tangent. It started with watching a movie called *2012.* It got him thinking and contemplating things out in the world. He then found out about the militia and what they were doing. The more he read and listened to the information, the worse he got. He started talking about the New World Order plans for mass genocide, the dollar collapsing and the H1N1 flu virus and how the vaccine was meant to kill off the earths' population.

He always joked about the environmentalist and animal rights folks. He felt they were just a bunch of dope smoking hippies that were stoned one night and figured out a plan to make a living without working by bilking money out of women and children. They used women and children's caring nature for animals and the environment to evoke an emotional response from them measured in how much money they could donate to the causes and to pay themselves a high salary. The hippies cried about animals being mistreated, the trees being cut down, bad water or whatever they could think up. The donations flew in from suckers all across the nation and the free loading hippies got set up in a great lifestyle. Of course, it was non-profit, but the salaries and expense accounts of these people were right up there in the six figures for most of them. How these people slept at night having school kids donating their lunch money for their fake causes was beyond Joe. What really upset him was most of the people believed them with a religious zeal. They preached it and shunned anyone who had a different view point. They often labeled those nonbelievers as evil.

Joe was now turning into a full time survivalist. He researched a lot of things on the internet. He worked on wind and solar power. He bought bulk grains and stored them in fifty-five gallon drums. Before he had become more survival minded, he used to collect some of the spilled over grain at the local grain mills to feed his chickens. He would collect a few buckets each year and now he was collecting as many fifty-five gallon drums as he could get. He stored some gas with preservatives. He switched their electric cook stove to a propane cook stove. He bought a huge propane tank to store a few years' worth of propane. He also stored some heating oil for the diesel generator he bought. He was buying up guns and ammo like mad. His reloading room for ammo looked like he could make enough bullets for an Army. He bought up some gold and silver to store for currency when the dollar finally collapsed.

Joe's old Army buddy, Preston Riley, had just retired in Madison, Wisconsin. They had stayed in touch with each other through emails when he couldn't visit. Preston had been a helicopter mechanic and was now working at a small airfield. His wife had divorced him a few years ago and now he was living with a woman named, Sharon. He should have known better after his first wife not to get involved with another city woman. Sharon loved the bright lights and fancy restaurants and parties.

Preston was an outdoor person like Joe. He liked to hunt and fish. Preston had bought twenty acres of land right next to Joe and Jane when they bought their farmstead. He bought and set up a small two bedroom trailer for deer hunting on it. He came around once a month to visit and check on his property. Joe and Preston had hand dug a well. They added a few solar panels to the trailer to run the lights and radio, nothing fancy at all. Preston had found a wood burning hot water heater on the internet and installed it. It was his one luxury for hunting season. Nothing beat a hot shower. A solar panel with a twelve volt pump pressurized the house system. Joe joked it would have been easier to run three hundred-foot-long extension cords out to the trailer from his property. Preston always worried about security; he'd take down the solar panels and store everything inside the trailer out of sight when he was gone. The trailer was grounded on two ends and the metal sides and roof gave plenty of protection from the elements.

After listening to all the information Joe picked up about the things going on in the world, Preston decided to make this his SHTF (When the Shit Hits The Fan) retreat, too. Preston felt it couldn't hurt to be prepared for a disaster or whatever. One thing the military had taught him was to cover your ass. If nothing ever happened, he had a cool hunting camp. It was a win-win situation as far as he was concerned. Another thing the military had taught him was to not trust politicians. He felt with politicians running the world, anything could happen. They didn't always have the people's best interest in mind.

Jane put up with these two, thinking of them as boys playing end of the world games. Kind of like a mild mid-life crisis. They weren't city type people, so instead of flashy sports cars and fashion clothes they played 'what if it was the end of the world.' When Preston came up once a month to visit, most of the time it was fun. They had good times and laughed a lot. But lately the talk had gotten out of hand, she thought. Way too much about the New World Order and stuff about the powers that be trying to crash the whole financial system and releasing a biological weapon to kill off 90% of humans on the planet. This kind of talk gave her the chills. She was remembering the recent biological training she had under gone. All of this was running through her mind, giving her lightning-like glimpses of the horrible pictures and video evidence she had been shown of the horrible results of biological attacks.

That is just way too much crazy talk. She felt no one in their right mind would ever conceive or execute a plan or idea like that. Sure the world was pretty messed up but it was just human error and learning from our own mistakes. She also felt that with technology advancing at such a fast rate, terrorists around every corner of the globe causing havoc and death was just a sign of their times. People couldn't keep up emotionally and so they had invented a bogey man they could put all their fears into. It was their way of handling way too much change in their daily lives. With all the social structures and cultural changes that have happened in the last fifty years, it was a wonder that the world wasn't an even crazier place. The breakdown of the family unit from a mother and father and grandparents for emotional support and stability is at the heart of everything she felt. Today the norm is a single parent with no close family for any kind of mental or emotional support. They become a single digit unit to handle things that it used to take two parents and two sets of grandparents to handle with aunts and uncles thrown in the mix too. She felt so sorry for the kids of today's generation. She felt they really didn't stand a chance for any kind of a good life. No supervision and no one they could talk to that would understand their situations or even to know what they are talking about. Yes, the world was a very much messed up place. There is no need for a suicidal phantom New World Order to kill us all off with a bio weapon. We are doing it to ourselves without any help from them she darkly thought.

Joe had started doing deep research into the top ecology people. Those no good hippie people were on a power trip. He wasn't sure if they were really insane or started to believe their own press or what. They were openly calling for a mass genocide of people to save the planet for the animals. How insane was that? Even some people like Patrick Geryl in his book, *How to Survive 2012,* had a real crazy out there stuff like that in it. In his book on page 184, a heroic battle for the wisdom cult had the legend of the rainbow warrior. Under the symbol of the rainbow all races and all religions of the world will unite. Together they will proclaim the great wisdom of living in harmony with each other and creations of the Earth. The ones who are teaching this will become know as the rainbow warriors. Although they are warriors, they will have loving hearts and carry the spiritual way of living and knowledge of the "Old Ones" with them. And they will do no harm to any living creature. The legend tells they will be a FORCE of peace and harmony.

On page 185 in the author's own words, it said: 'We will conquer. We simply have to. ONLY WE WITH A WELL ORGANIZED VISION WILL BE ABLE TO RE-ESTABLISH CIVILIZATION. And like a phoenix, we will arise from our ashes, ruling the world in an ecological way with an essential message for all future generations.' There is a lot more of the same kind of thing, but it was clear in his writing what he was saying. The eco-cult warriors will make everyone become vegetarians or they will kill you. That was the message, loud and clear.

This is some whacked out stuff, Joe thought. *You have got to be kidding if anyone really would believe this crap.* He found so many more books, articles and manifestos with the same kind of theme through them. They were about death to the humans and a worshipful idealistic attitude to the animals. There were thousands of them all over the place. This was some crazy, scary stuff. He did more research and found that this stuff was being taught in colleges. It was being taught in grade schools, too. Remember the kids giving up their lunch money to save the animals? *Oh boy,* he thought.

Joe shared all his research with Jane and Preston. He wanted to believe this was just some ranting from a far left wing extremist, but these folks were organized, and may number in the millions. What was truly scary is that these people were so far out in left field that they hate their own species. *How crazy are these lunatics? How much power do they really have? Are they collecting guns, ammo, and bomb making information? Are they studying bio weapons to release on the public?* These were his concerns. *And how serious were they, really?*

Just how far out there were these crazy people? Pathological human haters were what they truly were, and like the movie, *The Body Snatchers,* their madness spread around the world. How often do you hear people say that there are too many people in the world? Really? Who promoted them to God to say and judge when there are too many people? They say everything is mankind's fault. We are in the middle of the fourth mass extinction. Well, that was a theory better known as a lie. You see, some academics with too much time on their hands and not enough brain power made up a computer model and said mankind was wiping out five thousand species a year. They were gone, completely extinct. A reporter back in the 1990s called up the "so called" experts and asked for a list of the top 100 animals that had gone extinct in the world. They said, "Sorry, we don't have that list." The reporter said, "Okay, how about the top ten?" They said, "Sorry, we don't have that list." The reporter was now getting desperate for facts to write the story. The reporter said, "Can you name one species that has gone extinct in the last year because of mankind?" They answered, "No." The reporter asked, "Why not?" They answered, "Because it is a computer model and not based on what is really happening in the world."

Then really crazy stuff came out later. Joe found this on the internet:

From: Keith Arnett Sent: Sunday, April 2, 2006 5:22:25 PM Subject: Dr. Pianka's FINAL SOLUTION

While Heinrich Himmler's "final solution" was limited to exterminating the Jews, Dr. Eric R. Pianka promotes a FINAL SOLUTION for 90% of earth's population. In accepting the 2006 Distinguished Texas Scientist award, Herr Pianka was interrupted with applause and received a standing ovation.

"Soylent Green is people." And the way cinema's futurist society dealt with over population was through the "Renewal Ceremony," where the inductees were secretly turned into FOOD for the remaining citizens.

AT LEAST THEY WERE TURNED INTO FOOD! Unleashing the Ebola virus on humanity, as publicly advocated by reptilian advocate Dr. Pianka, would result in billions of excruciating deaths and rotting corpses in the streets. Does such a position increase the esteem of the Texas Academy of Science? Does the Academy deem such a colleague as a visionary, exemplar, and eloquent representative?

THIS IS AN OUTRAGE! For a scientific community, however provincial, to recognize Dr. Pianka sublimates wholesale genocide. His advocacy of the extermination of most human life on the earth flies in the face of natural selection, and is so patently absurd as to defy logical challenge. The Texas Academy of Science, her directors, fellows, and members, is DIMINISHED through close association with, and its elevation of, Dr. Eric R. Pianka.

If the Academy is to maintain public and professional credibility, it must censure Dr. Pianka and rescind his "Distinguished" status. Please use your personal and professional influence toward that immediate end.

Sincerely,

Keith M.

Joe and Preston talked about this crazy professor a lot. Dr. Doom received a standing ovation for openly talking about a bio weapon that could wipe out 90% of the human population. He was advocating killing billions of people. How insane was that? The nutcases must surely be running the asylum in America. This comes right back to the bunny and tree hugger crowd, who openly bragged about wanting the same thing. Surely Homeland Security was watching these crazy academic communists in America, right?

No, they weren't. The Body Snatchers have their own people in charge of Homeland Security. In a twist of irony, Homeland Security ignores the reality of real American haters. They are real people haters. They target instead the so-called right wing extremists, like Christians who home school their children, and our Veterans. It is like the Nazis' final solution with America in charge instead of Germany. How crazy was that? Who would have thought this could ever happen here in America? The world had really gone truly insane.

Joe ran across this: 'Homeland Security on guard for 'right-wing extremists.' Returning U.S. military veterans singled out as particular threats.

"Returning veterans possess combat skills and experience that are attractive to right-wing extremists," it said. "DHS/I&A is concerned that right-wing extremists will attempt to recruit and radicalize veterans in order to boost their violent capacities."

Why would DHS put out a report against our veterans? The most deadly threat known to mankind had just been made by Dr. Eric R. Pianka, who promoted a FINAL SOLUTION for 90% of earth's population. He accepted the 2006 Distinguished Texas Scientist award. How in the world had this happened? A man stood up and advocated killing off 90% of the earth's population and he gets an award? Didn't we kill Hitler and fight against genocide in the Second World War? Now, we're giving awards for the same thing? It reminded Joe of a Mark Twain quote, "Suppose you were an idiot, and suppose you were a member of congress; but I repeat myself." *Sometimes I wonder whether the world is being run by smart people who are putting us on, or by imbeciles who really mean it. How in the world could this possibly be true?* But, there it was in black and white, living proof before him.

Joe was now firmly in the camp that our Government was being run by imbeciles that really mean it. How far out there could these people be? Some lunatic professor wants to have a final solution, and not only that, he receives a standing ovation and awards? Any thinking American should see the writing on the wall with this one. This was the final solution for Americans? Unfortunately, with imbeciles, crazies and far left lunatics all over our Government, that outcome was becoming easy to see and believe. They wanted 90% of all people on the planet dead. They were following some type of cult thinking that was immediately apparent in their writings. These were our leaders and thinkers of solutions? What kind of crazy crap was this kind of thinking?

Jane came home from work and Joe was busy working in the garage workshop. She thought, *I bet he was too busy working to make dinner again.* She sighed and tried to think of what was easy and fast to cook for dinner. She realized she would have to check the freezer and pantry before she could decide what to make. To her surprise, a note was on the table. It said, 'Check the microwave.' She looked inside. There in front of her was one of her favorite meals: Sliced fresh garden tomatoes, steaming hot corn on the cob, baked beans and a grilled pork chop. She smiled and chuckled. *What a wonderful husband I have*, she thought.

As she was eating, Joe came rushing into the house. He stopped in his tracks, seeing her, and smiled. He said, "Good; you found dinner. How was your day?"

She smiled back at him. "Long. Glad to be home. What are you working on?"

Joe smiled "A new deer stand." The phone rang. Joe answered.

It was Preston. He said, "Did you hear about this strange flu overseas?"

Joe answered, "No, I've been busy with plans on the new deer stand."

Preston continued, I just heard about this myself. There's a serious illness in the Ukraine. They're saying this mysterious illness is known as the 'Ukrainian Plague.' It has now affected approximately one million, three hundred thousand, with approximately seventy thousand hospitalized in serious to critical condition. There are reports that suggest the total deaths could be six thousand or higher."

Had someone really gone and done it? Was this natural or man made? Could this be a test run?

Chapter 2

21st Century Mountain Man

"Excellence is not a singular act, but a habit. You are what you repeatedly do."
Shaquille O'Neal

George Johnson was divorced. His wife had left him when he was in the Navy for an officer. Their two children, George Jr. and Alicia, stayed with their mother. The court gave her custody and told him he was free to pay child support. It was a rotten deal as far as he was concerned. He would rather have his children. He didn't get to see them or talk to them much anymore. They were always too busy doing other stuff. He missed them. Fortunately for him, he bought his ten acre hunting property before they were married. This was his salvation, his peace on earth. With thirty-five percent of his pay taken out for child support, he was left with only nine hundred ten dollars a month to live on. He was a retired Chief Mechanic. Luckily, he had a plan. He had been preparing for the end of the world his whole life.

His property was in Northern Wisconsin. It was prime property in his eyes. It had plenty of oak trees to keep the deer in his area year around. But his cabin was really great. It was built into the side of a hill with ten yards of gravel and drain pipes to pull the ground water away from the cabin. It had double walled ten inch logs, with sand filled in between. He smiled and thought Ole Ned Kelly from the 'Fifty Most Dangerous Men' would be proud of him. The roof was metal and covered with 6 inches of topsoil, then grass seed was planted on top. He built it in the late 1980s as a hunting camp/nuclear fall out shelter. The front was hidden from view with a huge brush pile. He had his solar power panels set at the correct angle to catch the sun's rays, but you could not see them if you were just walking past. To see them, you had to be almost on top of them.

George had a great life. His small twenty four by twenty foot camp had everything he needed to survive. He had a propane cook stove with twin one hundred pound cylinders, which provided all his cooking needs for about fourteen months. Four spare cylinders stored in the garage. But being part boy scout, he always refilled the empty cylinder as soon as possible. Always be prepared was his motto also. Nobody knew when the SWHTF (Shit Would Hit The Fan). He was smart and had a thirty foot well dug right under the cabin lined with 3 foot cement culverts. A twelve volt DC water pump provided the cabin's water needs. He didn't need much water just for the shower, toilet, washing dishes and clothes. He had a small apartment-size washing machine. He dried his clothes on a clothesline outside in the summer, and over the wood stove in the winter. Not that he needed much wood for winter. Three cords was more than enough to keep the cabin toasty warm. All his doors and windows had built-in double steel one quarter inch plates welded together. A trip cord was set to drop these into place from the inside. Once dropped down in place, they could be bolted from the inside into the reinforced logs of the cabin. It could be secured from just about anything.

Above each door and window was a steel pipe with small holes drilled in it to spray liquids out to soak any person trying to break in with homemade lye. His wood stove had eight inch heavy walls, with one quarter inch thick piping that ran underground out the back and up to a fake hollow tree. Amazing what a person can do with paint, glue and scraps of bark. The ground cooled the heat and the smoke was all but invisible when it came out the top. When it was sealed up, the cabin would be invisible to the world. You could walk right by it and not notice a thing.

He was still bitter about the divorce. The old saying that rules and regulations were only for the enlisted and not for officers sure came true for him. His wife was having an affair with an officer, a Lt. Commander.

When he tried to press charges against him, the military turned on him like a shark at a feeding frenzy. You see, officers are above the rules in the military. Any E-7 that stood up to them was quickly reminded it is not about right and wrong, but about officers couldn't do any wrong. He was sent to anger management classes. The military reviewed his travel records. They transferred him to a new base. He was to be given no responsibilities and to be watched every second. He was not to be trusted with anything now. They even tried to force him into alcohol rehab. It was not alcohol that was the problem, it was the fact that his wife was sleeping with an officer and they were not doing anything about it. All they did was keep him moving around and treat him like he had a disease.

In the end, he was given a choice; take retirement or press charges against the Lt. Commander. He might've won that case, but he was told in no uncertain terms that he would be targeted and they would make sure he ended up in Leavenworth. He knew all about the corruption in the Military. He had seen and heard about bogus charges brought against those that didn't play the game and go along with what they wanted. So, he took his retirement. He felt that he really didn't have a choice in the matter. He had to be around to protect his children.

You can't live in the past, he kept telling himself. He had been betrayed by his wife and the military. For the first few years he tried to get his head back on straight. He had to start thinking about the future. The past was dead and gone. He felt he learned a very valuable lesson in life. You can't take anything for granted. Life can change in a blink of an eye. You also can't live in the past; there is only today and the future. He was determined that he would not be an embittered man and go around blaming others for his misfortunes. It happened, leave it in the past and get on with life. Bad stuff, unfair crap happened to people all the time. So, he concentrated on that. He would make whatever effort he could to stay as close to his children as possible. He was firm in the decision that he would not lose his children, too. He still had his health and the cabin, so he would be okay.

He met a woman named Marion. She was a widow and he visited her in town once or twice a week. Her husband had managed a cattle ranch. He had been killed by a bull in a freak accident. He was moving the animal into a new field during breeding season. The bull must have been mad about being taken from the cows that were ready to breed. The bull charged the poor man, who was on a four wheeler trying to get him into the new field. The engine stalled and the bull ran him and the four wheeler over. The bull, the man and the machine went down in a confused heap. The bull ran off. The man was left pinned under the four wheeler. The bull came back and charged him again. They think it was the second charge of the bull that killed him. The bull's hoof hit the man in the head, which killed him instantly. The other workers tried to get to the man, but the bull was just too fast.

Together, George and Marion made a great couple. They helped each other through the emotional time of mourning. She helped him to understand that he was mourning the death of his marriage and career. She explained it would just take some time and to talk about it and not keep everything bottled up inside. He told her the same thing. She could talk to him about her husband, too. They understood each other. He helped her to see life is for the living. She told him everyone needed someone to talk to. Someone that you could say whatever was on your mind to. Not the polite chit chat that most people go through, but the real honest sharing of feelings and thoughts.

He thought about what she said and came to realize that was something he really missed. Someone you could speak your mind to. He didn't even realize how much and what he had lost with the divorce. He was really glad that he had met her and that they were together. She had a depth to her that his ex never had. He also came to realize that his marriage hadn't been all he thought it had been. All his married life he had been gone for long periods of time. He thought about how little time his ex and him had really spent together. They had never just sat and talked by the fire like Marion and he did. They had always been busy with other things. His job and the children took all their time. He was starting to understand how much had really been wrong or missing with his marriage. Before the divorce, he had just been too busy with everything to have time to think about stuff like this. None of this would have ever crossed his mind. He was coming to understand that in many ways he had a much better life now than he had before. This life was much more real and rewarding.

In the fall and winter, he set steel traps and professional grade cable snares. It was a hobby, a supplemental income. Not that the furs were bringing in much money these days. He tanned the furs himself over the winter and sold them under consignment to the Native American smoke shop on the reservation. He put beaver pelts on a wooden hoop in the old Mountain Man style. He steamed alder branches to make a nice round hoop. It was a favorite souvenir to the tourists and hunters who used them for cabin decor.

He also had coyote, fox, mink, muskrat, otter and weasel pelts. It gave him something to do on the long, cold winter nights. Plus, he was in the woods each and every day. What a way to enjoy life. He learned the deer patterns and found the bear dens. He helped out a few local farmers to thin out the deer herds that were destroying their crops. He hunted them on block permits issued to the farmers. He took four deer a year. It was his main source of meat. He also had beaver, raccoon, duck, goose, ruffed grouse, smoked muskrat, smelt, walleye, trout and pike to round out his meat supply. He ate better than he ever had before. He thought with a smile, yes, this was the good life.

With his trapping and snaring skills, he knew he could weather just about any economic storm that hit this country. He remembered a lot of the tales of the Great Depression. He sewed his own fur hats and mittens. He lined his coat with beaver furs. God created the warmest coats in the world, he thought. In those cold January days when the temperature dropped way below 0 with wind chill making it minus twenty, minus thirty, or minus forty degrees outside, he sure was glad for the warmth of the furs.

His gun collection was modest. He had a 12 gauge Remington 870 shotgun for bird hunting, a Ruger 10-22 for varmints, a Browning .22 Buckmark pistol for the trap line, a 30-06 Remington 700 topped off with a Leopold 3 x 9 scope, and two semi-automatic SKS with ten thousand rounds of ammo for it. He had twenty thousand rounds put away for his .22, most were his favorite small game round, the Remington Yellowjacket. It was an amazing round for small and medium game animals. It took a few years of losing wounded rabbits and grouse before he understood the solid point bullets were just ripping through the animals and not transferring the energy to the animal to bring them down. Once he switched to Yellowjackets, his take of birds and rabbits went up. Now, he was almost guaranteed to bring home the meat.

He was rich beyond money; something people who lived in the city never could understand. Their judge of success was fancy cars, big McMansions and ten credit cards. Most people were living way beyond their means. Many had learned a very hard lesson in 2008-2009 when the economic crash came. They lost their jobs, houses, and then their fancy cars. Some people ended up living with relatives. Many ended up living in tents. Obamavilles were popping up all over the country. Like the Hoovervilles of the Great Depression. The grand American experiment was coming to a close. The American dream had died. The U. S. dollar was about to collapse.

Little did George know how vitally important his lifestyle was soon to become. George's job now was to get his children there to the cabin and protect them. It was a job he took very seriously.

Chapter 3

The Day Everything Stopped

"A common mistake that people make when trying to design something completely foolproof is to underestimate the ingenuity of complete fools."

Douglas Adams

There is a hidden agenda here in America. It is a lot scarier than we could ever think or imagine. The people using the teachings and ideals of this agenda are everywhere. Everyday people like you and me use these things we've been taught by it without ever knowing that it is part of a hidden agenda.

These people teaching and using the things appear to be following the 1928 manifesto of the Frankfurt School. The people who started the Frankfurt School were Marxists. They came from a Marxist organization based in Germany in the '20s and '30s. When the Nazis came to power, the Marxists had to flee Germany. A good question to ask is why did they have to flee and go somewhere else?

The Marxists had been in power in the U.S.S.R. They were the government in Russia. They were known as the Marxist Communist or the Marxists Socialist government. Their form of government said that all people are equal. No one person should have more than anyone else. All things were shared. The government controlled everything, food, health care, what work needed to be done and when it would be performed. All things were controlled by the government and distributed by the government. This system failed miserably. Their people were starving. Their health care was a joke. Work was not being done as it should. Everything fell apart. They sent their agents to subvert Germany. These agents are the Marxists.

When they fled from Germany and Hitler they brought all their beliefs and ideals with them. They came to America and started a school. It was called the Frankfurt School. This school taught how to use mass manipulation to control the populace, among other things. To further the advance of their 'quiet' cultural revolution – but giving us no ideas about their plans for the future – the School recommended (among other things):

1. The Creation of Racism Offenses.
2. Continual Change to Create Confusion.
3. The Teaching of Sex and Homosexuality to Children.
4. The Undermining of Schools' and Teachers' Authority.
5. Huge Immigration to Destroy Identity.
6. The Promotion of Excessive Drinking.
7. Emptying of Churches.
8. An Unreliable Legal System with Bias Against Victims of Crime.
9. Dependency on The State or State Benefits.
10. Control and Dumbing Down of Media.
11. Encouraging the Breakdown of the Family.

With Key People in our Government given positions by President Obama, the Marxist plan of the final takeover of America was on. Since Obama's election, America had been heading down the tubes. A food crisis developed in the fall of 2009.

"The nation's economic crisis has catapulted the number of Americans who lack enough food to the highest level since the government has been keeping track, according to a new federal report, which shows that nearly fifty million people — including almost one child in four — struggled last year to get enough to eat... Several independent advocates and policy experts on hunger said that they had been bracing for the latest report to show deepening shortages, but that they were nevertheless astonished by how much the problem has worsened. 'This is unthinkable. It's like we are living in a Third World country,' said Vicki Escarra, president of Feeding America." The promise of green shots (jobs promised here in America, alternate energies, etc ...) was falling down, especially after the Climategate Scandal. Once and for all, Americans were waking up to the fact that peer reviews meant bribes were accepted from the colleges. Yes the reality is the Gullible Green Groups had donated money to a college. A Ph.D calls his friends and says, "Give me a peer review study to support this supposed fact and there will be all kinds of grant money for your college, too." That is how peer reviews works these days in America.

It was crystal clear this was what happened to anyone who studied the wolf reintroduction issue. It was the same as the corrupted lies and manipulation as seen in the Climategate Scandal. It was all corruption and greed and to the hell with the peoples' welfare. It is all about keeping the grant money flowing in. Real scientific studies be damned, just support the agenda and take the bribe, oh sorry, the grant.

By September 30th, 2015, the beginning signs of the end of America were clear to those paying any attention at all. Something big was in the works. Gold shot up to two thousand dollars an ounce, silver was near a hundred dollars an ounce. Oil hit two hundred dollars a barrel. Gas at the pumps was five dollars and seventy five cents a gallon. Bread was five dollars a loaf. This happened almost overnight. Ammunition was crazy. A box of 30-06 was a hundred dollars for a box of twenty shells; if you could find them. .22 ammo was just plain insane to buy. It was two hundred dollars for a five hundred round brick. Back in the '30s, the powers that be could make moves buying into gold, silver, wheat and oil behind the scenes where the public could never find out about. This extreme buying caused shortages of these products. What products were left were usually very high priced. Today with the internet and information being put out in seconds, nothing was hidden from public view for long, not if they knew where to look.

With prices rising so rapidly people started buying food and other essentials like mad. In the panic that followed, the shelves were stripped bare. The National Guard had to be called out to patrol the stores and to protect the semi-trucks bringing food and supplies in. Los Angeles, Detroit, Chicago and Atlanta turned into open riots. People in the know hit the road, running to their retreats. Many of those retreats were family farms. The smart ones that had stored gas for the trip generally made it if they went right away. Others, who didn't leave at the beginning, ended up trying to walk where they were hoping to go. With all the rioting and mass chaos going on, the gas trucks weren't able to get through to the cities' gas stations. In one day, cities ran out of gas. Many people took off on foot to get out of the chaos of the cities. Most of these people were robbed and murdered for their possessions in the dark of night.

There were three hundred seventy nine major cities in America. One hundred cities were in open revolt, rioting and chaos; the other cities still had problems with distribution of some items, but they were spared the rioting and insanity. The mass exodus from the troubled cities had begun. Traffic was backed up in some areas for miles and miles. Most people across America were shocked at how this had happened so fast. They were glued to their TVs, watching the latest events. The people that weren't in rioting cities had the attitude that everything would work out eventually. It always works out someway or another. They got on with their everyday lives. They knew the government would step in and make everything as it was.

The Chinese Military was watching the events in America intently. They had cracked the codes into the European banks and found documents of a top secret plan by the heads of these financial institutions to bring the whole world under their influence and control. First, they would crash the American economy because most things were based on the American dollar, and then they would release a mutated Ebola virus on the world's populace. Then, what was left of the world would be under their control. They had plans to rebuild everything their way. The Chinese found out that this biological weapon they were going to use was stored in an underground bunker in America. This virus would be transported to American planes, then be distributed all around the world. The pilots would not know that they would be releasing a deadly virus.

The Chinese realized their country was in grave danger. They needed to do something immediately to prevent this from happening. According to the documents, there were several people in high offices in America that were helping the banks carry out this plan. They were not sure who they could trust in America. They contacted Russia and showed them the proof of what the European Bankers were planning. Together, they came up with their own plan.

As soon as they were sure the European plan was going into effect, they would make their move. The Chinese would release several high altitude nuclear blasts above America. Russia would take care of Europe. The EMPs would shut off the lights for many years to come in America and Europe. China, fearing a double cross from the Russians, planned to send up EMPs across Russia. In truth, it was in retaliation for past grievances. The other fear China had was that India and Pakistan had nuclear missiles and might retaliate. EMPs were planned to be sent over their countries, as well. The world was going to be a very dark place soon. Russia, fearing that China would double cross them, had EMPs ready to strike over China. China would join the rest of the world in darkness.

October 7th, 2015, was the day the world was changed forever.

To understand what an EMP really does, all you need to understand is why your computer needs a surge protector. An EMP is a giant surge of power running down the grid, frying the transformers, which are the switches that power the national grid. The banking systems, debit cards, credit cards, checking accounts, everything needed electricity to work. Stores are all set up with an electrical system. To get some cash registers to work, some stores have a system to scan the prices right off of the items.

The term electromagnetic pulse, sometimes abbreviated EMP, has the following meanings: A burst of electromagnetic radiation that results from an explosion (especially a nuclear explosion) or a suddenly fluctuating magnetic field. The resulting electric and magnetic fields may couple with electrical/electronic systems to produce damaging current and voltage surges. It is a broadband, high-intensity, short-duration burst of electromagnetic energy.

The Chinese had studied this and figured they could do it with a single bomb three hundred miles above America. Russian and Chinese military scientists in open source writings described the basic principles of nuclear weapons designed specifically to generate an enhanced-EMP effect, that they term "Super-EMP" weapons. "Super-EMP" weapons can destroy even the best protected U.S. military and civilian electronic systems. The Obama administration fell right into the hands of the Chinese completely. The Chinese demanded missile technology in exchange for buying U.S. bonds. Like a bad poker player, Obama agreed and handed over the plans that helped bring America down.

The Chinese knew this was the time for the plan to go into effect. They contacted Russia. The time had come to release the EMPs. Both sides pressed the buttons that brought darkness to the Earth. The U. S. Army, having supposed EMP proof vehicles, soon learned that cheap contractor's equals shoddy work. The EMP shielding only protected 15% of the vehicles and equipment. They were commandeered to protect the White House. Northcom in Colorado was activated. The President flew in. Luckily, the EMP shielding had worked for Air Force One. The bureaucrats were scuttled off to the underground caves prepared for them with taxpayer money, it was stocked with food, water, power and had a hydroponic growing system. They would sit out the END OF THE WORLD in comfort, leaving the American people to fend for themselves. No help was coming. The American people didn't know yet that most of the world was now in darkness.

Soon the Army, Navy, Marines, Air Force and the Coast Guard were overwhelmed. People were going AWOL, there was open warfare everywhere, and the troops were being slaughtered. No comms, no backup, it was clear to most of the soldiers to frag their officers and head home. What was there left to fight for or defend? Even the President was holed up somewhere. This was survival of the fittest time.

Police couldn't show up for work with disabled cars. Some walked and tried to make it in. Many died on the way. There were open fire fights going on all over the place. They only had so many bullets. Most of the officers in disabled cars simply walked home to protect their families. It was a nightmare on the streets.

At the end of the week, there was no such thing as an anti-gun liberal left in the United States of America. The women that worked so hard to get the guns off the streets soon understood what gun control really was all about. They soon realized they had a helping hand in the destruction of America.

The people of the Christian churches that taught the rapture were sitting in shock, waiting for the grand lie to happen. No rapture came; no escaping the chaos, the four horsemen of Revelation was loose upon the world. Only years later would some unravel the truth of what Revelation really meant. Once the war had started, twenty-five percent would die a violent death, twenty-five percent would die from disease, twenty-five percent would die from famine and the reminding twenty-five percent would rebuild. Until that time, five to ten years of chaos would rule the world. Because of poor record keeping, no one knew if there was truly twenty-five percent left, maybe there was less.

If FOX, CNN, or MSNBC were still around, it would be major story time. But the EMPs took them out right along with everything else, and for once in many generations, people had to talk to each other to find out the truth.

The U.S. Army War College warned in a 2008 November monograph titled *Known Unknowns: Unconventional 'Strategic Shocks' in Defense Strategy Development" of crash-induced unrest.'*

The military must be prepared, the document warned, for a "violent, strategic dislocation inside the United States," which could be provoked by "unforeseen economic collapse," "purposeful domestic resistance," "pervasive public health emergencies" or "loss of functioning political and legal order." The "widespread civil violence would force the defense establishment to reorient priorities in extremist to defend basic domestic order and human security." "An American government and defense establishment lulled into complacency by a long-secure domestic order would be forced to rapidly divest some or most external security commitments in order to address rapidly expanding human insecurity at home," it went on. "Under the most extreme circumstances, this might include use of military force against hostile groups inside the United States. Further, Department Of Defense would be, by necessity, an essential enabling hub for the continuity of political authority in a multi-state or nationwide civil conflict or disturbance," the document read.

The grand cleansing of the world had begun. This was the modern day Dark Ages. Chaos would reign for the next five to ten years. Who would survive? Who would die? It was all up to God now.

Chapter 4

The Wonders Of Chaos

"The difference between school and life? In school, you're taught a lesson and then given a test. In life, you're given a test that teaches you a lesson."

Tom Bodett

Throughout history, during times of social unrest, women and children paid the greatest toll. This time of unrest in the world was no exception.

She had no idea what time it was when she woke up. She was in shock. She hurt everywhere. She could only see a little out of one eye. She looked around her bedroom as best as she could. She was alone. She laid there for a long time, praying they would not come back. She finally realized one of her wrist straps had loosened up some. She slowly worked her hand until she could pull it free. It took her a long time to work the rest of the straps free. She tried to sit up. Slowly, she got out of bed and stumbled to the bathroom, barely making it by holding onto the walls. She was bleeding everywhere, including her vagina and anus. *So much blood everywhere. Does the human body even have that much blood?* she thought. She looked around the dimly lit bathroom. Looking down at her body, there was not an inch of her that didn't have blood, or a bruise or something. Nothing was really registering in her brain. She stayed in the bathroom a long time before she finally realized the house was quiet. Either that, or she was deaf now, she didn't know which. *Does it really matter?* she thought. She shivered in her nakedness. *Was it cold out? It doesn't feel cold,* she thought. She finally made her way back to her bedroom. It looked like a tornado had blasted through it. Things were broken and thrown every which way. She grabbed the first thing on the floor that looked like it would cover her. She was shivering, so she must be cold, right? It was flannel nightgown. *This should be warm,* she thought. It took her awhile to get the nightgown over her head. She kept losing her balance and stumbled around. She fell a few times and it took some time to get back up again. She could hear herself gasping for each breath. *At least I know I'm not deaf,* she thought.

She slowly staggered out of her bedroom and inched her way to the top of the stairs. She looked long and hard with her one eye. She listened for any sound. All she could hear was occasional snoring. *They were still here.* She shivered more violently as she waited at the top of the stairs. She knew she had to go get help. But where could she go? And who would help her? She didn't really know the neighbors that well. They hadn't lived here all that long. She felt she had to do something, anything, or she would start screaming and never stop. *I'll try to get outside, then I'll ... no matter what,* she thought, *I have to get down the stairs.* Oh, how she didn't want to go down those stairs. They were down there. She took as deep a breath as the pain would let her and took a step. She took another and another until she reached the bottom. Hesitating on that last step, she shook violently. She was so afraid they would hear her or see her. She stepped down from the last stair, inching her way as silently as possible down the hallway. She looked both ways. The snoring was louder now, it sounded like it was coming from the living room. She could see some of them asleep on the floor, the couch and the chairs. It looked like they had found her mother's liquor cabinet.

Bottles of liquor were littered all over the place. She looked the other way down the hall. Silence from the kitchen. She strained with every fiber of her being for any sounds coming from that way.

Nothing, not one sound could she hear. She turned and slowly moved along the wall into the kitchen. She could see the back door … it was right over there. She took a couple of deep breaths to get up her courage. She walked straight to the door and slowly opened it, walking through to freedom. Slowly, she shut the door. It had grown completely dark. She hadn't noticed until she stepped outside. She resisted the urge to run screaming into the night. She had no idea where or which way to go. She stepped around the side of the house by the garage, praying she was out of sight. She had to think but her head was so foggy.

She tried to remember where that hunter lived, the one she and her friends had protested against for having guns and murdering innocent animals. Where was it? Where was he? He had guns. He could come and kill those awful men, those monsters. She remembered he said he was a Christian. She hadn't been raised with religion, but remembered something about forgiving those who sin against you. Maybe he would forgive her for being so wrong. She would beg him to please forgive her. She was so very sorry. She remembered some of the things she and her protest friends had yelled at him and felt ashamed. *Please, please God. Please let him forgive me.* She prayed and hoped there was a God. *Please help me,* she wept silently. Without the street lights, it was so much darker than she remembered. She took a couple deep breaths and told herself to calm down and think. Suddenly she remembered where the hunter lived. His house was a couple of blocks away. Her prayer had been answered. She walked as quietly and as quickly as possible, skirting the edges of the other houses. Her heart leaped in fear every time she had to cross a driveway. She was so sure they would see her and drag her back. She stopped to listen for noises every couple of steps. Her whole world was focused and existed in those two steps she took. The world appeared shattered and splintered to her now. Life had turned itself upside down. She didn't know who to trust. If she could get a gun, she would go back and kill every one of those rabid monsters in her house.

She thought, *Oh dear God, my mother. Will I ever see her again? What have they done to her?* She was silently crying, barely feeling the warm tears as they rolled down her face. The tears were making it harder for her to see out of her eye. She tried to pull herself together. She had to go on and get help. Her mother was depending on her to rescue and help her.

She was creeping around some hedges when she heard a noise behind her. She stopped, and as quietly as possible, bent over to crawl on the ground. Intense pain wracked her body. She kept thinking, *Ignore it, just ignore it.* She clenched her teeth trying to keep the darkness from stealing her mind and finally made it to her hands and knees behind the hedges. Her consciousness wavered a few times, but caught herself before she fell down. There was the noise again. She tensed up. All of sudden she was cold, so very cold. She was exhausted physically, mentally and emotionally. She didn't know if she could go on anymore. She could smell the earth. Slowly, she lay down on the ground, her energy just seemed gone. There it was again, the noise. Footsteps. Coming up behind her. *How can they be tracking me at night?* she thought. *Please God, please don't let them find me.* Her trembling grew so strong she felt unsteady. She resisted with every fiber of her body not to scream. Her breathing increased, her heart pounded wildly, like a beating drum. It was beating so hard and loud she wondered if it could be heard. Would it give her position away? *Calm down and stop breathing so fast,* she thought. *Just calm down,* she kept repeating in her head like a mantra. *You got this far, don't give up hope now.* She looked up, and suddenly in the starlight, she could just make out a figure in front of her. She held her breath and closed her eyes, saying a silent prayer, *Dear God, please don't let them see me. Them?* she thought. She heard footsteps coming up on the other side of her. All too soon, another figure walked up to the first.

They whispered back and forth in hushed voices. She strained her ears to hear what they were saying. Her lungs were screaming … she hadn't realized she had been holding her breath. She was so scared. She didn't take a breath. She just kept holding it in. She needed to breathe. *Move on, you two, dear God, please go,* she prayed. She could not wait any longer; she had to breathe. They were close enough now that she could tell the two were men. They were only six or seven feet away. Slowly she released her breath. She started a new mantra in her mind, *Quiet, just be very quiet.* She slowly drew a breath in. The two figures bent down and she heard one of them say, "How do we get out of town?" Then they clearly were not the thugs. *Oh thank God. Please help me,* she said over and over. It sounded to her like she was screaming, but it came out just barely a whisper. The two figures jerked and turned toward her, startled. They weren't sure if they heard something or not. A flashlight clicked on, aimed right at her. It blinded her. She closed her eyes. It felt like an electric shock of pain went straight through her brain. One of the figures gasped at the sight of her on the other side of the hedge.

"Oh my God, what happened to you?" Suddenly they heard a loud bang and a 9mm bullet ripped through the hedge above her head. The two men instantly rolled and dropped into a prone position. They both had guns. One had a short rifle with a flashlight attached to the barrel. They heard the next bullet and saw the dirt kick up in front of them. More bullets came their way. Then the deafening reply from the Remington 870 12 gauge shotgun roared and flames came out the barrel. *Surely this is hell,* she thought. The next shot they heard was fired from a loud cannon. The blast echoed off the houses.

She heard grunts and two bodies hitting the ground. Then they heard the rack-rack sound of the 870 being reloaded and the click-clack of the 30-30 being reloaded. She heard one of the men whisper to the other, "Both down." She could not take it any more. She could not just lay here and not do something. Slowly she stood up and started to run as fast as her body would let her. She was screaming as loud as she could and she didn't hear the bullets that whipped past her head as she ran. Three of the brutal thugs that had broken into her house started rapidly firing a semi-automatic 9 mm in her direction. The echoing across the houses deafened the replies from the 12 gauge and the 30-30. She stopped and hid behind a tree.

One of thugs screamed in pain. He yelled, "Kill those mutherfuckers."

Another one said, "Ahh, damn it, I'm hit. Help me."

Good, I hope it hurts like hell, she thought. She screamed out as loud as possible above the noise, "There are seven of them. They have my mother at 17282 Oak Lane." Suddenly bullets were erupting everywhere again. One hit the tree she was hiding behind and she started crying. The shotgun roared, the triple 000 buckshot skipped off the brick wall, hitting the thug hiding behind the porch. He died with a very surprised look on his face.

Suddenly she was red hot mad. She was remembering all of the things that had happened to her, all of the things that had been done to her. All of a sudden it was just too much. A rage built in her and she charged back towards them yelling, "Kill all of them … they're rapists! Shoot them! Kill them all! Kill them! Shoot them!" She raced forward. A 9mm hollow point caught her square in the chest. She fell backwards by the hedge she had been hiding behind earlier. She heard the roar of a shotgun and rifle return fire. Her last whispered words were, "Save my mother." Then the darkness closed in on her forever.

One of the thugs yelled out, "I'm gonna kill you two mutherfuckers!" Mark turned off the flashlight. The world became very dark. Everyone's eyes struggled to adjust. Shadows soon looked like some insane thing or person charging you. One of the loud mouthed punks started shooting at nothing but imaginary men charging him. Mark and Eric watched him. It would have been quite amusing if it wasn't such a deadly situation. As the thug was firing, Mark saw an opportunity to crawl over to the porch. He peeked over the edge and saw the punk's raised hand and the flash of the gun. He smiled and turned on his light, knowing full well the bad guy would be blinded. He stood up and the 12 gauge roared, then silence swept through the dark night. His partner, Eric, stood up and walked over to Mark. He shut the light off. They both bent down. They were not sure who was hit and who was dead. They thought four of them were hit and most likely dead, but they could only see three bodies. They had lost the element of surprise to try and take the house and rescue the girl's mother. Eric whispered to Mark, "What do you want to do?" Mark said, "Let's go check on the girl." They snuck back along the edge of the house until they were even with hedge and the girl. Mark said to Eric, "Stay here and cover me. I'll check on her." He took his backpack off and laid it on the ground.

He could barely see her lying on the ground in the darkness. If it wasn't for her light colored nightgown, he might not have found her without a light. He crawled up to her and whispered, "Are you okay?" No response. He reached out his arm and found her hand. Her fingers felt cold. That didn't mean much. People who are in shock are usually cold. He had learned this from an EMT course he took to prepare for the worldwide collapse he knew was coming. He then reached up and felt for her neck. He found the proper place for her pulse point … nothing. He reached up and held his hand around her nose and mouth for a couple of minutes to feel if any breaths were being taken or exhaled. He felt nothing. She was dead.

He crawled back to Eric. He whispered to him, "She's dead." There was silence for a few moments while they thought about this situation.

"Let's finish this and kill the rest of them animals," Mark hissed between clenched teeth.

"No," Eric said. "Use your head. We don't know this woman from Adam. We only saw three bodies down. That means four are left. We are outnumbered two to one. It would be insane to go after them. Besides, her mother is probably already dead."

Mark wanted to burst out yelling that it didn't matter. But then he stopped and thought, *No, Eric is right. What kind of sense would it make to chance their lives when the girl was already dead?* He agreed with Eric. Chances were, so was her mother. He turned to Eric. "It's time to get out of town. Let's get back to the escape plan and get out of this hell hole," Mark said instead. The two had been good friends since college. They found they had a common interest. They both were concerned with the world's condition and were preparing for the end of the world as they knew it. The two of them had many late night talks about it. They established a survival retreat with the help from Mark's dad.

It was just up the coast if they could reach it. They had it fully stocked and Mark's dad was retired from the railroad and lived there full time to guard it and to do maintenance. They had fifty pound packs with them. It was enough gear and food to last for five days. They were lucky in this firefight. Neither one of them had been hit or wounded. That might change if they didn't get a move on. It was time to leave this disgusting place and get going.

It was the right decision for them to make, after all. Pam's mother was already dead by then. She had been beaten to death. Mark and Eric had hit and killed three of the brutal thugs and wounded another. The thugs were waiting at Pam's house. They set up an ambush for anyone who would be stupid enough to come after them. They had also heard Pam yell the address to the two people who had shot at them. They laid in wait, hoping someone would come after them. The thugs were looking forward to the confrontation. They wanted to take out the two people that had tried to help the girl so they could even the score for their dead and wounded. Mark and Eric would have died walking into that ambush.

Eric and Mark put their backpacks on and checked the straps and flaps. They didn't want to lose any of their equipment or make any extra sounds as they ran. They looked at each other's backpacks when they had them on just to be sure everything was secured right. They both took off running across the street. They passed through a back fence gate and entered a back yard, then jumped a low fence. They were back on the track of their pre-scouted escape route. They headed for the interstate, deciding to only travel at night. It would be safer that way. They figured they could make at least ten miles a night. They had two hundred miles to go. Two hundred miles would be twenty days. They would need to get more food along the way or go on quarter rations. Luckily, they had purchased for their supplies an Emergency Snare Kit. They, of course, had it with them in their bug out pack. With a little luck, they would snare a deer and smoke the meat. That would give them plenty of food to make it up to the retreat. When they reached the interstate, it looked like they were in a scene of a zombie movie. Dead, useless cars blocked both sides the road. Some cars had the doors opened invitingly, like they were just waiting for the owners to get in. A few bonfires could be seen in the distance.

Mark turned to Eric and said, "This looks really bad. What was Plan B?

Chapter 5

Nothing Works

"Whatever course you decide upon, there is always someone to tell you that you are wrong. There are always difficulties arising which tempt you to believe that your critics are right. To map out a course of action and follow it to an end requires courage."

Ralph Waldo Emerson

Jane was an avid bow hunter. So was Joe. It was an activity that they both looked forward to and shared as a couple. Plus, they both loved deer meat. They always called venison deer meat. It was a joke between them. They would freak out some of her friends when they came to visit by presenting them with a meal made out of deer meat. Even if it wasn't, they'd say it anyway, just to hear the comments and complaints. And they looked forward to the "Oh, how could you kill those cute little Bambi's?" It gave them the opportunity to educate the guests all about hunting, and about deer in particular. They had guests that felt so strongly against hunting that they had walked out without listening to what they had to say or eating, either. Joe and Jane would look at each other and one of them would say, "More for us to eat."

One thing both Joe and Jane disliked intensely were people who were ignorant of something and wouldn't take the time to educate themselves before forming an opinion on a subject. Most people who are against hunting and wildlife control do not know the facts. They just spout off slogans and other people's opinions like they were a parrot instead of an intelligent, thinking human being. The internet is a wonderful information highway, full of free reference libraries and statistics. There are no valid excuses in this day and age for people not to be fully informed on whatever subject they feel passionate about. But, without fully researching both sides of a subject, how can anyone form a truthful opinion of one's own?

Every year since Preston had bought his place by them, he had been there for hunting season. He also looked forward to educating the guests about hunting at dinnertime with anticipation. He called it putting in his "one cent worth."

He had called the day before and said he wouldn't be up this year. Joe and Jane were shocked. Preston had never missed a hunting opportunity that they knew of. He hunted on several occasions even if he was sick. He would do so against Jane's advice. The only thing Jane and Joe could think of that would keep him away was the new ditzy woman in his life. Preston had brought her by a few months ago so they could meet her. They felt justified in giving her that nickname. They joked that the term 'air head' would have been an educated version of her. It was shocking that he was letting a woman interfere with his hunting. He had never let his ex influence him about it, in fact, it was a sore spot with her and caused a lot of friction in their marriage. No matter what she did or said, he went hunting every year as usual. He was a very serious hunter. She also gave him a lot of crap about spending so much time with them doing it, too.

They knew that the divorce he went through had really messed with his mind. His ex had not been a very nice person and she really showed her true colors during the divorce. Joe and Jane didn't care for her and the feeling was mutual. They had nothing in common at all. All she ever talked about was fashion, or the sales at the upscale department stores, or the trendy clubs and restaurants where she ate out with her friends and gossiped about everyone she knew. She also went to fashionable clubs with her friends when Preston was gone. In fact, they couldn't remember her ever saying a nice thing about anyone and mean it. She would say something nasty about someone and then say, "But she's really a sweet and thoughtful person, really. I just love her to death."

During the divorce, Preston had found out that she put him thirty thousand dollars in credit card debt. He had to get a job to pay them off. Now that he was paying her alimony, too, he didn't have enough money from his retirement to pay for it all and live. They did not ever think any kind thoughts about her. They resented the fact that Preston wasn't there enjoying his retirement with them because of her. There really weren't any jobs where they lived in his field of expertise. He was a highly experienced helicopter mechanic. There isn't much about a helicopter that he didn't know. That is why Preston wasn't there and had to live in the city. They would miss him a lot this year. They always joked about being "The Three Musketeer Hunters."

Every year during bow hunting season, Jane would take one week of her vacation time. Bow hunting in the fall was her peaceful and quiet time. It was her time to absorb the feelings and the smells of the woods. It was a time for her to be able to really relax and enjoy just being and not doing. By this time every year, she really needed to get away from the intensity of her job and the pressures of everyday life. She and Joe had tree stands on a friend's farm, Jim and Marge Johnstone. Their farm was about five miles from their own place. The month before she would have her quiet time in the woods, she would count the days down with excited anticipation. This time was no different than all the other times she had used one week of her vacation time for bow hunting.

They had no idea the world as they knew it was about to come to an end. There were no signs, no predictions, no warnings, nothing. This day started out the same as any other day. The alarm woke them up so they would have plenty of time for a leisurely breakfast and not be hurried as they went out for the morning hunt. After a peaceful morning and watching a beautiful sunrise, at mid-morning it was time to climb down and meet each other at the truck. Joe was always playing practical jokes on her. He would sneak out of the woods to get to the truck first. He would hide in the woods and start snorting like a deer or acting like bear was there, so that when she walked past it would scare the heck out of her.

This year, she thought, *I'm going to sneak back first and surprise him.* She looked at the sun to judge the time and decided it was a bit earlier then she usually left to go to the truck. Now was the time to leave her stand and beat Joe. She climbed down and started to walk quietly through the woods. As she walked toward the truck, she thought about how much she loved the woods and how beautiful they were. The trees changing color and the leaves falling and making a colorful path to walk on totally delighted her. But, the color change had not really started yet this year. She thought, *Maybe next year I'll take off the third week of October instead. The color changes will be in full display by then.* She was really enjoying herself.

She came around a bend on the path and heard a slight noise. She stopped to look around and listen. As she looked forward, right there on the trail, was a nice eight point buck. He was looking towards where the truck was parked. She slowly grabbed an arrow in the quiver and drew it out as quietly as possible. She told herself, *Take your time. Slow down all movement.* She notched the arrow and looked up at where to buck had been. She was elated. The buck was still standing there. She smiled to herself and thought, *Ah, Joe must have got down earlier than I thought for his practical joke and pushed the deer right into me.* Her smiled got bigger. *The joke is on you this time, Joe.* She drew her arm back. She picked the thirty-five yard pin. She relaxed, steadied the arrow and released it. The arrow shot down the path, heading exactly where she had aimed. It was a perfect double lung shot. When it hit the buck, it made a funny sound. Thunk. *What the heck? Did the arrow go underneath the buck and hit a tree?* It had looked like a perfect shot. She popped another arrow from the quiver, aimed and shot at the buck again. This time she saw the arrow hit, but it had made another thunk when it had hit the buck. Then she heard Joe laughing like a little boy that had pulled off the best practical joke in the world. He was hopping around doing a victory dance and singing gleefully, "Got ya. I got ya again!"

She jerked around to where Joe was and said, "Very funny. You're a jerk." She pointed her finger at him and continued, "You are buying me new arrows and broad heads for that stunt, Mister."

Joe had set up a buck decoy and covered it with a real deer hide that he had tanned. It looked pretty real unless you were standing right next to it. She was mad. Joe kept smiling just like a little kid and chuckling. He pulled the stakes out that were holding the buck in place, then walked with it in his arms up to the truck. She came stomping up and said, "You are a jerk. That's so not funny." Joe just kept laughing. They loaded up the bows and their other equipment. They got into the truck and Joe turned the key. No sound, nothing. She couldn't resist herself and said, "Left the headlights turned on, didn't you, jerk?" She smiled and started laughing so hard. "Ha, ha, the joke's on you," she said.

Joe turned and faced her. He said, "No, I didn't leave the lights on. See, they're turned off." She looked over at the light switch, and sure enough, it was turned off.

"Well, any idea what is wrong with the truck?"

"I'll take a look. It's probably just a bad connection on the battery or something like that." He got out of the truck and popped the hood open. He yelled for Jane to get in the driver's seat and try to start it. He tinkered with everything he could think of that could cause the truck not to start. He kept telling Jane, "Try it now." Finally after several minutes he said, "This is just not working. I give up. I don't know what's wrong with it. Everything looks fine. I can't find any reason for it not to start." He shut the hood.

He walked over to the driver's side of the truck and motioned for Jane to roll down the window. He said, "Well, let's just head over to the Johnstone's. Get what you need for right now out of the truck. We'll get the rest of the gear after we tow the truck back home." Jane gathered up what she thought she might need for a short while and got out of the truck. She was looking forward to seeing Marge. She didn't have the chance to visit her neighbors very often. They talked on the phone a lot, but just never seemed to have the time to just go over to each other's house to visit. It would be great to just sit and drink coffee and talk for awhile.

Joe was hoping to borrow Jim's beater farm truck to tow his truck home. He also hoped that Jim was around and had not gone into town for a part or something so he could help Joe figure out why the truck wasn't starting. Maybe Jim could come up with something he hadn't thought of. It sure was weird that the truck wouldn't start. That truck always started no matter what. He had always referred to the truck as 'Old Reliable.'

It was only a mile walk to Jim and Marge's farm house from where they were. They set out down the path. It was a great day for a walk. The air was crystal clear and crisp smelling; the sky was such a beautiful shade of blue with only a few wispy clouds here and there. The day was warming up and it just felt so good, so right to be outside enjoying it like this. All was right with the world, Jane felt. Well, except for the truck. But if the truck hadn't broken down, they would not have had an opportunity to have this enjoyable walk. *Everything works out one way or another. It is a wonderful day just to be alive,* she thought.

The path ended as they came out of the woods. They saw the farm house a few hundred yards away. They walked up the driveway towards the house. Their dog was barking, so it had alerted them that someone or something was outside. It could have been a wild critter. You just never know when you lived out in the country. So, it was no surprise that Marge was at the door to greet them. As they approached the house, Joe noticed Jim coming out of the barn, wiping his hands on a rag. They greeted Marge and waved to Jim. They waited for Jim to catch up to them before telling them why they had walked out of the woods instead of driving up. Jim came up the steps onto the porch. Jim and Joe shook hands.

Jim asked with a chuckle, "Lost your truck?" They all laughed. Every year they had hunters and hikers and nature lovers knock on their door asking for assistance in finding their lost vehicles. They all had some wild stories about crazy city slickers to share with each other whenever they did get together to talk. Marge said, "Come on in and I'll get you both a cup of coffee."

"Marge, is it okay for Jane to go in and have coffee? I need to talk to Jim if he's not real busy with something right now," Joe said.

Jim answered with, "I was just tinkering with the tractor. It wouldn't start. Let's go to the barn and we'll talk."

Jane went into the house with Marge. Jim and Joe walked down the porch stairs together. As they were walking over to the barn Joe asked Jim, "What's wrong with your tractor? You just got that one, didn't you?"

"Yes, it's brand new and it won't start." Joe turned and looked at Jim. Jim noticed the look Joe gave him. "That's one of the reasons why I asked you to come out to the barn with me so we could talk away from the women." That definitely got Joe's attention. "Let's wait until were in the barn and I'll tell you about it."

Jane walked into the kitchen with Marge. Marge said, "Have a seat and I'll warm the coffee up on the wood stove." She sighed. "The power is out again and Jim couldn't get the generator to work this morning.

Joe and Jim reached the barn and walked over to the tractor. Joe looked around and noticed the two cars had their hoods open, as did both of Jim's trucks, his newer one and the old beater. The riding lawn mower had its compartment open, too. Joe turned and looked at Jim and said, "What the heck is going on?"

Jim said, "The power went out, so I thought I would go get the new big tractor and haul some hay bales to the other barn for winter. It wouldn't start. I looked it over, but I couldn't figure out why. I thought, 'well, I'll just go get the smaller tractor and use it. It will take more time, but it needs doing. I'll mess with the big tractor and fix it later.' I walked over to the other barn and my other tractor wouldn't start, either. I looked at the engine and I can't find a reason why it won't. So I walked back over here. I tried my newer truck and it wouldn't start. I thought this was mighty strange. So I decided to try my old beater truck. It started right up. I was going to just go ahead and use it to move the hay bales, but curiosity got the better of me about the cars. I started wondering if they would start or not. It was about this time I realized that my watch wasn't working. There was no display lighted up, no numbers or anything on the face of it. Then I shut off the truck and went over to the cars and tried them. They won't start. I tried the lawn mower and it won't start, either."

Joe sat down heavily on the side of the tractor and thought, "Oh God, it's happened. They went and done it. They really did it. Don't panic. Stay calm." He looked up at Jim and said, "We were out hunting this morning. When we got back to the truck, it wouldn't start. We walked over here to ask you for a tow. I couldn't figure out why the truck wouldn't start and was going to ask you to help me figure out why." Jim was thoughtful for a minute. Joe decided to wait and see what conclusion Jim came to.

Jim looked over at Joe and said, "This is bad, isn't it? It's real bad, huh?" Joe just nodded his head yes. "Do you know what happened?"

Joe stared at Jim for a few seconds, thinking about how to explain it and how much he should say. "I only know of one thing that could do this. A high altitude nuclear blast, an EMP. It fries all electrical circuits."

Joe waited to say anything more to give Jim time to digest this information. Jim looked hard at Joe and said, "That's what I figured, too. I was hoping I was wrong. I thought at first that I had watched too many movies on the SyFy channel and was jumping to way out there wrong conclusions." Joe was quick to reassure Jim that this was a way out there conclusion. But it was real. Things would never be the same again.

Jim and Joe remained quiet for a few minutes, lost in their own thoughts. Jim finally asked, "What do you think we should do?" Joe had decided that it would be best to go get his truck and then to get Jane and him home. Preston would be showing up and they had better be there when he did. Now that the time had really come, he wanted to take everything with other people real slow. Let them get a bit over their shock of the situation first before he came up with any suggestions for them. He wasn't at all sure if he wanted to come up with any suggestions. He wasn't sure at the moment how involved people would want him, Jane, or Preston to be in their affairs. Time will tell. It would give them all time to come up with a plan of action. In all the scenarios they had talked about and all the plans they had sort of made, being a leader in this community hadn't really been one of them.

Joe looked at Jim and waited until he was sure he had his complete attention before answering him. "I'm not real sure just yet. But I do know two things right now. The first is we had better go in and tell the women what has happened. The second is I still need you to tow my truck to my house. I would sure appreciate it if you could do that. Afterwords, we can take things real slow and decide on what needs to be done one thing at a time, okay?"

Jim looked relieved. "That sounds like a plan to me. Of course I'll tow your truck to your place. We're friends and neighbors, aren't we?"

Jim and Joe walked into the kitchen. Marge got up to get them coffee. The two men sat down on the opposite side of the breakfast bar. They had a serious, worried look on their faces. Jane thought, *I wonder what happened? The way their luck was going this morning, maybe they couldn't get Jim's old truck to start, either. But, that wouldn't be so unusual. Jim was always tinkering with it for one thing or another. No, it has to be something else, something more serious for them to look like that.* Marge set the men's coffee cups down in front of them. Both men gave their thanks to Marge.

Marge looked closely at Joe. "Are you all right? You don't look so good." She completely ignored Jim. Obviously, she was still mad at him about the generator not starting.

Joe waited a few seconds to see if Jim would say anything. Joe turned and looked at Jim. He just sat there looking at the breakfast counter and didn't say or do anything. He didn't even look like he was breathing. *Okay, then, it's up to me.* He looked up at Marge and said, "I've had better mornings, that's for sure. I'll be fine. Thanks for asking." He turned to Jane. "We think something terrible has happened. Something we all were hoping would never be a reality. The only vehicle that will start is Jim's old farm truck." He felt in some part of his mind like this was a dream, a real nasty dream. The worst nightmare he could imagine. "I think what happened was someone set off a high altitude nuclear bomb, an EMP. It has fried everything electrical. Nothing that requires electricity will work. Not the lights, not generators, not cars or trucks, nothing will work unless it is old, like the farm truck. The farm truck has different parts than the newer ones do."

Joe looked at Jane. He got up from his stool and walked around the breakfast bar and sat down next to her and pulled her into his arms. Jane was glad he had come over next to her. After a few minutes, she drew back. Joe just looked at her. She finally said, "I need to get to the hospital. They'll need me there to help with everything. Oh dear God, Joe, there is no electricity. The back up generators won't work now, either. What about the patients on life support? Who could have done this crazy thing? Why would someone do this? Is this a terrorist attack? I have to go. I have to get there now, Joe. They'll need me now more than at any other time." She stood up and faced him. "How will I get there? Do you think Jim would take me to the hospital after he drops you off at home?"

Joe stood up, too and looked hard at her. "Calm down. Take a deep breath. Think about this situation for a minute. It may not be safe for you to go there. We shouldn't separate ourselves from each other right now. That would not be a smart thing to do at all. We don't know what it will be like in the city or at the hospital. Everyone who lives close to the hospital will have already gone there to help. What can you do that isn't already being done? If you go into the city, how will you get back home? Think about this. The roads will be clogged with vehicles. How will Jim even be able to get through to get you to the hospital? Let's just get home first. Then we can talk about it."

"You folks ready to get your truck and go home?" Jim asked. They both answered in the affirmative. They gathered their things up, put their coats on and walked to the front door. Joe reached for the door handle first and led them all outside.

They walked into the barn and got into Jim's old truck. It was a 1972 half ton Ford pickup. Jim started it up and it was a happy sound. It was a sound they were not going to hear much in the future. Jim drove out of the barn and down the driveway towards the old road on his property where Joe had parked his truck that morning. After a few minutes, they spotted Joe's truck on the old road. Jim pulled ahead of it, stopped and didn't even think about turning the motor off. He just didn't want to chance the truck not starting again. He felt a bit superstitious about it, since it was the only vehicle that would work. Joe jumped out the passenger side door and Jim got out on the driver's side. Jane got out last. Joe had already grabbed the tow chain out of the back by the time Jim and Jane got to the back of the truck. Jane walked on and got into Joe's truck. They hooked the chain up and Joe climbed into the cab of his truck to steer it as Jim towed them. They drove back down the old road to Jim's place, then up the driveway to the road that would take them home. It was not easy for Joe to steer his truck. No power steering. *Wow, you don't realize how great power steering is until you don't have it anymore,* Joe thought to himself with a chuckle.

"Good thing you're in good shape or your arms would be stiff and sore tomorrow," Jane said. They shared a look and a smile. The world as they knew it might have ended, but life goes on. Life was what you made of it.

They were traveling at about twenty miles per hour. Two miles down the country road, Jim slowed down and stopped. Joe thought to himself, *And you thought the steering was bad.* Using power brakes without power was not an easy thing to do either. He just barely managed to get his truck stopped without bumping into Jim's old truck. Once Joe had the truck stopped, he was able to look around and see why Jim had stopped.

There was old Fred standing by his mail box. Jim got out of his truck walked over to him. Before he could say a word, old Fred said, "She's suppose to be here with the mail at 10:30. Here it is, 11:15." He was looking at his watch. "She's forty-five minutes late. I tell you, when I ran the mail, I was never this late. Not ever. I made sure of it because people are always waiting anxiously for their mail. It's important to be on time. People appreciate it when you do your job right and are on time. What's wrong with this younger generation? Can't they get anything right?"

Jim smiled at Fred. "Hey Fred, is your car running okay?"

Fred stared at Jim for a few moments like he lost his mind. Then Fred said, "Of course, my car is running fine, you damn fool. How do ya think I got it up here? You think I pushed it?" Jim smiled, thinking what a sight that would be. Seeing old Fred, who was eighty-one years old, pushing his car uphill using his cane. Jim laughed. Then he asked, "Have you tried to start your car since you've been waiting here?"

"What for?"

Jim sighed deeply. "Fred, could you please try to start your car?"

Fred looked at Jim strangely and said, "Why do you want me to?"

"To see if it will start, of course."

"Why wouldn't my car start?"

Jim was getting a little exasperated by this time and said, "Fred, would you please go try and start your car? I will explain after you try it, okay?"

Fred looked at Jim like he was dealing with a mentally defective person and said, "Okay, I'll try to start my car." He slowly walked over to his car and opened the door. He got in and sat down. He put the key in the ignition and turned. Nothing. No sound, no clicking, nothing.

Fred looked over at Jim. "What in the heck did you do to my car?"

Jim turned around and looked at Joe and Jane, sitting in their truck waiting, then turned back around and looked at Fred. Jim didn't say anything for a few moments and Fred spoke up again. "Jim, what did you do to my car? You know I can't afford another one. You had better fix it right now or I'll get the Sheriff on you."

Jim had his hopes dashed. He had hoped they had been wrong and what happened to their vehicles was just some bizarre, unexplainable thing. But this, this confirmed what they thought had happened. Jim started to feel sick to his stomach. He reached out his arm and braced himself on Fred's car. His knees were feeling a little shaky.

Joe saw Jim reach out to grab Fred's car. He turned to Jane and said, "Stay in the truck. I'll see what has happened. No matter what, just stay in the truck."

Jane said, "But this is just old Fred. He might need something after he is told about the EMP. He might have a heart attack or something."

"I'll call out to you if he needs your help all right?"

Jane looked at him with a pinched look on her face. "Nothing will ever be the same again, will it?"

Joe reached out and caressed her face for a moment. "No, it won't." He got out of the truck and walked over to Jim. Fred was asking Jim if he was all right. Jim looked real pale and was just staring at the fender. Joe said, "Jim?" Joe said louder in a firmer voice, "Jim."

He reached out and shook Jim's shoulder. Jim looked at him. "What?"

Joe said, "Fred has been talking to you and you didn't hear a word he said."

Jim looked at Fred. "I'm sorry, Fred. I didn't mean to ignore you. You just don't understand yet about what's happened."

"I know what happened. You did something to my car and now it won't start. I'm going to call the Sheriff on you," Fred declared.

Jim and Joe exchanged a look. Jim said, "Go ahead, Joe, maybe you'll have better luck getting his attention and explaining what has happened then I've been able to."

Joe turned to Fred. "Fred, my truck won't start, either. All of Jim's vehicles except this one won't start. The power is out, too. Jim can't get his generator to work. And his watch is dead. All electrical and computerized things have stopped working. We think an EMP has been set off. If it was an EMP that went off, we're all in big trouble."

Fred asked, "Did you say a TNT went off? Is that like a bomb? Are the Russians invading?"

"I said an EMP went off," explained Joe.

"That's what I said, A TNT went off."

Joe looked at Jim and then looked back at Fred and said, "I said an EMP went off. An EMP is an electronic magnetic pulse bomb. A high altitude nuclear bomb was set off. It fried all electrical circuitry. Nothing electronic will work. That's why Jim's old truck will work when your car won't start."

Fred said, "Oh, one of those. So, we don't have any electricity and our vehicles won't start."

"Yes, one of those. And no, we don't have any electricity."

Fred asked, "Are the Russians invading us, do you think?"

"I don't know if they are or not," replied Joe.

Fred said, "When I was real young, we lived with no electricity, you know. I guess I'll just have to live without it again."

"That's right, that's the attitude to have," said Joe.

"Fred, you live quite a ways back. Do you want me to give you a lift home before I tow Joe and Jane home?"

"Thank you, Jim. I would appreciate a ride back to my place. It would take me a long time to walk home these days. I'm not as young as I used to be, you know."

Jim and Joe walked back to the trucks. Jim unhooked the chain from the back of his truck. He turned to Joe and said, "I'll be right back as soon as I get old Fred home."

"We'll be right here waiting for you." The two men smiled at each other.

Jim went over to old Fred and helped him get up into the truck. They drove away down the road. Jane got out and walked over to Joe. "How did he take it?" she asked.

"A lot better than any of us have. He said when he was younger he lived without electricity and can do it again. Not that he's really going to have a choice in the matter," Joe said.

"Good attitude to have."

Joe smiled. "I said the exact same thing." Joe grabbed her hand. "Let's wait in the truck." They walked towards the passenger side door and Joe opened it for her.

"Thank you, kind sir."

Joe smiled and bowed. "You're welcome, my lady." Jane giggled and got into the truck. Joe walked around to the driver's door and climbed in. Jane started to say something, but changed her mind and stopped. Joe was looking all around, on the alert. Now wasn't the time to talk about things. Joe would just be distracted and this was not the time to have a serious conversation. Jane waited in silence. Joe would let her know if he saw something. He'd talk when he had something to say.

Jim's truck rattled towards them. Joe looked over at Jane and saw that she was deep in thought. He could just imagine what her intelligent mind was coming up with. *I bet she figures it out before too long.* He said, "Jim's back." Jane looked out the windshield and saw Jim pulling up. Joe got out of the truck and waited for Jim to position the truck to reattach the tow chain. Joe called, "Everything go all right?"

"Yeah, I got him home and he was going on about needing some things from town. I told him I would be back tomorrow and see what I could do for him. Right now, I need to get you two home."

"Thanks. I am kind of anxious to get there."

"It's not even noon yet and it has already been one hell of a long day, huh?" commented Jim.

"That's an understatement, for sure." The two men reattached the chain and then got into their trucks. They were on their way home at last. When they rounded the last bend in the road and saw their place, Joe was relieved. They made it. He let out a sigh in relief. Everything he needed was there. Not knowing that everything was undisturbed and safe was had really worried him. This is what he had been preparing for. Well, not this exactly, but he knew something was going to happen eventually. It had to because they had all been living on top of a house of cards that was gradually getting more and more unstable. It was just a matter of time before things started falling down around everyone.

They all got out. The men unattached the chain and Joe put it in the back of Jim's truck. "Thank you for the ride home, Jim. I hope Marge is feeling better soon. Please keep in touch with us and let me know if there is anything I can do to help," Jane said.

"You're welcome. Marge will be all right. It was just a shock to her, you know. I'll keep in touch, don't you worry about that."

Joe said, "Thanks Jim. Let me know if there is anything I can do for you. I owe you one, neighbor." They shook hands, then Joe walked with Jim back to his truck. Jim opened the door and sat down. "You should go home and button everything up tight. It could get real nasty, real soon around here."

"No way, I'm going into town and see what has happened. Maybe they have some news there. I'll let you know what I find out." Joe watched as Jim drove away. When he was out of sight, he went into the house.

Joe paced from one side of the kitchen to the other. He had kept all his emotions and feelings under control until now; he hadn't wanted to scare everyone to death with the true reality of the situation they were in. He lifted the phone receiver and looked at it. Jane looked at him strangely and said, "Its dead, remember? Duh."

He slammed the phone down. He yelled, his voice shrill, "I have to talk to Preston. I have to tell him The Shit Has Hit The Fan. That it has really happened. I need him here. Now." He started pacing back and forth again. He stopped and turned to her and said in a very tight voice, "This is a Red Alert. This is no joke. I am not overreacting or anything like that. So get that out of your mind right now. You just don't understand yet. But, I'm going to explain it to you. All it takes is one EMP to take out the whole United States. Just one. Some other country did this. It doesn't even matter which one. But what it does mean is that we would have retaliated back with an EMP of our own. So we now have two countries without power. Do you think that it will end right there? No, it won't. Everyone will get in on it. Any country that has EMPs will be taking this opportunity to retaliate against any country they have a grievance against. And the next thing you know, the whole damn world will be in darkness. Before this day is over, there probably won't be a civilized nation left with power. Only things that have the proper shielding will still work, and let me tell you, that will be such a small amount that it isn't even worth mentioning at all. The whole world will be in darkness by the end of this night."

He paused for a few moments. "It means there is no stock market anymore. No credit cards, no bank cards, money means nothing now. What can people do with money when there are no banks? There will be no way to buy food or anything. Hell, the food can't even be delivered to the cities now. No delivery trucks will be working. So what good is the money they have in their pockets, if there's nothing to buy? Look at the big picture here. This is like dominoes. Everything is falling down. There is no way to even fly in care packages and food to the cities if it could be done. Airplanes don't work anymore. Well, maybe Air Force One does. But that isn't going to help us any. Can you imagine the riots? The chaos this is going to cause? I bet there was fighting everywhere on the freeways and highways after all the vehicles stopped working. People always have to find someone to blame. Look at all the cities that were already undergoing riots and fires and just plain down right chaos. All hell is breaking loose right now.

"But it is nothing compared to what is coming. What do you think is going to happen when the people understand that this can't be fixed? That things aren't going to get better? That there is no government left right now to help them? What are they going to do? And even if there was, they would have no way to help them. The shit has really hit the fan. No if's, and's, or but's about it. This is it. There is no going back now that someone pushed the first red button." He took a deep breath. "That is why I need Preston to get here now. In a few days, it might be too late for him to make it out of the city. Remember how quickly those other cities ran out of food? The stores were emptied out in one day. One day. And that was with the power working. Well, imagine what it will be like with no power, no vehicles working and no food."

Jane got paled at the picture Joe was painting of the situation. She felt her stomach rolling. She was going to be sick. She had tears running down her face. "Oh my God, this is hell on earth," she whispered.

Chapter 6

Reality Sucks

"Don't wait. The time will never be just right."

Napoleon Hill

Preston was at work when everything electrical went dead. He couldn't finish changing the fuel pump he was working on without proper lighting. Regulations say no light, no work. He took a break and waited for the power to come back on. It didn't matter to him if he was working or not, he still got paid. At least this was a break from the normal routine. Things had been dull around here lately. Work had been kind of slow the last few weeks. Usually the noise of the crew and helicopter engines being turned on and off was an occasional sound in the background. There was only a few of them left here to finish up. There were a couple of suits upstairs, three clerical workers, him and another mechanic. The other mechanic had called in sick today, so, for today, he was working alone. The place was almost as quiet as a tomb. The company he worked for was moving to a new, larger hanger several miles away at a small airport. It definitely was a step up from the size and location of this place. He was finishing up the last few jobs they had at this location. He and the other mechanic would be joining the rest of the crew next week. It sure will be nice working at the new place. The move meant when they had to take a chopper up and test it, they wouldn't have to get permission. That was the main reason they were moving. In cities, there were noise laws that had to be obeyed. At the new place, it wouldn't be a problem anymore.

He had just grabbed a Coke out the refrigerator that the crew used for their lunches when one of the clerical guys came in with a shocked look on his face. Preston asked him what was wrong.

"I was going to take an early lunch, since the power is out. I went out to my car. It wouldn't start. I was going to come in and ask you if you could take a look at it to see what was wrong when I noticed several cars out on the road. The doors were open on the driver's side. I looked around, but I couldn't see anyone. I walked around the side of the building to see if anyone was there when I noticed that it was real quiet. There was no traffic sounds, nothing. I thought how odd that was. When I reached the back of the building, I saw a whole lot of cars just sitting there. Both sides of the freeway are clogged with them. They looked abandoned. I looked and looked and I couldn't see anyone inside of the cars. I thought maybe there had been an accident and traffic was backed up, but it was kind of eerie. There were no sounds. Usually, you can still hear the car engines and what not. But I couldn't hear any of the normal sounds. Then I noticed that down a ways it looked like some people were standing around, arguing and yelling. At least that's what it looked like from here. People's hands were gesturing all around wildly. Then several people started fighting. I got scared then. I thought, 'oh no, we could have a riot right here like is happening in those other cities that have been on the news lately.' I thought I'd better call 911 and report this before it gets out of hand, but my cell phone is dead. It was fully charged this morning. I glanced at my watch and it's dead, too. See?" He showed Preston his dead cell phone and watch.

The breath Preston was about to inhale stuck in his throat. His stomach clenched in fear. He felt like he had an electrical shock go through his body.

The clerical worker went on with his report of events. "Then I looked far down the freeway and I saw a lot of people walking down the off ramp. I turned and saw a few people standing out behind one of the buildings down the road. They were watching what was happening, too. One guy turned and noticed me and jogged over here. He asked if my car would start. I said 'no, I have a dead battery or something.' He said the same thing. Their cars won't start, either. We compared notes and none of their cell phones or watches were working, either. He was as worried about a potential riot as I was. He said he had to get back to his co-workers. I then starting thinking about how strange all of this is and I realized this could be something else. Like a terrorist attack or something. But this is Madison, Wisconsin. Why would a terrorist attack us here? What do you think it could be?"

"I'm not sure, but I do know that this isn't anything good, " Preston said. He walked over to the wall and picked up the landline phone. It was dead, too. He noticed that his hand was shaking. The phone system used to be shielded. Too bad it still wasn't. He would like to call Joe and Jane and tell them what had happened here. He thought, *Damn, damn, damn it. This had to happen when I'm all the way over here. Why did it have to be right now? Why not next week when he would've been at the new building? It would be five miles closer to my apartment.*

Preston turned around to face the clerical guy and said, "I'm leaving. You should start walking home to check on your family, too. This could get ugly real quick. It may not be safe for long out there. Imagine New Orleans and 9-11 all rolled into one." The other man got paler listening to Preston's advice. Preston turned and gathered up his coat and what not that he had lying around and headed for the outside door. When he reached it, he turned around and told the man, "Good luck."

Preston understood immediately that it had to have been an EMP. It was the only thing that would cause the power, cell phones, watches and all the vehicles to go dead at once. His Army training was about to pay off. He hurried over to his truck. He pulled his bug out bag from behind the seat. He took off his work boots and put on his hiking boots. He pulled out his special belt. He checked his 1911 Colt 45 and made sure it was loaded and ready to go. He secured it. He then checked his two extra clips he always had on the belt. He thought, *Yup, they're full, just like they're supposed to be.* He then grabbed the bottled water he kept behind the seat for emergencies and filled his camel pack. He had added this to his Alice pack just last week. He thought to himself, *Good move.* He carried enough gear and supplies to live for three days in it.

It was eighteen miles to his apartment. He had already mapped the shortest route that he felt would be safe to travel. It kept him out of the main part of the city. He would keep to the wooded areas as much as possible. The clerical guy must have told his story to the rest of them in the building. He saw everyone coming outside to try their cars. None of them started.

One of the other clerical workers came up to him and asked, "Why in the heck do you have a gun?"

Preston replied, "You had better start to understand what all of this means real quick. We have been hit with an EMP. We are at war with some other country.

"From this moment on, everything will be different. You all will be walking unless you have a bicycle. People will not be in their right minds. Most people won't understand what has happened. From this moment on, it will be pure survival of the fittest and smartest. It will be like New Orleans and 9-11 rolled into one. Trust me on this. I'm retired from the military. I know what I'm talking about. You had better get home to protect your family."

The guy shook his head and said, "You're nuts. They will have this all fixed in a few days. The power goes out and you freak out. You are so overreacting."

Preston looked hard at the guy and said, "Listen, genius, there is only one thing that will take out the whole power grid, cars, cell phones and watches. In other words, everything that is electrical. That's an EMP. Period. There is nothing else that could do this. There is no quick fix for this. If the device wasn't shielded properly, then it's dead." Preston gestured all around them. "Just like this."

The guy said, "I don't believe you. You are just overreacting. There is no way this was an EMP. Our government protects us from stuff like that. This is America. We are the number one super power. No one would dare do something like this. Our government makes sure of it. It always has, and it always will. You're just plain nuts." The guy turned away from Preston and walked over to one of his coworkers and started talking.

Preston thought, *Well, I tried to warn them. It's all up to them now. They're morons. Overwhelming evidence smacks them in the head and they just flat out refuse to believe it.* He turned back to his truck to check if he had everything that could be useful. He would not be coming back this way. Not ever again.

Preston took off towards the wooded lot across the street at a jog. One of the bosses called out to him, "Hey, where are you going? Wait up. I want to talk to you." He stopped and turned around. It was one of the executives in a suit, tie and dress shoes. The man approached Preston and said, "It is against company policy to have a gun on the premises."

Preston just shook his head. He looked at him standing there all spiffed out in his suit and said, "You're brain dead, aren't you? You don't like me carrying a gun on company grounds? Then fire me. I'm going home." Preston was done talking to these morons. *They won't listen. They won't even consider the facts of the situation. Granted it was not something that they had ever been faced with before. But still they were acting totally brain dead.* He turned and started jogging again. He could hear the executive mumbling about something else as he left. He thought, *Good luck, moron.*

Preston smiled as he jogged. He was picturing the executive walking home in his spiffy suit and dress shoes in his mind. *I hope he has blisters on top of blisters when he reaches home—if the suit doesn't run into any kind of trouble. I wonder if he can make it home. That is the most important question right now.* That thought wiped the smile off his face and sobered him right up. This situation was no laughing matter. He came out of the wooded area right where he should be. He started walking down the street. It was filled with abandoned cars. He had three blocks to go before he would need to turn to make it to another wooded area. He had gone three miles already. He was making excellent time. Only fifteen miles to go. It normally took twenty minutes to drive ten miles. Walking was three miles per hour. He had another six hours to go before he would make it to the apartment. It was a whole new world out there to get used to. He had to make it home before everyone's confusion wore off and they started to understand the reality of the situation. Then people were going to be mighty angry.

Preston's new woman in his life was named Sharon. They were living together in his apartment and had been together for five months. He had moved to the city ten months ago to get a job, while she had been born and raised in the city. Sharon liked to socialize. She liked going out at night and she loved parties. They had met at a singles bar downtown. She had her hair done twice a week at the salon and her fingernails done every week. It was a ritual for her. To his knowledge, she had never missed an appointment. No matter what else was going on in her life, she made sure to never miss pampering herself. She deserved it. She worked hard and had earned it, at least, that's what she was always telling herself. People liked her now. She would not be like her mother.

Sharon was at work when the power went out. An hour later, her boss told her to go ahead and go home. They were up on the fifth floor, so she had to walk down the stairs. The elevator had stopped working. She walked out to the parking lot outside and saw all the cars still there. *That's strange,* she thought. She had seen and heard people leaving the building; a few people at a time for the last hour as their bosses told them to go ahead and go home. She didn't know what to make of it, but it didn't really concern her. She got into her car and it wouldn't start. She kept trying and trying and it still wouldn't start. *Damn Preston, I knew I should have taken it to a real mechanic last week,* she thought. She pulled out her cell phone to call him and give him a piece of her mind, but her phone was dead. *I know I charged it last night,* she thought. She got out of the car and walked back into the building. She looked at the stairs and sighed. *If I ruin my new designer shoes, I will just have to kill him. This is entirely his fault. If he would have let me take her car to a real mechanic this wouldn't be happening.* She climbed the stairs and went back into the office. Her boss wasn't there. He must have left the back way. He parked his car down the street at a parking garage. *Damn,* she thought. And the phone isn't working either. Well, she would just have to get out to the main street and see if she could get a cab. She thought, *Preston is going to reimburse me for that cab fare. He is also going to pay for whatever he did to my car, too.*

She left the building. She had a passing thought that it was strange she hadn't seen the security guard, either. He usually was always downstairs in the lobby so he would be available for whatever he was there for. She started walking down the street, her stride showing her anger at Preston. She noticed all the cars. They were just all over the place, every which way. She walked further on. She got to the main street and people were standing around all over the place ,blocking the sidewalks, too. She had heard the people long before she got there. Everyone was talking. It sounded like a gigantic bar with everyone talking at once. They were all standing in little groups. It kind of looked like a church social or something, except the language definitely wasn't anything you would hear there. She looked around. *What on earth is the matter with them?* She joined the people on the sidewalks, trying to go with the flow of foot traffic. She kept looking around to see if she could see a cab, but all she could see was cars stopped everywhere … and people. People were everywhere and acting kind of strange.

She pressed on. After seven blocks, her feet started to hurt. There were already several blisters that had formed. She noticed a shoe store up ahead. *I'll stop and get me a pair of running shoes. He's going to pay me for them too, the jerk.* She limped up to the store and went inside. The lone clerk was just closing up. She looked at the running shoes and chose a pair. She grabbed a pair of socks, too. She went up to the clerk and said, "I'll take these."

The clerk looked at her and said, "Do you have cash?"

"No. I have a credit card."

"The credit card machines aren't working. I can only take cash right now." He turned away.

"You can run my card on one of those machine things and then run it through when you get the power back on." Her patience was beginning to wear thin.

"I can't do that. I don't know that your credit card is good."

"It is good. Of course, it's good."

"No, I can only take cash right now," he insisted.

"Fine. How much is it?" she said, exasperated.

He pulled out a tablet and pencil and figured it out. He turned to her and said, "That will be one hundred forty-two dollars and fifty-one cents."

She looked in her purse and she only had a hundred and ten dollars on her. "Will you take this and put the rest on my card?"

He laughed at her. "Look, lady, I told you I can only take cash."

"My car won't start, I can't find a cab and I might have to walk home. I have already ruined my designer shoes. I need these so, can you please make an exception and put the rest of it on my credit card?" she begged.

He just stared at her. Finally he said, "No. Cash only. Go to the bank and then come back when you have the cash." The bank was back three miles the other way.

She started to cry. This was just getting to be too much for her. She looked at him and pleaded, "Please?"

He rolled his eyes. "Fine, if it will get you out of here." He took the cash and her credit card and then asked for her license. She gave it to him. He copied everything down and then had her sign the credit card slip. "I know where you live now. If this doesn't go through, they will take it out of my salary and I will hunt you down to get my money. Understand?"

She said haughtily back to him, "My credit is good." He asked her what size shoe she wore. "A five and half." He went into the back of the store and returned with a box. She grabbed the shoe box and socks and went over and sat down to put them on. When he saw the blisters on her feet he started to feel a bit sorry for her and was glad he decided to help her out. He offered her a few band aids to help. She smiled at him and said, "Thanks."

He thought, *Wow, she really is pretty. I wonder if she has a boyfriend or husband. Maybe I should ask her out.* He cleared his throat. "Do you have a boyfriend or husband?"

She had finished putting the new shoes on. She stood up, holding her ruined shoes. Her feet still hurt, but it was a lot better than before. She smiled at him and said, "I have a boyfriend, but maybe not for long. He's a jerk."

He smiled at that comment and asked, "Would you like a bag for your old shoes?" They wouldn't fit into the running shoes box.

"Thank you, that is very nice of you." He brought her a plastic bag with the shoe store logo on it. She placed her ruined designer shoes in it. She walked over to the door and then turned back to him. "Call me next week and see if I'm available." She then rejoined the people walking down the sidewalk. The clerk finished locking up and then realized he didn't have her phone number. She never gave it to him.

As she walking home to the apartment, she was disturbed by all the abandoned cars. There were no normal city sounds, either, just people talking, arguing and she saw a few fist fights. But everyone was on foot. You could actually hear their footsteps. It was pretty eerie. There had been a few police officers here and there, surrounded by people asking questions. They all looked pretty upset. All anyone was talking about was the power blackout and that their cars didn't work. She thought with a flash of anger, *Did they let Preston work on their cars, too?* Maybe he had lied about being a helicopter mechanic. She had never seen him at work. Maybe he was really a car mechanic. If he was, he was a very bad car mechanic. Her car had been running fine. It was just making a little noise somewhere under the hood. He said he could fix it right up. She had wanted to take it over to Max, her regular mechanic, but he insisted he could fix it up in a few minutes. He got under the hood and did something or other, and now it wouldn't run. Maybe he had lied about being a mechanic and didn't want her to know about it or where he really worked. People lied all the time. *You can't trust anyone,* she thought. She was going to give him hell when he got home. All of this was his fault. He owed her a lot of money for all of this. She would make sure he paid her back too. She turned the corner and there was the apartment down the street. She was relieved to be home. Her feet hurt so much. Thank god she had only had to walk three miles. She wasn't sure if she would have made it if it had been any farther away. She was tired, thirsty and panting to get a breath. Preston was always telling her to get into shape. Maybe she should think about joining a gym.

Everywhere Preston went, he saw people walking around the dead cars. Most people were still just standing around, trying to figure out what to do. He avoided as many people as he could. To anyone watching, it would seem that he would just disappear. He would be there one minute and gone the next. He came out near a park, and just down from where he was, a guy was trying to get a bicycle away from another man that had been riding down the trail. A fight broke out. He stayed in the woods across from them and went down farther to cross the trail. He just shook his head. It was a miracle that this was the only violence he had seen so far today. He really hoped it would be the last. But he knew better. It was just a matter of time. *I wish I had my mountain bike right now,* he thought, then realized he would probably spend more time having to defend it than ride it. It was better that his bike was at home. It would be really useful in getting out of the city now that vehicles were a lost cause. He had to get home and get on the road to his retreat. Joe and Jane were counting on him getting there. They had to get survival and protection plans started as soon as possible. He hoped Sharon made it home okay. She only had three miles to walk. She should have been there hours ago. He only had two miles to go now. *Best get on with it. Time is a wasting and I'm not getting any younger,* he thought with a smile, remembering Jane's favorite phrase. She was always saying that. It was starting to get dark. Night was coming, bringing a lot of new troubles and worries all by itself. He was sure of it. He started to jog again.

Sharon had soaked her feet, then bandaged them up. She wasn't good at this sort of thing. The bandages looked like they would fall off before too long. She put her thick, warm pajamas and slippers on, then pulled on her fleece robe, too. It was getting cold in here. The apartment had electric heat and the power was out, so, there was no heat. She kept walking over to the thermostat and tapping it with her fingers saying, "Come on, come on. It's getting cold in here. Turn on." She was getting hungry. She had missed lunch with all the stuff that had happened to her today. She just completely forgot to eat. She went over to the cupboard and got out some crackers and her specialty cheese she bought at the wine and cheese shop. She ate a few pieces, then decided that it had been one hell of a day and she would open a bottle of wine, too. She deserved it. When she finally got the wine opened she had chipped a nail and broken another clean off. She was pissed. She always took care of her nails. It was important to her to have long, pretty nails. She would have to replace them with fake ones now. She hated to do that. The glue always made her fingers itch.

She grabbed a new magazine off the coffee table and looked through it while she drank her wine and waited for Preston to get home. She had several subscriptions to fashion and makeup magazines. She had to keep herself up and look her best at all times. It was very important to look your very best no matter what. The longer she waited, the madder she got at Preston.

For the last mile to the apartment, Preston kept seeing more and more people that were angry or confused. Most had a dazed look on their face. Who knew how far they had to walk to get home? It was dark by this time. Preston had the .45 colt very close and ready to use. Dark was when the predators came out in the cities, and tonight was going to be very bad. There were so many victims ripe for the picking. All of them were just trying to get home. They had no way to protect themselves. *It's going to be a blood bath,* he thought. His next thought chilled him to the bone. *The streets tomorrow morning are going to be littered with the dead and dying.* It felt like he was in a horror movie or back in some third world country again. He had seen this before. He knew what it was going to look like. The thought made his stomach turn over. To know it was happening right here in America just broke his heart. He had fought to keep crap like this from happening here. Many a good soldier died to keep the average person here from knowing the horror of what people can do to other people when civilization goes down the rabbit hole. Everything from this moment on would be a whole new way of thinking through situations. There were so many things to consider. He was starting to get upset and his breathing increased. He told himself, *Just calm down. Take slow breaths. Control the situation; don't let the situation control you.* That was his old sergeant's advice he gave all of the new recruits. It was sound advice. He just never really expected everything to fall apart quite like this.

Preston crept around some cars, staying out of sight as much as possible. He made it to the back alley. He didn't want to confront all the people standing around outside the front door to the apartment building. There was glass littered all over the place. It looked like someone had been beating on the cars and the lower floors of the apartment buildings along the street. Some of the vehicles even had slit tires. He could see it clearly in the moonlight. He wished there was some cloud cover. If he could see them, then they would be able to see him, too. He stayed in the shadows as much as possible, but he would have to break cover to cross the alley. He could see a gang of seven kids down the alley at the opposite entrance. They were drinking. He could see the beer bottles in their hands. There were several broken beer bottles there, too. One of the kids threw his beer bottle at the wall and laughed. He grabbed another beer out of the bag on the ground. *Oh this is just great. I don't need a bunch of drunken kids right now*, Preston thought.

He hoped they didn't have any weapons or decide to prove how tough they were with him. He really didn't want to hurt them. Or kill them. He took a deep breath and calmly walked across the alley. When he got halfway across, the kids spotted him and yelled, "Hey." He turned and looked at them. They started toward him. He thought, *Here it comes.*

When the first two got up to him, they stopped. "Did you come from the other side of the city?"

"Yes," he answered.

The rest of the kids caught up with the first two. They stopped and stood next to their friends. One of them asked, "Is it like this there, too?"

"Yes."

"Do you know what happened? Why everything isn't working?"

He thought for a few moments, deciding what and how much to say to them. He decided to tell them the truth. "We were hit with an EMP and it fried everything electrical."

The kids thought this over for a few moments then one of them asked, "You mean like a bomb?"

"Yes."

Another one asked, "How long till it can all be fixed?"

"As far as I know, it will probably be five years or more before things can be repaired enough to work again. That is if there are enough technicians left in the world to do it," Preston said. The kids stared at him in shock.

Another one of the kids asked, "Do you think this is like World War 3?"

He answered, "Yes. We were hit with an EMP; we would have retaliated against whichever country that did it. We either sent back an EMP of our own, or we sent enough nukes to bomb their country into glass and deep craters. But, it won't stop there. Every other country that has the capabilities to send an EMP or bomb will get into the act, too. They'll send out bombs to whatever countries they don't like. The only thing keeping the stability was that no one was insane enough to push the first button to do this. Well, someone went insane and did push the button. By the end of this night, most of the world will have been bombed into the dark ages."

All the kids looked pretty scared at this statement. The apparent leader of this group then asked, "You were in the military, right?"

Preston answered, "Yes. I know what I am talking about, if that is what you're getting at."

The leader then asked, "What should we do?"

Preston thought for a few moments and said, "If I was you, I would be securing as much water, food and first aid supplies as possible. I would get my family to a secure place that can be easily defended. I would then go to the library and get as many books as possible on building windmills and other power sources and learn how to make and maintain them; all energy sources, like steam power and solar, too. That is a commodity that will be in high demand in the future." The kids looked pretty uncertain by this time. "I have to go now. Good luck to you all."

"Yeah, good luck to you, too." They turned and started back down the alley, deep in conversation.

Preston took a deep breath and let it out slowly. He thought, *I tried, that's all I can do. They were good kids. I hope they make it. The world is going to need resourceful kids in the very near future*. Preston walked up to the gate and climbed over it. He didn't have a key. Only the landlord did. He walked up to the back door to the building and got his key out. The door still looked secure. No broken glass or anything yet. He unlocked the door and stepped through, securing the door behind him. It wouldn't stay secure for long. He stayed in the shadows as he crept along the hall and up the stairs.

His apartment was on the third floor. There was debris lying on some of the stairs. It looked like someone's suitcase had popped open and spilled everything out as it tumbled down the stairs. There was a man's shaving stuff and a woman's makeup scattered all over the place. Clothes were hanging all around. He walked over as much as he could. It would be good to leave this stuff right here. It could be a good noise maker to alert him if someone was coming up the stairs. He could hope, anyway. He got up to the apartment and he put his key in the first lock and unlocked it, then the deadbolt. He turned the handle and pushed against the door. The handle turned, but the door wouldn't open. Sharon must have put the secure bar in place. He tapped lightly on the door with his fingers and said, "Sharon, it's me, open up." He could hear her moving around some and then the sound of the bar being removed. He could now open the door. He entered the apartment.

Sharon was standing there in her pajamas and slippers. She had a wine glass in one hand. She was staring daggers at him and pointing her finger at him with the other hand. "Nice of you to show up. It would have been even nicer if you would have come home on time. I have had one hell of a bad day, thanks to you." She paused to take a breath. "What I want to know is, what in the hell did you do to my car? You said you knew what you were doing. Well, obviously you don't know squat about cars." She gestured broadly with her hand. "Look at all the other cars that don't work, either. What did you do to them? You said you were a mechanic. I think you're lying. I think you've been lying to me the whole time. You know what you did? You made me have to walk home. Walk. You owe me, mister. You owe me a lot. I have blisters because of you. I have a ruined pair of designer shoes you owe me, too. I had to stop and buy a pair of running shoes. The clerk was a creep and kept giving me a hard time about paying with my credit card, as if my credit isn't any good. Do you know how being treated like that made me feel? Then the jerk comes on to me. He was an asshole. He was a complete asshole. Just like you. Then I get here and the place is cold and dark. I have to bandage my feet because of you. I have a headache trying to read my magazine by candlelight because of you. I broke a fingernail and chipped another one opening the wine. I deserve a little wine after the day I had. This wouldn't have happened if you were here to open the wine. But, were you? No. You were God knows where while I'm left here to suffer alone. This is all your fault, mister, and I won't put up with it at all. Get your shit together and get out of my apartment." Preston reached out and took the wine glass out of her hand. She yelled right in his face, "Don't touch me, you asshole. I mean it … get your shit and get out. Now." Preston opened his mouth and before he could form a word, there was a loud banging on the door.

He looked at the door, and then at Sharon, and then at the door again. Another louder, longer knock on the door rang out. He told Sharon, "Shut up." She just kept screaming at him. "I said shut up. Right the hell now." Sharon wasn't paying any attention to him at all. He grabbed her arms and shook her and said in a loud voice, "Sharon, shut the hell up!" That got her attention.

She pulled away from him and screamed, "Don't touch me, you asshole. You're all alike, just lying assholes." He grabbed her and held her with one arm and put his other hand over her mouth. She struggled to get away. The hand over mouth was still holding the 45. It was right there in front of her face. She started trembling and breathing fast. She was afraid of him now.

He said by her ear, "Shut up." He held her more tightly. Whoever was outside was literally banging on the door by this time. He said in a very low threatening voice, "Stop struggling."

Her body stiffened in his arms. "If I let you go, will you stop screaming?" She nodded her head yes. "I'm going to take my hand off your mouth. If you start screaming again, I'm going to lock you in the bedroom. Do you understand me?" She nodded her head yes again. He took his hand off her mouth. She stayed silent, just breathing with heaving gasps and sobs. "Stay right there while I see who it is."

He walked over to the door and leaned on the wall besides it. He didn't even try to look out through the peep hole in the door. He knew it was too dark to see anything. The banging was continuous by this time. "Who is it?"

A quivering female voice answered him saying, "It's me, Amy, your next door neighbor. Are you two okay?"

Sharon swayed drunkenly. "Are you going to shoot her?" she slurred. Her eyes were opened wide in shock. No one had ever treated her this way before. She didn't know what to do. She didn't want him to hurt her. She whispered, "You know I don't like guns."

Preston ignored Sharon and said loudly to Amy, "Step back away from the door." He heard her move.

"I stepped back. Now what should I do?"

"Are you alone?"

"Yes, I'm alone."

"Where is your boyfriend?"

"Gone for the last month. I kicked him out."

"All right, I'm going to open the door just enough for you to enter. If anyone else tries to come in, I will shoot them. Do you understand?"

Amy hesitated and then said, "Yes, I understand. It's just me. I'm by myself."

Sharon started screaming out, "He's got a gun. Oh my God, he has a gun!"

"Shut up, Sharon," he said, turning to her. She kept screaming and crying loudly. He took one threatening step towards her; she backed up and put her trembling hands tightly on her mouth as if to hold in any sounds that might escape. She stood very still. She was crying hard, her body shaking with the effort to stay silent. Preston opened the door and Amy walked in.

As soon as Amy was through the door he quickly slammed it, locked it and dropped the bar into place. He holstered the .45. Sharon's volume increased. All she could say was, "He's got a gun," over and over.

Amy looked at Sharon and saw the red marks on her face. She turned around and stormed over to Preston like an avenging angel bent on dealing out the wrath of God. She demanded in a loud angry voice, "What did you do to her?"

Preston sighed and said, "It seems this is entirely my fault, at least according to Sharon. She was just telling me to get my stuff and get out of her apartment."

Amy looked at him with her eyes flashing a wrathful gleam and said, "This is your apartment."

"I know," he said.

"That isn't what I asked you. Did you hurt her?"

He answered her with a sigh, "I was just trying to explain what happened to you. Do you want to know or not?"

Amy said firmly, "Answer me, did you hurt her?"

Preston paused to think back through the last few minutes and what he had done to make Sharon shut up. "I guess that would depend on your definition of hurt."

"What do you mean? It is never called for to be violent to a woman," Amy said.

He said, "I wasn't violent. I was trying to get her to shut up so I could hear out in the hall. I had to know if it was safe to open the door."

Amy remembered seeing some fighting here and there and other violent acts today. Humanity hadn't been at its best today that was for sure. Yes, people had gone completely nuts today. As she was jogging home, she saw down a side street where a guy had taken a tire iron and beat another man with it. She said, "I guess I can understand about the being safe part. People weren't very nice today, were they? But you didn't have to be mean about it, did you?"

"I might have been a little more forceful than I meant," he admitted.

Amy let out a relieved sigh. "I'm sorry I didn't mean to barge in here and start yelling at you. I just got scared when I heard all the yelling start." Before he could reply, he noticed Sharon starting to fall; Preston grabbed her just in time before she hit the floor.

"Sharon, I'm going to put you to bed. We'll talk when you wake up, okay?" She was still crying. He carried her out of the room and Amy could hear the rustling of the blankets. She could hear him tell her, "You're just drunk right now. I'm sorry if I hurt you, but you wouldn't stop screaming. I'm sorry if I scared you, too. I didn't mean to. Go to sleep and I'll wake you up later when I get everything ready to leave. It will be all right. Just go ahead and rest for now. I'm sorry."

That statement got Amy's full attention. *Leave? And go where, I wonder? And how was he planning on getting there?* She heard his footsteps coming back. As he entered the room, she said, "Is she okay? She looks pretty out of it."

"She'll be all right."

"Can you finish telling me what happened?" she asked. "I'm sorry; it's really none of my business."

He said, "I might as well tell you everything, since you heard most of it."

Amy blushed. It's not very nice to know that your neighbors are listening to your private conversations.

"Well, Sharon was accusing me of manufacturing all of this crap today for her misfortune. She wouldn't be quiet. She became hysterical and I had to subdue her to get her attention. It was a matter of security and safety. I can't protect her if I can't hear if there is danger out there. Anyway, she's drunk and had a bad day, and basically just blamed me for all of it."

Amy said, "Didn't we all have a bad day?"

"Yes, we all did. Anyway, that's all that happened. Then you showed up at the door. You walked in like a woman on a mission and started yelling at me, too."

Amy blushed again and said, "Sorry about that. I thought you were hurting her. I thought that you two had gone nuts like everyone else today."

Preston realized that she must have seen some awful things today, violent things. They heard Sharon calling out. He said, "I'll be back. I'll go see what she needs." He turned and headed to the bedroom. Amy just waited in the living room for him. Preston walked into the bedroom and softly called, "Sharon, did you need something?" No answer. He called again. Still no answer. She hadn't moved, so he walked around to her side of the bed. She was still asleep. It must have been a bad dream that made her cry out.

As soon as he was back in the living room, he said, "Amy, you have to go back to your apartment and fill every single water container you have, including the bathtub and all of the sinks. Every single glass you have, anything at all that will hold water. Go now. This is the most important thing to do right now."

Amy looked at him seriously for a few moments and then said, "After I do that, can I come back over here? It's scary right now without the power and everyone going nuts. I really don't want to sit over there by myself. Do you know what happened?"

"Sure, come on back over and we'll talk when you're done."

"Do you have a flashlight I could borrow? It will go a lot faster than to try to do this by candlelight."

"Sure, I do," he said. He walked over to the door and grabbed his pack. He reached in a compartment and pulled out a flashlight and handed it to her. She tested it, then said, "I'll be right back as soon as I have everything filled."

"Okay." They walked to the door and Preston let her out.

As soon as Amy was gone, he went around the apartment and made sure all the blinds were closed. He took sheets, towels and some old blankets and covered all the windows securely. He was going to light the Aladdin lantern he had and he didn't want any light to leak out and let people know that there were people up here and that they had a light source. And, it would help to warm it up a little. He got out the two burner propane cook stove he had. It was attached to a twenty pound propane tank. He'd gotten it for camping and for power outages. His whole apartment was electrical. He got out the old metal percolator he had and got coffee going, then he lit the Aladdin lantern. He started filling up the bathtub, sink and every container he could find.

Amy walked into her apartment. She immediately went to the bathroom and turned the faucet on to fill the tub. She went into the kitchen next, and started filling everything she could find that would hold water. She started thinking about Preston and Sharon. She didn't know either of them that well. She was already living in her apartment when Preston moved in. *What a hunk,* she thought. She sighed. It seemed to her that all the great hunky men were either married, gay, or already had girlfriends. Here she was, twenty-nine years old and no prospects for Mr. Right. All the men seemed to go for the dainty types like Sharon.

It's not that she had trouble attracting a guy, it was just that she seemed to attract all the wrong types. Take her last boyfriend, for instance. He had turned out to be a lazy bum. She found out he was a gamer. He sat around all day and did nothing but play games. The Sharon's of the world would win hands down every time. She sighed again. Sharon was a dainty, tiny blue-eyed blonde. She had an athletic type body. She probably wore a size zero or a size one.

Now she could stop thinking about Sharon and Preston. *Reality sucks,* she thought with a smile. *I have successfully avoided thinking about this situation. Now back to the real world. What in the world could have caused all this to take place?* she wondered. *It's like Twilight Zone creepy.* She went into her bedroom and put on long underwear and extra socks. She gathered up her comforter and wrapped it around her and decided she had stalled long enough. It had scared her tonight to hear the yelling coming from Preston's apartment. It also made her mad. She thought Preston was the greatest and it would have killed her find out he was an abuser. She had never heard anything like that from over there before. She was greatly relieved to know it had just been Sharon getting out of hand. She had heard the sneer and contempt in her voice when she had been yelling at Preston. How could Preston even think that Sharon had any true feelings for him? Her voice said it all. It was just as she had expected all along. Women like Sharon only thought of themselves and nobody else. That was the beginning and end of the story. Sharon had had a bad day. What a laugh. What about what had happened to everybody else, for Christ's sake? Did she think it had been a picnic for everyone? It was time to go next door and find out what had happened today. What had caused of all of this. She had a very bad feeling about it. She had had it ever since she discovered her watch was dead. Then she found out her car was dead and then her cell phone. She remembered her grandfather telling her when she was young, 'Stiff upper lip, my dear girl.' She missed him a lot. She looked around and decided that she had better blow out the candles and get on with it. *Stop being a silly goose,* she thought. Besides, she was wasting the batteries with all her avoidance. Who knew how long the power would be out? Preston would not appreciate her wasting his batteries. She opened her door and walked a few steps over and knocked a lot quieter than she had earlier.

Preston said through the door, "Who is it?"

She smiled. "Your friendly neighbor who just got water logged." She heard the locks opening. Then the bar was drawn up. The door opened and there was light. "Wow," she said. "Did the lights come back on and I didn't notice?"

Preston smiled and said, "No, but I have a lantern."

She laughed. "It's like real light."

"It is real light."

"Ha, ha. You must think you're a very funny guy, huh?"

He smiled and said, "I have been known to tell a joke or two."

"I meant it's like a light bulb bright," Amy explained.

He said, "I know. That's probably why it was invented. People got tired of being in the dark."

"Well, it works really well. What does it run on?"

"Kerosene or lamp oil."

"That's great," Amy said. "I have some lamp oil over at my place. Someone gave me this tiny, little bitty lantern for Christmas one year and it ran on lamp oil. I had to ask the clerk at the discount store what it ran on so I could buy whatever it was to refill it. It seemed they only sold it in half gallon jugs. My little tiny lantern only takes about a tablespoon full to fill it. I didn't know that the bigger lanterns were so bright or I would've bought one of those. I have almost a full half gallon of oil left."

"That will be a good thing to have," Preston said.

The aroma of coffee filled the air. "Is that coffee I smell?" Amy asked.

"Yup. I put a pot on to perk after you left. It's almost done now. Would you like a cup?"

She sighed and said, "I would kill for a cup right now."

"Whoa, I'll have to remember not get in the way of the lady and her coffee, then," he said with a smile.

She asked him, "How did you make coffee if the power isn't on?"

"I have a propane cook stove. I bought it when we had the first power outage. I had a smaller one I used when I went camping. They're real handy to have around."

"I would say so. You can cook on that stove, too?"

"Yes, just like a real stove," Preston said.

"I'm starved. Are you hungry? I'll cook."

"Yes, it was a long, stressful walk home."

"Tell me about it. I had to walk fifteen miles. How far did you walk?" Amy flexed her feet to relieve the stress.

He was impressed. "Eighteen miles."

She said, "Wow, that's a really long walk, too. It's a good thing I jog every morning or I don't think I would've made it." She went back to her apartment and got some food to cook.

She smiled. "Okay, dinner will be ready in about ten minutes, then, man of many words."

He laughed as he walked away. He was beginning to like her a lot. The only other woman he knew of that was a bit like her was Jane. He had always envied Joe having a woman like Jane. His mother had been a petite southern woman. She died when he was ten. His wife had been interested in her shopping most of the time and gossip. She didn't cook. Sharon didn't cook, either. It was nice seeing a happy woman in his kitchen cooking. It was a novel idea to him. The only other happy woman he knew of was Jane. If only Amy wasn't just so damn young. He sighed.

He went into the hall and opened the closet door. He took out the two packs he had put in there for just such an emergency as this one. He went through them. He then went around the apartment gathering up things to put into them. He was deciding how many razors he should pack into one of them when he heard Amy call out that dinner was done. He had been trying to ignore the wonderful odors coming from the kitchen while he was packing. He dropped all the razors into the pack and said, "I'll be right there." He would finish figuring out how many razors later.

She had set the table for three. She looked up at him when he walked into the dining room. "Are you going to wake up Sharon to eat?"

"No. Not right now."

"Oh. I thought she might be hungry and it would help her sober up faster if she ate something. I cut my steak in half to share with her."

"She won't eat it," Preston said.

"What? Why?"

"She doesn't eat meat."

"Oh, I should have figured that," Amy said.

Preston looked at her., "Figured what?"

"That Sharon doesn't eat meat."

"Why?"

She sighed. "Because she is so dainty."

He laughed and said, "You think she's dainty?"

"That is quite plain to see."

"She hardly eats at all. A salad or cheese and fruit are what she usually eats."

Amy said, "I know the type. Now sit down and eat your steak before it gets cold."

He said, "Yes, ma'am."

She laughed, pointed her finger at him and said, "That, soldier, is a direct order from headquarters."

Amy sat down and picked up her fork. "Okay, hit me with it. I know it's going to be bad, very bad. I can feel it. I figure the only thing that could do this is an EMP bomb. Am I right?"

He looked at her with amazement, his fork stopping in midair. "Yes. It was an EMP that did this."

"That's what I thought. I figured it out on my jog home today. So do you know which country was the first idiot to push the button?"

He said, "No. There is no way to tell."

"So, do the movies have it right? Will we really be in the dark ages again for years?"

"Yes."

She sighed. "I thought so." He just looked at her with a puzzled expression. "What? You thought I was dumb? I watch the SyFy channel. I've seen the movies about the end of the world. An EMP was the only thing that fit all of this together into one package." She looked at him with a very serious expression. "The way I figure it is that it is going to be like a barbarian movie, with a zombie movie mixed together with modern weapons thrown into the mix. Am I close to reading this situation right?"

He thought for a moment and said, "Yup, that about covers it." He popped a piece of steak in his mouth, savoring the nourishment.

"What should we do now? What's the next step? I think it's getting out of the city. We need to get away from the little zombies as soon as possible. Because in all the movies, the little stupid zombies die pretty quick and then the big bad zombies come out to play."

He said, "That's about it."

She said, "So, how do we get out of the city? Vehicles don't work anymore. Walking would be insane. The only thing left is bikes."

He was fascinated with the way she worked through all this. The way her mind was right on target. "Yes, that is what I was going to use. Mountain bikes."

She said, "Do you have some place in mind to go to? I don't know of any place around here. My uncle had a hunting camp up north in the mountains, but, that's too far away. Plus, it's winter. There will be snow everywhere soon. That means a person is limited to places that can be reached in a short amount of time." She looked at him intently. "You know, you can jump in anytime with some ideas or suggestions of you own." He laughed real hard at that comment.

"Why should I? You're doing fine on your own." He washed down a bite of potato with his coffee.

She said drily, "Thanks a lot."

He set down his fork and looked at her. "Do you have a place in mind to go?"

She thought for a few moments and then looked up at him sadly. "No. I never believed they could be so stupid as to push the button that would end the world. I guess I gave them credit for being smarter than they are. I don't have any place to go to at all. Not without a vehicle." She looked at him and said, "I probably wouldn't make it even with a vehicle. You know all those little zombies. I don't have a gun. I would have to stop to pee or to sleep sometime and that's when the zombies would get me. It would be inevitable. Every movie I've ever watched shows the stupid, or the tired, or the people without weapons dying first. That will be me."

Preston was deep in thought for a minute. "If you had a place to go to, what would you bring?"

She said, "Whatever I could carry that would be of use for the future. But none of that matters, because if you didn't already have a place stocked with food, it would be useless. There is no way a person could carry enough food for a lifetime on their back. Even if you had vegetable seeds, it still wouldn't matter. There is no way to carry enough food to get through a winter, spring and summer till the vegetables could be planted and then matured enough to eat. And that isn't even taking into consideration all the other things that you would need, like tools and books on how to do things." She was feeling more and more scared as she talked. She had held it together all day long, but now, after really thinking about it, she realized there was no way to survive what was coming. At least not for her. Preston saw the look in her eyes and knew she'd just realized the gravity of the situation. About who would survive and who wouldn't. Possibly. You could be as prepared as anyone could be and still not survive.

He said, "That was really intelligent, the way you worked through this whole situation. That is very surprising coming from someone as young as you are."

She looked puzzled at him and said, "As young as I am? How old do you think I am? Twelve?"

"No, not twelve. You're what, twenty or twenty-one?"

She laughed and said, "It would be nice to go back to that age and do this all over again. I would save every itty bitty scrap of food I could get my hands on. Do I really look that young to you?"

"Yes."

"I'm not sure if I'm supposed to take that as a compliment or an insult. I'll be thirty in January."

A look of shock crossed his features. "Really?"

She said, "Have you ever known a woman to lie about her age to be older than she really is?"

'No, no I haven't," he admitted. *Wow. I should have asked her out months ago.* Then he remembered Sharon was in the bedroom and started to feel a bit guilty. Preston had known for the last month that his relationship with Sharon was going nowhere. He was ready to call it quits with her, but she was living with him and it was his duty and obligation to see to her safety.

Preston said, "I've never been a good judge of a woman's age. I'm sorry if you feel insulted. I didn't intend it to come out that way." In his mind he was thinking that he wouldn't leave Amy here, either. An intelligent woman like her didn't deserve to be abandoned. Besides, Joe had said they would need people to form a small community. Joe wanted more people there with them to share the work of raising food. Well, if she was willing to go, he would bring her. Gladly. He already knew Jane would like her. It was just going to change the situation. Now, he would have two women to look after.

It wouldn't be easy, that was for sure.

He looked at Amy and smiled. Amy just looked at him questionably. He cleared his throat. "I have a place to go to that is stocked with food. I have two really great friends that are there now. We have room and supplies for more people. You are welcome to come with us when we leave if you want to." He waited for her answer.

She looked thoughtful for a few moments., "Yes, I'll come with you. Where is it?"

He said, "It's in Minnesota. I have a retreat there. We'll have to get you a bike. That won't be easy now that all the vehicles are dead. Bikes will be premium possessions now, better than gold or silver. Out of all the situations that Joe and I came up with, we never seriously considered that this would be the one that would bring the world down. We thought that the dollar would collapse and that would cause the world's economy to collapse with it. Then everything would go downhill from there. I guess you could call Joe a survivalist. Me too. We got into this after Joe retired from the Army three years ago. He started to hear some really disturbing things and he started to do research on them. What he found out just blew us away. We realized we were all living in a house of cards and it was about to get blown down by a big evil gust of wind. So, we started to prepare for a collapse of some kind so we could survive. We have just about everything we could think of."

"You're a survivalist?"

"Yes."

"That's a good thing. Right now we're going to need a whole lot of them. If the movies and books have it right, that is the only way mankind will be able to survive to have a future so we don't die off like the dinosaurs," she said. "At least it will provide some sort of a social structure so we can have a future that won't make us go back to the caveman days."

"We can only hope."

He paused for a few moments and then looked at her and asked, "What about your family? Do you have someone that you want to be with?" He was worried that she had family close by and would want to bring them along, too. Protecting the two women was going to be hard enough. He would not add to their numbers. That would be insane right now.

Amy looked down for a few moments, thinking how she really didn't want to admit that she was such a loser that she had no close family or friends that she would want to be with. She worried that he would not want to take her with him if he knew. Should she lie to him? No, she couldn't do that. She dismissed that thought as soon as it entered her head. It was always best to remain honest and truthful. She took a deep breath and then looked back up at him and said, "I don't have any close family anymore. My grandfather raised me after my parents died in a car accident when I was eight. He died when I was twenty. I had a great uncle, too; my grandfather's brother. He died a few years ago. He left his hunting camp near Lake Superior to me in his will. I don't really know any of my father's family. They lived in another state. We didn't visit them very often. We sent Christmas cards, but that is about it. My mother's side of the family lives in England. After my grandmother died, my grandfather and his brother decided to move to America. My mother was four years old then. He never remarried, so she was an only child. So, I really don't have any family left that I would want to see." She had a very sad look on her face now.

He said, "I'm sorry. I don't have any close family left, either." He was greatly relieved that he wouldn't have to explain to her why they couldn't bring anyone else with them. He asked her, "You do understand that this invitation to my retreat is just for you … You don't have any girlfriends or anyone else you would want to bring along, do you?" He wanted to make sure she understood about this.

"No, not really. I have friends, but not anyone I would trust right now. And I can't think of anyone I would want to be with me in a survival situation. They wouldn't be able to understand the seriousness of this situation. I tried to talk to a few of them about survival and preparing, but they didn't want to hear about it at all. They thought I was nuts to even be thinking about stuff like that, even after 9/11 and New Orleans. They just don't understand how anything could happen to them. So, my answer to your question is no, I don't have anyone who would even believe us to want to come along. They will probably think the government will come and save them to the bitter end."

He went over to his desk and pulled out a pad of paper and a pen. He handed it to her and said, "Write down everything you have that we might need that can be carried in backpacks. Only put lightweight items on the list. After a few hours, you will feel like you are carrying around a backpack of rocks. Even with being on a bike instead of walking, your back will hurt. But they won't hurt as much as your shoulders will if they are unaccustomed to carrying a pack."

"I jog every morning with a pack."

"Does it weigh at least twenty-five pounds?"

"No."

He said, "Then you really aren't carrying a real pack. You'll find that out soon enough for yourself." She took the pad and pen from him. She looked thoughtful for a few moments and then started writing. Preston walked away and went down the hall to the bedroom. It was time to wake Sharon up and explain the situation to her. Hopefully, she would be sober by now.

Sharon was still in the same position he had left her in. He walked up to her and shook her shoulder. "Sharon, wake up." Sharon moved and mumbled, but did not wake. He tried again. She yelled, "Get your hands off me, you asshole." He sighed and thought, *This is going to be a very long night.* "Sharon wake up. We have to get ready to leave to go to my retreat. We have to get out of the city before morning."

"I am not going anywhere with you. Why are you still here? I kicked you out, so go. Get your stuff and get out and leave me alone."

"Sharon, this is my apartment," he said.

"I don't care. Get out. I don't want you here. You hurt me. You threatened me with a gun. A gun, for God's sakes, you know I hate guns. You abandoned me today and made me walk home. Nobody does that to me, do you hear me? Nobody. I won't be treated that way by anyone. Do you hear me? Get out or I'm going to call the cops on you. You abused me. I will send you to jail." She reached out and grabbed the phone and put it up to her ear. There still wasn't any dial tone. She threw the phone at him. He dodged it easily. She said, "Leave me alone. I'm going back to sleep. If you're still here in the morning, I will call the cops and have you arrested."

"All right, get some more sleep."

He thought, *Well, there is just no way we're going to be able to leave tonight. How in the hell could he make Sharon understand the seriousness of this situation? They had to leave ASAP. The longer they waited, the harder it was going to be. The longer they stayed here, the more people he was going to have to kill to get them out of the city. How was he going to make her understand that? By tomorrow night, people were going to be aware that this was a complete break down of everything. No police. There would only be people taking what they wanted because they were stronger or had weapons. Amy was right; all the little zombies will be out in force soon. They had to be gone before the big zombies got organized and took over the city.*

He turned towards the dining room table and looked at Amy writing on the pad. "We are not going to be able to get out of here tonight. Sharon won't get up and she's still mad at me. We should get some sleep. Tomorrow we can gather together what we'll take with us. We have to find you a bike. Sharon and I already have one. We'll leave tomorrow night."

Amy looked at him for a long time before saying anything. A million things were flying through her mind. She finally said, "Okay, tomorrow night it will be. How long before the zombies will get to be a real problem, do you think?"

"They're already a problem," he said seriously. They had been hearing gunshots and other loud noises off and on all night.

She said softly, "I was afraid you were going to say that."

Chapter 7

The Best of Plans Have Flaws

"When all's said and done, all roads lead to the same end. So it's not so much which road you take, as how you take it."

Charles de Lint

George Jr. was in his beat up twenty-year-old Chevy truck. It was the only kind of vehicle he could afford. He insisted that he had to have a truck when he went looking to buy his transportation. Trucks were handy for just about anything. They were a lot better than getting some beat up old car. Trucks had class. His dad drove one. Now that he was eighteen and in college, he felt he should make his own decisions about things. The truck was his very first major decision. It would have to last him all through college. After he graduated and had a good job, he could buy a better one. Until then, this would do just fine. He thought for a while on what life would be like after he was an engineer. He imagined all the things he would design and build after he got his degree.

He also thought about college as he drove down the highway. It certainly was different than high school. College seemed to be a world into itself that was not touched much by the outside world. It was a lot harder, too. There really wasn't anyone around to make sure you got up on time to get to class. It was up to you to make sure you did it. And there were a lot of other things you had to make sure you did, too, like laundry and studying. You had to remember what times meals were served, if you got busy doing other things and missed getting there on time, well, it sure wasn't a pretty sight seeing all the leftovers that others had handled and mangled up. He had ended up missing a few meals because he wouldn't touch those leftovers with a hundred foot pole. He shuddered with disgust just thinking about it. Some of those guys he had seen touching the food were real dirt bags. They probably hadn't washed their hands in years. It was a whole lot harder being a grown up than he ever thought it would be.

He smiled just thinking about the first time he did his own laundry. His mother had never taught him how to do it. He thought it couldn't be very hard. People did it all the time. *You just put your clothes into the machine, added some laundry soap and presto, clean clothes, right? What's so hard about that? Any moron could do it.* He laughed at himself. He had bought a new red hooded sweatshirt a few days before he had to do his laundry. Well, he had to. He didn't have anything clean left to wear. He just put all of his clothes into the machines like everyone else. He ended up with pink socks and underwear. He still remembered the shock and outrage he had felt over that. No way was he wearing pink socks and underwear. A girl named Gayle he had a crush on had seen what happened and explained to him about separating the colors and things. She also had him rewash the pink stuff with some bleach. They came out almost perfectly white. A few more times with bleach would do the trick, she told him. He had been so embarrassed over his ignorance.

It seemed everyday brought new things to his attention that he had to make a decision about. It sure was hard being an adult, but it was fun, too. He could go to parties and not have to worry about a curfew anymore. His whole dorm was a party sometimes and there were lots and lots of girls. He had his eye on a pretty blonde named Gayle down the hall from him. She was his dream girl. It had been so nice of her to help him with the problem of his pink underwear and socks.

She hadn't tried to make him feel like a moron for not knowing about separating the colors. He was working up the courage to ask her out. He kept kicking himself for not having the courage to ask her out when she helped him with his pink laundry. He wasn't sure how he would be able to take it if she turned him down. Maybe it would be better if he didn't ruin his dream of her. Maybe he shouldn't ask her out after all. Maybe it was better to just leave things as they were. She did say hi to him when they saw each other in the hall. They also shared a couple of classes. He wasn't sure if she even knew that. He sighed. Sometimes things just seemed so complicated. When he was in high school, if you asked a girl out and she said no, it was no big deal. The guys would rib you about it for a while, but that was it. This was way different. This was the big leagues. If he got shot down now, everyone in the dorm would find out about it. They would label him a stupid loser. He wasn't sure if he was ready to face something like that. He had seen how a few other guys had been treated after they had been shot down. Oh well, he would leave that alone for now and make a decision about it some other time.

He was looking forward to seeing his dad; he hadn't seen him since he started college. His father had come to his high school graduation, and Junior was very glad he had. There had been a few awkward times between his dad, his mom and his stepfather. He chose to spend as much time with his dad as possible; his mom and stepfather hadn't liked that at all. They had made plans for dinner and such after graduation. Well, that was just too bad. They hadn't asked him what his plans were. They just made the plan without consulting him, as usual. His mom always resented the time he spent with his dad. He was glad that his stepfather got transferred to Hawaii. Now they were far enough away that he could breathe. They were always telling him what he was going to do. No asking him what he wanted or anything. Now, they were far enough away that they couldn't call him all the time, either. The time difference definitely worked to his benefit.

Earlier this morning a main water pipe had broken in his dorm and water was everywhere. It had flooded the carpets in the halls before they had been able to get it turned off. What a mess. Some rooms had water a couple of inches deep in them. They closed the whole dorm down. Told the students they had to leave for a week so they could repair it. They were going to have to tear some walls down while doing the repairs. They were afraid that there might be asbestos in the walls. They would have to get someone out to inspect them and everything. They were excused from classes for this week, too. He had called his dad and asked if he could come out and hunt with him since it was bow-hunting season. He thought he would miss out, being in college this year. He had been planning on coming out for Thanksgiving to hunt this year instead. Now, he would be able to do both. He was very happy the way it had worked out. He loved being with his dad.

He saw the road sign for his turn to get to his dad's place. He turned and drove down the two-track dirt road that led to his house. His house was so cool, too. His dad had all this stuff hooked up to be self-sufficient. He loved looking at the systems his dad had rigged up. His dad was really smart. Someday he was going to find out how his dad had done it all. He had been asking him for years and his dad just laughed and said he had done a little of this and a little of that and put it all together to make this. He was curious about how it all worked. He was determined that one day he would find out. He was really curious about why his dad was so mysterious about it all. That made him more determined than ever to find out. He had inherited his love of tinkering with things to see how they worked from his dad. He parked his truck by the garage entrance and turned the engine off. He gathered his stuff and walked to the front door. He set his stuff down and went over to the rock his dad hid the key under. He moved the rock and there was a single key lying there. He picked it up and walked back to the door. His dad had said he would be out on the evening hunt by the time he got here. He had said to go ahead and get comfortable. He would be along as soon as it was dark, unless he got his deer, then he would be back sooner and expect him to help haul it out of the woods. He smiled at that thought. Just like old times. He hoped his dad did get a deer.

He went into his bedroom and set his stuff down on the bed. He grabbed one of his textbooks. He would read while he waited, he didn't want to fall too far behind in his classes. He was engrossed in his book when he heard a key turning in the lock on the door. He closed his book and stood up.

His dad came in with his bow. They hugged and his dad said, "It's good to see you, Junior." Junior was what his dad always called him. It was ridiculous to call him George Junior all the time. Sometimes he called him son, too. Those times just made Junior's day.

Junior said, "Did you see any deer out there?"

"Just one little doe. I'm still waiting for that old monster buck to come by. I saw him just before hunting season opened up. I just haven't figured out what time he is coming through. I'll get him yet."

Junior looked around the living room at all the deer racks his dad had and said, "I bet you do get him."

His dad took off his coat and boots off. "You hungry? I made venison stew and baked some bread for dinner."

"I know, I can smell it, and I peeked in the kitchen at what you had cooking. I'm starved … when can we eat?"

His dad laughed and said, "Boy, you are always hungry. When I know you are coming, I make sure to go into town and stock up on food or you would eat me out of everything with those two hollow legs you have." Junior laughed. It was an old joke between them.

After cleaning up from dinner, he went into the living room and sat down in his favorite chair. It was a chair he had found one day at the Goodwill when they had been browsing around town. He asked his dad if he could have it. It was a recliner like his dad's. After hunting, they would take naps in them. Junior smiled at the memories. He had so many good memories with his dad. He found his dad more interesting than his mom and stepfather. His dad was watching the news.

George Sr. did this everyday at this time. It seemed like the world was going insane. Another city had started to riot and burn things down. *Why are people doing this?* he wondered. What a nightmare. Why would they burn their own neighborhoods down? It all sounded nuts to him. Had the people in these cities contracted some kind of disease or alien virus like in the movies? They sure were acting like it. Maybe it was even something like in the movie, *The Body Snatchers* or something. Maybe they aren't even real people anymore. They sure were acting like something other than human. Maybe they had been turned into animals.

George Sr said, "Things are getting real bad. These people are so stupid. The more they riot, the longer it's going to take to get food to their city. I don't think they even have an intelligent thought in their heads. Look at how they are acting."

"I was just thinking the same thing," Junior replied. "They aren't even acting human anymore. It's like they have some kind of sickness or something that is making them crazy."

His dad sighed. "You're not too far off. They have what is called 'mob fever.' They work themselves up into a frenzy until they start hurting each other and burning things down. Just remember all the things I told you and showed you about surviving. The way things are going, these people may cause some kind of a money collapse that will take our government down with them. The total of rioting cities is well over a hundred now. You still have your bug out bag with you?"

"Yes, Dad, I don't go anywhere without it. I've kept my promise to you."

"Good. Keep it that way. I think this could be it. I can't see how we will recover from all of this. The monetary amount is in the billions now. With the businesses that were destroyed because they couldn't get supplies, the trucking companies going broke, the food distributors going out of business because they can't get their supplies out to the restaurants and what nots, the property damage; the list just goes on and on. If things get bad, Son, in the city where you are going to college, you immediately get into your truck and drive straight here. Okay?"

Junior said, "Count on it, Dad. I'll be up here as soon as possible if anything happens there." Junior was thoughtful for a few moments. "Dad, on the way up here, I saw several fast food places that had signs up saying they were closed until they could get a delivery."

"I was expecting that to happen sooner or later around here. The fast food places are franchises; they only sell the supplies they buy from the franchise company. They can't just go to any store and buy what they need. With the trucking companies going out of business, they might not be able to find anyone who can move the supplies to the places that need them. Just remember what I said, Son. These are dangerous times we're living in."

Junior said, "I won't forget. I have all of that to remind me." He gestured at the TV. "They aren't really talking about any of this at the college. I think that's kind of weird. There has never been as much civil unrest as right now in our country and no one there even mentions it." He was thoughtful for a few moments. "Now that I think of it, it's kind of creepy. In a way, it's like one of those Twilight Zone episodes."

His dad smiled at Junior and said, "Life does seem that way sometimes. I've had a few days that I thought would make a good episode."

They sat for a while, just watching the TV. "People react in strange ways to these kinds of things. Most people just want to stick their heads in the sand like an ostrich and pretend none of this is happening," George Sr said. "They feel that if they don't think about it, it will just go away all by itself. The rest of the people react like they're spectators at the Roman Coliseum. They are panting in anticipation of the next spectacular gory thing that will happen. They cheer for whatever side they are on, too. It will either be for the police and the violence they have to use to try to stop these people that are rioting or for the rioters and the violence they are just plain doing to each other. I think they are sick in the head. This is an awful thing to have happened and you don't hear anyone really wanting it to stop or even do anything to help it to stop. It is completely out of control. Our whole society is really messed up." The telephone rang. His dad got up to go answer it. While he was gone talking on the phone Junior decided to get back to his textbook. He picked it up from where he had set it down earlier and started reading.

They both went straight to bed a little while later. When you get up before the chickens, you tend to go to bed pretty early. In the morning, they were both up and eagerly looking forward to getting to their tree stands. It was a typical hunting day. They had no idea what this day had in store for them. They met back at the fork in the trail at mid-morning, like usual. They ate breakfast and had their nap. They did a few chores around the place. After lunch they decided to go into town. They got into George's truck and drove to town. On the way, they saw a few cars and trucks broken down along the way. That was not unusual enough to capture their attention. George Sr told Junior about the woman he had been seeing in town named Marion that he really liked. Marion's daughter was up visiting her mother this week, too. They were all supposed to get together sometime this week so everyone could meet each other.

As they approached the town, they could see something was wrong. The street was clogged with cars. People were standing around all over the place, talking, shouting, and they could see a fistfight had broken out down the street. Did some kind of accident happen? Something was terribly wrong. The traffic lights were not working. Power was down in the whole town. George inched his way closer to the grocery store. They got out and walked up to the front and saw that the store was closed.

They were walking back to the truck when a woman stopped them and asked, "How come your truck was running?"

"What do you mean?" George Sr asked. The lady explained that all the power in the whole town was out and that the vehicles had stopped working all at the same time. George got a sick feeling in the pit of his stomach. "Do you have on an electronic watch?"

The lady was looking at him strangely, trying to figure out why he wanted to know what time it was when much more important things needed their attention. "I don't know what time it is. My watch stopped working at the same time as everything else. Why do you want to know what time it is? The cars are a more serious problem than what time it is." She stomped angrily away.

George Sr turned around and saw someone trying to steal his truck. He grabbed Junior's arm. "Come on, hurry, someone is trying to steal the truck." They ran back towards the truck as fast as they could. The guy trying to steal it saw them and backed up with his hands spread out in front of him, showing that he was not a threat. He turned around and ran away. "Get in the truck," George said. "Hurry. Lock your door, too." He got in and pushed the lock button.

Junior looked at his dad and asked, "What's wrong? What has happened?"

George Sr looked at Junior hard and said, "This is the worst day of your life. This is the day the whole world will be without power."

"What do you mean the world will be without power?"

"Someone set off an EMP."

Junior stared at his father in shock, then shook his head. "I couldn't have heard you right. Someone was crazy enough to push the button?"

"Yes, that's what I said."

Junior sat silently for a while. He looked at his father and said, "Everything electronic is fried, right?"

"I'm afraid so."

"Shit."

Someone pounded on the driver's side window. They both whipped their heads around to see who it was. It was the mayor. They couldn't make out what he was saying. George rolled down the window an inch and said, "What do you want?"

"That lady over there said your truck is still working," the mayor said. "Is it?"

"Yes, my truck is still working," George replied.

The mayor said, "Get out of the truck. I am taking this truck over."

George and Junior didn't budge. They just stared at him.

The mayor started beating on the window again. "Get out of the truck."

"No."

The mayor's face turned an ugly shade of red. He beat on the window again, then stopped and grabbed a guy who was walking by. "Get the sheriff. I have a job for him."

George and Junior looked at each other in panic; they weren't armed. George started the truck up. The mayor grabbed the door handle and tried to open the door, but it wouldn't budge. He grabbed onto the top of the window so fast his hands were a blur. "Get out of this truck right now!"

"No." George started moving the truck forward. A crowd had appeared around them. He slowly pressed forward.

"I'm not letting go, so stop the truck right now!" the mayor threatened.

George gunned the engine and moved faster. The mayor tried to push the window down. George really gunned the engine and the truck jerked forward. The crowd parted like the Red Sea. Most of them were staring at the mayor like he had lost his mind.

"Let go of my window," George said to the mayor.

It was the mayor's turn to say, "No."

"You have been warned." The truck sped up. "Reach across me and roll up the window. It will cut off the mayor's fingers," George instructed Junior. Junior reached across his dad for the window handle to roll it up, when the mayor let go. They both watched him bounce around and come to a stop with one boot missing. As they rounded the bend in the road, he was blocked from their view.

George Sr cut down a side street that looked pretty empty. He swung the truck around so they could get onto another street. "I'm heading for Marion's to get her and her daughter and bring them with us to the house. It won't be safe here for long." They pulled into Marion's street and stopped at her house. The whole block looked deserted. It was so very quiet. They approached her door; it flew open and Marion looked out at them and smiled.

"Get in here you two, and hurry," she said. "You're letting the cold inside." She stepped back and they entered the house.

George Sr shut and locked the door. Marion looked at him and raised an eyebrow in question. George said, "Marion this is my son, Junior."

Before she could say anything George Sr said, "Where's your daughter?"

"She's downstairs in the basement, getting the wood stove going so we can get the house warmed up. We waited over two hours for the power to come back on and it hasn't yet."

"That's what I wanted to talked to you about. Can you please call your daughter up here?"

"What in the world is going on, George?"

"Just tell her to come up here," he insisted.

Marion could hear the seriousness in his voice. "Okay. Have a seat while I get her." She walked away and went through the doorway into the dining room. George and Junior both sat down and waited silently, thinking of the implications of what happened and what this all meant. They heard both of the women coming, and stood up.

As they came in, Marion's daughter looked at George Sr and said, "What do you need me for? I need to get back down there and get the wood stove going. It's a temperamental beast and it's being real stubborn today." Junior's heart shipped a beat. There standing in front of him was Gayle the girl he a crush on and had helped him with his pink laundry. He said, "Gayle, what are you doing here?"

Gayle looked at him and then his father and said, "I live here. What are you doing here?"

Junior gestured towards his dad and said, "This is my father."

George Sr cut in and said, "You two know each other?" They both answered "yes" at the same time.

George said, "Imagine that. I'm sorry but we don't have time for this right now. Can we all sit down for a minute?" Marion and Gayle shared a puzzled look, then sat down. "We were just in town and things are not going too well there."

Marion said, "What do you mean, George, not going too well?"

George sighed. "Let me tell this as it happened and you can judge for yourself, okay?" They explained all that happened.

Marion starting laughing. "I swear I would've paid a thousand bucks to have seen that arrogant, obnoxious, jerk bouncing around. But George, this will get you in trouble with the law. That jerk of a mayor holds a grudge. He'll probably have you arrested. You'd better go some place and hide out for a while. Oh, you're an outlaw now. I'm dating a bad boy."

"Marion," George said, "please listen to me very carefully. An EMP has been set off and this is the start of the world being without power. This date will remain in everyone's mind for generations to come."

"What do you mean an EMP was set off? What is that exactly?" George explained patiently.

"Someone set off a nuclear bomb here?"

"Yes."

"Where? Where did they set it off at?"

"Over the United States Of America."

"Wait a minute, I'm confused now. How can you set off a nuclear blast all over America and we can still be here alive?" she asked.

"It was a high altitude blast way, way up in the sky. It won't do anything to us except fry the electronics."

Marion sighed. She threw her hand over her heart and said, "What are you trying to do, give me a heart attack? You said a nuclear blast."

"That means a bomb," George said. "It was a bomb."

"But we're still here. How can that be, then?"

"Marion, you watch too many movies. An EMP is made to destroy electronic components only, not to kill people. Indirectly, an EMP going off will eventually be responsible for killing most of the world's population."

Marion laughed again. "George, you're confusing the hell out of me. If it doesn't kill people, how can it kill off most of the world's population?"

"It will happen because the world will become a very dark place. No power, no lights. It's electrical power that keeps everyone in line. It's the light that keeps most of the monsters hiding in the shadows. Without lights, how can we scare away the monsters?"

Marion shook her head and said, "I'm not understanding anything you're saying here."

"Marion, listen to me. You and Gayle go pack a bag and come back to the house with Junior and me. Things are going to get a little out of hand now. Without the police around to help with the monsters, it is going to get very bad for everyone, but, it will be especially bad for women. I know what I'm talking about. I'm retired from the Navy, Marion. I've seen this before."

"But you drove here. How come your truck is working when you said everyone's vehicles won't work? I tried my car earlier and it won't start, just like you said."

She looked at George, awaiting his answer. "My best guess on that is it might have been because my garage is a metal building that is grounded on all four corners or it was the hilly terrain that stopped the blast affects from reaching my garage. I'm not really sure."

"What does that mean? You are guessing at this?"

George sighed again deeply and said, "Okay Marion, I'll start over and try to help you understand what this entire situation means."

****

Tim was jogging down the road that led to town. The angry rhythm of his feet hitting the pavement echoed loudly in his ears. He knew that his old chief was responsible for this mess. He vowed to get even with him. He would do whatever it took. He wanted him dead for everything he had done. His feet seemed to echo dead, dead, dead, with each step. He started thinking of his favorite daydream. He walked up behind his old chief and turned him around quickly and slammed his fist into his face, making him fall to the ground. He would jump down and straddle him and put his hands around that bastard's neck and squeeze as hard as he could. He would watch until he saw the fear in his eyes as he realized who it was doing this to him. He would laugh and tell him, "I told you I would kill you, you bastard."

He could feel the delicious sensation of having the power of life and death over someone. When you take someone's life you realize that you are a God. He laughed again, thinking, "Yeah, I'm the reaper God of death." He got close to town and noticed all the cars clogging the roads. The stoplights weren't working. He began to wonder if they had lost power, too. He headed down the street and was just about to turn the corner and go to the repair garage when he noticed that three guys were dragging the mayor between two cars. The mayor looked like he had been dragged behind a horse or something. One boot was missing and he was screaming. He couldn't make out what he was screaming about. Everything looked strange. There were people standing around huddled by each other in groups. He wondered idly what could have happened as he headed to the garage.

When he arrived, the door was locked. He knocked and called for Wayne. He couldn't see or hear anyone inside the building. He was really getting curious now about what could have happened that Wayne wasn't there, but his tow truck was. Tim was going to explain to him about what happened, and he could come see for himself that the vehicles were not starting. It just might save his brother Phil's job. He at least owed Phil that after the way he jumped him this morning. He felt a little bad about turning on his brother like he had before he left. But Phil just didn't understand what happened wasn't his fault, and that stupid chief was responsible for the mess his life was in these days. That girl had asked for it. Everyone said so. Everyone except his chief and the officers. Of course, they had a holier than thou attitude. Their word was law and anything anyone else said was a lie, no matter what. They didn't believe him that she asked for it. They were just useless assholes, anyway.

He walked over to Main Street and looked around to see if there was someone he could ask about Wayne's whereabouts. He decided to go to the courthouse to find out what had happened. Everyone was looking pretty bewildered and confused. *What was up with that? And why were all the cars just left like that everywhere?* Whatever happened must have been pretty big to cause such a reaction.

He was a block from the courthouse when he spotted a guy he had gone to school with. He hurried up to him. "Hey, Brian. What happened?"

Brian turned to look at him. "Hey Tim, how are you?"

"I'm fine. Do you know what happened?"

"I'm not really sure. Everyone is saying we were hit with an EMP and that's why nothing is working. I'm on my way to the courthouse to find out what they know about all of this."

"Do you mind if I come with you?" Tim asked. "I was on my way there myself to see what happened."

"Of course, I don't mind. Do you know anything about EMPs and what this means?"

"If we were hit with an EMP," Tim said, "we're screwed, completely and truly screwed."

"What do you mean?" Brian asked.

Tim explained what he knew about EMPs. "Like I said, we'll be screwed."

Brian looked shocked. "How long until they can fix it all and get everything working again?"

Tim said, "I don't know. But it won't happen quickly, that's for sure. Do you realize what they would have to do to fix everything in the whole country?"

"That would take about fifty years," Brian said. "So, what do we do now? How do we get to work and home and everything?" He started panting and looked like he was going to pass out.

Tim grabbed him and shook him a few times. "Brian, get a hold of yourself. You had better get what you need right now in town and get home with it before everybody else takes everything and you're left with nothing of value to survive with." Tim turned around and said, "I've got to get home right now." He took off running.

Brian called after him, but he ignored him. The implications of the situation were starting to dawn on him, too.

Tim saw the sporting goods store up ahead. He ran along the building and around the side to the back. He looked around. He tried the handle on the back door. It was locked. He looked around again. Still no one around. He stepped back and raised his foot. He aimed to kick the door beside the door handle to break the lock. The door swung inward. He waited a minute to see if anyone was coming to investigate the noise he made. He saw no one. He went inside. He knew no one was inside the store. He saw how empty it was as he passed by on his way to the back. He went straight to the backpacks. He picked out as big a one as he could find. He went over to the counter where the ammo and guns were kept. He broke the glass and reached inside and grabbed all the ammo that was there. He made sure to take only the boxes that they had guns for. He next ran around the store and threw this in here and that in over there. A little bit of everything he thought might be useful. They could come back and take the rest of the stuff later. He put the backpack on and looked out the back door. All clear. He stepped out and pulled the door closed as far as it would go, then took off running. He had to get home and explain the situation to his pa and brothers. They had things to do to assure their survival. He smiled. This was a golden opportunity to take out that bastard, Johnson. *Oh yeah*, he thought. A plan was forming in his mind. *I will get you and your place, too.* He laughed and ran faster, knowing this was the best thing that could have happened for him.

****

"And that is the situation we are in, Marion," finished George. "Now, will you please get some things together so we can leave before things get even crazier out there?"

Marion smiled at George. "I thank you for your concern, but we will be fine here. My family has never run from trouble, not ever. I'm not going to start now. We stick like glue and don't let trouble make up our minds for us. My family survived the Civil War and stuck together. We will stick together now, too. I will not just run off and abandon my house to whatever might happen. *Might* happen, George. You don't even know for sure if it was an EMP or not. I will not leave, absolutely not." She stamped her foot and glared at him. "I've made up my mind and that is that. There is nothing that you can say that will make me change my mind, either. I can't even believe you would suggest such a thing to me. If we have hard times coming now, my place is here in town. I will be needed here to help with this emergency, whether this is an EMP thing or not. You expect me to just abandon my friends and neighbors? I can't do that. I will not do that. I can't believe you are selfish enough to even suggest that I abandon everyone and save myself and Gayle. That would be a horrible thing to do. I am a Christian woman and I will not abandon anyone who may need my help. I will thank you to get out of my house now!" she yelled at him. She pointed to the door. "Get out!"

Junior and Gayle had sat through this whole conversation between their parents and just looked back and forth as each of them spoke. Now they looked at each other. Gayle just shrugged her shoulders at him and said, "She's my mother."

Junior looked at his dad. "Dad, you can't just leave them here."

George looked at his son, and then at Gayle. He finally said, "Gayle, the invitation is open to you, too. I hope you come with us now." Gayle looked at her mother standing there and saw how angry she was.

She sighed and said, "Thank you, George. That is very kind of you to invite me after the way my mother's treating you. I can see that you have her welfare and safety in mind and that you care what happens to her. But she is my mother and I can't just leave her here." She turned to her mother. "I say we should go with George and Junior."

Marion huffed out, "Absolutely not. We are staying here together. We will help our community through whatever crisis this is. We will never abandon our friends and neighbors." She glared at George. "I told you to get out of my house. I mean it. Go. "

He turned to Gayle and started to open his mouth to tell her to be careful when she jumped up and said, "I'll walk you out to your truck. You're lucky your vehicle still works." She walked over to the coat rack and grabbed her coat and scarf and went out the door. Junior looked at Marion and his dad, and then followed her outside.

Gayle was pulling her gloves on as he walked up to her. He didn't quite know what to say or do. He looked earnestly at her and said, "Gayle, this is a very serious thing that happened.

You both are not safe here. It was really bad when we were in the middle of town and it's going to get worse."

Gayle sighed. "Don't worry, I'll work on changing my mother's mind. Why don't you see if you can talk your dad into coming back in a few days? I'm going to wear her down. I'll be relentless in my pursuit to change her mind. I've seen all those end of the world movies, too, you know. I have a basic idea of how this could play out. The whole world will be murder, rape and mayhem, with everyone running around, gathering up as much food and supplies as they can. I can't believe it just yet. It seems like a nightmare that you know you might have, but it hasn't caught up with you yet. Sorry, I'm so shook up I'm not even making sense." She gave a nervous laugh.

"Don't worry about it," Junior said. "It does seem unreal, like a bad movie or something." He paused and looked at her intently. "Gayle, I'm really worried. Believe my dad. He has never been wrong about what the military or government will do. He's told me many times how situations will play out about things you see on the news and the internet. He was always right."

George walked out the door and saw Junior and Gayle talking. He headed straight for the truck, got in, and shut the door. Junior nodded to Gayle. "I have to go now. Take care. I or my dad will be back in a few days, if we can, to check on you." Junior walked over to the truck and got in. George started the truck and drove down the street. "Were you able to change her mind at all?" he asked.

His dad sighed. "No. She's a very stubborn woman. She says I'm overreacting and I'm an unfeeling, cold, heartless bastard to abandon everyone. I asked her how I can be both at the same time and she just screamed at me to get out."

"Don't worry, Dad," Junior said. "Gayle said she's going to work on changing her mind. Gayle seems to be very determined. She asked me if we could come back in a few days. She feels certain that she can change Marion's mind about this."

His dad said, "I'm glad Gayle is optimistic, because I'm not. I really don't think she can change her mind. This situation that we're in will change every single person on this planet. No one will get by without seeing, hearing or feeling something horrible at one time or another. It will affect us all. It will cause us to think differently, to react differently than we have ever had to before."

They drove in the back way this time. His dad stopped the truck and turned off the engine.

There were noises coming from the front of the place. It sounded like they were trying to be real quiet. There was some whispering, but they couldn't make out what was being said. George said quietly, "We'll go in through the garage and see what's what." Junior followed his dad and did everything exactly like he did. His dad stopped at some shelves and gently pulled them out towards himself. He then reached back and worked the paneling out and set it aside. He reached inside and removed two SKS rifles, two chest pouches and two ammo cans. He handed one of each to Junior, then whispered into Junior's ear, "Chest pouches have two hundred rounds for stripper clips, ammo boxes have sixteen hundred rounds." Junior was surprised. He hadn't known there was a secret hiding-hole in the garage. His dad looked at him seriously, then bent over and whispered in his ear again, "We may have to kill whoever it is out there. We'll give them the chance to leave peacefully, but don't count on it. Do you remember how to use the stripper clips?" Junior nodded yes.

"Load up your clips and put ten rounds in the rifle." They both got busy getting everything ready. George Sr could see how nervous and alarmed Junior was, so he leaned over and whispered, "I got these two as back ups at a gun show in the 1990s. I paid only $79.99 for each of them."

Junior gave him a nervous smile and whispered, "I'm impressed."

"We can't let them get in the house and seal it up. Even I couldn't get in if someone did that. We would be left out here in the cold with no real supplies. You do understand why we have to stop them, don't you?"

Junior nodded yes.

His dad smiled at him. "You do remember how to use an SKS?"

Junior smiled more easily and whispered, "Of course, they are a blast to shoot."

His dad reached into his chest pouch and pulled out the camo face paint and started applying it to his face. He motioned for Junior to apply some to his face, too.

Junior whispered, "Why are we using face paint?"

"So we can sneak up real close before they will be able to notice us."

Junior nodded and started applying the paint to his face too. "What's the plan?"

"You need to get higher than me so you can cover me. I need you to sneak up to next year's wood stack. You remember where I cut that maple down on the little hill?"

Junior nodded yes.

His dad continued, "Get behind the stack and put the gun over the top of it. It will help you keep it steady. That should give you a clear view of the area, too. I'll come up on the left side down in the low area. If this turns into a shooting match, don't hesitate at all and aim for the center mass of each target. Okay?"

Junior nodded yes.

His dad reached out and put his hand on his shoulder and gave it a squeeze. He whispered, "Son, if anything happens to me, the keys are under the front tire of the truck. You get in the house and shut it down tight. Don't come out for six months. The main chaos will be over by then. I left the manual for the house in my desk drawer. It will explain everything to you about all the systems of the house."

He looked around and listened for a moment. He smiled and whispered, "They're sure having a hard time getting in, aren't they? Now, when you hear me yell out that you are covered by five guys, I want you to shoot in front of one of them. Hit the dirt. That will be their one and only warning. If it goes bad out there, put them down just like you do a deer. Hopefully, we can convince them to move on without bloodshed. I'm going to go take a look out the window. Stay here. I'll be right back." His dad moved silently to the window. He stood with his back to the wall. He slowly turned around and peeked out. He drew back and waited for a reaction. After a minute, he decided that they hadn't seen him. He came back over to where Junior was and squatted down.

"Do you think they saw you?"

His dad shook his head no. "The sun is shining right into their faces. I would've looked like a shadow if they saw me at all. There are three men out there trying very hard to get in the house. Let's go ruin their day and make a statement that they definitely picked the wrong place to try to break into." They quietly left the garage. George Sr relocked the door.

They both snuck into their positions. George hid behind a large rock that was fifty yards from the front door. He looked up at where his son should be. He could just make out the tip of the barrel on top of the woodpile. *Good, he got there safely.* One of them was trying to kick the door in. The other two were standing back and talking quietly. He couldn't make out what they were saying. All three of them were armed and had hunting knives in a sheath on their belts. These guys were serious. This wasn't a normal break-in, either. They wanted in very badly. What could they possible want all the way out here? He started to get an uneasy feeling about all of this. *Shit,* thought George. *I should have left Junior at Marion's.* He wasn't ready for the big time just yet.

The guy at the door was getting pissed. He was screaming and yelling and cussing up a storm like some demented, insane creature. That made George smile. If he were alone, he would've just stayed hidden in the woods until they gave up and left. But Junior was here and he didn't know if he would be able to handle the pressure of staying in that position for hours without knowing where his dad was, or even if he could stay still for that long without giving himself away. Better not take the chance of losing his son. That was one thing he couldn't live with. Just thinking about it brought a cold shiver down his spine. He slowly moved a little closer around the rock to see if he could hear what they were saying.

The guy trying to kick the door down was screaming at the top of his lungs, "You son of a bitch, open this door!" He turned to the other two and said, "This isn't Fort Knox, you know. Why the hell doesn't this door open?" He motioned to the other two guys. "Get over here and help me kick this door down. Get over here." The other two hesitated. The first guy screamed at them, "Now!" They hurried over.

Man, that guy is really pissed. George was quite pleased with the way his defenses had held up. He sighed. It was time to end this nonsense. He stepped around the rock and yelled, "Freeze! Turn around." They abruptly stopped what they were doing and whipped their heads around to look at him. They didn't move. He repeated, "Turn around slowly and keep your hands away from your sides. If you don't move slowly, I might mistake that for a move to go for a weapon. You three don't want me to think that, do you?" All three of them had long hair. Two of them had their hair tied at the back of their necks. The third one's hair was all over the place. His hair was covering most of his face and clung in sweaty clumps. It was hard to see what he looked like.

George Sr said again, "I won't tell you again, so you had better comply this time or your blood will be soaking into the dirt by my front door. Turn around slowly. Keep your hands out away from your body. You're covered by five guns." A shot rang out and the dirt kicked up in front of the one in the middle. They turned around slowly. George said, "Turn your weapons around to face you and slowly lay them down on the ground."

What happened next is hard to explain, it happened so very fast. A woman stepped out from the woods ten feet from George and said, "Drop the gun, old man." She was holding a Ruger 10-22 on him.

George wanted to laugh. He replied, "Your friends will be let go just as soon as they place their weapons on the ground. Young lady, put that gun down before someone gets hurt."

"Shoot that son of a bitch Carol, right now!" yelled the punk on the left. He lunged forward onto his left shoulder, reaching under his coat.

George was already swinging his rifle towards the young lady and didn't see him lunge forward. Junior, up on the hill, couldn't see what the guy was doing because the other two blocked his view.

Damn, George thought. He didn't want to shoot a woman. He felt a tug on his jacket and a 40 SW slug caught him under the right arm. He didn't feel any real pain. It was more like a stinging, burning sensation. He turned his head and saw the handgun in the hand of the guy on the left. Before he could react to the new threat, the young lady started firing at him. He quickly dropped her with a double tap. He turned back toward the thugs. The one on the ground kept firing at him and yelling, "I told you I would kill you!"

He felt like he was in a dark void. The only thing he could see was the SW semi-automatic kicking up as the thug shot at him. He felt another hit and a stinging, burning sensation in his stomach. Why didn't he shoot? His finger was on the trigger wasn't it? Then he realized that he was shooting. He got the thug on the left, the one that kept yelling something at him about killing him. He shot him twice in the chest. He aimed at the next one and his vision started to blur. He wasn't sure if he got that one at all. He could feel something warm and wet running down his right side. The other two were scrambling around, trying to aim their guns. *Why wasn't Junior shooting? Oh my God, what happened to Junior?* Then he saw the dirt kick up behind one of the thugs. *Junior. Thank you, God.* He was all right. He had to drop those two fast before they could get to Junior. He tried to raise his rifle up to aim at the two thugs, but his arm wouldn't move. Everything felt like it happened in slow motion. Why was he moving so slowly? He fell to the ground and never even realized it. He looked at the sky and thought what a beautiful day it was. His last thought was, *Oh God, Junior, I failed you*. He saw the darkness closing in.

Junior was shocked when his dad fell. Rage built in him until he couldn't breathe. The second guy that his dad had shot at and missed when he fell to the ground fired at him, sending splinters flying all around in the air in front of him. That broke him from his rigid shock. He quickly swung the rifle at the guy that shot at him and fired one shot. The guy went down. His rage kept building until he felt it would fill the whole world. He let loose a bellow of rage, a primal instinct in him that he thought he could never feel. He spotted the other guy running for the hills. He started pouring lead in his direction. He fired four shots. Three of them hit his center mass and he went down. His breach locked open. He bent down by the woodpile and reloaded the stripper clip. The click, click, click of it sounded very loud to him. When he had the last one in, he yanked back hard on the lever and let it go. The bolt slammed forward, putting a fresh round in the chamber. He popped backed up, swinging the rifle and looking for threats.

He strained his ears to hear every sound that was out there, but all he could hear was moans. He ran down the hill and over to his dad. He lay motionless. He felt for a pulse. It was very faint. He was still breathing. One of the intruders moaned. If these four assholes hadn't showed up, he and his dad would be locked together in the house. They would have been safe from killers like them. His rage built until he couldn't contain it anymore.

He stood up and calmly, deliberately, walked over to each of the killers and shot them in the head. He looked at the woman who had shot at his dad and caused him to be hit. She was coughing up pink foaming blood. That was good, it was a lung shot. He walked over to her and kicked her rifle away. "I hope you suffer a long, painful death, bitch," he screamed at her. He could hear her straining for a breath.

Junior ran back over to his dad and checked his pulse. It was still faint, but it was there. He was still breathing. "Hang on, Dad. I'm going to get the truck to take you to the hospital. I'll be right back." He took off running. He grabbed the keys from under the wheel and jumped in. He had it started almost before he was all the way inside. The door was still open when he put it gear and took off. The door swung closed. He drove over the intruder that he had shot running away. He didn't even give it a conscious thought. He pulled up next to his dad and jumped out. Junior picked him up and raced to the other side to put him in the passenger seat. He got the door open and set his dad on the seat. That's when he saw the blood. It was everywhere. Both of his hands were colored red. His dad wasn't breathing. Quickly, Junior felt for a pulse. Nothing. He tried again. Still nothing. He stood there and stared at his bloody hands. His dad was dead. He was all alone. His legs gave out and he slid to the ground. Tears leaked from his eyes. *When did I start crying?* he wondered. He held his head in hands, feeling so very lost. The full impact of what had just happened hit him then. The world was coming to an end. His dad was dead. What was he supposed to do now? He was in a very dark, lonely cold place and just wanted to let go of all the confusion and pain he was feeling.

Many hours later, after darkness had long since fallen, he stirred. He stood up and walked like a zombie to the front door. Oh right, the keys were in the ignition of the truck. He slowly walked back to get them. He saw his dad's body and started to cry again. Great wracking sobs shook his whole body. He grabbed for the keys and kept missing them. Finally, he grasped them in his hand and stumbled to the front door. He had a hard time seeing the keyhole through the blur of his tears. He couldn't seem to get the key to go into the door handle. He threw the keys down in frustration and started to kick the door and beat on it with his fists. He was screaming and beating on the door until he could hardly feel his hands. He lost his balance and fell down when he tried once more to kick the door. Junior just lay there, staring at the sky. He really didn't notice the stars or the moon or anything else. He just lay there in misery, staring at nothing, lost inside himself.

Junior regained awareness a lot later that night and realized he was lying on the ground. He rolled over slowly and got to his feet. He looked around for the keys and saw them next to the rock that his dad had placed a key under just two days before so he could let himself into the house. He reached down to grab them and had a hard time getting his fingers to close around them they were very swollen and stiff. After several attempts, he was able to snag them. He stumbled once again to the door. This time the key went right into the lock. He had difficulty turning the key to open the door. His fingers were so swollen and numb he couldn't feel them. He just kept applying pressure downward and eventually he heard the lock click open.

He pushed on the door with his shoulder and stumbled inside. He looked around for a few minutes in the dark and kicked the door shut, then walked into the kitchen. He knew where everything was in the house. He reached up above the refrigerator to the cupboard and fumbled around, trying to grab the bottle of Canadian Mist. His fingers weren't cooperating, and the bottle started falling out of the cupboard. He caught it and pressed it to his chest, holding it very tight. This was all that there was right now. Nothing else mattered. He dragged his body to the living room and sat down on the couch. He opened the bottle with his teeth. His fingers were too swollen and would barely move. He held the bottle up with his palms and took a long, deep drink. When he brought the bottle down to rest on his lap, he noticed his dad's recliner. He sat in the dark just staring at the empty chair.

Chapter 8

Silent Game Getter

"It is not the critic who counts; but the man in the arena; who knows the great enthusiasm, the great devotion, who spends himself in a worthy cause, who at the best knows in the end the triumph of high achievement and who at the worst, if he fails, at least he fails while daring greatly. So that his place shall never be with those cold and timid souls who know neither victory nor defeat."

American President Theodore Roosevelt

Eric and Mark just stood there, looking around. The scene before them stunned them into absolute silence. It was straight out of any zombie movie they had ever seen. Nothing in life had ever prepared them for something like this. Movies are a fantasy of someone's imagination, not reality. They exchanged a shocked look. Finally, they were able to take a breath. Many a night they had sat up, discussing what the end of the world would be like.

They tried very hard to be reasonable and practical about their expectations of what it could be. They both had come to the conclusion that they would have plenty of time to get to the retreat. People would not react as fast as they would. People would not understand what the event, whatever it was, meant. With everyone being confused about whatever had happened, they figured they would be able to get safely away before the realization of the situation became apparent. At the first sign of trouble, they would head straight to the retreat. They would get the retreat secured and that would be that.

And now here they were, days later, looking at the zombie movie scene. They both thought of what they had been through to get to this point. All the things that had happened and all the horrible things that they had seen went through their minds like a slide show. The future looked mighty dim. They were still a long way from the retreat. Mark hadn't said anything to Eric, but he was really worried about their ammo situation. After their very first firefight, they were down by twenty-five. He had one hundred and three bullets left for the 30-30, and Eric had sixty-seven shotgun shells left for his 12 gauge.

They were going to have to avoid people and shootouts as much as possible. Not that they were looking for any situations like that, but now it was a top priority to avoid them at all costs. Well, not at the cost of their lives, but just about anything else. If they ran out of ammo, they would be dead meat, literally, no question about it. This scene proved it beyond a shadow of a doubt. There were some people walking around in a daze. A lot of them were just staring straight ahead. Most didn't even notice Mark and Eric at all. They just looked right through them. It was down right creepy. No one spoke. They just stared at nothing. It was like these people were dolls or mannequins or something not alive. It sent a chill up their spines. Bonfires and cars were burning. Up ahead, they could hear some yelling and screaming by a large bonfire.

They stayed about five paces apart. They staggered apart to make themselves harder targets to hit. They were disciplined and had practiced this many times. They stayed in the shadows as much as possible, trying to avoid getting to close to anyone. No telling how people would react when they encountered them. They had already witnessed many scenes straight from hell. This was a very uncertain world now.

Eric was in the lead when he stopped abruptly and looked at the overpass ahead. His spidey senses were tingling. He smiled, thinking of a moment in the Spiderman movie. What he felt was kind of like that. He had learned years ago to listen to his senses, but he had learned to pay special attention to this kind of a danger tingle. He moved over to the ditch and used hand signals to Mark to indicate what he was doing. When Mark reached him, they both bent down, looking all around.

Mark asked, "What's up?"

"Not sure. But something doesn't feel right." Eric looked around for a minute. "We should cut out into the field and go up on the hill over there, then cross the road. This side doesn't have enough cover for us."

"All I can see is the bonfire there with punks hanging out, being stupid. They're just punks acting like they have the situation under control."

"We can't afford to fight too many battles," Eric said. "We can't keep getting lucky. It's better to be safe than sorry." Mark nodded his head in agreement. They made their way about a hundred yards from the highway out into the field. They started slowly towards the hill. They paused when they reached it, straining their ears to hear any sounds that they could. They strained their eyes, trying to see anything that represented danger of any kind. When they reached the top, they stopped and did the same thing again. There had to be something that gave Eric a sense of danger. Nothing. There was nothing unusual at all.

One at a time they crossed the road. Like a well-oiled machine, each man knew what to do. The point man ran across the road first, while the remaining man covered him. Once the point man had reached the other side and taken cover, he was ready to provide fire support for the remaining man to come across the road. They made it across without a problem. They stayed low and headed out into the field. When they had gone about a quarter mile, they swung back to the highway. Mark sighed, thinking, *It is going to take forever to get to the retreat if we have to keep doing things like this.* But he reminded himself it was better than walking into a trap. They had seen the evidence of others that had. It had been pretty bad. They walked in the darkness, trying to get as far as possible before the sun started to rise. The darkness was their cover, concealing them from curious eyes. The real problem was the bad guys used the darkness as cover, too.

Sunrise was near. They stopped to find a safe concealed place to hole up during the daylight hours. They walked about a quarter of a mile from the highway into the shrubs and low bushes, looking for just the right spot. They found it. They both would fit comfortably. It had a place they could climb into and be concealed from prying eyes. One thing they had decided when they made their plans to walk to the retreat was that they would make sure to get enough rest so they could stay alert and not have tired, sluggish minds and bodies for their trek. They had to be able to think quickly on their feet. Each night brought more and more situations that needed fast thinking, stealth movements, and reactions. Even though it was going to make it a very long trip with each of them sleeping a good five to six hours a day, it would be worth it if they could reach there in relativity good physical shape. Their only real concern was food. They weren't carrying enough to make it up there.

They quickly made camp. As the sun got higher in the sky, they made a small fire. A fire was harder to detect when the sun was brighter. The brush also helped conceal it. Besides, there were so many fires burning everywhere, no one would pay attention to one more. They made oatmeal and coffee. Mark put the rest of the leftover coffee into a thermos for the rest of the day. It was Eric's turn to sleep first while Mark was the guard. Mark got comfortable against a large shrub and Eric settled down to sleep. He reached into his backpack and took out his journal. He was writing everything down that happened so he had a detailed account of events. He wanted the future generations to know what this situation really was like. Mark felt they had a right to know exactly what it was like out here now. He wanted them to understand the chaos, the confusion, and helplessness that everyone felt when they realized no help was coming. *We were all on our own now. It was up to each and every one of us to make this a livable, workable situation or a living hell.* He realized that the old sayings of only the strong survive or that it was the survival of the fittest were not quite right after all. It was the smart ones that had good equipment and could think fast on their feet that were going to survive. At least, it seemed that way to him after going through so many bad situations already, and the trek to the retreat was just beginning.

After five days of travel they were getting concerned about their food supplies. Reducing their portions to half rations would make the food last longer, but leave them vulnerable. That was something they had to avoid at all costs. Every day more and more dangerous situations developed. The bad guys were banding together to form large gangs that could afford to be bolder. It was a game of playing king of the hill, only more deadly. The losers didn't survive for long. Like rabid dogs, the pack would turn on the weak. They had seen this up close and personal. The loser of one of those takeovers almost ran into them while they were hiding in the bushes. Mark and Eric's hearts leaped up into their throats and the adrenaline was pumping through their veins so loud they could feel it. When the bad guys finally tackled the loser, they were close enough to reach out and touch. They dragged him away. It was a horrible sight to see. The thing that was hard to grasp was the savage way they seemed to enjoy it. It was plain to see that every single one of them got off on it, too. In many ways it was like watching a movie or playing a video game. Mark and Eric decided they would take out as many of these psychos as possible if they could. They didn't deserve to live. They forfeited that right as soon as they started killing with such gleefulness and malicious aforethought. They weren't killing to defend themselves or property, they killed because it gave them a thrill. That realization sent a primal chill down their spines.

They had settled in a concealed place for the day and Eric was on first watch this time. He was thinking about their food situation and decided they needed to find some place farther away from the road to hole up in for a couple of days so they could hunt some meat. It couldn't be helped that they were going to get way behind schedule to do it. They needed food. He would discuss this with Mark when he awoke. Eric was leaning against the branch of a pretty large shrub contemplating the food situation when he heard a twig snap. He looked over at Mark. He was still asleep and hadn't heard it. He looked all around their concealed spot, trying to see what was out there. He had a clear view of three sides. The brush behind them was really thick and he didn't think anything could come at them from that way. He could feel that something was out there. He held the shotgun in his lap so it would be ready if he needed it.

He strained his ears to hear any little sound. Then he heard what sounded like two steps, then silence. He looked around frantically to see what or who was sneaking up to them. His breath panted in and out in his desperate attempt to see. Finally, he realized that the sound was coming from behind him. There were two more footsteps. Someone was out there for sure. He waited for a clue to alert him to this person's intentions. He could hear nothing. *What the heck? This person really knows how to come in real slow and quiet-like.* It made the hair on the back of his neck stand straight up. This was someone smart and dangerous. He brought the shotgun up higher. Steady steps headed right for them. He slowly turned his head so as not to alert anyone to his presence. He finally turned far enough around to be able to see in the direction the footsteps were coming from. Peering around the bush, he spotted what had been stalking them. It was a doe sneaking along a trail in the ditch below them. He smiled, relieved that it hadn't been a person coming after them for their stuff.

He raised the shotgun up took aim at the deer. He clicked the safety off as quietly as he could. It made a small click, just loud enough to spook the doe. The last he saw of her was her white tail flashing as she ran out of sight at warp speed. *Oh well, at least I tried*, he thought. He sighed. It would not be good to make that much noise and alert anyone in the area that they were there, anyway. It was better to keep a low profile. He felt bad about spooking the deer and missing a chance to get more food. They really needed to think about some way to stock up before their situation turned critical. He thought about that for a while. *How do you get food and not make noise that alerts others of your presence? How can it be done so you don't spook the deer, too?*

It finally hit him right between the eyes and he softly smacked himself. *How could I be so stupid to forget? Oh yeah, I know how to get that deer.* He quickly pulled his pack over and pulled out his Emergency Snare Kit. He opened it up and took out one of the camlock snares. They could be used as an Emergency Deer Snare. He quietly snuck down the trail to a narrowed area. That was the best spot. He quickly set the snare up and placed a large stick slanted up above the snare. That would ensure that the next deer would duck their head down under the stick and walk right into the snare. The deer wouldn't see the trap because it blended right into the surroundings. Hopefully, they would have fresh meat to eat tonight. He quickly made his way back up to their camp to await the results of his efforts. He had been gone a total of two minutes. Why take the chance of giving away their position to others if he didn't have to? The snare would work silently and effectively to take down that deer. No one in the area would even know anything about it.

He was thankful he had run across that "Buckshot" guy on the internet. He knew what he was talking about. Every time Mark or he had researched survival stuff, they kept coming across references to him. They started reading his articles. It taught them both a lot about getting food quietly and with equipment that would work for them 24/7. This method was silent and he didn't waste valuable calories while doing it.

About an hour later he was sitting in his lookout spot enjoying the sun when he heard a lot of thrashing around. He looked over towards where it was coming from; he could see a deer caught in the snare. The deer was twisting around and its legs gave out. There were a couple of more kicks, and then it lay still. By the time he got over to it, the deer was lying still with the snare around its neck. It was dead. *Oh my God*, he thought. He had no idea snares were so effective. They were more effective than hunting. That had just been proven to him. He was so very thankful he had learned this life saving skill. He had watched Buckshot's Survival Snaring DVD and learned how to set the snare properly. The deer did exactly what he said it would do. He smiled and his heart filled with relief. The food crisis was over. The deer should last them until they reached the retreat.

He walked back up to their camp. He shook Mark's shoulder. Mark sat up real fast, looking around.

"Relax," Eric said. "I woke you up so you could help me drag a deer back here. Our food crisis is over. We'll be eating real food. We're having fresh venison steaks today." He smiled hugely at Mark.

Mark blinked at him a few times trying to make sense of what Eric had said. "How did you get a deer? I didn't hear any shots. I wasn't that deep asleep. I would have heard if there were any shots." All of a sudden Mark's brain went into high gear. He tried to get out of the sleeping bag too quickly and all he did was tangle himself up in it and the zipper got stuck. He looked frantically at Eric. "Eric, we agreed not to make any noise when the other one was asleep. We have to move right now. Someone will be coming to investigate the shots you fired. How far away were you?"

Eric was busy pouring Mark a cup of coffee from the thermos. He turned to him and said, "I told you to relax. I did it silently. No one heard a thing." Eric handed Mark the cup of coffee.

Mark took it and gulped down a big swallow. Mark was totally confused now. *How did Eric kill a deer silently? Did he jump on the back of a deer and slit it's throat or something? Like you see in the movies? How in the hell did he do that? No way,* he thought. He looked hard at Eric and tried to figure out how he could possibly take that deer silently and not have blood all over him. Finally he asked, "How in the world did you take it silently? This I have to hear." Eric explained all that he did. Mark looked at Eric incredibly and said, "No shit? It really works just like the DVD said?

"Yup, exactly like it said."

Mark finally got himself out of the sleeping bag. They went down the trail to the deer. Mark gutted it. They dragged the deer about a hundred yards away from their camp. They put a slit in each tendon of the back legs of the deer. They lifted it up and tied each leg to a large branch to hold the deer up off the ground. They skinned it together. They decided to eat the heart and liver first to celebrate. Mark told Eric, "Good job. Now we'll have enough food to make it to the retreat."

"We have to stay here an extra day to dry the meat to preserve it for the trip," Eric said.

"You mean after we stuff ourselves full a few times, don't you?" Mark replied with a laugh.

Eric joined him in a quiet laugh and said, "Most definitely, that is what I meant." After being on the road for over a week they were ready for some fresh food and rest.

Mark busied himself with making a small fire to cook up the heart and liver. Eric started making a woodland smoker to dry the meat with. He had learned how in Buckshot's Wilderness Survival DVD Volume 3. He made a teepee-style smoker with branches about six feet around and about six feet tall. He then covered the outside with long grass he cut with his knife, along with leaves and weeds. He interwove branches that circled the teepee from bottom to the top. He started cutting long thin strips of meat and hanging them on branches of the teepee. He had to be careful of the fire he made to dry the meat with. He wanted a little fire that smoked a lot.

Man, these are going to be real tasty, too, Mark thought. His stomach growled from the smell of the cooking meat and Mark laughed and said, "Food will be done in a few minutes."

Eric's mouth watered just at the thought and smell of the fresh meat cooking. When Mark said the food was done, he covered the meat with a garbage bag to keep the flies off. He washed up in the river that was a few hundred yards away.

Eric sat down and Mark handed him a plate piled with half the liver and heart on top of rice. They both ate quickly. As they ate, they both sat silently with their thoughts of relief that they had more food. There was plenty of rice and oatmeal left, but they'd run out of just about everything else. Now they would have venison to go with it. They were going to make it. They were confident about the trip now. They dried the meat all that day and the next. When darkness started to fall on the second day, they were packed up and ready to hit the road. There was nothing like eating real well and getting plenty of sleep to freshen your outlook on life. They approached their trek north with a bit more of a spring in their steps.

It was a little over a week since the lights went out. The thin veneer of civilization was gone. By now everyone had realized and understood that the world had radically changed forever. There was no authority, no one in charge of things. There were no rescues or anyone left to come to the rescue. No relief from the horror that each new day brought. There was no word from the government. Even if there had been a way for the government to give help to the people, they would first have to go in and establish order.

How would they get to the cities to do that? That was on the minds of almost everyone. They hadn't even been able to do so when the cities had been rioting and this, this was a thousand times worse. Everyone everywhere was on their own to survive in any way they could. There were no laws nor were there any rules to guide people through the things they faced each day. This world that they lived in now was a crazy dangerous place. It was like the mask of humanity had been torn off and a rotten evilness underneath had been exposed into the air, affecting everyone everywhere. Mark and Eric found out later that night just how crazy and radically different and evil this world was compared to the one they had lived in before. They were approaching another overpass on the highway. They followed the same plan as before. They moved off the main road about one hundred fifty to two hundred yards farther out from the highway. It was way safer this way to get by them. They had seen people up on them just shooting for no reason. This world they lived in now was a very strange and alien place indeed.

The bonfire by this particular overpass was a very large. They were all standing outside of a mobile home a little way down from the overpass. They could see about twenty to twenty-five in the reflected light from the fire on their faces. They were all men of mixed ethnicities. There were a few black men, some white, some Asian and Hispanic men. They were drinking and passing bottles of liquor and shooting toward the road. They were yelling and screaming and having one hell of a party. They all wore a green patch on their jackets. They couldn't quite see what was on the patch, just that it was green and that they all had the same kind sewn on their jackets. They must be a gang or something. Mark and Eric wanted to avoid them. They started to creep even farther out from the road. They didn't want to be hit by a stray bullet.

As they were slowly and quietly making their way farther away, they heard a few women start screaming in terror. Mark and Eric stopped and exchanged a look. Mark said, "It sounds like they are torturing the women." Eric nodded his head in agreement. Mark whispered, "We should go take a look."

"Yes, we should. Maybe we can help them." Both of them remembered what had happened to Pam. They started making their way out onto the overpass quietly, staying in the shadows. They reached the side and looked down on a horrible scene. There were six women of various ethnicities tied up to the front of a car. They were all strung together like a chain gang. They were mostly naked, their clothes hanging in tatters. They were dirty and several were bleeding from various cuts and wounds. When they saw the condition the women were in, it hardened their souls and gave them the fortitude to help.

One guy was near the women with a knife in one hand. His other hand had a bandana wrapped around it. He was cutting the face of one of the women and laughing. He told them, "I told you not to bite me. I told you I would cut you into little pieces and feed them to the fish in the river if you did it again. Now are you going to be polite and not bite me anymore?" He laughed again evilly. Some of the other women were crying and screaming. He reached over with the hand that held the knife and slapped a woman, saying, "Shut up, bitch." He left a bloody trail across her face. He said to the women, laughing, "Be nice to me, bitches. Remember you can and will be replaced. There are plenty more where you came from."

Two other guys came stumbling over, grabbed two of the women and untied them. They wrapped leashes around their necks. They were smiling drunkenly as they dragged the screaming women along the ground towards the mobile home. Mark and Eric exchanged a disgusted look.

They backed away slowly. When they had gone a good distance, they stopped behind a truck and bent down. Eric whispered to Mark, "There must have been a lot of food stored in that mobile home for the thugs to stay here."

"They could have carried some with them when they left the city. But I don't think so. They aren't the type. These kinds of men just take what they want."

"I agree. But we have to help those women," said Eric.

"Yes, we will. We have to come up with fool proof plan." They remained in thought for a few minutes.

"The two of us can't take on thirty guys. We'll have to wait until the party winds down and most of them pass out. I'll sneak down and cut the ropes on the women and lead them up ahead. We'll sneak out into the field. You stay up here and cover me with your rifle," Eric said.

"Okay, sounds like a good plan. Just remember not to get yourself killed trying to save them. If it comes down to saving them or yourself, please pick yourself. I won't be able to make it to the retreat alone."

Eric smiled at Mark. "Well, at least I know where your priorities lie. I can't die so you can make it to the retreat."

Mark smiled back. "Yeah, and don't you forget it, either." They settled down to wait for the party to die down and the men to start passing out. They did their best not to think of what was happening to the women in the meantime.

As they waited, Mark thought about his poor man's night sight on his rifle. He had bought glow in the dark red paint to put on his front sight and green for his back ramp. In the moonlight, he could make the shots if the figure was in the open and not in shadows. He should have spent the money on a real night vision scope when the world was still together. Well, it was too late now.

Eric had made his way slowly down into the ditch earlier. He had waited until it was time. It had been an hour since things had settled down. All the women were back in front of the car, tied up. It was 4:00 am. He was about fifty feet from the girls. Eric made his move. Staying low to the ground, he slowly crawled his way over to the women. The sound of his clothes scraping across the pavement seemed very loud to him. It surprised him that the sound didn't alert the women that he was there. The women were huddled together for warmth and they were dozing. He approached the one on the end closest to him. He reached up and put his hand over her mouth and whispered in her ear, "Shhh, I am here to let you all go. Quietly wake up the other women. Make no noise. We don't want to wake those men up or draw attention to what we are doing. I'm going to remove my hand now and cut the ropes that bind you. We'll make our way out to the field up ahead. Do you understand me?" The woman nodded her head. Eric released her and started cutting the ropes.

The woman nudged the woman that was beside her and whispered, "Some guy's behind me cutting my ropes. He said he's going to let us go. Tell the others quietly." She could feel Eric cutting the ropes that connected her to the others. The third one down nudged the next woman and that woman jerked and screamed out, "Leave me alone." Eric dived flat on the ground. They all heard someone in the distance yell for the women to shut up.

Eric lay there gripping the shotgun, ready for anything. He waited for a few more moments, listening for approaching footsteps. None came. He carefully cut the ropes from the women. He whispered to all of them, "Come with me if you want to live. But don't make a sound." They started to make their way across the pavement to the ditch when one of the women spotted a guy asleep in a sleeping bag on the hood of a car not far from where the women had been tied up. She freaked out and grabbed a good-sized rock, and running back to the sleeping man, she screamed, "I'm going to kill you!" She brought the rock down on his head over and over again.

Eric quickly jumped up and told the others to run into the field, then make their way to the top of the hill. He jumped over a fence and lay down to give the women covering fire.

The camp woke up real quick. A guy ran to the woman who was beating the sleeping guy's brains out with a rock and grabbed her by the hair and yanked her down. A 30-30 shot rang out and the man fell to the ground. All of a sudden the camp was alive with the men running around screaming and yelling all over the place. Wild shots were firing everywhere. The traumatized woman that had attacked the sleeping guy was scrambling around like a deranged animal and ran straight up to another guy to bash his head in with her bloody rock. The guy fired at almost point blank range. She stopped, slowly fell to the side, and dropped down to the ground. The 30-30 fired again and Eric heard a grunt of pain. A few of these guys were so drunk or disoriented that they were firing on their own guys. It was time for Eric to make his escape. It was past time to get out of Dodge. This Wild West show was over.

Eric couldn't believe it. None of them had seen the other women getting away. There were no shots fired in their direction. He stopped at the bottom of the hill to listen for any pursuit. He heard a lot of shots, but couldn't tell who was shooting at whom. The darkness bred confusion. He headed up the hill towards the women.

Mark, up on the overpass, watched as Eric stealthily made his way over to the women. After a minute he heard one yell something. He couldn't quite make out what she had said. He held his breath thinking for sure they were all going to wake up and start shooting. He couldn't see Eric. Then he saw Eric's head pop up, as he started moving down the line, cutting the ropes. Nothing moved. They took off across the pavement. He had just thought, "It can't be this easy," when one of the women bent down and grabbed a rock, yelled something he couldn't make out and attacked a guy sleeping on the hood of a car. Then all hell broke loose. There were guys running around all over the place shooting, yelling and screaming in a matter of moments. A guy grabbed the woman who was beating the sleeping guy's head in by her hair. Mark aimed and fired. The man dropped to the ground. The crazy woman ran back towards the guys instead of taking off to be free. She attacked another guy with the rock and he shot her almost at point blank range in the chest.

Mark couldn't shoot because she had been in the way. As soon as she dropped, Marked shot the guy. He fell straight over. He saw the other women and Eric heading for the hill. It was time to leave this party. He swung around his gun arm holding on to the rifle and turned to leave when he felt his rifle jump in his hand. He instinctively gripped it tighter. It had almost been ripped out of his hand. He thought, *What the hell was that?* There wasn't time to look. He just took off, going as quickly as he could, but staying in the shadows. He wanted to go down and see if any of those guys were following Eric and the women.

Eric reached the women up on the hill. He said, "We have to keep going. They will come looking for us. Follow me. We have to get off the road and into the woods up there." He pointed towards north. "It is your decision to come with me or not." He took off walking real fast. The women looked at each other and then started to follow Eric. When they had gone about a half mile, Eric stopped. He turned around and saw that all of them had followed him. He said, "You can rest now. We'll wait here for my partner." They all dropped to the ground like a puppet whose strings were released. He walked around, checking the area out.

When he got back, they were all lying down except one. She was sitting up against a tree. He walked over to her. She didn't look up or anything. Eric's heart lurched in his chest. *Had she been hit with a bullet he hadn't seen come their way? Was she dead?* He reached down to feel for a pulse on her neck. She grabbed his hand and threw it away and screeched, "Don't touch me. Don't ever touch me again." Eric was so startled that he had jumped back when she grabbed his hand. She looked at him with fire in her eyes.

Eric backed up even more. He thought, *Oh wow. Is she going to go crazy like that other woman had and try to kill me?* Then he thought of what she had been through and realized she probably didn't want any man to get near her. He understood as best he could. He opened the backpack and took out the clothes and laid them on the ground, he added a bag of dried venison, then laid down two blankets, the first aid kit and at last, he set down his canteen at her feet. "Can you please give some to the other women?" he asked her. She stared at him for a few minutes not moving.

Eric could see she was thinking real hard. She picked up the canteen with shaking hands opened it and sipped a little water. Eric could see that her lips were bleeding. He wondered how long she had been without water. She then took a little longer drink. She reached down and grabbed a pair of socks. She took one and poured some water on it and crawled around and used it to wet the lips of the other women. They were whimpering for more. She lifted their heads and gave them a little water. She had to fight with them to keep hold of the canteen, because they were trying to drink all the water. Eric felt sick to his stomach at how these women had been treated. He snapped out of his daze and told her, "I have to go find my partner. He should have been here by now." He turned and walked away.

She said real quiet like, "Are you coming back or are you going to leave us out here by ourselves?"

Eric stopped for a moment. "I'll be back as soon as I find my partner. I would not leave you out here alone in the condition you're in by choice. I guess the question is more like, do you want me and my partner to come back and help you?"

She looked steadily at him as if she was judging his words. "I can't care for these women on my own."

"Then I'll be back to help you," Eric said. She nodded and turned to pick up the bag of jerky. Eric headed back the way they came.

Mark had been taking his time, sneaking around, seeing if any of the scumbags were around. The last he saw of them they were shooting at shadows. He couldn't help but laugh. Some were yelling that they got one and then they would run up and it would be one of their own guys. He deduced that they had trained themselves to always wear their patches so they could see who to shoot and who not to shoot. Most were running around without their jackets on, so that meant they didn't have their patches on. He was slowly making his way up to the hill. He would stop every couple of steps and listen to see if any were coming his way.

So far, none were following them. He stopped to listen and heard a faint sound. He waited to see what it was. After a couple of minutes, he didn't hear anything else. He decided it was probably a rabbit or something. Just as he was going to take a step he heard a sound again. He waited. He looked around and could see someone slowly making their way towards him. It couldn't be one of those scumbags. Besides, they were traveling the wrong way. He watched this person came closer. Damn, they were good. They went a few steps and stopped to listen, too. As this person got closer he finally realized it was Eric. He could tell by the way he walked and carried himself. He stepped out of the dark so Eric would be able to see him. Eric whipped around to him, aiming the shotgun. He saw it was Mark and lowered the gun.

When Eric reached him he said, "What took you so long?"

Mark said, "I was making sure none of those scumbags followed you and the women."

"Well, did they follow us?"

Mark smiled. "No. They were too busy shooting each other to worry about you. They were totally confused about who or what was attacking them. They never even noticed that you took off with the women."

"Good. Let's get back to the women. They are in pretty bad shape."

"How is the one with the cut face?" Mark asked.

"I don't know. I don't think they're going to let us get near them to look at the cut."

"Why not? We saved them didn't we?"

"It is going to be a lot more complicated than that, I think," said Eric. "They were brutalized and raped. They're not going to trust us because we are men. I was thinking about this on my way to find you."

Mark grunted, "Oh that is going to be just great. How in the hell are we supposed to help them if they won't let us near them?"

"This is a delicate situation, Mark. We don't want to make it any worse than it is. One of them talked to me, sort of. I got too close and she almost took my hand off. But I left her caring for the others. We need to get back and get them moving before those bozos realize we took the women and decide to look for us."

"Right." They headed back up the hill.

Mark showed Eric his rifle. Eric said, "What happened?"

"One of those assholes shot the stock. The bullet was aimed at me and the stock got in the way. It saved my life."

Eric was amazed. "I thought that crap only happens in the movies?"

"So did I."

"Are you all right?"

"Yes, it will keep," Mark said. "Nothing serious."

They reached the spot where the women were. They were all sitting up and chewing on the dried meat. Some were gorging themselves. Eric and Mark looked at each other in amazement. They had never seen women eat so fast. They looked back and then Eric stepped over and grabbed the rest of the dried meat. As soon as he stepped closer, the women screeched and crawled backwards to get away from him. He stepped away. He sat down, thinking maybe he would look less threatening that way. He spoke softly so he wouldn't startle them again. "Calm down. We won't hurt any of you." He noticed that several wounds and cuts had been covered with bandages. He was glad for that. "I didn't mean to startle you. I was just getting the dried meat so you wouldn't eat anymore of it." They looked upset at this statement. He and Mark exchanged a look. Eric sighed. "That didn't come out quite the way I meant. If you eat too much too soon, it will make you sick and give you really bad stomach cramps. I was just trying to help you not to over-eat at first. Do you understand what I meant? I didn't mean to scare you." They looked at each other and then one by one they nodded their heads.

Mark bent down next to Eric and said, "We have to go. They'll come looking for us." The women started to whimper at that news and some started to cry. Mark looked at Eric as if to say, *What did I say that upset them?*

Eric closed his eyes and said, "Ladies, help yourselves to the clothes that are on the ground." Some of them were trying to hold what was left of their clothes together to cover themselves. They were all shaking. Eric didn't know if it was because they were cold or if it was from nerves or what. He slowly scooted over and grabbed the two blankets. The two that hardly had any clothes on looked really cold. He threw each of them a blanket down by their feet. The two women snatched them up so fast it was almost a blur. They helped each other to open them and put them around their shoulders. Eric and Mark exchanged another look. It was real hard not to feel sorry for these abused women.

Eric said, "I know you're not really up to this, but we have to leave here. Those scumbags may come looking for us. We have to get farther away from them before you can really rest." Eric stood up and took off his coat. He placed it on the ground and said, "One of you are welcome to wear this. Walking will keep me warm."

Mark stood up and took off his coat, too. He placed it on the ground. He looked at the women and said, "One of you can wear my coat, too. I don't really need it."

"Ladies choose quickly who will wear what. We have to leave." Eric turned around and motioned for Mark to do the same. He didn't know what to do, but figured they would not want them watching their every move.

He heard whispering and some rustling of fabric. They waited for it to quiet down before they turned back around. When they did, all the clothes were off the ground and on various ladies. They were wearing the coats, too. "We have to leave. Do any of you need me to carry you? Or help you to walk?" They all looked at each other, then back at him and Mark, and they shook their heads no.

Eric and Mark looked at each other and Mark said, "I'll lead and you bring up the rear, okay?" Eric agreed. Mark started walking away from the road. He was heading at an angle, trying to find the easiest places to walk for these women. They all followed. The women started to stumble when they only had gone about a half-mile. Mark stopped. He said, "Sit down over here." He pointed to a place that had a lot of bushes growing together. He took a drink from his canteen and then capped it and set it on the ground by the women. They each took a drink. When it got to Eric, it was almost empty. He got a couple of sips and that was it. They let the women sit for fifteen minutes, then Mark said, "We have to go again." The women helped each other up and took off after Mark. Eric trailed behind.

They had gone about another quarter mile when the women started slowing down. Mark stopped and found a place for the ladies to rest. He indicated where to sit. They all sort of flopped down. Eric thought, *They aren't going to be able to go much farther.* They looked all done in. "Rest," Mark said. "I'll be right back." He took the canteens and walked off. Mark remembered from the map that there was a stream over here somewhere because the river was on the other side of the road. He hoped he could find it quickly because they had to find somewhere to bed everyone down for the day.

Morning was going to be here real soon. He almost walked right into the stream. He filled the canteens up and added some germicidal drops to sterilize it. He walked back to the place where everyone was waiting for him. He passed them a canteen and they all drank deeply. He handed the other one to Eric. Eric took a long drink. It had been a long night and it wasn't over yet. Mark said, "I know you all are exhausted. We have to go only a little farther, and then we should be far enough away to find some place to bed down for the day. Does anyone need any help?" They all shook their heads no. They stood up and Mark led them out again.

He was looking for the perfect spot to be safe for the day. The sun was starting to rise. At least it made it a littler easier to see what was what. But it also made them stand out like sore thumbs, too. He saw a spot up ahead that looked like it could be good for all of them. He walked over and peered around. Eric looked around, too. They looked at each other and grinned. It was a perfect spot.

It was a large stand of bushes and shrubs all around with a little hollow in the middle. There was another little hollow part a few steps away from the first one. Mark opened up the sleeping bags and zipped them together to make a really long blanket. He put a tarp on the ground and laid the sleeping bag on top of it. There wasn't anything left to make a pillow out of, so this was going to have to be good enough. He turned to the ladies and said, "You all can sleep here for the day. We will move out again when it is night." They looked at him and then at the bed he had made for them and then one asked, "Where will you sleep?" Mark showed them the other little open spot and said, "Eric and I will take turns sleeping there. One of us will be awake at all times to keep watch for anyone coming near us. It's not safe out here now." They all fell down on the makeshift bed and were soon asleep.

Eric and Mark stood there, looking at the ladies sleeping. They looked at each other with real concern in their eyes. Mark asked Eric, "How are we going to get us all to the retreat now?"

Chapter 9

Silence Is Golden, Duct Tape Is Silver

"You should always tell the truth, because if you tell the truth you make it the other person's problem."

Sean Connery

While Amy had been making her list, Preston had been getting the couch made up into a bed. He put clean sheets, a couple of wool blankets, and her quilt on top with a pillow. He figured he would grab his mummy-style sleeping bag and sleep across the room by the door. Not in front of it; that would be a stupid thing to do. But near enough in case there was trouble. He went to set it up.

"I'm done with my list," said Amy.

"I'll look it over tomorrow and we can decide what we have room for in the packs," answered Preston.

"Okay. I am a bit tired. It has been a Twilight Zone day. Maybe after some sleep I'll be able to think a little clearer. My mind has been all muddled up today. Tomorrow I'll be able to help you prepare for the trip." She turned, went into the bathroom and shut the door.

Preston focused on preparing his sleeping area. He was laying out his weapons and ammo, his flashlight. He thought about what Amy had said about tomorrow. He smiled. *Wow, if all she had said and done tonight was with a muddled mind, what was she going to be like clear-headed?* If she thought any clearer or assessed situations any better, she would soon be out-thinking him. He chuckled to himself. Boy, was she out of his league. He shook his head and smiled. She was a real find. She was a diamond hidden in a sea of pearls. He had never met a woman quite like her before. She was just so, so practical. The only other woman he knew of that was sensible and practical most of the time was Jane.

Amy shut the bathroom door and thought, *Oh my God, he's making a place for me to sleep.* She had thought that she would go to her apartment to sleep for the night. No one since her uncle died had ever done something nice like that for her. She knew she probably wouldn't get any sleep over in her own bed in her apartment. She would be worrying about all the little zombies walking around causing havoc and terror and what kind of problems they would have to face tomorrow. It was really nice of him to actually make a place for her to sleep. She might be able to get some sleep tonight after all.

Not being alone was really great. This whole thing today scared the hell out of her. Everything from this point on would be so very different. Uncertainty hit her. Why had Preston asked her to go with them to his retreat? She pondered that for a few minutes. She couldn't come up with a good reason. She was nobody special. She didn't really have any special skills at the moment that would be an asset to them at the retreat. She planned on having some skills in the future. She had a lot of information about snaring and trapping for food she would learn to use. She loved to learn new and interesting things. But she had to admit to herself she had no real experience yet.

Tears formed in her eyes and her breath hitched. What if these other two people at his retreat didn't like her or didn't want someone with no real skills there? What would she do then? Everything she had read about said only people with real skills would be let into survival groups. She realized that she really didn't have a choice in the matter; she couldn't stay here and hope to survive with no real supplies or skills either. Her tears ran down her cheeks and she wiped them away; she hated crying. Crying never solved anything. Thinking and working through a problem was when a solution would be found. Crying about it never solved anything; it only made her feel worse, gave her puffy eyes and clogged her sinuses. She looked around and noticed some antibacterial wipes. She took one and washed her face.

She finished up in the bathroom and returned to the living room.

Preston looked at her. "You look tired. I made you a place to sleep on the couch. It's a pretty comfortable couch, too. We'll talk tomorrow after some sleep. Things are just," he paused and smiled at her, "a bit different now. I hope you don't think that I am presuming anything. I made up the couch for you without really thinking about it from your point of view. We really don't know each other very well and I didn't give a thought that maybe you wouldn't want to stay here. I just did it and was thinking about your protection. I wouldn't be able to protect you from the little zombies running around out there if you are over in your own apartment."

"Thank you," Amy said. "That was very kind of you to think about protecting me at all. I appreciate all that you've done. I wouldn't be able to sleep if I went home. I would be too worried; I'd be up all night, so thank you again."

Preston was puzzled a little by her answer. "You're welcome."

Amy sat down on the couch. She took her coat off and laid it at the end where her feet would be. She removed her jogging shoes and lay down, pulling all the blankets over her. She turned on her side, facing the room. It felt cozy and warm. She snuggled down, closing her eyes and releasing a sigh. Preston turned off the lantern. Without it, the noise outside seemed much louder. He got into his sleeping bag and lay facing the door. He sighed, too. It felt good to just be able to relax for a while. This might be the last time he could do so until they reached the retreat. He intended to get as much sleep as he could. He closed his eyes.

Preston was the first one up in the morning. They had a relatively decent night's sleep. He was woken up a few times by noise, but nothing that was close enough to make him have to get up. It was now 6:00 am. He had overslept; he was usually up at 5:00. He got up and removed the sheets and things that he had covered the windows with the night before. It made it a little brighter inside. He didn't want his windows to look any different than the others and bring attention to this apartment. He looked out the sides of the windows. It looked like a war had taken place out there. He shook his head and put the coffee on. He checked the water at the faucet. Nothing came out. He hadn't expected it to; it had stopped last night. He was just double checking. Without the pumps working at the city water building, there would be no more water coming out of those pipes. He went into the bathroom to wash up and shave.

Amy woke up to the smell of coffee. She sniffed, appreciating the scent. She stretched and looked around. Preston was not in his sleeping bag. She hadn't really thought that Sharon, the princess, would have been thoughtful enough to put coffee on for all of them. Of course not, it had been Preston. She got up and put her shoes on. It was cold. She walked into the kitchen and saw the coffee pot perking away. It looked done, but she didn't want to turn it off, maybe he liked really strong coffee. She rinsed out the cups from the night before so they would be ready. She held her hands out to warm near the flame of the propane stove. Preston stepped around her, reaching for the coffee pot. She jumped in surprise, she hadn't heard him come up behind her. He filled both cups and handed one to her. She mumbled a thank you. He reached down and turned the burner off. She looked at Preston all cleaned up and thought how unfair that was. She figured she looked like something out of a horror movie about now, hair all over, probably lines on her face from the pillow and puffy eyes from crying last night. But wow, he looked good. She could get used to looking at him first thing in the morning. She realized what she just thought and blushed, reminding herself not to go there and remember the princess named Sharon in the bedroom that was living with Preston. There was no way to compete with a dainty petite perfect woman like her. She sighed then turned and headed for the table to enjoy her coffee.

Preston smiled at Amy's back as she headed to the table. She didn't look like a morning person. She was cute with her shiny, light brown hair pulled out of her braid and hanging around her face. She looked young, real young. She had blushed, and had a scowl on her face. She didn't look like her usual bubbly self. It was quite attractive, really. She was human after all. He still had a hard time believing she was as old as she said she was. He was just reaching for the coffee pot when he heard Sharon mumbling and moving around in the bedroom.

He turned and walked into the hall, seeing her disappear into the bathroom. He sighed. Sharon would be all put together when she came out. She always was. He realized how unnatural that was, like a mannequin or something. He looked over at Amy and saw how real she looked in her rumpled, slept-in clothes and uncombed hair. She was much more beautiful in a natural way than Sharon could ever be. Sharon worked hard to keep looking good every day; but it was just an illusion. That thought shocked him. He realized that he had never seen Sharon in a natural state like Amy was right now, with no makeup on or in rumpled clothes. He wondered if he would think she was attractive without makeup, probably not. He had seen her a few times in the morning with her hair a little messed up and it had never struck him how attractive she was at that time. He shook his head. What in the hell was the matter with him? The world they knew had ended and here he was comparing these two women. He took a deep breath, shaking his head at himself and poured more coffee into his cup. He kept telling himself over and over again, *get your priorities straight right now.*

Preston was going through the things he had set aside in the spare bedroom to put in the packs. Space was really limited in the packs for the two women. He knew it would be a losing battle to try to talk Sharon into leaving any of her makeup or hair stuff behind. But, she would have to carry it on her back herself. He smiled at that thought. *I wonder how long before she starts to throw some of it away?* He hated the thought of wasting the very valuable space they had with that kind of stuff. But Sharon was Sharon, after all. He doubted he would be able to reason with her about it. He finished his pack and set it aside. He would carry all of their essentials in his pack and the saddlebags he had made for the bikes.

Sharon was just about done getting herself put together to face the day. She was frustrated and upset because she couldn't shower or wash her hair. She debated whether she should wash her hair anyway with the water in the bathtub. She decided that wouldn't do, because with the power out, she wouldn't be able to style it properly without using her hot rollers. She sighed and swore. It was very important to her to look her best at all times. Now, how was she going to accomplish that without the power to do so? Hopefully, the power would come back on soon. It made her feel dirty to not follow her morning routine, especially after walking all the way home and perspiring yesterday. She shuddered at the thought all that had happened to her the day before.

She left the bathroom and walked back into the bedroom. She went over to the dresser and grabbed her cell phone. It still didn't work. Well, just as soon as the power was on again that problem will be solved. She walked into the kitchen, ignoring everything around her. She reached inside the refrigerator and grabbed a bottle of water. She went back into the bedroom and got out a couple of tablets of pain reliever from her purse to help with the headache she had. *That was also his fault,* she thought angrily. She was going to finish getting ready for work. As soon as the power came on while she was at work, she would call the police and have him arrested. How dare he treat her like that? She decided to wear a business pants suit. She'd have to wear something soft on her feet because they still hurt and were a bit swollen. The pants suit would cover that fact up. She was looking in her closet, deciding what pair of shoes would do when Preston walked in. She ignored him. He was a problem that soon would be gone.

Preston heard Sharon in the bedroom and wondered what she was doing. He walked in. She was dressed to go out and standing in front of her closet.

"Sharon, what are you doing?"

She ignored him.

He tried again. "Where do you think you are going?"

She ignored him.

He touched her on the shoulder and she turned around and pushed him away, screaming, "Don't touch me, you asshole, don't ever touch me."

Preston looked at Sharon. "Fine. But answer me this, where do you think you're going?"

"I don't have to answer you. You don't exist to me anymore. Do you understand me? You do not exist. Get out of my apartment. Go. Go. Just leave me alone." She angrily grabbed a pair of flats and shoved her feet into them. She winced. "Shit, that hurts!" She adjusted the shoes and walked out of the bedroom with her head high, her body tight with anger.

Preston got up, sighed, and went after her. He ran into the living room and almost knocked Sharon over. She was standing there with an angry look on her face. She turned to him and slapped his face real hard, screaming, "How dare you? How dare you sleep with her here in my apartment? You bastard. Get out now. Get the hell out and take that slut with you." She pummeled his chest with her fists.

Preston grabbed her hands. "Sharon, calm down. Just calm the hell down."

Sharon continued to screech at him. He didn't let go of her. She started kicking him with her pointed shoes. He was hopping around, trying to avoid her kicks while explaining why Amy had stayed the night. Sharon was past hearing anything he could have said in his defense. Preston saw Amy walk up behind Sharon and stand close to her. She grabbed Sharon and shoved her right at Preston. Preston was able to get her turned around so he could hold her still with his arms wrapped around her. Sharon's volume increased. Preston couldn't do a thing about it; it took everything he had just to hold her. Preston saw Amy coming with something in her hands and smiled at her. She maneuvered around to get close to Sharon and Sharon reached out and slapped her and scratched her face. Amy didn't even look mad, just a bit surprised. Sharon tried to slap her again and Amy lunged right at Sharon, knocking her hands away and applied what she had in her hands across Sharon's mouth, finally shutting her up. It was a piece of duct tape. Sharon had a shocked look on her face and stood absolutely still in Preston's arms. They all panted for breath for a few moments. Preston and Amy were enjoying the quiet.

Amy was the first to move. She grabbed the roll of duct tape and came back to Preston and Sharon. She showed the roll to Sharon and said, "Do you want me to tie you up with this?"

Sharon looked at the roll of duct tape, then looked at Amy, and then back to the roll again.

"Shake your head and tell me if you want me to tie you up or not? I won't wait very long for your answer, Sharon. I'll just tie you up and be done with this, this..." Amy paused, not even sure what to call it, "this fit of yours. Do you comprehend me?"

Sharon looked at Amy with fear in her eyes and nodded her head yes.

"If Preston releases you, will you sit down so we can have an intelligent conversation about your wrong impressions?"

Sharon was shooting daggers at her with her eyes, but nodded yes.

Amy looked up at Preston. "Okay, let her go, but if she starts her crap up again, I'll duct tape her up into a little ball. This is ridiculous."

Preston let go of Sharon and took a couple of slow steps away from her just in case she did something again. She didn't. She marched over and sat down in a chair, not making a sound. Amy let out a relieved breath. Sharon took off the duct tape and threw it aside.

Amy sat down the closest to Sharon. She looked up at Sharon with a hard look in her eyes. "Sharon we will get one thing straight right now," Amy said. "I will not put up with your fits. Get that into your head right now."

Sharon huffed. "Who the hell do you think you are to tell me what to do?"

Amy sighed again. "Sharon, this is Preston's apartment. This is not your apartment. He lived here long before you came along. You are a guest here in his apartment and you had better start acting like one. I will not permit you to treat him like you do. He doesn't deserve it. Do you understand me?" Sharon was outraged at what Amy was saying. She opened her mouth to speak, but before she could, Amy said in a threatening voice, "Before you say one word, you had better think long and hard about your answer to me.

"You will treat Preston and I with respect, Sharon. You will talk nice and calmly to us about any concerns you have. We will answer you in the same way. But, I am warning you right here and now, I will not put up with your shenanigans, your screaming, cussing and hitting. Do you understand me? Those are the ground rules we will abide by. In times like these, we must have some kind of order and respect between us. If you get out of hand with Preston again and attack him, or even don't talk to him with a respectful voice, I will tie you up in a little bitty ball of duct tape. If you ever raise your hand to hit me again, I will punch your lights out. You have been warned, Sharon. I will not warn you again. Preston is too nice of a guy to make you behave. I am not as nice as he is. Now, think before you open that big mouth of yours." Amy rubbed her temples to ease the headache Sharon had given her. It was way too early in the morning to deal with this shit.

Sharon pouted for a while. Amy sighed once again, irritated with Sharon. She said, "Sharon, I stayed overnight here because it isn't safe out there. I don't have any way of protecting myself. I don't have a gun and I don't know how to use one. I slept on the couch and Preston slept in his sleeping bag over by the door to keep us safe. Preston was a perfect gentleman last night. None of this had anything to do with sleeping with each other or anything like that."

Sharon looked at Amy and then at Preston. "Are you going to let her talk to me like that?" she demanded. When Preston didn't do anything or say anything, she said to him in a shrill squeaky voice, "How dare you let her talk to me like that. You let her in here and you are letting her treat me this way." She started to cry. Amy sighed again. Sharon sounded broken hearted. Preston moved to go to Sharon and Amy grabbed his arm and pulled him back down on the couch. She shook her head no at him.

She turned back and looked at Sharon. Sharon was obviously faking it. Amy turned to Preston and looked at his face. He was feeling sorry for Sharon. He wanted to go to her and comfort her. Oh boy, did he need to be educated. After a few minutes of fake crying, she got up and dramatically ran from the room, slamming the bedroom door.

Preston let out a shaky breath. "Sharon is delicate and can't handle things like this. I thank you for helping me with her, but I don't think you were right to be hard on her like that. She's just upset right now and got the wrong impression about us. She's crying, and I should go and reassure her."

Amy sighed and thought, *oh brother.* She looked at Preston. "You think she was really crying?"

Preston looked at her, shocked that she would say such a thing. "Yes, she was. You were really hard on her and she can't take being treated like that. She has a delicate constitution."

Amy laughed. "Why are you laughing?" asked Preston. "This isn't funny. You were very mean to her."

Amy said, "Preston, she has you wrapped around her finger and can make you do anything she wants. All she has to do is look up at you with one of those delicate expressions in her baby blue eyes or cry and you cave in like an earthquake hit you." He didn't quite know what to say to that statement. She continued, "What do you want to bet that she isn't really crying?"

Preston stared at her. "I know her better than you do and I know she's crying. She can't handle situations like this. She's too delicate."

Amy was getting irritated at Preston's innocence of what Sharon was doing. "Okay, I'll prove it to you. I'll go into that room and accuse her of faking it and let's hear what she says to me. You sneak up and listen by the door, okay? Don't make a sound or anything. I want her to think it is just her and me. Okay? Is it a deal?"

Amy's attitude toward Sharon angered Preston. He said firmly, "Okay, I agree. But this is my apartment, as you said earlier. Don't think you can come in here and tell me what to do. You understand that?"

Amy looked at him with amusement dancing in her eyes. "Absolutely. I agree with you. But we'll talk after we check if Sharon is really crying or not. When I motion you with my hands, come in and see for yourself."

Amy walked down the hall. Preston kept his word and stealthily made his way to the door, leaning on the wall where he would be hidden from sight. Amy softly knocked on the door, then opened it up and said, "Sharon?"

Sharon glanced at Amy out of the corner of her eye and saw that she was alone. Sharon faced her with her hands on her hips and said haughtily, "Get away from me, you bitch. You think you've won Preston with your tough attitude? I'll show you how little effect you'll have on him. He loves me. Me. Not you. Just look at you. You're a fat cow. I'm beautiful. You have an ugly face and body. Who would even talk to you? People walk right by you and don't even see you. You blend into the walls. He'll come in here and I'll make him not listen to you. I'll make him get rid of you. All I have to do is cry again and he'll do whatever I want to make me stop. You'll be out on your big tramp of an ass, you cow slut. How dare you come into my apartment and tell me how to treat him? I'll treat him however I want to, and there is nothing you can do about it." Sharon had a very smug look on her angry face. She reached up and smacked herself on the side of her face and started to cry. Amy never moved from the door right next to Preston.

Preston stepped around Amy, pushing the door open all the way and saw Sharon crying on the bed. She looked up at him with tears falling down her face, the reddened slap mark showing up very prominently. "Oh Preston," she complained, "she was so mean to me; she hit me. Help me, please, help me. Get her away from me. Please, please get her away from me. She was hitting me." She cried like her best friend ever had just died. She leaned over, hanging onto Preston and looking up at him with those pretty blue eyes of hers.

Amy started to laugh so hard she almost choked. "Now do you believe me?" she asked. Amy walked away, laughing.

Several minutes later, Preston walked out into the living room looking a little lost. Amy had spent the time straightening everything up and folding the blankets.

He looked at her and started to say something, then changed his mind and shook his head. He sat down at the table and looked down at his hands. Amy felt sorry for him. It was a hell of a shock to find out you were a sucker when it came to the Sharons of this world. She had seen other men when they realized they were just being played.

She went to the bedroom and knocked lightly before she opened the door. Sharon was straightening her clothes in the drawers. She didn't even look up. Amy set the tray down on the dresser and said, "I brought you something to eat. Preston said you don't eat any meat, so I brought you some fruit salad, cheese, and crackers, and bottled water to drink." Sharon still didn't acknowledge that she was there. Amy tried again. After all, they would be going through all of this together and she was trying to make the best of the situation. Amy moved closer to Sharon. "What are you doing?" Sharon ignored her. Amy sighed. "We're all going through this together. Can we please try to at least be civil to each other and get along?"

Sharon turned to Amy. "You don't exist. I am not talking to a fat cow like you. You were mean to me and I'm having you arrested as soon as the power comes back on."

Amy smiled and thought, *That's the best you can do?* She said, "Sharon, the power is not coming back on for many years to come. Everything changed because we were hit with an EMP bomb. Nothing electrical will work. We all have to start over from scratch. Nothing will be fixed for at least five years."

"You're as crazy as he is," she replied. "He's just a conspiracy nut. Don't believe him when he says this stuff. He's wrong. He's so very wrong. You both will feel pretty stupid when the power comes back on. But what can you expect from morons and fools like you two?"

"You really think the power will come back on?"

Sharon just looked at her, rolled her eyes, and continued to straighten a dresser drawer.

Amy thought for a few minutes and then asked, "What do you think happened when the power went out and the vehicles, watches and cell phones stopped working for everyone out there? Everything stopped working at the same time, Sharon. This isn't just some power outage for a few days. This is permanent. This can't be fixed easily. "

"You're crazy. I'm not listening to anything you say," Sharon said. "What do you know?"

Amy had just about enough of Sharon burying her head in the sand and not accepting what had happened. She reached out and grabbed Sharon and dragged her over to the window. She opened the blind and said, "Look at this, Sharon. Does this look like a typical power outage to you? Those are dead bodies out there, Sharon. If this was just a temporary thing, don't you think the police or an ambulance or someone would have helped those people? There's no one left out there that can help anyone. This is something none of us have ever seen before. You'd better wake up and accept this situation for what it is. It is complete chaos out there. Look at those fires burning everywhere. We have to get out of the city tonight, Sharon, before the bad guys that killed those people come here to kill us, too. Because they will come and kill us, that's what they do and there isn't anyone left to can stop them. They'll hunt us down, rape us women, and then kill us. If you have a gun, you might be able to make it out of here. This is the situation we're facing. Do you understand what we've been saying now?"

Sharon just stared, a shocked look on her pale face. Her eyes were glassy. She wasn't blinking right. Amy realized she might have been a bit too plain speaking to her. Well, tough. They didn't have time for anymore of her tantrums or her inability to really look at this situation. Amy reached up and closed the blind. Sharon just stood, staring. Amy led Sharon over to the other side of the room and sat her down on the bed. She got down and looked Sharon in the face. Sharon was still not seeing her. Amy clapped her hands in front of her face. Sharon blinked a few times and then reached out and pushed Amy away.

"Get away from me. You're crazy. The power will come back on. You wait and see. The power will come back on. What happened out there is just a … a … a … riot or something. Get out of here. I don't have to listen to you."

Amy couldn't believe it. Sharon still refused to believe it. Amy threw her hands up in the air. "I tried, I really tried." She turned around and walked out of the room.

She found Preston in the second bedroom. Preston had his head stuck in the closet, doing something. Preston turned and looked at Amy. "I heard what you said in the bedroom. I didn't think she'd change her mind and believe what we've been saying to her. But please, don't open the blinds again. We don't want anyone to see that people are up here in the apartment. Okay? It will let the bad guys know where we are."

"I'm sorry for doing that," Amy replied, "but I couldn't think of anything else that would make her face what's happening. I won't do it again."

In the afternoon, Preston looked at the list Amy made. He was surprised. She had listed:

Survival Kit
Folding Stove With 36 Fuel Tabs
16 Energy Bars
2 Space Blankets
1 Tube Tent
First Aid Kit
2 Light Sticks
50 Germicidal Water Purification Tablets
2 Tubes Of Fire Starting Paste
Picked Up At The Discount Store
Hand Cranked Radio
2 Hand Cranked Flashlights
1 Pound Of Vacuumed Packed Coffee
2 Key Chain LED Small Flashlights
Knife With Compass On It
1 Shake Chemical Flashlight
Swiss Army Knife With A Lot Of Neat Tools On It
Water Bottle With Filter On It
36 Fruit & Peanut Bars
6 Boxes Of Waterproof Matches
24 Packages Of Freeze Dried Soups
2 Cases Of Beef Jerky
1 Case Of Salted Peanuts
4 Cases Of Cup Of Noodles
36 Bags Trail Mixes
6 Bags Of Snack Sized Chocolate Bars (A Must Have For The Trip!!)
Bought At The Military Surplus Store
Key Chain Can Opener
24 Various Colored 12 Hour Light Sticks
4 – 120 Hour Candles
Canteen
5-Gallon Collapsible Water Container
Mess Kit
Stainless Steel Chow Set With A Can Opener
4 Flints To Start Fires With
Picked Up At Garage Sales
Sterno Stove With 4 Cans Of Fuel
Small Metal Coffee Pot
2 Wool Blankets
Small Water Purifier With A New Filter Still In The Box
2 Hand Cranked Egg Beaters
1 Hand Cranked Apple Peeler
3 Hand Cranked Can Openers
1 Tiny lantern
½ Gallon Lamp Oil
Buckshot's Complete Survival Trapping Guide
Buckshot's Basic Survival Manual
Buckshot's Emergency Snare Kit

2 Snare Repair Kits For The Snare Kit
2 Dozen Small Game Snares
2 Small Snares Repair Kits
2 Dozen Medium Game Snares
2 Medium Snares Repair Kit
2 Dozen Camlock Snares (Emergency Deer Snares)
2 Camlock Snares Repair Kit
1 – 4 Ounce Bottle Of Muskrat Lure
1 – 4 Ounce Bottle Of Raccoon Lure
1 – 4 Ounce Bottle Of Beaver Lure
1 – 4 Ounce Bottle Of Predator Lure
1 Dozen #110 Conibear Traps
6 Yo Yo Automatic Fishing Reels
2 Mora Of Sweden Survival Knives
Buckshot's Survival Snaring DVD
Buckshot's Advanced Survival Snaring DVD
Preparing Game For The Table DVD
Beginning Trapping DVD
Buckshot's Predator Trapping DVD
Animal Skinning DVD
Ultimate Survival Trapping Tips & Tricks DVD
Seven Day Deer Camp DVD.

Preston thought, *Wow, she has been preparing for a survival situation.* He smiled and thought no wonder she didn't think he and Joe were nut cases. He laughed softly. He had no idea his neighbor was a survivalist, too. He would have to think about all of her supplies and what they could take with them. His stuff was already packed up. He'd look over her stuff and decide what could be brought and what would have to be left behind.

Preston called Amy out to the dining room; she came out of the kitchen, wiping her hands on a dishtowel. She saw he was looking at her list. "Ready for some coffee?" she asked. "I just heated the pot up."

"Yes, thank you. I wanted to talk to you about your list."

"Okay, I'll get the coffee and be right back." She returned with the coffee, filled the cups, and sat down across from him at the table.

"Were you preparing for an emergency situation or a disaster?"

"Yes, I was. After New Orleans," Amy stopped a moment to take a sip, "I got to thinking what could happen here. So, I started preparing. I looked things up on the web and learned about survival. The things I read scared me, too. I saw how easily we could just fall apart like a crumb cake if something serious happened and we weren't ready. I've only been doing this for about a year now. I didn't have that much money, but I did what I could afford to do. I just didn't have enough time to get all I wanted to. I know it's not much, but I did what I could. I was buying a gun and taking a shooting and a safety course for the next item. Then I was going to get non-hybrid vegetable seeds and so on till I had a large stash. I was going to take a survival course for trapping and snaring to provide meat and animal skins to tan. I was going to prepare my uncle's hunting camp up north for my retreat." She looked down at the table with a sad look on her face. She then looked back up at Preston with a very serious look on her face. "There just wasn't enough time for me to do it all. That is why I said I didn't have any real skills yet. I had planned on having several skills to offer a group and we would go to my retreat and somehow survive together."

Preston was really blown away from her answer. She was so far ahead of the game for the average person. He looked at her and said, "The first thing we'll do when we get to my retreat is run you through a shooting course for handguns, shotguns and rifles. You'll learn gun safety at the same time. I can teach you that. I've taught shooting before, so we can take care of that. You'll then have a very valuable skill. You'll be able to protect yourself and others."

Amy smiled. "Thank you, Preston. I really want to learn to protect myself and others. I hate the idea of being so vulnerable right now."

Preston looked down at her list. "What do you feel you must have with you? I need to know what you won't part with as I calculate what will fit in your backpack."

Amy immediately said, "All the things listed under for the future. They'll be valuable to have. I'll learn those skills from the books I have. I'm taking the DVDs with me in case sometime in the future I can run across a working DVD player. I figure there has to be one working someplace. I also want to take my two egg beaters, the apple peeler, the three can openers, the radio, the flashlight, the key chain LED small flashlights, my survival knife with a compass, the shake chemical flashlight, my Swiss Army knife, a flint and the six bags of chocolate bars."

Preston had been checking them as she named the items. He looked up at her. "How big of a pile is this and how much does it weigh?"

"I really don't know how much it weighs," said Amy, "but the pile will be about this big." Amy showed him the size of the pile with a box she had emptied. Well, it would be doable, but he had to find out how much all this weighed first.

"Could you go get it and bring the items here before dark so we can get packed up?"

Amy grinned when she heard this. "I'll get my stuff right now."

"Okay." Preston got up and let her out the door.

That afternoon they had all of Amy's things packed up and ready to go. Preston told Amy he was going out to see if he could find her a bike. He took some things with him in a small shoulder bag to trade for the bike. Amy barred the door. Preston had told her he would come back and knock on the door. Before letting him in, he wanted her to knock back on the door, then he would knock three times. That would let both of them know that everything was okay. Preston asked Amy if she would please get Sharon ready while he was gone. He was anxious to head out as soon as it got dark. He had already spray painted Sharon's ski jacket. It had been yellow and pink. Now it was a matte black color. Amy's coat was a dark navy blue, so he didn't need to do anything to it.

Amy walked to the bedroom door and sighed. She reached out, tapped the door, and then opened it. Sharon was sitting on the bed, looking through a magazine. Amy stepped into the room carrying Sharon's backpack. She had noticed that while Preston had a very large backpack, her and Sharon's were quite a bit smaller. Amy dropped the backpack on top of Sharon's magazine and said, "Get this packed up with what you're bringing with you. We'll be leaving soon. I'm giving you about fifteen minutes to pack this up. If you don't do it, I'll come in and do it for you. You probably won't like what I would pick, so you had better get busy."

Sharon said, "I am not going anywhere, you stupid cow." Amy turned around and left the bedroom.

Amy went into the kitchen to get a few more things ready, then she sat down at the dining table with a cup of coffee. She was thinking about all that happened today. What a day. It almost matched yesterday for weirdness and distress. Sharon was lost in her own little world, refusing to believe anything was wrong. All afternoon she had kept saying the lights would be on soon. They could hear her moving around turning the lights on and off, testing them. Every time either of them had checked on Sharon, she would refuse to talk except to say that she was not going anywhere and called them names. Amy sighed. She was a hundred and twenty-five pounds, and the doctor had told her that she was a little underweight for her bone structure and height. She was five feet six inches tall and wasn't fat either. Sharon was just trying to get to her by calling her a fat cow. She sighed. It was time to go find out what Sharon had put in the backpack.

When Amy went into the hall, she saw the backpack lying empty on the floor outside the door. She rolled her eyes and picked it up. She opened the bedroom door and went inside. Sharon had finally eaten some of the fruit from the fruit salad, and the cheese and crackers were gone. Amy started opening drawers to go through Sharon's stuff and pack.

"Get your fat cow hands off my stuff!" Sharon screeched.

Amy ignored her, continuing to go through the clothes, separating them. The next thing she knew, she went flying into the wall, dropping the backpack. Her head bounced off the wall. She lay there, stunned and dizzy.

Sharon jumped on her, pulling her hair, screaming, and slapping her. "You are not touching my stuff, you fat cow. Get out of here. I will kill you. Don't ever touch my things again!"

Sharon slapped and scratched Amy a few more times in the face and on her arms, leaving bloody scratches behind. Amy felt like a tornado had just hit her. She reached up and pushed Sharon off. She tried to stand up, but her knees were too weak and her head was spinning. Sharon jumped on Amy's back, pulling her hair again, and trying to knock her head into the wall again.

That's it, Amy thought. Amy reached back and grabbed Sharon by the hair, lowering her upper body and throwing her over her shoulders. Sharon landed with a loud thump on the floor. Amy crawled over to the wall and stood up on shaky legs. Sharon was still lying on the floor trying to get a breath. Amy made her way over to the bedroom door and left. She walked a little steadier the farther she got down the hall. She went into the dining room and grabbed the roll of duct tape. She made her way back to the bedroom. Sharon was neatly putting all the clothes back into the drawers.

She turned and saw the duct tape in Amy's hand. Sharon's eyes got big. She backed up to the bed. Amy just kept coming. Sharon fell back on the bed and rolled over to the side nearest the bedroom door. She took off running. She plowed into Amy, but Amy was ready this time. She grabbed Sharon and both of them swung around in a circle. Sharon was able to elbow Amy in the stomach in an attempt to get away. Amy huffed out a breath, but kept a hold on Sharon, swinging her around again. They swung around by the doorway and Sharon shoved Amy at the door. Amy's head banged into the door and she lost her hold on Sharon, falling down on her knees. Sharon took off running down the hall. Amy stood up on shaky legs again and raced after her. Amy rounded the hall into the dining room and flew though to the living room. Sharon was at the door trying to open it. Amy took a flying leap and tackled her. They both went down to the floor in a jumble of legs and arms, but Amy was on top. Amy grabbed Sharon's head and banged it a few times on the floor, then pulled her hands up and ripped a strip of duct tape free. She grabbed Sharon's arms and tried to tie them up, but Sharon got one hand free and scratched Amy's face again.

Amy drew back her arm and punched Sharon in the face. Then she grabbed Sharon's arms and pulled them down, rolling her over on them after tying her hands together, then pulling them down close to Sharon's body. Amy tore some more tape free and started tying Sharon up. Sharon started screaming. Amy started rolling Sharon across the floor, taping her up into a tight bundle. She then tore a strip off and taped up Sharon's mouth. Sharon was lying, squirming on the ground with her nostrils flaring out. Amy sat there for a few minutes to get her breathing under control.

She finally stood up and pulled Sharon over to the corner and sat her upright. She got into Sharon's face and said, "I warned you that I would duct tape you up if you got out of hand again." Sharon's eyes were very wide and glassy. She was shocked senseless. *Good,* Amy thought. She sat down on the couch and assessed the damage Sharon had done to her.

There was a knock on the door. Amy raced over as fast as she could and knocked once on the door. Three more knocks came from the other side.

"Who is it?" asked Amy.

"The bike guy." It was Preston. She moved to open the door, hissing in pain. When she finally got the door open, Preston quickly entered, wheeling in a mountain bike. He took one look at her and did a double take. He noticed Sharon taped up in the corner. Amy was having a hard time getting the bar back down into place. Preston stepped forward and grabbed the bar. "Let go. I've got it." Amy let go and stepped aside. Preston secured the bar. Amy walked slowly over to the couch and sat down.

Preston went over and looked at Sharon sitting in the corner. She was staring at him with shocked, wide eyes. She kind of looked like she had last night when he had to be rough with her to get her to shut up, except she now looked like she would have a real shiner tomorrow on her left eye. It was red and puffy. He took a step back and really looked at her. Her arms were taped to her chest, and all the way down to her waist. Her legs and feet were taped together snugly. He wondered how Amy was able to get the tape so tight. Sharon had to have been squirming around. Maybe she had knocked her out first. He turned and looked at Amy. She looked like she had just had a fight with a wildcat. She had scratches all over her face, arms, and hands. Her hair was out of her braid and hanging all around her. She was leaning back on the couch with her eyes closed, deeply breathing. She had smeared blood in her hair on the right side. He turned back around and looked at Sharon. Wow, he must have missed a hell of a fight. He walked into the bathroom and gathered supplies up and got a basin of water and a washcloth. He shook his head at the scene before him in the living room. No one would believe it if he told them. Nope, no one would believe it. He went over to Amy and set everything down on the coffee table.

He gently touched her arm were there were no scratches to get her attention. She opened her eyes and looked at him. He noticed that her pupils seemed to be dilated more than they should be. He reached up and felt her head where her hair was streaked with blood. She hissed at him. That was a painful bump. He dipped the washcloth in the water and gently patted the area. It came away with fresh blood. He cleaned the blood out of her hair, then applied light pressure to stop the bleeding.

When it stopped, he looked at it and decided it would be fine. There was just a small scraped area on the bump. Head wounds always bled a lot. He applied triple antibiotic ointment to it. He knew he should cut the hair around the area, but women were picky about their hair, and after seeing what she been through and the shape she was in, it was not something he wanted to approach right now. If necessary, it would be done later. He then cleaned the cuts and applied more ointment and bandages. He asked her if she was hurt anywhere else.

"No. Thank you. I was resting first, then I would have cleaned them up."

He said, "That must have been some fight you were in."

She smiled. "Yeah, you should have seen us rolling around the floor. You would have liked that scene. That's how I duct taped her up."

Preston laughed at that. He would have really liked to see that happen. He gathered everything up and walked out of the room. Amy stared at Sharon. Even with all the aches and pains she had, she still felt a bit sorry for her. She looked so pathetic sitting in the corner with her wide, shocked eyes.

Amy walked into the bedroom and Preston was there looking at some of Sharon's belongings. He turned and faced her. "You should be resting. I think you have a slight concussion. Your pupils are a little dilated."

"I said I would help Sharon pack up and I'll do it," she said.

"Okay, tell ya what. You sit down on the bed and tell me the items to put in the pack. Okay?"

"I'm not delicate, you know. It'll take a lot more than that to put me down for the count."

He smiled. "I don't doubt that at all." Amy turned and started to sway with dizziness. Preston caught her and said, "You're lying down on the couch and resting. No complaints. You need rest."

"Okay, twist my arm," Amy said. "I won't complain at all." Preston led her to the couch. Amy lay down and Preston took the sheet and the other two blankets and pulled them over her. Amy shut her eyes to stop the room from swaying. It felt good to rest for a few minutes.

Amy woke up with a hell of a headache. She tried to get up, but felt nauseous. She lay back down. Preston had the lantern on in the dining room. She looked around and saw that the sheets and things were back up on the windows. She also noticed that her comforter was on top of the two blankets covering her up. She started to feel really bad that they hadn't been able to leave when it got dark. She vaguely remembered Preston waking her up a few times. She wondered what time it was. Slowly, she sat up. It wasn't as bad this time. Her stomach was still upset, but not too bad. But boy, her head was really pounding in time with her heartbeats. The light was making the headache worse, too. She was thirsty. She got up to get a drink. She noticed that Sharon wasn't in the corner any longer. *I wonder what Preston did with her?* She moved slowly to the kitchen. She grabbed a glassful of water and took a drink.

Preston walked into the kitchen. "Don't drink that too fast or you'll be throwing it right back up." Amy turned around and looked at him. "How's the head doing?"

Amy said, "A heavy metal drummer is in there rehearsing for a concert."

"That good, huh?" He held out his hand and said, "Take these. They should help. Then you need to go lay back down. Rest is the best thing for you right now."

Amy took the two tablets from him and placed them in her mouth, swallowing them with another drink of water. "Thank you," she said. "I'm sorry we couldn't leave when it got dark. Do you know about what time it is?"

Preston said, "It's about 11:00 pm. Sharon wasn't in any shape to leave, either. Can you tell me what happened this afternoon?" Amy told him all about it. He smiled. "Wow, that was some fight. I was wondering, because you had a lot more damage than Sharon."

"What can I say? I underestimated how tough she could be. She fought like a wet wildcat. She attacked me when I wasn't looking; I wasn't ready for that. After the first surprise attack, I got her under control."

Preston chuckled. "Yes, you did. I had a hell of a time cutting her out of the duct tape."

"You undid her? Why?"

Preston looked at Amy for a while before answering. Then he said, "She was traumatized by it all and in shock. I cut her out of the tape and got her into bed. She hasn't spoken a word to me or even looked at me. I found her a little while ago going around the apartment, trying the light switches again. She saw me coming and ran back, got into bed, and buried her head under the covers." He sighed.

"I'm sorry. I didn't mean to do that to her, but she crossed the line."

"Don't worry about that right now. We'll have to leave tomorrow night. We can't put if off anymore than that or we won't have much of a chance to get away. You lie back down and rest and gain your strength so we can leave tomorrow." He took a small flashlight and shone it into each of her eyes. She flinched and closed her eyes. "Your pupils look normal now."

"Good, but my head is really throbbing right now."

"That should be gone by morning."

It was just getting light out when Amy opened her eyes. She looked around and saw Preston asleep in his sleeping bag. She stretched, then flinched at the stiffness and soreness that seemed to be everywhere on her body. She got up and put coffee on. She went into the bathroom and got cleaned up and put clean clothes on. There was nothing like washing your face and body with icy water to wake you up. The coffee was done. She poured a cup and sat at the dining table. She felt really good. She just had a small headache and a tender sore spot on her head. She was clear headed. She had felt so groggy last night. It had been really nice to have someone to take care of her. She wondered what this day would bring. Ever since the EMP had hit, it had been nothing but one thing after another. She sure hoped they would be able to leave today.

She heard Preston stirring in the living room. He came into the dining room, running really fast; he looked at her, then headed on through down the hallway. He came back and said, "The door was unbarred and Sharon is gone."

"What? Where would she go?"

"I don't know."

"When could she have left?" she asked.

"I don't know that, either," he answered. "I must have slept harder then I thought. I didn't hear her open the door." He walked over to the window and looked to see if he could see Sharon anywhere. He turned to her and said, "I'm going to get ready to leave. If someone grabs her and makes her talk, they could find out that we have food, water and lights and they'll be coming to take it from us. We'll take the bikes and our packs and go out in the woods over there." He pointed to a woody area. "We'll wait and see if she comes back or if anyone has forced her to tell them we're here."

She looked at him seriously. "And then what?"

"If she doesn't come back," he said, "we'll just head out without her. I don't even know where we could look for her or which way she went. If she comes back with someone, we'll have to play that one by ear and decide what to do." He turned and walked down the hall. She prepared to leave.

****

Sharon lay in bed for about an hour after she heard Preston settle down and turn off the lantern. She silently crept out a few times to make sure they both were still asleep. She put her good wool winter coat, gloves and hat on. She walked slowly and quietly into the living room and went to the door. She took a long time opening it so she wouldn't make any noise. Slowly, she made her way out of the apartment building. It was so very dark out there. She felt her pocket to make sure she had the little flashlight that Preston kept in the bedside drawer. She was going to need it to see the street signs. She had decided after Preston had cut her out of the duct tape that she wasn't staying there anymore with those two crazy people. They were trying to kill her. At least that bitch would. She just knew it. How dare Preston leave her alone with that bitch and go off to who knows where while she had to fight for her life? Her whole world had turned upside down. She still couldn't believe that he would believe that bitch over her. That had never happened before. He hadn't been very nice, either.

She decided to go to her Cousin Monica's house to wait it out until the power came back on. Then she would have them both arrested at the same time for the horrible things they did to her. How dare they treat her this way? Well, she would show them just as soon as the power came back on. She'd been checking the phone and the light switches all day and night, because she was calling the police as soon as the power came back on. She made her way along the highway. She had a long ways to go. Monica lived about eight miles away. She made sure to wear her new jogging shoes so her feet wouldn't hurt too bad, remembering the horrible walk home she had to do. It was creepy out here. You could see fires burning all over the place in the distance. The cars were just sitting there. Some of them had the doors open. She stopped to rest frequently. Boy, this walking stuff was hard. She took out her bottle of water and took a drink. She recapped it and placed it back in her pocket. The small bag she carried was getting very heavy. She was still pissed at that fat cow bitch and Preston because she couldn't find some of her makeup or her good hairbrush. God only knew what they had done with her stuff. That cow bitch probably stole them and Preston let her do it.

Who did they think they were? Nobody treated her like that and got away with it. Yup, just as soon as the power came back on, they were going to jail and out of her life for good. Good riddance. She still couldn't believe that cow bitch had hit her and given her a black eye and tied her up. Half her face was swollen up and she couldn't even open her eye on that side of her face. It hurt, too.

Sharon remembered she had to go up an overpass to get to Monica's house. It looked different walking than it did when she was driving. It was pretty high up, too. She came to an intersection and got her flashlight out to read the street sign. She must have made a wrong turn back there; she was on the wrong road. She walked back and looked around and went the right way. She kept stumbling over things on the sidewalk. She had to stop to rest more often; she was so tired. The sun was rising. It was scary out here. She knew she had to keep going. She could hear weird scuttling sounds and a few times she thought she heard footsteps. She hid in a doorway for a while and the sounds went away. She was walking past an alley when a hand reached out and grabbed her. She screamed. She felt herself being thrown into the wall. She heard laughter.

****

Preston and Amy got everything together they were taking. "I'm going to take this bike over to the location we'll be spending the day. I'll be back in a few minutes. Then we'll go down in storage and get the other two bikes and take them over, too." Amy nodded. He looked at her and said, "Lock up and wait for my knock."

Amy walked to the door. "Be careful. Watch out for all the little zombies." He smiled and nodded his head as he stepped into the hall. Amy barred the door. She went into the kitchen to check one more time for anything they said they were bringing that might have been left by mistake. She sighed deeply as she went back into the living room and watched the wooded area for signs of Preston. It was a scary thing happening. They were taking off into the wild blue yonder together and just leaving everything behind. She wondered how long it would really take them to get to the retreat. What would the retreat be like? Would his friends there like her? She was more worried about that than anything else. She closed her eyes and sighed. Take one day at a time and deal with it before worrying about what the next day after that would bring. Deal with one problem at a time, too. There would be a lot of problems on this trip to get through. What had Sharon been thinking of to take off like that? If she thought being tied up with duct tape was bad, what in the hell would she think of what the little zombies would do to her? There was a soft knock on the door. Amy turned and walked to the door.

****

Sharon woke up feeling really cold and hearing more laughter. Someone poked her. She looked over and one guy was going through her bag, throwing stuff all over the place. She tried to get up and realized someone was holding her down.

"Get your hands off my stuff," she yelled. They laughed harder. She struggled to get up and couldn't do anything but wiggle.

"She doesn't have nothing good in here," said one of them. "There's no food or water." The other one held her bottle of water in the hand that wasn't holding her down. They both took a drink. Sharon kept squirming around, trying to get free.

She was saying over and over, "Get your hands off me."

Finally, the one that had been going through her stuff looked over at her and asked, "Where did you get the water?"

Sharon just said, "Get your hands off of me."

He reached out and hit her in the face on the side that was already bruised. Sharon screamed. "Answer me right now. Where did you get this water?" he demanded. Sharon struggled with all her might. She was scratching and kicking as hard as she could. He reached over, grabbed her throat, and yanked her up so he was face to face with her. "Tell me where you got the water from." She started crying. He shook her. "Tell me where this water came from!"

She barely could get a word out. "My apartment."

"Do you have more water there?" She tried to shake her head yes but could barely move at all. She was trembling in terror at the look in his eyes. He tossed her back on the ground. "Where do you live?"

"24012 Maplewood Drive," she whimpered.

"What else do you have at your apartment?"

"Some food and a lantern."

He stood up and dragged her up to her feet. "Let's go. Lead the way." The two men started laughing. One reached out and pushed her. She stumbled and fell to the ground. He yanked her up again and said, "Get up and get moving."

****

"Who is it?"

"It's me."

"Me, who?"

"Very funny." Amy was already opening up the door. He stepped into the living room, looked around and said, "Let's go." Amy picked up the backpack and got the rest of her things. Preston led the way down to the storage area. He went over, unlocked his storage space, and brought the bikes out one by one. They walked them over to the door. Preston looked around and said, "It's clear. Follow me." Amy walked closely behind him, steering Sharon's bike. He would stop behind things or beside them and look around before proceeding. When they got across the road and into the wooded area, Amy saw where Preston had the other bike. It was hidden in a little space underneath some trees. Preston motioned her to lean the bike by a tree. He took the saddlebags and secured them to the bikes. He then pulled out a tarp and put it on the ground, then opened up two sleeping bags and indicated for her to sit down on one. He sat down on the other. "We'll stay here today and wait to see if Sharon comes back. We'll only wait until dark for her. Then we leave." Amy got them a couple of sandwiches and poured them some coffee out of the thermos she had filled. They sat quietly and ate their breakfast.

Amy was looking at his bike now that it was a little lighter out and she could see things better. "What is that on your bike?" she asked.

He had rigged up a mount for his bike. It was a swivel that held a 20-gauge semi-auto Charley Daley shotgun. He had sawed off the stock so it had a pistol handle and sawed off the barrel down to fifteen inches. "That's a shotgun. It will cover any head-on assault we run into." He held up an AR-15 and said, "I'll carry this on my back." He laid the AR-15 back down and patted his 45 his side. "And I have my trusty .45 Colt on my side."

"Cool," Amy said. She indicated the shotgun on the bike. "How did you get it up there like that?"

"I used the swivel part from a boat oar. I modified it and locked it down. It worked like a champ. I took a bike air pump clip design to snap and hold an air pump on the bike frame and modified it to hold the handle of the gun. It worked really well. I simply pull up and the gun will be free to swivel around where I need it to point to."

Amy smiled at him. "Wow, that's going to work great. Good thinking."

He smiled back. "Thank you. We should get as much rest as we possibly can today while we're waiting. We don't know how long we'll have to go until we can find a safe place to stop for the day after we leave here tonight. Later this afternoon, we will go over a little gun safety and you can practice going through the motions. I have a 9mm Hipoint with a shoulder holster and two extra magazines that you can carry for personal defense."

"Okay." She thought for a while and then asked, "How long do you think it will take us to get there?"

"We should be able to cover about eighty to ninety miles a night. The trip is going to take three to four days, maybe more; it will depend on what we run into between here and there." They sat in silence, deep in their own thoughts.

Amy had practiced with the handgun all afternoon. She felt comfortable with it now. She didn't know if she would hit anything she was shooting at or not, but she would give it her best effort. They took turns lying down and having a nap. The other would stay up and keep a look out for anyone coming near them and to keep an eye out for Sharon. When the sun started to set, they got everything ready to leave. There had been no sign of Sharon. When it got dark, Preston sighed. "Okay, it's time to go."

Amy looked at him. "Are you sure you don't want to wait a little longer to see if she shows up?"

Preston said, "No, we've waited long enough. I don't think she's coming back." They left the third bike and Sharon's backpack there. Preston had Amy take Sharon's bike because he had equipped the bikes with tubeless, airless tires. That reduced the weight they had to carry. No need to carry patches and air pumps. They climbed on the bikes and started riding. Preston led the way with Amy following.

****

It was about a half hour after full dark when Sharon and the two guys finally made it to the apartment building. They pushed Sharon up the stairs. She was freezing. She had lost her hat on one of her many falls. She hadn't even realized it. She had seen so much today that made her climb inside herself and refuse to see anything else that was out there. The smell of rotting meat was everywhere. She stopped at the apartment door and fumbled to get her keys out of her pocket. Her hands were cold and her palms were bloody from the pavement. She had lost her gloves, too. She didn't remember when. The one guy-standing behind her had a gun pushed into her back. Finally, she was able to get the door open. No one was there. They went inside. The guys commented on what a nice place it was. They walked around and saw all the water and searched the cupboards for food. One of them grabbed a bottle of wine and ate some cheese as he walked around. Sharon was still standing in the middle of the living room.

The two guys came back and looked at Sharon. "Now we can party. We have everything we need. Food, water, wine and a woman to entertain us." The one guy set his bottle of wine down and went over to Sharon, taking her coat off and whispering in her ear, "It's party time."

Chapter 10

Starving Hunters

'Doubling down on stupid is not a particularly good idea.'
Breitbart

Junior was up by next year's woodpile, holding the rifle tightly aimed at the three bad guys by the front door. He was waiting to hear his dad say there were five guys out here with him. That was the signal to shoot in front of one of them. Why won't they just leave? Why are they here? What could they possibly want? None of it made any sense at all. The world had just ended. These guys couldn't need anything yet. It had only been a couple of hours since the EMP had hit. The sun was shining brightly, making all the colors of the leaves and trees vivid and vibrant. What was taking so long? Then he heard the words he was waiting for. He squeezed the trigger and a loud bang echoed through the woods. A small amount of dirt in front of the three bad guys shot up into the air. All three of them reached for their guns and started shooting at his dad. He aimed and shot each of them twice, making them fall in slow motion. He looked over at his dad; he was on the ground and a woman was lying there moaning not too far away, with a rifle on the ground next to her. Next thing he knew he was running down the hill towards his fallen father, but he just couldn't seem to get there. He was running and pumping his legs with everything he had, but it just seemed that no matter how hard he tried he couldn't reach him. He screamed out, "Dad, dad!" There was blood splattered everywhere and running down like little streams. The red color was splashed here and there, overshadowing the whole clearing, shining clear and bright like in a painting. He reached down and touched his dad, then drew his hand back at the cold feeling of his body. Blood was dripping off his hand. The tear shaped drops shined with a brilliance like phosphorescence red paint crystal clear and large. He screamed out, "No, oh God, no!"

He jerked and sat up, looking at the clock by the bed. It was 11:30 pm. Sometimes his dreams were of what happened in a very weird, distorted version of the events. They always consisted of him trying to kill the bad guys before they could shoot his dad. It never worked no matter how hard he tried. It didn't matter what order he killed the bad guys, they still managed to kill his dad before he could shoot them all.

He sighed deeply. The only thing that could have changed the events was if Marion and Gayle had been there with rifles, too. Then it would have been a more even firefight. If Marion would only have listened when his dad had pleaded with her to come with them, he might still be alive today. *Marion deserves whatever happens to her in town*, he thought, feeling anger and bitterness towards her. Well, Gayle didn't deserve to have anything bad happen to her, but she had stayed with her mother, so whatever happens is her own fault. He had decided that it would be better for all of them if he didn't go check on them in town at all. He wasn't sure he could control himself from doing something he might regret later to Marion. *Might regret was the key phrase*, he thought with anger. If he saw her now, there was no telling what he might do to her. It is just better for everyone if he kept his distance from them. Who knows, maybe someone will get tired of her big argumentative mouth and take care of the problem for him. That would be poetic justice. Like life was ever fair or filled with justice. He snorted at that thought. He'd known that all his life. His dad used to tell him, "Life is not fair. Anyone who says different is either in la la land or they are just plain outright lying. Life and the word fairness should never be used in the same sentence. It can never be."

It had been ten days since the world had ended and his dad had died. Feeling clear headed for the first time since it happened, he started thinking about what he should be doing. Realizing what needed to be done, he planned to set out some muskrat traps and get a small trap line going for meat and animal fur to tan. It's what his dad and he would be doing if he hadn't died. He was feeling more human right now than at any time since it had happened. The last ten days felt more like being in a waking dream or a robot programmed to go through the motions of getting up and going to bed than anything human. His dad would be very disappointed in him at the way he had been acting since it happened. This was the busiest time of the year. There was hunting and trapping for meat and fur that needed to be done. Looking seriously at his dad's chair setting there, he vowed he would make his dad proud and use the skills and knowledge he had taught him to survive.

Going to the garage and getting his traps ready to set first thing in the morning was his top priority now. After all, he felt he had already done the hardest thing he possibly ever could by burying his Dad. He stared at the clock for a long while, lost in his thoughts of better times. All of a sudden it dawned on him that the lights were working. They shouldn't be. An EMP should have taken them out. Now that it came to his attention, he realized that everything was still working in the house. It must be like his dad had said. The house was built into the hill. The hill must have protected the house and garage from the EMP. He shook his head in amazement. Wow, his dad had built one hell of a place. Needing a shower very badly, he got up and went into the bathroom and jumped into the shower. The water really felt good. Afterwards, looking at himself in the mirror, he didn't recognize his reflection. A stranger stared back at him from the mirror; some kind of a deranged person from a B grade movie. He chuckled a bit at that and thought of the things his dad would have said if he could see him now. That thought sent a shock through him. He had better get his act together and show that he was worthy of the time and knowledge his dad had given him. His stomach growled and he realized he was very hungry. How long had it been since he'd eaten anything? He couldn't remember the last time food had mattered to him. It must have been before all of this had happened. It's time to eat a real meal. As he prepared something solid to eat, he made a mental list of what needed to be done before he could set out traps tomorrow.

Junior went into the garage, checking the walls to see if there were anymore hidden surprises his dad had in the walls. So far he had found a few things, but nothing like the hole that his dad had stashed the rifles in. Refilling the ammo pouches and cleaning the rifles made him feel like his Dad would be proud of him. He decided to put one rifle back in the hole for a backup and he would carry the other rifle all the time, just in case he needed it. You just never knew when you might need the semi-automatic SKS. Events had already proved that fact to him.

At first light he gathered up everything needed to go to the lake and start his trap line. His first job was to find the active muskrat huts. It felt good to be out in the crisp autumn air again. The leaves were changing and the brilliant yellow and orange colors brightened his mood a little. The Canadian geese were overhead honking, and looking up, he saw the V high in the sky. They were heading south. For a quick moment he wondered if that was a good idea. Maybe he, too, should be heading south before the winter snows come. Upon reflection and respecting his dad's survival instincts on picking this location, he decided it would be better to just stay put right here, where everything was located. In fact, he had more than most people did right now. Not only was there a working truck, but power for lights and things. His dad had spent many years getting this place ready for any type of a disaster. He had done an excellent job, too.

He approached the marsh like an old friend. He felt at home here. The smell of fresh mud and the sight of the first muskrat hut caused excitement to build inside of him. The first one was a large round mud and cattail hut. It was built about three feet tall and about four feet around at the base. There was fresh mud and a slide off the top heading into deeper water. He had only twelve traps to set. He took six Number 1 Long Spring Traps and six Number 110 Conibear Traps with him this time.

The leg hold traps were set up with drowning slides and needed two stakes. One stake was necessary near the trap and one stake would be out in the deeper water. He remembered when he was little, his dad tried to explain to him what deeper water meant. He chuckled at the memory, thinking it meant over his head in about five or six feet of water. He smiled, remembering the look on his dad's face. It was one of those looks dads give their sons when they are thinking, *He can't really be my son.*

He set the first leg hold trap at the right side of the slide where the muskrats would climb out. He staked it in water that was about three feet deep. The drowning swivel was an ingenious invention. It only allowed the trap to go down to the deeper water. Once the first set was finished, he started to feel a whole lot better and more like his old self. As he walked in front of the hut, he hit a deep trench, almost falling into the water. Stopping, he realized he found the entrance run to the hut. Using the hip boots, he felt in the mud and traced the trench right up to the underwater entrance. Grabbing one of the Number 110 Conibear Traps and stakes, he set the trap on the run quickly and quietly. Once the trap set was completed, he walked off looking for the next hut. He found a huge feed bed. In the cattails, he set two leg hold traps, one trap for each trail leading up to the feed bed would do the trick. He remembered his dad had him watch Buckshot's Water Trapping DVD before he would let Junior put out some traps of his own when he was young. It was so he would understand what he was doing and not just copying his dad. Looking the sets over, a feeling of confidence overcame him. They were pretty near perfect.

Before long, he finished setting the rest of his traps. He looked around and decided it was clear; the marsh had plenty more huts to set. But it wasn't wise to be away from the house too long. He would just keep moving these traps every fourth day, just taking the cream of the crop of muskrats. Seeing a Mallard duck swim by, he considered shooting him but changed his mind. No sense telling the world where he was with the noise of a bullet. The whole idea of using traps and snares was to be silent but effective.

He was averaging about four muskrats a day. He would gather up the guts, tail and feet and set them out about three hundred yards from the house to bring the predators in close. His dad had always harped on the myth of the hug a predator crowd that believed nature was somehow perfect without mankind interfering with it. They didn't understand that Mother Nature wasn't a kind old woman that loved animals and trees. Mother Nature was a very hard and unkind mistress. Mother Nature's way of dealing with overpopulation of animals was to use disease and starvation to skim down the herds to manageable proportions for each area. The animals suffered horrible deaths. Mankind, by harvesting each fall the meat and fur of animals, makes healthier herds possible. This way there was enough food to go around for all of them and they would be healthier.

Mankind was much kinder and more humane than Mother Nature could ever be. Nature actually thrived from mankind's involvement in managing the harvest of furs. Anyone who studied ecology knew that fact, too. His dad had no tolerance for fools who refuted this fact. Every time he thought about being a modern day Mountain Man, an image of a coyote mountain man style hat came to mind. This was the year he was going to catch the coyote that would be volunteering for his new hat. The plan was to tan and sew it by hand.

The day started with waking up before daybreak and going out to check his muskrat traps. He would change the location of the traps that were not producing much fur to a new area with more active signs. Going home and bringing the day's catch, always being careful to watch for intruders, could be a bit challenging at times. It was easy to forget that it wasn't safe outside. He would skin the day's catch and put the guts and unused parts out for the predators in the bait pile, then eat and go to bed. It became a routine for him and kept him busy doing something productive.

After the chores were done, it would be time to check the garage for intruders. There was a nice hiding-hole built into the brush where he could watch the road safely and no one would notice if anyone was there. "Work the plan," his dad always said. That meant waiting for at least six months before venturing out to the town to see what was left. It had now been three weeks since the world ended and his dad died. Those two events would always be side by side in his mind together. So, he had five months and one week to wait out before going anywhere. He checked the radio for a signal every afternoon. At night, he watched DVD movies or the movies they had made as a family and remembered what life used to be about.

He had plenty of food, water and warmth. He only burned a small fire at night in the wood stove and let it go out as he slept. With only one wall exposed to the elements, it was a brilliant plan on his dad's part for holding the heat inside. He was enjoying going out now in the fall while he still could, because once the snow started, he wouldn't be leaving the camp. It was much too dangerous to leave a snow trail right to his door.

In the morning, when he was checking his traps, he heard the sound of two people coming towards him long before there was any sight of them. City people always sounded like a freight train going through the woods. Sitting down at the side of a muskrat hut, he watched and listened for them. Cattails were all around him and whoever they were, they wouldn't notice him sitting there. The two people stopped about fifty yards away. They could be seen clearly and their loud argument could be heard for a long distance. *What morons*, he thought.

"You said you knew how to hunt and we would have no trouble surviving in the woods," the first one complained. "That's why we came here. I'm starving! We only had one rabbit to eat in three days. I'm losing weight like mad. We can't go on like this much longer."

"Well, if you wouldn't have missed that deer yesterday we would be eating real well right now," said the other.

"Well, you missed that deer last week, so you have no room to talk."

"I'm starving. What the hell are we going to eat when winter comes? Tree bark?"

"We'll have to give this hunt up and go back to my dad's house" said the first one. "Maybe they got some emergency supplies from the government or something. I agree we can't live like this much longer. There's no food out here."

"I'll tell you what, if we don't get a deer in two days, we'll head home, okay?"

"Okay."

The second one said, "Let's hunt around this lake here and maybe we can get lucky." They took off through the trees.

Junior kept his eye on them. There were still a few traps to check before heading home. He finished up as quickly and quietly as possible so those two men wouldn't see or hear him. As he threw the four muskrats for the day in his pack, he was careful leaving the marsh not to toss any mud or leave tracks that others could see that would lead them back to the house. Arriving home and hurrying inside, he kept to his routine. As he was skinning the muskrats, he was thinking about what those two men had said. They were stupid fools. They were surrounded by food. They were so blind to everything around them. They were in hunter mode. They could have cooked up the cattail roots and caught a few muskrats to eat. Did they even look around the area and see what was available to eat? No, they did not. They were stuck in the mighty hunter mode. He figured they had to be acting like backpack survivalists.

That's the only idea that made sense. His dad had warned him about those kinds of people and their mentality. Their way of thinking was to fill up their backpacks with mostly useless equipment and head to the woods with no food and magically they would be able to hunt enough to survive. Like walking out in the woods is like going to nature's supermarket. Like anyone can just walk out in the woods and the deer or whatever will just appear right in front of them for them to shoot and eat. Nothing to it. Nothing at all. Anyone can do this. They are the mighty hunters. Don't they realize how many times they've gone out hunting and not returned with any game to eat? Or went a whole deer season and not been able to bring one deer home? How would they eat in the meantime? They had no cabin. He bet they were living in a tent, too. Yup, they were morons.

Well, hopefully they would be gone in a couple of weeks anyway, one way or another. He was really hoping they would leave in the next two days, like they suggested. Snow was coming soon. They wouldn't survive out there when the snow started to fall. He took his skinned muskrats and put them on stretchers, thankful there would be plenty of fur to tan this winter. He needed to get out and collect three buckets of acorns to use to tan the hides with. He'd boil them down for tannic acid. That should keep him busy this winter and keep him from going stir crazy when he was housebound.

He gathered up all the guts and parts and went outside. The coyotes and raccoons had been getting into the bait pile. There was evidence of this as he tossed the new guts into the pile. *Good*, he thought. A few days after those yahoos leave, it will be time to set out some snares for the coyotes and raccoons. On the way back to the house, he kept thinking of those two guys. *Why do people think they can head off into the woods and survive? They have no skills and no experience.* He shook his head. He was so glad his dad had taught him how to survive out in the woods from as far back as he could remember. Even with all of his experience, he wouldn't be foolish enough to just head out in the woods and survive with just a backpack. It took planning, equipment and a whole lot of experience. He shook his head again. The sooner the backpack survivalists leave, the better it would be for him. He figured that as soon as the snow started falling there would not be many of those kinds left around in the woods. Well, at least not alive, anyway.

The next day he was very cautious as he headed out to check his traps, walking a little bit, then stopping to listen and make sure it was clear. Getting into the cattails as quickly as he could was his first priority. They would hide him from sight. Slowly, he would step in the water, making sure not to make a splashing noise. Today he was armed with a Ruger Mark 11. It was his .22 pistol. He walked around very slowly so as not to cause ripples in the water and give his position away to anyone that might be around. He wanted to keep as low of a profile as he could. He needed to move some of the traps to better locations, but was worried about the two guys from yesterday. He decided to wait until tomorrow to move them. He had gotten only three muskrats today. Carefully, he made his way out of the cattails onto dry land.

He stepped out and heard a voice say, "Freeze." Junior reached his hand slowly down to get the Ruger and the voice said, "Don't try it kid. I will shoot you." The two yahoos from yesterday walked out of the brush towards him. They both had rifles with scopes mounted on them.

"We saw you leaving this area yesterday from across the lake," said the other one. "We waited this morning to see if you would come back today. What are you doing? Duck hunting?"

"No," said Junior. He looked them over and saw how unkempt they were and how unhealthy they looked. He hoped they wouldn't notice that he had on clean clothes and that he didn't smell like they did. He hoped the hip boots and his old Army field jacket covered up this very obvious fact. If they were the least bit observant, it would be as clear as day to them. They seemed as oblivious to this as they had been to the fact of food around them yesterday. Junior asked them curiously, "What do you want?"

"We want to know what you are doing here on our lake," said the first one.

Junior's eyebrows lifted in surprise at that answer. He said, "Your lake? The last time I heard, the State of Wisconsin owned this lake." Junior was starting to dislike these two arrogant yahoos. "You guys from the city?"

The second one said, "Yes, but we come up here hunting every year. So this is our lake now."

"So, what are you doing?" Junior pressed. "Are you trying to rob me? What is it you want?"

"Nope, we aren't robbing you. We're not criminals. We're just telling you to stay away from our lake from now on. We own it now, not the State of Wisconsin."

Junior was disgusted with them at this point. "Fine, whatever. I will be on my way, then."

He took a step and the second one said, "Wait a minute. What do you have in that pack?"

"None of your business," replied Junior. "Unless you're lying to me about being criminals and intend to rob me."

"If what you have in that pack has to do with this lake," said the first man, "then we aren't robbing you, seeing that we own it now. So it is very much our business to know what's in that pack."

Junior said, "Fine, lower your rifles and I'll show you." They cradled their rifles in their arms. Junior took the pack off and pulled three muskrats out of the pack.

"Rats. You're eating rats. You must be starving, too."

Junior wanted to scream at them that they weren't rats. Morons. Instead he said, "I'll give you each one so we all have something to eat. It's better than nothing."

"Rats. Well, why not?" said the second man. "I'm starving and the thought of eating a rat is better than the nothing we've been eating. In fact, I never thought I would say this, but they aren't looking all that bad at the moment. It must be the hunger talking."

The first one said, "Wait a minute. How did you catch these rats? I don't see any bullet holes and we didn't hear any shots."

"I caught them in rat traps. My dad has a dozen of them." Thinking real fast on his feet, Junior added, "My dad should be watching you two right now." Both of them looked around real quick in all directions.

"You're bluffing," said the first one. "We don't see anyone but you."

Junior smiled at them. "That's the plan." It was as if the Grace of God had shined down on him at that very moment. They had all heard a very loud cracking behind them in the woods.

"Okay. We don't want any trouble," said the second one, "and if you don't mind, we would like to have a rat to eat like you offered. Is that okay? We're starving."

The other one agreed. "Yeah, please, we don't want any trouble, okay? One of them rats to eat will be right down neighborly of you. We meant no real harm to you and your dad." Junior looked at them and then tossed each one of them a muskrat. He put the other one back in his pack. Both men thanked him.

Junior started walking away, then stopped and turned around. He'd been thinking as fast as he could about what he could do to scare them away. They were holding on to the muskrats as if they had never seen food before. They looked up at him. "For your own safety," Junior said, "don't try to follow me. My dad is a real security conscious type of guy, know what I mean? He's retired from the military and set traps all over the place around here. For your own safety, don't try to follow us. I don't even know where he set up all the traps." He turned around and continued down the trail at a normal speed, making sure not to show any concern.

Both men again said, "Thanks for the rats. We appreciate it." He didn't acknowledge them at all and kept on walking. As soon as he knew they couldn't see him or hear him anymore, he took off at a fast trot. It would be hard to run all out when he was wearing hip boots, but he wanted to put as much distance as he could between them and him before he stopped. He wasn't taking a chance of tripping with these hip boots on. That was all he needed right now.

After he had run past the second hill, he stopped and got off the trail to keep watch to make sure they hadn't tried to follow him home. He found a comfortable spot, sat down and waited for two hours. He decided that tomorrow night after dark he would return and pull all of his traps until these two yahoos left the area. He was thinking about the two men and how lucky he'd been with this situation. Tomorrow he had better scout around and find where these two were camped and keep a watch on their activities until they left the area. The house was just a mile down the trail. It wouldn't be too hard for them to find it if they were determined to do so. Yup, the house was too close for comfort with these two clowns trampling around the woods. It would be better to just pull all the traps tomorrow night and seal the house up tight and wait them out. He wouldn't be able to keep up the story that his dad was around if they watched the house.

He got home, sealed everything up tight, and pulled all the metal shutters down on the windows and secured the bolts down tight. That way no one would see any lights or anything. They'd walk right by the place and not notice anything. He grabbed some brush and swept out all the tracks from the trail and outside the house. He scattered leaves all over. It looked natural and untouched. Yup, these two would walk right on by and not notice anything at all.

He skinned the muskrat and put it up on the stretcher. He was getting tired of eating fried muskrat anyway. He had smoked up a lot, too, and stored the smoked pieces in airtight containers. They would be a good source of meat throughout the winter for snacks, soups and stews. Thinking of food made him hungry. He decided to make an early dinner and save some to eat later tonight. His appetite was back. After he ate and cleaned up, it was dark. He decided to go get the traps and not wait until the next night. It would be better to get this over with.

He'd seal the house up and that would be that. He started to think about the two morons and their rifles. One man had a .300 Weatherby Magnum Rifle with a Leupold Mark 4 Extended Range Tactical M1 Rifle Scope. Their accuracy had been proven in the field. Their rugged and absolute waterproof integrity was unquestionable. They were everything a tactical shooter, long-range shooter, target shooter, or hunter could ask for. Just the riflescope, mounts, sling and ammo he spent well over $4000.00. The other man had a Ruger M77 Hawkeye Bolt Action Rifle 7164. What a fool the one who bought the Weatherby was. He could have bought a Remington SPS Tactical 308 Black Hogue Stock with V-II Leopold for under $1,500.00 and saved almost $3,000.00. He could have spent that money on food. Those two would be well supplied right now. But the fantasy of a backpack survivalist has nothing to do with reality. Their mentality is it is better to say 'I can hunt and fish to survive instead of getting properly prepared to really survive.' Living in a tent come January with no food … that rifle is going to look pretty useless. As Duncan Long said in his book, *Survival Rifles*, "A good garden and traps will feed you better than a wealth of hunting rifles." Unfortunately for many people, the truth of that statement had to be learned the hard way with deadly consequences. Junior thought the Remington was a much better outfit for around $1500.00 with sling, scope mounts and ammo.

He went outside and stopped to listen and sniff the air. If they were upwind of him, he would smell them long before they got close. Those two were pretty ripe. He made his way as slowly and quietly as the heavy frost would let him. Each step he took was followed by a crunch. He certainly hoped those two wouldn't be around and cause any more trouble. He still shook his head at them telling him they owned the lake. What arrogance and nerve they had. He neared the lake. It took him over an hour to get there. He went at a snail's pace. There was their fire across the lake. Well, that explained why he ran into them twice in a row. He approached the cattails. Walking in the swamp was hard enough in the daylight, and doing it by the light of the moon was even more challenging. He had to keep feeling his way with his foot before he could take a step forward. There were some deep holes around here, and if he wasn't careful, he could fall into one by accident. He went to take a step and a muskrat dove in the water right in front of him, scaring the crap out of him. He stood there for a few minutes waiting to get his heartbeat and breathing down to a normal level from the adrenaline running through his body. He found all his traps; only one had a muskrat in it. Well, the most important thing right now was to get the traps and get home, not worry about how much he caught. He tried to stay calm and keep an eye on the two men at the campfire. He kept telling himself to remain calm, get done, and go home.

He was just making his way out of the cattails when the wind shifted and he could faintly hear the two men talking. He couldn't understand what they were saying. He gave them a glance then started for home. The voices must be coming with the wind across the lake. Those two had no sense at all. *If I was intent on harming them they'd be very easy targets.* He shook his head and continued on. He was bone tired and the night air seemed so very cold to him. He made it to the house and waited a few minutes, listening to see if anything was amiss here. Everything seemed to be fine. He went inside, sealed up tight, and heated up what was left from dinner. He kept yawning. He decided to finish everything else tomorrow. He was too tired right now to deal with anything else. He made his way into his bedroom, grabbed an extra blanket and threw it on the bed. He was just too tired to make a fire tonight. He climbed in and closed his eyes.

****

The two men sat by the fire trying to keep warm. It was very cold out tonight and the wind really chilled a body to the bone. They could feel the dampness coming off the lake. They got into their sleeping bags to get warmer. Neither man felt very good. They had eaten the rat the kid had given them, but they were still hungry. They hadn't seen a deer or rabbit in days. If they didn't get something more to eat in the next couple of days, they'd have to head back to the city and see if there was any government help with food. They didn't know what else to do. They had always hunted and they didn't know what else to do to get meat. Never once did it cross their minds to get some traps or snares. Each time they went out hunting, they burned up more calories they couldn't replace. They were starving.

Glen sat in his sleeping bag, trying to warm up and stop the shivers. Carl was shivering just as much as he was, too. Glen, the shorter of the two, said to Carl, "That rat sure tasted good, didn't it?"

"It tasted better than I thought a rat ever could," said Carl.

"I wonder if that kid will be coming back to the lake tomorrow?" wondered Glen. "Maybe we can get another one of those rats from him. Hell, we'll take them all from the kid, because this is our lake now." He laughed and Carl joined in, too.

"Yeah, we'll take all he's got because this is our lake. We'll let him do all the work and we'll eat everything he has. I wish I knew when he was coming back. I'm still hungry." Carl tried to burrow deeper in his sleeping bag.

"Yeah, me too."

They both thought for a while, then Carl said, "We should go around the lake in the morning and hide. Then when he tries to leave with the rats, we'll take them from him again. What do you say to that? Is that a good plan or what?"

Glen thought a moment. "We'll follow him back to where he's from and take that over, too. It will get us some shelter and heat. Maybe there's some food there. That's a better idea, don't you think?"

"Yeah, that's a much better idea. I like that one the best. We'll just follow him to his place, and then if that kid's father shows up, we'll just have to kill him so we can take it over.

We have to so we can survive. We'll make that kid keep providing us with food, too. What do you think about that?"

"That's a very good plan." Glen grinned at Carl in the firelight. "We better get some sleep so we can be up before the sun and get into position before that kid shows up."

****

Junior woke up and it was dark. But with the house sealed up tight it was always dark in here; the steel plates bolted down over the windows and door effectively blocked all light in and out. He looked at the clock. It said 10:00 am. Wow, had he overslept. He went into the kitchen, got his traps, and skinned and gutted the single muskrat. He took the guts and unused parts out to the bait pile. He covered the bait pile with leaves. He had the strangest feeling he was being watched. He quickly made his way back inside. He dropped the steel plate into place over the doors and windows. He grabbed the bolts, and using a socket wrench, he tightened them down into the solid wood frame. Now he needed to stay sealed in for two weeks or so just to be sure the two guys were gone before he emerged outside again. He really didn't keep track of the days, but glancing at the clock would tell him what day it was. Each day he grew more and more restless.

****

Marion was standing by the living room window keeping watch while Gayle gathered up the things they had decided to take with them. She packed their items in the backpacks they were taking to George's place. He must still be mad at her, because he and Junior hadn't come back for them. She sighed deeply, feeling like such a fool for staying here. She was really sorry for the things she'd said. He was right about the situation. Everyday it had gotten worse and worse. There was so much violence; stealing and true down right evil going on that it had shaken her belief in humanity. They had gathered all the available food and supplies together as a community and put them in one place. She and several others tried to keep everything together and ration foods and goods out as needed. They were trying to have some sort of order until the government could get things running again and help them out. It had been going pretty well at first, then people started breaking into the storehouse and stealing food and things. If that had been the only problem, she wouldn't be leaving now.

People who were sick started dying. At first they didn't think much of it, because people get sick everyday and some do die, after all. The situation they were all in wasn't the best for sanitation or cleanliness either. Then her best friend, Katie, came down with pneumonia and died. Katie had been fine with just a little cough and Dr. Anderson gave her some antibiotics to clear it up. Katie was fine for a few days, then she started to get worse and Dr. Anderson gave her an IV with antibiotics in it twice a day. Katie was getting better and improving. The fever disappeared, she just had a small cough and had said she was feeling much better. Then yesterday morning, she went to check on Katie and she was dead. She went to Dr. Anderson's office to tell him and heard Dr. Anderson and the Mayor arguing. Dr. Anderson had discovered that the Mayor was injecting the sick people with a lethal dose of something as soon as he could get them alone. The Mayor didn't want Dr. Anderson wasting the medicine on what he called second hand citizens. The sheriff had arrested the Mayor and took him to jail. It was a nightmare.

Then this morning, when she was on the way to the storehouse to do her shift watching and handing out necessary supplies, there was a shootout. It seemed her neighbors and friends had enough and they stormed the jail to kill the Mayor. The talk had been all over town about what the Mayor had done. When it was all over, twenty three people were dead, including the Mayor, the sheriff and the two deputies, and she didn't even know how many were wounded and hurt. Some people had stormed the storehouse, too, and taken most of the supplies they had gathered there. The thieves had killed Dr. Anderson, Stuart the pharmacist, three other people who'd been there to get supplies, and her friend Henry, who had been on shift. She came home and talked to Gayle about the situation. They decided it was time to get out of Dodge before anything else bad happened. It had been hard for Gayle not to say, 'I told you so.' Gayle had been saying several times a day that they should get out of town and go to George's place before people got out of hand. Marion just hadn't been able to believe people could act like this. She sighed again deeply and tears welled up in her eyes. George and Gayle were right; the world they had known was forever gone and people had gone insane, completely and truly insane.

Gayle handed her a backpack. She looked around at everything, wondering when or if she would ever see her house again. She picked up the double barrel shotgun cocked it open to make sure it was loaded and then walked to the door with Gayle right behind her. She turned and looked at her house from the road as tears rolled down her face. Gayle grabbed her arm, gave it a squeeze, and said, "The first step of a journey into the unknown is always the hardest." Marion smiled at Gayle, remembering the day Gayle got that quote from a fortune cookie. Gayle was always using that quote. It had become a joke between them. She nodded at Gayle, then turned around and started walking down the road.

****

Junior felt he should be out there trapping and snaring the predators. He was pacing around the living room. He was going crazy being cooped up. He needed the hides he would trap so he could tan more at a time. He really wanted to make that coyote hat this year, too. He kept thinking about those two clowns saying they owned the lake. It was just him, so he couldn't take a chance of opening up and going outside. What if they broke in while he was gone? It was a chance he couldn't take. He paced some more. They'd be gone soon. They'd run out of food and go back to the city, where they belonged. He just needed to be a bit more patient. A lot was at stake. Correction, *everything* was at stake here, including his life. He had to remember that. After a week of pacing around and bemoaning the fact he couldn't go outside, he was thinking of taking a chance and doing it anyway. He was going to go insane if he stayed inside any longer. He started pacing again. It had now been one month since the world had changed. He felt very alone and needed to have a conversation with someone, anyone. He'd never been on his own this long before. He was starting to dislike his own company. He chuckled at that thought. A psychologist would have a field day with him. He paced some more.

Little did Junior know that the two survivalists had followed his footprints in the frost right back to his door. Those footprints had stuck out like a neon sign that said 'follow me home.' They'd started watching the place. They shot a deer the afternoon after he'd given them the muskrats, so they had food to settle in and wait until he came out. They thought they were quite clever finding his footprints to follow. They had been waiting for him or his dad to come outside so they could take over the house. They couldn't figure out how to get in. They'd tried a few times, but everything was shut down tight. They hadn't tried real hard yet. The two men were trying to be quiet so they could surprise them. They'd have to come out eventually. It was getting real cold out, too. Well, it was just a matter of time.

Junior was pacing again and had just decided to go reheat the coffee when there was pounding on the door. The noise startled Junior, and he jumped a few feet into the air. He quickly went to the door, thinking it must be the two hunters. His dad had put in a cool spy camera so he could see who was at the door. Marion was standing there, carrying a double barrel 12-gauge shotgun and Gayle was carrying an old Marlin bolt-action eight shot .22. He unbolted the door and used the pulleys to raise the steel plate up. He invited them in. As soon as they crossed the threshold, he practically pulled them the rest of the way to get them out of his way so he could reseal the door up behind them.

When he had the door secured, he turned around to face them. Only Gayle was standing there looking at him. It hit him then that they didn't know about his dad.

Marion walked back into the living room. "Where's George? Is he outside trapping or something?" Junior gave Marion an angry glare. Gayle sat down on the couch. Marion just looked at Junior. As he tried to move past her, Marion reached out and grabbed his arm, and looked him straight in the eyes. "Tell me where George is. I have to apologize to him right now. I was so wrong."

Junior looked at her, tears welling up remembering that if she and Gayle would have come with their guns, maybe his dad wouldn't be dead right now.

Marion stepped back from his look. "Don't tell me he is still mad at me. Did he say he never wanted to see me again?" she asked. "Is that why you're acting strange and angry?"

Junior shook his head no. The tears started to roll down his face. Marion looked at him, then over at Gayle, and then back at him. Junior wiped his eyes with his hands and said resentfully, "It would be a little hard to apologize to him now. He's dead. He died as soon as we got home from your house. Three bad guys were waiting here to rob us. We could have handled them, but they had a woman hidden in the woods. She stepped out and surprised my dad. That's what got him killed. No, I correct that statement. My dad died because you didn't come with us and bring your guns. If you would have come with us when he asked you, none of this would have happened." He turned from her and walked angrily away before he did or said something that he would possibly regret later. He went to his room and slammed the door.

He knew he'd have to face them. Not like he had much of a choice in the matter unless he wanted to throw them outside and tell them to get lost. Even as mad at Marion as he was, it wouldn't be right to do that to her, and he especially couldn't do that to Gayle; if Marion left, Gayle would go with her. That much was pretty well guaranteed. But, that didn't mean he had to be nice to Marion, and he wouldn't be. There would never be any forgiveness for what she caused to happen to his dad. The best he could come up with in regard to Marion was to pretend she wasn't even there. If he started yelling at her and got really angry, he didn't know if he could prevent himself from hurting her, and he wasn't going to cross that line and start hurting women. He walked into the living room and saw the bolts lying on the floor where he'd put them after letting them in. He had secured the door but hadn't sealed it up tight. He grabbed the socket wrench and starting tightening the bolts down. Marion was crying and Gayle had her arms around her mother on the couch, talking quietly to her.

After Junior walked away, Marion had just stood there in shock at the words he'd said and the angry way he'd delivered them to her. George was dead. He'd been dead for over a month now. That couldn't be right. She looked at Gayle to see if she'd heard the same thing she had.

Gayle got up and came over to her, giving her a hug. "I'm sorry, Mom, I know you really liked George."

Really liked, she thought. No, she had fallen in love with him almost from the first moment she had seen him. He couldn't be gone. Gayle led her over to the couch and sat her down. Gayle handed her a tissue and she realized tears were running down her face. She wiped her face, but the tears wouldn't stop falling. She sat there and thought about the all things they had shared together and said to each other. *There was no way in hell George was gone. No, not again.* After losing her husband, she had made sure not to get too close to anyone, because it was just too painful when they were gone. George had slipped right through all her defenses as if they weren't even there. He made her feel like a teenager again. They just clicked in every way. No way could he be gone. Deep sobs escaped, shaking her whole body. Gayle rocked her and held her tight.

Gayle looked up from embracing her mother when Junior came into the living room and moved past them as if they weren't there. His grief was deep, too. It was etched all over his face. He looked a lot older and sadder than he had the last time she'd seen him. He blamed his dad's death on her mother. *Oh my God,* she thought, *he must have buried his father by himself.* She didn't know what to do. She had liked George. She thought he had been gallant in his efforts to get her mother to change her mind. What should she do? What should she say? She made up her mind to just play it by ear. After all, what else could she do? Later that night, Gayle got her mother calmed down enough to go lay down on George's bed.

Hopefully, she'd be able to rest for a while. She went into the kitchen to see what was there to make. She started dinner and put more coffee on. She grabbed a cup for her and one for Junior and knocked on his bedroom door with her foot as softly as she could. He told her to go away and leave him alone. "Okay," she said, "I just brought you a cup of coffee and I'm making some dinner. It'll be ready in about fifteen minutes."

She set the coffee cup on the floor and was turning to leave when Junior opened the door. He looked both ways and saw she was alone, then reached down and grabbed the coffee cup off the floor, taking a sip. "Sorry, I thought you were your mother and I don't want to talk to her," he said.

"I can understand needing to be alone at a time like this. I was the same way after my father died. I didn't like talking to anyone. I just wanted to be alone and remember all the things we did together. I felt no one could possibly understand how much I missed him and how my heart felt like a big empty hole without him around." She reached out and touched his arm. "I'm sorry you lost your father. I liked him. I thought he was quite gallant. But, I know how it feels, and I'm here if you need to talk about it. I just wanted to let you know that. You don't have to be alone anymore. I can't imagine what you've been through, doing all of this on your own with no one to talk to or help you. I'm here if you need me. I'll leave you alone now and stop bothering you."

She stepped back to leave and Junior reached out and pulled her into a hug. He hugged her real tight. They stood in the hall for a long time. Junior finally released her and said with a ragged breath, "You have no idea how good that felt. I always thought I was a loner and enjoyed being by myself. I've come to realize it's not that I'm a loner. It's that I didn't want to be around the people that were in my life before, except my dad. Thank you. That meant a lot to me. It has been real hard getting used to being without my dad."

She smiled at him. "You're welcome, anytime. You need to talk or a hug, just let me know. I'm available. It's not like I'm going to be going anywhere." He smiled at that statement. She looked at him seriously and asked, "Do you feel like living dangerously?"

He looked at her for a few moments considering what she could mean. "What did you have in mind?"

She smiled. "Are you hungry? I'm cooking. Dinner will be done probably right now. I'd better go check on it." As she walked away, she heard him chuckle just a little bit. It was a start. It was a small step, but a very important one.

The next morning while Gayle and Junior were eating breakfast, Marion walked into the kitchen and said in a very raspy voice, "Junior, I need to see George. Please take me to see him." Junior looked over at her; she looked terrible. It kind of reminded him of what he'd seen when he looked into the bathroom mirror when he had finally woken up after his intense grief and taken a shower. He nodded his head yes. They got up and prepared to go outside to the grave site. Gayle put her arm around her mother as they walked down the trail. Junior noticed how Marion kept stumbling and seemed unsteady on her feet. He didn't notice it was the tears in her eyes that made it hard to see where she was going.

When they reached the tree, Marion saw the marker and let out a sob. She held her hand up to her mouth as if to hold in any noise she might make. She slowly walked up to the grave, sat down, and placed her hand on the dirt. She hung her head, crying. Junior didn't know quite what to do. Gayle sat down next to her mother and put an arm around her shoulder, hugging her. Marion didn't even seem to notice. They stayed like that for a while, then Marion said in a low whisper, "Leave me here for awhile. I want to be alone with the man I loved."

"No mother. I will not leave you here alone."

"Go. Just go and leave me alone with George." Gayle looked to Junior as if to say, *what should I do?*

Junior walked up by the marker, looked at Marion down on the ground and said, "Gayle, let's go."

"No. I'll stay here with you, Mom. I won't leave you alone here."

Marion reached out and grabbed Gayle in a tight hug. "I need to be alone with George for awhile. I ... I have to talk to him. I don't want you here. I need to be alone with him. Go to the house. I'll be all right." Gayle got up reluctantly and turned to Junior. She didn't want to leave her mother here by herself. Junior reached out, took her arm and led her down the trail. Gayle kept looking back at her mother. She seemed so small and alone next to that big grave.

"She'll be all right," Junior said. "It just hasn't sunk in yet. I was the same way. I used to come and spend hours sitting next to the tree, just to be close to him." Gayle stopped, reached out and put her arm around him and hugged him. He hugged her back. They stayed there for quite some time. Then they heard Marion start to talk to George. They stepped apart and hurried down the trail. Neither one of them wanted to hear what she had to say. It was a private conversation not meant for anyone to hear but George.

Gayle finally asked the question that had been on her mind since they got back to the house. "How long should we let her stay out there?"

"If she isn't back by the time it starts to get dark we will go get her, okay?" Junior said.

Gayle, feeling reassured, said, "Okay. But should we leave her out there that long?"

"Yes, she'll come back when she's done. Don't worry too much about it."

Gayle said, "This has hit her real hard, you know. She was sort of like this when my dad died, but not this bad. At least I don't remember her being hit as hard as she is now, but I was lost in my own grief at the time, too, and maybe I just don't remember it right. We've gotten closer since then. I'm worried about her."

"I don't know the right thing to do," Junior said. "I've never lost anyone close before except a grandfather I didn't know very well, until now. I guess she'll grieve as much as she needs to. It's hit her harder than I thought it could. She said she loved him. I didn't know that before. But I think my dad loved her, too." Gayle felt a little better since Junior wasn't so hostile towards her mother right now. She decided a change of subject was in order before they both ended up crying.

She looked around. "When is the last time you cleaned this place up? The dust must be a half inch thick." Junior looked around as if just now noticing how dusty and messy the place was. He was a bit shocked that he'd let the place get so dirty. He didn't know what to say in answer to Gayle's question. She realized this and said, "I'll tell you what. We'll split the chores up and have this place spic and span in no time." Junior looked relieved and agreed. They both got up and got to work on the house.

When Marion got done talking to George, she was emotionally spent. She just sat there for a while, convincing herself to go to the house. She was so very tired and her heart hurt. It hurt to breathe. She slowly got up and stood there, looking around at George's most favorite spot in the world. She touched the grave marker, gave it a kiss, and slowly made her way down the trail towards the house. She knew Gayle was worried about her, but she had important things to say to George, things that were none of those two kids' business, things that were just for George to hear and no one else. Things she had to say to him. Personal things she needed to express to her lover. She felt so bad that the last time they'd been together they had argued. Time to head back to the cabin.

She was almost at the fork in the trail when a man jumped out and grabbed her. "You are my ticket to get inside that place," he said. "Walk real careful-like or I will shoot you. Do you understand me?" She nodded yes, thinking how bad this man smelled. "Good. Just keep walking and go up to the door and tell them to let you in. Then we'll go into the place real nice and friendly-like. You got that now?"

"Yes, I got that." He pushed her in the back with the rifle he was holding. She started walking, thinking at light speed on how to warn the kids that something was wrong. Then and idea formed in her mind.

There was a man off to the side in the trees on the right, and the guy behind her hung back. Maybe she could get inside before they reached her. Well, she would try, anyway. She walked right up to the steel plate that covered the whole doorway, because the outside door was already left open for her, and she stepped as close as she could, almost hugging it and said, "Susie, tell your father to unlock the door and let me in."

Junior was speaking when they both heard Marion outside. He and Gayle shared a puzzled look. Then it dawned on Gayle that something was wrong.

She said very quietly, "Junior, something's not right."

"Yeah, let's look outside and see what's going on," Junior said. He looked out with the spy camera and saw the two yahoos that had told him they owned the lake. One was back on the side, and the other one was a little way behind Marion. He had forgotten all about them. Junior thought real fast.

"Shit, two guys are out there with my mother and they both have rifles." Gayle looked worried.

Junior said, "I saw that. Now listen to me very carefully. Tell her that your dad can't get the door open just yet or something."

"Okay, Mom," called Gayle. "I'll tell Dad. He'll be here in just a minute."

Junior whispered, "I'm going to stand right by the door; you pull on the rope to raise the door up, and I'll yank your mother in here. As soon as I do this, let go of the rope and the three hundred fifty pound steel door will slam down closed. We'll put the bolts in it and secure it so they can't get in. Now, while I'm getting everything ready, tell your mother that your dad can't find the socket wrench. I'll signal you when I'm ready to grab your mother. Okay?"

Gayle nodded. "Mom? Dad can't remember where he set down the socket wrench. It'll just be a few minutes until we find it. Okay?"

Marion said, "Okay. Just hurry; it's cold out here."

Junior had an idea and motioned to Gayle to come closer. She leaned in close to him. "You raise the door halfway up and we'll pretend it's stuck. When the door is half up, call out to your mom to bend down because the door is stuck. After you see me yank your mother in, just let go of the rope. Okay?"

Gayle looked at him strangely. Junior just motioned for her to do it. Gayle raised the door up halfway and said, "Mom, Dad can't get the door all the way open, so you're going to have to bend down to get in. Okay?"

"Okay, I'm bending down now," Marion called. As soon as Marion bent down in the doorway, Junior reached out, grabbed her and yanked hard. Gayle let go of the rope. It happened as fast as a blink of an eye.

Marion went sailing across the floor and Junior was trying to get the bolts lined up to tighten them. There was a loud pounding on the door that made all three of them jump. Junior looked at the spy camera; both men were standing right in front of the door.

"Hey buddy," one of them said, "you got any more spare food for us? How about you give us one of those women?"

In his nervousness and anger at the two men, Junior couldn't get everything lined up straight. In frustration he whispered to Gayle, "Push the button down and I'll talk to them. Marion, help me get these threaded through so I can tighten them up." The two women scrambled around, doing what he said. Gayle pushed the button down and Junior said, "Get the hell out of here or this woman here will shoot your dumb asses."

Gayle grabbed the shotgun and racked a shell in the chamber. "That will be a cold day in hell before either one of us goes with you," Gayle said. "I'll shoot your asses before you even get close to the door."

Junior finally got the bolt lined up right, reached for the socket wrench to tighten it, and then moved to the next one.

One of the guys outside said, "That isn't very nice. We come up here all friendly-like, and you treat us like this. Hey, we can make a deal. You can let us inside and we'll help you defend this place. What do you say about that offer? We're good shots, you know."

Junior started to crank the bolts down tight and the other man outside, hearing the noise, said, "I take it you don't want us to come in, huh?" They both backed up a little way and shot at the door. A bullet ricocheted off the door and hit the one on the right in the stomach. The man bent over and fell to the ground.

The other bent over his friend. "What happened? Are you okay?" He then turned to the door. "Why in the hell did you shoot him?"

Marion rolled her eyes and yelled out, "You moron. You shot him. The bullet ricocheted off the steel."

The man just stood still and silent for a few moments. "It never would have happened if you would have opened up the door. This is your fault," he said through the door. "Now, I'm going to kill each and every one of you." He backed up further and started shooting the door again. He was acting like a mad man. His face was screwed up into a grimace and his teeth were tight against his mouth. His neck was sticking out and bulging, the veins stuck out clearly. Another one of the bullets ricocheted off the door, hit his injured friend in the head and killed him instantly. In his rage, he never even noticed. He reloaded and emptied the gun into the double fourth inch plate steel again. The ringing inside the house was very loud. The man backed away from the door, turned and left.

Junior wasted no time in getting the rest of the bolts down tight. He let out a relieved sigh when the door was secured once again. He turned to the two shocked women and said, "I met those two yahoos last week. We were lucky this time." He told them everything that had happened. He then thought for a few moments. "I don't know how he found this place. Maybe they followed you two here." There was silence. There wasn't anything to say to that statement. There was no way to know for sure.

Marion glanced at the spy screen. "Look at what that crazy fool is doing." She pointed to the screen. The man was marching back up to the door with his arms full of wood and brush. All three of them looked at each other. Marion gestured up to the loft area. "There's a shooting port up there. It's twelve inches by eight inches. Your dad used to shoot deer from it. You're going to have to kill that crazy man out there. He isn't going to stop. Did you see his eyes? You better do it now before he sets this place on fire. You have no choice. He's acting insane. He'll kill all of us if you don't stop him now."

Junior looked at Marion. "I don't know if I can just shoot him."

"You have no choice now," Marion said. "He's crazy and won't stop unless you stop him. Do you understand that?"

Junior grabbed the Remington 870 that was loaded with three inch magnum triple ought buckshot. He climbed up to the loft and slid the panel back as quietly as he could.

He could just barely see out, but he could see the rage-filled man coming with another armful of wood and brush. The opportunity to take the shot quickly passed.

The man banged on the door. "This is your last chance. Open the door or I'm going to burn you out and kill you all." The man marched back out to the woods again. Junior couldn't shoot him in the back.

A few minutes later, the man came back into view with his arms full of sticks and brush. Junior aimed at the center of the man's chest and yelled out, "Stop right there and drop the brush. Turn around and leave or I will shoot you." The man ignored him and kept walking to the door. Junior pulled the trigger. The barrel was outside and it wasn't as loud as Junior had thought it would be. The pellets tore through the sticks and brush right into the center of the man's chest. He arched back a bit, then fell to the side and lay on the ground. This was not like a Hollywood movie where you shoot someone and they fly back ten feet and fall over dead. They use pulleys and a harness to make it appear like that in a movie for a special effect. This was real life.

Junior waited to make sure he wasn't getting up again. He could hear moaning. He climbed down from the loft. He walked over and put the shotgun away. He grabbed his .22 pistol that was in a holster on a belt and strapped it on his waist and leg. He pulled the tabs tight.

"What are you doing?" Marion asked. Junior ignored her and got the socket wrench and opened the door. He went outside, shot the moaning man in the head, and dragged the body over to the area he had used before to burn bodies. He walked over and shot the other man in the head just to be sure he was really dead. He holstered his .22, grabbed one leg and one arm, and started dragging the body over to the first. He then got two old tires from the garage and threw them on top. He gathered up brush, wood, and sticks and covered the bodies up.

He walked back into the house. He looked around and the two women were just staring at him. "What did you do?" Marion asked.

Junior looked at her and said clearly and expressionlessly, "I dragged the bodies over to the burn pile. We have to burn them. You have to keep the fire burning hot. It's best not to leave it too long or the smell gets really bad."

Marion looked shocked. "What do you mean, burn the bodies? What are you talking about?"

Junior explained. "You have to burn the bodies. You don't want them rotting, stinking bodies around the place spreading disease. They could contaminate the ground water. So, you burn the bodies to keep the place clean." He looked at them. "You two are going to help me, right?" Both women backed away from him, shaking their heads no with a look of horror on their face. He shrugged his shoulders, turned around, and hooked the door open. He went outside to start the fire.

As he tended the fire, he was cold inside. Survival of the fittest lowered these bodies to two-legged predators that needed cleaning up. They were no longer people, just predators. They were pests that had to be taken care of. He looked around and thought with a worried expression how the area was starting to look like a battlefield. Burned areas, bullet holes in trees, and now the door was looking a bit worn, too. He sighed. *We need spring to get here so the fresh new grass can grow and hide all of this. In a couple of hours, there were just some bones left in the pile. He went and got the wheelbarrow and shovel. He scooped up the bones and dug a hole to dump them into. He returned everything to the garage and went back into the house. He secured the door.*

He turned around and looked at the two women sitting on the couch, huddled together. "This door stays secured at all times," he said. "I will be the only one to open it up. I don't intend to open it until spring." He started towards the kitchen, then stopped and looked at them again. "I'm going to go clean up and get some coffee. Would either of you like some?" The two women just looked strangely at him and didn't say anything. Junior shrugged his shoulders and left the room.

Chapter 11

Ungrateful Woman

"There is nothing more frightful than ignorance in action."
Johann Wolfgang von Goethe

Eric took the first watch and let Mark get some sleep. Every once in awhile, one of the women would cry out, whimper or jerk awake and cry. The other women would scoot closer and give her comfort. They'd also look around and see where he and Mark were. Eric had quietly crept down to the stream earlier and refilled the canteens. They were going to have to find some kind of containers to carry water for these women. They could check out some cars for water containers, and maybe some clothes and things for the women. He was really worried about how they were going to get everyone safely to the retreat. Two guys sneaking around silently was one thing, but trying to sneak around with injured, untrained women was whole different story. How would they be able to do this? That was the question that they needed to figure out real quick. He kept pondering this question.

One of the women cried out and woke Mark up. He hadn't been sleeping very deeply, anyway. His right leg was stiff and sore. It was cold on the bare ground and his stomach growled. He got up and joined Eric. Eric asked him if he was hungry. "Yeah, I could eat a horse right now."

Eric laughed quietly and offered some dried venison. They were fresh out of horse meat. They shared a smile as they sat there and ate.

"What are we going to do?" Mark asked.

"I have been thinking about it all morning," said Eric. "We'll need to check the cars we pass for clothing and one liter bottles to carry water in."

Mark nodded. "This is going to slow us down." Eric nodded in agreement. "As soon as they wake up, we need to talk and set up some rules."

Eric looked at him. "What kind of rules?"

"Like they need to do what we say immediately and not ask a lot of questions, for one. For two, they need to understand that there may be times when we have to grab them or touch them to get them out of the way or to get their attention, and we can't have them freak out every time we do so. Third, they'll have to learn to be quiet and walk a lot more silent than they're used to. Things like that."

Eric nodded his head and said, "Good idea."

"Go ahead and get some sleep. I'm awake now; there's no use in both of us being up."

"Okay." Eric went over to the spot Mark had been sleeping, laid down and closed his eyes. Mark decided to use this time to plan what needed to be said to the women for all of their safety.

Later that afternoon, the ladies started to wake up. The rustling of the tarp woke Eric up, too. He joined Mark by the fire. Nothing like the smell of coffee. Mark had made a pot of oatmeal for the ladies to eat. Eric noticed a small pot of water sitting off to the side with a cup by it. He looked over at the women; they were all awake now. He picked up the pot and the cup and took it over to the women and set it on the ground. They just looked at him.

"This is for you all to drink," he said.

The blonde woman who'd spoken to him the night before reached out, took the pot and cup, and said, "Thank you." She took a drink and passed it along to the others. In no time, the water was gone.

Mark and Eric exchanged a surprised look. "I made you all some oatmeal," Mark said. He took the pot over to them.

One dark haired woman picked up the pan and ate a few bites before passing it along. After they'd eaten all of the oatmeal, the blonde woman thanked them. She looked around at the other women and then asked, "Do you have any toilet paper we could use? And where should we, you know, go?"

Mark and Eric looked at each other again. Eric rubbed the back of his neck, thinking. "We have one roll of toilet paper," Mark told them. "It has to last the whole trip up north. Do not use it unless you have to take a crap. I have a shovel that you'll use to dig a hole with to crap in, and then you cover it up. And don't get any on the shovel or you'll be the one to clean it off. When you have to go, always let us know first, don't just take off. Right now, go out about fifty feet that way, and do what you need to do." He pointed where he wanted to direct them. The women looked at each other, then started to get up. They covered themselves as best they could. Seeing them in daylight showed how dirty and abused they really were. Eric got the roll of toilet paper out, Mark got the shovel, and they set them on the ground. The women left to do what they needed to do.

Eric laughed. Mark said, "What?"

"Is this part of the rules?"

"Damn right it is," Mark said. Eric laughed some more.

The women returned, sat down on the tarp, and covered up with the sleeping bags. One of the women asked, "Are you the police, the Army or what?"

Eric and Mark shook their heads no. "We're just two guys trying to survive long enough to get to our retreat up north," Mark said.

"Do you know what happened?" one woman asked.

"When are the police coming?" asked another.

Mark held his hand up and said, "The police won't be coming."

"Why not?"

Mark said, "We think we were hit with an EMP. It's the only thing we can think of that can take out the power grid and everything electrical. Do any of you know what an EMP is?" Three women shook their heads no and two nodded their heads yes. "An EMP is a high altitude nuclear bomb," Mark explained. "It fires out all electrical parts. Everything we use today has some kind of an electronic component in it. That's why clocks, watches and cars aren't working. There's no power for lights, either. There are no police or government to help us. They have no way to communicate or to get emergency supplies to people that need it. We don't know if we're at war with another country or will be invaded or not. There's no way to know right now. We're on our way to our retreat up north. We bought a place, stocked some supplies and my dad is up there right now, waiting on us to get there."

All the women were shocked at this news. One finally asked, "What are we supposed to do? Where should we go?"

"You're welcome to come with us," Mark said. "It's pretty dangerous these days, as you've already found out. People are acting crazy, strange, or violent. There is no law and order out there. My name is Mark." He pointed to Eric. "This is Eric."

The black woman spoke up, saying very quietly with tears running down her face, "My name is Channon. My husband and I were walking after all the cars stopped and those animals came and grabbed me. They killed my husband right in front of my eyes."

An Asian woman hugged Channon and said, "My name is Abhita, but everyone calls me Abby. I was hiking on the trail back that way." She pointed back the way they came from. "They surrounded me and said I was their property now. I fought them, but there were just too many of them." She hung her head down.

The woman next to her was white with reddish colored hair. "My name is Katie," she said, "and they killed my boyfriend when he tried to protect me. We were on our way to the mountains for a short trip." She sobbed and covered her face.

A Hispanic woman said, "I was trying to get to town and they grabbed me. My name is Maria."

The last woman was white with blonde hair. She cleared her throat and said, "My name is Lisa Marie. I was just trying to get out of the city and find somewhere there wasn't too many people. I was hoping to find some friends that lived close by. They weren't home. Those nut cases grabbed me when I was walking down the road."

"Do any of you live around here?" asked Mark.

Katie spoke up. "My parents live about forty to forty-five miles from here. It's over that way." She pointed northeast.

"We're going north."

"I want to go to my parent's house," Katie said.

"Okay, but we can't take you there," explained Eric.

Katie said, "I'll walk."

Mark and Eric looked at each other. Mark replied, "Okay, we'll be leaving here when it gets dark." Katie nodded. Mark said, "Anyone else have anywhere to go?" The other four women shook their heads no.

Mark said, "Okay, listen up. I have some rules for you to follow. If you can't agree with the rules, then you're on your own." He listed them for the women, then added, "Just remember the two most important rules. You have to do what we say exactly the way we say immediately, and you have to be quiet. No loud talking. Do any of you have a problem with any of the rules?" They shook their heads no. Mark said, "Two of you will be with Eric and the other three will be with me. As soon as we get close to the turn off for Katie, she'll go out on her own. Then it will just be two of you with me. If you hesitate even once in obeying an order, then we'll have to leave you behind. You will be endangering the rest of us. Is that understood?"

Abby asked, "What if we don't understand what the order is? You may use terms or say something that we don't understand."

Mark thought about that for a minute. "I'll make sure to speak as plain as I can. Do you all agree?" The five women looked a little uncertain, but nodded their heads yes. "Okay. Channon, Abby and Katie, you'll be with me. Maria and Lisa, you go with Eric." He picked the groupings because Channon and Abby were hugging, and Maria and Lisa were sitting near each other. Katie was on the end by herself, a little way apart from the rest.

What's up with that? he wondered. "We'll look in abandoned cars when we can to see if we can find you some clothes, and we'll be looking for one liter bottles that you can carry for drinking water. Maybe we can find a few backpacks in the vehicles that were used for kids' books or something so you can all carry things we may find. We'll look for any useful items. Rest for now. We have a long walk ahead of us. We'll be traveling at night and sleeping in shifts during the day." The women lay down to rest and gather strength for the coming night.

Lisa wondered if they had traded one hell for another one. Could they really trust these two men? That Mark guy seemed pretty hyper and military-minded. Definitely a no-nonsense type A personality, although she couldn't find any fault in his rules. They did seem to know what they were doing. They had rescued them, after all. She was very grateful for that. The world had really turned into a horrible nightmare place. If it had been an EMP that hit them, what was the future going to be like? She was glad that Maria would be with her. They had gotten pretty close the last few days. And now these two men had said this type of thing has been happening everywhere. What happened to civilization and being civilized? How had everything fallen apart like this so fast? She shivered and scooted down farther under the sleeping bag cover and turned on her side in a fetal position.

Maria lay down next to Lisa. Lisa was on the outside, just as she'd been when they were tied together. She put her arm around Lisa when she curled up, giving her a reassuring hug. *Are we at war?* That's what kept going through her mind. Maybe that was why everyone had been acting crazy. When the cars stopped, she had heard a few people say it was Judgment Day. That scared her more than even an EMP. She had said a prayer and wished she had her rosary. It just seemed that when she prayed with her beads, it was more likely God would listen to her. Now she would never see her beads again. She sighed. It wasn't that she was that religious, the beads had been a gift from her Nana, that is what she called her grandmother. The last week had been a blur of abuse, hunger and thirst. She thought for sure she'd die. In fact, she had prayed for death a few times. That wish and prayer had not been granted. It just seemed that the horror would go on forever. Then their two white knights showed up. They had not ridden up on their steeds with swords swinging around like avenging angels. No, they had shown up like ghosts in the night. Her lips curved into a small smile. The smile felt unnatural to her lips. She didn't think there could ever be a reason to smile again. She didn't know what the future had in store for her, but it had to be a lot better than the last week had been. The two men seemed to know what they were doing. She would trust in that fact. Any more trust than that would have to be earned. She did sort of have a feeling that she could trust them. After all, they had put their lives on the line to rescue them. Those two men were nothing like the animals that held them captive. It felt important to remember that.

Abby thought about what it could mean to the world if the U. S. had been hit with an EMP bomb. It would be devastating to the financial stability of just about every country out there. Almost everything was based on the U. S. dollar. It would eventually cause a global collapse. What would the effects of Wall Street shutting down be? Oh, shit. All of her investments would mean nothing now. Everything tied up with Wall Street would mean absolutely nothing. No Wall Street. That was a hard concept to wrap her mind around. That would mean no commodity trading, either. That in itself could cause mass starvation. She wondered if the world had figured that out yet. Who could have been so stupid as to make a decision that would end the world as we know it?

Channon was just plain tired. The grief for her husband was clawing her insides. Nothing that had happened to her physically could even compare to what she felt on the inside. They had known each other since they were young kids. His little sister was her best friend. She couldn't imagine a life without him. She kept praying that those animals would just kill her, too, so she could join him. It would be such a relief to just let go of all of this. But God was not paying attention to her prayers and granting her heartfelt desire to join him. And those two men were talking about an EMP bomb like it was a very important thing. Who cares about any of that? And talking about rules. Who in the hell cares about rules? The only thing that mattered to her was joining her beloved. She didn't even get to tell him her news before they killed him. That must be why God wouldn't let her die. She had been waiting until they got to his grandmother's house before telling them all at the same time. Even all that had been done to her physically, the rapes, the beatings, hadn't changed it. Maybe it was a mistake. Maybe it hadn't been real. But the stick had tuned blue and the instructions had said if it turned blue, it was positive. Why now? Dear God, why did it happen? They had waited for two years saving up a down payment to buy a house. They had bought the cutest three-bedroom house.

Katie lay there thinking about the walk to her parent's house. She should make it, no problem. With having food, water and a gun to protect herself, she'd be there in no time.

She was just going to forget about everything that had happened to her. It was over. End of story. She couldn't wait to see her mother. She'd never tell them. They wouldn't understand. She didn't even understand this, so how could they? She didn't believe this EMP thing. It couldn't be true. Just the other day she had heard a helicopter or a small plane, she couldn't remember which. So, if everything wasn't working how come that did? She just knew her parents had called the police when she didn't show up; they were looking for her. It had probably been them in that plane or helicopter. Boy, were the others going to be surprised when they got to wherever they were going and found out how wrong they were. That man saying no police were coming was full of it. There was no way the police weren't looking for her. She'd been trying to figure out what kind of game those two were playing. Maybe they were just taking all of those other women someplace so they could be sex slaves again. You heard about that sort of thing happening every once in awhile. Who did they think they were to do that? Tell her she couldn't talk, well, she'll just see about that. No one bossed her around.

When it was about an hour until dark, Mark and Eric cooked up some rice to go with the dried venison to eat before they started out for the night. When they'd packed everything up, Mark said, "Look around here carefully to make sure we have everything, because we can't afford to lose one single item."

"Ladies, please be quiet," said Eric, "you're making too much noise. You have to be quiet all of the time. Sound carries a long way when there isn't any background noise to interfere with it. You can't let anyone know that you're out there. All of our safety depends on you being silent. If you have something really important to say to us, please whisper as quietly as possible. Otherwise, just don't talk at all."

"You have to walk silently," Mark reminded them. "Don't scrape your heels and make noise. Look where you're going so you don't kick anything. Don't step on anything. Step over it quietly. If you can't do that, go around it, but stay in the shadows and move slowly so you won't make any noise. Be as silent as ghosts, ladies. All of our lives depend on it. Remember that at all times. Be as silent as a ghost.

Okay, Channon, Abby and Katie, you come with me. We'll walk about five or six feet to the side and in front, leading the way. Each of you, listen very closely to what I'm going to say next. When we walk, we'll stagger our steps five paces apart, because if we walk in a straight-line, one bullet could kill us all. Lisa and Maria will be with Eric to the rear. Remember, be silent ghosts. Make your steps like our steps. Stop when we stop. Duck down when we duck down. Pay attention to us every single second so you know what to do. Eric and I will be looking in as many cars as we can for clothes and water containers. Stay several paces back when we do this. Let's go."

Mark started off and Channon followed right behind, then Katie, then Abby brought up the rear on their little group. Eric started out with Maria after him, and Lisa in the rear of their group. Mark sighed. He had a feeling it was going to be a very long night. Training to walk properly was not an easy thing to do and these ladies were not in good shape. If they could keep moving, even if it was slowly, it would be about as good as it was going to get. It was going to take a long time to cover a hundred and fifty miles to the retreat. The goal was ten miles a night, at the bare minimum. Thankfully, Katie wasn't going with them all the way. That Katie had a real bad attitude. Just looking at the set of her mouth and the arrogant expression on her face told him that.

Eric took off about five paces behind Abby and four paces to the left. He kept his eye on Lisa and Maria to make sure they were not walking in a line and were at least four or five paces apart, one to each side of him. They stopped and looked in the cars as quickly as they could. So far they had found two t-shirts, a sweater and four containers to use for water. There was a stream not too far ahead, and he knew Mark would be stopping to clean out the containers and fill them up with water. It would be time for a rest, too. The women were getting tired and their steps were shortening. At least they were finding some clothes for them. It was getting pretty cold at night and they were going to need them the farther north they traveled.

Mark led the way off on the right when they got to the stream. He stopped about two hundred yards from it and told them to be still and silent. He listened for about five minutes and heard nothing unusual. He walked over to the stream and looked slowly around. It was all clear. He signaled for them to come closer.

Katie walked off by herself and started to throw water on her face, loudly saying, "Oh, that feels so good to get clean."

Mark walked up behind her and grabbed her arms to silence her. She screeched and fought him. He grabbed both of her hands in one of his and put his other hand over her mouth and whispered in her ear, "I told you to be a silent ghost. What part of that did you not understand? You're making way too much noise. If anyone is around, they'll hear you and come investigate. Now we have to leave immediately. I'm going to let you go now. You'd better remember to be a silent ghost or you will be left behind. Do you understand me?" Katie nodded her head yes. Mark let her go.

"Who do you think you are to tell me what I can and can't do?" Katie said loudly. "I will do as I want. If I want to make noise, I will."

Mark was taken aback. He whispered, "Be quiet. Noise carries over water for a long way."

"I'll talk as loud as I want to," Katie said even louder, standing with her feet apart and her hands on her hips.

Mark walked up and glared in her defiant eyes. "Shut up right now, or I'll knock you out and leave you here on your own. Do you understand me?" They glared at each other for a few moments before Katie looked away. "Now get your ass moving if you're coming with us, because we can't rest here now because of you."

He turned around and started walking. Eric took his place and led the group. Lisa, Maria, and Abby had cleaned out the water containers, drank their fill, and refilled them during the confrontation.

Abby had two containers to fill up and she'd done so. She handed one to Channon and told her to hold it tightly. Mark led them back over by the road, walking pretty fast. He was pissed at Katie. He had just known it would be her that would cause trouble. If someone started following them because of her he'd be really pissed. What was so hard to understand about being silent? She walked the loudest out of them, too. He couldn't wait for her to be gone. He told himself just one more night and she'll be going off on her own. After they'd gone three miles and not seen anything, he headed off toward the stream again. When he signaled for them to come closer, he waited for Katie. He held her back and said, "You wait until everyone else is done. That way, you make any noise, we'll just leave you here by yourself and everyone else won't have to suffer for your selfishness." Eric and the women went down to the stream and Eric stood watch while the ladies washed up as well as they could. He handed them a towel to dry with. It seemed to brighten them up some.

Eric and the women went over to some brush so they would be concealed from sight and sat down and rested. The women had given the sweater to Channon to wear. The two women with the most tattered shirts were given the t-shirts to wear. He'd wondered how they would divide up the clothes they found. The ladies looked after Channon because she was kind of out of it. She stared a lot at nothing, and you had to wave your hand in front of her face or touch her to get her attention. Then his thoughts switched to Katie. He wondered what was up with Katie acting like that. What an ungrateful bitch she was.

Mark and Katie came over and joined them and sat down. Mark and Eric remained alert to danger. Mark whispered, "We will sit here for fifteen minutes, then we have to go. We're making good time tonight. Hopefully we can go a lot farther before we have to stop for the day." Eric nodded at Mark. Eric thought how weird this felt with five women with them. He smiled to himself, thinking how they had a problem getting one woman to go with them on a camping trip to rough it. Now they had no equipment and there were five of them. Life can sure be truly weird and turn everything upside down. He wondered how they were going to be able to make it until tomorrow night with Katie with them. Well, at the rate she was going, that wouldn't be a problem for long. They had all heard what Mark had said to her. None of the ladies had looked concerned about leaving her.

Mark signaled it was time to go. Eric took the lead this time. They found two cars with kids' backpacks in them. They emptied them out, giving one to Lisa and one to Abby. Those two seemed to be a bit stronger than the others. They'd carry the water containers and whatever else they could find for them. He was watching the overpass up ahead carefully when he felt a touch the back of his arm. He looked down at the hand on his arm; it was Lisa. She dropped her hand and whispered, "Mark and the rest of them are way back there, I think. I can only see Channon standing by a car." She pointed back the way they came.

Eric could see Channon, but there was no sign of Mark, Abby or Katie. Eric whispered, "You and Maria move off to the bushes over there about fifty yards and I'll go see what's going on." Lisa nodded. She silently went up to Maria and whispered in her ear. Eric waited until they were concealed in the brush before going to see what was going on.

Mark had been walking along when he felt a slight touch on his side. He reached down to feel what it was when something hit him hard on the back of his head. He staggered to his knees. Someone tugged on the rifle in his hands. He held it tighter. He was pushed down on the ground from behind. Losing his grip on the rifle, he fell to the pavement. Then he heard a lot of noise. He turned over as best he could with the backpack on and saw Katie pointing the rifle at him. He thought, *Oh shit, she's really trying to shoot me.* He wasn't that worried because the hammer was still in the up position. She obviously didn't know how to cock the rifle.

"Give me the backpack," she said.

What? Mark thought.

Katie kicked his foot. "Take the backpack off."

"No."

"I will shoot you. Don't doubt me about that. You're an asshole," Katie said. "Now give me the backpack now."

Mark could see Abby creeping up behind Katie. "All right," he said, "but I have to get up to get it off." It was the only thing he could think of to distract Katie from Abby's approach. What did Abby think she could do anyway? He turned onto his hands and knees and reached up to a car bumper to help him get up with the heavy backpack on. He heard a whacking sound and a few thumps; Katie cried out. He turned around to see what happened. Abby stood over Katie, holding the rifle at her side. Katie was lying on the ground, holding her arm. Abby walked over to Mark and handed him the rifle. Mark took it with a lifted eyebrow.

Abby gave him a small smile. "I don't think she'll try that again. Bend down and let me see your head."

"We'll do that later," he said. He didn't see Eric anywhere. Where in the hell was he and the other women? He smiled at Abby. "I don't know what you did, but thank you. We've got to move right now in case someone heard us."

Abby nodded and walked over to Katie, grabbing her arm. Quietly, she addressed Katie, looking her straight in the eyes. "Get up. Be quick and silent. Don't test me or I will break your arm next time." Katie got up with Abby's help.

Eric stepped up beside Mark, almost giving him a heart attack. "What has she done now?"

Mark said, "We need to go ahead a few miles and make sure no one heard anything. Then we can take a break and we'll tell you what that bitch did."

Eric nodded. "What are you going to do with her in the meantime?"

Mark looked to Abby and asked her quietly, "Can you keep an eye on her for a few more miles?"

Abby nodded yes, then said to Eric, "But I'll need you to take Channon up with the other women while I handle this." Eric agreed.

Eric stepped over to Channon and softly said, "Channon, you need to come with me for awhile. Okay?"

Channon looked at him. "Where? Where are you taking me?"

"Just up ahead a little way to be with the other women for awhile. Okay?"

"Why?" she whispered.

Eric tried to smile to reassure her. "Because Abby has to watch Katie so she doesn't do anything else that might put us in danger; she can't take care of you right now."

Channon looked at him for a few moments with a puzzled expression. "Lisa and Maria are up there?"

"Yes, they are hiding in the bushes."

Channon looked relieved and quietly said, "Okay, take me to them." They headed out, Channon let him get a little ahead, then followed him about five feet back, off to the right. *Well, she had been paying attention, then.* Eric was relieved. They reached the other two women, who came out to meet Eric and Channon.

Lisa asked softly, "What happened?"

"I don't know. We're going a few more miles, and then we'll take a break and find out." Lisa and Maria nodded.

"Is Channon going to be with us now?" Eric nodded. Maria said quietly to Channon, "Okay, you stay in between Lisa and me."

"Okay." When they had gone a little over two miles, Eric started looking around for a place they could rest. He decided to go by the river, because the noise of the flowing water might cover up any noise they might make. He had to find a spot big enough for all of them, but it had to conceal them from sight and give Mark and him a clear view to watch for danger. Sometimes that was a difficult thing to find. They had traveled over three miles when he found the perfect spot to rest. It wouldn't do as a spot to spend the day in, but it was perfect for just being concealed enough for a short rest. He was a lot more confident about the women keeping up now. They had slowed them down, but not too badly.

When they got rid of the troublemaker, Katie, they would probably make even better time. Eric had a feeling that event was fast approaching. Mark had no time or patience for fools and morons. He looked back to Mark and signaled that he found a spot. Mark looked around and nodded. They all sat down. Abby pushed Katie down on the ground, not very gently. Katie made a painful cry and Abby bent down to whisper to her again. Eric got the germicidal drops out and asked Lisa and Maria to get the water bottles so he could make the water drinkable.

They looked at him kind of weird and Maria said, "We drank some of the water in the river. Are we going to get sick?"

"I didn't get a chance to put anything in the containers because we had to leave so fast," Eric said. "From now on, don't drink any water that we haven't treated first, all right?" Both of them nodded and handed him the containers. He treated them and handed them back.

"We'll rest for a few more minutes," Mark said, "then we'll have a small discussion on what happened back there." Everyone nodded. The ladies were glad to rest; it was hard to keep up with the men. They had much longer legs than they did. Sometimes they took two steps to the men's single step. After a few more minutes, Mark said, "You all are wondering what happened back there. I'll tell you. I was walking and someone hit me in the back of the head with something, knocking me down to my knees. Then someone tried to get my rifle. I held on tightly. This person pushed me in the back, making me fall down on the pavement. I let go of the rifle to catch myself." Lisa and Maria gasped. Mark continued, "I turned around to see who it was, and it was Katie."

Lisa, Maria and Channon made little shocked noises and turned to glare at Katie. Katie was staring out at the river. They turned back to Mark. "Katie told me to give her my backpack, or she was going to shoot me." The women looked outraged at that statement. "Abby sneaked up behind Katie. I saw her coming, then agreed to give Katie my backpack to give her time to do whatever she was going to do. I had to turn back around and grab a car bumper to get up with the backpack on, and when I did, Katie was lying on the ground with Abby standing over her, holding my rifle. Abby gave me back my rifle. You all know the rest. I asked Abby to keep an eye on her so we could leave. If someone heard or saw us, we could be in danger." Silence met those words.

Eric said quietly but firmly, "She's an ungrateful bitch." He was outraged that Katie had hurt his friend and endangered them all, trying to steal their supplies and equipment. He glared at Katie. She ignored them.

"I warned her," Mark said. "I don't want to leave a woman out here alone, but we can't trust her now. We're going to have to leave her here on her own." He looked around at the other women. "Do any of you want to stay with her or have any problem with this decision?" The other women shook their heads no.

Katie looked around at them. "Give me some food and a gun and I'll be happy to get away from all of you," she said loudly. "You're all stupid losers if you believe them about this EMP stuff and no police. How stupid can you be?"

Everyone got to their feet.

"You're just going to leave me here with nothing?" Katie said. "Don't listen to them. They're just conspiracy nuts." Mark and Eric headed out, and the other women followed. No one said anything.

When sunup was close, Mark started looking for a safe place. They'd traveled a little over five miles. That made thirteen for the night. Not too bad, even with all the stops they had made. He was happy about that. There was only about one hundred thirty-seven more miles to go. Well, if they could increase the mileage to at least fifteen miles a night, then it would take them eight or nine more days to get there. *We'll run out of food long before that.* They were going to have to stop somewhere for a day or so and rebuild their food stock. Hopefully, they'd be able to snare another deer or two. Then they'd be all right. There, up ahead looked real good. He looked around and found a pretty large area that just might fit all of them. He had decided to stay as close to the river as they could when it was daytime so any noise the women made while sleeping might blend in. At least it sounded good in theory. He had kept his eye out for anyone following them. He especially looked around for Katie. He hadn't seen her since they all had left. He would mention to Eric to keep a look out today when it was his watch to see if she came this way or not. Damn, he was tired. His head hurt and his right leg still hurt from when the gun stock splintered when a bullet hit it. Eric and he hadn't gotten much sleep yesterday, with the rustling and whimpers from the women. He kept thinking someone was going to hear them and come after them for their stuff. And now, of course, some men would come for the women, too. It just seemed like everything was conspiring against them to get to the retreat as fast as they could. He sighed. He was hungry again, too.

They got the camp set up. Eric decided to get a rice soup type recipe going for all of them to make everything last longer. He got the two camel backs from Mark's and his backpacks, the two canteens, a two quart pot for cooking and the coffee pot gathered together to fill them up when Maria approached him and said she'd do that. Abby said she'd go along to help and keep an eye out for anyone. Maria grabbed the two small backpacks to take with them, too. Channon was already asleep on the tarp with a blanket thrown over. Mark was sitting down on the ground, resting his head back against a branch.

Lisa walked over to Eric. "Mark was hit on the back of his head and he's limping on his right leg. Can I have the first aid kit to treat him?"

Eric was surprised that she would volunteer to touch one of them after her reaction two nights ago. "Sure, it's in my pack over there. If you need more assortment, Mark has a better one in his pack."

"I want to thank you for rescuing us and taking care of us. I just wanted you to know that." She turned, got the first aid kit out, and went over to Mark.

Lisa got down on her knees by Mark and he startled awake. She jumped a little. He grabbed her because it looked like she might fall over, she tensed up and gasped with a look of terror on her face.

He let go of her arm after righting her and said, "I'm sorry. I didn't mean to touch you. I was just trying to keep you from falling over."

Lisa slowly relaxed and then looked at him. "No, I'm the one that's sorry. You just startled me is all, and it's hard right now to trust any man. It's nothing personal. I just came over to look at your head and leg." He looked at her with a funny expression. She blushed. "I mean, you were hit on the head, and you were limping with your right leg; I just wanted to tend to any wounds you might have."

He looked at her thoughtfully for a few minutes. "I'm fine." He leaned back and closed his eyes again.

Lisa softly cleared her throat. "I can see that you aren't fine. I don't know how far we're going, but you need someone to look at your wounds or you might not be able to make it to this retreat of yours. If you have a wound and it gets infected, how are we going to get antibiotics for you?"

He thought about what she said for awhile. It was hard to admit that his head was killing him and his leg hurt. "Okay, fine, look at them." She smiled a little bit at how hard it was for him to admit needing help of any kind.

"Scoot over here with your back to me, so I can see your head." He scooted over, careful not to get too close. She had to lean forward. He had some dried blood on his scalp and hair. "I'll be back in a few moments," she said. She went down to the river and got one of the pop bottles they used for water and walked back up to the camp. She approached Eric. "It seems to me that if the water isn't safe to drink, that maybe using it to clean a cut out it might not be safe to do, either."

"Good point," he said. Eric got the germicidal drops, put some in the container, shook it up, and handed it to her. She went back to Mark and cleaned his cut out. It should probably have stitches, but she didn't know how to do that. There was a large bump, too. She was as gentle as she could be. She looked for a pair of scissors but didn't see any. Well, she'd just have to apply the triple antibiotic ointment to the split skin, anyway. When she was done she said, "Okay, now I need to see your leg."

Mark looked at her like she was crazy. "You want me to drop my pants?"

She gulped. "Yes."

"I thought that would be the last thing you would want a man to do," he said.

She looked at him and raised an eyebrow at him. "I'll be looking at your leg for wounds and nothing else, got it?"

He shrugged. "Got it." He undid his belt and pulled his pants down. Lisa struggled with a tight feeling of panic in her chest. After she got control of herself, she looked at his leg. There were several areas that were bloody and some had red all around them. Two looked really bad by the back of his knee. They had pus in them. She sighed.

"I'll be right back." She got up, grabbed a sleeping bag and dropped it on the ground. "Lay down on your stomach. You have several areas that look pretty bad." He had a hard time getting down, so Lisa helped him. When she had him settled, she started cleaning the bloody spots that were seeping. She knew this had to hurt. It took awhile to get them all cleaned. There were some splinters. She wondered how the hell he hadn't said something before now. She shook her head at his machismo for silently suffering in pain.

She heard the other women coming back from the river. She looked over and said softly, "Eric." He came over and looked at Mark's leg. His eyes got big.

Lisa said, "Do you have a sewing needle or something I can use to take out the splinters with?"

"Hold it right there," Mark said. "What do you need a sewing needle for?"

"You have splinters and pieces of wood embedded into your leg; I need to take them out so it can heal."

Mark sighed and lay back down, resigned to the fate of being poked with a needle.

"Yes, I have one, but I've something better. A Swiss Army Knife with tweezers."

"Okay. Put it in the fire for a few moments to sterilize it, then please bring it to me." Maria came over and asked if she could help. "Sure." Mark grumbled that he wasn't a circus clown to be the day's entertainment. Both women quietly laughed. Lisa told Maria that she'd get the splinters out. While Lisa was doing that, Maria would wipe all of the other wounds and put ointment on them before covering them with band-aids. Eric brought the hot tweezers over and they got to work.

Eric made a great soup. He took the two-quart pot and filled it as full as he could. He added one cup of rice, one package of onion soup mix and eight pieces of venison jerky, broken up. He brought it to a boil, put the lid on the pot, then turned the small stove down so it could simmer for ten minutes. He planned to let it sit for ten more minutes, and it would be ready to eat. He added some salt and pepper. It should be done about the same time Mark would be done getting patched up. He felt bad, he'd forgotten that Mark said it would keep when he asked him if he was hurt. Damn, those two deep wounds behind his knee looked pretty bad.

"Chow's done," Eric said. They ate. The pot was scraped out clean. It had been a long night and they were all hungry. Time to sleep. "I'll take first watch and you get some sleep." Eric woke Mark up every hour to check on him because of his head wound. He seemed to sleep better today than the day before. Eric kept looking around with his small mini Nikon 6x20 binoculars to see if there were any game trails, but he didn't spot any. *We are going to need more food before long again.* Those four extra mouths made a dent in their supplies.

Mark woke up and felt refreshed. His head still hurt, but not too bad. His leg was stiff and sore, but felt better than it had before Lisa and Maria played doctor on it. He got up and poured a cup of coffee. There wasn't much left in the pot. He looked around and noticed that everyone was up, including Channon. They were down at the end of the brush, cleaning up. Man, he needed to brush his teeth. It felt like an army of ogres had marched through and left little pieces of them behind in his mouth. It looked like the ladies were sharing Eric's spare toothbrush. Eric was looking at the road with his binoculars. He walked up to join him and peered out at the highway. There were several people searching the cars as they passed by.

Eric said, "They've been up and down here a few times today. Looks like they're searching for something or someone."

"Oh, great, just what we need. Do the ladies know they are out there?"

"Yes, Abby saw them earlier and we watched them for awhile." The ladies finished cleaning up and sat quietly where they had slept.

"Go ahead and get some sleep," Mark said. "I'll take over for now." Eric handed him the binoculars. Mark watched the people going up and down the highway until they were out of sight. *That was just plain weird. What were they looking for?* Mark decided to make more coffee. He turned around and saw Maria making another pot. They were learning to be extremely quiet. He hadn't even heard her pour the water into the pot.

Abby asked, "Are they gone?"

"Yes. Any idea of what they are looking for?"

"No. They just keep showing up every couple of hours, checking all the vehicles and then head back south. It makes no sense."

Mark said, "Maybe they're just looking for someone that's supposed to meet them here. It doesn't really matter. It has nothing to do with us unless you recognize any of them. Do you?"

"No, I've never seen them before. Besides, they don't have the Green Rainbow Warrior patch on their coats."

Mark said, "Rainbow Warrior? What's that? Is it a gang?"

"It's what those assholes had on their green patches. It's supposed to stand for warriors of every nation on the earth. Every creed and ethnic group is part of them. They were very weird. The questions they asked us as they were beating us were insane."

"What kind of questions?" Mark asked.

"They asked us if we ate meat, chickens or birds, eggs or drink milk. Did we eat cheese, things like that. It made no sense at all. I think they were just looking for any excuse to do what they wanted. They asked questions that everyone would say yes to eventually, and it just gave them an excuse to beat us even more."

Mark wondered about that, it did seem very weird. "It sounds like they are an animal rights group that only believes in eating grains and vegetables," he said. "Well, maybe, anyway. There are so many of those groups out there, it's hard to keep track of them. I never heard of Rainbow Warriors before. It could be a new group just starting up."

Abby said, "I thought animal rights groups are the ones that believe in loving nature and animals, you know, like hippies. Love, peace and hate war, that kind of thing. The Rainbow Warriors were nothing like that. I've never seen such violent people. I've heard a lot about the Triads, you know, growing up in my neighborhood. Those guys get off on being angry and insane. They enjoyed it."

Mark said, "Is that all they asked you? Anything else?"

"Yes, that's all they asked about. The other stuff they said was completely insane." Abby wrapped her arms around herself.

"What did they say to you?"

Abby sighed. "Every morning and afternoon, they ranted and gave us lectures. They probably would have at night, too, but they were too drunk by then. Sometimes, they'd ask us about what they said, and if we didn't answer right, they'd cut us and do even more hurtful things."

"I'm sorry," Mark said. "If you don't want to talk about it, I understand."

Abby hesitated and then said, "It's not just that. It's that the whole thing was like being in an alternative or parallel universe. I'm afraid if I tell you the things they said, you might think I'm insane for even repeating them. None of it made any sense."

Mark's curiosity was up now. "I know they're not your words, but their words. You can tell me and I won't think you're insane."

"All right, but don't say I didn't warn you. They told us we were practicing speciesism. I don't even know what that word is. It was like they thought we had something against them. I told you it sounded insane. They said we should worship and honor them, not to eat or harm them. That it would be a great honor for a wolf, a bear, or a cougar to eat them. But that people should not eat them. Not ever. It was evil to do so. If you loved them, as you were supposed to do, you would honor them, and worship them and that the earth would heal from the evil blight of mankind. We didn't deserve to have the earth. Animals are much more important than people. They were going to cleanse the earth of the six billion evil people who prey on other species; but they said it in a way like we prey on other intelligent species. They would go on like this for hours at a time about what an honor it was to cleanse the world of evil animal eaters. I warned you it was insane. None of it makes any sense unless you believe they're aliens from another plant and we hunt and eat them."

Mark was trying not to laugh. He smiled and said, "I'll tell you what speciesism is, and then it will make a weird kind of sense to you. It means that you hate other species and treat them accordingly."

Abby thought for a while. "I still don't understand. What does that have to do with them being eaten by a bear or whatever, and honored to have it happen, or about honoring them and worshiping them?"

"As I was saying earlier about animal rights groups, this fits right in. They basically believe that animals should be worshiped. They feel that people don't belong on the earth, only animals belong here. That animals are majestic and godly. Only humans do harm to things, and that when a wolf eats a newborn calf as it comes out of a cow, it's okay. True speciesism is supposed to be about discrimination, not one species killing and eating another one. Nature is built on one species hunting another. These people, however, say it's okay when wolves attack and eat your child, but you can't do the same to the wolf. We shouldn't have been where the wolf was, regardless where it happened, even if it was in your own yard. Coyotes, mountain lions, and so on... We shouldn't be in their territory. Whatever animals do is fine. It's we humans that are wrong for being here on the earth. We're always at fault. They say this propaganda crap all the time, but you don't see them committing suicide to rid the earth of their harmful presence, now, do you? They are nothing but human haters. They're hypocrites because they don't do what they preach."

Abby was shocked. "People really believe this stuff?"

"Yes, they do. They preach that it's wrong to hunt or fish. You should eat nothing but beans, vegetables, alfalfa sprouts and the miracle soybean. To eat anything else is a sin of the highest order, according to them."

Abby laughed. "Do they think by eating those things they aren't killing or harming anything?"

"Yes."

Abby laughed harder and covered her mouth to be as quiet as she could. "I read a research study once on plants. They feel pain. They hooked up different vegetables and fruits to monitors to register if they feel being picked or eaten. The study clearly showed that they did. When you pick a fruit or vegetable, the sound captured on the monitor was equivalent to a high, piercing scream. I wonder what they'd think of that?"

Mark joined in the laughter. "They wouldn't believe it even if they did read it. If it doesn't support their theories, it can't be true. That's their philosophy. They'll continue to say that whether science supports their viewpoints or not. After all, look at Climategate and the falsified studies. Even after showing them the truth, they still don't believe that it was all just a scam to raise research money. They're zealots, and like other cult members, they're brainwashed. It is as sacred as their religion to them. In fact, it is their religion." Abby just shook her head.

Channon was sleeping again. Lisa and Maria left her alone to rest, and went apart a little ways so they wouldn't disturb anyone with their whispering. Lisa said, "Okay, what did you need to talk about?"

"Do you think we can trust them?" Maria asked.

Lisa looked intently at Maria. "I think we can. They've treated us very well, like real men should, and not like we were nothing but dirt or a slave."

Maria nodded, then looked down at the ground with a pained expression on her face. "What if they're taking us to a camp full of men? I mean, what if we just jumped from the frying pan right into the fire?"

Lisa was thoughtful for a few moments. "You might be right. But they risked their lives to free us. I believe them when they said they just wanted to help us. I think they are decent guys. They're a little rough around the edges, but they're our best bet so far. I don't know what happened to the world, but our options are thin to zero. They have food and a plan to survive. What else can we do?"

Maria thought about it for a few seconds. "You're right. Who knows what's really going on out in the world? We might be at war, for all we know. But one thing we do know for sure is the cars all died and the lights are out. And look at how we were taken and treated. No one came for us, like the police, or anyone. Mark and Eric did rescue us. No one else even bothered to try. They are heroes for that fact alone. Abby seems to trust them, too."

"Abby is really very smart, and if she trusts them, we should, too, at least until they give us a real reason not to. Let's try not to judge all men by those creeps we were taken by, okay?" Maria nodded. "My thoughts about all of this is wherever they are taking us," Lisa said, "has to be better than where we were."

Lisa was tired. The future was very uncertain about so many things, everything, really. When she tried to sort out her thoughts, she would get a tight, constricting feeling in her chest that made it hard to breathe. It felt like she was drowning in a sea of doubt and uncertainty. Mistakes could mean the difference between life and death. Especially with the way the world was now.

Maria lay there and wondered why Mark and Eric had rescued them. What did they want with them? What were they planning for the future? She agreed with Lisa that they didn't have a real choice right now. In a world without police or government, anything could happen. The future didn't look like it was going to be a very nice place to be. Would it be whoever had the biggest gun and was toughest would win? No police or government meant there weren't any rules. It was going to be a free for all out there. *I don't want to think about this right now.* She remembered what it had been like when she was a kid and her family had been alive and together. All the love and happy memories she had. That was, until a drunk driver had killed them when she was nine. She had been sick with a sore throat, so her Nana had stayed home with her while her brother, mother and father went to church that Sunday morning. They hadn't come back. Then it had been just her and Nana. Nana had died when she was in college. Now it was just her. Well, she had a lot of cousins, but didn't know them very well. They were all so poor they couldn't afford to visit much.

Abby joined the rest of the women and lay down to rest for a while. She was still trying to figure out how people could believe it was wrong to eat meat or fish. *Are they stupid or what? You need animal protein to rebuild the cells in your body. Everyone knows that.* Plant protein for fiber was great to round out a diet, but you needed animal protein in order to be healthy and keep a sharp mind. As soon as she had the chance, she'd share her knowledge with the other women about the wackos who had held them captive. Maybe they would understand it better than she could. It just totally mystified her that people could believe crap like that.

Eric let the women know it was time to break camp and get ready to hit the road. Everyone, including Channon, helped pack. The women refilled all the water containers earlier, so they were all set to go. Mark got everyone's attention. "We'll go over some hand signals so you'll know what to do in a hurry if the need arises." He held his hand up, bent at the wrist, and said, "This means to stop." He clenched his fist and said, "This means drop to the ground and crawl to the closest cover." The women nodded. He held his hand in the up position, but turned around the opposite way, and said, "This means to back up." He looked around at the women and they nodded. "But always keep foremost in your mind that no matter what, you are to be silent ghosts while doing anything. That's the most important thing. Got it?" The women nodded yes. "I don't like that group of people that have been looking into the cars all day. We don't know if Katie has been captured by someone else and told them about us. It's very strange behavior. So, we're going to head out a little way from the river for a few miles before we turn onto the road so we will hopefully avoid them. We'll change our pattern from what we used when Katie was with us. That way, whatever she has told them about how we travel will be different, and the likelihood of us running into them will be reduced." They all nodded that they understood. He started off, with everyone falling into their places.

After traveling about three miles, Mark turned towards the road and angled his path to take them to the highway. Once there, they again resumed looking into cars for useful items for the ladies. They'd been lucky so far, they hadn't seen anyone else. They found two hooded sweatshirts, a pack of gum, two opened containers of breath mints and a woman's coat. After two more miles, Mark headed towards the river so they could take a break. He intended to give everyone a snack. They deserved it and they were making good time. When he found the perfect spot, he checked it out and then signaled for everyone to come. Things were sure going a lot smoother now that the ladies understood the basic hand signals. Later on, he'd teach more of them. They had gone about six miles now. He was satisfied with how well things were going. They all sat down gratefully for a rest. The ladies drank all of their water. Mark guessed it would be awhile before they had hydrated their bodies enough and would be drinking more water then normal. He told them quietly that they could go wash up and get more water. When they were done, he instructed them on how to keep watch. They had a lot of ground to cover to the retreat. After fifteen minutes, they set out again.

The clouds had been steadily moving towards them; it looked like it might rain. The wind was picking up. They only had two Swiss Army camo ponchos with them that they'd ordered from Major Surplus. They had gotten a complete battle dress uniform with long johns, gloves and the rain ponchos for only $24.95. It was a great deal of supplies for the money and worth every penny. They had two heavy-duty lawn-sized trash bags with them that they could make into rain ponchos, but that would mean they were going to have to find some shelter somewhere.

Eric thought that they could find a van, motor home or a pickup with a cap and use it to hole up in until the rain stopped. Mark was looking around for something they could use for shelter, too. They didn't see anything suitable at all. There were only cars. As they walked on, the rain started. Mark had them stop and bent down between two cars. He looked at the women, evaluating their sizes. He looked at Eric and said, "Get your trash bag out and cut it along the seams." He took his trash bag out of his pack and did the same. He now had two large pieces of plastic. He went over to Abby and placed one over her head to measure it. When he had it adjusted just right to fit her front and back, he cut a slit that she could stick her face out of, but it would be tight enough to keep her hair dry. He then got out a roll of camo cord and cut a long strip off it and showed her how to make a belt to hold the bag closed so the wind wouldn't blow it around. He next went over to Channon to do the same thing. Eric was doing the same for Lisa and Maria. Mark said, "Stay closer from now on. It will be harder to see the hand signals." They all nodded. When they had everyone covered, they started out again. The rain would pour down and then a light mist would drizzle for a while. This went on for hours. The tennis shoes the ladies had on were not made to be waterproof. They were wet and cold. It was about fifty degrees out, but felt much colder with the wind whipping around them, robbing their body heat. The ladies' teeth were chattering. Fog was setting in too. It was getting real hard to see, and that, in itself, could be very dangerous. They could bump into a gang and not even see it coming. Mark estimated they had gone about six or seven miles since the break they'd taken.

They were going to have to find some place to hole up until the rain stopped. They needed to get the women out of the rain and get them warmed up. Mark signaled to Eric. Mark said, "We have to hole up. It's too dangerous in the fog to keep going. Start looking for two vehicles that aren't too far apart. Let's try for mini vans or trucks. I'll take one and you take the other. That way if we run into trouble, we can cover each other."

Eric nodded. "Good idea." It was his turn in the lead, so he started looking for two vehicles that were close together, but not too close. He spotted a mini van up ahead and they had just passed by another one back there. He stopped and signaled to Mark to take that van. Mark and the two women went towards the van. Eric turned around and headed for the other van up ahead.

When they were settled inside the van out of the rain, Eric lit up the stove for ten minutes to warm it up inside. He hadn't known how to put the seats in the back down, but Maria said she knew how. The women climbed in the back and Eric sat in the front seat. He told Lisa and Maria that they would all take watches so the others could get some rest while they were holed up. He quickly showed them how to use the shotgun. He had them practice holding it in the shooting position and loading it and unloading it. He had them practice until they were comfortable handling it. There was enough room for the two women to lie down in the back comfortably. Eric took the passenger side and reclined the seat back. Wow, this was comfortable. It felt great after all the days of sleeping on the hard ground. He was taking first watch to allow the ladies to get dry and warm before their watches. *We'll probably be here only for a couple of hours.* He looked around and couldn't see anything but fog. He couldn't even see another car. He got comfortable. The plan was to stay here just until the rain stopped and they could see better.

That was the last thing he remembered thinking. The cushioned comfort of the warm van surrounded him like a cocoon. He quickly fell asleep. He woke up with a crick in his neck. He looked around and didn't recognize where he was for a moment. *Oh shit, it's full daylight outside and the sun's shining.* He hissed, "Lisa, Maria wake up. Wake up right now." His seat was in a reclined position so anyone looking at the van would think it was empty. He slowly lifted his head up. *Damn it,* he ducked down fast and hissed to the women, "Stay down," in an urgent whisper. Lisa woke up totally at the urgent sound of Eric's voice.

"Oh my God, they found us?"

"No, I don't think these are the ones that had you two," Eric replied in a soft whisper. "There are some people in front of us. I saw three of them for sure. They might just be scavengers looking for food. Stay low. Get your shoes on and pack everything up. Be ready to move out of here quickly." He peeked up over the dashboard very slowly. There they were, just two hundred yards away. He didn't see any guns. They were carrying stuff in a bundle. There were three guys and two women now. *Damn, what a bad fighting position to be in.* The windows to this van were power, and couldn't be rolled down. He would have to open up a door and swing the gun all the way out before he could even get it pointing in the right direction. *Damn it, damn it, damn it, this really sucks,* he thought. How could he have been so stupid to have fallen asleep? *Where the hell was Mark?* He turned and couldn't see the van Mark and the other women were in. He looked at the two women and asked, "Can you open the back door up? If you can, then we can escape out the back."

The two women turned and looked at the back of the van. Maria said, "Yes, there is a handle back here. Let me see if I can get it to open." She scooted down to the back and turned the handle, the hatch started to swing up. She held onto it and turned to look at Eric.

Eric turned and looked forwards. They were about a hundred yards away now. That is too close for comfort. The lead person was walking fast, not really searching the vehicles, just giving each one a quick glance inside. He whispered to the women, "Climb out the back and make sure you have everything. Stay down out of sight." They both quietly climbed out. Maria held onto the door so it wouldn't swing up. Eric slowly crawled over the seat and out. He closed the door just enough so it would latch.

The lead guy must have seen the movement or heard the click of the latch, because he yelled out, "Problem."

That was a weird code word, Eric thought. The guy took cover in front of a vehicle, but kept watch for them. The rest of his group scattered outside and worked their way up to the front. Eric quickly got behind the van and took aim forward. They retreated back a couple of cars, anyone coming would have to get by his 12 gauge.

Lisa whispered to Eric, "I didn't see any guns on them. What's the problem?"

Eric said, "If they were unarmed, they would have retreated and scattered. They didn't. Instead, they advanced on towards us. You better believe they have guns. Stay down and out of the way. Be ready to move in whatever way I signal you to go." Lisa and Maria looked worried, but they both nodded. They had taken cover behind a white Cadillac. Eric moved up to the driver's side door and slowly opened it up and then yelled out, "What do you want? We're not looking for any trouble."

Laughter answered him. A man's voice said, "Trouble? You aren't looking for trouble? There will be no trouble at all. What you fail to understand is, you see, we own this road now, and you have to pay a toll to use our road."

Eric answered, "Then we don't have a problem. We won't use your road. We'll walk into the woods. We aren't paying any toll."

Eric's statement was met with more laughter. "Well, you'll have to walk off our road to get to the woods," said the man, "so you'll still owe us a toll."

Eric thought, *well, buddy I tried to be nice about this.* He flipped off the safety of the 12 gauge. He was down on one knee with the shotgun aimed right at Mr. Loud Mouth. The others in his group were moving closer. He saw they were all armed with handguns. Eric yelled out, "That's far enough." He only saw five, but there could easily be more of them hidden from sight. Eric was thinking that the longer he could keep them talking, the better it would be for all of them. As far as Eric could tell, there were only teenagers here. They wore hooded sweatshirts and they seemed to be between sixteen and twenty years old. They must be a gang. "What's your toll?" He thought it would be food, money or something like that.

"Well, I'm glad you want to be reasonable with us about this," the man called out. "That's a good idea on your part. We just want your guns."

Eric smiled. "That's a good idea. How about you give me all your guns and I'll let you live?"

"No, no, my friend, you don't understand," said their spokesman. "We own the road and you pay us the toll." Eric thought this clown must be the leader of the gang. It was time to end this. He'd give them one last chance, then he was going to drop him like a bad habit.

Eric yelled out, "All right, last chance, kid. You back off now and you can live."

The kid he'd been talking with was leaning over the hood of a car, aiming his 9mm pistol at Eric. The car was kitty-corner to Eric. He aimed at the kid's chest. Eric saw the kid turn and point to someone and signal them to weave forward. Eric had enough of this nonsense. They weren't going to let them get past without a confrontation. He couldn't wait any longer or it would be too late. He squeezed off the shot. The kid disappeared from sight and left a lot of blood dripping off the hood of the car. He racked another shell in the chamber, looking for a new target.

There was complete silence for a few seconds. The silence was louder than the roar of the shotgun. Eric's mind was racing. Clearly, the gang was surprised and not used to people fighting back. Then the bullets starting flying towards him, homeboy style; they were all shooting at him. All that could be heard was clunk, clunk, clunk. One bullet hit the door by Eric as a kid charged up on his open side. Eric could see the kid firing the handgun as he raced towards him. Eric leaned out a bit and pulled the trigger, dropping him at thirty yards out. There was another kid charging up on the other side by the mini van. Eric looked again and saw more kids firing at him, and off in the distance, a lot more were coming his way. Eric thought, *oh shit; this is going to get really bad.* He felt a tug on his left thigh and didn't think anything about it. The next bullet hit the glass of the door he was hiding behind, showering him with shattered glass. He ducked down and came up shooting mad. He quickly fired three shots at the kid hiding behind the Dodge caravan, but the engine was stopping the pellets from penetrating.

He ran back to the ladies and said, "Retreat a few more cars back and keep a clear view so no one can sneak up behind you. If it gets real bad, get out into the woods and find Mark." He grabbed more shells and loaded the shotgun, putting more in his pockets. He didn't notice the frightened looks the two shared before doing what he said.

Pulling up the 12 gauge, he felt much more confident now with more shells. There was nothing like a little 00 buckshot for a close in firefight. Every time he saw movement, he fired. Now there was only an occasional shot fired his way, but the last two were hiding real good. Obviously, they were waiting for reinforcements to arrive. He watched for a few moments and then decided it would be better to head for the woods. He was a bit worried because he hadn't seen Mark, or heard his rifle, either. He signaled for the two women to come up to him. "Listen to me. I'm going to shoot a lot of shells at these guys; while I'm doing that, I want you two to stay low, but hurry to the woods and hide. Don't stop for anything. I'll be following right behind you. Ready?" The two women nodded. "Go." He started shooting, and was just starting to make his way over to the woods when he saw one kid running like hell, full out aiming at the women. He walked up to the front of the vehicle, slowly crossing in front towards the women. They were running full out now. He saw one of the kids raise his gun up, aiming at them. He fired at the kid. His shotgun blast took out the window in the side door and the windshield of the car the kid was near. The kid dropped down for cover. Without even thinking about it, he worked the pump action automatically when he heard the empty shell hit the pavement. He saw the kid on the ground behind the door. He rolled out from in front of the car to the next one over. His mouth was completely dry and his left leg ached a little. He quickly made his way up to the front of that car and stepped around, aiming the shotgun. In front of the vehicle a young girl was hiding. He stepped behind her, pointing the 12 gauge in her direction. She looked back over her shoulder at him and dropped her gun. She put her hands out to the sides palm up so he could see she was unarmed and took off running. He bent down and picked up the Glock 9mm and stuck it in his coat pocket. He ran for the fence by the woods. He heard shooting behind him, saw the dirt kicking up in front of him off to the side just as quick as 1-2-3-4-5. He stopped at the fence and turned back to look. The girl was bent over, firing one of her fallen comrade's guns at him. He fired a quick shot at her and she fell over.

He jumped the fence and took off running. With his fifty-pound pack on his back, it was more like a fast trot. He was thanking every single minute he and Mark had spent out in the woods, training with a full pack on. He never would have made it if he wasn't in shape. He felt a tug on the pack, but just kept going. He cleared the field. When he entered the woods, the ladies were waiting for him. He made it.

Lisa gasped. "You're hit; you're bleeding.

He looked down at this thigh and saw the blood. It didn't feel badly hurt. *I must still be running on adrenaline*, he thought. "More are coming. We have to keep moving. Where's the river?" He spotted it not too far away. *River, perfect*, he thought. *It will hide any footprints we make.* He just kept moving straight for the river. The women followed him at a trot. They hit the riverbank and headed north. They kept going for about two hundred yards. When he found the spot he was looking for, with a high bank with a just enough room to walk, he slid down it and whispered, "Come on." They slid down the overhang along the brush. "Get under, quickly." He looked back at the trail they had made; grabbing a branch, he smoothed over their tracks. Hopefully it was not enough to give them away.

He walked up to them. They were huddled underneath the brush. "We've got to get closer to the top." He pulled out his entrenching tool and dug a spot so it was flat for each of them to sit on when they reached the top. He instructed them to quickly pull out the poncho to cover up an enclosed space. He showed them how to use the dirt, brush and mud to pack the sides down with. They quickly got it done. He pulled out some 550 cord and cut a few small lengths, giving it to them to tie the tops on each side down. He walked in the water around on the left side; There were some tree branches overhanging the area. He grabbed some dead ones, set them up in a tangle to break the outline of the poncho so they'd blend into the scenery. He stuffed more brush around the area to make it look natural. He was looking the area over when he heard some twigs breaking. It sounded close. No time to worry about if it looked right or not. He slowly lifted his foot out of the water and climbed under the quickly made hut. He made a zipping motion with his hand and lips.

They could hear more branches breaking all around them. It sounded like twenty or more people up there. A voice said, "Come on, they can't be too far." He sidestepped in the little hut, picking up the 12 gauge. They could hear them coming closer now. Eric thought about whether this would work or not. One thing he knew was they'd know for sure in a few minutes. He could hear them coming closer and closer. His mouth was so arid that he couldn't even swallow and his heart was loudly drumming in his ears. He heard one run past them. Another one walking by. The tension built with each footstep.

He looked over at Maria. Her eyes were closed and her lips were silently moving. She was shaking. No doubt she was saying a prayer. He glanced over at Lisa; her eyes were opened wide and she was breathing in quick little gulps. She was going to hyperventilate at the rate she was going. He leaned over to her ear and whispered, "Its okay. Just calm down and breathe slowly through your nose." She was scared and shaking. The footsteps were almost directly overhead now. Eric readied himself. He would have to step down, spin around, find the target and fire. It would be tough to do, but better than doing nothing.

The footsteps stopped almost directly above them. All three of them were looking up at the top of the little hut. Eric held his breath as he waited to see if he would need to jump into action. He heard a male voice shout, "Keep looking. They have to be here somewhere." Both the women jumped a little at the voice ringing out. The footsteps started up again, each step taking the man farther and farther away. Maria let out a bit of air and took a big gulp. She obviously had been holding her breath. Eric looked at her and smiled. She tried to smile back at him. The mud on her face and wild-eyed expression said it all. It was hard to calm down in an insane world like they were living in. Lisa sat absolutely rigid. You had to really look to see that she was even breathing.

They sat like that for a long while. After about ten minutes of not hearing another sound, he relaxed a little and whispered to the women, "We have to stay put until darkness."

Lisa took a couple of deep breaths and relaxed some. She reached into Eric's pack and pulled the first aid kit out. "Drop your pants and let me patch you up." In all the excitement, he'd forgotten about being hit. He looked at it and figured it must be from the broken glass. He pulled his pants down. After all they'd been through together, there was no time to be modest now. He had a bloody torn piece of flesh about two inches long. It looked like a bullet had skimmed along his leg. "You got lucky," she whispered. Taking an alcohol pad, she cleaned the wound. It took three pads to get it cleaned up from the crust and mud. She put some triple antibiotic ointment on a 3x3 band-aid and applied it. "Okay you can pull your pants back up now." He wanted to say something funny, but thought it wasn't the right time.

He pulled his pants up and buttoned them. Lisa gave him a small smile and whispered, "Good, now maybe you'll slow down so we can keep up with you." He gave her a weird look like he didn't understand her at all. Maria and Lisa both chuckled quietly at him. The look on his face was priceless. He decided the best thing to do right now was ignore both of them.

The ground was wet from the rain. He realized they were going to get very wet and cold if he didn't do something about it. He reached over and untied his sleeping pad he had for the ground. He had them scoot around so he could get the pad underneath them. At least that would stop them from getting a wet butt. They huddled together on the pad. *Two women*, Eric thought, *one on each side*. This was every guy's dream come true. And it would be, if the world weren't falling apart. Now it was practical and a matter of survival.

He wondered what had happened to Mark, Abby and Channon. He sure hoped they got away and were okay. What if Mark needed him and he'd left him there, needing help? What if Mark was wounded? He hadn't heard Mark's rifle. But maybe with all the firing going on, he'd missed hearing it. How would he be able to find him now? What if they got captured or killed? How would he know? Eric knew he had to be strong for these two women. They were both looking to him to know what to do and how to do it. He would have to put all of that at the back of his mind for now. He had to take care of Lisa and Maria. After all, it was Mark who picked what women would go with each of them. So, in a way he was doing what Mark had wanted him to do. He missed his friend. His eyes filled with tears that he could not shed. He didn't want to scare his companions. He blinked the tears away and took a deep breath. He would be the rock of Gibraltar for these two women. He was all they had. He thought, *Well, best get on with it.*

Chapter 12

Fly Like The Wind

"You see, in life, lots of people know what to do, but few people actually do what they know. Knowing is not enough! You must take action."

Anthony Robbins

Amy's bike followed wherever Preston led them. He could see more clearly where they were going. He had instructed her on how he wanted her to follow him before they'd left. She was to stay at least four to five feet behind him and three to five feet to the side, if possible. That way one bullet wouldn't take them both out. When they were traveling through debris or between vehicles, she was to follow his path exactly and do everything he did. She was a bit nervous. It had been years since she rode a bike and she'd never even been on a mountain bike before. He had explained the gears and how they worked. He said the trip should take no more than three days at the maximum, but to prepare for one week. The unexpected always cropped up, she should also remember that no plan survives contact with the enemy; in this case, the little zombies. He also reminded her that ordinary people who were desperate for food or water could be just as dangerous as the zombies. It was vital to stay alert and on guard at all times and not let your mind wander. He explained that out of everything they had to do for their survival, this was the most important and hardest thing to do. If your mind wandered off, it could get you killed.

She was to be the eyes in the back of his head, just as he was the eyes in front. They had to work as a team, keeping constantly aware of what was around them. She was jumpy and nervous because they couldn't see sometimes because of the smoke they rode through. He had given her a bandana, tied it around her neck, and told her to pull it up over her nose and mouth when they rode through the smoke so she could breathe and keep from coughing; that could give their position away. She wasn't used to wearing camo paint on her face, either. Every couple of minutes it seemed she had a spot on her face that itched. She kept looking around and running these facts through her mind to keep herself alert and commit them to memory. He told her a lot of things before they left. She hoped she could remember all of them. There were a lot of new things for her to get used to now that the world had become a very chaotic place to live in.

She found herself tensing up as they approached another smoky place up ahead. Every time they rode through one, she kept expecting someone to jump out at her or grab her. They hadn't seen anyone yet. They had just heard noises off in the distance. It was really eerie. At times it seemed like they were in an episode of the Twilight Zone or a horror film. She couldn't make up her mind which one suited this situation. They should soon be on the outskirts of the city. It couldn't come fast enough to suit her. She was afraid of running into people that would ask for their help. She knew Preston was right when he said they couldn't stop to help anyone. Logically, it made a lot of sense, but the humane part of her felt they should stop and help people as much as they could. Right now people needed as much help as they could get. But, back to the logical part again, what could they do to help them that would make a difference? She couldn't come up with anything and that upset her. She felt that the whole world was falling apart and there wasn't anything she could do about it. The situation was hopeless. She sighed. Her emotions were on a roller coaster. It didn't help knowing she was going to start her period in the next couple of days, either.

Boy, was it going to be tricky changing a tampon on this trip. She didn't know how to tell Preston that they were going to have to make more stops so she could check on her tampon. What a time to have to deal with all of that. She usually had bad cramps, an upset stomach and a backache with it all for at least three to four days. Plus, she felt bitchy. Right now, if someone jumped out at her, she'd probably rip their head off and spit on it. She leaned forward to ease her back because it had started to ache.

They were occasionally seeing people here and there. They didn't seem to even notice them going by. That was really creepy. Most of them were walking with a purpose, as if they were heading to some place important. The others were just shuffling along in a daze. There really wasn't time to observe them for long. But that's what it looked like. It was like her and Preston were invisible or something. It gave her the chills. What a weird night.

She knew that Preston wasn't stopping until they were way outside of the city. He had told her they could make about twelve miles an hour on the bikes, but to expect somewhere around eight to ten miles an hour with weaving around obstacles and debris. He also told her that when they got to the hills, they'd go down to about five miles an hour, but would gain some speed back going down the other side of them, so it would even out depending on how many of them they had to ride over. He had smiled at her when he said he had never really counted how many hills there were between here and his retreat. She had laughed. Who would even think of doing such a thing as count the hills between places? Well, maybe cross-country bikers would or someone who planned a trip on a bike. She realized with a shock that she'd done exactly what Preston had warned her of, her mind had wandered off on its own. She admonished herself about being alert and being the eyes behind Preston. *Get your head on straight or you might loose it permanently and get Preston killed, too.*

Preston was glad to finally be on the road. He was ever watchful of the surroundings. Amy was new to all this, and the chances of her not letting her mind wander were slim. She'd do it and not even realize it. So, he had to see for both of them. There hadn't been time to train her properly in catching movement out of the corner of her eyes and recognizing danger signs.

He had made sure to give Amy easy things to say so he'd know what she meant when she needed something. If she needed to stop, obviously, she would say 'stop.' If she saw something he didn't, he told her to use the numbers of the clock. If she saw something on the left and he was looking to the right, she was to say 9 o'clock, or 10 o'clock and so on. He would then know something was happening that he hadn't seen. But what was even more important was he would know exactly where it was happening. Then he'd be able to respond faster. At least he hoped it would work that way. She'd stayed right up with him and not one complaint out of her yet. It was quite refreshing after the Sharon fiasco, so far, so good. They had passed people, but they hadn't paid any attention to them at all. The people hadn't even given them a second look. Conditions didn't look good out here. Almost everywhere they had passed by cars and buildings with bullet holes in them. That was plain to see in the light from the fires. There were bodies lying around here and there, too. They were almost to the highway now. They'd make better time and it should be safer the farther out they went. He sure hoped that Amy would be good to travel all night tonight. He had to remember that she was recovering from a slight concussion and might not be feeling very well.

The highway was just a few miles up the road now and looked like a prime ambush spot. It was really dark with deeper colored shadows. It looked like no one was around. He had a bad feeling about this. He really hoped Amy was paying attention. Sure enough, three punks came running out of the alley, shooting homeboy style. Bullets and flames flew out from the barrels of their pistols, standing out from the darkness in a brilliant flash of fireworks. Without really thinking about it, he'd already pulled the handle of the shotgun up to release it from its holding position and hit the brakes on the bike. He swung the bike a little to the side and zeroed in on one of them and pulled the trigger. The roar of the 20 gauge in reply to their little weapons was very loud and flames shot out in a blinding flash. He missed. He quickly zeroed in on another one and the #3 copper plated buckshot put a quick end to him. He aimed at the first one again and pulled the rigger. The punk fell to the ground. The last punk was coming straight for him. Preston was unable to see him and swung the shotgun towards him, firing the shotgun twice. He heard the breach lock open and knew he was out of shells. The punk had seen his two friends go down, so he dropped to the ground, firing at Preston.

Amy had not been blinded by the flashes and could see what was going on. She had pulled out the 9mm when the firefight first started and clicked the safety off. Two bad guys were down almost before she could blink and she saw the third one dive to the ground, still firing at Preston. She saw Preston reach down for his .45. She wasn't able to see the sights on the 9mm in her hand, it was too dark. She pointed where she thought the shot would go and pulled the trigger. She saw sparks ricochet off the pavement too far to the right. She adjusted her hand a little more left and pulled the trigger; it sparked again. She was a foot off and a little high. She adjusted her aim once again and pulled the trigger. She had over compensated and the bullet hit about a foot in front of the bad guy. She saw the sparks and thought she'd missed again. But the bad guy dropped his gun and grabbed his throat with both hands after her last shot. Preston had the .45 out, and before he could pull the trigger, he heard the 9mm fire three shots.

The firefight was over. There were no more targets. He could see the guy on the ground now in front of him. He got off the bike and walked over to the guy that Amy had shot. He intended to put a bullet in his head if he wasn't already dead. He bent down a little to get a closer look and the guy was clearly dead. He turned the guy over with his foot and the guy's hands fell away from his throat. There was blood everywhere and a neat 9mm bullet hole in his neck. He thought, *I'll be damned a ricochet bullet killed him.* He turned and looked at Amy. She was still looking around for threats, holding the 9mm in her hands in the shooting position he had her practicing earlier in the day. It looked like it had paid off. He was amazed that she had entered into the firefight. Firefights were fast and confusing. She had kept a calm head when he had missed with his last two shots. He hadn't realized the punk had dropped to the ground. She'd saved his life and had her first kill. He got back onto his bike.

"Are you okay?" Preston called to her. "Are you hit?" He could see she was crying. "Amy, are you okay?" She nodded her head yes. "Did you get hit with a bullet?" She shook her head no. He backed the bike up a little to be alongside her. He reached out and touched the side of her face to get her to look at him, not the dead man she had just killed. When he had her attention he said, "You did good. You did real good." She just looked at him with misery in her eyes. She then looked down and took a deep breath; she shook her head yes. He waited until she looked at him again and then he said, "Thank you. I didn't see that punk drop to the ground. The flashes blinded me for a few moments. You saved my life."

She stared at him and finally said in a soft whisper, "You're welcome."

He looked straight into her eyes. "We can't stop now. It's too dangerous. More might be on their way after hearing the shots. Follow me, and as soon as it's safe, we'll stop for a break and talk about this. Okay?"

"Okay." He let his hand fall from her face and he sighed deeply. He reached out, grabbed the shotgun and turned it over. He grabbed one shell off of his twenty-five round bandolier and he pushed it into the tube. He then hit the release button and fed in a fresh shell.

He fed more shells until he had four in the tube. He pushed the shotgun down and locked it in place. He settled into his bike seat and started out, making sure Amy followed.

She felt kind of numb; everything around her felt unreal. In her mind, she was saying, *I killed him* over and over again. Tears blurred her vision. She knew he was a bad guy. He would've killed Preston if she hadn't shot him. She knew this with every fiber of her being. But she had taken a life. Someone was dead because of her. Where was this righteous feeling she was supposed to feel, knowing what she had done was the right thing? In the movies, the good person was supposed to walk away from a shootout with their head held high and blow the smoke off their gun. They were the good guys, right? If they were the good guys, why did she feel so bad? She had to stop. She was going to throw up. She called to Preston and pressed her brakes. As soon as she got off the bike, she got sick, right there by the side of the road. She heaved and heaved until there wasn't anything left, then she got the dry heaves.

She finally became aware that Preston was holding her up with one arm and holding her hair out of her face with his other hand. She straightened up a little. He asked if she was all right; she nodded her head yes. She thought, *what a stupid question. Of course I'm not all right. I killed a guy. How could I be all right?* She didn't know the words to say to make him understand how she felt. He probably thought she was a weak female and might faint or something. He stepped away from her and her heart rate sped up. What if he just left her right there for acting like such a baby? She started to cry again. *God, why can't I stop crying?* He came back and patted her face with a wet cloth. He handed her a bottle of water; she tried to take it, but her hands were shaking so hard she couldn't grasp it. He wrapped her hands around the bottle of water so she could hold it. She rinsed her mouth out a few times, and then drank some. She kept spilling it all over the place. Finally, he took it and put the cap back on. He walked away from her again.

She just stood there, not knowing what to do. He came back. "Amy, we're going to go off into the woods over there and find a spot to sit down. Follow me and walk carefully, so you don't fall. Okay?"

"Okay." Preston started off slowly, and she guided the bike, stumbling along behind him. He found a spot that was very secluded. He took the bike from Amy and hid it beside his in some brush. He took the tarp and a pad and put it on the ground under some low tree branches. He spread out both sleeping bags side by side and guided her into one, helping her to sit down. He climbed into the other one and sat beside her. She felt like such a fool. She just wanted to go to sleep and never wake up again.

They sat in silence for a few minutes, then Preston softly said; "The first time I killed someone I didn't have time to think about it until later that night. I got sick and threw up all over the place. Then I got drunk. A buddy of mine helped me that night just by being there and understanding what I was going through. His name is Joe. I had just met him a few days before it happened. We were in some foreign country, supposedly restoring order and delivering relief supplies at the time. His unit was low on men and they asked for volunteers to go out on patrols. I, of course, volunteered for some action. I had visions running through my head of being a hero or something. Being a helicopter mechanic, I hadn't seen much action up until then. He's a few years older than I am, and had seen a lot of action. The man I killed would have killed Joe if I hadn't fired first. We were checking out a building because we got a report of suspicious activity going on. Joe was leading, and this other guy was watching behind us. I was in the middle. They put me there because I didn't have any experience. We came around a corner of the building and Joe was looking around to make sure the way was clear for us to go forward. There was a shed not too far from us. I had this weird feeling that someone was watching. I was trying to see everywhere at once. I caught sight of movement and something shiny out of the corner of my eye, raised my rifle, and shot four times. Joe was a few feet ahead of the other guy, and me almost at the corner of the building. A body rolled down off the shed. At the time, the only person the man could have seen was Joe. The other guy and I hadn't stepped around the side of the building yet. I only hit him once. The bullet went in below him on an angle and went right through him. It was not a pretty sight. Joe thanked me for saving his life. We never figured out where the other bullets went."

Amy started to cry again. She felt bad for killing the bad guy, and she felt sorry for Preston having to shoot bad guys, too. He reached over and pulled her close to him, held her tightly and just let her cry it out. He figured she had been through hell the last few days and was entitled to a good cry if it would help her to feel better. If he had some whiskey or something with them, he might have tried to get a few drinks into her to help numb the mind until it could deal with the situation. He hadn't thought to pack any. He sighed. She had been so brave tonight.

Preston held Amy tightly, rubbed her back and her hair some, and told her over and over he was there for her. He understood what she was going through. When she had cried herself out and just lay in his arms, still and loose like a rag doll, he laid her down on the sleeping bag. He got up and wet a cloth for her face and dabbed at the smeared camo paint. Acceptance would come in time. He knew she would dream of this incident over and over until her subconscious had dealt with it. He had helped a few others deal with their first kills, too, just as Joe had for him. It wasn't easy to take a life. It shouldn't be. When it became easy, you knew you had turned into a psychopath. He had never helped a woman through this experience before, though. He wasn't sure exactly how to help her except to give his constant support, to let her know she wasn't alone, and that he was grateful for what she had done.

Amy was just numb inside She wasn't sure she could have found the right words to explain what she felt in her heart. She was glad she hadn't had to explain, because Preston got it and understood. They could relax here for a while until Amy felt a little better and was able to go on.

She said, "We better leave and get as far as we can tonight. I'm sorry about falling apart and making us stop. I don't think I've ever fallen apart quite like that before. I'm sorry."

Preston looked at her and smiled. "You're entitled to have a bad reaction to killing someone. You would be a sociopath if it didn't affect you. I'm glad to know you're not a sociopath."

She just shook her head at him. He really was crazy. Well, judging from the reaction she had over killing that bad guy, she guessed she was about as far from being a sociopath as one could get. She helped him pack and decided to take some ibuprofen for her headache and backache. They steered the bikes back to the highway, looking all around to make sure they were alone.

Preston reached over and touched her face and hair. He smiled at her. "You did good. Real good. I'm glad to have you with me on this trip to the retreat." Preston took off and she followed.

After they got out of the city, the vehicles thinned out on the highway. They were making really good time. They had seen a few small campfires out in the woods when they were closer to the city, now, it was just the darkness and them. One thing was really good; light was visible from a long way away. Their eyes had adjusted to the darkness and they could see really well. They passed by lots of deer by the side of the road, and saw a few other critters cross the road in front of them. It was peaceful and beautiful. They both appreciated it after all the chaos in the city. The beauty of the countryside soothed Amy's soul. It reminded her a little of the woods where she had grown up. The only difference was the pine trees here were mixed with hardwoods. She kept noticing the animals and thinking about what she had learned about taking them for food. Yup, that guy, Buckshot, had been right; animals were all over here and there was no reason to starve. She started to feel more optimistic about learning the skills to trap and snare them for food.

They saw a bonfire up ahead, close to the highway with two guys by it. One was lying on the ground, maybe sleeping, and another one was standing by the fire, keeping watch. Preston had noticed that the guard had a rifle on a sling over his shoulder. They worked up their speed to about twenty-five miles an hour to pass the bonfire. There was a whooshing sound as Preston flew by. A couple of seconds after, another whooshing sounded. The man looked around as they passed by, then up at the sky, like maybe there was a bird or something out there. Preston smiled and thought, *I can tell how this story will go: Hey dude, I was standing watch and two ghosts flew past, or maybe it was a couple of big birds diving down to the road or something. They were gone before I could even swing my gun around.* The man couldn't tell what they were, because he hadn't been able to see them. He was standing too close to the fire; it ruined his night vision. What a stupid thing to do. It was one mistake that Preston took advantage of.

They had no further incidents or encounters that night. Preston had estimated that they'd traveled about sixty miles. It had been twenty-five miles to the highway that would get them to the retreat. They'd traveled about ten miles of it when Amy had broken down. At around midnight, they started out again. It was now almost dawn. That meant approximately six hours of averaging about ten miles each equaled sixty miles. He figured he needed to start looking around now for a place to hole up for the day. This was the perfect place because they were between two towns. They'd be less likely to run into anyone out here. He watched the woods on the left for a good spot because both towns were on the right side. This was farming country, there were likely less people on the left. He spotted a good-sized wooded area and headed for it. There was a dirt road almost to the woods. He signaled to Amy that they were turning to the left. He looked back to make sure she had seen him. She kept right up with him. They climbed off the bikes, steering them into the woods. When they had traveled about three hundred yards, he looked around for a spot they could secure with bushes for cover. There it was. There were low pine branches, almost to the ground, with a lot of brush in the back. They could scoot down under them to sleep and pull brush up close to hide them in plain sight. He'd throw his ghillie suit over some branches above their sleeping spot and they'd blend right in with the environment; that way, if they moved around in their sleep, it wouldn't disturb the ghillie suit and wouldn't show movement. It would be like a little hut, almost like a deer blind that hunters used to hide themselves from animals. He explained to Amy what he was doing and what needed to be gathered together to do it. After they were set up, Amy made them some apple and cinnamon flavored oatmeal for breakfast. She used a cup of water and sprinkled in some powdered milk into it to pour over the oatmeal. They each ate two packets of oatmeal. It was good and they were hungry.

Bike riding was hard on the muscles. Before they settled down for the day, Preston took some Aspercreme and rubbed it into Amy's shoulders. He had her rub more on her legs and arms. She asked him to please rub some on her lower back, too. It was really killing her. She took a few more ibuprofen caplets. She wasn't sure if it was because she was on her period, or if it was the backpack or the way she had to lean over on the bike, but her back hurt a lot. They snuggled down in their sleeping bags. Preston would go into a light sleep and doze on and off all day. He was used to it. He was a light sleeper, anyway. He'd let Amy get some much deserved rest and deep sleep today. She had earned it. It was light out now.

Amy woke up feeling quite refreshed. She ached a little, but nothing bad. *Thank God,* she thought, *I'm used to jogging or this trip would be holy hell.* She looked around and realized that it was late afternoon. She looked over at Preston and saw that he was turned on his side, facing her, asleep. He never woke her up to keep watch. Well, there couldn't have been that much danger out there or he would never have gone to sleep. Of that fact she was sure. She realized that the sleeping bags were right next to each other. In fact they were almost over lapping and Preston's arm was across her stomach. She vaguely remembered having some really weird dreams about shooting the guy. She couldn't really remember them, just a big jumbled mess of fragmented pictures and feelings. She must have been tossing around and Preston put his arm over her to keep her from rolling into the sticks he'd placed around them to help hold up that camo thing over them. Well, she had to go find a bush. She slowly scooted out from under his arm so as not to disturb him. Holy cow, it was cold out today. She quickly put her boots on and moved a bush in the back and crawled out.

She got coffee going and heated some water for more soup to go with the sandwiches. She had seen a big pond out the back way. They would be able to refill all the water pouches after dark; it was pretty exposed all around. They both had a thermos, and she'd fill them up before they left for the night with hot coffee. Maybe for their one long stop they'd make tonight for a meal, she'd make some hot chocolate for them as a change of pace. Preston had told her the plan was to stop only three times a night. They would stop half way for a meal and twice for snacks, something hot to drink, and for a bathroom break. They would stop for other bathroom breaks only if necessary. That was fine with her. The more they traveled, the sooner they'd get to this retreat of his. Then they'd be a lot safer than they were now.

Preston heard her silently moving around, making coffee. She was the quietest woman he had ever known. He peeked at her. She set out sandwiches and cups, then poured a cup of coffee. He thought she intended to sit back and enjoy it like she had the other morning. To his surprise, she brought it over to him and said, "Good morning."

He was busted. She'd known he was watching her, so he sat up and took the cup. "Good afternoon. Thank you." She poured herself a cup and leaned on her backpack to enjoy it. She looked cute. She had leaves and small sticks stuck in her hair. He'd been smart and wore his knit hat on his head because he'd been cold. He guessed with all that hair, it must help keep her warm. Her hair was pretty, even with leaves in it. He couldn't get over how quiet she was. All the women he knew, except Jane, had to be talking all the time. She seemed to actually like the quietness. She also seemed comfortable all rumpled up; she didn't take time to straighten her hair and all that other stuff women did all the time. She reached over, grabbed the coffee pot, and refilled their cups without saying a word, just like it was a natural thing. They had a lot to learn about each other. He smiled. He looked forward to getting to know her a lot better.

They got everything packed up and the water containers ready to be filled up. They decided to use her germicidal tablets because Amy explained that she'd read about animals causing diseases if they urinated or defecated too close to water. This was farm country and there were cow patties around, so it couldn't hurt to be careful of disease right now. In fact, he knew for certain that Jane would agree with Amy. As soon as darkness settled in they went down to the pond and filled everything up. Amy had already figured out how many tablets for each container before it got dark. When they were done, they uncovered the bikes from the camo tarp he'd placed over them. They had blended right in. She would never have known they were there if he hadn't showed her. She smiled at him and remarked on his cleverness. She made him feel good about the smallest, stupidest things. He was beginning to understand that she appreciated everything he was doing, just as he appreciated her quietness and the way she was so practical. And of course, for all the food she had prepared. That deserved special thanks. She was a good trooper. This was one woman he wouldn't mind going camping with. He had never ever considered taking a woman camping before. Well, except Jane. He couldn't wait for Jane to meet Amy. She was going to love her. He could just image the shocked look on her face when he came up with Amy and not Sharon. He couldn't wait.

Amy was waiting for him to get going so she could follow. They set out towards the dirt road. They got to the ditch on the side of the road and settled down to watch for a while to make sure it was safe to travel. He was thinking about how Amy just pulled out the 9mm to clean it like it was no big deal last night. He had hoped she was not against using guns now after what had happened. It was a relief to know she was okay with it. The question was, would she be able to draw it and shoot again if necessary? She now knew what it was like to take a life. *I'm sure the opportunity will arise to find out before we get to the retreat. Badness in the world never seemed to end, no matter what part of the world I'm in. It must be an integral part of human nature or something,* he thought. It was the same everywhere as far as he could tell. As soon as law and order went out the window, badness came in and took up residence.

They had been studying the road for about fifteen minutes when they faintly heard what sounded like singing off in the distance. Preston and Amy exchanged puzzled looks. The singing was getting closer to them and they could see a brightness surrounding the people. They must be carrying flashlights or something. Then they spotted about fifty to sixty people coming, decked out in camo and armed to the teeth. An older woman was leading these people down the middle of the road. Preston pushed Amy down gently so she couldn't be seen. One of the people walking had spotted him and said, "Come join us."

Preston whispered to Amy, "When they get even with us, I'll go up and talk to them to find out what's going on. Stay here and stay low so they don't see you or the bikes." Amy nodded okay.

Preston climbed out of the ditch and approached the woman leading the people. They were all carrying a lit candle. She smiled at him and said, "Brother, come join us. We are headed to the church and Preacher Jim is giving a sermon on the Sins of America. If we pray hard enough, Jesus will come and Rapture us out of here and take us to heaven to be with Him and His Father. You are welcome to join in our prayer for deliverance from this evil, sinful world."

Preston said, "Thank you for inviting me, but I don't believe in the Rapture. I'm just passing through and will be on my way peacefully."

A man a few rows back said, "Brother, you are on the wrong path. You need to come with us to save your very soul from the evilness of the world."

Another man spoke up. "You will come with us. We can't leave you here in this sinful world. That would be a sin against us."

Several amens were said. Preston knew this could get out of hand real quickly. There was nothing worse than a believer of a religion who thought he knew the right path for everyone else. The world was filled with them. They hadn't helped the world, not one little bit. All they'd done was spread prejudice and hatred against anyone who believed differently. Yeah, like they were real, true Christians. Their actions proved beyond a shadow of a doubt what God they really followed. It sure wasn't the Almighty God of Heaven, that was plain to see.

"I have to get going," Preston said, "some people depend on me and my friends to arrive and help them through this. I forgive you for leaving me here. You will not carry a sin against me for this." *Honesty was always the best policy. Let's see how they like that.*

A woman said, "We should take him with us and let Preacher Jim decide what to do with him. He seems to lack faith."

The older woman who was leading them said, "Yes, we should take him and his friends to Preacher Jim. He is more qualified to deal with a lack of faith than we are." She turned to Preston. "Tell your friends to come out here and join us. Let them make up their own minds if they want to come with us or not. I think you'll be surprised at what they decide. We have food to feed them, too."

Preston thought, *oh great... what were you just telling yourself about honesty? See what happens when you stretch the truth?* He thought real fast. "Okay. I'll ask them. They are free to come out and join you if that's what they want." The crowd looked satisfied. Preston yelled out, "If you want to join these people here and go pray for the Rapture, come on out." Out of the darkness across the road, three men, a woman and two children appeared. Preston's mouth dropped open a little. *Who the hell are they? Where did they come from?*

The woman said, "We would like to go to church with you and pray for the Rapture." The crowd of people surrounded them, welcoming them into their group. Preston was still in the *huh* stage of shock at their appearance like phantoms out of the darkness. Amy, in the ditch, put both hands over her mouth to make sure no sound escaped when she saw the expression on Preston's face. She wasn't close to the crowd with their lit candles. She still had her night vision and saw them approach and listen. *Oh, this was just too funny*. She wondered what Preston was going to do now.

Preston said to the new group that appeared out of the darkness, "The word 'Rapture' is not in the Bible anywhere. If you go with them, you are condemning those children to starvation when this Rapture doesn't take place. Don't go with them. This is not what the God of Heaven would want you to do. You'll be following a false preacher and false teachings of the Bible. Think about those two children, because whatever you decide affects them."

Two men stepped up to Preston. "You have said enough. You said they could decide for themselves what they wanted to do. They have. Leave them alone."

The lead woman said, "May God strike you dead for those blasphemies you have uttered out of your filthy, evil mouth. You are evil, and to evil, we say, 'Get behind me, Satan.' Go on, get away from us, you evil, unbelieving creature."

"Now that is a real Christian attitude to have," said Preston. "You call me evil and tell me to get behind you because I don't believe as you do. Yeah, I can see you are real Christians." Some of the men raised their rifles at him. Preston held up his hands. "Fine. I'm going." He shook his head in disgust, turned around and walked off into the night.

Amy watched him walk out of sight of the crowd. He turned to watch them. They started singing a hymn as they walked down the road. Preston headed back to Amy. She thought he was one of the bravest men she'd ever seen. He'd taken on a group of religious fanatics when the world as they knew it had ended. That took real guts. She learned a long time ago that you couldn't reason with zealots and fanatics. All you'd do was frustrate yourself and anger them. No good ever came from it. Most people believed what they wanted to believe, whether it was based on fact or not. It didn't really matter to the believer, because as they say, they have faith. Amy always wondered how people could believe and have faith in something they didn't really know or understand. Yes, Amy believed in God and Jesus.

Preston was climbing down into the ditch. He didn't look very happy.

"I'm sorry they wouldn't listen to you," Amy said, "and that they chose to go with those fanatics."

"Well, I tried, anyway. Where in the hell did those people come from?"

Amy laughed. "I almost couldn't hold in my laughter at the look on your face. It was priceless. They must have been approaching before that group reached us. We were so intent on this group that we didn't see them coming. They had stopped to listen to what was being said. They looked relieved when they realized this was a religious group on their way to church. They didn't even hesitate to walk out when you yelled. I'm sorry they didn't listen to you."

"Their church must be around here some place close by. Come on, we'll follow them back here just to make sure they turn off this road. I don't want to run into them again. Then we'll take off." They followed them for about four miles and then the group turned off the road and headed in to some little town. The sign said 'Granger, seven miles.' As soon as they got past the turn off, they got on their bikes and took off down the road.

They stopped for a break. Preston came up close to her. She had fantasized about this so many times since meeting him. She reached out and pulled her ski mask off her face and let it fall to the ground. She reached up and grabbed his head and pulled him down and kissed him. She thought this was heaven. *Oh yeah*.

Preston was glad she made the first move. He had wanted to kiss her for a long time now, but thought it would be too soon after what happened last night. He deepened the kiss. It was everything and more than he had thought it would be. He ended the kiss and smiled at her. "I've been wanting to do that for the longest time."

Amy raised her eyebrow. "Really? What took you so long? I've been waiting for almost a year now. I've wanted you to kiss me since the first time I saw you standing in front of your apartment door."

It was his turn to raise an eyebrow. She laughed and he joined in. "I thought you were too young for me and I was being a dirty old man, thinking you were sexy and cute."

She said, " Time to go" She bent down and picked up the ski mask and pulled it over her head and adjusted it. Preston smiled at her, looked around, and then they took off.

They stopped for their third break and went off into the brush together. She kept chuckling softly. He was looking at her as if she lost her mind. When they reached the spot he had in mind, he put the bikes in the brush. She had just taken her pack off and was reaching for the thermos when he grabbed her and kissed the daylights out of her. *Wow*, was all she could think.

"Now tell me why you were laughing."

"I felt like I was a teenager again, trying to find a place out of sight to neck with my boyfriend. It just struck me as funny with as old as we are that we're out looking for a secluded spot." She was smiling.

He shook his head at her and laughed, then poured them both a cup of coffee. "It does feel like that in a way. Did you do this kind of thing very often?"

She turned and looked at him. "So, we're at that stage already, are we?"

"What stage?"

"About our past affairs and what we have been up to since puberty."

He laughed. "No. I was curious if you spent much time making out with your boyfriends when you were a teenager."

"No, not really." She sipped her coffee. "I had three boyfriends before I left for college. My grandfather and uncle scared off most boys before I even got a date." He stood up and she put everything back in the packs. They got the bikes and he leaned over and kissed her. She was getting used to it now. She sighed. *Wow. I could get used to this.*

They got on the road. They hadn't seen anyone at all since the zealots. That still kind of left a bad taste in her mouth. She just didn't understand people who thought they had the right to tell other people what they could or could not believe. *That was what free will was all about. How could they not get that part of the Bible?* It just didn't make any sense to her. Surroundings, remember the surroundings. Boy, Preston had been so right when he said this was the hardest thing to do. *How do you keep your mind from wondering off?* She had no clue.

When it was time to start looking for a place for the day, Preston estimated they had traveled about a hundred miles. That made it one hundred sixty miles they had traveled. They had about ninety miles to go. They would be there tomorrow night sometime. If it wasn't so dangerous, he would try to press on further, but that would be stupid. They would be sitting ducks out in the daytime. Maybe it was because he was older now, but it sure would be great to sleep in his own bed, or any bed for that matter. The ground seemed to get harder every time he tried to sleep on it.

He found a large wooded area ahead and signaled to her that they would be stopping. They got off the bikes and walked them into the woods. Preston walked around a bit before he found a spot good enough for them to spend the day in. They got busy setting up camp. They were both pretty tired. Amy made up a quick breakfast. Afterwards, Preston rubbed her down with Aspercreme again. Her shirt was already open, she undid her bra and let it fall down. She turned to Preston with a smile. They became one in a tangled heap as they fell onto the sleeping bag. Afterwards, they fell asleep.

Preston had awakened a few times when the wind blew hard, making the tree branches sway. He sure hoped that it would settle down or they would not be able to ride safely tonight. He drifted off back to sleep, holding Amy close. She had snuggled right down into the sleeping bag, making sure her head was covered. He had smiled at that sight. When it was late in the afternoon, Preston woke up. He felt Amy stirring in her cocoon. He saw an arm and felt her shift around.

Amy peeked out. "Wow, it really got cold. I'm glad we'll be there tonight." Preston yawned and agreed. She got the coffee going and went off into the bushes. He did the same. They chatted a little and ate. There were still a couple of hours before darkness would fall. They were getting restless to be on the road. They still hadn't seen anyone. Preston debated about leaving here early or just waiting until dark for sure.

Finally he decided that it would be all right to take off early because they had about two to two and a half hour's ride to the turn off. If they saw someone, they could just disappear into the woods. He asked Amy what her opinion was.

She said, "Let's go now." They'd been watching the road and still hadn't seen anyone. They'd seen a lot of animals. At night, it was kind of tricky riding by the deer along the roadside because they had a habit of jumping right out in front of you, just like when you were driving a car. It was easier to stop with the bike than it was for a car, that was one advantage.

They were on the road in no time. It was getting dark and they had a few miles yet until they reached the other highway. The timing had worked out perfectly. She followed right behind him, a little to the side. They got on the new highway and immediately noticed more cars. Preston had warned her that they were going into a more dangerous area now and to keep her eyes out for anything. She made sure to look around and keep her mind on what they were seeing and going by. They turned off the highway onto a two lane road. They had agreed to keep going, but she had to pee like right now and her throat was very dry; she kept coughing a little. She finally got close to Preston and called, "Stop."

Preston looked around and headed off the road some and stopped. He looked at her. "What's wrong?"

"I need a drink and I have to pee really bad."

"We're almost there, can't it wait?"

"No."

"Okay. Let's just pull off here and we'll have a cup of coffee and you can go use the bushes." They leaned the bikes up against some brush and went off into the woods. Preston didn't go very far. He was just on the way back when he heard voices. He thought, *shit, the bikes.*

He took off running holding the AR-15 out in front of him.

A young voice said, "Hey Mom, what great luck. Look, there are two bikes, just sitting there."

A woman's voice, obviously the boy's mother, said, "Michael, don't. Michael, come here this minute!"

Preston came racing around the side of the brush near the bikes. The kid was running up to the bikes and didn't have eyes for anything else. Preston quickly looked around and only saw the two of them.

The woman was now running up after her son. "Please, don't shoot him. Please. Please, Mister, don't hurt him."

Preston pointed the rifle at the ground and stood still. The kid finally noticed him and visibly jumped.

"I'm sorry, Mister, I thought maybe someone just left them here or something. I didn't mean them no harm." Both of them were scared shitless and shaking.

Preston said, "It's okay, just relax. I'm not going to shoot you." Amy came around the side of the bushes and both the mother and young boy huddled together, shaking in fear.

The mother said in very shaky voice, "We'll just be on our way. We didn't mean you two any harm. Come on, Michael." She grabbed his arm and started to pull him along.

Amy and Preston shared a look. Preston said, "Do you have time for a cup of coffee? We have plenty. We also mean you two no harm." The mother and boy just looked at Preston, not knowing what to do.

Amy dropped the pack on the ground. "I have some hot chocolate we could make for your son. Are you hungry? We have some extra food we could make for you. We mean you no harm. Please, we have plenty." She reached into her backpack and pulled out a wipe and started wiping her face off. She smiled at them. She set the stove up and got some water out to boil for hot chocolate. "Really, we mean you no harm. Come and join us for a meal. I know things are crazy out there right now, and it it's real hard to trust people because they're acting weird and crazy, but you can trust us. Please, I would feel just awful if you walked away from us in fear."

The woman looked very uncertain. The boy said, "Please, Mom? Please, I'm hungry. Can we please eat something?"

Preston walked up to Amy and sat down. She handed him a wipe so he could wipe most of the paint off his face. Amy said, "I'll tell you what. I'll make the food and hot chocolate, and we'll leave it here for you. Okay? Then you won't have to come any closer to us." She got busy making soup. She made up a cup of coffee and a cup of water for the boy, took them over to the road, laid them down and walked away. She said over her shoulder, "This is just to get you started. You must be thirsty." The woman and boy walked over to the cups and picked them up. The boy drank the water straight down. Amy walked a little way and put Preston's canteen on the ground and went back to the stove. "You're welcome to drink as much as you want to. We have more water." They each took a long drink of water from the canteen.

The water started to boil, so Amy put some in the cups and added some soup. She looked up and the boy and woman were approaching them. They sat on the ground across from them. The woman said, "Thank you. Thank you very much for being so kind." She then took the cups of soup. She relaxed some and they started to eat. The woman finally got her nerve up and asked, "What's with the paint on your faces?"

Preston said, "It's dangerous out there right now. Many people are playing around like they're bringing the Wild West back into style." He hadn't wanted to say something with the boy sitting right there. He went on, "The paint is to hide our faces in the dark to blend into the shadows so we won't be a target." They were eating pretty fast. They must have missed a few meals. "I'm Preston and this is Amy."

The woman asked, "Are you two married?"

Amy blushed and Preston said, "No. I have a hunting camp we're going to. It was pretty rough in the city where we were." The woman nodded her head at that statement.

"Do you know what happened?" the mother asked.

"I am retired military," Preston said, "and I'm pretty sure we were hit with an EMP bomb that knocked out everything electrical. Where are you headed to?"

The woman looked at them. "We were heading to my father's farm in Iowa."

Amy and Preston exchanged another look. Preston said, "Where is your husband?"

"I'm divorced. We've been walking for two days. We'll make it. It'll just take some time to get there, is all."

"You won't make it," said Preston. "I can tell you that right now. You have no weapons and no survival gear. Where is your food for the trip? It will be snowing before too long. Are you prepared for that?"

The woman looked down. "I don't have any food."

Preston said, "How did you think you could go so far without any supplies?"

The woman looked resigned. "I have no idea. I was doing the only thing I could think of for my son. To have stayed where we were would have been worse than taking off without anything." Preston and Amy looked at each other again.

Preston said, "I have some friends about fifteen miles down the road. My hunting camp is there, too. You are welcome to come stay the night and have a hot shower and a hot meal. We can at least do that for the two of you."

The woman looked at them with a puzzled expression. "If nothing electrical works, how can you provide a hot shower?"

Preston smiled. "My place is solar powered and I have a wood-heated hot water tank."

The boy spoke up. "Please, Mom. It's better than trying to sleep with a blanket and freezing. Please, please."

The woman looked at them. "All right. We'll come for one night. Thank you for having us and helping us."

Preston and Amy smiled at them. Preston said, "Amy and I will go ahead and drop off our gear, and we'll be right back to get you two. Then we'll have room for you to sit on the bracket back here to ride to our place." The woman and young boy looked relieved at that news.

Amy asked, "What's your name?"

The woman looked flustered and said, "Please for give me. I have forgotten my manners. My name is Joan Jakabowski, and this is my son, Michael. We both thank you for your kindness."

Amy and Preston got up to leave. They got on the bikes and waved back at them. They rode as fast as they could on the country dirt road. They stopped and pulled up to a chained gate. There was a farmhouse and barn and other buildings that Amy couldn't make out in the darkness.

"Stay here. I'll go and let them know we're here." He took off the backpack and placed his guns and bandolier on top of the pack.

"What are you doing?"

"I want to live through the encounter, so I'm disarming myself." Amy raised her eyebrows. He turned, climbed over the fence and called out to the house in a loud voice, "Joe, you lazy good for nothing grunt. I'm home." There was no answering response. That was really weird. He walked up to the door and opened the storm door.

Before he could reach for the door handle, he heard, off to the side, a shotgun rack a shell in the chamber and a voice said, "Freeze right there, Mister." Preston turned to the side and there was Joe with his Remington 870 in his hands peeking around the corner of the house.

Preston yelled, "Knock it off, you bonehead. It's me."

Joe smiled and laughed. "Gotcha." Then he laughed harder.

"Go unlock the gate and let my new girlfriend in."

Joe looked at him. "What happened to Sharon?"

Preston said, "It's a long story and we have a woman and her son waiting for us to go get them down the road. So, let Amy in and we can get on with it."

"Okay, but you have a lot of explaining to do." They walked over to the gate and Joe unlocked it and pulled it open. He looked at Amy and thought, *She doesn't look like the typical Preston girlfriend.* Well, they would find out soon enough.

They all made their way to the house; Jane had the door open for them. When they went inside, Preston gave Jane a hug and told her about the woman and boy. He introduced them to Amy. Jane gave Amy a long look and thought, *Wow, this one might have possibilities.* She wasn't anything like Preston's ex or his other girlfriends.

Joe said, "I'll help you unload the bikes and I'll go back with you to get the woman and boy."

"Great." He turned to Amy. "I'll be back as soon as we get Joan and Michael back here." He kissed her and ran his hand down her hair to reassure her that everything was all right. He turned and walked out the door, leaving her with Jane.

Amy said, "I'd better go help them unload the bikes."

She turned to go out the door, too, when Jane said, "You really shouldn't. You would just be in the way out there. Believe me. When those two get together they are like children. You will find that out for yourself. Come on and take your coat off and have a cup of coffee. You can sit by the wood stove in the kitchen and get warm."

"You may not want me to be too close. I haven't had a shower in three days."

Jane laughed. "I know that. I have been camping with them before. They believe in going totally primitive and sleeping on the ground, too."

Amy chuckled. "You have just described what it has been like since the EMP hit us. Except Preston had a propane two burner cook stove so I could cook for us."

Jane said, "You cook?"

"What is it with this cooking stuff? First Preston, and now you act surprised that I can cook. Don't you cook? I mean, I wouldn't mind cooking for all of us, if that's what you'd like."

Jane laughed and said, "Did you ever meet Sharon?"

"Yes, I lived next door to Preston and the Dainty Princess."

Jane laughed so hard when she heard that. She was finally able to get out, "How long have you and Preston been together?"

"Since last night."

"Oh."

"Why 'oh?' What does that mean?"

Jane smiled. "You're going to fit in around here, I can just tell. Welcome to our humble abode."

Amy looked around. "Wow, you have a beautiful house. I love your wildlife decor." They started talking about everything as if they had been friends forever.

Preston and Joe had put a warm hunting seat on the back bracket of the bikes for Joan and Michael to sit on for the ride back. They used two bungee cords to hold the hunting seats in place. They rode down the road, side by side. When they got to the pair, they showed them how to sit so they wouldn't fall off. Preston had the woman ride with him because Joe wasn't as familiar with riding the bike, and with the extra weight of an adult woman, it would just be better for them if Preston took her. Preston introduced Joe. They made it back without encountering anyone. Joe locked the gate up. They put the bikes into the barn and then walked up to the house.

They went inside and Preston told everyone that he'd promised them a hot meal, a shower and a good night's sleep. Jane smiled and made them feel welcome. She asked if she had any clean clothes with them.

"No, we donn't have anything clean, but we had some dirty clothes," explained Joan.

"Well, you'll just have to stay a day longer, then, so we can get your clothes washed up, too."

Joan started to cry. "I don't know how to thank all of you for your kindness."

Jane smiled at her. "You just did. We're glad to have you. I have some clean clothes you can wear after you take a shower. Now, finding something for Michael to wear will be a bit of a problem, as we don't have any children. But we'll find something and make do. All right?"

Joan said, "Thank you." Jane went and got some clothes for her and showed her where the shower was. "Everything you need is in there. Help yourself to shampoo or anything you may need." They could hear Michael entertaining them in the kitchen. Jane smiled. "As soon as you're done, come into the kitchen and get Michael. There should be enough hot water for both of you to take a shower. We've been expecting Preston to show up at any time and kept hot water ready. Go ahead and indulge yourself." Jane went back into the kitchen. She was just in time to hear Preston say that Amy and he were taking off for his place to shower and sleep.

Jane said, "Go ahead, we will take care of Joan and Michael. We'll all sit down tomorrow and have a long talk. I know you two and plans have to be made, but we won't do them until you both are rested and have clear heads. Got it?"

Preston laughed. "Yes, Mom, I got it." Jane laughed too.

"That sounds sensible, thank you," said Amy.

Joe groaned. "Oh no. We have another Jane around here." Jane reached out and smacked him on the arm.

Joe yelled, "Ouch. That's abuse you know."

Jane shook her head and said to Amy, "See what I mean?"

Amy just laughed and went and got her coat and picked up her pack. Preston laughed. Amy called out good night as they left.

Chapter 13

High Emotions End in Disaster

"There are no mistakes. The events we bring upon ourselves, no matter how unpleasant, are necessary in order to learn what we need to learn; whatever steps we take, they're necessary to reach the places we've chosen to go."

Richard Bach

Junior made dinner and set the table. He told Marion and Gayle that dinner was ready. Both women were still huddled on the couch looking a bit dazed. He told them to hurry it up or dinner would get cold. He went back into the kitchen and put the food on the table. Gayle told him Marion had gone to lie down for awhile. Junior shrugged his shoulders defensively, feeling like they were treating him as if he were a monster for what he had to do. He'd done what his dad had always told him. Maybe they just didn't understand how things were now that the world had ended. They were women; he didn't understand women at all. He wasn't sure how to deal with this kind of thing. He started eating, ignoring the whole situation.

Gayle sat down at the table. "Junior, I'm sorry I couldn't come help you with what you were, er, doing. I just couldn't do it." She shuddered.

He looked at her. "Do you think I liked doing it? Or that was easy for me to do it?"

Gayle looked down at the table and sighed deeply. She thought for a few moments and then looked him in the eye. "I'm sorry you had to do that by yourself. I do understand why you had to do it. I'm sorry, I just couldn't make myself do it. I'm sorry." She got up and walked out of the kitchen. He continued to eat and thought about what she had said. Maybe he was expecting too much from them. They were women, after all. But, they didn't need to make him feel bad about doing what had to be done. He laid his fork down losing his appetite and sighed deeply.

He got up and went into the living room. Gayle was sitting on the couch, her arms wrapped around her knees, holding them next to her chest. Her head was resting on her knees. She was crying softly. He went over and sat down next to her. He was so out of his depth with this whole thing. He just didn't know what to do. He didn't want to hurt Gayle. He felt bad that he'd made her cry. He reached over and pulled her close. She kept saying over and over, "I'm sorry."

"I'm sorry, too. I didn't mean to make you cry. Please stop. You're getting my shirt wet." She looked up at him with a surprised gasp. He smiled at her. "Look at that huge wet spot you put there." She looked at his shirt and then back up at him. She looked away from him, not knowing what to say.

He got up and moved to her other side and pulled her close again. "There, now you can put a huge wet spot on this side and they'll match."

She looked at him as if he had two heads. He started to laugh at her expression. She shook her head at him and said, "You're crazy. You have completely lost your mind." He just laughed harder. She smiled and then she started to laugh, too. They laughed until their sides hurt and they were gasping for breath. "You're looney toons."

Junior just smiled at her. "Yup, I am." That made both of them start laughing again. It was several minutes until they could get themselves under control. It felt really good to laugh.

Marion had been lying on the bed thinking about George when she heard the laughter from the living room. It was good to hear them laughing. At least those two were getting along okay. She was glad because it sure would've been hell if Junior resented both of them. It was hard enough to deal with his feelings about her without compounding it with resentment for Gayle, too. She was sure glad that if the world had to end, that Gayle had been at home at the time. She would've had to go out and get her. She wasn't sure if she would have succeeded in getting her here to safely. Not with the way people had been acting in town. *If it was that way here, what had the big cities been like? I'm sure it was horrible, too.* Probably much, much worse than anything she could imagine. It was still hard to believe that the world had changed. It seemed everyone was out for themselves and the hell with anyone else. She wasn't sure she was cut out to live in a world like this one, especially alone. George was gone. It still seemed like a living nightmare. All of this did. If those two kids out there didn't need her so much, she'd just give up. As far as she could see, there really wasn't much reason to keep going now. She sighed.

Gayle walked into the bedroom and turned the light on. Marion blinked against the brightness. Gayle sat down on the bed. "How are you doing?"

"I was fine until you turned the light on."

"Do you want to talk about what happened today?"

Marion looked at her. "Which part would you like me to talk about? The part when some wackos captured me to get in here or about the part when Junior burned their bodies to ashes?"

Gayle sighed. "Whatever you want to talk about."

Marion let out a bitter laugh. "I really don't need to talk about any of it. I'm just trying to come to terms with the way things are now. I feel really bad that Junior had to burn the bodies. I feel doubly bad that he had to do that by himself. I should have been strong enough to help him. I'm the adult here. But I just couldn't. I thought I was a strong woman, but this showed me that I'm not. I just let Junior do it all. George probably hates me now. His son has turned into, uh, I don't even know what, and I let him have to deal with this, too. I just don't like myself very much at the moment. I'm not the person I thought I was. It's a hard thing to face up to." Gayle was holding her mother's hand, rubbing it gently. She had never seen her mother this way before. There was silence for awhile as they thought about what Marion said.

Junior walked into the room and knelt down by the bed. "I heard what you said. It's okay; I only did what I had to do."

Marion reached out and put her hand on his face and said through her tears, "It most certainly isn't all right. You shouldn't be left to deal with things like this alone. I'm so sorry for my weakness. I feel so ashamed of myself. I wish George were here to help us. He would know the right thing to say or do. I feel so out of my depth."

Tears filled Junior's eyes and ran down his cheeks. "I wish with my whole heart he was here, too." Marion grabbed Junior in a hug and the two of them cried together over the loss of a great man they had both loved. Gayle quietly got up and went into the other room, leaving them alone to share their grief. They needed each other.

Gayle reheated a plate to eat and put the rest of the food into the refrigerator. She went into the living room, picked up a book she'd brought with her, and started reading. She could vaguely hear them talking in the bedroom. They both needed this. She was glad they'd be able to understand each other a little more now. After a couple of hours, she got tired, pulled a throw blanket over herself, and fell asleep. She woke up in the morning and immediately felt the lack of tension in the air. What a relief. She looked up at the clock and saw it was almost 6:00 am. She went to the bathroom. She smiled as she went by the door to the bedroom. They'd both fallen asleep in there. They must have talked for a very long time last night. She made coffee as quiet as a mouse. She wanted them to get a good night's sleep. Neither of them had been sleeping well and they needed this, too.

It was about 10:00 am when Junior came into the kitchen. Gayle was sitting there eating a bowl of oatmeal. She'd made a pot of oatmeal for them to have as they got up. She felt it was safe to make ... nobody could make bad oatmeal. Maybe she just needed to cook more often to get better at it. Junior got a cup of coffee, sat down at the table, and yawned.

"Did you sleep well?" she asked.

"Yeah." He wrapped his hands around the mug.

She finished eating and put her bowl in the sink. "I made a pot of oatmeal for breakfast." Junior looked alarmed. She laughed. "It came out just fine, you know. I can cook some things. Not everything I make is tough and burnt." Junior just raised an eyebrow. "Well, it's true. Not everything I make tastes terrible."

"Okay. But are you going to hit me if I tell you that it has to be proven before I'll believe it?"

She glared at him. "Fine. Go ahead and see for yourself, then."

"I will in a bit. I have to wake up first." She glared at him for a couple more moments, then walked out. Junior hoped she wasn't mad at him. He'd been partly joking. The meal she had cooked had been terrible. The meat had been dry, tough, and burnt on one side. The fried potatoes she made had been burnt and as hard as a rock on the outside. They hadn't been too bad once you got to the middle, but getting there was a real effort. He was glad he had good strong teeth or they would all be broken stumps. He couldn't remember ever having to work his jaws so hard to eat before. Even the sweet corn she'd cooked had been brown on the bottom. He sighed. He'd make sure that either Marion or he cooked from now on. Well, at least until she had some lessons, anyway. He and Marion had made their best effort to eat as much as they could; it's the thought that counts, but they could only survive through that kind of thing so often.

She paced around the living room for a while, waiting for her mother to wake up. She finally decided to take a shower. There wasn't much to do to keep busy. It wasn't like she could turn the TV on and find something interesting to watch to occupy her mind. She thought with dread of the endless days stretching before her without much to do. She was getting bored and bit depressed. That was a new experience for her. She had always felt that there would always be something she could do. She sighed deeply. She had to find something to occupy her mind or she'd go stir crazy. Maybe she could go clean the garage or something. Usually there was something that needed to be done in a garage. Yup, that's what she'd do. She sighed again. Now, how was she going to convince Junior to let her out so she could get to the garage?

Junior got brave enough to try the oatmeal after he smelled it and found that Gayle hadn't burned it after all. Nothing could taste as bad as burnt oatmeal. He heated it up, adding a little water so he could stir it. It was good. He decided to check the weather outside today and haul in more firewood if it was real cold.

Junior raised up one of the steel window plates to look out at the weather. The snow looked to start early this year. It was pretty dark out and it wasn't even noon yet. Yup, those looked like snow clouds out there. He was thankful. He wasn't sure he could have taken another encounter with more yahoos right now. He was stupid to think they could all stay inside until spring, too. He wouldn't have been able to endure it. Just the short time he'd been holed up in here waiting for the yahoos to leave almost drove him batty, and now to be confined inside here with two women? No, he didn't think he could take that. He'd haul more wood inside today even if they didn't need it.

Gayle came over and looked out the window, too. "It looks like snow."

He smiled. "I was just thinking the same thing. I'm going to haul some wood in today and get my traps and snares ready to set out as soon as it falls. The danger will pretty much be gone by then. Anyone left out there in the woods would die of exposure, so my guess is they'd head back to a town to hole up for the winter."

"Thank God," Gayle said. "Can I go out to the garage for a couple of hours and clean out there or something?"

"Why do you want to do that?"

"I'm going crazy in here with nothing to do and winter hasn't even set in yet."

"Okay." Junior shrugged. "When?"

"Like right now."

"Right now this minute?"

"Yes." She paced.

"Sure, yeah, okay. Let me unbolt the door and look around first, and if it's safe, then you can go to the garage for a couple of hours." He totally understood the desire to get out for awhile. He got the door unlocked, grabbed his SKS and went out to look around. Gayle waited impatiently for him to finish.

Marion walked up behind her and looked out the window. "It looks like snow."

Gayle jumped in surprise. She looked at her mother and gave her a hug. "Are you all right?"

Marion smiled at her. "Yes, I'm all right. How is Junior this morning? I must have fallen asleep while he was talking to me. I feel so embarrassed. He's not mad at me again, is he?"

Gayle laughed. "No, he isn't mad at you. He fell asleep, too. Imagine my shock this morning walking by the bedroom door and seeing my mother in bed with an eighteen-year-old boy. He's a year younger than I am, mother. I almost had a heart attack." Gayle dramatically put her hand over her heart and looked solemnly at her mother.

Marion looked confused a moment, then burst out laughing. "You had me going for a moment there, young lady." She reached out to smack Gayle's butt. "Remember, you're never too old for me to spank, either." Gayle laughed.

Junior came back inside. "I think its okay to go to the garage for awhile. I unlocked it for you. As soon as you're inside, lock the door again. I have my key to get in with. I'll be out there in awhile to see to the traps and snares." Gayle wasted no time getting ready to go out. She told her mother she'd be back in a couple of hours and walked out the door.

"Junior," Marion said, "I'm sorry I fell asleep last night in the middle of our conversation. I didn't mean to."

He laughed. "I think I'm the one that fell asleep. You were talking about the time my dad took two deer in one day from the peep hole up there." He pointed up.

Marion laughed. "I thought you were the one talking last and I'd been rude and fallen asleep."

Junior said, "It doesn't matter, I guess, who fell asleep first. I'm sorry for my rude behavior towards you before."

Marion reached over and patted his arm., "There's nothing to forgive. You had a right to feel that way."

Junior smiled. "Gayle made oatmeal for all of us this morning. I left you some on the stove. It came out fine; she didn't burn it or anything."

Marion laughed. "She can cook a few things that aren't too bad. Oatmeal is one of them. I'll make dinner tonight, okay?"

While Gayle was in the garage, she looked around at all the neat stuff there. There was a foot pedal sewing machine. She tried it and it worked. She smiled. *This is great.* She found some patterns for coats, hats, gloves and other things. She found one pattern that looked like maybe they were boot liners. They didn't look like they were supposed to be made into real boots, but she could be wrong. She'd ask Junior about it later. She kept exploring and forgot all about cleaning. This was the cleanest garage she'd ever seen. On one side, there were animal skins on stretchers, drying. They had a musky, pungent smell. Not exactly a bad smell, just different than anything she was used to. She kind of liked it. There was a lot of stuff stored here. It would take weeks to go through it all. She found a zipped canvas clothes bag lying on a table in a corner and unzipped it. She was delighted. It was filled with animal furs that were tanned. They were so soft and silky. There were all different kinds stretched out, lying in a flat bundle. She kept running her hands through them. She had never really felt real fur before and fell in love with the feel and warmth.

She remembered the patterns she'd found and laughed in delight. If there was one thing her mother had made her learn, it had been how to cut out a pattern properly and how to sew clothes. She was thinking of all the cool things she could make with these furs. She was imagining gorgeous fur hats, hand warmers, and leggings. The possibilities were endless. She was in seventh heaven. Then she remembered that these furs weren't hers. She lost her smile and stopped rubbing and admiring the furs. She straightened them and zipped the bag closed and backed away from them before the temptation got to be too much to resist. She turned around and Junior was standing there, watching her.

She blushed. "I'm sorry. I was being nosy and looking at things. You have some really cool stuff." Junior had seen her lose her smile and put the furs away. He wondered what had made her do that.

"My dad has been collecting things from estate sales for many years," he said. "He never threw very many things away. He felt people overlooked treasures all the time. A lot of what he collected will now be very useful. He believed in doing things the old-fashioned way."

"Do you know what the items are in these boxes and containers?"

"I know some of the things, but most of it, no, I don't know what is in everything. It will be an adventure going through all this stuff. I was planning on doing it this winter when it gets too cold to be outdoors doing anything else. I can make a fire in the wood stove over there; it warms this place up really fast. This garage is well-insulated. I was kind of dreading doing it. It will remind me of him so much. He always saved the best stuff to show me when I came up here. He handpicked every single item stored here. It will be a hard thing to do. Would you help me go through it all?"

Gayle smiled at him. "I would love to. I can't wait to see what's in all these containers. I already found so many cool things. It will be an adventure. I was always going through all the pictures and old clothes and things in our attic. I loved rainy days, because it gave me an excuse to go up and look through them again." She laughed and Junior smiled at her.

Sharing these things with Gayle was helping him to remember the great times he had with his dad. When they shared memories or talked about their fathers, it didn't hurt quite as much as it did before. He was grateful for Gayle and now for Marion, too. Last night had made him think about Marion in a different way.

Junior got the wood stove going in the garage. He set a big pot of water on it to bring to a boil. He poured in about a gallon of black walnut husks. After bringing it to a boil, he would move the pot off the direct heat and let it simmer for about thirty minutes. It would turn a purple-black color. He would then simmer the leg hold traps in the solution for thirty minutes. He and his dad had collected the walnut husks in the early fall when they fell off the tree on the ground. They would crack them open and leave the nuts there for the squirrels. Some people liked to save the nuts and dry them out; around Christmastime, they would be dry enough to grind into flour for bread. He would use this solution from the walnut husks to darken the leg hold traps and to free them from any odors left on them. The walnut smell was natural to the coyotes he planned on trapping and it would blend in to the natural environment. He would then cut a few strips of odor-free wax and apply it to the mixture and dip the traps, covering each trap in a light coat of wax. He would hang on to the chain attached to the trap with the metal stake that would hold the trap in place when he set it. He'd do this because the wax would seal them and make them scent-free and it would help preserve them. It also kept the trap from freezing to the ground. He would store the leg hold traps in Rubbermaid containers lined with leaves and sticks until ready to use so they wouldn't pick up any odors.

He got another pot and filled it half full of water. He would boil the water, then lower the heat to simmer. He would slowly stir in one cup of baking soda, being careful not to let the bubbles and foam spill over the top of the pot. He would keep this pot at a light boil for about twenty minutes with the snares in it. He'd then put the individual snares outside on the ground. He would let them set outside for seven to ten days. They'd turn a dull gray color, which blends in with the surrounding area more naturally.

He would use conibear traps for his water trapping. His dad had found the best thing to prepare them was to spray paint them a flat black color. It lasted the longest and held up best. He got everything going and set to work. He'd done this so many times that it became second nature to him. Gayle asked what he was doing. He explained each process and why it was necessary.

"Can I go with you on the trap line?" she asked.

"Sure, but it's hard work and you'd better dress real warm." Gayle was excited about learning to trap and snare. She couldn't wait to get to the tanning part. Those furs were so beautiful. She still had visions of making things with the furs in her head.

Snow started to fall while Junior and Gayle were in the garage. They discovered this when they were setting the snares outside to cure. Junior got excited. He would be able to start trapping in a day or two. Gayle was just as excited. She had something to do now that was new and interesting. They'd spent about five hours out in the garage. They had been gone longer than they both had planned. With Gayle's help, he had gotten all the traps and snares ready to go. He was deeply satisfied with the day's work. He would start the tanning process tonight. It would give Gayle something else to do, too.

When they got into the house, the first thing that hit them was the smell. Marion had baked an apple pie. Junior's mouth watered. They had missed lunch. They put their coats and gloves away.

Marion said with a smile, "There is fresh coffee. Come have a cup while I get dinner served."

"Yes, ma'am," Junior said. Gayle and he went and washed up and came into the kitchen. It was nice having someone else do the cooking for a change. After dinner, they washed the dishes, then they played cards for a while.

Junior said he was going to get the tanning process going.

"Can I help?" asked Gayle.

"Sure." Junior got out a special pot his dad used for tanning. He filled it up with water and put it on to boil. He explained they needed to go back out to the garage and get a bucket full of acorns. He had forgotten to bring them in when they came in earlier. When they had, he poured about a gallon of acorns into the pot. He explained to Gayle that they collect as many acorns as they can find. He had showed her a lot of five gallon buckets full of them. When the pot started boiling, he turned it down to a light boil for thirty minutes. He let it cool a bit, and then he strained it and poured the liquid into an empty five gallon plastic bucket. Plastic worked best, because the solution ate right through anything else. Immediately, he rinsed the pot and washed it good so the tannins wouldn't eat through it. He did this process twice, giving him about three gallons of tannic acid. He explained to rinse the acorns off really good and let them dry. When they were dry, he would smash them up and make it into a paste for squirrel bait. Or, he said, they could be processed further and then dried, so they could be ground up into flour for bread. His dad didn't believe in wasting anything.

The tannic acid solution had to get to room temperature before the hides could be added. A wooden tree branch made a good utensil to push the fur down and stir it up. This had to be done everyday. They had to be real careful not to spill or drip any of the solution on anything. A wooden block worked well to rest the wooden stir stick on so it wouldn't eat through the carpet. It took between seven and ten days to tan a hide, depending on the size of the hide and on how well it was skinned and fleshed for thickness. If the skins weren't tanned thoroughly, they'd rot. They'd know they were done when the hides had turned a uniform color. Patience was the key, Junior explained to Gayle as they were putting the muskrat hides into the solution. Gayle was excited. Junior laughed and thought, *just wait until its time to break the hides, then she won't be as excited.* It took a lot of hard work and time. It was worth it, but it was a long process.

Junior got everything ready to start setting traps. The snares wouldn't be ready for a while yet, but he could get the traps out now. Marion made them both a lunch to take with them. He wore his insulated hunting suit and had Gayle wear his dad's. They had to roll it up and tape the legs some, but they made it work so she'd be warm. They used trap baskets to carry all the traps and the tools they'd need. They did real well the first day; they set out two dozen traps. They had a great time. He explained everything as they went along. On the way home, Gayle got into a goofy mood and started playing around. She was running and sliding on the trail when she fell and slid over the side. She wasn't hurt, but her legs got wet from a little stream. She got pretty cold and they were about two miles from home, so Junior made a fire to warm her up. She was shivering. He held her close to help warm her. The next thing he knew, they were kissing. He pulled away and looked at her. She was looking back at him. He wasn't sure where they were going with this, but decided to enjoy it anyway. He kissed her again. After awhile, Junior said they needed to get back. They held hands on the way back and kept looking at each other and smiling.

Things went this way for a couple of days. They both weren't sure how to approach Marion with the idea that they really liked each other. Gayle told Junior that they would play it by ear. Later that evening, they all played a game of Scrabble, then Marion went to bed. She usually went to bed early. Gayle said she'd always been like that. Her dad and her would sit up and watch movies after her mom went to bed. It was a secret they kept between them.

Every couple of days when Junior and Gayle were out checking traps they would find a trap set off. You could see the area was all tore up from a caught animal that had been in the trap. But there was no animal by the time they got there. They looked around for tracks to see if someone was out there stealing the animals. There were no tracks, no nothing to give them a clue to what had happened to the animal. Junior explained to Gayle that sometimes you would catch an animal by the toes and they would work themselves out of the trap. But again there were no tracks leading away from the trap. You could see the tracks of the animal coming up to the trap and getting caught but nothing else to explain where the animal had gone off to. Junior scratched his head over this dilemma. What the hell was going on here? He didn't have a clue, but it made him uneasy. Someone had to be around here somewhere. That was the only thing that made sense. He had to make sure the women were never outside alone. Obviously, this person, whoever it was, meant them no immediate harm, but he didn't trust anyone's intentions at all. He didn't say anything to Gayle. He didn't want to spook her.

A few days later he stood over the trap of another missing animal, thinking about the implications. This was setting into a pattern. He didn't like it at all. It wasn't that someone was stealing an animal that upset him. It was the fact that this meant for sure that someone was out here somewhere, watching them. Whoever it was had to be watching them because they never would have found where he'd placed the trap sets any other way. The sets he made blended into the surroundings. He left no disturbed dirt or any other clues that anything out of the ordinary was out of place in the area he made a trap set at. How else could a person know there was a trap there? That person had to be watching them to know. He wasn't sure what to do about it.

Gayle smiled and laughed at Junior's perplexed expression and said in an eerie voice, "I tell you it was the aliens that did it. Yes sir, it was the aliens."

Junior looked over at her and raised an eyebrow. "Aliens. You couldn't come up with anything better than the aliens did it? I could come up with a lot better stories than that. Like it was a Native American that is out here living off the land and he sensed that a trap was here. He guided an animal into it so he would have something to eat and leave a puzzle for the stupid white man to figure out. Something like that."

Gayle scowled at him. "I like my idea of aliens better."

Junior laughed. "Come on, we have to move this trap now. Let's get busy." Gayle wanted to make Junior a fur coat because he got cold sometimes. She could tell when they were out together on the trap line. She thought she could make her mother a fur hat, too. She had asked Junior if she could make a few things with some of the furs that were already tanned and he'd said yes. She'd looked at his coat for the size and found a pattern that would work. She found five beaver hides that were pretty close in color, and a real pretty black beaver hide for her mother's hat. There were a couple of beautiful white weasel furs she was going to use for trim. She decided to make them as Christmas gifts. She had Junior help her bring the sewing machine into the house and place it in his dad's room so she could sew. She told her mother and Junior they couldn't see until she was done. She would keep stringing them along until Christmas time. She was happy with the idea of making useful gifts.

A few days after Gayle had started her sewing project, they were out on the trap line again. She had learned it was a little harder working with furs than regular cloth, but she was enjoying the challenge. They came up to an area with several animal trails. They had made a few double sets in this area. Gayle was checking on one for weasels and Junior was checking on another about a hundred yards farther down the trail for coyotes. They had gotten one weasel and Gayle was resetting the trap when she heard Junior call out. She quickly walked over to him. He was standing over a set holding an animal fur in his hands. She thought, *wow that's a neat trick. No carcass or guts around just an animal fur.*

She got close and could see the fur was stiff. "What did you do with the rest of it?"

Junior looked at her. "This was already lying here when I arrived to check the sets." She looked at him with a tilt of her head. Junior finally said, "This must be from whoever is taking the animals out of the traps."

Gayle looked around. "I told you it had to be aliens. Now they're bringing them back. I guess they don't understand that we need the whole animal back, not just their stiff skin. They must have been conducting experiments." She laughed at Junior's expression.

"Knock it off about aliens. Whoever took the animals quick tanned the hide and brought it back to us."

"Maybe they feel bad about stealing from us and are returning what they don't need or something," said Gayle. Junior just shrugged his shoulders. It sure was a mystery. He put the skin in his pack basket, re-set the trap and they went on to checking the rest of the traps.

Junior had been spending a few hours every night out in the garage. Gayle was curious about what he was doing. She asked him, but he told her he was organizing things and skinning the days catches. Gayle didn't believe him because he would skin almost everything in the afternoon when they got back. She would ask to go with him, but he always made an excuse. Maybe he was regretting kissing her and didn't want them to be together. She wanted to be with him. She thought she was falling in love with him, but maybe it was still too soon for him. She wasn't sure how to approach the subject.

They were sitting on the couch and got into an argument over which actress had been in the movie they were discussing. They started horsing around and ended up wrestling on the floor. They had a hard time containing their laughter so they wouldn't wake Marion up. Gayle was on top of him, pretending to choke him. He pushed her down and rolled on top of her. They kissed. Junior felt intense desire for her, but wasn't going to push it. He got up and said he had to go out to the garage and finish up for the day. Gayle was a bit stunned. Was she making him draw away? Junior went out the door. After a few minutes, she decided the only way she was going to know was if she went out there and asked him. She thought about it for awhile and decided it would be better to know now rather than later, when she'd fallen even harder for him. She made up her mind to do it now before she lost her nerve.

She put her boots and coat on and went out to the garage. The door was unlocked. That wasn't like Junior.

She crept in and he was skinning an animal. She couldn't see what kind from the door. She turned and locked the door, just like told her to every time she went out here. "Is it me you don't like? Is that why you keep pulling away from me?"

"What? What are you talking about?" Junior didn't look at her.

Gayle sighed. "Every time we kiss or get the least bit close, you pull away from me. I just want to know if you don't like me, or if it's something about me that turns you off or what?" Junior was washing his hands now and didn't say anything. "Can you at least look at me and tell me what makes you turn away?"

Junior turned, grabbed her, pushed her up against the truck door, and kissed her hard, pressing his whole body against her. Gayle thought, *wow*. Junior stepped away from her. "That's why."

Gayle felt that he obviously desired her, so that wasn't the problem. "And that's a problem how?"

"How far do you want to take this?" he asked.

"I really like you a lot, Junior. I like kissing you. I want to do more, but how can I when you keep pulling away and confusing me?" Junior stepped closer and kissed her again. She returned his kiss. He fumbled around for the truck door handle and finally found it. He pulled the door open and picked Gayle up and set her inside, then he climbed in beside her.

A few days later, the snow was really flying hard. A lake effect storm had moved in across Lake Superior. It looked like they were going to get several inches. Junior sighed. They were going to have to pull the leg hold traps now. Winter had come early. He could still snare the beaver under the ice and thin the coyotes down, too. He explained to Gayle that they would have to pull the traps, but they'd be putting out the snares. Junior still carried the SKS as his trap line rifle and Gayle carried her Marlin bolt action .22. It was hard to see very far because the snow was blowing so hard.

The snow was wet and clung to their boots. Junior was thinking that maybe they should have used the snowshoes, but that would have slowed them down even more. The wind was blowing about ten miles per hour and straight out of the north. It was bitter cold out; neither one of them enjoyed being out in all this white stuff. It sure slowed them down. They didn't get back until late afternoon. They both were exhausted. It felt like they had run the trap line and then ran for ten miles straight carrying a heavy pack. They took care of everything they had to and left the rest for later. Gayle had been visiting Junior in his room at night, and neither one of them had been getting much sleep lately. They came inside and ate some homemade soup and bread. Junior went into his room to take a nap and Gayle settled down on the couch with a comforter over her for a nap. Marion read a book on tanning. They had all been spending at least an hour at night breaking the hides in, and she hoped to pick up some tips. She had added wood to the stove earlier; it had gotten a little chilly when Gayle and Junior let in the cold air. Those two looked exhausted. She knew about trapping, but never really gave much thought to how hard it was. She was glad she was inside today. It looked really nasty out there.

Later that night, when they'd gotten all the fur on stretchers, it was time to grind up the week's worth of flour. It was a slow process. The wheat berries went into the hand grinder. Then they set the screen sifter on top of a bowl and cranked the grinder. The large pieces were collected and put back in to be reground again. This process had to be repeated four times until the flour was piled up and finely ground. They all took turns turning the crank on the grinder until they had enough for the week. They went to bed exhausted, their arms sore from turning the crank.

Marion woke up early in the morning. She went into the kitchen and started coffee. Junior had said last night they wouldn't be going out today on the trap line. The major part of the storm had hit last night, but there was no telling how long the snow would keep up. It was a bit chilly in here this morning and she was wearing thermals under her clothes. She put a couple of pieces of wood in the wood stove, then looked over at the couch to see if Gayle was covered up against the chill. She realized with a startled gasp that Gayle was not asleep on the couch. She walked down the hall and Junior's door was closed. Marion stood absolutely still while she absorbed the meaning of that closed door.

Marion went into the kitchen and poured a cup of much needed coffee. Her hands were shaking. She sat down. *Oh isn't this just great,* she thought. *All we need is a baby right now. Wow. Oh God, they would be trapped here all winter and their hormones are running wild. Gayle will get pregnant for sure.* She hung her head down. *Oh dear God, I wish George was here. He would know what to do about this.* Her mind raced trying to come up with a solution. She was out of her depth here. Well, there was only one thing they could do. They had to get married and fast. They needed to find a minister or priest or someone to marry them. She wasn't picky now that the world had ended. She would take whatever or whoever was available to marry them. It was time to go talk some sense into them. She stood up and took a deep breath.

Marion walked to Junior's door and hesitated for a moment in indecision. Then she stiffened her spine and opened it up. Gayle and Junior were asleep, entwined together with their arms around each other under the covers. She almost backed out of the doorway, afraid to go on. She took a deep breath, took a few more steps into the room and said, "I see you both had some fun last night."

Both Junior and Gayle's eyes flew open. Gayle gasped and she realized she must have fallen asleep last night, not gotten up and left as she'd been doing. *Oh shit,* she thought. Junior and Gayle looked at each other and then looked away real fast. They were busted. Well, it was better that it was out in the open. Junior had wanted her to tell her mother that they were getting serious, but she'd said no, not yet. She liked keeping the secret. She only wanted to keep it a secret for a little while longer. *Here we go,* she thought. This is why she hadn't wanted to tell her mother. The questions and judgments would start now.

Junior could tell that Marion was ticked off. He had warned Gayle that Marion would be upset if they weren't straight with her. Gayle had said her mother would make their relationship difficult; she wanted to keep it a secret for a short while so they could enjoy it in peace before the fireworks began. She'd tell her, but not yet. Well, it looked like it was too late to keep it a secret now.

"Well, don't either of you have anything to say for yourselves?" Marion waited briefly, and when neither of them said anything, she said, "You stupid kids. What do you think you are doing? You're going to get pregnant, Gayle. How did you think we would manage this with no doctor and no hospital? Did you think to wear protection?" They still hadn't moved or said anything. Marion put her hands on her hips and screamed at them. "What in the hell were you thinking?"

Gayle turned over and glared at her mother. "That is quite enough, mother," she said icily. "We're both old enough to make up our own minds if we want to sleep together or not. You have no say in this decision."

"You two are getting married if I have to take the bible in my own hands and hear your vows myself as you pledge yourself to each other as God is your witness," declared Marion. "Do you hear me?"

"You can't tell us what to do as if we were young children needing to obey you. Do you hear me?"

"Did you at least use protection?"

"I have a diaphragm, and you know it mother. I'm not pregnant."

"Maybe not yet," Marion said, "but you will be. Women get pregnant with a diaphragm all the time. I told you to get on the pill. Do you ever listen to me at all?"

Gayle sighed. "The doctor said I shouldn't use the pill, Mother. We have a history of strokes, blood clots and heart attacks in our family. Even my doctor said it would be asking for trouble to use the pill."

"Fine. Then you're getting married."

"Mother, just stop this. This is totally ridiculous. The world has changed forever and we don't need to be married."

Junior spoke up. "Don't I get to have an opinion on this subject?"

Both women turned to him. "NO!"

Gayle closed her eyes, took a deep breath, and said, "This is between my mother and me." She put her hand on his face and then reached over and kissed him.

"You are getting married," insisted Marion. "I mean it, too."

"Mother, give it a rest. We're not getting married because you told us to. Get that into that thick skull of yours. We're not getting married."

Junior reached around Gayle and grabbed his pants off the floor. He pulled them under the covers and put them on. He climbed out of bed and stood in front of Marion. "I wanted to tell you about us but Gayle didn't want to just yet. I'm sorry you found out this way. I know it must be a shock. Is there anything I can do to make this up to you?"

"You can keep your pants zipped up, that's what you can do. Stop sleeping with my daughter, for another." Junior turned away from Marion and walked out the door. Marion was hopping mad now.

Gayle gasped. "That was an awful thing to say to him. How dare you?"

Marion was getting madder by the second at Gayle's attitude. "Just never mind that. We're leaving here right now and going back to our own house. It was a big mistake to come here. I was right in the beginning to just stay there."

Gayle looked at her mother with fire coming out of her eyes. "You're crazy. You have completely lost your mind. You have done nothing but insult Junior and George ever since the world has changed. I will not have you talk like that about the man I love. Do you hear me? He took us in and gave us food and everything we need, and this is what you say to him in return? Only a damn fool would leave here with the way the world is now."

Marion really lost her cool. "You're my daughter and you will do as I say. We are leaving here today, whether you like it or not. Get ready; we are leaving now."

Gayle was angry, too. She was so tired of being treated as if she were a child. She glared at her mother. "I am nineteen. I am quite old enough to make up my own mind about what I want to do. You are insane to want to go back to our house. We don't have any food there, Mother… nothing. Remember? We were almost out of wood, too, for the wood stove. I'm not going anywhere. I'm staying here."

Marion screamed back at her, "I am your mother and you will do what I say. We are leaving here now. Get ready, damn you."

"Fine. You want to leave and go commit suicide? You go right ahead. In fact, that is a good idea, because then Junior and I can run around here naked all day long without you around."

"Fine. That's the way you want it, little girl, then I'm out of here." Marion turned to leave, but Junior was standing in her way.

"Will you two please calm down so we can talk about this and work it out?" he asked calmly.

Marion was too mad to reason with. She said nastily, "You just want to get rid of the old lady so you two can screw like rabbits all winter long, don't you? Well, you get your wish. I'm out of here." She stomped off.

Gayle climbed out of bed and looked around for her clothes. The sight left Junior completely stunned. He couldn't think or speak. When she finally had her clothes on, he shook his head to clear it and said, "You have to calm her down. It's not safe for her to go off on her own, Gayle."

Gayle looked at him. "Once she gets like this, there's no changing her mind. Remember the scene at my house with your father? That's just how she is."

The noise of Marion yelling and hitting the door startled both of them. They raced out of the bedroom into the living room. "Junior, unlock this door. I'm leaving!" She had her backpack filled and ready to go.

"Marion, please think about this first." he said reasonably. "The safest thing for you to do is stay here with us. You know that. Please calm down. Control your anger; don't let it control your reasoning. Please, Marion. Listen to me."

Marion wasn't hearing anything Junior had said. "Unbolt this door or I will. Do it now." Junior was afraid she would hurt herself if she tried to do it in the mood she was in. He looked over at Gayle, questioning her with his eyes.

"She's fired up now. There's no reasoning with her when she gets this way. Just unbolt the door. That's all you can do. Who knows what she'll do if you don't. You're talking about Mrs. Mulehead, the most stubborn woman in the world."

Junior said the only thing he could think of to Marion to calm her down. "I will marry your daughter. I want to marry Gayle. I love her. Please stay. It would be suicide for you to leave. Please, just stay."

Gayle yelled at Junior, "What? I'm not marrying you just to keep her happy. No way."

Junior was hurt by that and looked over at Gayle. "What's the matter? Am I not good enough for you?"

"That has nothing to do with this," said Gayle. "That is a non-issue. The point of this is," Gayle pointed her finger at her mother, "she is not going to order us around like children. We are adults and we will do what we please without asking her permission. If and when the time comes for me to marry someone, it will be because I love that person and want to marry him. It will not be because my mother told me I have to."

Junior walked over and unbolted the door. He could still hear them arguing behind him and just blocked the words out. It seemed there was no reasoning with either one of them. He had a lot of practice doing that with his own mother.

When he had the door unbolted, Marion walked over and said to him in nasty voice, "She really can't cook at all, you know. She'll probably poison you."

Gayle yelled, "That's because you're a lousy teacher!"

Marion grabbed the double barrel shotgun. Junior raised the door, and Marion stomped outside and kept going. There were eight or nine inches of snow on the ground and new dark clouds were heading their way.

Junior tried one more time to diffuse the situation. "Marion, go for a walk and cool down and think about this. Please, come back." Marion stopped, turned, and said in perfectly calm voice, "Okay, you two have fun now." She turned around and headed out.

In a shaky voice, Gayle said, "Mom, please stay. Please, don't go." Marion just kept going and waved her hand back at them. Gayle and Junior stayed like that until she was out of sight.

Junior turned around to find Gayle crying. Junior sighed. He had wanted someone to talk to when he'd been all alone and going nuts. Well, at least it had been nice and quiet without all the drama of these two. He sighed again. He lowered the door and bolted it. He pulled Gayle into his arms and rubbed her back while she cried.

After about five minutes, Gayle straightened up and said, "I'm going to go get her. I can't let her be out there all alone."

Junior sighed again. "Why couldn't you two have come to some agreement before she left?"

"I couldn't let her get away with treating us like children. If I wouldn't have stood up to her, it would only have gotten worse. She'd be telling us what to do about every little thing and expect us to obey her, or she'd pull a stunt like this. You don't know her like I do. She's been like this my whole life. Why do you think I'm nineteen and a freshman in college? I should be a sophomore. She kept using the 'I'm your mother' and guilt about my dad dying and her being alone. At first it was so I could help out at the pottery shop and be around for her. I was supposed to only miss half a year. She kept stretching it longer and longer, claiming that she needed me there. I finally had to put my foot down and go through half a dozen scenes like this before I was even able to leave this year for college. If you just ignore her, it only gets worse. She takes it as agreement and starts planning your life for you. I finally figured out the only way to handle her was to completely stand up for myself and not give her an inch, because she takes ten miles every single time. Yes, my life would have been a lot easier if I just agreed with her and do whatever she wants me to do. I'm sorry, but I can't do that. I'm an adult now and I make my own decisions. Can you understand what I am saying?"

Junior remembered his own mother and stepfather making plans and telling him about what he was going to do, too. He also remembered he had to make the decision to stand his own ground to be an adult and not just do what they wanted. He kissed her and said, "Yes, I do understand. I just feel so bad about all of this."

Gayle kissed him back. "I do, too. I'd love it if she would just be halfway reasonable about things. She constantly refuses to meet me halfway. It is all or nothing with her." She sighed. "I have to go find her and convince her to come back here where it's safe."

"You don't know this area well enough yet to be out there traipsing around in a snow storm," Junior said. "You'd probably get disoriented and lost yourself. I'll get bundled up and go look for her. You need to stay here in case she comes back. If she comes back here and we're both gone, she might not stay here and wait for us to return. Besides, if we both left, we'd have to leave the place unlocked and whoever it is out there that's been taking the animals out of the traps might come in and lock us out. Then what would we do? Someone needs to be here all the time to guard the place, okay?"

Gayle sadly said, "I understand. But you be careful out there, all right? I don't want anything to happen to you, either."

Junior smiled at her. "I'm always careful."

He put thermals on and then his insulated suit. He put his winter parka on over the top. He used his dad's rabbit and leather hat to keep his head and ears warm. He used his dad's good winter gloves for his hands. He had good insulated leather and rubber boots for his feet. His dad had made sure to outfit them both with good quality items for the winter. When he was done, he grabbed his SKS and four extra stripper clips and put them in his pocket. He didn't think he'd need them, but it was always better to have extra than to run out and need more. He kissed her at the door "It'll be all right. I'll find her. Lock up after I leave so I won't worry about you, okay?"

"Okay. Just stay safe," she said. Junior smiled and walked out the door.

Junior followed Marion's tracks. They were already filling in with snow. The falling flakes and wind did their best to cover them up. Junior thought, *just great. We are having a hell of a snowstorm and I'm out chasing down a stubborn woman too stupid to stay where it was safe.* He sighed and hurried to catch up. He couldn't believe how far she'd gotten. She was really moving at a fast pace. After an hour, he stopped for a few moments to catch his breath. He looked to the north and the heavy dark clouds were still moving towards them. That meant even more snow was on the way. He picked up his pace. He had to reach her soon or he would lose her tracks altogether.

She must still be really mad. Her steps hadn't slowed down, not once. After two hours, she was still not within sight. The snow was falling faster with bigger flakes. The new storm was hitting them now. He had passed a couple of houses that looked abandoned. There was no light or movement around them. He wondered where the people had gone. He walked on, steady against the wind. Off in the distance he heard a shot and then another shot. It was maybe a half-mile ahead of him. He quickened his pace. He thought, *I sure hope she isn't in any trouble; maybe she's just shooting a deer or something.* He was trotting along the road to get to her. He came around a curve in the road, and up ahead in the distance he could see dog-like figures coming up to a bundle lying on the road. As he got closer, he could see that something was lying on the road with some of the dogs standing over it while others came up and sniffed at it. He was now about two hundred yards from whatever was lying on the road; it looked like a blurry scene from a dream. It was hard to see. The snow was falling pretty thick and his eyes kept blurring from the wind and cold.

He kept up his pace to get to whatever it was there. He was about a hundred yards away from it now. There were a lot of dogs here, maybe twenty or thirty. He didn't really think much about it and figured they'd run off when he got closer. At thirty yards, he could see two dead dogs lying in the snow. He looked a little farther and saw the shotgun lying on the ground next to the bundle, almost completely covered with snow. A shock went through his body as he realized that the bundle on the ground was Marion. He looked closer and saw a large husky was eating her neck and a big black lab was chewing on her legs. He looked over and a beagle was chewing on one of the dead dogs. *Oh my God,* he thought. The dogs must be starving, and had attacked her. Without forethought, but more of an instinct, he raised the SKS up and shot the husky in the side, then sighted in the black lab and shot it, too. The full metal jacket ripped right through them. They both howled a mournful sound, running off, biting at their sides. The rest of the pack looked up at him and then charged. In the lead was a huge German shepherd. He couldn't believe how fast they were moving. He dropped the German shepherd with a head shot. It fell down and slid to one side. He quickly aimed at the next dog in the lead. It was an English setter. He hit it and it ran off. He fired two more shots and the breach locked open. He reached down into his pocket with shaky hands and pulled the stripper clip out and quickly reloaded. The rest of the pack had run out into the trees when he had started shooting at the charging dogs. He could see them circling him. He walked closer to Marion. He had to see if she was still alive. He already knew the answer, but he had to make sure. He bent down, looking at her neck and the huge amount of blood that was lying in the snow around her. Her eyes were wide open, but she wasn't seeing anything. She was dead. The area smelled of fresh blood and he could see the steam rising up from the warm blood. Just then, the little beagle charged him. He ignored it and quickly looked all around. More dogs were slowly making their way closer. The little beagle got a hold on his leg and started chewing on his boot. The other dogs waited to see what Junior was going to do.

Junior kicked out his leg and the little dog went flying. He quickly aimed at it and missed. The little bastard charged right back at him and grabbed onto his overalls, ripping right through them. He swung the gun over and gave the dog a solid whack with the rifle stock. The dog yelped and fell away, rolling about three feet. He quickly raised the rifle again and shot it. *Enough of this nonsense. No sense in getting some infestation or disease from these dogs. Who knew what they'd been eating?* The beagle howled in pain and started a death kick with its legs. The rest of the pack backed off. They had started to move in closer during his fight with the beagle.

He started back tracking. He could see their dark shadows moving off through the trees. The shadows stayed with him, but kept their distance as he made his way back. He thought, *Damn this is bad, real bad.* These dogs weren't afraid of people or gunshots. When he'd gone about two hundred yards, he turned and looked back. Some of the dogs were eating the dead ones. The snow was coming down faster and he couldn't see as well as he could a couple of minutes before. This was about as bad as it could get. He had to get back to Gayle.

He'd traveled about two miles, with the pack trailing him the whole way. About every ten to fifteen minutes, one of the braver dogs would run across the road in front of him to distract him and two or three dogs would run up and try to bite, snapping their jaws. He would shoot one or two, and sometimes knock one down with the rifle when it lunged at him, and then shoot it. This happened over and over again. It seemed the pack never got any smaller, no matter how many of them he killed. When he looked back at the largest part of the pack, they'd be eating the dead dogs. *They are testing my reflexes,* he decided after awhile. The sound of a hound howling startled him. *This is like a nightmare you can't wake up from.* He hurried his pace. He had to get home or they'd eventually wear him down, or attack him with more than two or three at a time. He couldn't hold out forever on his own. After another hour, he thought he saw an abandoned house. He decided to head for it. Maybe he could get to cover and kill them off, or maybe they'd give up on him and move on. The house was just up ahead. He thought, *Thank God.*

As he approached the house, they attacked again. He was ready for them. He quickly dropped two of them, but missed a third one. *A charging, fast running dog was hard to hit,* he thought. He jumped up on the porch and opened the unlocked door. He was relieved it had been unlocked. He felt more secure in the house. He walked over to the front windows and looked out. Dogs had surrounded their dead packmates and were eating them already. These dogs had to be literally starving to behave this way.

He looked at his watch. It would be dark soon. What a strange, horrible day this had turned into. Last night everything had been just fine. He and Gayle were getting along great. She was interested in the things he was. He never thought he would be able to find a girl that would like the things he liked. She wasn't stupid like the other girls he knew that only cared about their hair or fashion. She was someone his dad would have liked, too. That was important to him. He sat down in a chair. Why did Marion have to insist on going out? How in the hell was he going to be able to tell Gayle? The dogs were circling the house now. His stomach growled loudly. Great, he should have at least eaten breakfast before taking off. But how in the hell was he supposed to know this would happen? *Shit, Gayle.* How could he tell her dogs attacked, killed and ate her mother? But, first, he had to live through this. He rubbed his hands over his face in frustration. Right.

****

Gayle was pacing the living room like a caged lion. She had been doing the same thing for hours. Pace one way, turn, and pace back to where she had started from. She'd been doing this over and over. She wanted to scream. What could be taking them so long? She dressed to go outside. She opened the door, went outside, and closed the outside door to keep the house from getting too cold. Junior had left the outside door open. She walked over by the garage. She couldn't even follow them. There were no tracks left in the snow. They had filled in a few hours ago. It was really snowing hard now. She looked around, noticing it would be dark soon. *Where were they? Damn you mother, why did you have to take off like that? Everything was going great and you just had to do this now during a snowstorm. Everything was fine and you had to ruin it.* She was really worried about them. They'd been gone much too long. What if they both were lost? Or injured? She wouldn't know where to go to help them. *Please come back, Mother, please,* she prayed. *Junior, please come back to me safe.* She started to cry.

Junior had taken off and hadn't even eaten first. *Why? Why did this happen?* Why couldn't her mother just be reasonable? She shouldn't have let Junior open the door and let her leave. She felt so guilty. This whole mess was her fault. She should have just told her mother and had it out with her days ago. *Where were they? Please,* she prayed, *please.*

****

After pacing around the living room for a while, Junior decided to look around and see if he could find something to eat. He checked all the shelves in the kitchen and they were completely empty. He got his small flashlight out that he kept in his overalls pocket and checked out the pantry. There was a jar of peanut butter that had some left in it. He grabbed a spoon and sat down to watch the dogs while he ate it. It was better than nothing. He had to really work at getting the peanut butter out of the jar. It was frozen. He had to chip off a piece and then suck on it. He thought about killing some more of the dogs, but decided against it because it would just give more food for the dogs that were left out there and keep them around longer. He sat there and intently watched them. There were still about thirty dogs out there. He had greatly underestimated the amount of dogs in this pack. How was he going to get out of here without the dogs seeing and hearing him? He paced around the living room again, sucking on a chip of frozen peanut butter.

He decided to check out the rest of the house before it got too dark for anything useful. He went down the hallway and the doors were closed. He opened up one; it was a boy's bedroom with spaceship pictures and mobiles of the Challenger. He opened up another door across the hall; it was a little girl's room. It had mermaids and underwater pictures. He opened up the next door on the same side as the little girl's room; it was a bathroom. He went over to the last room across the hall, opened the door, and got the shock of his life. There were three bodies on the bed. There were two children, a boy, a girl, and a woman lying there. He looked around the room again and stepped closer. They had been shot in the head. There was a man lying on the floor in a frozen pool of black blood on the other side of the bed. There was a Glock 9 mm lying a few inches away from his hand on the floor. Junior noticed a box of shells for the 9 mm on the nightstand. He picked the gun up and put it in his pocket. He gathered all the shells that were scattered around and put them in his pocket, along with the rest of the box.

He noticed an envelope propped up by the lamp with the words, 'This is for whoever finds us,' wrote on it. Junior picked it up and stepped over the man on the floor and walked out of the room and shut the door.

Junior sat back down in the chair, opened the envelope, and pulled out several pages of stationary with handwriting on them. He started reading. It seems the man, a Dave Owens, his wife, Joanne, and his two children, Brandon and Crystal, were starving to death. He had done everything he could think of to find food for his family. He had listed all the ways he had tried and failed. Finally, in desperation one night, he couldn't take it anymore and shot his family and then himself. He couldn't watch them starve anymore. He left the letter so anyone that found them would know who they were and what had happened. Junior thought how sad it was. This man had been surrounded with food and hadn't even known it. Junior would have helped him if he had known. *Those poor kids*, he thought. He couldn't even imagine what it would have felt like for Dave Owens to watch this happening before his eyes. He thought about Gayle; about how they were now sleeping together and were sort of a couple. What if they had children, as Marion predicted? He hadn't even thought of that.

What would it be like to be a father? Well, he knew one thing for sure. His children would never starve to death. He would try his hardest to be a good father, just as his father had been to him.

The dogs started barking and growling outside, saving him from thoughts of the future. Well, he was going to have to live through this first before he could worry about what kind of a father he'd be. A few of the dogs were at the door, growling and scratching. He got up and moved a big, heavy side table over in front of the door to help secure it tighter. It sounded like some of the dogs were throwing their bodies against the door. Great, how was he going to get out of here? That was the question. He realized he'd better secure the back door, too. He went into the kitchen, and sure enough, the dogs were trying to get into the house in back. He put a chair under the door handle and made sure it was snug and couldn't be moved. He noticed a closed door off the kitchen and opened it up. It went to the garage on the side of the house. He hadn't even realized there was a garage here. It had been snowing so hard he hadn't been able to see the whole house. He brought out his flashlight and looked around to make sure it was closed up tight. It was, thank God, or he would have had another door to secure. He found a roll of duct tape and smiled. In the letter, Dave Owens had said to take anything useful with his blessing. Junior went back inside the house with the duct tape. He could tape his boots and legs and arms up and make it harder for the dogs to bite him. An idea was forming in his mind about how to safely get out of here now. He would have to wait for morning. It would really be stupid to try it now in the dark.

It was completely dark outside now. He could still see movement around the house. The dogs were not leaving. He guessed the most he could hope for was that some of them would freeze to death tonight. That would just give more food to the dogs that were left. *Great, just great.* The dogs were still trying to get in the door. He could hear howling, growling, and sometimes fighting. Now, he just had to make it until morning. He settled down for a long, impatient night. He hoped Gayle had stayed inside were it was safe. His dad had not ever warned him about dogs going feral. He'd never thought about it, either. That must be where all these dogs came from. People are always going out to the country and letting their pets go when they didn't want them anymore. They though they'd be able to survive, like a coyote or something. Most of them just starved to death because they didn't know how to hunt for food. Some did turn feral and had to be shot.

Now that he thought about it, he remembered reading something about a pack of feral dogs that had terrorized a small community somewhere. They finally had to hunt them down and kill them. The feral dogs had been attacking and killing people's dogs and cats. They also attacked children playing outside. Wow. When the world had ended, people must have let their pets go in the woods because they could no longer feed them. Now, they were Junior's problem. *Gee, thanks people*, he thought.

****

Gayle stayed outside, shaking the snow off of herself every once in awhile. It was full dark now. *Where were they?* She shoveled some in front of the door to be able to open it up. She was trying to keep it cleared for them when they returned. The wind kept blowing the snow back against the outside door. Her heart constricted in fear. What if they never came back and it was just her left here to survive on her own? *Oh God, please don't let that happen. Please come back.* She was numb with fear and cold. She kept looking down the trail, hoping to see them coming. Her breaths puffed out in the cold and snow as she waited and watched.

Chapter 14

Split Up

"Many times a day I realize how much my own life is built upon the labors of my fellowman, and how earnestly I must exert myself in order to give in return as much as I have received."

Albert Einstein

Mark, Abby and Channon climbed into the van. He told the women to go ahead and lay down in the back. Abby put the seats down and spread out a sleeping bag so they could lay under it and get warm. Mark sat in the passenger seat to have more legroom to stretch out. He had long legs. Both women were shivering. Mark said he'd light the small stove for ten or fifteen minutes and warm it up. He felt really bad. His head was pounding hard and he was a bit sick to his stomach. He felt he might be coming down with something because he was shivering, too. He shouldn't be that cold, but he was. He explained to Abby that they'd have to each take turns to keep watch. He didn't even try to include Channon for a watch. She wasn't up to it. He told Abby to go ahead and get some sleep; he would take the first watch. He lit the stove and after a few minutes, the women stopped moving; all he could hear was even breathing. He put the stove away. He leaned his head back and thought about taking something for the drum pounding in his head, but couldn't make himself reach over to his pack and do it. Instead, he pulled the lever so he could lie down more and relax. He could peek out the window and see, if it would ever stop raining.

Abby and Channon were awakened by the sound of a gun battle going on in front of them. Both women jerked awake and looked around. The sun was shining brightly. Abby realized Mark hadn't woken her up for her turn to watch. Abby looked around intently and couldn't spot any immediate danger. All the sounds were coming from up ahead. She noticed that Mark hadn't moved at all. The sound of the battle going on should have had him jumping up to help Eric, Lisa and Maria. Abby scooted up to look at Mark. He wasn't awake. She reached out to shake him and felt how hot he was. *Shit, he has a high fever.* She shook him again, harder, and he blinked up at her with glassy, bloodshot eyes. He closed his eyes again. Abby shook him again and he looked at her, not really seeing anything. Abby grabbed Mark's rifle from across his lap and looked at it, trying to figure how to shoot it without a stock. She didn't think she'd be able to fire it in the condition it was in. She quickly looked around, assessing the situation. She still didn't see anyone out there. They were going to have to get out of the van before they were discovered. It was just a matter of time before someone would notice them.

Abby grabbed Channon's arm, getting her whole attention, and whispered urgently, "You have to scoot down and open the back door. We have to get out of here. Mark's real sick and has a high fever; he's out of it. We have to find some bushes to hide in and wait for Eric, Lisa and Maria to find us."

Mark softly moaned up front. Abby quickly pushed Channon towards the back and said, "Open it up right now." Abby scooted up to the front again and hurriedly whispered to Mark, "We have to get out of here right now. I'm going to need your help to get you out of here. Hand me your pack. Mark's hand fumbled around and tried to lift it up. He finally got it up enough for her to grab it, and Abby pulled on it with all her weight. She and the pack went over in a pile. She looked over the pack and saw the back door was open. She shoved the pack down her and it slid out the door with a thump. The door didn't open upward as she thought it would. This door opened sideways. Channon just stood there looking terrified.

Abby said, "Channon, get down out of sight before someone sees you." Abby scooted back up to Mark and shook him. Mark moaned. She reached over and gave his face a smack. Mark jumped and looked at her. "Come on. Climb over the seat. We have to get out of here right now." Mark just blinked at her, not understanding what she'd said. Abby shook him again, and then pulled on him to get him to move. She was finally able to get him turned around and started to pull him towards the back of the van. He helped her as much as he could. He must have finally understood. She stepped down out of the van and told Channon to help her with Mark. They got him on the ground. Abby looked around and saw a big clump of bushes over on the west side of the road. It was the closest cover they had.

She quickly got Channon's attention and explained what they were going to do. She showed Channon how to hook her arm under Mark's to help pull him along with them. She put the pack on Mark's back. It would be easier to drag it with him wearing it than to try to drag it along with them using another hand to hold it. She reached in and grabbed Mark's rifle, handed it to Channon and said, "Hold this in your other hand and don't let go of it for anything."

Abby pulled the small backpack out of the van and slipped it on. She then grabbed the sleeping bag and yanked it out. She rolled it up and tied it to Mark's pack as quickly as she could. She bent down on the ground and motioned for Channon to do the same. They dragged Mark between them. It was about a hundred feet to the brush. They got into the brush in no time. Adrenaline is amazing stuff. Mark was moaning and saying, "What?" and calling the women Eric. Abby kept shushing him. They crawled under the brush pile, dragged Mark in after them, and lay still, gasping for breath. Abby was on the north side, closest to the shooting. The sound of a shotgun was almost the only sound they could hear now. Abby heard a rattle, looked up, and came face to face with a rattlesnake. She froze. It was coiled up, ready to strike. Channon let out a small scream and slammed a hand over her mouth as if she needed the help to stop. Abby slowly inched her way backwards in very gentle, smooth moves.

She kept her eyes on the rattlesnake, not even blinking. When she was back a few feet and prayed it was enough, she whispered to Mark, "Give me your knife." Mark had passed out and hadn't heard her. He didn't even move. *Oh shit*, Abby thought. Channon heard her and slowly reached across Mark to his other side, unsnapped the Velcro strap on the sheath, and pulled a four-inch knife out. She slowly placed it into Abby's outstretched hand. Channon slowly moved back, giving Abby room to move if necessary. Abby saw a forked branch next to her head. She leaned a little back and quickly sliced through it, holding the forked stick in her hand. Before she could move to do anything else, they heard voices and footsteps coming towards them. Abby froze.

She quickly went over in her mind what she knew about rattlesnakes. This one looked about three feet long. They could strike two thirds of their body length. She slowly scooted back a little more to make sure she was far enough away, because the footsteps kept coming their way and they might startle the rattlesnake and make it strike at her. The steps kept coming closer and closer and voices were softly talking. Abby remained intensely focused on the rattlesnake in front of her.

The voices and footsteps were just about even with them when the snake gave a little rattle of its tail. A girl's voice said, "Did you hear something?"

A boy's voice said, "No, I didn't hear anything."

"Did you see anyone else around here?"

"No. I haven't seen anyone," said the boy. The snake shook its tail louder now, making it clear to everyone it was getting agitated.

Both voices stopped talking immediately. The girl said in a startled voice, "This isn't a good place to be standing. Let's go."

Footsteps and voices grew farther away, going south. Abby slowly lowered her arms to get into a better position, holding onto the stick tightly. She sat absolutely still, waiting patiently for the snake to move. It didn't even look like she was breathing.

Abby had just remembered something else about rattlesnakes. They liked to curl up on hot rocks to bask in the sun. They searched out warm areas with their tongues; that's why they would sometimes slither into sleeping bags with people sleeping on the ground, to get next to the warmth. Mark was the hottest thing around right now with his high temperature. She grew worried that the rattlesnake would slither over to Mark and curl up on his chest. She carefully eyed the snake for any movement. The gun battle out there was long over now. All Abby could hear was an occasional voice in the distance. She still waited patiently for movement from the snake. The rattlesnake finally started to uncoil itself and slither away. It headed straight for Mark. Abby moved so fast she was a blur to Channon, who watched her every move. The movement was so fast that Channon at first thought she had imagined it. But no, she hadn't imagined it at all. In one quick move, Abby had pinned the snake to the ground right behind its head with the forked stick in one hand, and with her other hand, she sliced its head right off with Mark's knife. Channon blinked in surprise and disbelief at what she had seen. Nobody moved that fast. But here was the evidence right before her. Abby stabbed the snake's head and flicked it off farther into the bushes and reached out and grabbed the long body and opened the small backpack and put it inside. Channon just blinked at her in amazement. *Wow, that was really some move.* She eyed Abby more closely, wondering where she'd learned to do that.

Abby looked over at Channon. She still had tears running down her face. Abby said to reassure her, "Piece of cake, nothing to it. We'll wait here until we can't hear them anymore. We'll move to a safer place if we can. Keep an eye out for Eric, Lisa and Maria, okay? They're around here somewhere." Channon nodded yes, wiping her tears away. They waited for an opportunity to move, but kept hearing sounds and shouts off in the distance, and a few times people traveled up and down the road.

Abby got the pack off Mark and took his rain poncho, coat and t-shirt off. She worked the rain poncho under him so he was lying on it. She got the first aid kit out and made him swallow three tablets to reduce his fever. She grabbed his t-shirt, soaked it with water, and put it on his chest. She took off his boots and socks, then wet his socks, wrapping them around each foot. She rubbed his face down every few minutes and poured more water onto the various cloths to keep them wet. She made him sip water every ten minutes or so. She didn't know how high his temperature was, but she was afraid he would go into convulsions. There wasn't a thermometer in the first aid kit. She thought it was stupid not to have included one.

After a few hours, Abby got his temperature down and he became semi-aware of his surroundings and recognized his companions. He wanted to know what happened. Abby explained. Abby got another drink ready for Mark.

Channon whispered to him, "Abby pinned the rattlesnake down with a stick and cut off its head just that fast." She snapped her fingers. "If I would have blinked, I would have missed it."

Mark looked at Abby and said in a hoarse voice, "How did you do that?"

Abby just reached out and raised Mark's head up. "Don't talk. Drink. When it gets dark we can move farther down and cross the road so we'll be by the river. We need more water."

"What is wrong with me?" he asked.

Abby sighed. "I won't know for sure until I can examine you properly, but I suspect that your leg wounds are severely infected, and it's poisoning your whole body. I wish I'd been the one to tend to your wounds. I don't think Lisa and Maria got all of the infection and debris out of them before applying that ointment that caused the wounds to close. You have a dangerously high fever. I know you're shivering now, but we have to get your fever down or you could go into convulsions. They can kill you or cause brain damage. I also think you have a slight concussion. You're pupils are not dilated the same. You just need to rest right now. Later, when it is safer, I'll make you a tea that will help."

"Any idea where Eric went?"

"We haven't seen him, Lisa, or Maria." Abby made him drink more water. He looked at her and said in a soft voice, "Thank you."

"You're welcome. Now go to sleep. You need the rest." He closed his eyes and fell into a deep, fevered sleep.

Abby looked over at Channon. "I am going to need your help. Mark's very sick. I'm also going to need you to be able to take a watch and be aware of what's going on around us constantly, because I can't be on watch all the time. I know you've been through hell. All of us women have. But I need you to put that aside for now and concentrate on the here and now for our safety. We don't want to get caught again. I need you to pull yourself together and help me. Do you think you could do that?"

Channon considered this for a few moments. "I don't know if I can, but I'll try. I want to help." Abby smiled and then reached over and patted her arm. Well, it was a start, anyway. Channon needed to have a reason to live. Maybe this would help her to pull herself together. What a mess they were in. She knew they were headed north, but where up north? Where were Eric, Lisa and Maria? She hadn't seen or heard them since they'd divided to rest in the vans. Were they all right? Had they been killed? After she got Mark and Channon settled into a new place farther north, she'd come back and see if she could figure out what happened to them. She wanted to know if they were dead or not. Had they been captured? She needed to know so she could figure out her strategy. If they were captured and made to tell their habits, she wanted to be able to change their pattern. It would reduce their chances of getting caught just like Mark had said and done before. Once she knew what happened to them, she wanted to get further north before looking for a place to hole up to care for Mark, putting as much distance as she could between them.

Traveling was not going to be easy with Mark out of commission. She thought about what she needed to do to treat him. She'd make a bitter tea to reduce his fever; it would help with the infection, too. She'd do this before she left tonight to find Eric, Lisa and Maria. When she got back, she'd need the rest of the night to find a spot for them to hole up for a few days. The reality of the situation was Abby didn't really have a choice. If she had to do everything, she would manage somehow. Her grandfather always told her there were no such things as problems, just puzzles to solve. She just had to look around and find the pieces that were needed to complete the puzzle. Solutions were all around. She thought, *Oh yeah, Grandfather, you haven't looked at what I'm looking at.*

****

Eric, Lisa and Maria were packed and ready to leave as soon as it got dark. All they had left to do was fold the poncho and tarp and put them in the backpack, then they'd set out for the night's adventure. That was the way Eric had started to think of the trek north. It was either that, or to lose his mind. It just seemed every night something new happened. It was like being on an African safari without a guide. You just never knew what would jump out at you.

He just wished he knew where Mark was. He whispered to the women, "You ready?"

They both whispered, "Yes." He waited a good five minutes observing all around them to be absolutely sure it was clear.

That gang had looked for them a long time. They'd been up and down the river all day. They could hear them. He took five steps and then stopped to listen. The women followed his example. They took five steps and stopped to listen, too, just like deer do. There were a couple of bonfires up ahead about a quarter mile. He stepped up on solid ground out of the river, and the women followed him, making little noise. They were getting good at this stealth stuff.

They traveled for a while, and then Eric stopped and motioned for the women to come up to him. He whispered, "I know we're not going very fast right now. After we get past the bonfires, we can head over to the road and make better time. We have to get away from here as silently and quickly as we can. There are a lot of them; we don't want to run into any of them in the woods. Those by the fire won't be a problem; their night vision is destroyed from being next to the fire. We'll sneak right by them and keep on going. Watch for my hand signals in case we have to drop to the ground and crawl. Okay?" Both women nodded.

Eric started off and the women took up their positions on his sides. When they were getting close, Eric signaled for them to come up beside him. They could see the gang clearly, even from where they were. They were all talking in little groups huddled around the fire. They caught snatches of conversations. Most of them were talking about how creepy the woods were at night and horror movie scenes. Eric smiled and thought, *just keep believing that.* They didn't have any patrols out or guards or anything that Eric could see. They crept silently by and kept going. The gang never suspected a thing. When they were a good distance away, Eric stopped again and motioned the women to spread out and take up their positions again. They quickened their pace.

He headed out for the road and stopped at the ditch. They had gone maybe a mile and a half over the past three hours. What a waste of time. But it was better to be safe than sorry. If this trip up north had taught him anything, it was that. "Okay, we'll take a small break, and then head out and try to make up some time."

Lisa poured Eric a cup of coffee, then Lisa and Maria shared a cup. Eric had been watching for movement on the road.

Lisa asked, "How's the leg?"

"Fine. You're a good nurse."

"Thank you." They started out again, walking up an incline. It was hard on the legs. They would soon be in the real mountains. He had no idea how long it would take them to climb the mountains on foot. He sighed. It was just going to get more difficult. He looked around at the vehicles they passed. They were empty of anything useful.

The women had each taken a wool blanket and wrapped it around themselves to keep warm. He had to find them some clothes and coats or they'd freeze to death pretty soon. The higher they climbed, the lower the temperature was. At least they were walking all night and keeping warm from the exercise when it was the coldest. The sun was still shining most days and it kept them warm when they were sleeping. Maria coughed again. Eric didn't like the sound of it. What in the hell could they do if one of them got sick? Maria's cough had gotten steadily worse since they'd gotten wet and cold in the rainstorm. She mostly kept her hand and the blanket over her mouth to keep the sound of coughing down to a low noise so as not to give their position away. They went up one side of the incline and then down the other, just so they could start to climb upward again. They were all going to be in excellent physical shape after their journey to the retreat. Remember, no pain, no gain. He laughed quietly. He was worried about the ladies being half-dressed. He had to find clothes for them. He looked into all the cars they passed. Nothing. The vehicles were getting farther apart.

The next night, and it was almost time for a meal break. Eric was trying to find a natural concealed area for them to rest.

He'd just taken a step when a voice said, "Freeze. Don't move a muscle. Slowly put the shotgun on the ground. Be real careful about it." Seven men appeared out of thin air, closely surrounding them with their rifles pointed at Eric.

Lisa and Maria gasped and let out a small surprised squeak. They started trembling, their eyes wide with terror. Eric slowly lowered the shotgun to the ground and straightened up. A man pulled it towards him and laid it on the ground at his side, aiming his rifle back at Eric.

"It's all right, ladies. Step over to us, away from him," a man said. Both Lisa and Maria stepped closer to Eric, looking at him with terrified eyes. "You women come over to me now. Get away from him," he commanded. Lisa and Maria crowded still closer to Eric, visibly shaking in terror. These men looked like military or something. A few men were wearing something over them with bumpy, feather-like things sticking out all over in some kind of camo material and had some weird goggles on their faces. The other men had some kind of face paint streaked across their faces. The women crowded even closer to Eric, almost knocking him over. Eric didn't know what to do. The man who had spoken was now getting frustrated. "Move away from him right now." Maria pushed up against Eric. He was already off balance; he fell over in a sprawled heap with arms and legs sticking outward.

Lisa was knocked off balance and fell to the ground on her hands and knees, right at the feet of the man that had taken Eric's shotgun. Lisa grabbed the shotgun, flipping the safety off and racking it. She pointed it at the man that had taken it from Eric.

Eric yelled out, "Lisa, no! Drop it. Just drop it."

Lisa said to the men, "You all put your weapons down now." They didn't move. Lisa screamed like a wild insane woman. "DO IT NOW OR I START KILLING YOU!"

The men exchanged glances, not sure what to do. The leader looked at her. "Lady, I don't know who you are, but know one thing. Before you can move your finger, you'll have a lot of lead headed your way."

"Go ahead and kill me," she screamed. "I'd rather die than let you take me captive again."

There was silence for few moments. The man replied, "What do you mean, you won't be taken captive again?"

"Already done that, and I won't let myself be taken again, do you understand me? I will die first."

There were a few more moments of silence. "We were rescuing you from this man, here. Look at how he's treating you. You two are wrapped in a blanket and don't even have proper clothes, for God's sake. How could you want to stay with him?"

Lisa said, "Rescuing us? This is supposed to be a rescue? We were already rescued by Eric. Eric, you tell them."

"I think there's been a misunderstanding here. I'm not holding these women captive, if that's what you think." Eric looked over at Lisa. "Lisa, put the safety on and put the shotgun down."

"No way in hell. I don't trust these men. Look at how they've treated us already, holding us at gunpoint. No way. I am not going to be anyone's sex slave again." Lisa was shaking her head.

Maria spoke up. "Everybody, just stop right this minute. Just stop it. This is insane." Maria looked over at Eric. "Do something."

Eric said to the man in charge. "Can I get up and approach her?"

"Okay."

Eric stepped over to Lisa. "Lisa, give me the shotgun."

"No. I won't let them take me again."

"Lisa, they had the wrong impression about our situation. They thought I was holding you and Maria captive."

"That's not true; you weren't holding the shotgun on us or anything. I think they're lying to you. Don't believe them."

"If they were evil, Lisa, they would have killed me right off the bat. We didn't even know they were there. If they were evil, like you say, they would have just killed me and taken you and Maria. Think about that, Lisa."

"That's not true," Lisa maintained. "Maybe they want to torture us. You can't trust them, Eric."

Eric said gently, "Lisa, all men are not like the ones that tortured you. These men thought they were rescuing you from me." He paused for a moment, then decided to approach this problem from another angle. "Look at it from their point of view. A man and two women are walking in the forest. The man has a shotgun and the two women are wrapped up in blankets and don't even have proper clothes. Now, be truthful with me, Lisa. What would you think?"

The leader said in a quiet voice, "Lower your weapons. They are not a threat." All the men lowered their rifles, pointing them at the ground uneasily. He realized from what Lisa had said that these women had been horribly mistreated, tortured and raped. This woman wasn't going to trust them when they were pointing rifles at Eric. She thought they were evil. He didn't like that she still had the shotgun pointed at his brother. But someone was going to have to take a leap of faith in order to diffuse this situation. He said, "My name is Chuck. We noticed you three walking back a few miles. We really did think this man here was mistreating you. We decided to rescue you. We weren't trying to capture you or anything. My wife would have my head if I even considered that. Is your name Lisa?"

"Yes, it is. I don't trust you."

"I've figured that out. I'm sorry we've started off on the wrong foot. Let's start over and do this right this time, okay?" He held his hands out in a non-threatening manner. "My name is Chuck. Lisa, you are holding my brother, Tim, at gunpoint. Can you please lower your weapon?"

"Lisa," pleaded Eric, "please listen to what he's saying. I'm not asking you to trust them. Have I led you wrong yet? Haven't I looked after you? If you trust me, then please lower the shotgun." Lisa looked at the man standing before her, watching him intently, trying to see if he was evil. The problem was, evil didn't always use a face you could recognize. Eric was right, though. She did trust him. And he was right about what she'd think if she saw a man with two women in blankets like they were. Did she dare lower the shotgun? That was the question, wasn't it? Should she or shouldn't she? She realized in a moment of total clarity that she was the aggressor now. They had lowered their rifles. If she were to shoot this man, it would be in cold blood. She would kill this man out of revenge and fear for what other men had done to her. She started to cry. Eric reached out and took the shotgun, flipping the safety on and pointing it at the ground. He patted her shoulder in support and understanding. Lisa fell to the ground in a crying heap. An audible sigh could be heard around them.

Maria came over and hugged Lisa, whispering to her.

"Now get back to your posts," Chuck said. "Are you three hungry?"

Eric said, "We were just about to stop and make something to eat when you guys jumped us."

"Andy, go get three MREs." One of the men left.

Chuck and Tim approached. Lisa was looking down at the ground, but finally got her courage up and looked up at Tim."I'm very sorry I almost shot you. I feel horrible about it."

Tim looked at her strangely. "You don't have to apologize to me. We should apologize to you. We didn't mean to scare you like that. That wasn't our purpose. We thought we were doing a great thing by rescuing you and never even gave it another thought about how it would look to you. I'm sorry to have scared you."

Lisa was embarrassed now. "Don't apologize for trying to be the good guy. If that's how it looked. You would have done a great heroic thing by rescuing us. Please don't let this horrible experience stop you from future rescues because of my reaction. I would feel awful if I knew I'd stopped you from doing the right thing."

Tim laughed, and with a twinkle in his eyes and a raised eyebrow said, "Well, maybe next time I'll be sure to wear a white hat so the women know I'm the good guy." Everybody chuckled.

Andy brought back three MREs. Chuck said, "Here you go. Why don't we sit down and you can eat while we talk."

The women looked at the brown package in front of them on the ground; they'd never seen one before. They watched Eric to see what he did. Eric reached into his pocket and pulled out a pocketknife and opened his up. He passed the knife to Lisa, who was sitting between him and Maria. She copied him and passed the knife to Maria. Maria opened hers up and passed the knife back. Eric reached in, grabbed the main entree, and pulled it out, then reached in and pulled out the fork, knife and spoon. The women followed his lead. Eric had frankfurters and beans. Lisa had beef stew. Maria had chicken à la king.

As they ate, Eric said, "About a month ago, my friend Mark and I headed up north. We had to fight to get out of the city. When we reached the main highway, it looked like a scene from a zombie movie. We traveled at night and hid during the day. We ran into violence everywhere we went. We found a gang of about thirty guys holding some women captive; they were abusing them. We rescued six of the women. One died in the fight to free them. We gave the women the choice to go where they wanted or come with us. One we left behind a few days after rescuing, because she tried to steal our stuff and attacked my friend. We got into another firefight with another gang. We escaped. My friend, Mark, was with two other women and we got separated. He'll be heading this way, too. About twenty miles back, we ran into the last gang. There were fifty or sixty of them. They wore hooded sweatshirts and carried pistols. We've been traveling ever since. Do you know what happened?"

Chuck said, "As a matter of fact, we do. We have a short-wave radio and picked up a broadcast from New Zealand. It appears that Russia or China set off an EMP that took out our whole electrical grid. The EMP got most of Mexico and Canada, too. Alaska and Hawaii weren't hit. I guess they figured they'd just starve with no supplies coming in.

"Thank you for sharing the news with us," Eric said. "Do you know what our government is doing?

"The best we can tell, the government, or what's left of it, is hiding in bunkers, surviving with food and supplies taxpayers paid for. They're just waiting it out. It's now up to everyone to stand tall and make it on their own. What kind of skills do you have? We have room for three more if you're willing to pass our tests to join us."

"That's a very generous offer," said Eric, "but I'll be heading out. It's up to Lisa and Maria to decide if they want to stay here with your group or not." He looked over at Lisa and Maria. "Well? They have food and shelter. It's up to you if you want to stay here." All eyes turned and were staring intently at the two women.

Lisa grabbed Eric's arm, holding it so tightly he thought it would snap in half. She said in a panicked, high-pitched voice, "Eric, what are you saying? Do you want us to stay here? Are you tired of looking after us? Is this what you want?"

Maria stood up. "I'm not staying here. Eric, can I please go with you? Please, don't leave me here." She looked around with wide eyes.

Eric reached out and patted Lisa's hand. "Calm down, both of you. Maria, sit down and we'll talk about this." Maria looked like she was ready to dart off into the forest. Eric said firmly, "Maria, sit down." Maria looked at him with indecision in her eyes. "I won't make you do anything you don't want to, okay? Now, please sit down and we'll talk." Maria took a deep breath, nodded, and sat down again.

Eric said, "Think about this. Don't just make a snap decision based on your emotions. I don't know if they have a doctor or not, but you two need to be looked at by someone who has some knowledge about these things. You might have been damaged in some way from the abuse you suffered. They also might have medicine that can help you with the cough you have, Maria." Maria had been coughing on and off all evening.

Lisa asked, "If we want to remain with you, can we? I mean, are we welcome to go with you? Or are you just politely telling us you want us to stay here with them because you don't want us slowing you down? We need to know before we can make a choice."

Eric was taken by surprise. "Yes, you are welcome to come with me. I thought I'd made that plain."

"I'm staying with you, Eric," said Maria.

Lisa, after a long look at Eric, said, "If we are really welcome to go with you, I want to go with you, too."

The other men looked disappointed. Eric turned to Chuck and Tim. "We thank you for your hospitality and the MREs. We'll be leaving now."

Chuck and Tim had stood up. One of the other men that had been standing back a ways said, "We can give you some clothes to wear, Lisa and Maria."

"Thank you that would be wonderful." Maria nodded in agreement.

"What size do you wear?" asked Chuck.

"Size 6," the women chorused.

The men looked puzzled over this answer. "Medium," said Eric. The women looked at Eric with a puzzled expression. "Trust me. A medium size would be best."

"What kind of clothes are we talking about here?" asked Maria.

Chuck gestured around him at the men. "Clothes like what we're wearing."

"Oh. Then we should get a small size," Maria suggested.

Chuck started to say something and Eric broke in quickly. "They need a medium." Both women looked at Eric like he was crazy.

Chuck said, "Bring them a complete set of Swiss camos in medium."

It was just as Eric had suspected. He thought they'd be European made, and the sizes tended to run a bit smaller than American sizes. Chuck, being the leader here, would keep any and all American-made camo clothing for his group and not give them away freely. The man came back with a bundle of clothes and handed one set to each woman. There were pants and a jacket-type shirt, a camo rain poncho, thermal pants and top, and pair of thick brown socks setting on a brown t-shirt.

Both women looked up at the men around them and smiled. "Thank you very much." Chuck just nodded his head. The women hadn't smiled at all since they'd been here. He felt good about doing something nice for them. The men had been a bit dazzled by how pretty they were, even if they were unkempt.

Maria and Lisa walked off a little way. Maria untied the blanket from around Lisa. "You go first and I'll hold up the blanket while you get dressed." It was heaven to have full clothes on again that weren't dirty and torn up. They were almost warm now. They still wrapped the blanket around them as a coat, but doubled it up and tied it with the cord Eric had given them. Their feet were a little warmer, too, now that they had socks. It was a good thing their tennis shoes had expanded some from the walk or they wouldn't have been able to get the thick socks on their feet. They walked back to the men with a bit of a spring to their step.

"Do they fit all right?" asked Eric.

Lisa smiled. "They're fine."

Eric turned to the men. "Thank you. We'll be going now."

"Thank you for the food, and especially for the clothes," said Lisa and Maria.

One man walked up to them and handed them the MRE packages. "More food is inside. You should take them with you." They put the MREs in their packs.

"Thank you," said Eric. Chuck and Eric looked closely at each other. Eric was watching his body language closely. He seemed relaxed, but ready.

"We'll send an escort with you to the end of our territory," said Chuck.

Eric nodded at him and asked, "We're heading north from here. What can you tell us about what's up ahead? Are there any problem areas?"

"Where are you going?"

"North to Oregon. We're going to my uncle's ranch."

Chuck nodded. "We sent out a scouting party for about ten klicks. It is pretty clear of anyone up to there. You might run into a few stragglers here and there. There aren't many people left from around here."

Eric said, "Thank you." He turned and started towards the road.

A man ran up to Maria. "Here, this is for you." He handed her a plastic grocery bag tied up with some softball-sized things in it.

She couldn't tell what they were. She blinked at the man and then slowly reached out and took the bag from him. "Thank you."

"Go in peace," he said. "I hope things work out for you. Stay safe." She turned and hurried up to Lisa and Eric, holding the bag tightly.

Chuck called out, "You sure you won't change your mind and join us?"

Eric turned back for a moment. "No. We have to go on and get to my uncle's place."

He turned and started walking. Two men walked ahead of them, leading the way. Lisa started to say something, and Eric stumbled into her on purpose. He whispered real low, "Don't give any information to them."

She just looked at him, and then said, "Have you been drinking? Did you have an Irish coffee when we weren't looking?"

Eric laughed and righted himself. "I wish, no, I stepped on a rock and it threw me off balance."

Lisa huffed. "Hum, that sounds like denial to me. Shame on you. You didn't share with Maria and me." She threw her nose in the air and marched on in pretend indignation. Eric smiled at her and laughed.

Eric was sure there were men following them, too. *They were a careful bunch. Can't really blame them for that.* Eric turned to Lisa and Maria. "This is probably the last chance you both will have. Are you really sure you want to leave with me? They probably have a lot of food and clothing stocked." Both women shook their heads and kept on walking.

The sun would be coming up soon. Eric thought about what Chuck had said about it being clear for about ten klicks. That was a little over six miles. So that means a six mile circle they would be patrolling. That's a big territory to watch and protect. They must be a really big group to have that kind of manpower. Those guys were prepared for a long time, considering they had spare clothes they could give away. They had top-notch gear, too. They had camo face paint, military clothing, ghillie suits, good rifles and night vision. They worked well as a team. Obviously, they work in pairs. It is easy to take out a lone man; not so easy to take out two. They weren't amateurs by any stretch of the imagination. He figured they wouldn't really be out of reach for probably ten to eleven miles. He was itchy to get out of their territory as fast as they could. People had been known to change their minds.

****

Abby had kept watch on the road and the surrounding area. It had been a long time since they'd seen or heard anyone. Eric had mentioned that there were streams all over the place around here. She was desperate to get some water for Mark. He would die for sure if she didn't find more water. It was still a few hours until the sun set. She was going to have to go out on this side of the road and see if she could find some. It would be insane to try to make it across the road to get to the river. She looked around and noticed Mark's camo coat lying on the ground. It was big enough to be a dress on her. She could pull it over herself and keep low, hopefully blending into the surroundings while she looked for water. She touched Channon's arm. Channon turned to look at her with a questioning expression. Abby thought, *good. She's still alert.* She said, "I have to go look for some water. I don't have a choice. He'll die without it. I'm going to put his coat on and blend into the bushes here. We have one container of water left. You'll need to keep wetting the cloths and rubbing him down. He needs to drink some water every ten minutes or so. Can you do this for me?"

Channon looked alarmed. "Okay, but don't be gone long, just in case." Abby nodded her head. What a mess they were in. She sighed and grabbed Mark's coat and quickly put it on. She bent down and the coat dragged on the ground. It would have to do. She grabbed the water containers and held them close as she made her way from bush to bush. Soon she was out of sight.

Abby found a stream running between rocks. It was small only about three or four feet deep, and maybe six to seven feet across. She observed the area for a while to make sure no one else was around. After about ten minutes, she slowly crept over to the rocks. This was going to be a bit difficult. She was going to have to climb up on the rocks and reach down and fill the containers with water. She hoped she could reach, or else she was going to have climb into the stream. She didn't have time to look around for a more accessible way. She lay down on the rocks on her stomach and reached down. She inched forward a bit more. She slowly reached her hand down and found she could reach the water. *Thank God,* she thought. She grabbed the smaller water containers and filled them up and set them down beside her in a crevice. She reached down with Mark's camel back to fill it. When it was full, she almost fell into the stream trying to pull it up. She held on and slowly inched her way back until it was safe to lift it up. She rested for a few moments when she had it beside her. She climbed back down, moving the water containers with her. Carrying it back was awkward, since she had to hunch over to stay hidden. When she got close, she looked around and realized there were three different places that looked almost the same from this side. Which one were they hiding in? She hoped Channon was watching her or she was going to have to search each one.

She slowly moved towards one possible area,when she noticed movement off to her left, out of the corner of her eye. It was farther down. She froze in place, hoping whoever it was wouldn't notice her. She looked down to make sure the water was covered up. She looked back and saw a slow moving hand going back and forth. It was a black hand, so it was probably Channon. She had greatly misjudged how far she'd traveled looking for water. This whole area looked pretty much the same from this side. She slowly made her way over. Channon took the water containers from her. "What were you doing down there?"

Abby shook her head. "Looking for our hiding spot." She quickly grabbed some water and tended to Mark. She'd been gone a long time. She got some more fever reducer out of the first aid kit and gave them to Mark, making him swallow the caplets by rubbing his throat up and down. "Get some sleep, because I'm going to need you tonight to watch Mark while I find us a place to hide for a few days." Channon looked at her for a long minute, then nodded and laid her head down. Abby got comfortable and waited for darkness to come.

When it got dark, they had everything ready. Mark was semi-conscious and helped a little with getting him up. Abby had showed Channon how they'd help him to walk. It was very slow going. They were all exhausted; worrying about being seen was stressful, and helping Mark took a lot of strength. She hoped they'd covered at least two miles. It was hard to tell in the darkness, stumbling around rocks and bushes. She found a place that was up a bit that had several shrubs and bushes in a tight clump on pretty even ground. This would be good enough for them; she needed to check if she could find their companions' bodies or clues to where they might have gone. She quickly explained to Channon what she was going to do.

Abby had grabbed some herbs when she'd gone out for water she planned to use for Mark's fever and infection. She made sure the stove couldn't be seen from the road, and boiled some water to make the bitter tea. After it had steeped and cooled down, she made Mark drink some. He fought her because it tasted terrible. She told Channon to keep giving the tea to him on and off until she got back.

Channon grabbed her. "Don't go back there," she said with a panic-stricken voice. "You might get captured or shot. Don't leave us alone. I can't help him. I don't know what to do."

Abby said, "Shhh, not so loud. It'll be fine. I'll be a ghost. Don't worry. I'll stay in the shadows. Now pull yourself together and take care of Mark while I'm gone. Okay?" Channon started to cry again. Abby patted her. "You are stronger than you think you are. You'll do fine; I have confidence in you."

Channon sniffed and wiped at her tears. "I'll do my best."

"That's good enough for me. You'll do fine, I'm sure of it." She had not taken Mark's coat off, so she was all set to head out. She grabbed one water container and a couple pieces of venison jerky and put them into the pockets to carry with her. She patted Channon's arm and stepped out into the darkness.

She quickly moved from bush to bush back the way they'd come. She was looking for the two vans they had taken refuge in from the rain. She started running into smelly bodies and knew she was close. She was real careful moving from shadow to shadow, making sure the way was clear so she wouldn't be bumping into things and making noise. She tried stay clear of the bodies. Sometimes the stench was so bad her eyes would water and she'd gag. She was determined to find out what happened to them. She looked at each body she went by, looking at the clothing to find them. They weren't there. She noticed a couple of bodies over on the slope leading to the river. She slowly looked around. She hadn't seen anyone or anything yet. She went over to the bodies. They weren't anyone she knew. It looked like they had made their way to the river and Eric had shot these on the way. So, they had hopefully escaped. Well, it was time to get back to Mark and Channon. She saw what she had come back for. At least they weren't dead.

Abby made her way silently back to Mark and Channon. She had turned around as she was leaving and looked the area over really well this time so she would be able to find it again. She still had a little trouble finding them, but at least she'd been closer to them. She smiled at Channon.

She quickly explained to Channon what she had found, and that as far as she knew, they weren't dead and had gotten away. Channon actually smiled a little. That gave Abby hope. Mark was thrashing around and Abby knew she had to get them some place concealed so she could take care of him. They lifted Mark up and started out again.

After awhile, they could see the bonfires through the trees and faintly hear some of the noise of the gang across the road. With it being so dark, the gang stood out like a sore thumb. They'd have to be blind to miss them. Abby didn't think they were in any danger, but intended to get as far away from them as possible. They just kept putting one foot in front of the other, dragging Mark along with them. Abby would stop every now and again and apply more water to Mark's skin with a wet cloth and make him drink more of the bitter tea. When it had been a long while since they could see the bonfires, she found an area they could rest. They all thankfully sank to the ground.

After they rested for a few minutes, Abby said, "Channon, take care of Mark. I'm going back and see if they are holding them captive or not before we go any farther."

Channon looked at Abby. "If they're captives, what are you going to do? They'll kill you or we'll be in the same situation as before."

"I won't be seen," Abby said. "I won't go close. I'm just going to look around quickly and see if I can spot them or not. I just want to know, so when Mark is better, we can tell him if they were there or not. Then he'll know what to do about any of it. I'll be back as soon as I can."

****

If Abby had crossed the road and walked on the riverside, she would have run into Eric, Lisa and Maria. Abby was on one side of the road going silently from bush to bush towards the bonfires, and Eric, Lisa, and Maria were heading up the ditches along the road on the other side away from the bonfires.

****

Abby crossed the road a bit down from the bonfire, looking all around to make sure the way was clear. She found a spot where she could observe them from. She couldn't see Eric, Lisa or Maria anywhere. It didn't look like they had any captives. She watched them huddle around the bonfires. Why didn't they find houses to stay in somewhere? Staying out in the open like this was stupid. She'd seen what she needed to. She turned around and headed back to Mark and Channon.

They got Mark up and they slowly started out again. Abby was so tired. Finally, she felt they had gone far enough to cross the road and find a place to hole up. They made their way across as quickly as they could, then got out of sight in the bushes. Now she had to find a place to stop. She found a small area where they could take a break. She went over and filled the water containers; they were running low again. Finally Abby said, "I'm going to go ahead a ways and find us a place where we'll be able to take care of Mark. Then we can set up camp. Take care of him. I'll be back as soon as I can. Keep alert and watch for danger." Abby headed north with the river.

She looked around, constantly assessing the area for what she needed. She came around a small bend and found the perfect spot. There was fast water running over rocks, making loud splashing sounds. It would cover up Mark's moans, hopefully. She walked over to the bushes and shrubs, and down a little way were some trees and shrubs, surrounded by bushes. They'd have to clear a spot in the middle for them to be out of sight. She hoped it would work. She trampled down some of the plants and found that the ground was solid and sort of flat. She turned back to get Mark and Channon.

She gave Mark some more fever reducer caplets and tea before they started off slowly. The sun was coming up just as they finished setting up camp. It had taken awhile to clear the spot in the dark. Abby had used the weeds and bushes she cut as more cover for them along the sides. She had made a little sleeping area apart from Mark. That way they'd be able to get some rest, too. Now that it was light, she could see they were in a good area. They would be able to see someone coming.

Abby sat down and made a pot of coffee. At least Mark had the coffee pot in his pack. They were getting low on coffee, though. She thought maybe she would gather some dandelions and make a tea for them to drink instead. They all needed the vitamins and minerals, Mark most of all, so he could fight this infection. This would be the last pot of coffee she made. She'd save the rest for when Mark was well. She made a small pot of oatmeal, and she and Channon ate. "I'm going to go collect some herbs to help Mark. Watch him. I'll be gone for just a little while." Channon nodded.

Both women were exhausted already and they had a long day to go yet before Mark would be out of danger.

When she had gathered what she needed, she took a pot of water and set about making a poultice for his infection. She took another pot to make bitter tea. She set these aside to cool. She grabbed the sock she'd been using to wipe him down with and washed it and the t-shirt she'd been wearing with a bar of soap to make sure they were as clean as she could make them. She wrung them out and set them on some rocks to dry in the sun. She went back over to Mark and checked on him. Channon was half asleep and she asked for her help in getting Mark's pants off.

Channon looked at her. "Why are you taking his pants off?"

"Because his leg is infected and we need to see it to treat it. So help me," Abby said. "When I'm applying the poultice to the wounds, you can go down to the river and wash his jeans out and make sure you scrub the area where the infection was rubbing against his skin really well. Then put them on some rocks to dry. Okay?" They got his pants off. It had been a real effort. Mark had moaned and fought them. His knee was swollen and it pulled and rubbed as they removed the jeans. It didn't smell so good, either. Abby and Channon turned him over; holy cow, did it look bad. Channon gasped. Abby handed her the jeans and motioned her to go wash them. This was even worse than she had thought. Abby made him swallow a whole cup of tea. He fought her the whole way. It tasted terrible, but since when did medicine taste good?

When Channon came back, Abby asked her to help drag him over to the river so she could clean him up. They found a spot that had some sand and rocks and it was about eight inches deep to submerge him in. Abby stripped down to nothing and held his head up out of the water and washed him. He would open his eyes every few minutes and look at her. She washed the infected parts really well, and once they got the gunk out, it didn't look quite so bad. It was hard to hold him and wash him at the same time. He was a large man and kept slipping away from her. Channon helped as much as she could. Abby ran water over his face and washed his hair. They pulled him up out of the water and laid him on the rocks to dry off. She tied the almost dry sock around the bad wounds to keep them clean while he dried off. They got him back to the little camp by placing him on the tarp and sliding it over. They turned him on his stomach so she could work on his wounds. She told Channon to take advantage of the nice weather and wash the sleeping bag, the two blankets, and everything else, and to climb into the river and wash up herself. She would do it herself later in the day.

A lot of stuff was drawn out of the wounds and some more small pieces of wood, too. She applied the poultice to all of the wounds on his leg because they all were infected. It was amazing how many tiny pieces of wood came out. When she had drawn all the infection out, she applied the triple antibiotic ointment to them and bandaged all of them up with gauze to keep them dirt free. His fever broke the second night they were there. He had fought Abby and Channon applying the poultice, thrashing around, moaning and groaning loudly. He woke up for short periods now, but would fall back to sleep quickly. His body needed to rest. He didn't fight her anymore about drink the bitter tea. He understood that he needed it. On the third day, he appeared to be more alert and could move his leg without groaning in pain. On the fourth day, he could get up with help and walk around some. In one more day, he said they had to get moving.

Abby had cooked up the rattlesnake and they'd eaten it. She found six Yo Yo automatic fishing reels in Mark's pack, so she caught fish every day. She had been drying some of the fish to make soups with later on when they traveled. She had a nice big bag full now. She told Mark they would have to stop every hour and he'd have to rest for ten minutes or so. She kept collecting herbs and making teas for all of them to give them much needed vitamins and minerals. Every night Mark was able to walk a little faster and farther. Now he was almost back to normal and his leg only occasionally bothered him. He kept wondering were Eric, Lisa and Maria were. He thought they'd run into them by now. He had thought that maybe Eric would have found a place to hole up and wait for them to catch up with him, but he must have headed straight for the retreat, knowing Mark would catch up with them there.

Abby kept saying, "Just place one foot in front of the other; that's how we're going to get to the retreat." So, that's what they did. They hadn't run into anyone since the gang. They found a spot that looked like a couple people had used it for sleeping. They figured that it had been used by Eric, Lisa and Maria. It gave them hope and a purpose to keep going faster to catch up with them.

****

Eric, Lisa and Maria were almost to the top of the incline when it was time to find a place for the day. There was a rest stop up ahead at the top. He wanted to get them off into the forest and hidden before they got close to it. There might be people who have taken up residence in the buildings. They might do this if they didn't have anywhere else to go. He wanted to be able to sneak by them in the night. It was his turn to have first watch today. It seemed that with the cold season almost here, everybody had headed south. That was fine with him. They had watched a few people here and there make their way south. He was worried about having another shootout. He was down to thirty shells for the shotgun. He hadn't said anything to the ladies. They had enough to worry about. They set up camp and cooked a rice soup with dried venison in it. He was going to have to find a place to hole up for a couple of days and snare some food. They were getting real low on supplies again. He remembered the delight the women had shown at all the little treasures they had found the night after they'd left Chuck and his group when they had opened up the MREs and dumped them out. They had practically jumped up and down over the bag of M&Ms that had been inside. They had traded their jelly and cheese spread with each other. They were also in heaven with the toilet paper and wet wipes. Maria had shared with them the bag of apples that nice man had given her.

When the ladies were asleep, Eric stealthily moved off into the forest to check out the rest stop. It was better to find the danger now and make a plan than to try to improvise as he went along. He pulled his binoculars out and observed the whole area for an hour and a half. He hadn't seen anyone at all. He went closer and waited for fifteen minutes. He was listening for any sounds that people would make. He heard nothing but the faint sound of wind going through the trees. He slowly crept closer and checked the place out. No one was there. It looked like a few people had been through there, but no one was there now that he could see. There was dust and dirt all over the place and no footprints. The place stunk like a sewer. He quickly left. He looked around at the mountains surrounding them. He sat down beside a post by the road and observed it for a while. No movement that he could see either way. He was looking at the road and wondering what was up ahead for them. Well, since he was here he might as well go look and see what was on the other side. He could observe for while and see if there were any people that way. He got up to see what was over on the other side.

He found a place he could be concealed and still look with his binoculars. He scanned the sides and didn't see any wood smoke or any sign of people. This was clear. He looked at the road and slowly looked down it for shadows. He saw something moving in the breeze. He stopped and observed it. He realized it was a camo coat, just lying on the ground. He looked around and there were all sorts of camo clothing and camping things strung out all over the place, then he saw the Wal-Mart truck about a third of the way up the incline with the back doors opened up, swinging in the breeze. *Holy cow,* he thought, *this must be the first truck for the hunting and camping season.* The one responsible for everything camo for hunting and camping appearing on the shelves of the store overnight, almost like magic. He knew this because he had watched the shelves for bargains, and it happened over night. The truck must have been on the way to the store when the EMP hit. *I wonder what's still in the truck. Probably not many useful things left. Everybody had most likely cleared it out by now.* But from what he could see strung out all over the place, he would be able to outfit both women with gear of their own. Then they could all eat at the same time with their own plates, bowls and cups. *And look at those warm clothes. I've got to get them.* It would be best to do this in the daylight when they could see sizes and such. He told himself to calm down and watch for a while. This might be a trap and those items might be the bait. He watched for about an hour. Nothing else moved, except the door swinging and the clothing moving in the breeze. He felt it was safe to wake up the women and get them outfitted. He hoped they would have day packs in there somewhere. He quickly made his way back to camp.

The women were delighted. They stood in stunned disbelief looking at all the items scattered around. Lisa found a box that contained one black snowmobile boot in her size. She looked around for the other one. She found one, but it was also a right boot, and not in her size. She kept looking around for the one that matched. She finally found it under a car. She sat down on the ground, pulled her tennis shoes off, and slipped the boots on. They fit perfectly and her feet were warming up. She laughed in total delight at having warm feet. Maria kept looking around at the boots, but couldn't find her size. She finally found a brown left boot that was her size. She looked all around and couldn't find the matching right boot. She found every size but the one she needed.

She climbed up inside the truck and started throwing things out the doors, looking for more boots. She was opening up boxes and pulling them around and making room to get to other boxes. She threw some stuff that was in the way out the door and Eric yelled, "Hey watch it. I was standing there you know."

Maria paused and looked back at him, muttered sorry, then turned around and continued throwing things out of her way, but out the other side. Lisa found two winter parkas in her and Maria's size and put them in a pile to save. She walked around and looked at items, but didn't know what to keep. She found two mess kits still in the boxes and brought them over to the keep pile.

Something flew by her head. She looked up and things were flying out of the truck at her. She stepped back quickly and fell over something just as a bunch of small boxes landed on her with a thump. She yelled out, "Knock it off, Maria."

Maria peeked out at her. "Sorry. I'm trying to find some boots. All this stuff is in the way." She turned and went farther back in the truck. Lisa shook her head at Maria behavior. She had seen this behavior before in stores at Christmas time. It was the 'get the hell out of the way or get run over and stomped on' syndrome.

Eric called out, "Are you all right?" He was wondering since she was still lying on the ground with the boxes on top of her.

The boxes started moving, and then Lisa sat up and looked at him. "Do I look all right? I was just run over by a crazed shopping woman." She looked around. "Wow, do you think its Christmas time and this is an inherited trait or something? I think I got run over last year by her sister."

"I know what you mean," Eric said. "I learned a long time ago to get the hell out of the way when a woman has that crazed look in her eyes. It was bad enough when women were restricted by society rules and the amount of money she had to dictate their shopping manners. Now there are no rules and money is worthless, so we had better get a full catcher's outfit with a mask to safely go shopping with Maria."

A box flew by his head. A mysterious voice from inside the truck said, "I heard that."

Eric said, "I know, that's why I said it."

Another box flew by, just missing his head.

Lisa laughed. "You better quit while you're ahead. Her aim is improving."

Eric laughed. "Maybe we'd better join her in the truck and help control her violent impulses."

The disembodied voice yelled back, "I heard that, too." Lisa and Eric just laughed and climbed into the truck.

After spending half the day getting supplies together, they decided to head on out. They were all too keyed up to sleep now. Eric still laughed remembering Maria behavior over the boots. She had been just as bad when it came time to look for pants. They had to be a certain length because she was shorter than Lisa. He shook his head. They got some really great equipment, too. He had found a box of scopes and picked out three Leupold's. One was an M4 Extended Range Tactical, the second one was a VX-ll 3x9x40mm Duplex Reticle and the third one was the 66310 Boon & Crockett matte. It had an extended twilight lens system. He sighed in happy pleasure. He could never afford one of them before, and now he had three of his favorite kind of scopes. He had found some day packs. He'd taken four of them and tied one on top of the other one for Lisa and Maria. On the bottom one he had cut and tied two strips of paracord to the bottom of the pack on each side to hold a sleeping bag. On the bottom pack he had put all the equipment they would need and left the top one for their clothes. But the real bonus had been when he had found the box that had Pellet Guns in it. He picked two Ruger Air Hawk Elites. And there had been a box with lots of pellets for them. They had the new ones, too, that traveled at 1,200 feet per second. Each woman now was armed with almost a .22 rifle.

The women had spent almost forty minutes alone picking out the clothes they would put in the packs. He had gone outside to keep watch, bored with their comparing one thing to another that looked the same to him. And they were talking in woman speak, too. This one has a scooped neck. What in the heck is a scooped neck, anyway? It seemed like it really couldn't be that important if he didn't even know what it was, and had gotten along just fine his whole life without one. He shook his head.

He couldn't complain about the amount of time they were spending on deciding those scooped neck things, though. He had spent almost an hour comparing scopes and narrowing it down to just three of them. He smiled just thinking of the scopes. He couldn't wait to show them to Mark. *I sure hope he shows up soon.* Then he remembered how indignant Maria gotten over the fact that the only toothbrushes they could find were camo ones the store sold as a novelty item to hunters every season. He quietly laughed over that. They found some combs that come with cases for campers and backpackers. But now they all had knit hats and insulated gloves, and the women had picked insulated hunting suits to wear over their clothes and under their coats. They would be good and warm now. He had picked out two insulated wool shirts and two pairs of pants, because he had given his clothes away to the women when they first rescued them. And socks, they had all picked out thick warm socks and a couple of t-shirts, too. The women had found some camo underwear and bras that sportsmen always buy their wives and girlfriends because they feel guilty about spending so much money on all their things and equipment. The women were happy now that they were warm and had proper clothes and boots. He was happy, too. Now they just needed to find somewhere to hole up for a couple of days so he could snare them some more meat to dry. He still didn't like the sound of Maria's cough, but maybe now that they were warmer she would get better.

They had been traveling now for two days with the women carrying their own packs and equipment. They hadn't complained, not once. He told them he was going to start looking for a place they could stop for a few days to get more food. It was getting a lot colder at night and there was frost on the ground. They had been steadily climbing in elevation. Maria's cough was getting worse, and the colder air they were in all the time seemed to make it worse. He was going to start looking for an abandoned cabin for them to stay in while he set some snares out. They could make a fire in a fireplace and warm the place up and maybe that would help Maria's cough. He didn't know what else to do. She didn't have a temperature. At least, it didn't feel like it. He had checked her out after a long coughing spell she'd had last night. They were almost at the top of another rise. He was going to start checking out the roads that had mailboxes on them to find an abandoned place. They came around a bend in the road, and there was a mailbox up farther. He could just make it out up ahead. He told Lisa and Maria to wait for him in the trees off the road while he went down and looked at it to see if it was abandoned or not. It was hard to see if there was any smoke coming out at night with the wind blowing around. It was about an hour until daylight.

He walked down the road and it curved to the left. He walked on for awhile and the road ended. There was a driveway there. He walked up the curved driveway around a lot of trees and there was a large log cabin that had a triple garage off to the side. It didn't look like anyone had been here in a long time, but it was better to be safe than sorry. He watched it for a while and still hadn't seen any movement. He walked around the whole place and it still looked deserted to him. He noticed the solar panels on the roof. He decided to go get Lisa and Maria and they would make a camp under the trees out back and keep an eye on the place with the binoculars all day and see if anyone was around. They were waiting for him and they all walked through the forest way back from the house. They made their camp and he moved some brush and downed tree branches to make a little secluded place to hide them. Lisa had the first watch today and then it would be Maria's turn. He would go last. She would wake them up if anyone was there and got close to them.

When it was finally his turn for watch Maria reported that the only thing she had seen were a few deer and some rabbits. Both women had been excited with the prospect of staying indoors somewhere and possibly sleeping on a real bed. They said this had to be a rich person's place, because look at how secluded it was and how big the cabin was also. Well, he would give it another hour, and if no one showed up, they would get inside and see for themselves. Lisa woke up and kept watch with Eric while Maria dozed and coughed some. When the hour was up, he said they could go see about getting inside. They packed everything up in case they had to leave in a hurry and walked around to the back of the cabin. The blinds were closed, so you couldn't see inside of the house, but Eric was interested in looking inside the garage. He could see a door inside on the house side, so it probably let into the house. That's what he had wanted to know. Now the problem was the window size. He wouldn't fit through the window. Lisa volunteered to climb in and unlock the outside door. Eric broke the window and cleared all the glass out with his shovel. He boosted Lisa up through the window. She looked around and then went over to the door leading outside and unlocked it. Eric and Maria came in and they locked the door again. Lisa walked up to the door that led inside the house and turned the knob. It opened. Eric stepped in front of her and said he would check it out.

The women waited for him in the garage. He came back after about five minutes and said no one was there. They all went inside and locked the door. Eric grabbed a chair out of the dining room and put it under the door handle, along with turning the dead bolt on the door. He put a chair under the other two doors leading outside, too. The women looked around, marveling at the beautiful place. *Wow. It was as beautiful inside as it had been on the outside.* Eric came back and said he was going outside again for a few minutes and would be right back. Lisa and Maria smiled, thinking he had to go pee. They took their backpacks off and sat down in real chairs. It was a lot warmer inside than it had been outside. They took their coats, hats and gloves off and hung them on the coat rack in the foyer. Eric came back inside and went into the kitchen, then came back and did something to the heater on the wall. He went down the hall and was gone for three or four minutes. He then went up stairs and the women followed him. There was a wide-open area that had chairs and side tables, and books lined the walls on three sides. There was a hallway leading off to the left. They walked down it and there were five bedrooms and four bathrooms. There was a main bathroom in the hall and three of the bedrooms had bathrooms, too. Everything was as neat as a pin with hardly any dust. At the far end of the hall was a study that had more books in cases along the walls, with the fourth wall being glass from top to bottom.

As they went from room to room Eric had been messing with the wall heaters on the bottom. The women hadn't paid any attention to him as they looked around the rooms, admiring them. Eric told them to pick the rooms they would be staying in. He went downstairs and checked all the pipe fittings for the house. He already checked the upstairs fittings. Everything was hooked up. He found the basement door and pulled out his flashlight and went down the stairs. He looked around and found a small room off to the side and saw the unions and hooked them back up. He looked around and saw the breaker box; he flipped the main switch, holding his breath. He got lucky because the inverter lit up. He found a very large hot water tank and it was heated by propane. He lit the pilot light. They would have hot water. Well, if the pump was working. He walked out of the little room and looked around and saw more doors down here. There was probably a laundry room here somewhere. He needed to find it to test if they had water or not. He found it on the right of the little room. It had a washer and dryer. The dryer ran on propane, too. He got down and lit the pilot light. There was a small sink and he held his breath and turned the faucet on. Water ran out; he laughed.

He wanted to tell Lisa and Maria, but he thought he'd better check those pipe fittings again for leaks first. He checked out the downstairs and then went upstairs and checked them once again. No drips and no leaks, yahoo.

Both women were still upstairs looking around. Lisa was in the study at the end of the hall. "There are wooden blinds in almost every room in this house; the rest have insulated shades, and they all have insulated curtains that can be closed against the cold or the heat. I've closed them all to keep anyone from seeing us. The wall of windows was beautiful, but we shouldn't leave it open. The windows are tinted and I don't know if they would keep anyone from being able to see us or not."

Eric said, "Good thinking, Lisa. Now come with me. I have something to show you."

Lisa eyed him curiously. "What?"

Eric was excited and practically hopping around. He just smiled and laughed. "It's a surprise."

Maria walked into the room. "What's a surprise?"

"Come on and I will show you," said Eric. He turned and walked down the hall.

Maria and Lisa exchanged a look and shrugged at each other. Maria said, "Maybe he found a pool table or something."

"Well, there is only one way to find out," Lisa replied. The women smiled at each other, then turned and went down the hall. Eric was waiting for them in front of one of the rooms. He stepped inside when he saw them coming. The women stopped and looked into the room. It was the hall bathroom. *What was he doing in there?* both women thought as they watched to see what he was going to do. He looked at the women, smiling, and then reached out and pushed the toilet handle down. The toilet flushed. Both of their eyes got as big as saucers as they realized what this meant. They exchanged a look. Lisa reached her shaky hand into the shower towards the water tap and slowly turned it on. Water flowed out. Both women started jumping up and down, squealing and screaming at the same time.

Lisa screamed, "We can take a bath," at the same time as Maria screamed, "We can take a shower."

Eric wanted to put his hands over his ears at their high-pitched screams. He said, "And that ain't all." He walked over to the wall heater and turned it on. Heat flowed out of it. The women just stared at it for a few moments in awe as the heat flowed over them. "The stove in the kitchen works, too." He turned the light switch and the light came on. The women looked at him like he was a god or something. Eric laughed at their expressions. "There will be hot water for a bath or shower in about thirty minutes." Lisa's mouth opened in surprise and she just gaped at him.

Maria fell down on her knees, laying her body on the floor in front of Eric in supplication. "Oh great and powerful leader, we pledge our allegiance to you, oh great one. You are a god among mere men. You are our hero forever for this great and wondrous thing you have accomplished."

Lisa fell to her knees and bowed before him. "Oh great one, you are our hero forever for this miracle you performed."

Eric blushed and looked at them with stunned disbelief. "Cut it out, both of you." Both women started to giggle at his expression. The next thing he knew they were kissing his cheeks, laughing, hugging him, and telling him how grateful they were. Not only had he rescued them, he'd given them heat, electricity, water and a real stove to cook on. He looked at them jumping up and down again and said with a raised eyebrow, "There's a washer and dryer in the basement, too."

Lisa looked at him, threw her right hand across her chest and holding her left hand out in a stop gesture and said, "Stop, stop, Eric, or you're going to give me a heart attack or something."

It was Eric's turn to laugh at them now. Maria said, "Well, I'm going to go down to the kitchen and make us something to eat while we wait for hot water."

Lisa said, "Good idea. I'll come with you." Lisa turned to Eric. "Thank you, Eric. You're a hero and a genius." Both women walked out of the bathroom and went downstairs to the kitchen. Eric stood there for a few moments and sighed. He could get real used to this hero stuff. He'd better not let this go to his head and get any ideas, though.

None of them had thought to look in the cupboards yet. Maria dragged Eric's pack into the kitchen and got out a few pieces of dried venison. There wasn't much left. The same with the rice, there was about a large handful left. They'd been rationing it out to make it last longer. Lisa was looking for a pot to cook in and found one. She opened up a top cupboard, looking for a glass for a drink of water. The cupboard was filled with boxed and canned food. The two women exchanged looks and looked over at the door to the pantry. They raced over and opened the door. It was fully stocked. They squealed again and jumped up and down. Lisa grabbed a can of coffee and Maria grabbed two big cans of beef stew. They stood there looking at each other with tears in their eyes. Then they both smiled. Lisa made coffee and then grabbed a box of Jiffy mix and a box of powdered milk and made some drop biscuits. She put them on a cookie sheet and stuck them in the oven and turned the timer to fifteen minutes. Maria used the electric can opener and opened up the beef stew and put it on the stove to warm.

Eric walked into the kitchen just as the timer went off. His stomach growled loudly. They all laughed. "What is it I smell? It doesn't smell like rice soup. Is that coffee?"

Maria said, "Sit down at the table." She had rinsed out some bowls and small plates for the biscuits and stew. Lisa bent down and pulled out the biscuits with a potholder. Eric's eyes got real big and both women laughed. "Come here and look at this," Maria said.

She opened up several of the cupboards and Eric gasped. "Food."

Maria and Lisa laughed. Maria said, "Come look at this." She opened up the walk-in pantry's door and gestured for Eric to look. Eric almost fell over. He looked at Maria and then back at the filled shelves. He didn't know what to make of this. It was like a miracle.

Lisa called out, "Food's ready. Come on, let's eat." They sat down and ate everything the women had prepared. All three of them were all thankful to have plenty of food to eat.

They had a cup of coffee after eating and sat in real chairs, enjoying drinking out of their own cups and not having to share and pass it along to someone else. They hadn't had any coffee since they'd gotten separated. Mark had the coffee and coffee pot in his pack.

Maria said, "Don't forget to rinse your dishes off and put them in the dishwasher." They both turned and looked at her. She laughed. "Yeah, a dishwasher, too." Eric shook his head at her and smiled.

Lisa said, "Did we die one night and maybe don't realize it and this is heaven?"

Maria laughed. "It's a good heaven, too. I want to stay here. We have water, heat, electricity and food. Lots and lots of food."

Eric looked at her. "The food won't last forever."

"Don't burst my bubble yet. Let me enjoy this for awhile, okay?"

"Okay." Both women got up, rinsed their dishes, and put them in the dishwasher. They said they were going to take their baths and would see him later. He watched Lisa walk away with a wishful expression on his face. He sighed. *Better not go there.* This was a great place, but the propane and food wouldn't last forever. But, he could enjoy it while it lasted, too. He got up to take a much-needed shower. He needed to pick a bedroom, too. He was getting ready to go out and spend a few hours on guard when Lisa came downstairs. Wow, she was beautiful. Her hair was all shiny and clean.

The mountains must have protected this place from the EMP. "Where are you going?" Lisa asked.

"To find a place to sit and guard this place."

"Good idea. Can I come along with you for a while?"

Eric smiled. "Sure."

"Let me tell Maria and I'll be right back." She went up the stairs and came back down a few minutes later. She put her insulated suit and boots on. Later that night they decided to watch a DVD on the TV before going to bed. Eric wanted to watch *Tombstone* and the women wanted to watch *Sleepless In Seattle*, so Eric was out voted.

When it was over, Eric said he needed to talk to them about watches. He asked them if they wanted to have two four hour watches a day or to go for one eight hour shift. Both women promptly said, "Four."

"Okay. We will start tomorrow. I'll take the ten to two shifts twice tomorrow. Lisa ,you'll take the two to six shifts twice. Maria, you'll take the six to ten twice tomorrow. Then the day after, we switch. I'll take the two to six shift. Lisa, you take the six to two shift. Maria, you take the two to six shift and so on. That way no one gets stuck with the bad shifts all the time. Okay?" Both women agreed. Eric said, "Get a good night's sleep tonight. I'll see you tomorrow." Both women said good night. They went upstairs together, talking.

The next morning, all of them were up bright and early. Lisa started washing all of their stuff and getting things ready for when they had to leave. Both women knew this was just temporary and planned on taking advantage of it while they could. Sleeping in a bed again was wonderful, but being clean was the best thing of all. Maria found a bread machine in the kitchen and made bread. This one made two loaves at once. She thought that was the greatest thing. Eric got the refrigerator going. It ran off propane, too. Eric was on watch when lunchtime came around. Lisa had sliced up a canned ham for sandwiches to go with the bread Maria had made. She told Maria she would take a couple of sandwiches out to Eric as soon as the bread was done and a thermos of fresh coffee for him. It was so great having food again and planning meals. Maria planned on making some chocolate chip cookies that afternoon. She knew Eric would love them, but she loved them, too. She had found some powdered margarine in the cupboard to her amazement, and thought, *what will they think of next?* The ding of the bread machine sounded and Maria took the loaves out of the machine. Lisa cut up one loaf and made sandwiches. She already had the coffee ready to go. She got her coat, boots, hat and gloves on went and outside where he was on watch. The bread was still warm in her hand and it was steaming.

She handed the sandwiches to Eric on a plate and poured him some coffee. "Thank you," he said. "That smells wonderful."

He picked up a sandwich and was about to take a bit when a small voice said, "Can I please have some?" Eric and Lisa quickly looked around, and standing at the edge of the trees was a little girl wearing a pink coat and a pink hat with a white tassel on it, looking at them with beautiful blue eyes. They had dropped their guard. That could be dangerous.

Out of the trees behind the little girl came two boys. The oldest one said, "Come on, Amanda, we have to go. I'm sorry, Mister, we didn't mean to bother you. We're just passing through. Come on, let's go."

Little Amanda stood fast in her need of some of that sandwich, stomped her little foot. "No. I'm hungry. We haven't eaten in a long time. You promised me we would eat soon. Well, it's soon now."

"Where are your parents?" Lisa asked.

"Mommy went to get food and didn't come back," Amanda said. "I don't know about my daddy. He's gone; I don't know him. Have you seen my mommy?"

Eric and Lisa exchanged a look. Lisa said, "No, sweetie, we haven't seen your mommy." Lisa looked over at the boys; they were skinny and looked hungry, too.

Eric looked at the two boys and realized these children were starving. "What are your names?" he asked.

The oldest said, "We're sorry for bothering you. We're leaving now." He reached down and took Amanda's hand and started to pull her along. Amanda started screaming and kicking, crying out, "I'm hungry. I'm really, really hungry. You promised me. You promised me we would eat today!"

Lisa, with tears running down her face at this heartbreaking scene, said, "It's okay. We won't hurt you. We'll give you something to eat." Eric got up and started to walk over to the children and the oldest boy pulled on Amanda's arm harder dragging her away. Eric stopped and said, "I won't hurt you. I understand that you can't trust anyone right now. I'll place this on the ground. You all go ahead and eat the sandwiches." He placed the plate on the ground and walked away. Amanda was trying to get away from her brother and get to the sandwich. She hadn't taken her eyes off it since she'd laid eyes on Eric. She twisted this way and that, finally, in desperation, she kicked her brother in the shin, making him cringe and drop her hand. Amanda ran over to the sandwich and picked up the top one. She proceeded to eat it one small hungry bite at a time. Eric and Lisa watched in amazement that she could get her little mouth around any part of that sandwich. The boys looked on with fear on their faces.

Lisa had enough of this. She marched over to the boys, who only had eyes for Amanda and that sandwich, and didn't pay her much attention. She stood in front of them. "You children are starving. We have food. We are going to feed you. We won't hurt you."

The oldest boy looked up at her. "Why would you feed us? We aren't your kids."

"We'll feed you because you are hungry and your mother isn't here to do it for you. That is why we would feed you." Then her tears got the best of her and she said to the boy with a shaky voice, "We'll do it because you need help and it's breaking my heart knowing you are hungry and are so afraid of us that you won't take the sandwich and eat it." The boy just looked at her with a puzzled expression, not understanding what she had said.

Eric said in a soft and gentle voice, "We won't hurt any of you. We know people are acting really strange now and it might not be safe to trust strangers, but you need some help and we're the only ones around right now. You are going to have to trust someone to help you. At least take the other sandwich and let your brother eat it. Okay?"

Lisa grabbed the other sandwich and put it into the other boy's hand. "Please, eat it, please."

The boy looked to his brother to tell him what to do. The oldest boy hung his head and nodded. The boy ate half the sandwich quickly and then handed the other half to his older brother. He shook his head at his brother. "Eat it. Eat all of it."

"No," said the younger boy. "You eat some, too. You didn't eat any of the apple we had yesterday. You gave all of it to Amanda and me. Here, you eat it." He tried to get his older brother to take the half sandwich.

Lisa asked, "Why don't you trust us?"

None of the kids answered her. Eric walked over closer and put his hand on Lisa's shoulder. "You're cold and hungry. Where are you going?"

Amanda stopped eating long enough to say, "To look for our mommy."

Lisa looked at the oldest boy and said, "I know about being mistreated and not being able to trust anyone. So does my friend, Maria, who lives with us. When all the cars stopped working, some bad men took us and hurt us. Eric and his friend Mark rescued us from the bad men. Eric and Mark had to fight them to save us. They were starving us and didn't give us any water to drink. We would have died if Eric and his friend hadn't rescued us. Everywhere we've gone, we've run into bad people who are violent and hurt people. That's why we came up here. To get away from people like them. You can trust Eric. He's not a bad man. He's a very good man. He's a hero. We'll help you. That's the honest truth." She stared into the boy's eyes as she talked. The older boy's eyes filled with tears and he blinked. Lisa reached out and hugged him to her as he cried. She rubbed his back consolingly. "It will be all right now. You're with friends. You don't have to be strong all the time. There is no shame in needing a helping hand. Come on inside and we'll get you all warm and fed." She led all the kids inside.

Maria had seen them and heard some of what was said out there; she had fresh chocolate chip cookies waiting for them. Eric just shook his head at the sight of seeing the other two follow her and the oldest boy into the house. Amanda was still carrying the sandwich. He didn't think anyone would be able to get her to let go of it. It made him think of a mother duck and her little chicks, or maybe the pied piper. The youngest boy had stopped and picked the plate up to take it inside the house. Someone had taught them very good manners. Eric followed them inside.

Maria had found some kids' clothes upstairs in the two kids' bedrooms. The oldest boy was too big for them and too small for any of their clothes. They made do with a combination of what Maria and Lisa had. Lisa and Maria got them into the tub and washed up. They finally got the whole story out of them. Their mother had taken off over two weeks ago to go find food for them. When she didn't come back, they had gone over to a couple of friends' and neighbors' houses for help and were turned away at the door. They were not even allowed inside because they weren't their kids and not responsible for them. They had seen some people acting strange and violent, too. The oldest boy, Chris, was thirteen and decided to go look for their mother because one night someone had broken into their house. Chris had gotten all of them into a closet as several people were searching and ransacking the place. There had been gunshots. It scared him to death. He decided they couldn't stay there anymore after the intruders left. So, he, his ten-year-old brother, Ryan, and his five-year-old sister, Amanda, headed out on the back roads to go look for their mother. They hadn't found her and now they were hopelessly lost. They had been wondering around the forest for several days.

Four days later, Eric was on watch in the morning. He had taken to patrolling around the area every hour or so. He was thinking about how disappointed he had been to not find any batteries in the Wal-Mart truck. He had found some in the house, so they were good for a while. He was also thinking about how Maria's cough was getting better. How lucky they were to find this place. He just wished he knew what had happened to Mark, Abby and Channon. He wished they would hurry up and get here to enjoy this place, too.

Lisa wasn't sleepy, and Maria was busy doing something with the kids, so she decided to go join Eric outside on watch for a while. She carried two cups of hot chocolate. It was very cold outside now. Snow would be coming soon. She was so glad they all had warm clothes to wear now.

Eric saw her coming and smiled. She handed him a cup. "Thanks."

Lisa said with a smile, "It's the least I could do for my hero."

Eric scowled at her. "I wish you and Maria would knock that off."

Lisa laughed softly. "You are our hero for many things, Eric, so how can we knock it off? Besides, I brought you something."

He didn't say anything at first, just drank his hot chocolate. After a few moments he said, "Okay, what did you bring me?"

Lisa pulled a plastic bag out of her pocket and handed it to Eric with a smile. He smiled back at her. "I'm in paradise. We have hot chocolate and chocolate chip cookies, too. It doesn't get any better than this." He offered her a cookie and she took one out of the bag and started eating it. They munched in silence.

When they were done, they both started out on patrol. They went out a little further than normal, just checking the area out. They would walk for ten steps or so, then stop and listen if they could hear anything moving around. They had just started moving again when a voice softly called out, "Eric?" Eric and Lisa quickly turned around and both of their eyes went wide with shock. Abby stood there by a tree, decked out in a camo outfit with a knit cap on her head.

Chapter 15

Travel or Stay

"Most survivalists are independent types that simply want to be left alone."

Anonymous

Amy walked with Preston to his trailer. He told her about some of the things he and Joe had done to their places to prepare for the end of the world. Amy was truly amazed. He had a regular stove to cook on that ran off propane, or he could cook on the wood stove. He had lights hooked up, hot water, a washing machine and a toilet that flushed. She laughed in delight at the thought of it all. She had thought that they would be living in pretty primitive conditions; lanterns, and cooking on a little stove, maybe like the one he had back at the apartment. Kind of like they'd been living before they left. When he said it was a trailer, Amy thought it was some little tiny camper-like thing that they'd be living in. She didn't mind. She was completely surprised when they came out at the end of the path and there sat a mobile home. It must have been seventy or eighty feet long by about twelve or fourteen feet wide. It was just a single wide, but still it wasn't some little thing, either. It was very nice. There were steps leading up to a deck that connected to a big, closed-in porch. Wow. Preston told her he'd paid under $3,000.00 for it. Wow, had he gotten a bargain or what? He walked up the steps and unlocked the door, then did the same with the interior door.

He lit a lamp, then said he had to take care of a few things so they would have hot water. When he returned, he'd get a fire going in the wood stove. Amy said, "Okay." She sat down in the living room and looked around. It was very nice. It wasn't dusty, like she thought it would be. The wood stove was between the kitchen and dining area, almost in the middle of the trailer. The living room was on the end. Preston went outside. Amy saw wood and kindling stacked in a box next to the wall by the wood stove. She decided to get a fire going. She had grown up with using a wood stove for heat, she knew how to build a fire. She opened the stove up and got to work. They still had some water in their packs. He'd told her the propane cook stove was ready to use, so she got some coffee going, too.

Preston came in and said, "Wow, you got the fire going."

She rolled her eyes at him. "I'm not totally helpless, you know."

He laughed. "I can see that. We'll have hot water in about thirty minutes or so."

"It should be about time to add some logs to the kindling," Amy told him.

"Okay, I'll do that."

"Are you hungry?"

"Yeah, I am. Are you going to perform some more magic and whip us up something great from your bag of tricks?

She laughed at him. "That depends on what you have in here to cook on."

He smiled. "I have pots and pans, plates and glasses, and even things to use to eat from them with."

She put her hands on her hips. "Very funny. Ha, ha, ha." She started opening up cupboards, found a couple of frying pans and got to work. Everything was done in no time. "Where do we get water from to wash our hands?"

He raised an eyebrow at her. "Where do you normally get water from?"

She looked at him for a few moments, then turned around and tried the water tap. Water came out. She laughed. "I didn't think I'd see that again for at least five to ten more years."

He tipped an imaginary hat at her. "Ah, shucks, ma'am, nothing to it."

She laughed and curtsied. "Thank you, cowboy." They washed up and ate. Preston explained that he'd loved going to the alternate energy fair they used to host in Wisconsin every year. That was where he and Joe had bought their solar panels, charger, controller, fluorescent lights and twelve-volt water pumps. They were using one now. The batteries had been topped off with one lone solar panel as a trickle charge.

"Water should be hot now. Go ahead and take your shower, then we'll get some sleep." He showed her where the bathroom was. She got out some clean clothes from her pack and went into the bathroom. This was heaven, absolutely heaven to have a shower again. She had thought they'd be warming up water over a fire for a tub or something. He hadn't told her, and she couldn't blame him because she hadn't asked him, either. The water was super hot, too, just as she liked it. She didn't want to get out. She sighed. She'd better ,so he could have some hot water. She hadn't washed her hair because she didn't want to go to sleep with a cold, wet head. She felt great. It was amazing how everything seemed brighter after you washed off a few days' worth of dirt and grime, not to mention brush your teeth and rinse with real running water..

She came out to a warm trailer. Wow, this place must be really insulated to heat up that fast. She had put her dirty clothes in the hamper in the bathroom. She felt a bit awkward doing it, but after all, she was going to be living with him now. It felt a bit awkward because she'd never done that before. She had two guys that lived with her, but they had moved into her place. She was new to all of this.

Preston was sitting at the table drinking coffee, he smiled at her. She smiled back. "It warmed up in here fast. I'm impressed."

He said, "No, it doesn't take too long. This isn't too big of a place to heat up." He got up. "Do you want to go to bed right now or wait for me to get showered first?"

"I'll wait right here." He walked down the hall. She got some more coffee and realized he'd turned on some lights. This was great. She felt like doing a happy dance, but was too tired. She could hardly believe they were really there. Wow, he came back into the dining room and sat down. Yup, his hair was wet and he looked and smelled clean, so he must have taken a shower. What was he gone, maybe five minutes?

"Why are you staring at me like that?"

"That had to be the fastest shower in history."

He laughed. "It's the military training. Have to do everything fast."

She chuckled. "Is that why you eat so fast, too?"

"Yup," he said, "been doing it for over twenty years." She shook her head at him and yawned.

He stood up. "Come on, it's bedtime. We get to sleep as long as we like today. Joe said we don't have to do anything but rest up from the trip. We'd better take advantage of it. He can be a bit of a slave driver, Jane, too."

She said, "Put my pack out on the porch, okay? It still has some perishables inside and it's too warm in here to leave them just sitting in the heat."

"Okay. I have to stack the stove for the night, too."

"Okay, I'm going to the bathroom. I'll be back shortly."

They met in the dining room. He kissed her and then looked into her eyes. "The sleeping arrangements are up to you. I only have one big bed in my bedroom. The other rooms are full of supplies. If you want, I'll sleep on the couch. It's up to you."

She raised her eyebrow at him. "Don't you want to sleep with me anymore? So, what, was I a one night stand?"

He got a bit flustered, not sure how to answer that.

She laughed and kissed him. "I'm kidding. I don't expect you to sleep on the couch, if that's what you're saying. If you don't want to sleep with me, I can sleep on the couch and you can have your bed. I wouldn't want to take your bed away."

"I didn't want to presume anything. I didn't want you to feel obligated to do anything, either, since I was the one that took liberties and held you close when we slept. I wanted it to be your decision."

She touched his face tenderly. "You are really something, Preston. Something very wonderful and special. I am privileged to know you and to be here with you. I would like nothing better than to be held in your arms as we sleep." He smiled and kissed her.

He turned on the hall light and showed her which room they'd be sleeping in.

"A bed, a real bed," she said.

He laughed. "I agree." He turned off the hall light, then they climbed into bed and snuggled. She was asleep in about thirty seconds flat. He lay there thinking of things for a while, just enjoying holding her in his arms. It was a novel thing for him. Both his ex and Sharon didn't want to be held by him. It might mess their hair up or something. He liked to touch her silky hair. She didn't seem to mind at all.

They woke up late in the afternoon. Amy lay there for a while, enjoying the feel of Preston running his fingers through her hair. She turned around and kissed him. It was much later when they finally got up for the day. They spent their time getting to know one another, just as all couples do. Towards evening, a ringing phone startled her. She jumped in the air and whipped around.

Preston laughed. He went over to a cupboard, opened it, flipped a lid up, and picked up a phone handle out of a boxy looking thing and said, "Yes, Jane, what do you need?" Amy just stared at him in shock. It must be a wind-up phone was all she could come up with, the kind seen in World War II movies. Wow, they had everything. Preston hung up the phone and looked at her with a twinkle in his eyes. "I guess I forgot to mention the phone." She started laughing and couldn't seem to stop. "Are you all right?"

She had tears running down her face she was laughing so hard. She finally was able to gasp out, "The look on your face." She continued to giggle.

He kept staring at her like she had two heads. "What's so funny?"

"You looked like a little boy that was going to get his hand smacked for taking a cookie out of the cookie jar." He couldn't figure out what she was talking about. She just shook her head at him and continued to giggle.

He decided to ignore it and go on. "Jane wanted to know if we were free to come over for dinner. Do you want to?"

"Sure, why wouldn't I want to?"

He was relieved. "I don't know. I was just asking. I didn't want to make a decision without asking you first."

She kissed him. "Thank you for considering if I wanted to go over there or not. I really like Jane. So, if you want to go, we will, unless you have something else in mind for this evening?"

Preston sighed. "I'd rather stay here with you, but we should go over and find out what's up. Jane said she'd really like us to come over. She emphasized the really part." She reached over and patted his face. "Maybe something is up with Joan and Michael. We are kind of responsible for them since we brought them here. We'll have other nights together, I hope.

I know we'll have to start standing watches and such, and I want you to teach me to shoot properly."

He kissed her hand. "We'll start your real training tomorrow."

She smiled and turned to get her coat and hiking boots on. She also strapped on the 9mm. The world wasn't a safe place anymore. It wasn't really safe here, either, she reminded herself, no matter if it felt sort of normal.

Preston smiled when she grabbed the 9mm as if it was the most natural thing in the world. It was a habit she needed to keep. As soon as she got familiar with rifles, she'd be carrying one of those around, too. You never knew when you might have to jump into action immediately. He looked up at the ceiling and said a thank you to God for sending her to him. So far, they made a good team. He had his .45 Colt strapped on already. He grabbed his coat and the AR-15 as they walked out the door. Amy didn't even blink, but he knew better now. She was very observant and intelligent. He couldn't wait to get Joe alone and tell him how great she was.

They both kept a look out as they walked. Preston pulled her close. "You are beautiful. I'm very glad you're here with me."

She smiled at him. "Me too." He laughed softly and they continued to walk. She was constantly surprising him. He never knew what she was going to say. It made him feel glad and happy inside. He couldn't think of the last time he'd felt quite like this. Didn't matter, though; only now mattered anyhow.

They got close to the house and he pulled his radio out of his pocket . "Bravo Team, this is one three. We are at the door. Out."

"Roger that, one three. Out." The door opened for them and Jane was standing there, holding a rifle and the radio. She smiled at them. "Come on. Don't let the cold air get in." They quickly stepped in. "Coffee's hot and I made some cinnamon rolls this morning. Dinner won't be done for about an hour." Amy and Preston took off their coats and hung them on the coat rack by the door, then followed Jane into the kitchen where Joe, Joan and Michael were sitting.

Joe sighed, then turned to Preston and Amy. "Maybe you can talk some sense into her. We don't seem to be getting through to her at all about how dangerous it is to be traveling alone with a child." Preston and Amy exchanged a serious look, then turned to look at Joan.

"I have to get to my father's place," Joan said. "He's elderly and will need us there to help him."

Preston and Amy sat down. "If you're dead, how would that help him?" Preston asked.

"You don't know that I would die. Look at how nice you've all been. I'm sure I'll find others that can help us along on our trip, too."

Amy said, "I wouldn't count on that, Joan. You haven't seen what we've seen."

"I have to go," she said. "That's all there is to it."

Joe, Jane, Preston and Amy all exchanged looks. "Let me tell you what our trip was like," Amy said. "If we hadn't been armed, we would have been dead the very first night." She told them what had happened. She left out some things because Michael was there. But they understood what she was saying.

Joan said, "We'll take the back roads. We'll stay away from the main highways, because that's where most of the people will be."

"You don't know that," said Preston. "How many other people do you think might come to the same conclusion and use the back roads?"

"I thank you for everything you've done for us, but we're leaving in the morning. We have to."

Michael spoke up. "Mom, I want to stay here. They have chickens and everything. I like it here. I don't want to leave."

Joan said firmly, "We are leaving in the morning, Michael." Michael just hung his head down and sighed. He knew better than to argue when she used that tone of voice.

Amy reached over and touched Joan's arm. "Joan, you are making a big mistake. If these people have offered to let you stay here, you should. To go out again on your own would be insane. You two were already out of food and water. Think about Micheal's welfare. Do you want him to starve to death? What if no one else helps you? You can't carry as much food as you would need, even if you had it. It would weigh too much. Think about this logically, please. Think about what you'll be doing to Michael."

Joan drew her arm away from Amy and shook her head. "We are leaving in the morning. My father needs us. We'll go to him; that is final." Amy looked at everyone else; they looked as upset as she felt. But realistically, what could they do? Hold her here at gunpoint? Kidnap Michael? She was open to just about any suggestion to help Joan change her mind. No one said anything.

"Let me get both of you a cup of coffee," Jane said. She poured them each a cup.

Amy said, "Thank you, Jane, but you don't have to wait on us. We are quite capable of getting our own. You have too much to do around here to be waiting on anybody. We have to pitch in and do our fair share."

Joe laughed. "I like you, Amy. I like you a lot. I like the way you think."

Jane sat down and smiled at Amy. "You're welcome."

"I appreciate you making me feel welcome," said Amy, "but don't go to any extra trouble, okay? We're all adults, so we can do things for ourselves. That's my thoughts about it. I don't want to offend you or anything. I just think we should be practical." Joe and Jane were beaming at each other and they high-fived each other.

Preston smiled at Amy and kissed her. "You did good."

Amy looked at him like he lost his mind. "What are you talking about? Did good about what?"

Joe said, "Amy, I'm glad you are here."

"Dinner should be ready in about ten minutes," Jane announced happily.

Amy got up. "I'll help you get everything set up, Jane."

Michael and Joe kept everyone entertained throughout dinner. Preston and Amy didn't say very much. They both felt a bit let down that Joan was insisting on leaving and putting Michael into danger. They had rescued them from starvation and thirst. How many times did she think that was going to happen? Amy figured if someone was very lucky, they'd get helped or rescued once. Just once. Most people that she'd seen hadn't even been helped once. She couldn't believe that Joan thought other people would offer to help her. *How stupid could you be?* She was obviously not in her right mind. Anyone would think she was an unfit mother, taking her child into danger deliberately.

She felt like telling Joan that she could leave if she wanted to, but Michael was staying here. She knew she couldn't really do that, but where do one draw the line? She didn't know. When was it rescue or force? She didn't know. She needed to talk with Preston and see what his feelings were. Her heart ached at the thought of Michael suffering some of the things they'd seen.

After dinner, Joan and Michael went to the room they shared. The four of them sat and had another cup of coffee.

Preston said, "I hope she changes her mind."

"We tried everything we could think of to change her mind," Joe said. "Nothing reached her."

Amy said gloomily, "Not even Micheal's welfare seems to concern her."

Jane shook her head sadly. "Exactly my thought. She doesn't believe they'll run into danger out there. That everyone is going to be nice and kind and give them food and clothes everywhere they go."

Amy said, "I know. I'll just be sorry to see Michael leave tomorrow. I don't think she realizes how people can change when there is no law and order to call on."

Preston wanted to change the subject and get them all thinking of something else. "Amy wants to learn to combat shoot." He knew that would perk everyone up.

Joe looked excited. "We have to start training her tomorrow."

"Are you sure you want to do this?" asked Jane. "Do you know what you're getting yourself into?"

"Yes, I want to learn. I was saving up money for a gun and planning on taking a safety and shooting class; and a combat shooting course after I practiced, of course."

Joe rubbed his hands together, practically jumping up and down in his chair. "Damn, Preston we have our first student post EOTW."

Amy looked at Jane with confusion; Jane mouthed "End of the World." Amy nodded.

Preston laughed. "I knew that would perk you up."

Jane said, "Oh Lord, help us now. Amy, I hope you live through this. You have no idea what they'll put you through. Maybe you should let me show you how to shoot."

Both Preston and Joe practically shouted at the same time, "NO!"

"No way, Jane," Preston said.

Joe said, "She's our student. Amy said we would teach her, didn't you, Amy?" Preston and Joe waited, holding their breath and looking at her intently.

Amy looked at them all and wondering what was going on. She could tell Preston was leaving it up to her, but really, really wanted her to agree with Joe. "I want to be able to defend myself and all of you. Preston promised to teach me." Before she'd finished her statement, Joe was practically jumping up and down with glee.

"Yes!" Joe yelled.

"I hope you know what you are doing," warned Jane.

"Breakfast is at oh four hundred tomorrow morning, and your first class starts at oh five hundred," Joe advised. "I suggest, recruit, you get some rest, because you're going to need it."

Amy looked at Joe, and then at Preston, wondering what they were going to do to her. Shooting wasn't that hard to do. "Okay. I'll be there. Now, I'll help Jane with the dishes, since everyone else is sitting around on their butts being lazy and letting her do all the work. We also need to make out a rotating schedule for cooking and cleaning so we all do our fair share around here." She thought to herself, *now put that in your pipe and smoke it, Preston and Joe.*

Jane laughed really hard. "Amy, I really like you." Joe and Preston exchanged a confused look. How had they lost the upper hand of the conversation so quickly? Both men said they were going out on patrol.

Joe wanted to know what had happened to Sharon and how he got hooked up with Amy. Preston explained everything. He told Joe about the useless boyfriend Amy had broken up with, too. Joe laughed so hard when he heard about Amy tying up Sharon with duct tape. Preston told him all about the shootout and what Amy had done. Joe said they were going to have to train her hard to help her get over this. Now that she knows the reality of killing someone it might make her hesitate. With training, she'd react as she was taught; she wouldn't hesitate when it was time to shoot someone. Joe thought she might be made of the right stuff because of the logical way she had adjusted her aim. He mentioned it to Preston, and Preston agreed.

Later that night before Preston and Amy went to bed, she asked him about this oh four hundred thing and exactly what they planned on teaching her.

Preston said, "We'll teach you to combat shoot, but you have to learn a lot of other things first."

"Oh, okay. I like to learn new things."

Preston just smiled at her. "This may seem a little strange to you, but when I'm teaching you, I'm not your boyfriend, okay? I'll just be your instructor. Do you understand?"

"No. What do you mean?"

"I'll instruct you in all sorts of things and I'll correct you and criticize you. It won't be personal."

"Oh," said Amy. She was still confused.

"Okay, let me put it like this. As a boyfriend, I think you are great in everything you do and say. Do you understand that?

"Yes, I do. Thank you."

"As your instructor, I'll think you're an untrained greenie that is armed and dangerous. So when I criticize you, I'm criticizing an untrained greenie, not my girlfriend. Do you understand now?"

"I think so. You mean you'll yell at me and tell me I'm a stupid person, but I'm not supposed to take it personally, as if it was my boyfriend saying that to me. I'm supposed to pretend you're just some guy teaching me. Is that it?"

"Exactly. I won't yell at you unless you do something really dangerous and stupid. But Joe and I will criticize you on everything. Please don't take it personally, that's all I'm trying to say."

"Am I supposed to call you sergeant or lieutenant or something? Is this like Army training?"

Preston sighed. "Well, it will be a little, but we'll treat you a lot better than if you were in the Army."

"Okay. I'll remember that my instructor is an asshole and my boyfriend is wonderful. Does that cover it?"

"Ahh, yes," he said, chuckling. "That about covers it."

The next morning Amy was there, right on time. Joe said they'd start with the 9mm because she was familiar with it. They went over all the pieces on the pistol. Joe explained where they went, what they did, how to clean it, take it apart, and put it back together again.

Wow, Amy thought. She learned how to clean the clip and everything. Everyday she'd practice this before going out to shoot, and again after shooting. She needed to know how to do this even in the dark. When she got good at it, they'd move on to another weapon. It was a little after seven that morning when Jane walked Joan and Michael down to the gate. She called everyone on the radio and they came over and said goodbye.

Joe asked, "Is there anything we can say or do that will help you change your mind about leaving?"

"No there isn't," said Joan. Joe and Jane had made them up a small kit. They put in two pounds of rice; twelve assorted flavored bouillon cubes, a small bag of navy beans, four tea bags, and several small packets of salt and pepper they had collected from fast food places. They put it in a small bag and added one plastic container of water and a small pot from one of their mess kits. They stood there for a while and just watched them walk away. They all sighed, turned around, and went back to what they were doing. There wasn't really anything to say that hadn't been already said.

Joe and Preston took Amy out back to the shooting range for practice. They set up some targets. She got good pretty fast. Once she made the connection between the hand and eye coordination to the sight, she was good to go. She wanted to learn to shoot in the dark, too. Next time she was faced with shooting someone and couldn't see the sights, she wanted to do a lot better than she had before. They hadn't yelled at her, either. They just reached out and moved her hand or elbow, or said 'don't lean or stuff like that.' She had a lot of fun. Joe said she'd practice in the morning and the afternoon because they needed her up to speed fast. Everything they taught her would work towards the goal of combat shooting, to determine targets and non-targets in light or darkness. She'd be judged on timing and her choices of targets. But that would be after she learned the various weapons. Joe explained how important it was to know what each weapon could do, then you could plan your attack or defense accordingly. His motto was, "Know your weapons well." He explained that speed would come only with practice, practice and more practice. Then accuracy and speed could be worked on together. He said graduation would come when she could do all of this, work as part of a team of two and a larger team, and know the various positions, what the responsibilities of each were, and could do them proficiently.

Wow, her head spun, but she was excited. It was hard work holding your arms in the same position so long. Joe and Preston explained that working around the homestead will help her with the upper body strength that she needed. They'd teach her to shoot a compound bow, too. There would be times when stealth and taking out targets as silently as possible were very important. The exercise from all of this would enable her to have the muscle control to hold her weapon for long stretches of time and not over fatigue her muscles. She would be combat ready for whatever came their way. In the afternoons, after shooting practice, she'd use the bow and arrows for an hour. Jane came by in the afternoon and demonstrated a few things to her, too. Jane shot ten times in rapid succession with her pistol. She hit the kill zone almost dead center nine times, only one was a little apart from the others, but it was still in the kill zone. Amy sighed. She'd be happy if she could just learn to shoot as good as Jane. Ammo was precious and not too much could be wasted on practice. Jane told her she'd improve with practice. Jane also demonstrated to her how to shoot the bow while Preston and Joe explained.

When it was her turn to try, there had been a few mishaps that had everybody laughing. Amy had a big bruise on her right cheek because she held the string too close to her face and it smacked her. She learned real fast how to hold it close properly so that wouldn't happen again. This was a lot harder than she thought it would be. Her arms hurt long before the hour of practice was up. When she was done for the day, Preston took her inside the house and rubbed Aspercreme all over her arms and shoulders to help with the pain and stiffness. The women then prepared the evening meal together and it was decided that they would all eat at one place from now on except on special occasions. There was no sense in cooking at the house and at the trailer. It would save on supplies, too.

Amy got her backpack and emptied it of the leftover food. There was still quite a bit left since they'd arrived faster than they thought they would. Joe was as amazed as Preston had been. He loved that she had packed so well and crammed things all over the place. There wasn't one inch of wasted space. There was every kind of trail mix, and beef jerky. A lot of beef jerky. Amy explained the equipment she brought for the future and Joe dismissed it. He felt she'd wasted space with useless stuff. Amy didn't know how to explain that this equipment was important. She just let it go. She'd think about some way to use it to help them. Then maybe they'd change their minds.

Joe smiled with pride at Amy. They all had a very good chance of making it here. They had stocked up with supplies and equipment. They had chickens and a pig to slaughter. In one freezer, they had about half a cow left, and they'd hunt for more meat. They had buckets of fresh potatoes, carrots, onions and apples stored down in the basement. They did this every year, so they knew how much to store and were experienced in doing it. They always stored a lot more than they could use. Jane had canned a lot of things, too, with help from Joe. There was still a lot of food to dehydrate and can.

Joe and Preston sat down and worked out a watch schedule. They needed more people, and fast. More people increased their chances of survival. Doing this everyday for six hours was going to get old real fast, with no breaks or days off, because this had to be done along with all the other chores, too. The men decided to take the night watches because they were more experienced. They'd take turns for the 6:00 pm to midnight and the midnight to 6:00 am every other day. Amy and Jane could work out who got the 6:00 am to noon and the noon to 6:00 pm shift. This would have to do until they got more people. It would also work out better so that Jane could teach Amy and Preston about canning and dehydrating foods. They had to get ready for winter.

Both women spent the rest of the evening and night canning and dehydrating. The men went out and put up remote driveway sensors all over the place so they had a warning system and alarm if something got close. Joe and Preston had already reinforced the loft in the barn in preparation for the EOTW. The barn loft was the watchtower for the whole property. They had second-generation night vision to see in the dark. They placed a receiver for the driveway sensors in the loft, the trailer and the house. Each person was issued a radio and would listen to the watch person in the loft to learn what had set a sensor off.

Joe and Jane had already reinforced the house. They had quarter inch steel plates for the windows and doors on pulley systems that could be locked into place quickly if the need arose. They left one small window per room raised up for daylight to get inside. All other windows were already secured down tight. The men went into the barn and got the wheel barrow and the quarter inch plates for the trailer and secured it. They'd ended up making special frames sunk into the ground to support the weight of the steel. They made special supports out of two by tens to hold the sand bags. Cut into the walls beside the windows were a twelve-inch by twelve inch shooting hole that could be opened. These were covered over with steel wire like a cage trap, very strong and would keep out any grenades or anything else that someone might attempt to throw inside. When they were done with the trailer, they went back to the barn and grabbed a lot of sand bags, making several reinforced areas to observe from and be protected from bullets.

At about 8:00 pm they decided to take a break and went into the house for coffee and a cinnamon roll. The women had just finished cleaning up from canning thirty quart jars of tomatoes and had the dehydrators filled and going. Everyone sat down for coffee and a cinnamon roll. It had been a long day. Joe picked up his cinnamon roll and was about to take a bite when the alarm sounded. Someone was here. Preston grabbed his AR-15 and Joe grabbed his Remington pump with the extension tube. He had nine rounds of double aught buckshot. It would be a great deterrent to anyone. They both raced to the door and Preston jumped out to the right behind some sand bags. Joe jumped out to the left behind more sand bags. A stray cat was in the driveway frozen in fear. They both started laughing at once. They went back inside the house. Joe said, "I'm glad the watches start tonight. Then we'll be able to enjoy a meal or a snack in peace without stray cats wandering onto the driveway." Everyone laughed at that.

Preston said he was going to take the midnight to six watch shift that night. Joe protested and Preston told him that he was too keyed up to sleep anyway. Preston told Joe he'd better get a lot of sleep because he was old and needed the rest; they'd be cutting firewood the next day. It was an old joke between them, Joe was a few years older than Preston. Joe said he'd head up to the loft right now and Preston could come and relieve him at midnight. Preston and Amy headed back to the trailer. Jane had told Amy that she'd take the six in the morning shift to noon watch until Amy got familiar with everything, then they could switch off watches.

Preston had a few wind up clocks around that he'd picked up at flea markets so they knew what time it was. He also had a wind up alarm clock that he used to take with him when he was on assignment in the military. Amy had her grandmother's wind up watch, too. They each had a radio and a number to identify themselves with. The call sign for the loft was tower, the call sign for the house was Bravo Team and the call sign for the trailer was Delta Team. Joe's call sign was one one, Preston's call sign was one three, Jane's was one two and Amy's was one four. That would identify who called and from where to avoid confusion.

At a quarter to midnight, Preston filled his thermos up and kissed Amy goodbye. He grabbed his radio and said, "Tower, this is Delta Team one three, ETA in five minutes, over.

Joe picked up his radio and said, "Roger that, one three. Tower out." Preston went into the barn and climbed the stairs to the loft. Joe was sitting by one of the windows looking out. "It's been really quiet tonight. I started the log book."

"Good idea," Preston said. "It'll help us to keep track of how many animals are around, too. Might help us to fill the freezers up with meat."

"Yup, it will. I'm going to head on to bed. Amy will be up for her lesson soon. We can't forget about that, even with all the watches."

"Sleep good, old man."

"You keep that up and I'm going to have to whip your ass."

Preston just laughed as Joe left. It was a cool, but quiet night. Preston hoped it would hurry up and snow. That would cut the chances of most people traveling, especially way out here off the beaten path. Then he remembered they had a lot of wood to chop for winter. That would be easier without the snow. Oh well, can't have everything. He made a round, looking out of the shooting holes with the night vision goggles. They had two shooting holes on each side, reinforced by sand bags. Their night vision was powered by AA batteries, as were their flashlights and radios FRS. They recharged the batteries with a small solar charger.

The radio squawked, "Tower, this is Bravo Team one one. Anything going on?"

Preston picked up the radio. "Tower here, one one. Seen a couple of coons run through the yard. We should clean them out before they break into the chicken coop. We'll have roasted coon and make a Daniel Boone style coonskin hat."

Laughter came out of the radio. "Good idea, one three. I'll set out the cage trap tomorrow. See you in the morning. Bravo Team out."

Preston said, "Tower out."

Preston spent about ten minutes at each shooting hole, watching the property. He saw a couple of deer in the field. He also saw a coyote trot by. He recorded everything in the logbook. The logbook had a small blue LED light attached to it so you could see to write everything down. It would record the time the animal was seen, where the animal was seen, which way they came from and which way they were going. It was to keep a record of the wildlife, but it also kept the night from becoming too boring. About three in the morning, he saw a lone figure walking from the west heading towards the farm. This could be a scout or decoy. He quickly ran to the other areas and looked out. Nothing was there. He ran back and looked out front again. The figure was gone. *Was he seeing things?* He was sure he had seen someone walking. He continued to scan the area, *okay, there he was.* The brush had blocked his view for a few minutes. The figure was walking fast. *Better get Joe up.* He picked up the radio and said, "Bravo Team, this is Tower. Come in." He repeated, "Bravo Team, this is Tower. Come in." And again, "Bravo Team, come in."

Out of the radio came a rough reply, "What?"

"One lone figure turned into the driveway and is headed towards the house."

Joe said, "On the way. Stop him."

Preston yelled out, "Freeze!"

The figure froze in place, standing in the dark. The figure looked all around. His voice must have echoed off the house.

A voice called out, "It's me, Michael. Don't shoot."

Preston called out, "Michael, what's going on? Never mind, just stay there." Preston came down from the loft and went to Michael. Joe was on the porch behind the sandbags with the Remington in his hands, covering the figure.

They met in the driveway. "Michael, why are you here? Where is your mother?"

Michael, with tears in his eyes, screamed, "They got her! They took her! They got her!"

Joe said, "Who's got her?"

Michael was almost hysterical. "Two men. You've got to help her. Please, please help her. They got her."

"Damn it, I knew this was going to have a bad end to it," said Preston.

"Never mind that now," said Joe. "Get back up there in case they followed him." Preston turned around and ran back to the loft. Joe brought Michael inside. Joe said, "Okay, now calm down. What is going on?"

Michael took a deep breath. "We left, and about eight miles from here, two men invited us to lunch. Mom said okay. They seemed friendly. We followed them and walked into this yard; there was junk everywhere. There was this yucky looking bright orange truck and two trailers together. There were cats running all over the place. They grabbed my mom and threw me into the root cellar. They took her into the trailer. She was screaming and screaming." He put his hands over his face and cried. "They were hurting her."

Joe thought, *Damn those two white trash scumbags, Dan Wizel and Randy "Joey" Belimore. Randy was a useless asshole living off Social Security disability for being an alcoholic. Dan was a useless freeloader making his wife support him by working in the old folk's home. Randy had been married once but his ditzy wife finally smartened up and divorced him.*

Michael said, "I heard the fat one say he had someone to keep him warm now this winter."

Jane set down a cup of hot chocolate in front of Michael and put an arm around him. "Don't worry, we'll take care of this. Drink your hot chocolate now." She looked hard at Joe.

"Michael, stay here with Jane. I'll be back." Joe stepped out of the house and headed for the loft. He clicked his radio. "Tower, this is Bravo Team. ETA two minutes."

"Roger that. Tower out." Joe stomped up the stairs trying to contain his anger at those scumbags. He had been trying to remember what guns those two had. A Marlin semi-auto .22 and a 12 gauge single shot, maybe a 30-30. They were always out poaching deer while collecting food stamps. They were nothing but white trailer trash. When he entered the loft area, Preston asked, "Who has her?"

"Remember the two moron poachers we chased off the property last year? You remember the idiot with the blaze orange jacked up Ford pickup truck?"

"Oh yeah, the welfare queens?"

"Yeah, those two."

"What are they, about eight miles away?" asked Preston.

"Yup, those are the two losers."

"So, what's the plan?"

Joe pointed to the radio. "Wake Amy up and have her meet us over at the house at daybreak. Cancel training today. We have a plan to make."

Preston thought to himself, *we'll be doing the town a big favor by taking those two morons out.* He spoke into the radio. "Delta Team, this is Tower. Come in."

Amy's voice answered. "Tower, this is Delta Team one four. Over."

Preston said, "Delta Team, meet Bravo Team at daybreak. Training canceled. Tower out."

"Copy that, Tower. Delta Team out." Preston was ready to go over there and kill them both just on general principles. They were both society leaches and good for nothing scumbags. They were close to them, way too close for comfort. Eight miles wasn't far enough. Especially, with how many deer they poached a year.

Jane finally got Michael settled down and asleep. She had given him a mild sedative to help calm him. He was very worried about his mother.

Amy called on the radio. "Bravo Team one four is at the door. Over."

Joe answered, "Copy that, one four. Bravo Team, out." He opened the door and let her in. She was early. All three of them made a big breakfast while they waited for Preston to join them. Joe and Jane filled Amy in on what happened. Amy was pissed as hell at those scumbags and at Joan for leaving. Preston came in and kissed Amy good morning. Jane said they would eat and then have their meeting. There was very little talking as they all shoveled their food into their mouths with anger-filled eyes. When Amy had poured everyone more coffee, they started the meeting.

Joe presented all the known facts about Dan and Randy, as well as what had happened with Joan and Michael. "Each of you state your opinions about this situation and what we should do."

Preston said, "We have to rescue her because Michael is depending on us. We don't want or need those two that close to us, either. They've shown they are a danger. We need to take them out before they cause even more damage to someone."

"If Randy has raped Joan, which seems likely," said Jane, "with how much time he's had her now, we should cut his balls off as an example to other men. It will let everyone know that people around here will not put up with that kind of behavior. Dan should die for helping him kidnap Joan."

Amy asked, "Are they single men? Do they have family around here that could maybe go inside and get Joan outside for us?"

"Randy's wife divorced him," said Joe. "Dan has a wife and three children. He has two boys; I think they're about fourteen and twelve, and a ten-year-old daughter. I think Dan and Randy are distant cousins or something. There's another cousin that lives a couple of counties away, but we don't know him and he has nothing to do with them."

Amy said, "If we decide to kill Dan, what are we going to do with his family? We can't leave them defenseless without a man around to protect them and provide for them. I think we need to decide this first."

"Good point," said Jane.

"I guess we could give Dan a strong warning not to do anything like this again," suggested Preston.

Joe said, "They are pretty stupid, but I agree we can't just leave the wife and children out there to fend for themselves, even if they are trailer trash. We aren't bringing them here, that is final."

Everybody agreed.

"Randy will have to die," said Joe. "I can't see any other way to keep him from doing this again. He and Dan have been arrested more times then anyone around here for one thing or another. I believe, as you do, Jane, that he has already raped Joan."

"If he hurt her or raped her, he deserves death," said Amy. "It's not like we can have him arrested and sent to jail anymore. It's kind of extreme, but I see no other choice. We can't let this go on or more people around here will start doing things like this if they know they can get away with it. I'm not saying we should become the law around here or anything, but we should take care of this situation in a way that will make someone think twice."

"Okay, Preston, we'll use the bikes and get Joan."

"Wait a minute. What's the plan?" asked Amy.

"We won't know for sure until we get there," said Joe. "Our objective is to get Joan and deliver justice to Randy."

Amy said, "That's it? That's the big plan?"

"Yes, that's the plan." Amy looked at all of them as if they were insane.

"Joe and I will know what to do when we get there and assess the situation."

"How close do Dan and Randy live to each other?" Amy asked.

"They all live together," said Joe. "They took two trailers and put them together to make one big one."

"What do you think the wife and older children will do while you're delivering justice to Randy and a big warning to their father? Do they know how to shoot a gun? Do they have guns of their own? Who's going to cover them and keep them out of this if they do have guns? And who's going to guard the bikes? What if they take off on the bikes? Then you two would be stranded there with a hurt woman that may not be able to walk if she has been brutally raped."

Jane looked at Amy with a thoughtful expression, considering what she had said. Joe stared at Amy, thinking.

Preston said, "Joe, I told you she has a good brain."

Joe looked at Jane. "Will you go and guard the bikes and keep the others out of it?"

Before Jane could say anything, Amy volunteered. "I'll go with you and do it." Everybody looked at her. "I won't let them get near the bikes. I can protect them." She didn't want to put Jane in a position that she might have to kill someone. She knew what it was like. She would protect her from it as long as possible. "My aim has gotten good. I can hit what I aim at, especially since its light outside."

Joe said, "If one of the kids had a gun on Preston or me and intended to shoot us, could you shoot them?"

"Yes, I could. I'm not letting anyone shoot either of you. We need you around here way too much to let some low income trashy people who think they can do whatever they want get away with something like that. If it comes to that, I will shoot them. I won't like it, but I'll do it." That was good enough for Joe. He looked to Preston for his opinion on the matter since he knew Amy better than he did.

Preston stood up. "Let's go get Joan."

They put on camo face paint, pants and shirts. Joe grabbed the Remington; Preston had his AR-15 with a holographic sighting system and Amy had her 9mm. Amy grabbed a blanket for Joan in case she was injured. They got on the bikes and headed out. All three of them were intent on dealing out justice for this horrific crime. Jane said she'd get some supplies together for when they brought Joan back and she could examine her and assess the damage.

They stopped about two miles from the place. Joe said, "We should hide the bikes in the brush away from the driveway. Amy, you come closer to the trailer, but stay out of sight. Don't show yourself unless you have to. You can keep an eye on what's going on. Always stay between the bikes and the trailer and make sure no one gets by you. Preston and I will make our way around and come in from the other side. We'll do what we have to and get out of there fast. Agreed?" They both agreed with him. They got back on the bikes and headed towards the trailer. They stopped a ways down from the trailer on the dirt road. Trees and brush hid them. They stashed the bikes. Preston and Joe took off to the other side and Amy headed towards the trailer. She watched Preston creep up to a woodpile and slip around the back. Joe went over to the root cellar and was crouched down by the door. They could see the board that Michael had kicked off to escape lying on the ground. They waited for quite awhile for someone to come out and make some kind of a move. Finally, the door opened up and a kid came out. They walked over to the root cellar and saw the missing board. They ran back inside yelling, "Dad, Dad, he got away." Soon Randy and Dan came outside, walking towards the cellar with rifles in hand.

When they almost got to the root cellar, Joe stood up with the Remington 12 gauge pointed at their heads. Preston stepped out from behind the woodpile and put the AR-15 barrel right against Randy's head and said, "Drop the guns right now." Both men froze in fear. They were not prepared for an unexpected attack. These two who had them in their sights were hardened men and were not playing games. The two scumbags recognized this right away and didn't move a muscle.

Joe said, "We want the woman you kidnapped yesterday."

Dan said, "You got the wrong place, man. We never touched no one."

Preston racked back the release bar so a fresh shell slammed home. "One more lie from either one of you and Randy's head will explode." Randy was shaking like a leaf in a strong wind.

Joe pointed the Remington 12 gauge at Dan's right eye. "That is a good idea. One more lie and we kill you both."

Dan said, "Okay, okay, okay she's inside. She's okay, really."

"Turn around real slow and tell them to let her go," Preston said.

Dan yelled out, "Let her go. Let her go right now."

Dan's wife stepped out on the porch with the 30-30 in her hands. Preston could just barely see Amy in the brush with her 9mm pointed at Dan's wife. Dan's wife said, "You let my husband go first." She whipped the 30-30 up and aimed it at Preston. Preston shifted his gun to cover her on the porch. "We don't want trouble with you. Just let the woman go or hell on earth will start. Right here, right now."

Dan's wife said, "Dan, what do I do?"

Joe jammed the barrel of the 12 gauge against the back of Dan's neck. "Tell her to release the woman or I swear to God you'll be the first to die."

Dan yelled out in a squeaky, high pitched scared voice, "Let her go. Let her go right now."

Joe whispered into Dan's ear, "Good job, Danny boy. You just might live through this after all."

The door opened up and Joan stepped outside. Her face was bruised; she had two black eyes that were swollen almost shut. A couple of the spots were still oozing blood and her lips were swollen and split open. She was holding her side as she slowly made her way down the stairs.

Preston was outraged. He jammed the barrel against Randy's neck and said through tight lips stiff with anger, "You're a real tough guy, huh? A real pussy beating up a woman, you piece of shit." Randy was silent and didn't even seem to be breathing. "Joan, come over here and get behind me."

Once she was past them, Joe said, "All right, Danny boy, you walk to the house and don't turn around." Dan started walking; every step was faster than the last one.

Randy started to take a step away. "Not so fast, you pussy. We're going to have a little talk."

Joe and Preston couldn't see Joan. They had their eyes trained on Randy. Joan grabbed Dan's .22 rifle off the ground, lifted it, pointed it at Randy's head, and pulled the trigger. Blood and brains splattered everywhere. Randy fell forward like someone had pole axed him.

Preston whipped around so fast it was almost a blur. He grabbed Joan's arm, trying to bring it and the rifle downward. "Enough."

Joan screamed, "No! They all have to die for what they did to me!" She kept trying to lift the rifle up to shoot at Dan. Dan, hearing the shot, took off running for the porch.

Preston said, "Cover me," as he yanked down hard on Joan's arm and dragged her behind the root cellar. Dan ran up the porch and was in the house in a flash, leaving his wife standing on the porch with her mouth hanging open. Joe didn't want to shoot her, so he fired twice quickly over her head. That definitely set her in motion. She ran inside the trailer. Joe took cover, too.

Joe yelled out, "Enough. No one else has to die, justice has been served." Silence came from the house.

Preston reached down and pulled the Marlin out of Joan's hands. She had pure hatred in her eyes. "We need to kill them all. The thing he called a wife is an evil piece of shit. Those… those evil spawn of the Devil's children of theirs… they all have to die."

Trying to break her out of this Preston said, "Justice was served. You are free now. The guy that hurt you paid the price. Now it's time to go before one of us gets hurt."

Joan screamed, her eyes wild. "Too late for that. I have already been beaten countless times and raped. Where the hell were you two when they took me and did this? Where the hell were you? If you are not man enough to do this, give me that gun back and I'll kill them all."

Preston shook her and got face to face with her. "We don't know you. We just barely met. We tried to tell you to stay with us, that it wasn't safe out here anymore, but you were too damn stubborn to listen to us. This is your own fault. So, don't you even try to blame us for this. Now, you want to go on a killing spree. Fine. Here's the rifle. Go ahead and kill them. The rest of us are leaving. We'll raise Michael without you." He turned and started to walk away.

Hearing her son's name snapped her out of her murderous rage. She started crying and fell down to the ground. Preston stepped back towards her when the sound of glass breaking was a sign to get the hell out of here. The 30-30 roared and a bullet hit the root cellar. Preston grabbed her arm and they all took off running, staying low. They heard the sound of two 9mm shots in return fire as Amy retreated back to the bikes. Joe didn't look back because he didn't want to kill Dan and leave his children fatherless. They all jumped on the bikes and were off. Amy sat backwards to cover them from the rear. The two men pedaled like mad for about a mile. They quickly stopped and Amy turned around so the bike would be more balanced. They took off again; about thirty minutes later they were back at the farmstead.

Joe called on the radio to let Jane know they were outside. The door opened and Amy helped Joan up the stairs to the porch. The women went into a room that Jane prepared and looked Joan over. Joan was pretty beat up. They got her into the bathtub and then Jane applied a few butterfly bandages where her skin had split. They helped her to the room where Michael was sleeping so she could see he was all right. Jane gave Joan something to help her sleep and got her tucked in bed. Jane and Amy went into the kitchen. They told Jane everything that had happened. Joe said he was way too keyed up to sleep and told everyone else to go to bed and get some rest. Joan and Michael would need them when they woke up. Preston and Amy headed to the trailer.

When they got inside, Amy put some coffee on. Preston just held her for a while. "What a morning," Amy said.

"Yeah."

Amy grabbed the gun cleaning kit and started on the 9mm and Preston started breaking down the AR-15. Preston asked, "Why did you fire at the trailer?"

"When you guys were getting away, that asshole swung his rifle around to fire at you. I just fired over the trailer to keep him from firing long enough to get you out of sight. I wasn't trying to hit him, because we had decided he would live for his children. After seeing Joan, though, I think I would have changed my mind."

"Thanks. That was good thinking. Don't think we didn't consider it, because we did. I was so pissed when I saw her. Did you see when she went off on me?"

"Yes, I did. She wasn't in her right mind, you know. So don't take anything she said personally. She'd been through hell." Preston started to say something and she held her hand up., "Yes, I know she brought all of this on herself, but don't you think she's been punished enough for it? I think she's a lot wiser now."

"Yes, she's been punished enough for her mistake."

"You can't blame her too much for wanting to kill them all. She told Jane and me some really disgusting things about all of them. I'm not sure we made the right decision, but it's too late to change that now. I just don't know about killing children, though. I don't think I can do that. Maybe wound them or something."

"Just remember that too kind of a heart may end up getting you killed," said Preston. "I wouldn't like that."

She looked up at him and smiled. "I'll keep that in mind."

"Smart ass."

Amy laughed. "There are other parts of me that are smart, too, you know, not just my ass."

Preston laughed out loud. "You are a laugh a minute. Aren't you done yet?"

She looked at him. "I was done first. I'm just messing around now, keeping you company while you slowly clean your rifle." He put the AR-15 down, stood up, and went to grab her. She giggled and ran down the hall with Preston close behind her.

Joan slowly recovered and healed. She was a little more serious and quieter now than she'd been before. Michael didn't like to get too far away from her. She was in the blue, purple and yellow stage of her bruises and looked awful. It was going to be awhile before she'd be fully healed. Emotionally and mentally, who could say. She didn't talk about it much. She pitched in and helped with chores. Michael learned to feed the chickens and collect the eggs. He started naming the hens and the two roosters they had. The chickens really seemed to like him.

Preston, Joe, and Jane started to hunt for meat. They'd been at it for two days. Joe missed a shot at a nice buck. No one else had seen much of anything. While they were out hunting, Amy spent her time re-reading *Buckshot's Complete Survival Trapping Guide* again.

Joan and Amy were in the house cooking dinner. Amy had some spare time while everyone else was out hunting. Jane had shown her a lot of game trails and the ones that they had their deer stands on. She decided to grab six camlock snares for deer and set them out. She didn't mention it to anyone just in case she didn't do it right. It might take awhile to perfect the skill. She had a nice time walking around and enjoying being outdoors. She stopped at the trailer and added some logs to the wood stove while she was out. She was back inside long before everyone else came back from hunting. Preston had the six to midnight shift tonight. He would be going to the loft as soon as he was done eating. They had taken to playing cards and other games in the evening to pass the time. She would stay for a while tonight, then spend some time with Preston on watch before heading over to the trailer. When Preston was in the loft, he wanted her to let him know when she was going out so he could keep an eye on her to be safe. She called him her "eye in the sky." She could always make him laugh. They had changed her class time to later in the morning because it was interfering with everything. Joe was disappointed that they couldn't make her start at oh four hundred hours everyday. He was in love with starting new recruits at that time. They all met at the house at 6:30 for breakfast. The person that had the midnight to six shift could go to bed after the meal. The others went out hunting. They were spending a lot of time and effort, but they weren't getting anything. This morning, after they got to the house, she remembered the snares. She told Preston she had to go check something and would be back in a while. He was helping Jane fix something on her bow. Amy headed outside with her flashlight.

It was a really cold morning. It would be time for snow before too long. She went down the first trail; that one was empty. She really hadn't expected to get anything. She checked the next trail, and there, right in the middle of the trail, was a dead deer. She jumped up and down and did a little happy dance. Now, she could prove what she brought hadn't been useless equipment and she hadn't wasted pack space. She went down the next trail and there was another dead deer. The next two were still set. She went and checked the last trail and there was another dead deer. She laughed out loud. She got three deer and hadn't even gone out hunting. She ran all the way back to the house and went inside.

Preston saw her standing there and she waved him over. "What has you so excited and smiley?"

"Come on, I have something to show you."

"What?"

She laughed and said, "It's a surprise. Come on."

They went outside and Preston said, "Is this going to take very long? I need to get to my tree stand. We really need the meat."

She smiled at him and didn't say anything. She bypassed the first trail since she hadn't gotten anything with that snare. They got to the second trail, and when they got close to the dead deer, she turned on her blue light and showed Preston.

"Is that a dead deer?"

"Yes, it is."

"How did you do that? I didn't hear you shoot it."

"You didn't hear anything because this kills them silently."

He looked at her. "What killed it silently?"

"My snare." He bent down and looked; sure enough, there was a twisted up snare around its neck.

"Holy shit. You got a deer with a snare."

"Come on, I have more to show you." She turned and walked away down the trail.

He said, "We have to take this back to the meat shed and hang it up."

"Come on. Follow me." She kept walking. She could hear Preston following. She showed him the other two dead deer.

He laughed. "I don't believe it. You got three deer and didn't even go out hunting. We've been hunting for days and didn't get anything. Come on, they aren't going to believe this. We need help dragging these back to the meat shed." They walked back to the house. Preston kissed her and said, "You did real good, babe."

Joe just finished eating his breakfast. Jane was picking up her bow to go to her deer stand. "Joe and Jane, we need your help with a few things," Preston said.

Both of them looked at them. "Help with what things?" asked Joe.

"Get your coat and gloves, because you have to see this to believe it. Just come on." Preston had their curiosity up now and they did as he said. They walked over to the first dead deer. Preston showed them what Amy had done.

Joe said, "I don't believe this." He looked all around the deer for a gunshot wound, thinking they were pulling a joke on him or something. He couldn't find one.

Preston said, "Just follow us now." He led them to the other trails and showed them the other two dead deer.

Joe was stunned speechless. He stood there and finally said with an incredible look on his face, "Let me see if I get this right. Amy had never ever gotten a deer before in her life. She had never put a snare out before, either. She watched a DVD and read a book from this Buckshot guy and put out six of these snares yesterday evening. She spent about half an hour walking around making these deer sets. This morning you checked them and you had three dead deer."

Amy said, "Yup, that's it exactly."

Joe blinked at her and then said, "I owe you a big apology. That was not wasted space or useless equipment. What the hell, we've just been wasting our time out here and you come along and get three deer after a half hour of effort. We've never gotten three deer at the same time, or even in the same day. You go out with six of these snares for the first time and overnight you get three deer." He shook his head. "We have to gut them." When they were done, Joe looked over at Preston. "Well, pick one and start dragging it. The women can drag one and I'll grab the last one. Let's get these to the meat shed."

Preston was smiling. "She's my girlfriend. My girlfriend did this."

Joe said, "Just shut up, grab a deer and start dragging."

"She's my friend, too," said Jane. "My friend did this."

Amy said, "Jane showed me where the game trails were." Joe looked at his wife and Jane stuck her tongue out at him. Preston laughed and laughed. Joe had been lording it over him for years that his wife hunted. Well, now it was Preston's turn to rub it in with what his girlfriend could do. They all heard Joe muttering to himself all the way back to the meat shed.

When the women were dragging the deer, Jane asked, "You read how to do this in a book?"

"Yes. I went over it again yesterday to refresh my memory before I went out and set the snares."

"Can I borrow the book? I have to learn how to do this. This is so cool. Good job, Amy, three deer." Jane laughed with delight at her friend.

"I also have some of his DVDs, too. We can watch them if we ever find a DVD player that works. I have some snares for raccoons, too. I want to put some out by the coop to protect the chickens."

Jane asked, "Can I come along with you and help?"

"Sure, it's not hard to do. One thing this guy Buckshot says over and over again is to study the wildlife around you and their habits. Learn from them; what they eat and what they do. That's the secret to catching them."

They got all three deer hung up. Joe said they'd start to process them in a few days. They'd show her how to cut them up and wrap them for the freezer in the garage. They had two freezers hooked up to a solar panel. She smiled and thanked them. She didn't say anything because she didn't want to hurt their feelings any more then she already had with getting the three deer in one night, but she already knew how, sort of. She had never done it but had watched the DVD *Buckshot's Preparing Wild Game For The Table* a few times. She had paid close attention to all the details for processing a deer because it seemed most likely that at some future time she would be processing a deer.

Amy was on top of the world. She felt like she was finally a useful part of this group with a skill of her own to share. All day long, Preston kept coming up to her and hugging and kissing her and telling her how great she was. Jane called everyone on the radio and said their weekly meeting would be starting in fifteen minutes. Amy and Jane had talked earlier that morning and came up with a few suggestions. The way they were doing things now was hard on the men, and they wanted to do more. Everyone got there on time and gathered around the table. Joe started the meeting. They'd do a weekly progress report to let everyone know what was what.

Jane reported that with Joan and Amy's help, the dehydrators and the vegetable canning was almost completely done. They were able to get all three of the canning pots going with all of them working together. They had made two extra homemade dryers to dehydrate with and had them going almost nonstop, so they were almost done. Now they were getting ready to make applesauce and apple cider, and then after that, they were canning pie and cobbler fillings. Jane said they were all going to have to take a few days off from other work to go pick apples and other fall fruits and process them. Everybody nodded. Wow, applesauce and apple cider, Amy couldn't wait. Michael seemed pretty excited about it, too.

Next, Preston gave a report on the progress of how much wood had been chopped and how much still needed to be done. Thank God, Joe and Preston had already cut up the downed the trees into chunks with the chain saw earlier in the year or this would be worse than it was already. There was a lot of wood to split for the various wood stoves. They were trying to get it all done before the snow started.

Michael was a big help. He put the split pieces into the wheel barrow, then stacked them in the woodpiles for the house and the trailer. He was definitely earning his keep. Everyone gave him a lot of praise for his hard work. Joe announced that they had all the meat they were going to need; it freed them up for all the other projects that needed to be done. Joe and Preston looked tired. With their weird watch schedules and sleeping times, they weren't getting enough rest. They were out chopping wood everyday. Amy said she had something to discuss with everyone about the watch schedule. Joe decided that they didn't need watches in the daytime because they were all out and about the farm all day long anyway, and they were all armed. The sensors were up and would notify them if someone approached. This way they could all help prepare for winter.

Amy said she thought they should include the women and Michael in the watches at night and change it to four-hour watches. Then all of them would be able to get more sleep, which would mean they would be more productive during the day. Joe and Preston started to protest and she held her hand up and asked them to please wait until she was finished, then they could voice their concerns were about what she was saying. Plus, this new schedule would give two women and one man the week off. It would be a morale booster because then everyone would have more free time. Plus, it would give everyone experience with watches and there would be three well-rested people that could take over if someone got sick and wasn't able to do their watches or they were attacked. She said one week Joan would have the 6:00 pm to 10:00 pm shift, Jane would take the 10:00 pm to 2:00 am shift, then Joe would have the 2:00 am to 6:00 am shift. They had given the men the most dangerous watch time because they were the ones with experience. Joe had told her that was the most dangerous part of any nighttime watch. They would have this schedule for one week. It would give Michael, Preston and myself the week off. Then it would be Michael's turn to have the 6:00 pm to 10:00 pm watch because everyone was still up at that time and could respond if he spotted anything. Then she would take the 10:00 pm to 2:00 am shift and Preston would have the 2:00 am to 6:00 am shift. They would do this and give Joan, Jane and Joe the week off. The men could spend the first week helping all of them learn how to do this properly. Joan, Michael and she would spend time each day learning to shoot; in the evenings, they'd learn about the responsibilities of being on watch. She told them she was done and sat down. Joe and Preston talked about the new schedule for a while, since they were the experienced security people. They agreed with Amy's reasoning and decided to go ahead and try it and see how it worked out. It would be better than what they were doing now. The men were tired. They had been running on three to five hours of sleep a night depending on what was going on. So, it was decided that Joan, Jane, and Joe would start tonight. They were all a bit excited. It would give each couple a whole week of nights together. Joan wasn't quite healed yet, but she wanted to do her part and she had the easiest shift, so it shouldn't be too hard. Jane and Amy had worked this out with Joan so she would be around during the nighttime for Michael if he needed her. Both Jane and Amy had read that it was important for children to have the security of a bedtime ritual with a parent. Michael hadn't been going to bed until 11:00 pm or midnight every night. Joan said he had always been a bit of a night owl. She had him read and do some scholarly lessons every night before bedtime to tire him out.

They had dinner and then Preston and Amy left to go to the trailer. Joe had slept for four hours that afternoon and said he would show Joan what to do. He was issuing Joan and Michael a radio, too, since they were officially part of the security team now. Michael was jumping up and down at this news. Preston and Amy laughed all the way to the trailer. When they got inside, Preston put some logs into the wood stove. They sat down and discussed making a schedule out that about every four to five hours one of them would need to come over to the trailer and add a couple logs to the wood stove. It was getting colder out and they didn't want any of the pipes to freeze. They had gotten involved in what they were doing around the place preparing for winter and had forgotten to come over to the trailer and add logs a few times. It was a pain in the ass to keep making a fire each time they forgot.

They sat drinking coffee in the living room and Preston said, "I didn't think you could do it. When you said you would figure a way for us to have full nights together, I thought that would be impossible until we could get more people here to share the watches. But you did it. It's a very good plan. I, for one, really appreciate it. A full night's sleep was something I thought I wouldn't be having for a long time."

Amy smiled at him. "You grumbled enough about it that I started to pay attention to how tired you and Joe really were. So, I approached Jane and we put our heads together and came up with this schedule. Besides, since we're all part of a group, we should all know how to stand watch and understand the security here."

Preston kissed her. "You are brilliant. Have I told you lately how wonderful you are?"

She laughed. "Not today." She stood up. "I'm going to unpack my backpack." Preston had a couple of drawers in his dresser that were empty and she finally had a little extra time this evening, so she wanted to get that out of the way. She took it into the bedroom and started taking things out. Preston came into the bedroom to talk to her.

She got her clothes put away and was putting her personal things into a small cedar box that Preston had given her. She pulled out a heavy bag of coins and was ready to put them into the cedar box when Preston asked, "What's in there?"

"My grandfather and uncle left these coins to me in their wills. They called them our insurance policy. I was never to sell them or cash them in. They could only be used if I was destitute or about to be thrown into the streets or another depression happened."

"Can I look at them?"

"Sure. They're gold and silver." She handed them to him.

Amy removed the rest of her stuff out of the backpack from all the pockets and found places to store things.

"Amy, you had a fortune here."

She turned and looked at him. "I know. But I promised I would never spend them unless there was a crisis of some sort. Now that money doesn't mean anything, they're only worth their weight in gold and silver."

He got up and went into the other room and came back with a coin book. "I thought so. These $5.00 gold coins are 1845 O Liberty Heads. They were worth $10,000.00 each." He started counting. Amy had twenty-one of them. They were all in mint condition, too. They were still in their square white cardboard sealed containers with laminated paper over the top. He guessed it was to protect them from the air and elements. They were all certified with dated papers of purchase. They were bought in the 1970s. Her family had bought them as soon as it was legal for Americans to buy and own gold. He continued to look through the coins and there were thirty-five Morgan silver dollars. They were certified and purchased in the 1960s. They were .77344 troy ounces of pure silver. They were $65.00 each and in mint condition. There were various other gold coins from several different countries, too. He didn't know what they had been worth, but if they were anything like the others, they would have been worth a lot. She handed him another little bag that had nine rolls of twenty-five each of Canadian Maple Leaf $5.00 silver coins. The appraisal receipt said one roll was worth $549.00; they were un-circulated and in mint condition. Their pure silver content was .9999. *Holy cow,* Preston thought.

She then handed him several rolls of nickels. He looked at her questioning. Amy said, "Nickels are worth about six cents of metal." She handed him several rolls of pennies. "Copper pennies dated pre-1983 have about three and a half cents worth of copper in them."

Preston asked, "How did your grandfather and uncle get into all of this?"

"When they lived in England, they inherited a book store from their father. They worked in there since they were small children and knew everything you could think of that had anything to do with rare or unusual books. After their father died, they ran it for a long time. They bought and sold rare books and first editions. When my grandmother died, they sold it and moved to northern Wisconsin. They opened up another bookstore there. When they were in England, they collected stamps. Well, when they got here, they decided to sell the stamps and buy coins instead. They always called it our insurance policy against anything happening and we would never be destitute or get thrown out of our house. They were big on worrying about taxes and not trusting governments. These coins were not to be used for anything else, no matter how much they might be worth to collectors or on the open market."

He said, "Your grandfather and uncle were smart men. I really would have liked them." She kissed him and smiled. "Well, I'm pretty sure in the future we'll have trading and a monetary system based on metals again. You will be one very rich lady."

She smiled. "That's the plan, anyway. These coins are only worth the metal now. It will depend on what it can get us in the future as to how rich we will be."

"I have a lot of silver coins, too. Both Joe and I bought bags of junk silver, so they are worth whatever silver content they have in them. Well, I don't think we will be poor, anyway."

"Well, maybe we can think about setting up a bank in the future. We'll have enough to do that with if you and Joe have a few bags of junk silver coins we can get into circulation from buying goods and maybe giving some loans out. It was just a thought, anyway. We can talk about it later, just an idea to keep in mind for the future."

Preston said, "I like the way you think. We could actually start an economy that is backed by something real."

"Maybe tomorrow you could find a secure place to put these. I would really be pissed if someone broke in here and stole them."

"Good idea. I'd be very pissed, too. I'd have to hunt them down and retrieve them. Very messy business doing that."

She laughed at his exaggeration and the menacing face he made. She put the bags of coins into the box on the dresser and her backpack into the closet. She turned to him with a pondering look on her face and put her hands on her hips and said with a southern drawl, "My, we have a lot of time on our hands. Whatever will we do with it?"

Preston laughed. He reached out and pulled her down on the bed and whispered in her ear with an exaggerated John Wayne type of accent, "Don't worry, little lady, I'm here to rescue you from free time and boredom." She giggled.

Chapter 16

Fight To The Death

"Dream as if you'll live forever, live as if you'll die today."

James Dean

Junior slept fitfully in the chair, waiting for morning. He kept dreaming of Marion lying in the snow surrounded by blood, with dogs eating their fill. Sometimes in the dream, his dad would also be lying on the ground, too. If it wasn't the dreams waking him up, it was the dogs outside, howling, scratching and throwing themselves at the doors. Every once in awhile, the dogs outside would get quiet. It raised his hopes that they'd finally given up and taken off. But, the growling, scratching and the sound of their bodies hitting the doors would start again and dash his hopes. He sighed in frustration. He'd come up with a plan. He was just waiting for dawn so he could get back to Gayle. He was worried about her. He still hadn't come up with a way to tell her about her mother—how did you tell someone something like that? He didn't know. He felt a bit guilty about his part in letting Marion out the door. His instincts had screamed at him that it was a big mistake, even as he was doing it. He should have refused to do it. He knew Gayle felt guilty about Marion taking off, too. How was she going to react to the news that letting Marion leave killed her? How in the hell had everything changed so fast once again? Is this what life was going to be like now? If so, he wasn't too sure he was up to the task of handling it. It seemed that every little decision you made had unseen and very unforgiving results.

It was a whole new way of looking at things. Going into town on the fateful day the world ended had caused his dad's death. The simple decision to set some muskrat traps had resulted in the death of two men. There was someone in the woods out there somewhere now, taking an animal out of his traps every few days. Whoever was doing it probably needed the food to survive. That might be a real danger in the future, too. What would this person do when he pulled all his traps and snares and there wasn't anymore free food to take? Would this person come looking for them and cause even more trouble than those other two hunters had done? And of course, letting Marion go outside to cool down from the argument had caused her death. He felt overwhelmed and uncertain about everything.

He was only eighteen and had no experience in handling things like this. It pissed him off. What the hell was he supposed to do? He slammed his fist down hard on the arm of the chair several times. Damn, and now dogs were forming huge packs and were a danger, too? Was there even anything left of the world that was worth going through all of this for? He'd been going through one thing after another ever since the world had ended. If the world was this bad now, what was it going to be like in six months, a year, or two years? Would the world ever be a good place again? Would he ever be able to go outside and feel happy and content again? Or would it be this way from now on until he died some horrible way, too? His stomach let out a hungry rumble. Damn, he was hungry.

His heart constricted in terror at the thought that he could lose Gayle, too. He would be totally alone again. But, this time it would be so much worse then it was before. He hadn't known what it was like to have someone live with you that shared everything like Gayle had done with him. He had to protect her no matter what. No way was he going to lose her. He had to get out of here. Someway, somehow he'd get back to her and keep her safe. He had to. The hell with everything else right now. Gayle was the only thing that mattered to him now. He started to pace the living room floor with determination, waiting for dawn to arrive. He kept his eye on the window facing east for the first hint of light.

Junior lined up the folded towels in front of him on the table. He wrapped two towels around the lower part of his leg and duct taped it. He made it loose enough that he could bend his knee. He did the same with his thigh. He did the other leg and his arms, too. He put two around his neck and taped them pretty tight, remembering how Marion's throat had been torn out. He was determined to live through this. He was tightening the duct tape on his upper right arm when he glanced out the window at the lightening sky and saw a figure coming down the road in the distance towards the house. He studied the figure intensely, trying to think why it looked vaguely familiar. When he realized who it was, it sent an electrical shock all through his body. He grabbed his rifle and ran outside, recognizing the danger she was in.

He jumped off the porch and ran as fast as he could. The roll of duct tape was trailing behind him, still attached to his right arm. As he got closer, he screamed out, "Gayle, shoot the dogs! Shoot them! Shoot them!"

Gayle stopped, looked puzzled, and then looked around at all the dogs that were everywhere. She turned back towards him and shouted, "What? Why?"

Junior screamed, "They'll attack you! Shoot them now!" The dogs had been slowly surrounding her and were moving steadily closer.

He got to her just as a dog lunged. He aimed and fired. Blood splattered everywhere as it dropped, squealing and kicking its legs out, before it lay still in a pool of blood. She looked down at the dog in shock.

Another dog charged. He yelled, "Shoot it!" She brought the Marlin bolt action .22 up and shot. The dog yelped, but kept on coming. "Keep shooting it until it stops attacking!" Gayle fired again and again, the dog's blood leaving bright red stains in the snow around them. Another dog charged at him; he shot it in mid-lunge. It skidded along the ground, leaving a trail of blood.

Gayle stared at the dogs in horror. "Why are they doing this?"

"They're starving and attacking people now. They have been eating the dogs I've killed, too. I stayed in that house over there all night and they had the place surrounded, trying to get inside to eat me all night long."

"Holy shit."

"Just keep shooting them. How much ammo did you bring?"

"I don't know. I just grabbed a handful out of the box and put them in my pocket." He hoped it would be enough.

Adrenaline was pumping through both of them in high gear now. They were faced with the age-old decision of fight or flight. But in reality there was no true decision about it at all. They had to fight or die. "Come here and stand at my back; keep shooting." Gayle stepped up close to him, turned and they faced down the dogs back-to-back, firing at any that came close.

What are you doing here? Why didn't you stay home where you'd be safe?"

"I couldn't wait there any longer, worrying about you and my mother. I had to come and find you. What if you were injured or needed help? It kept going through my mind all night long. I was going crazy wondering what happened to you both. Where's my mother?"

The moment he dreaded had finally arrived. He said in a hard desperate voice, "We'll talk about it later. We're a little busy right now. Just keep shooting." The dogs were coming in closer. One or two at a time were growling, snarling and snapping their jaws at them. Both of them were hitting the dogs and dropping them in bloody heaps. There was blood splattered all over the ground. It looked like a scene out of some B grade horror movie. The dogs just kept coming and attacking. It was taking Gayle three to five shots to kill them. She reloaded as fast as she could. Dead and badly wounded dogs were piled on top of each other in a circle around them. The live dogs were barking, growling and snarling; some were biting at each other, too. They shot at the dogs that were eating the fallen dogs, too. They were so close that there wasn't a chance in hell of missing them; some of them were almost at point blank range. Junior had blood dripping off the side of his face after hitting a dog that had jumped over several that lay dead at his feet. He hit it in the neck and must have hit the jugular vein. Now, another dead dog was added to the pile.

"Will you stop hitting me with that duct tape?" Gayle said. "You're knocking my aim off."

"Grab it and wrap it around your legs and arms. We're going to be out of ammo soon and we'll have to start clubbing them with the rifle stocks."

"How am I supposed to do that?"

He thought about it for a moment. "You're right, that was a stupid thing to say. Just don't worry about it now. I guess we'll be out of ammo soon and it won't matter then. We'll have to try and get back to the house over there." A Rottweiler on Gayle's side came in for the attack. Thank God she had just reloaded. She hit it with all eight shots and she was fumbling around in her pocket to reload again when it finally fell down and died almost at her feet.

Junior said, "I just reloaded; then I'll be out of bullets."

"I have enough for one or two more reloads, then I'll be out, too." They kept firing, but the number of dogs never seemed to decrease. The dogs were very loud; they were howling, barking, growling, whimpering and yelping all around them.

His SKS locked open and he didn't have any more bullets to put in. "That's it. I'm out." He turned the gun around to use it as a club. Gayle kept shooting. He whacked a few dogs that came close with the stock of the rifle on their heads. The cracking sound of skulls being hit reverberated around them.

Gayle said, "That was my last shot, too." She turned the rifle around to use it as a club. The roll of duct tape hanging off of Junior's arm was really swinging around and whacking Gayle now with his arm movements from swinging back and forth hitting the dogs.

She thought it was a good thing that she had her thick ski jacket and pants on or she'd be black and blue from that damn roll of duct tape. The dogs realized that they'd stopped shooting and came in closer, snarling and snapping. The pack was getting more daring. She swung the rifle up and hit another dog that was trying to bite her leg, when another dog lunged and grabbed her left arm and bit down hard, shaking its head back and forth. "Shit!" She was trying to whack it on the head with her other hand and couldn't get a good enough balanced grip on the rifle to swing it up and over. Junior reached over and whacked it a good hard hit on the head and almost broke her arm in the process. The crack of the skull breaking was loud, even over the other dogs. Her coat arm was ripped to shreds and blood was dripping off of her fingers onto the ground, mixing with the dogs' blood.

"Are you all right?"

"Yeah, thanks." She glanced at her arm, was amazed that she didn't feel it yet. She tested her hand to see if it still worked and her fingers moved. She could see the blood dripping on the ground but just ignored it, turning back to whacking dogs. She didn't have time to think about it anymore. Her left arm was feeling a bit weak, but she just ignored that, too. The dogs were coming in closer now, getting ready to attack en masse. The large circle of dogs around them was getting smaller all the time. More and more of them were coming in closer.

Gayle whacked another dog twice on the head. "If we get out of this, I'll marry you."

"Huh? What? You picked a hell of a time to mention that."

"I thought maybe it might boost your adrenaline and help get us out of this mess."

Junior laughed grimly. "I'm trying like hell. But it's too late to take back your promise now. I'll hold you to it." They were whacking dogs almost constantly. It was down to a matter of time now. They couldn't go on like this much longer. The smell of Gayle's blood was driving the dogs to more daring lunges on her side. "Get ready for a very bloody battle. They're getting ready to really attack us now."

"What do you think they have been doing up to now? Playing fetch?"

"This is going to be real bloody. Hit anything that comes close and don't stop until there are no more dogs left."

As she swung the rifle and whacked another dog she said, "No problem. Good thing I got into shape going on the trap line with you or I wouldn't have been able to go this long." A few more of the bigger dogs started coming in close, biting at them and jumping away before they could hit them with the rifle. What little strength and energy they had was being wasted in useless gestures. The dogs were fast and Junior and Gayle were slowing down.

Gayle had to hit one German shepherd three times before it went down and stayed there. She started to realize they were not going to get out of this. She kept thinking soon all the dogs would be dead or dying, but she realized that wasn't happening. More dogs kept coming out of the woods and joining the pack. Gayle said softly, "I just want you to know that I love you. I want to make sure you know that." She wasn't sure how much longer she could swing the rifle. Her left arm was getting weak and shaky, making it hard to swing the rifle up to bash in the dogs' heads. She wanted Junior to know she loved him before she died. She had no doubt that these dogs would kill her in an instant. Junior wouldn't be able to save her. They were out of bullets and hope. It was time to face up to the reality of what was happening. The cavalry wouldn't be riding up to save them. There was no cavalry anymore.

Junior heard what Gayle had said. He also heard how weak her voice was getting. "I think I fell in love with you the first day on the trap line," he said. "Don't give up, Gayle, just don't give up ever, we can get out of this somehow, just don't give up. If you give up, then all of this will have been for nothing." Terror that he was going to lose her after all overwhelmed him. He took a deep breath and shouted, "God damn it, don't you dare give up and leave me alone. Do you hear me? Do you? I can't do this by myself. I need you to live. Just keep hitting the damn dogs. Just keep hitting them. Do you hear me? Don't stop for anything."

Gayle swung at another dog. "Yes, I hear you and I'll keep hitting them as long as possible." Junior knocked her sideways because a Great Dane jumped up on the pile of dead dogs in front of him and lunged straight at them. He swung the rifle and cracked the dog's skull as it flew by. Gayle stumbled and almost fell, but Junior grabbed her coat and pulled her back up. He let go of her because the pack had crept up even closer. An all out charge was coming any second now. Junior could feel it.

Junior swallowed because his throat was dry. This was it. If more than a few charged them at a time, it was all over except the dying. There was just too many of them. They were standing now with their backs pressed up against each other, watching for the first sign of the mass attack they knew was coming. Both of them were gasping to breathe, leaving little puffs of steam in the air around their heads in the cold air.

Three dogs charged on Junior's side and two charged on Gayle's side all at the same time. Junior and Gayle raised their tired arms up, holding onto their rifles tightly waiting to start clubbing them again. As the bigger dog got close to Junior, a shot rang out, then another and another. The dogs that had charged them were falling. The rapid shots kept coming. The distinctive sound of an AR-15 rang out again and again. Soon the pack backed away and ran back to the woods. The shots kept ringing out until all of the dogs had disappeared. Junior kept looking around, trying to spot the person shooting the dogs. He could tell the shots were coming from the direction he'd last seen Marion, but he couldn't see anyone. This person was a damn good shot, too.

Gayle was looking down the road, trying to make out where this person was. She squinted her eyes, trying to find a person's silhouette against all the snow. Suddenly, an abominable snowman came into view, carrying a rifle. She backed up against Junior, pressing against his back tightly, eyes wide with shock and disbelief. Junior looked over his shoulder at what had made Gayle react like that and saw a man in a white ghillie snowsuit coming towards them. He turned around and said, "Thanks. We ran out of bullets."

Gayle squeaked out, "What are you?"

The abominable snowman said, "Quick, get to that house over there." He turned and started off. Junior grabbed Gayle and they ran after him.

Gayle gasped, "What is that thing?" Junior ignored her and ran faster, right behind the snowman. As soon as they were inside, Junior slammed the door clicked the lock and then shoved the table back in front it, making sure it was secure.

The man said, "Do you have a pistol?"

Junior remembered picking up the Glock 9mm from the floor and putting it into his pocket, along with a box of shells. He reached in and pulled the pistol out and said, "I forgot all about it."

Gayle smacked him in the stomach with her good hand. "How could you forget something like that? It's not like we needed it or anything." Gayle's left arm was hanging down by her side, dripping blood on her ski pants. Junior was stunned that she was hurt this badly and was still able to club the dogs.

Before he could answer, they heard several dogs growling and snarling. The realization hit all three of them at the same time. There were dogs closed up inside with them and they were coming straight for them down the hallway. Junior stepped around Gayle and turned towards the hallway. The man that saved them turned around and whipped his rifle up to face what was coming down the hall. Junior took aim. In a heartbeat, three dogs charged them. Shots were fired in rapid succession from the Glock and the AR-15, and all three dogs fell down and slid on the hard wood floor, leaving a bloody trail behind them. They came to a stop a few feet in front of them. One dog was still alive, snapping, whimpering and yelping mournfully as it lay in a bloody heap. Junior walked up to it and placed the barrel right next to its ear and pulled the trigger, putting an end to the sounds.

They were all a bit deaf now after the loud shots fired in a confined space. The man walked off down the hall and Junior followed him guarding his back. When they came to the last door at the end of the hall, it was all scratched up with claw marks and deep grooves dug into it. They had been trying to get in there to the dead bodies. The man opened the door up and Junior just stayed there in the hall, waiting for him to see what had happened. The man came out, closed the door, and they walked back down the hallway to the living room. They quickly looked around at the rest of the house to make sure it was dog free. They went back into the living room, where Gayle was sitting down on the couch holding her arm up to stop the bleeding.

Junior grabbed a towel and handed it to her to apply pressure to the deep wounds. "I'm going to check out the bathroom and see if there's something to clean that up with," he said. He quickly looked around in the medicine cabinet and finally, under the sink, he found some peroxide and cotton balls. He went back into the living room and helped Gayle take her arm out of what was left of her sleeve. "My name is George," he said, introducing himself to the other man. "Everyone calls me Junior. This is Gayle. We thank you for your help. You saved our lives."

The man pulled back the hood to his suit. "My name is Clint Bolan. I'm glad I arrived in time. I found a woman farther down on the road that had been killed and eaten by these dogs. I was following them to thin out the pack when I heard all the commotion. I knew they'd cornered someone by the ruckus. I got here as fast as I could." Junior had been pouring the peroxide over the deep puncture wounds on Gayle's arm and wiping them up with the cotton balls.

Gayle looked up at Junior and her eyes got wide with shock at the look on his face. No one had to tell her that the woman that was eaten by the dogs was her mother. Tears formed in her eyes and rolled down her cheeks. She choked out her misery with this news and realization, "Oh Mother, why did you have to leave? Why couldn't you just stay where it was safe?" She felt so guilty and miserable. She had no family left now. Her mother was gone. She sobbed against Junior's shoulder when he moved to sit next to her and hold her.

Clint sat down in the chair Junior had spent the night in so he could watch the dogs as he waited for them to collect themselves after this bit of news. If he'd known they knew the woman, he wouldn't have just blurted it out like that. He was curious what could have made the woman leave a safe place and go wandering off in a snowstorm. He was sure he would find out sooner or later what had happened. He usually found out what he wanted to know one way or another.

After awhile Junior told Gayle, "I'm sorry. I didn't know how to tell you. I was going to wait until we got home and then break the news to you about what happened. I heard two shots and ran as fast as I could to get to her, but she was dead by the time I arrived." He left out the part about the dogs eating her. He didn't want to repeat it to Gayle and make her think about it. He patted her back. "Gayle, you need to pull yourself together now. It isn't the right time to mourn her yet. We still have to get out of here. When we get home, then you can mourn her. Until then we have to keep a clear head and get out of this. Do you understand what I'm trying to say?"

Gayle hiccuped and wiped at her face with her other coat sleeve. Finally, she said in a tiny voice, "Yes, I do know what you mean. But, how can I forget I'm the one that killed her?"

Junior sighed. "You did no such thing. I won't let you talk that way. You didn't cause this to happen to her, Gayle. You want something to blame for this? Then put the blame where it really belongs: with the dogs. They did this, Gayle. The dogs did it. Get mad at them because they killed your mother. No one else was responsible except the damn dogs."

Gayle looked up at him in surprise with tear-stained eyes. She thought about what he said; he was right. Who knew this would happen? The damn dogs did this. They killed her mother. Her grief and guilt and all the other emotions paled in comparison to this one strong emotion that filled her. She screamed out, "Kill them! Kill every single one of them!"

Junior raised his eyebrows in surprise. "We've been trying. I'd say we killed more than a few of them already. When we get home, we'll put out snares and kill as many as we can. We'll shoot any dog we see. But first, Gayle, we have to get past them to get home. That's what we must concentrate on now. The rest will come later." He poured some more peroxide on the wounds and wiped away the white foam with a cotton ball.

Gayle thought about what he said for awhile. "Well, we'd better get out of here, then, don't you think?"

Clint said, "The dogs are back."

Junior said, "Great, just what we don't need."

"They're eating the dead ones now," Clint said.

Junior said to Gayle, "I'm going to get a small towel for your arm we'll duct tape it up tight. Maybe we can get away now while they're occupied with eating."

Clint said, "Where are you going? "

"We have a house about a mile and a half from here," Junior said. "You're welcome to come with us. We have everything we need there."

Clint looked at them. "Okay, get Gayle ready to go. She can carry her rifle and swing it at anything that might get by us." Junior went into the kitchen and got a clean kitchen towel and wrapped her arm up. He was helping her get her coat sleeve over it when Clint said, "What was up with the duct tape hanging off of you?"

"I was duct taping myself up with towels for padding against the dogs to make my way home when I saw Gayle out the window, coming down the road with the dogs surrounding her. I just grabbed my rifle and ran out the door and didn't give it another thought until Gayle mentioned it hitting her and knocking her aim off when we were shooting at the dogs."

Clint shook his head and looked outside. "It's impressive that you two held out as long as you did. They're fast and hard to hit."

"We had no choice but to defend ourselves or be killed."Junior was just finishing taping up Gayle's coat sleeve when they heard the dogs at the doors again, trying to get inside. This was a familiar sound to Junior since he'd listened to it ever since he took refuge in this house.

Gayle said, "My God. What are they doing?"

"Trying to get in and kill us." Gayle shuddered in fear.

Clint said, "When we go out the door, kill the ones in front of you and to the right. I'll do the same, but on the left. After that, kill anything that gets close to us. How many bullets do you have for the Glock?"

"Somewhere around twenty-five or thirty were left in the box."

Clint looked at him for a few moments, then nodded. Junior grabbed the Glock off the coffee table and reloaded it. They made their way over to the door and started to push the heavy table away. All of a sudden, the sound of breaking glass filled the room and glass shards flew everywhere. All three of them whipped their heads around and looked over just in time to see two German shepherds charging at them across the living room. Gayle screamed. Shots rang out as loud as thunder. Both dogs fell to their death just a few feet from where Gayle was standing. She looked around wildly for more dogs to come through the window.

Clint said, "I'll move the table. Cover the window, then get ready to move fast."

"Got it." Junior turned a little sideways to keep his eyes on the window. Nothing they did now would surprise him. He grabbed Gayle. "Stay between Clint and me at all times. Don't let yourself get separated from us, no matter what. Swing that rifle and hit anything that comes close to you."

Gayle said, "Okay."

Clint had his hand on the door handle and you could see the door moving some from the dog's bodies being thrown against it. Clint said, "Gayle when we are going out the door stay by Junior and keep your eyes turned inside here and let us know if another dog has gotten in through the window at our backs." Gayle said, "Right." Clint said, "Ready?" They both said yes. Clint grabbed the door and yanked it open with one arm and with the other he held the AR-15. He started shooting one handed and stepped around the door and outside. Junior was right by his side shooting at the dogs on his side.

They advanced over the bodies and reached the road. Gayle said, "Three are coming up on the back out of the house." Junior whipped around and fired at them. He missed one, Gayle swung the rifle and cracked its skull with a very loud crack.

Junior yelled, "I have to reload." Clint swung around and covered all sides as they made their way out. Junior pulled the slide back and it slammed a shell into the chamber. The pistol was ready to be fired. Clint swung back around to cover his own side, firing two shots off in quick succession. They hurried at a half trot. Some of the dogs were following them, but most had stopped to eat the dead bodies lying around. Clint and Junior kept shooting every once in awhile to discourage any from getting too close. The last half-mile to the house, they didn't seen any dogs. They must have all turned back. They finally reached the path to the house. "If we get separated," said Junior, "the house is at the end of this path, straight ahead."

Clint nodded and they kept going. When they reached the house, Junior opened up the outside door. "Hurry inside so I can secure this door." They raced inside and he shut the outer door, locked it, and then dropped down the metal plate. Gayle reached over with her good arm and turned on a light. Junior grabbed the socket set and the bolts and tightened them down.

Gayle stood there for a few moments, not sure what to do. Everything seemed so strange and different now that her mother was gone. She wouldn't ever be coming back. *Best not to think about it right now. I have to stay busy,* she thought. They had a guest, too. Her mother wasn't here to make dinner or to make the guest feel welcome. It was all up to her now. She took a deep breath. "I'll go make some coffee. Clint, go ahead and take your coat off and sit down. Dinner will be ready in a half hour or so. I took some stew out of the freezer to defrost before I left. There's plenty, so I hope you're hungry."

She walked into the kitchen. She stood at the sink a minute and tried to settle her thoughts. Her mother was dead. Somehow she'd known it deep down inside when she saw Junior was alone. She just hadn't wanted to acknowledge it. She knew her mother had been having a hard time adjusting to this new world they lived in. Especially since she found out that George had died. Had she done this because she no longer wanted to live in this world? Is that why she'd insisted on going outside in a blizzard? Is that why she'd turned and waved at them and said in a normal voice, "Have fun," when she was leaving? She didn't know. But it hurt, anyway. It didn't matter, not really. All that mattered now was that she was gone and Gayle had no one except Junior. She wasn't sure what to do with herself. She ached inside and felt like someone had squeezed her heart and wouldn't let go. She took her coat off and hung it on the back of a chair. She looked around at everything, trying to imagine what it was going to be like with just her and Junior now. She rubbed her chest with her good hand because it ached so badly, a lot more than her arm did. *Why am I not crying?* This hurt felt so deep that no tears could ever ease it. She realized that it really hadn't hit her yet. Not really. She never got to say good-bye.

She sighed deeply and realized she had two hungry men out there to feed. They both had given their all to keep her alive and deserved more than her standing there like she was frozen in place. Junior had to be starving. She went over to the oven and turned it on. She got a pot of coffee going. She reached down into a cupboard and grabbed a pot and poured the defrosted stew into it. She set it on the stove to simmer. She got the loaf of bread out of the bread machine. It was cold now, just as she knew it would be. She rubbed margarine all over it and set it in a pan to warm up in the oven. How many times had she seen her mother do this exact thing? She pulled out three fourths of an apple pie that was left over and put it in the oven, too. She set the table. Everything would be ready in about twenty to thirty minutes. She got a hunk of cheese out and cut some off and cut it into small squares. She grabbed a couple packages of crackers and put it all on a plate with some thick sliced ham. The men could eat this until everything else was ready for a proper dinner. She'd wait for the coffee and bring that into the living room, too. She decided to just get through this evening, then maybe she could have some time to think about all of this. She felt kind of numb and detached. She was just going through the motions on autopilot. A lot has happened since yesterday. All those dogs. *Man's best friend, my ass,* she thought. She shuddered and felt the bile rise in her throat, burning all the way back down as she swallowed. Just the thought of all those snarling, biting horrible things they had turned into. It was like some kind of a weird movie. Like a virus changed them. Maybe she was living in an episode of *The Outer Limits* or maybe this was a horrible nightmare. The coffee started to perk and she turned the burner down. She got out coffee mugs and got them ready. She watched the coffee pot perk for a few minutes and then turned it off. She poured the coffee and put the mugs on a serving platter with the cheese, ham and crackers and went into the living room.

Clint and Junior were in the bedroom going over some of the guns and things he had there. She said, "I made you two a snack to hold you over until dinner heats up. I brought coffee, too."

The men came back into the living room. Junior said, "Have a seat. Help yourself, Clint. I have to go help with dinner." He grabbed several crackers with cheese and ham and his cup of coffee and went into the kitchen with Gayle. "What are you making?"

"This morning before I left I took out some stew from the freezer to defrost for dinner. I got a loaf of bread going, too. I have it in the oven warming, along with the leftover apple pie."

He smiled. "That sure smells good. How are you doing?" He reached over and pulled her into his arms.

"I don't think it's hit me yet. With everything that happened today, everything is just sort of jumbled up in my thoughts. I keep thinking that my mother's dead and I should be falling apart, but I'm not. I just don't know what to do."

Junior rubbed her back. "Take it one day at a time. That's what you have to do. No one can tell you what to feel or how you should be acting or even what you should be doing right now. You just do what feels right to you, okay? There are many ways to feel grief and sorrow. I remember my dad telling me that after my grandpa died. You remember them and honor them in your own way; no one can say if it's the right way to do it or not because they aren't you."

She went over and stirred the stew "I just don't feel like crying. I feel hurt on the inside, like it's so deep that I can't cry. I'm not making much sense. But that's how I feel."

Junior hugged her from behind. "Then it's the right way for you. That's all that matters. I'm here for you."

She turned and smiled a little. "Thank you. You and Clint saved me today and I haven't even gotten around to telling you that."

Junior kissed her. "You're welcome. And the way I remember, you didn't sit around waiting to be saved. You did a whole lot of it yourself."

She patted his face. "I'd be lost without you. You know that, don't you?"

He kissed her hand. "Yup, that's me. I find the lost ones and keep them."

She gave him a weak smile and shook her head. "Go get Clint, smarty, dinner is ready." He chuckled and left to go get Clint.

Gayle hadn't set a place for herself at the table. She was sure she wouldn't be able to keep anything down with the visions of what must have happened to her mother, the horrible scene of killing the dogs dancing around in her head and all the blood. She couldn't get the smell of it out of her nose. She thought because they had a guest, to be polite, she could sit with them and have some coffee while they wolfed down the food.

Clint looked a couple of inches taller than Junior, so that made him about six feet three or four. He was a little heftier than Junior, too. He was more along the size that his dad had been, somewhere around two hundred ten to two hundred twenty pounds. In fact, she bet that Junior's dad's clothes would fit him, too. It would be up to Junior if he wanted to give away any of his dad's things or not. She thought about this for a while.

Later she planned on getting down the whiskey and getting good and drunk. The thought of why she wasn't crying kept going through her mind. *Is something wrong with me?* She remembered breaking down and not even knowing what day it was when her dad had died. The days had just sort of blurred into snatches of conversations and things people had done. *Why am I not falling apart now? I loved my mother.* It was true that she wasn't as close to her mother as she had been to her dad, but she should be crying at least, right? She rubbed her face and felt guilty because she wasn't falling apart like she had when her dad died. She felt a deep pain and tightness in her chest and numb at the same time. She was confusing herself. *I'm just going to forget about it for now and deal with it later. Think about Clint.* He was a safe subject that had no connection to anything else and maybe she'd be able to just get this day and night over with. She wasn't sure why it was so important to just get this day over with, but that's how she felt.

Clint and Junior came into the kitchen. Junior looked around at the two places set and realized that Gayle wouldn't be eating. He understood this. Food had been the last thing on his mind when his father had died. But at least Gayle wouldn't be alone. He'd do whatever he needed to help her through this. He said, "Clint, have a seat over there and I'll serve everything up." He brought the pot from the stove over to the table and got a ladle. He pulled the bread out of the oven; it smelled heavenly. He was so hungry. He contained himself and sliced it up and put butter on each slice, just as he used to do with his dad. He felt a deep sorrow that he wasn't there. He would have liked Clint. He left the apple pie in the oven to keep it nice and warm after turning the oven off. He turned around and Clint had waited for him to start eating. Junior brought everything over to the table. "Dig in, we have plenty."

Gayle was looking down at her coffee cup, lost in her own thoughts while Junior had gotten everything ready for them to eat.

Clint said, "Where can I wash up?"

"I'm sorry. I have completely forgotten my manners." Junior looked at his own hands and saw how dirty they were; one hand had dried blood on it. He closed his eyes, thinking that Clint must think he was a slob and a dirt bag for not washing up first. "Follow me and we can both go wash up." He got up and his stomach grumbled loudly in protest.

Clint laughed. Junior showed him where the bathroom was. Clint said with a wistful sound to his voice, "Nice bathroom. Does the shower work?"

"Yes, everything works here. My dad built this place to survive just about anything. I think the hills and the metal around the whole place protected it against the EMP because it was grounded." Clint shook his head in understanding. Junior turned on the water faucet and started to wash up. Clint did the same, washing his face, too. They went back into the kitchen and wasted no time in eating everything in sight. When they were done, Junior got up and said, "Now for the best part." He got the pie out of the oven.

Gayle smiled a little. "Junior loves his apple pie. He always says, 'It's my favorite' with a gleam in his eyes."

Clint laughed. Junior cut them all a piece of pie and set the pieces in front of them.

"I'm not hungry. I really can't eat this," Gayle said.

Junior looked at her seriously. "Please eat a little of it for me, okay? If you don't eat some, it will make me feel like a pig."

Gayle sighed. "All right. I'll try." Junior smiled at her and gave her a fork.

Junior handed Clint a piece. He said, "Thank you." He took a big bite of pie and sighed. Junior just smiled at him, happy that there was another person that shared his opinion of apple pie. He started eating his own piece. Gayle picked at her piece some and ate a couple of nibbles, but mostly left the rest untouched. When they were done, Junior got up and poured all of them more coffee.

Clint said, "I want to apologize to you, Gayle, for blurting out what happened to your mother the way I did. I didn't know that you two knew her. I would never have said it the way I did if I had known she was your mother. For that I deeply apologize."

Gayle looked at him for a few moments. "Don't worry about it, Clint. I would have found out sooner or later what happened to her. You saved Junior from having to tell me. It's best I deal with it right from the first and not get hit with this information later. I just can't believe it yet. Even after all that's happened, it still seems like a nightmare."

He nodded at her in understanding. "Can you tell me what's been happening around here since the EMP hit?"

Gayle and Junior told him everything. Some of it she hadn't even known and just heard about now. *Poor Junior,* she thought, *he's had to deal with so much all alone.* She reached out and held his hand. He smiled at her and it lifted her heart some. She loved him.

Junior asked Clint what had happened to him and where was he staying. Clint looked at them. "I was in the city when the EMP went off. I've been all over the world, and I knew what would be coming. I gathered up as many supplies as I could carry and headed out to the woods. I figured my chances of survival were much better out here than in the city with the MZB's running around."

Junior said, "What's an MZB?"

"Mutant Zombie Bikers."

Junior laughed. "Mutant Zombies are bikers?"

Clint said, "It's just another way of explaining how normally rational people react in an irrational world. They turn into Mutant Zombie bikers. Kind of like that movie that Clint Eastwood was in, *Any Which Way But Loose*, with Fido Bibo knocking some sense into most folks. But, unfortunately just as Fido implied, the orangutan was nowhere in sight to knock some sense into these people."

Junior laughed. "I loved that movie." Even Gayle smiled some at the reference to the movie. "Well, it hasn't been a piece of cake out here in the woods, either, but I can just imagine what it would be like in a big city. I wouldn't want to be there, either, in total chaos with everybody going nuts and turning into Mutant Zombie Bikers. It would be like a B grade horror movie of zombies just killing everyone and going crazy."

"Exactly. That's why I'm out here and not there."

"So where is your house at? Are you very far from here?"

Clint looked at Junior. "I guess I didn't say that plain enough. I'm living out in the woods. I built a shelter and that's where I'm staying."

Junior and Gayle exchanged an incredible look. "You've been out there surviving and living in the woods with just what you carried with you?"

"Yes."

"How?"

Clint smiled at the challenging look in his eyes. "Maybe I should tell you a little bit about myself so you'll understand how I was able to do it."

Junior said with a look of suspicion, "There's no way you could have been surviving out there this long with just what you carried with you. No way. I know about survival from my dad teaching me all my life and even I wouldn't be stupid enough to go out there and try to survive with just what I could carry."

Clint nodded, agreeing with Junior. "Have you ever heard of a SERE instructor?"

Junior looked at him, evaluating what he was saying. "Yes, I know what SERE means. It is Survival, Evasion, Resistance and Escape."

"Yes, that's what it means. I was a SERE instructor for the armed forces."

"Oh. Well, you would definitely know how to survive in the woods, then. I take back what I said about nobody being able to survive out there. Well, I meant normal people, anyway would not stand a chance of surviving out there."

Clint raised his eyebrow at Junior. "I agree with you. You think I'm not normal?"

Junior got red in the face and stammered out, "Ahh, I, ahh, I didn't mean that you were crazy or anything. I just meant an average person wouldn't be able to survive out in the woods this long."

Clint laughed. "Relax. I was just yanking your chain."

Junior looked at him. "Wow. My dad was in the Navy and he wanted to be a SEAL. but he hurt his knee in an accident and he couldn't qualify for the test because of it. He would have made a good SEAL. too. He knew survival inside and out. He could sneak up on anybody and scare the crap out of you. I always wanted to learn to do that. I keep trying, but I don't think I'll ever be able to be as good as he was. It was like he was a part of the woods or something. He could blend in and pop out and startle you."

Gayle said, "Yeah, just like the abominable snowman here." She pointed at Clint. "He just popped out of the woods carrying a gun and scared the shit out of me. I thought he was an abominable snowman with a gun." Clint laughed real hard at that one. Junior just looked at Gayle kind of weird.

Clint said with a smile, "I had on my camo snow poncho with my white ghillie suit over it and used the natural terrain to blend into the environment. I have to say, no one has ever called me an abominable snowman before." Junior was just shaking his head at Gayle, wondering how she could have thought that. There was no such thing as an abominable snowman. Everybody knew that.

Junior looked at Clint with a thoughtful look. "Would you be willing to teach me some skills?"

"What kind of skills?"

"Like camouflage techniques and improvised tools and weapons. Things like that?"

"What for?"

Junior sighed, then looked at him with intensity and said very seriously, "Because I'm out of my depth here with everything that's been happening. I have Gayle to protect, and my dad died before he could teach me everything he knew. I need to know more in order for us to survive now. Nothing is safe anymore. Look at what happened with the dogs. What about everything in the future? I need to know more in order to be able to handle everything. I figured that out last night when I realized that nothing would be the same. Nothing at all. I just don't know what else to do to prepare myself to meet these challenges except to learn more skills."

Clint looked at him. "I've taught many men; none have even come close to giving me as many valid reasons as you have to teach them. I'd be glad to teach you."

Junior said with relief, "Thank you very much. I look forward to learning from you. Would you mind moving in here with us? You can have your own room. We have a lot of supplies. My dad was always preparing and setting everything up for the end of the world. Plus, with Gayle and me trapping and snaring, we have plenty of fresh meat. Also, I could use someone else around here to help with security and things."

Clint looked at Gayle. "Would you mind if I moved in here, Gayle? After all, I am a stranger to you both."

Gayle said, "You may be a stranger, but you saved us today, and if you hadn't done that, we wouldn't be here right now. I want to thank you for your help today and getting us out of that house and home. You're welcome to stay as far as I'm concerned." She looked over at Junior, he nodded and smiled at her.

Clint thought for a few moments then looked at each of them. "I'll leave tomorrow and get the rest of my equipment. It will take me a little over a day each way, so I'll be gone about three days."

"That's great. I'm relieved to have you here. Would you like to take a shower?" He remembered the way Clint had looked wistfully at the shower.

Clint smiled at him. "Yes, I would."

Junior got up. "I think some of my dad's clothes would fit you. Come on and we'll go see if they will. Then you'll have some clean clothes to put on, too." Clint got up and put his dishes in the sink.

Gayle said, "Thank you."

"I wash dishes, too."

Gayle smiled a little at him. "That's good to know. But, do you cook?"

"Yes, I've been doing that for a long time. Never found a woman that wanted to wait around for me while I was out traipsing around the world keeping it safe, so over the years, I learned to cook."

Gayle looked at him. "Clint, it's their loss. You just haven't met the right woman yet. I'm sure a woman will come along and see what a great man you are and snatch you right up."

Clint said, "Thanks but, I don't see that happening now."

"Have a little faith. The right woman is out there, probably just waiting for you to show up."

"I highly doubt that." He walked out of the kitchen with Junior.

Junior took him into his dad's old room and realized that he and Gayle would be moving in here now. It felt a bit strange. This had always been his dad's room. He sighed. So much had happened since his dad had died. He went over to the dresser and opened up a couple of drawers. "Look through the clothes and pick something to wear. One thing my dad always did was buy good quality clothes because they lasted longer and held up under all the abuse he'd put them through. There are a lot of L.L. Bean shirts and pants. There's thermal underwear and warm socks in the bottom drawer, too. You already know where the bathroom is. Help yourself to anything in there. Clean towels are in the bathroom cupboard. Just put your dirty clothes into the hamper and we'll wash them for you."

Clint smiled. "Thanks."

Junior left him to it and went back into the kitchen. It was empty. He looked into the living room; it was empty, too. His heart started beating really fast as fear grabbed hold of him. Where was Gayle? He looked at the door, it was still bolted shut. He sighed in relief. He heard some movement in his old room and looked inside. Gayle was changing the sheets. He stepped up and helped her. She was struggling a bit with her hurt arm. When they finished, they walked into the living room.

Gayle said, "I couldn't let him sleep on those sheets that smelled of what we'd been doing in there."

Junior looked at her in alarm. "I didn't even think of that."

Gayle patted his hand. "That's okay. I remembered for both of us."

Junior kissed her and held her close. "I'm very glad you're here with me. I could have lost you today."

Gayle said, "I could have lost you, too. Later I'm going to get very drunk. I think I earned it today. I just want to drink until I can't drink anymore."

"I can understand that. I'll sit with you and you can drink all you want, okay?"

Gayle hugged him. "Thanks for being here with me. I'm so glad you're okay, too."

"We have to soak your arm in bleach water. No telling what germs and diseases those dogs have. We need to do this just to be sure. It will probably sting a lot, but it's necessary."

"It hurts a lot now."

Junior said, "I'm sorry, I forgot about it until now."

"I only remember when I'm moving it."

"As soon as Clint gets done in the bathroom, I'll get some bandages and we'll soak your arm; then you can drink, okay?"

Gayle nodded. Junior just held her. He wanted to keep Gayle close and let nothing ever harm her again. He had almost had a heart attack when he saw her standing there surrounded by the dogs. He closed his eyes and just thanked God that she was all right.

He felt bad about Marion dying. He didn't want to say anything to Gayle, but the way she had talked a few times made him think she didn't want to be here now, especially without his dad. Could that be why she'd taken off in a blizzard? He didn't know for sure. None of it made any sense. Why had she insisted on going out in the storm? He hadn't had time to even really think about this before. Too much had happened. There was always too much bad crap happening.

Clint came out of the bathroom and it made Junior's heart skip a beat for a minute. It had looked like his dad standing there out of the corner of his eye. He sighed. It was going to be hard getting used to seeing someone else wear his dad's clothes. He thought this was stupid. They're just clothes that anyone could wear. It was just hard seeing someone else in them. He got up. "I have to take care of Gayle's arm. Who knows what kind of diseases the dogs had."

Clint said, "Good idea. You should probably soak her arm in bleach water. Do you have any bleach?"

"I was already going to do that. Yes, we have bleach." He turned and went into the bathroom.

"Sit down," said Gayle. "You're going to give me a crick in my neck looking up at you."

Clint smiled. "Yes ma'am." He sat down in George's recliner. "It's strange sitting in a chair that actually fits me. I would be happy to just sit in any kind of a chair after being out in the woods for so long. I love being out there, but nothing beats a real bed, a hot shower and a comfortable chair to sit in."

"I can't even imagine going without those things for so long."

Clint said, "You get used to it after awhile. I'm just used to it more so than most people."

Junior came back. "We should do this on the kitchen table." He walked into the kitchen and Gayle followed him. He put down the bandages and antibiotic ointment and got a big roasting pan out and half filled it with warm water. He added one cap full of bleach and stirred it up. He unwrapped her arm and cringed at how bad it looked. It was swollen and bruising in several spots. There were multiple deep punctures. He went over to the cabinet and got down the whiskey and poured her a glass.

She reached out with her good hand and took a large swallow. She choked a little and sputtered out, "Wow."

Junior took her arm and gently put it into the water. He used some cotton balls to wash the punctures and to reopen them so the bleach could disinfect them. She hissed at him a couple of times. He hated hurting her, but it had to be done. He timed it, and after five minutes he took her arm out, gently patted it dry, and laid it down on on a clean towel. He used a two by two inch gauze pad and applied the ointment to the wounds. Then he used rolled gauze to wrap her arm up and taped it with athletic tape so it could breathe. He'd make sure to apply the ointment three times a day until it healed. Now, they only had to worry about rabies. Oh God, what if the dogs had rabies? He didn't know what to do for that. *Well, we'll just have to deal with it if it happens.* Gayle had finished the glass of whiskey and asked for more.

He filled the glass up again and set it down on the table. "I'm going to put this stuff away and then I'll be right back. Are you going to be okay until then?"

She said, "Yeah, I'll be fine. My arm feels better now."

Junior kissed her and tasted the whiskey. As he went by Clint to put the supplies away he said. "Right now I'm going to sit with Gayle while she gets drunk. I don't know how much more she can drink until she passes out, but I'm going to see if I can get her talking about her mother. I think she needs it, so don't mind us."

"She probably needs a few drinks after the day she had. I'm sorry for the way I told her about her mother."

"You couldn't have known it was her mother, so there's no need to feel bad. I'm the one that let her out the door, so if anyone is to blame, it should be me for doing that. None of this would have happened if I'd refused to open the door."

Clint said, "You couldn't have known that this would happen. Don't blame yourself. Blame the dogs for going feral. Or you could blame the people that just let their pets go off into the woods when they couldn't feed them anymore. They are all equally to blame for this situation."

"I'll try," said Junior. "But I feel guilty as hell. Well, I'd better get back to Gayle."

"I'll probably leave at first light."

"I'll be up, and if I'm not, just wake me up anyway, okay?"

"Okay."

Junior walked back into the kitchen and Gayle was sitting there, staring at the empty chair where Marion always sat. Junior knew how that felt, too.

He sat down next to her and pulled her into his arms. "I'm here for you, Gayle. You don't have to go through this alone. I love you." He kissed the top of her head and rubbed her back, holding her tightly. All of a sudden it was as if a dam had sprung a leak and she started to cry, softly at first, and then in great racking sobs that shook her whole body. Junior just kept holding her tight and rocking back and forth as tears welled up in his own eyes. A long time later, Gayle started talking about her mother. She told him about things that her mother had done. Sometimes she would laugh a little, remembering something funny. They talked long into the night, sharing good things about her mother and a little bit about his dad.

After another glass of whiskey, she finally either passed out or fell asleep against his shoulder. He wasn't sure which it was. He picked her up and carried her into the bedroom and laid her down on the bed. He took off her shoes and tucked her in. He went back into the kitchen and got out three ibuprofen tablets and a glass of water and put them on the bedside table for her to take first thing in the morning to help with the hangover he knew she'd have. Clint had long ago gone to bed. He turned out the lights, got into bed, and snuggled close with his arms wrapped around Gayle. It hurt him that she was hurting. He pondered on this for a while. *Is this what real love was like?* He fell asleep trying to figure that out.

Junior woke up abruptly. He got out of bed and looked around. Then he heard a noise. That must have been what had woken him up. It came from the kitchen. He then remembered that Clint was here and it was probably him. He slipped his jeans on and went out to take a look. The bed in his old room was empty, so it was Clint. Junior went back into the bedroom, got his shirt and made sure Gayle was covered up against the chilled air so he could shut the door. He didn't want to disturb her. She needed all the sleep she could get. He went into the kitchen and Clint was making coffee.

Clint said, "I hope you don't mind, I made coffee."

"No, I don't mind. Why would I mind if you made coffee?" This conversation was confusing him after getting a little over an hour's sleep.

"This is your home and these are your supplies."

Junior said, "You're a part of us now. Everything here is for all of us. As far as I'm concerned, you are no longer a guest here. We all have to work together as one team or this will never work. We'll equally share all that's here together. You can't go around thinking you're separate from Gayle and I or this won't work out. Am I making any sense?" Junior rubbed his face.

Clint said, "Yes, you're making sense, but I just wanted to be sure that after you thought about it you hadn't changed your mind."

Junior stared at him intently. "You and I both know that if you wanted this place or any house out there, you would have it without working up a sweat. None of us could stop you. I am not implying that's the case here. I'm just stating a fact. So, the real question is if you want to take Gayle and I on as trainees and teach us how to survive this hell. My dad taught me to be a thinker. I try not to be stupid. You popping out of the snow to rescue us was a gift. I'm just trying to come up with a way this will work to our mutual benefit. I need help to defend this place and survive like civilized people, not be like them out there. I just need your help." He gestured with his hand.

Clint smiled. "That was well thought out. Then I accept. I just wanted to be sure that you had thought this through. I wouldn't want to intrude here."

Junior laughed. "You wouldn't be intruding. We need you, Clint. I have no idea what I'm doing most of the time. Things just keep getting weirder and weirder out there. I need to learn how to handle these things and what to prepare for."

"You have been doing just fine. Don't think you haven't. Most people wouldn't have made it this far dealing with what you've had to."

Junior said, "Well, it's been hell. But I'm hoping with some training and instruction, it will help even the odds of surviving the end of the world as we know it. I'm going to make breakfast. We'll make you up a small bag of supplies to take with you so you won't have to worry and can just get your things and come back. I don't think we've seen the last of the dogs yet."

"I don't either. Thank you. Having some supplies will be great." Junior started another loaf of bread in the machine. It was a ritual they did everyday. He had some bannock mix that Marion had made up and would send along with Clint so he could make some bread, too.

"How much space do you have for supplies?"

Clint said, "I have just a few things that I thought I might need." Junior nodded his head at him and set about peeling potatoes for frying. When he got that going, he gathered up the bag of bannock mix that had the instructions written in Marion's handwriting on the bag, some margarine, a large hunk off the huge ham they'd been eating off of, three cup of noodles, three large potatoes, an onion, and three cups of long grain rice. He got a little baggie out and poured in some dried mixed vegetables. He grabbed some dried muskrat jerky he'd made and put it in a little baggie. He included some coffee and metal coffee pot to make it in.

Clint got ready to go and Junior unlocked the door. "Do you think you'll be okay out there with the dogs running around? I'd go with you, but I have to be here for Gayle right now. I know what it's like being alone after losing a parent. I can't do that to her."

"I'll be fine. Don't worry about me. You just take care of Gayle and yourself. Never go outside unarmed. Give Gayle a rifle to shoot that has some real knock down power to it. You would have done better if she'd had a more powerful rifle and a semi-automatic, not a bolt action .22 yesterday. When you have to go outside, one of you needs to stay alert and provide cover fire for the other one when you're busy doing something. Do you understand what I mean?"

Junior said, "Yes, I do. We'll do that. We'll need to go out and get some more firewood brought inside, and I want to go set out some snares for those dogs."

Junior raised the door up and Clint opened up the outside door and said, "Just take good care of yourselves." He stepped out into the darkness with dawn just starting to lighten the horizon a little. Junior watched him walk away, then shut the outer door and locked it. He lowered the metal plate and secured it again. He went into the kitchen to clean up and then he was going back to bed for a few hours, or at least until Gayle woke up and needed him.

****

As Clint walked back to his camp, he thought about what Junior said. That was one smart kid. His father must have been a good parent to teach him as much as he had. He was sorry he had died. Having more trained people around would be great, but not really necessary. Junior seemed eager to learn. He chuckled to himself. We'll see how long that lasts. He intended to train him hard and teach Gayle as much as she was able and willing to do. No telling when they would be attacked again, and by whom. It always happened. Most people were stupid and thought they could just take whatever they wanted whenever they wanted to. He'd been stopping people like that for a long time. He looked forward to the training and getting to know those two kids. He liked how they worked together as a team when they were out checking the traps. They were trainable. He was really glad he'd run into them and was able to help them.

Clint had been thinking about approaching them with an offer of his own. His offer wasn't as generous. He hadn't realized that they had a place that still had everything working. That was a real bonus. Junior's dad had been really prepared and lucked out with the EMP. He'd been thinking of taking over a small abandoned place and setting up some batteries, solar panels and things to be halfway civilized. He planned to start on that project in the spring. This deal with them saved him a lot of work.

Some dogs had been following him and were starting to come in closer. When he could see them out of the corner of his eyes, he quickly turned to the left and fired. He slowly turned around in a circle, dropping three of them. The rest quickly ran off. They wouldn't be back. They had learned to stay far away from him. But they tested his strength every time they saw him. He hoped Junior had listened to him about having one of them provide cover when they were outside. These predators would test them every time they saw them. He felt pretty confident that they'd do what he'd said. They'd found out the hard way what these dogs were like. Those two kids had done a really good job defending themselves against that attack. He was impressed with their determination to survive. That was the key to real survival. You have to have the fortitude to do whatever is necessary and meet each challenge with a show of force. Predators, whether they were human or of the four legged kind, only understood and respected someone who's smarter, faster, meaner and willing to kill them.

Clint stopped, made a fire, and melted some snow for water. He would save the gallon of water he had for when he really had to use it to save time. He'd have a cup of noodles and put some of that dried meat in it. He pulled out the thermos that Junior had loaned him and poured a cup of coffee. The smell alone was wonderful. It was great having coffee again. He'd planned on waiting for a few more snow storms and then he would venture out on a supply run and check abandoned houses to resupply. He didn't want to run into people because most confrontations would result in their deaths. He didn't like having to kill his fellow Americans. He had fought to keep them from knowing and experiencing crap like this. But realistically, it was bound to happen sometime. The whole world was a powder keg just waiting to explode.

Well, it did, and now it was up to each person to survive this chaos. Americans were not prepared for anything like this. They thought they were safe and snug in their houses. They would get up in the morning, go to work, and come home to their families. Maybe once in awhile they'd pay attention to what was happening on the global scale, shake their heads, and wonder how things had gotten so bad. They didn't understand the amount of work and lives that had been lost so they could sit in their houses and shake their heads at the news. They weren't experienced in any kind of survival for day-to-day living. It broke his heart to see it happen here. He gathered up his things and started walking again.

It was getting dark. Clint didn't stop, he'd use his night vision when it got dark. It would be a long while yet until he reached his camp. Then he'd make a proper meal and rest. He'd break camp in the morning and head out. He was a loner by nature anyway, and had always enjoyed his own company more than being around most other people. He had a feeling that Junior and Gayle were a rare breed and wanted to be friends with him, and that was okay with him.

He realized that Junior was using him to learn and train them, but he wasn't taking advantage. Junior offered a real exchange of services and goods. It was a rare thing to run into someone that offered such things honestly without a lot of ulterior motives attached to the deal. He'd made sure not to do anything that would intimidate them in any way when he was with them. He had a lot of practice at that. Junior had actually offered him a fair deal. It was a new thing for him. He'd just have to wait and see how it all worked out. He smiled. Life was definitely looking up.

****

Gayle woke up a little after 9:00 am. She got up slowly because her arm and head were throbbing. She was real quiet to let Junior get more sleep. She saw the tablets and water on the nightstand and took them. Her head felt like it weighed a few hundred pounds with a heavy metal rock band playing a concert. She'd felt Junior get up earlier and figured it was to send Clint off for his stuff. She hadn't intended on falling back to sleep, but that's what happened. She wanted to get up and see Clint off, too. Oh well, it was too late for that. She gathered up some clean clothes and headed for the shower to wake up. As she was showering, she saw her mother's bottle of shampoo, and it made her cry, reminding her she wouldn't be back to use it again. When she came out of the bathroom, she started a pot of coffee.

She cried off and on, feeling very strange about it all. It still seemed like some kind of a demented nightmare. Dogs had eaten her mother. She hoped that her mother had died quickly. It hurt to think what her poor mother must have gone through. The terror she must have felt. She hated them. She would kill any dog she saw from now on. They were acting just like any other predator, like a coyote or a cougar or a wolf, and she would treat every single one of them like they were from now on.

It was about 11:30 when Junior got up. He rushed out to see Gayle. She was sitting on the couch, crying. He rushed over and held her in his arms. He felt bad about sleeping so long. She looked at him with tears in her eyes and said, "I need to see her. I need to say goodbye to her Junior, I have to."

He said as gently as he could, "Gayle, we can't go out there. The pack of wild dogs is still out there. We don't know what kind of diseases they have. They might have rabies for all we know. It would be suicide to go out there now."

"We have to go get her and bury her next to your dad. We can't just leave her out there all alone." She started sobbing real hard.

"Gayle, we'll go outside and set up some snares to kill as many of them as we can. When it's safe, we'll go get her and bring her back here. We can't bury her, Gayle. The ground is frozen and we can't dig a grave."

She turned and looked at him with a horrified look. "You aren't burning her body, Junior. I won't let you. Oh my God. We have to bury her. We have to, right next to your dad. That's what she would want." She sobbed some more.

Junior rubbed his face. He didn't know what to do or say. There probably wouldn't even be a body left after the dogs got through with her. Just some bones strewn around. He couldn't tell her that. He thought real fast. "When it's safe out there, we can go get her body and put her in a box and leave it outside; we can bury her in the spring. Will that be good enough? I can't think of any other way to do it."

She sniffed. "Okay, but we are burying her right next to your dad."

He sighed. "Okay. But we won't do this until it's safe. We have a lot of dogs to kill before we can do that."

She reached out and ran her hand down his face and he kissed her. "Thank you. Thank you for understanding."

"I'm going to take a shower and make a sandwich, and then we'll go outside and set some snares to kill those damn dogs." He got up and walked out of the living room.

Gayle made him a couple of sandwiches while he was in the shower. She had found a smaller ski jacket in Junior's closet when she was emptying it. She'd have to wear that because her coat was going to need some serious alterations before she'd be able to wear it again.

Junior came into the kitchen and began to eat the sandwiches. He told her, "We'll have to work as a team when we go outside. We're going to the garage and getting the other SKS for you to use. You'll have to look carefully for dogs and shoot them if they show up while I'm setting out the snares. I will carry my SKS, too. We'll have to make our way back here as fast as possible. Do you think you're up to doing this?"

She said with a tightening of her jaws, "I will have no problem with that. I'll kill any dog I see from now on. They're killers. They killed my mother. They are predators now. I'll treat them as such."

He looked at her. "Yes, that's what they've turned into. They are canine predators." He suited up and Gayle did the same. He saw her put on his old ski jacket. "I saw all my stuff in the hall. Did you clean out my closet?"

"Yes, I did. I was trying to stay busy and not think too much. It needed to be done so Clint will have room for his stuff."

"We'll sort through everything later and put most of my dad's clothes in the closet for Clint to use. They fit him. Then we'll have room in the closet for our stuff." She nodded. He unbolted the door and they went outside. He turned to her after looking all around. "We'll need to grab some firewood while we're out here." They went into the garage and shut the door. He opened up the secret panel and handed the SKS to Gayle. "The SKS is a semi-automatic and uses ten shots before you have to reload. We'll both carry two hundred rounds each. We aren't taking any chances. This is no game." She nodded. He walked over and grabbed three dozen medium sized snares.

They walked out, not seeing any dogs. Maybe they'd taken off or not followed them all the way home. *One can at least hope,* he thought. As they took a step, they heard a dog howl off in the distance. Junior said, "Do you remember the movie *Mr. And Mrs. Smith*?"

"Yes. Why?"

"Just like yesterday, we need to be like they were in the movie if the dogs show up. Back to back and kill any dog we see. Even a little dog that might get by us and bite can have rabies. It would be fatal for us if that happens, so make sure to kill every one."

"No problem. I will."

"Let's move closer to the house." When they were halfway between the house and garage, like a silent ghost, the pack surrounded them and took up battle positions.

"Get behind me now," Junior said. Gayle quickly moved to his back and turned around and faced the dogs. He saw a huge St. Bernard peeking around some pine trees at them. That must be the Alpha male of the pack. He could see saliva dripping down from the dog's mouth. His head was huge. His growl was deep and loud. He sounded like a semi idling.

"They are moving closer," Gayle said, bracing herself.

He didn't say anything. His attention was on the St. Bernard. He thought, *hang on. Wait, do this slowly, don't spook him. I might get to kill the Alpha male right now.* He had tunnel vision solely on this St. Bernard. The air felt electric. Every sense he had was on heightened alert. He slowly raised the SKS. He would shoot this big son of a bitch in the head. Before the gun stock reached his shoulder, the Alpha male disappeared in a flash of snow, barking loudly.

The Alpha male had given the signal to start the battle. Gayle fired at a huge dog coming at her on the left. Another dog was coming up on the right. She tried desperately to shoot and drop the first one. The shot she fired kicked up snow to the right of the dog. It charged at her full speed and she fired again. Her shot was closer this time, but this dog was moving like greased lightening. She yelled, "Junior!" He looked and saw the one on the right coming at them at a full lunge, mouth gaping wide for the perfect neck grab. He didn't have time to aim, he just pointed the SKS at it and pulled the trigger. The dog was only two feet in front of the barrel and hard to miss at that distance. It fell off to the side, dead. Gayle shot again.

He felt snow pelt his leg going upward. He glanced to that side and saw a dog killed by a head shot lying at Gayle's feet. They each quickly shot two more dogs that died in bloody heaps on the snow. As fast as the attack had started, it broke off. Like silent, ghostly figures, the rest of the pack disappeared back into the woods. They both looked all around at the eerie scene. He said, "Get to the house." He walked backwards with Gayle leading the way. He constantly scanned the woods, straining his eyes, and caught glimpses of ghostly flashes of dark forms running alongside of them. This was like a repeat of the nightmare when he was trying to get away from the dogs and took refuge in that house. It gave him the creeps.

When they were inside, he slammed the door shut, locked it, and wasted no time in dropping the metal plate down and securing that, too. He turned around and said, "Damn, damn, who would have ever thought that such a huge wild dog pack would be in the north woods? You do know what they were doing out there, don't you?"

She looked at him. "Trying to kill us."

"Yes, they want to kill us. But what I mean is they were testing our reaction time shooting them. How long it took us and that kind of thing. That damn Alpha male is just too damn smart."

"Well, we're just going to have be smarter then he is," said Gayle. "And considering that we're talking about a dog, that really shouldn't be too hard to do."

"We need firewood. We have enough for maybe today, but we'll be out by tomorrow. We can't just lock ourselves in here and wait it out. If we don't have heat, the pipes will freeze. That would mean we wouldn't have any water. We have to get more wood in here. I swear I am going to kill every last one of them, so help me, God." He sighed., "We'll try again tomorrow, around noon this time. Maybe we'll have better luck then. My main worry is that they've done this before and learned from the experience. They might have trapped people inside and waited it out because sooner or later people have to go outside for something and then they'd rip them apart or break in and kill them. That's why they didn't give up when I was in that house. They just kept trying to get in and didn't give up. Then those dogs jumped through the window to get in. They didn't realize we were getting ready to come outside. We have to kill all of them, not just for our survival, either, but because they'll wipe out all the game in the area. That'll hurt our future chances of survival. It will also be a strain on our immediate survival to have to guard each step we take. Like now, with the firewood."

Gayle looked worried. "Do you think Clint made it out okay?"

Junior said, "Yeah, I do. There isn't much that can stop someone like him. He's probably got grenades or something to throw at them to keep them from bothering him. I'm glad we found him."

Gayle interrupted him. "Don't you mean he found and saved us?"

"Hmm, you're right. He's probably been watching us for awhile. Having him around increases our chance of surviving. He has skills we need in a big way. He can teach us some of these skills and help us learn how to survive. But we have to get the firewood in here. We don't have a chance without it. One bright spot in all of this is we only have to hold out until he gets back. If we haven't figured out a way to wipe these dogs out before then, he'll probably come up with a plan without even having to think about it." Gayle looked relieved.

Then he dashed her hopes. "But we have to survive between now and then. It's not going to be easy. We have three long days and nights to get through, and only one day of firewood with which to do it." She stood there looking lost and terrified. He put his hand on her shoulder. "Don't give up. We'll find a way to survive. We've been in worse situations and made it. Remember yesterday when we ran out of bullets and it seemed hopeless?" She nodded. "We made it, didn't we?" She nodded again. He hugged her. "We'll do it again. Somehow, someway, we'll make it through this." She believed him. She had great faith in him. He'd never let her down. They may not have known each other all that long, but she knew he wouldn't let her down. She hugged him back. She was so glad she had him in her life.

Later that night when they were snuggling on the couch talking quietly, she asked him, "What did you mean when you said earlier that Clint probably had grenades? Where would he get them from?"

He laughed. "He wouldn't need to get them from anywhere. He could make them from just about anything. He's an expert at making things he'd need to survive behind enemy lines. That includes explosives."

"Wow. He would be a handy guy to have around if we were at war."

"We are at war. Right now we're at war with those dogs. Besides, have you ever thought about the EMP going off?"

"What do you mean? The EMP destroyed our electrical grid and fried all of our electronic equipment."

"Did you ever ask yourself why?"

"Why what? You mean like some country was pissed at us and sent us an EMP and destroyed our electrical grid? Well, take your pick of which country that could have been. Just about every country hated us for one reason or another. It could have been any country that did this to us."

Junior said, "That's true, but the way these things usually work is that's just the first strike of an invasion. You take out the electrical grid and destroy all communications, then you invade and take over. We might be under invasion right now and wouldn't know it. We might be in the middle of a war. Why else would a country take a chance of doing this if they didn't intend on invading? Nothing else makes sense."

She said, "You think that might really be happening?"

"Yes, I do. Why bring so much misery to the world if you didn't intend on taking advantage of it? You know we must have retaliated. Why else would they do this? They'd have to know that our country would send over missiles to bomb their cities. The question I can't answer is, what country was desperate enough to do this? Both countries would be devastated. That's why I'm so glad to have met Clint. He can teach us how to fight."

She shivered. "That's a scary thought. Living out here, we may not even hear about it for years. I never thought about that part of this mess. That's all we need." She lay on the couch, thinking.

"It's something to keep in mind, anyway."

"I want Clint to teach me to fight, too," Gayle said. "I can learn to defend my country. No way am I going to sit here and let some assholes come over here and take us over. No way."

The next day, before they got ready to go out, Junior said, "I'll go out to the woodpile and get the firewood. You cover me with the SKS. We'll be real quiet and not make any noise. No talking and no bumping into the door. We don't want to let the dogs know we're outside. Your aim yesterday was a little off to the right. What you need to do is aim a little to the left of the target, that will compensate for the pull to the right and make you more accurate, okay?"

"Okay. How much wood are you going to bring in?"

"I was thinking about fifteen or so armfuls would get us through three to four more days. Then if Clint is a little longer than he thought, we won't run out before he gets back."

"All right. I just hope those damn dogs have left."

"I highly doubt it," Junior said. "But it can't hurt to hope for that." He kissed her and she hugged him.

They didn't really use much wood because three sides of the house were protected by the hill it was built into. Even the roof was covered with dirt and blended into the hill naturally. It kept the heat inside in the winter and kept the place cool in the summer. Junior unlocked the outside door and looked all around, making sure the area was clear of dogs. None were in sight. He signaled to Gayle that it was clear and he was going for an armful of wood. He had his SKS over his shoulder just in case. The woodpile was about twenty feet from the front door. He filled his arms up with wood, brought it to the house, and gently laid it inside to the left, out of the way. He went back out and grabbed more. Gayle was looking around for the dogs, keeping alert to the danger. So far they hadn't seen any live dogs, just the dead ones lying in the yard. They hadn't been eaten. Maybe they'd moved on to complete their travel cycle. All predators did that. He went and got another load of wood and turned around to head back to the house. He heard a deep, ferocious hungry growl that made the hair on the back of his neck stand straight up and an electric shock of fear ran throughout his body. He quickly looked up to where the sound was coming from. There was a Rottweiler up on the roof. It jumped and was in flight, coming straight for him with its mouth opened wide. The dog's large fangs stood out crystal clear. They were gleaming deadly white in the sunlight, drawing the eyes to them. The dog's jaws were ready and anxious to tear out his throat. The logs started to fall out of his arms and he thought, *Shit, we didn't think they'd be on the roof. This is going to be bad, real bad.*

Chapter 17

Reunion

"Faith is the process of leaping into the abyss not on the basis of any certainty about ~ where ~ we shall land, but rather on the belief that we ~ shall ~ land."

Carter Heyward

Eric and Lisa whispered at the same time, "Abby."

"Where's Mark?" asked Eric.

Lisa ran over to Abby and gave her a big hug. "I'm so glad you guys are all right."

All the noise they made woke Mark up. He peered around a branch above Abby's head and said in surprise, "Eric." Boy, was he glad to see him. Mark stepped around Abby. "How in the hell did you find us?"

Eric looked puzzled. "What are you talking about? Find you? You're the one that found us. We were just patrolling out a ways from where we're staying. Why did you guys stop here for the day?"

Mark said, "I don't know. You'd have to ask Abby. She insisted we stop here. We still had an hour to travel until daylight, but she insisted we stay here."

Everyone turned and looked at Abby. Abby smiled, shrugging her shoulders. "Call it woman's intuition." Lisa smiled at her answer. The men exchanged puzzled looks.

"Where is your camp at?" asked Mark.

Eric smiled. "We're staying in an empty log cabin." Eric and Lisa exchanged a smile because they both knew how excited they were going to be to find out everything worked in the cabin and that it was full of food.

"Where?" Mark asked.

"Up the road about two miles. Let's get your camp packed up." They followed Mark to a spot concealed with branches and brush.

Lisa asked, "How's Channon been?"

"Channon isn't with us anymore. She decided to stay with Chuck and his group. She was pregnant, you know." Lisa gasped at the news, and then horror filled her as she realized how she must have gotten pregnant. Abby explained, "She was pregnant before she was taken."

Lisa drew a breath of air in relief. "Why did she decide to stay there?"

"Because they have a doctor and can take proper care of her. Also, there were some black guys there and she felt a little more comfortable being with them. They treated her real well, just like she was a princess." She smiled, remembering how the three black guys had practically tripped over their own feet and swallowed their tongues when Channon had said she'd stay. All three of them had offered their places to Channon. They kept trying to outdo each other. Chuck finally told them to knock it off and to let Channon decide.

"Oh, I'm glad for her," said Lisa, "but I will miss her."

"I think it's for the best. They're a lot more civilized than we've been and can offer her proper medical care now for her and the baby."

"Well, just wait until you see where we're staying. We're being very civilized at the moment, too."

The camp was almost packed. "What have you been up to since we got separated?" asked Mark.

Eric said, "We'll talk about it once we get to the cabin. How much food do you have left?"

"Not much."

Eric said, "I decided to stop at an abandoned place to hole up for a few days so we could snare more food and rest up some. When we get to the cabin you can have a nice hot meal. Also, I stopped to help Maria. She had a very bad cough. Now that we have been staying inside, her cough has gotten better. It's not gone yet, but it's a lot better than it was."

Abby wanted details, but contained herself until she could see Maria for herself. She would find some dried herbs or some bushes around here that could help her with the cough. They all stopped and watched two deer eating something on the ground. They moved on when the deer walked off.

"Of course, now that we have met up with you we see deer," Mark said. "I was going to shoot one and dry it like we did before, because we are down to our last few slices of jerky. We've been keeping an eye out for deer and haven't seen one in days now." They got to the end of the path, but they still couldn't see the cabin yet. Eric and Lisa were excited to show them everything but wanted them to see it for themselves. They shared another smile. Then Eric remembered the three children they had with them and knew Mark wasn't going to be very happy. Children would just slow them down. Oh well, they'd just have to figure something out.

They came down the driveway and the cabin came into view. Abby's eyes got big and Mark just looked at Eric strangely. Eric must have lost his mind. It would take a lot of wood to heat that huge place up. Mark shook his head. They went around the back and came in through the kitchen door. The warmth hit them first, then the smell of something wonderful cooking. Then, they heard kids talking.

Abby said, "Children? You have children here?"

"What is that smell?" asked Mark. "Whatever it is, I want a lot of it." Both Eric and Lisa laughed.

Maria wandered over to the mudroom because she heard voices; she looked inside and squealed out, "Abby!" She ran over and gave her a hug, then she noticed Mark standing there with a very shocked look on his face. She reached out and touched his arm. "Welcome to our humble abode."

Mark walked into the kitchen and a little blur flew by him and jumped into Eric's arms. "I'm so glad you're back. I missed you."

Lisa reached out and straightened the little girl's collar on the cute blouse she was wearing and said, "We have guests. You have to be on your very best behavior now, sweetie."

"I'm always good. Isn't I, Eric?" Amanda said, her little arms wrapped around Eric's neck.

Maria corrected her. "You should say 'aren't I, Eric,' not 'isn't I.'"

"Okay. Aren't I, Eric?"

Eric laughed and gave her a peck on the cheek. "Yes, you are good. Amanda, this is Mark and Abby. They are going to be staying here with us from now on."

Amanda said, "Hi."

"Hi, Amanda," said Mark.

"Hi, Amanda. How are you?" asked Abby.

Amanda thought for a moment. "My brothers and me are good. Eric, Issa and Mia gave us food and let us stay here. But, you have to drink your milk or you don't get anymore cookies."

Abby laughed. "I can see that you are good. I'm glad to meet you. I'll remember to drink my milk so I can have more cookies, too."

Amanda said, "Yeah, me too." She leaned over to Abby and whispered, "It's yucky instant milk." She made a funny face. It made the adults laugh.

"Now run along and play because us grownups need to talk," said Eric. He bent over, put her down, and patted her on the head.

She streaked by the rest of them, running out of the kitchen. Maria called out, "Don't run. Walk." She stood there and shook her head; Amanda was long gone and hadn't heard a word she'd said. Maria turned to Eric. "Please don't tell her to run. She could fall and hurt herself."

"I didn't think of that. I'll be more careful how I phrase things. Thanks for reminding me. We don't want the children to get injured." Maria smiled at him.

Mark said, "It seems you've found a new little friend."

Eric laughed. "Yes, we have a few more of them, too."

Mark looked like he didn't like that idea at all. "How many more do you have?"

"Two more."

Mark sighed. "I'm starving. Can we eat? It smells absolutely wonderful, whatever it is."

Lisa laughed. "That's in the oven for dinner. We'll have it later. Sit down and Maria and I will make you something to tide you over." Lisa took her outer clothes off and hung them up. She went into the pantry and came back with another canned ham. Mark and Abby weren't paying attention to what Lisa or Maria was doing. They were in a deep conversation about all that had happened since they'd been separated.

Lisa put the canned ham on the counter and reached over to the sink and turned the faucet on to wash her hands. Both Abby and Mark jumped up out of their chairs. "Water!"

Maria reached over and turned the light on. Both of them gasped.

"Holy shit, you've got electricity!" Mark said. Eric grinned and didn't say anything.

"We have hot water for a shower or a bath, too," Lisa said. "And downstairs, there's a washer and dryer."

Maria said, "Come here. I want to show you something." She walked over to the pantry and beckoned Mark and Abby over.

They took a look inside. "Look at all that food!" Abby said.

Mark was stunned speechless. He turned around and looked at Eric. "How did you know about this place?"

Eric said, "I didn't. It was pure luck that I picked this cabin."

Lisa, in the meantime, had fried up some ham slices with honey on them and heated up some macaroni and cheese they had left over from last night, along with some green beans. She buttered a few slices of bread.

Maria set the table. She piled up a plate for Mark with a lot of ham and placed the rest on the table so Abby could eat as much as she wanted. Maria finally said, "This is going to get cold if you two don't get over here and eat." Mark and Abby quickly came over and sat at the table. Lisa poured them each a cup of coffee. Maria got them a glass of milk from the refrigerator.

Eric said with a smile on his face, "Don't you want to wash your hands first?"

Mark and Abby looked at each other, ignored Eric, and dug into their food. Mark thought, *Holy cow, this tastes so good.*

While Mark and Abby were stuffing themselves, Eric and Lisa told Maria how they'd all run into each other.

"It's by the Grace of God,"Maria said. "His guiding hand brought all of us together again."

Just then Chris walked in. "Amanda said someone was here. Who are they?" He looked at Mark and Abby suspiciously.

"These are our friends," Eric said. "The ones we've been waiting for. Come over and meet them."

Eric reached out and pulled him closer, putting his hands on Chris's shoulders. "Chris, I would like you to meet my best friend, Mark."

Chris still looked a bit suspicious, but he struck his hand out to shake hands with Mark. "Pleased to meet you."

Mark shook hands with Chris. "How's it going?"

"It's going fine now that we have Eric, Lisa and Maria."

"They are nice people."

Chris nodded. "Yes, they are. How long are you going to say with us?"

Mark looked up at Eric and raised his eyebrow at him. "Mark and I were together, making our way to a place we have up north. Then we acquired Lisa, Maria, Channon and Abby. We got separated when we ran into some trouble. Lisa and Maria were with me and Channon and Abby were with Mark. He'll be traveling with us to our retreat up north. He and Abby are part of our group."

Chris looked up at Eric. "Do you trust them?"

"I trust them. I trust Mark with my life. He has saved my life a time or two. I trust him more than anyone else alive on this earth. He's closer to me than a brother."

Chris relaxed. "Then I can trust him, too."

Mark sighed, shaking his head. "What is it with you, Eric? You're always picking up stray people and they automatically trust you and believe what you say is the gospel truth."

Eric laughed. "It's a gift." Mark rolled his eyes and everyone laughed.

"Chris, this is Abby. She's also part of our group and will be going up north with us."

Abby shook his hand., "Glad to meet you."

Chris said, "I'm glad to meet you, too."

"What are you and the others doing up there?" asked Maria.

"Ryan and I are playing a racing game. I'm starved. When are we eating?" Eric had set up the Nintendo PlayStation they found in the boys' room when Lisa and Maria were moving things around.

Maria laughed. "You're always hungry. But I guess that's what a growing boy does, huh?" She got out some of the chocolate chip cookies she'd made and poured three glasses of milk. It was nonfat instant milk and the children didn't care for it much. She made the children drink three to four glasses everyday. Mark and Abby just watched her as if they had never seen anything like it before.

Maria just smiled. "Go get your brother and sister and you can all have some milk and cookies to hold you over until lunch time."

"Okay. But we have to make this fast because I was winning. I don't want to lose my high score." He raced out of the kitchen. Mark and Abby looked kind of shell-shocked at this exchange. They both had thought they'd never see or hear anything that sounded normal like this again.

The children devoured their cookies and milk. Maria passed around a plate for everyone. Lisa refilled all the adults' cups with coffee.

Mark and Abby had several. It was hard for the adults to get a word in; the children dominated the conversation. Amanda totally wrapped Mark and Abby around her little finger. She was a beautiful little girl, very sweet and chatty. You could tell someone had raised her with security and love. The same was apparent with the boys, Chris and Ryan, but in a different way. Those two boys were going to be real heart breakers when they grew up. They were already good looking. Once the children accepted you into the family, so to speak, you were an immediate member and treated as such. They all had a lot of questions for Mark and Abby. They were all having a good time just being together and getting to know one another when Amanda asked a question that caused all conversation to abruptly cease.

She was sitting on Eric's lap and she asked Abby if they had seen her mother. Abby wasn't sure how to answer, so she decided to be honest. "I'm sorry, Amanda, but I haven't seen her. I don't know where she is."

Amanda said, "Our mommy went out to get us some food and she didn't come back, so we went looking for her."

Abby reached out and patted her arm. "We'll keep our eye out for her, okay?"

Amanda was quite satisfied with that and nodded. "Okay. Mia, can I have another cookie, please?" Everyone sort of sighed and started talking again. Maria handed Amanda a cookie. The adults turned the conversation on to other things.

Lisa and Maria had moved the little girl's bed into the boys' room because it had two captain bunks built into the wall. They rearranged all the furniture to make it fit. It was much easier to move one bed than to rip out two from the wall. They did this the first day when the children had become a part of their group. Chris was quite adamant about that. His mother had told him to look after his brother and sister and he wanted them close, so, all three children slept in the same room. That left one empty bedroom with no bed in it. They'd made it into a playroom for the children. The master bedroom had a king-size bed. The next bedroom had a queen-size bed. And the next one down from that room had two twin beds in it. Maria had chosen the room with two twin beds as her room. Lisa took the one with the queen size bed in it and both women had made Eric take the master bedroom for his room. Now they needed to rearrange the sleeping arrangements.

Lisa and Maria went upstairs and talked about this. It was decided to move Eric and Mark into the room with the twin beds. They'd give Abby the room with the queen-size bed so she could have the luxury of her own room, and they'd take the master bedroom. They changed the sheets and moved all their things. They told Abby and Mark to come upstairs and see their rooms; they could take a shower or a bath and get cleaned up. They quickly explained to Eric what they had done. He agreed that it was best. Lisa, Maria and Amanda showed them around. They were overjoyed to have bathrooms in their bedrooms. Amanda gave them all her opinions on things, too.

Mark and Abby were tired. They were going to clean up and then get some sleep in a real bed. Everyone promised to save them some dinner. Abby had heard Maria cough a few times and told her she'd look around and see if she could find something for her to take. Maria hugged and thanked her.

It was time for Amanda's nap. Maria read the kids a few stories at night and read to Amanda when it was her nap time. Lisa had a beautiful singing voice and if they got restless, she'd sing to them until they settled down. Amanda didn't have any nightmares. They weren't sure why.

Eric, Lisa and Maria figured that their mother was probably dead. They probably would never know what happened to her exactly. There really wasn't a way to find out. It seemed that the children talked about her less and less every day, and Amanda only asked about her occasionally, but every once in awhile, Amanda would say something that would make the adults think she understood more about the situation and the danger out there than they gave her credit for. Eric said he thought the boys knew that something had to have happened to their mother and that's why she hadn't come back, but were afraid to voice it out loud. Between the three of them, they had kept all the children pretty busy most of the time so they didn't have a lot of time to brood or think about it too much. They didn't know how else to handle this situation except to be around and available if they wanted to talk about it. But they all realized that the boy's fears and insecurities were coming out in the nightmares they had been having. Well, now they had Mark and Abby around to help, too. Eric looked at it like the five of them were pretty much parents to them now. He smiled, thinking back to his own childhood and teenage years. Two parents had been way too many as far as he'd been concerned. These poor kids were going to have five parents around all the time. He chuckled to himself and thought they wouldn't be able to get away with very much.

Mark and Abby got up after a while and ate their dinner. Mark was overjoyed at having coffee again. They had run out about four days ago. It was a relief not to be on watch all the time too. Neither one had realized how run down they were getting. They needed a good long rest. It was decided that they'd stay there for five days, rest up, eat real well, and fortify themselves for the trip north. Then they would all pack up and head out. They sat around and shared their stories of what had happened to them while they'd been apart. Eric was upset to find out Mark had been so sick. He felt bad for abandoning them when they'd needed him so badly. He apologized. Mark told him to just forget it. It worked out fine and Abby was quite a resourceful person. He told them the tea she made him drink tasted like poison, but it had worked. He wasn't totally back to one hundred percent, but he was getting stronger all the time and felt better each day. Abby said now that they'd be eating better and really resting, he'd be able to heal all the way. Eric, Lisa and Maria told them about how they had escaped and the guy that had stood practically on top of them. Mark and Abby were very impressed. .

Abby said to Lisa, "I have a message to you from Tim. I don't understand it, but he said you'd know what it meant. He wore a hat with some white cloth sewed over it and said to tell you he remembered to wear his white hat. Eric and Maria started laughing real hard; Lisa looked embarrassed. Mark and Abby asked what the message meant and why it was funny. Eric asked if Chuck or his men had said what Lisa did. They said no. He explained.

Mark raised his eyebrow to Lisa. "Wow, I am very impressed. You picked exactly the right man to point the shotgun at to make Chuck defuse the situation and give up his position of power at that moment."

Lisa, still embarrassed, said, "I reacted like some psycho is what you mean."

"No, Lisa, that isn't what I mean at all. You reacted like a warrior and were determined not to let them capture you again. You already had been a POW and tortured once, you were making sure not to let it happen again. We are at war with just about everyone. It's true. You can't trust anyone anymore. You did real well. Your instincts were in the right place." She sat up a little straighter in her chair, feeling better about what had happened with Tim and not quite as embarrassed about losing control.

Maria asked if Chuck and his group gave them one of those MRE things to eat.

"Yes, they did." Mark said that they came up a little rise and Chuck and a small group of men were standing there, waiting for them. "I was startled because Chuck called me by name. He said that you'd already been through their territory and they'd been expecting us to show up. They had an MRE right there to give each of us, and a bundle of clothes for Abby and Channon to wear. The whole encounter was strange. They shared news with us and treated us very well. I kept expecting them to do something, but they never did."

Abby said, "As we were leaving, a man gave me a bag of apples." Maria laughed and said the same thing had happened to her too. Lisa asked if she had a bag of M & Ms in her MRE. Abby said yes. They talked long into the night, just enjoying being together again.

Chris had taken to following Eric around, constantly asking his opinions on things as he helped Eric. Ryan had taken a liking to Mark and kind of followed him around and offered to help him with things. Mark would explain what he was doing and show him what needed to be done. Ryan would jump right to it and do his best to do it right. They became real pals. Amanda was in love with Eric. She loved the rest of them, too, but Eric was special. Usually, wherever Eric was, Amanda wouldn't be very far away. When they gathered together as a group, she always sat on Eric's lap or right next to him.

Mark decided to try to make a stock for his rifle somehow. He could fire the rifle if he had to, but it would be easier with a real stock on it again. He went out to the garage to see what was out there. He looked around and found a nice looking two by four. It was pine, but he thought it might work if he made the stock thicker where it joined the receiver. He needed a handsaw, a plane, some wood files and sand paper. That would work, but drilling the hole for the full length of the stock pretty much stumped him. He thought about it for a while. All the wood drills were only eight inches long. He needed the main hole to be a half-inch around and at least fourteen inches long. Well, he could drill the first part and that would be eight inches. He could then drill from the other side the four inches to make the five- sixteenth hole to support the bolt to attach the stock tight.

But, how was he going to reach the length of fourteen inches? That was going to be the most difficult problem to overcome. He'd have to figure it out as he went along. He gathered up the tools he needed and grabbed the two by four and cut a fourteen inch piece off of it. Then he traced an outline of the stock from memory. It was crude, but something to figure out where to drill the holes. He had to drill the holes for the stock first before doing anything else. Then he would form it to fit later. He found a hand drill and a vise on a workbench. He slowly made an eight inch long hole. How to get those last six inches? Maybe he could he make the stock only twelve inches long? Would that work? He thought a short stock would be better than no stock. No, he decided, that wouldn't work. He was going to have to come up with a way to do this. He looked around the garage for something useful. Damn, no survival manual he ever read talked about storing a long drill bit for making and repairing stocks. But, he was sure he was the first person in history to have a stock shattered by a bullet. He laughed. Of course, leave it to him to be the first.

He looked around at what was there in the garage. He found some three-eighths inch copper tubing. Was there a way to make a drill bit out of it? He looked over and saw a file. Maybe he could use it to cut teeth into the end of it to make it sharp. Well, there was only one way to find out. He did it and it seemed pretty sharp to him. Now, how was he going to be able to use it to make the hole the length he needed? He thought about it for awhile. He decided the best way would be to try the fire bow method and see if that would work. Abby walked by just then and he called her over and asked for her help. He explained what he was doing. Abby went outside and found a good size rock and Mark put some grease on it. She held on to the rock and pressed down hard as Mark worked the copper tubing back and forth with some string. This caused friction on both ends and burned the grease off the rock, so Abby had to replace it every few minutes to make it work. When she did that, Mark would remove the copper tubing and shake out all the wood shavings in the hole and the tubing and re-sharpen it. It was a slow process, but it was working. It felt like they did about a quarter inch every five minutes.

It took over an hour to finally reach those last six inches he needed. It was very simple then to drill the five-sixteenth inch hole from the other end, meeting the two holes together. He thanked Abby for her help and she smiled at him. "No problem. I'm all for getting your rifle ready to be used right. Never know when we might need it."

Over the rest of the day, he cut and planed his crude stock. He knew pine wasn't as tough as walnut, so he left the groove part extra thick. Before he realized it, the daylight started to fade. He had spent the whole day on this. All he had to do was attach it to the stock. He looked around and found a socket set. He again ran into the length problem. The three-eighth socket set didn't have a sixteen-inch extension. How frustrating. He put it down and walked away. He knew from past experience that if he didn't walk away from it, he'd end up ruining it somehow. Maria called to him that dinner was done.

As they were all eating, he mentioned to Eric how frustrating it was not to have the right tools. He explained about the length problem. Eric asked if he'd looked in the tool room down in the basement to see if there was something in there to help. He thought he had seen a few extension bars down there when he'd been looking for something else. Mark jumped up and went downstairs. He had to know right then. He found the room and looked around and sure enough, he found a one-fourth-drive socket with three extension bars. That would do the trick. He smiled and laughed. This was going to work out after all. He brought them upstairs and placed them on a counter. He sat back down and finished his dinner. When he was done, he grabbed the rifle, sat down, and lined the bolt up; it worked. His rifle was whole once more. He brought it over and showed everyone.

Maria said, "Isn't that color going to show up at night? It looks white to me."

Mark looked at it and thought about staining it. No, they didn't have time for that. Mark said, "I guess I could rub dirt on it to darken it."

"Maybe we can find some ashes to darken it."

Chris said, "Couldn't you paint it? There is a can of black spray paint downstairs."

"It will depend on what kind of paint it is," said Mark. "That's a good idea, though. Let's go take a look and see if it will work." They headed downstairs. It was a flat black color that would work just fine. He took it all apart again and applied a few coats, then left it to dry overnight. It felt really good to have his rifle whole again.

Each day the women gathered up the supplies little by little that they were going to take with them. Mark came up with the idea of using the wheelbarrow to put the food and supplies in. Eric said that would work great, because then Amanda could sit or lay on top when she got tired of walking. The women thought this was a great idea, too. Abby asked how they were going to get it up the mountains. Mark and Eric had to think about all the aspects of that before answering. They came up with the idea that they would all take a turn pushing it up and wheeling it down. Eric came up with the idea of using a large brick to place in front of the wheel if it became unstable. They could quickly put the brick down to stop it so they wouldn't lose everything over the side of the mountain if it started to get away from them. Each day they made sure to do the laundry and they started to pack some things away for the trip.

Mark was curious about what was in the basement. He decided to go check it out. He found some camping and hiking equipment in one of the rooms. Now they'd have enough equipment for the kids, too. Maria had found two kids' sleeping bags in one of the upstairs hall closets, so they'd use them for the two young ones. There were several small backpacks that were kid-sized, too, so they'd be able to pack the kids' things. Mark found a medium to large size navy blue pack in the garage that Chris could carry. He'd been looking for more water containers. Mark and Eric cut some cord to attach to the bottom of the packs for the sleeping bags. Lisa and Maria washed everything so they'd be fresh and clean. The next day, Mark found a brown sleeping bag rolled up in the garage when he was looking for some extra cord, so, Chris would have a sleeping bag. Eric found some ski pants and jackets in a downstairs closet and they altered them to fit Chris and Ryan. The boys just had their jackets, hats and gloves. It was going to get cold soon, so they were doing everything they could to make sure the kids would be warm.

The kids were excited about the trip. They didn't realize what a chore it was walking that far. They'd find out soon enough.

Before they went to bed on the last night, they packed up everything and had it ready. Tomorrow would be their last day at the cabin. Mark found some antifreeze in the garage and would put that down the drains and the toilets to keep the pipes from freezing. They planned to leave the place as clean as they'd found it and usable for others. All the women were busy making sure everything was clean. The kids were a big help with this. The boys had a hard time deciding what they wanted to pack in the bag Mark had given them to put extra things into to occupy them for the trip. Mark and Eric had tied two bags together just like Eric had done for the women, but this time for the boys to carry. Mark also came up with an idea of tying a couple of the small backpacks to the side and back of the wheelbarrow to carry more things in and to help stabilize it. They'd be using all of the small backpacks for one thing or another. Mostly they were used to carry extra water in.

It would be their last night for a while sleeping on a real bed. They'd be taking off tomorrow as soon as it got dark.

Lisa, Maria and Abby went into the master bedroom to talk. They did this every night before bed. Abby handed Maria a cup of tea. She made her the tea to drink three times a day for her cough, one in the morning, the afternoon and at night before bed. She no longer had a cough, but Abby was going to have her continue to drink it for a few more days.

Maria said, "Thank you. I just wish we could stay here. We have everything we need."

"Mark explained all of that. They have supplies at the retreat that will last for years. These supplies would run out a lot sooner than that. Besides, Mark's dad is up there; he probably needs Mark and Eric to help defend the place."

Lisa said, "I wish we could just teleport up there or something. I am not looking forward to sleeping on the ground again." The other women nodded.

"All that walking, too," added Maria.

"Well, the only other option," said Abby, "would be to stay here ourselves, and we already decided that would be stupid. We don't even have a semi-auto assault rifle to use to defend this place." The other women agreed.

Lisa sighed. "I know. I just hate to leave this place. Who knows what the retreat will be like or what will happen between here and there?" They wouldn't know until they got there.

Abby decided to change the subject. "So, Lisa, what's up with you and Eric?" Lisa looked at her with a puzzled expression. "What do you mean?"

"Maybe it's just me, but it seems like you spend a lot of time with him alone. Are you two becoming a couple?"

Lisa's eyes got big. "No. No, it's nothing like that. I just like being around him."

Lisa looked down at her lap. "There can't be anything like that between us. How do I know if I'm pregnant? Or if I have some horrible disease from what happened? I couldn't do that to him."

Abby nodded her head in understanding. "So, if you knew you weren't pregnant and didn't have a horrible disease, would you be a couple with him?"

"I'd like to, but I don't know if I can. I don't know if I could ever have sex again and not remember what happened."

Abby studied her for a few moments. "Why?"

Lisa looked startled and then got a little angry. "You of all people are asking me that? You know why."

Abby remained calm. "No, I don't know why. Explain it to me."

Lisa started pacing around the room., "Because every time I think about it, it makes me sick to my stomach, that's why. I want to throw up. That isn't a good way to set the mood, you know. It would be the foreplay from hell, don't you think? 'I'm sorry, but I have to go throw up, and by the way, you make me sick.' That isn't a very good start to a relationship."

Abby nodded her head. "I agree with you. That wouldn't be a very good start. But, what I want to know is why does the thought of sex make you sick? Was it because you didn't like it before we were attacked?"

Lisa looked at her. "I liked sex just as much as anyone else. In fact, I liked it just fine until this happened."

"How can you let those animals win?"

Lisa said, "Win? Win what?"

"Those animals did everything they could to humiliate and demean us. They wanted us destroyed completely, mentally, emotionally, and physically. They didn't want us dead, they wanted us destroyed. Those animals did that to make us less than human, to make us sub-human. If we can't have a relationship with a man and run scared every time a man gets close to us in that way, they've won and accomplished what they set out to do."

Lisa looked at Abby thoughtfully. "I never thought about it that way. That's exactly how I've been reacting, too."

"Good. Now you see what they've really done to us. None of it was about sex. It was only used as a violent tool to accomplish what they wanted. If they thought for one minute that beating us would have had the same effect, they probably wouldn't even have bothered with sex at all. So, being afraid of sex is stupid. Being afraid of a man is stupid. Being afraid of the ones that held us captive is a whole different subject. You have to separate that in your mind. Always remember those who abused us were animals, they were not real men."

Lisa said, "Wow. I never thought about it like that. But you're right, they are separate things. I see that now. So how do I separate them in my feelings?"

Abby said, "You have to come to terms with what happened to you. It was horrible. It was a nightmare. Then you need to think about those horrible things in a new light. Then you can separate them in your mind. Once you can do this, your feelings can be normal again. What happened wasn't done by a loving man or a man you had a sexual relationship with. Demented animals did those things. Big difference, don't you think? So you would be wrong to associate a normal loving man with them in any way whatsoever."

"I think I understand. I'm not sure I can do that yet. But I'm going to try."

"Every time you go over what happened to you with this new information, you'll start to understand how sick and demented those animals were. It has nothing to do with a normal relationship with a man." Abby reached out and hugged Lisa. "It'll get easier each day. You both are strong women or you wouldn't have lasted as long as you have. Just keep reminding yourself of that. One of these days you'll start believing it, because it's true." Maria came over and hugged both of them. She was thinking about what Abby said, too.

The next day they tried to keep everything cleaned up. They all took long showers, because who knew how long it would be again before they would be able to be really clean. Lisa and Maria got all the dirty clothes washed up and packed away. Abby filled all the water containers they'd found. Mark and Eric spent a lot of time making sure the supplies in the wheelbarrow were evenly distributed with the heaviest things in the middle on the bottom. The men had also nailed a board to the frame around the window they had broken to get in. They planned on locking the doors again and leaving just one door unlocked. The last thing they did was to run the dishwasher and put the dishes away in the cupboards. Eric and Mark went around and turned everything off, then poured the antifreeze. The sun was just starting to set when they walked out of the house for the last time. They got the wheelbarrow, then locked that door to the outside. Everyone started off down the road. The kids were skipping around excitedly, thinking it was a great adventure to be traveling at night. It was not going to be easy to teach them to be quiet. They were kids, it just didn't come naturally to them. Amanda especially was a chatterbox. The best they'd been able to do was to get her to talk quieter. Eric had made up a game to teach her to be still and totally quiet. They'd just have to wait and see how well that was going to work.

Amanda got tired after twenty minutes and wanted Eric or Mark to carry her on their shoulders. Mark and Eric explained to her that they had to be ready to defend them if they ran into bad people and couldn't carry her around. They put her on the wheelbarrow. She got her toy water pistol out and pretended to shoot at things. The women had practiced pushing the wheelbarrow around for a few days to prepare. They were all amazed that Abby seemed to have the best sense of balance with it. They thought it would be harder for her because she was so small. They stopped for a break and had a snack. When they decided to stop the next time they waited to reach a level part before they made a real meal. Amanda finally fell asleep on top of the wheelbarrow after they ate. Mark had moved some things around a bit so she could lay down exactly in the middle with the sides a little higher than she was so she wouldn't roll off in her sleep. The other two boys kept up with them, but the novelty of this adventure had worn off a few hours ago. Ryan occupied himself with looking around for wildlife. Chris was given the job of carrying the brick and being responsible for putting it down if the wheelbarrow became unstable.

About a half hour before sunrise, they started looking around for a place to sleep and hole up for the day. Mark walked up the incline into the woods and found a pretty level area where a few trees had fallen and there was some brush they could use to conceal themselves. That was getting to be a real problem. Pretty soon there wasn't going to be any brush left and they'd have to find downed logs instead. That wasn't always easy to find. The boys perked up again when it was time to make camp for the day. They thought this was really cool. Mark and Eric showed them how to make the area where they'd be sleeping more secure.

It was really cold. Everyone except Eric gratefully crawled into their sleeping bags to get some sleep. He had the first watch. Everyone fell almost instantly asleep. Even Amanda was still asleep. They had decided that when she woke up, one other would be awakened to keep her busy and quiet. The first shift had fallen to Lisa. When Amanda woke up, Eric would let Lisa know. The second shift was Maria's and the third shift was Abby's. They had decided that the men would stand watch and the women would take turns watching the children and sleeping in shifts. The women were going to be doing all the cooking and everything else to do with the camp. The hardest part for the boys to understand had been the fact that they couldn't have a fire for warmth. Mark explained that this was not a camping trip for fun. Fires were a danger for them. Smoke could be seen for miles around on a mountain and let other people know right where they were. So far, Eric and Mark hadn't seen anyone on their shifts.

Amanda had woken up about eight that morning and Lisa got up with her. She made some oatmeal for Amanda, Eric and herself and served it with buttered bread. Amanda thought it was a great adventure and quite funny to go potty in the woods. She'd been real quiet all day and played with her toys and colored in the coloring books. When it was nap time, she had crawled into the sleeping bag that Lisa was sleeping in. When Eric woke up, they both were still sleeping and looked like a mother and daughter. They looked a lot alike.

A couple of hours before dark, they were all up and getting a big meal going. Chris and Ryan were getting restless, so Eric took them for a short walk and showed them some animal tracks and explained what animals had made them. They were very interested in this. He had them look around close by and find more tracks and see if they could identify what animal had made them. He showed them how to hide behind a tree if they saw anyone. He said they needed to learn to be very quiet and to walk like a ghost. He had them practice walking, stopping to listen, and to identify the sounds they heard. That would tell them how far away they were from where the sound was coming from. The boys said this was like training to be a ninja. They liked that idea.

Abby spoke up. "Ninjas were hired assassins. That's not something you want to be." All three of them jumped when she spoke. They hadn't seen or heard her approach.

Eric turned to her. "I see you've been practicing to be a silent ghost. You're very good at it."

Abby said, "Thank you. I came to tell you the food will be done soon." She turned to the boys. "You two need to wash your hands and face. Come on." They all went back to camp. Eric had never really watched her walk before. He stared at her, trying to decide how she walked like that. She seemed to glide. He wasn't sure how to describe it exactly. He shook his head. He was getting fanciful now. It didn't matter how she walked as long as it was quiet.

They got the camp all packed up and set off. All of the adults' arms were sore from pushing the wheelbarrow. It was a lot harder than it looked. They were all going to get into shape, that was sure. It had turned into a routine once again. The kids were adjusting and they were quiet. Maria thought it was because it was dark. Darkness usually inspired quietness. When they were traveling, Amanda mostly slept. There had been a few times when she had wanted a story and the adults explained they had to be quiet. She picked up on their unease and had gotten pretty subdued, understanding that things were not the same as when they had been at the cabin.

Mark was getting worried about all the delays they seemed to run into. If they got caught in one of the passes and a blizzard hit them, it was going to be bad, real bad. They might not be able to go on. He was worried. He hadn't shared his fears with anyone, no sense in upsetting anyone else. He was worrying enough for all of them. Everyone was keeping alert because they weren't far from Redding now. Cities and towns meant people. The kids had picked up on the adults' tension and had hardly said anything. Even Amanda was a lot quieter.

Mark said, "When we're over this mountain, Redding will be on the other side." They'd been climbing for a long time now.

They came around a bend in the road and spotlights turned on, blinding them about a hundred yards ahead. A voice over a bullhorn said, "Freeze!" They heard a motor start up and a truck raced straight for them, coming to a screeching halt right in front of them. Five guys jumped out of the back, aiming their rifles at them.

Two men got out of the cab. One of them said, "Turn around and start walking. This road is closed. No one gets through here. Go back where you came from."

Mark said, "We're just passing through. We're on our way to Oregon."

The man said, "No one comes through here. Turn around and go back."

Eric stepped forward. "We don't want to stop in your city. We're just passing through. Send an escort with us to make sure we don't stop anywhere or whatever, but we need to get through. We have to make it to Oregon. We don't want any trouble."

The two men were getting mad now and the tension was building. The other man said, "Get going or we'll shoot."

Amanda started to cry. "I wasn't bad, Mister. Why do you want to shoot us?" She looked up at them with tear-filled eyes.

The two men felt bad and swallowed hard. The first man said, "Just turn around and everything will be fine."

Amanda started to sob really loud. "Please don't shoot us. Please!" Amanda looked terrified and tears were rolling down her cheeks as she stared at the men. Everyone just sort of froze and didn't know what to say.

Well, Lisa had enough of this. She stepped around Mark and Eric and put her hands on her hips and yelled with a hard look in her eyes and steel in her voice, "You should be ashamed of yourselves, terrifying these children. Telling them you're going to shoot them. How dare you? You are bullies, abusing helpless children, telling them you'll shoot them. Do your wives, girlfriends or mothers know how you're treating children?"

The two men exchanged glances. The first one glared right back and said, "Fine. Then we'll shoot you adults and take the kids."

Lisa grabbed Amanda and held her close. "You think I'd let you touch these children?" She turned and stomped away.

Eric and Mark exchanged a surprised look of their own. Eric said, "Calm down, everybody. Let's start over."

The man said, "There's nothing to talk about. Turn around and get going."

"I don't know what your problem is. All we want is to walk through your damn city," said Mark.

The other man said, "We have a city ordinance against letting anyone in, end of story. We have men stationed in the mountains all around here so no matter what you do, you will not get through. Now for the very last time, turn around and get going."

Eric started to say something and Mark stopped him. They had no choice. He grabbed the wheelbarrow and started walking towards the bend in the road. The others reluctantly followed. Amanda was still crying. Chris and Ryan seemed to be scared to death. Each of the adults were very angry, but not for the same reasons. Abby had armed herself with her knives before leaving the cabin. She'd been ready to start throwing them if necessary.

****

The men stood by at the truck for several minutes to see if there was going to be any more trouble. When nothing happened, they headed back to their command post. One of the men said, "Those women made me feel like a scumbag. Did you see the look on that little girl's face? Why do we always get the decent ones with the kids and the other guys get the real dirt bags and psychos?"

The other man said, "It doesn't matter. We have no choice. The city ordnance was put into place by the city council to keep all the whack jobs out of the city."

The first man said, "Then they should be the ones to tell these people and children they can't come in. I bet they wouldn't last one whole night up here doing what we do."

The other man said, "That doesn't matter, either. This is our job. We do it or someone else will do it for us. Either way, the end will be the same." The other man didn't say anything, just stared out the window. There wasn't anything to say. The world was one big screwed up place. But it was getting harder to go home and see his own children and not feel guilty. Who knows what they were sentencing these children to when they turned them away?

****

Mark wasn't sure of all the feelings he was feeling; there were so many of them and they were constantly changing. There were a wide range of emotions from anger, to helplessness, responsibility for the others, the need to see his father, despair and hopelessness. If they couldn't get to the retreat, they'd be in big trouble. They needed the supplies that were there. All of these emotions just kept circling around inside him and he didn't have a clue which one would win. One second he would want to stop and pound on something and the next he felt like they would be endlessly walking for the rest of their lives. He stopped when they reached the bottom. Everyone was disappointed they couldn't get through the blockade.

Abby asked, "How did they have a truck that worked?"

"It's because it was a 1972 Ford half ton pickup; it has points and a condenser. It wasn't affected by the EMP."

Lisa said in an angry tone of voice with a disgusted look on her face, "The least they could have done after scaring the children so badly and turning us away was give us a ride back to the cabin. I feel like going back and telling them off again."

All the adults said a very strong "NO."

"We don't want anyone to know where we are staying," said Mark.

"Don't worry, Lisa," said Eric. "Those men won't be forgetting what you said anytime soon. It doesn't matter now."

"We have to go back to the cabin and make it our retreat," said Mark. "We have no other choice now." The women nodded their heads. It was either that or take on a whole damn city. They started walking. It took them four days to get back to the cabin.

Mark and Eric had several discussions about training Chris. He was thirteen, and both men felt he was ready. He had learned an important lesson with the men that had made them turn back. He seemed to be a little more responsible. They reached the cabin on the fourth night, about two hours before daybreak. The men went around and checked it out to make sure no one else had set up residency since they left. They didn't find anything, but decided to play it safe. They got everyone settled into the woods, then the men worked the board loose and Abby climbed in this time. She let Mark and Eric in and they went inside and checked the cabin. It was just as they left it. Eric went and got the others.

They decided to leave the wheelbarrow to unload until later, after they all got some rest. They just brought their packs inside. Amanda was glad to be back. She loved it here. She demanded to sleep in her bed and not on the wheelbarrow. Everyone laughed. Maria said she'd make something for everyone to eat and then they could shower and get to bed. Eric and Mark hooked everything back up again. They only turned the heat on in the rooms they'd be using for now. They needed to make the propane last as long as possible. That meant using wood for heat. Abby gave Amanda a bath and the two boys were sent to shower. Lisa took a shower. She came back downstairs and relieved Maria of kitchen duty so she could go take a bath.

Mark took over looking after Amanda so Abby could go bathe. The water wasn't really hot. It was closer to room temperature, but none of them cared. It was great to be clean again. They sat down and ate. Amanda and Ryan thought the trip had been a great adventure and talked about it all through the meal. The adults got the children into bed. They sat downstairs for a while and relaxed over coffee and tea. The adults were yawning. Mark said they'd have a meeting later that night; they needed to make this cabin their retreat. Winter was almost here and they had a lot to do to prepare. They all went to bed. Every one of them smiled at the feel of a mattress under them once again before falling asleep.

The men got up in the early afternoon. The women had been up for hours. They had woken up around 7:00 am, hearing the children making noise downstairs. All three women met in the hallway and smiled.

Abby said, "We're acting like mothers."

"I feel like a mother," said Lisa.

Maria said, "Me too." They crept downstairs to see what was going on. The noise was coming from the kitchen. The sight that met their eyes made them stare with their mouths open.

There was powdery white stuff flung everywhere. There were wet streaks on the floor, making a paste of whatever the powdery stuff was. It looked like flour. Amanda was standing in the middle looking like a little ghost with an apron on, holding a glass of water. Chris was down on his hands and knees, trying to wipe up the white stuff with a wet cloth. Ryan was on the other side of the room with the broom and dustpan, trying to sweep the powdery stuff up, making huge dust clouds. The table and counters were piled with cooking utensils and bowls. There was a big bowl by the stove. Some white goop was dripping and running down the stove and the cupboard. There was steam coming from the sink, and it smelled like something had been overcooked or burnt. There was a chair in front of the stove and one in front of the sink. The white dust floating around was landing on Chris and Ryan, making them look like ghosts, too.

Lisa stepped forward. "Stop. You're just making it worse."

"What happened?" Maria asked. Abby started to laugh; She didn't stop until she had to hold her sides. All three children stopped what they were doing and stood absolutely still. Their eyes were big; they just stared with a look in their eyes that said they knew they were going to be tried, sentenced and punished for the rest of their lives. Even with Abby's laughter, they didn't move a muscle. Abby, still laughing, walked over to Amanda, picked her up and walked out of the kitchen. Amanda was still holding the glass of water.

Chris and Ryan started to talk at the same time. Maria held her hand up for silence. "Take a breath, and then one at a time, explain what happened here. Okay?" The boys took a deep breath and started to cough.

Lisa said, "Go take a shower and get the story straight between you two, then you can come back down explain what happened. I'm going to make some coffee." Lisa took out the can of coffee, grabbed the coffee pot, walked out of the kitchen and went down the hall to the den before she set everything down. She dusted the coffee pot off, went into the bathroom, and rinsed the pot out. After she started the coffee, she went back into the kitchen, grabbed some mugs and went back to the den. It was cold in there. There were some wood logs in the fireplace with kindling under them. She grabbed the long matches on the mantel and lit the kindling to get it going. She didn't know how to turn the propane heater on, and anyway, they were going to have to save the propane now. She rubbed her face and thought, *what a way to start the day*. They had gotten about two hours of sleep. She looked at her hands; they were covered with white powder, too. She looked down at herself and saw white dust everywhere. She sighed. Maria walked into the room, grabbed a cup of coffee and sighed. They looked at each other and started to laugh. They looked almost as bad as the kids.

After they'd cleaned everything up, they sat at the table and Lisa made pancakes for everyone. That's what started the whole thing. Amanda wanted pancakes, and no one was awake to make them. So, she decided to make everyone breakfast. She dragged the ten-pound bag of pancake mix out of the pantry to the middle of the kitchen. She put an apron on sort of; she couldn't get it tied right. She couldn't lift the bag, so she used bowls and other utensils to put the mix into the other bowls. She added water just like it showed on the big package. When she put it in the pan, it started to smoke. She tried to turn the pancake over and it was stuck. She went back upstairs and woke Chris up to come help her turn the pancake over. He ran downstairs to see what she was talking about. The pan was smoking, so he grabbed a mitten and quickly put the pan in the sink. Ryan had followed them downstairs. They'd been trying to clean up the mess so they wouldn't get into trouble when the women had walked into the kitchen. The women praised Chris for his quick thinking on getting the pan to the sink and turning the burners off. Yes, Amanda had more than one turned on. They explained to Ryan that sweeping powdery particles just sent them everywhere and made a bigger mess. They explained to Chris that you had to use a dry cloth to scoop up the powdery mess. Using a wet cloth just made a bigger mess.

The women said they were going to spend the rest of the day taking inventory of all the food items and try to figure out how much of everything they had and how long it would last.

Mark said, "That's a really good idea. Then we'll know what we'll be dealing with tonight when we have our meeting."

"We have to start using wood and save the propane," Eric said. "There is a very nice wood stove in the basement; we're going to have to start using that to heat the house. I'm going to spend the rest of the day chopping firewood."

"We'll have to look around and see if there's another ax so we can both chop wood. We need to spend some time taking inventory in the basement and the garage, too. We need to know what equipment is here and if there are any supplies anywhere else. Right now I'm going outside and scout around and be on watch. We need to start watches, at least until the snow gets here. After that, we'll be able to see tracks."

Everyone agreed with the work assignments and they all got started. Mark took Chris to start teaching him how to do things. Eric went outside, too. The women told Ryan to keep Amanda busy so they could work. There were two computers in the house and Abby suggested they use one to list all the supplies and she'd make up a database. Then they could quickly search for items or know how much of something was left. They'd have to update it weekly, but it would help them keep track of everything. They decided to make a hard copy, too, just in case they couldn't access the computer. It was decided that Abby would work on the computer and Maria would write down the list and Lisa would call out what they had. Maria and Lisa would take turns writing and working in the pantry and cupboards.

Ryan was in charge of watching Amanda while the adults were busy. He decided to take Amanda outside to play in the yard and be out of the adults' way. He was bored with being inside all the time. Their adventure had given him an appetite for outdoor activities.

Amanda thought this was a great idea and brought a jump rope with her. Ryan was looking around at the ground, trying to figure out if any animals were coming through the yard and what kind they were. His whole concentration was looking for animal trails, just like Eric had showed him. He was close to the woods and never saw the man who grabbed him. A hand clamped tightly over Ryan's mouth and he was lifted up off the ground. Ryan kicked the man and hit him as best as he could. The guy stuck to him like glue. Ryan tried everything he could think of to make the man let him go.

The guy whispered, "Stop it. Stop fighting me or I'll have to hurt you."

Ryan relaxed a little. His mind was racing, trying to figure out what was going on. He thought, *I wish Mark and Eric were here. They would know how to make this man let me go.*

The man dragged Ryan into the woods. He could no longer see the cabin. He started to get real scared. The man sat him down on the ground and removed his hand from Ryan's mouth. The man showed him his rifle and said, "We don't want to hurt you. We just want some food." The man was a nasty looking, dirty guy in a leather jacket. He had mud and dirt ground into his skin from sleeping on the ground.

Ryan stared at the man and said in a voice filled with defiance, "Mark is going to kick your butt if you don't let me go right now."

The guy laughed. "Who's Mark? Is he your dad?"

"Nope. He's a hero. He saved Lisa, Maria and Abby from fifty bad guys. He'll chew you up and spit you out." He had heard that in a movie once and thought that sounded mean enough to maybe scare this man. Four more rough and ragged men stepped out of the trees and came towards them. They looked meaner and even dirtier than the one that had dragged him here.

"How many are in that cabin?" asked one.

The first man said, "Shut up. I am trying to find that out right now."

The man turned back to Ryan. "Now listen to me, kid. We're going to trade you for some food. Now, tell me how many are in that cabin over there."

Before he could answer, he heard Amanda yell, "Ryan! Ryan, where are you? We're going to get into trouble. We're not supposed to go in the woods. Ryan! Ryan!"

The man with Ryan turned to the other men and said urgently, "Be quick now and go get her."

Ryan yelled out quickly before the men could stop him, "Amanda, run! Bad guys have me! Run and get the—oomph." He lay on the ground and couldn't breathe.

The guy had punched him in the stomach. Two men took off to grab Amanda. Ryan felt helpless lying on the ground. He couldn't even breathe, so how could he help Amanda? It was his fault they were outside. He could hear Amanda running and screaming. He kept praying, *Please God, save her. Please, don't let anything happen to her because I was stupid enough to take her outside.*

Lisa heard Amanda screaming like bloody murder was taking place outside. She ran outside on the porch. She saw Amanda running, then saw two men pop out of the woods and start chasing her. She thought, *What the hell?* She ran back inside, grabbed her pellet gun and yelled to Abby and Maria, "Trouble!" She charged out the door and jumped off the porch, racing off towards the two men. Her mother instinct was in high gear. She was as determined as a mama bear protecting her cubs. She would protect Amanda if she had to tear those two guys apart with her bare hands.

Mark was checking the different animal trails, pointing out important things to Chris. He wanted to know how far the trails went and where they were headed. That could be vital information and come in handy some time if they ever had to make an escape.

The men came from the opposite side. He hadn't seen anyone. All of a sudden, they heard some sort of a ruckus going on. He heard a child's high-pitched screams. The sounds were coming from the direction of the cabin. His heartbeat sped up. He looked at Chris and said, "You stay here in these bushes and don't come out until I come get you. Do you understand me?"

Chris looked scared. "Yes, sir."

"I have to go help and I can't be worrying about you, too." Chris nodded his head and sat down in some thick bushes. Mark whispered, "I'll be back as soon as I can. Don't move." He circled around, trying to find out what was going on.

Eric had been out back chopping wood. He heard a child's high-pitched, terrified scream.

Amanda, he thought. His heart jumped into his throat. Something was happening to Amanda. He grabbed his 12 gauge and ran around the back towards the screams. He was ready for war. He'd protect her as if she were his very own child. What he saw stopped him dead in his tracks. Lisa was holding her pellet rifle on two men, facing them down. His heart was thundering in his chest. *Oh my God,* he thought. Amanda was running towards Lisa.

Lisa said with steel in her voice, "Freeze! If you touch her, I'll kill you." Both men started laughing hysterically.

One of them was finally able to say through chuckles, "With what? You gonna use that pellet gun?" They started laughing again.

The other man looked at Lisa with lust filled eyes. "We're going to have a lot of fun with you tonight."

Eric was making his approach on the low side; they never saw him coming. The one on the left lifted his rifle and said with no humor left in his voice, "Drop that stupid pellet gun, lady, before I kill you."

The man next to him raised his rifle up and pointed it at Lisa, too. Eric was now thirty yards away. He stopped and lined up the 12 gauge on the closest man. He fired. The man fell and rolled over. He racked another shell into the chamber, taking aim again. The other man swung his rifle around to Eric. Before either could get a shot off, Lisa shot the man in the arm with the pellet rifle. That pellet hurt like hell and caused the man's aim to miss Eric. At almost at the same exact time, Eric's 12 gauge roared again, tearing the intruder to shreds with double ought buckshot.

Eric yelled to Lisa, "Grab Amanda and get into the house. Get her out of here!" Amanda had been running straight towards Lisa, and never looked back once. She flung her little body at Lisa, crying and screaming, half hysterical, almost knocking Lisa over.

Lisa grabbed her with one hand and didn't lower the rifle. She was looking off towards the woods and screamed at Eric, "They have Ryan in the woods!"

Before either one of them could say or do anything, a voice came out of the woods. "Drop your guns or we kill the kid." Eric had run straight towards Lisa and Amanda. He'd just made it to them when they heard the voice.

Lisa's heart leaped up into her throat and she thought, *Oh my God, Ryan.*

Eric said in a whisper, "Get her in the house right now before she sees any more." Lisa had been shoving Amanda's face and body against her legs, facing the other way, and was pretty sure she hadn't seen anything yet. She wanted to keep it that way.

Mark heard the shots and was making his way as fast as he could without giving his position away. When he heard the voice, his heart rate increased alarmingly. Adrenaline was rushing throughout his body, almost making him shake. His rage at these men tripled. He thought, *We'll just see about that, you scumbags.* Using a child as cover was a coward's way. He'd become very close to Ryan and felt like he was almost his own child. He hadn't wanted to, but the kid had wormed his way right into his heart.

He crept along quietly and came up on a small rise. He peered around a tree and saw the three men with Ryan. They were facing towards the cabin, away from him. The one that had spoken was obviously the leader. The man stood there with his left arm around Ryan's neck and with the other arm holding a pistol to Ryan's forehead. The man yelled out again. "You have five seconds to drop your guns or I kill the kid."

Mark steadied his rifle against a tree. He took a quick breath and let it out. He steadied his aim and squeezed the trigger. The man and Ryan had been only forty-seven yards away. It hadn't been a hard shot at all. The man's head jerked to the side and he and Ryan fell over. Mark worked the lever and yelled out, "You two drop your guns or you're dead. You're surrounded."

When Lisa had yelled into the house that there was trouble outside, Abby and Maria had been in the kitchen. Abby grabbed two knives out of the wooden knife block, turned to Maria and said, "Lock the doors. Stay by the front and only let us in. Shoot anyone else who gets in, either in the neck or the eye. Keep shooting them in the face and neck until they go down." She grabbed her coat and hat by the back door and silently went outside, making sure the door was locked. She crept around the cabin and slowly made her way into the woods towards Lisa and Amanda. After a few minutes, she saw Eric creeping along, real quiet like. She heard Lisa yell that they had Ryan. Her eyes got hard and she quickened her pace. She readied the knives. It didn't matter which hand she threw with, she was very good with both. She'd been practicing with knives and learning the art since she was a small child at her grandfather's dojo and also on Saturdays when her whole family practiced together. She'd been three the first time she'd broken a board with her hand. She had been five before she had enough muscle control to throw a knife. By age six she could hit any target she aimed at. Two hours' practice a day will do that for you. As she grew, so did the length of the knives she'd learned to handle. If she would've been someplace where a lot of knives had been available, those animals would have never been able to capture her. She sighed and pushed those thoughts aside for now. A child needed her help and she had best keep her thoughts where they belonged.

Eric was making his way towards Lisa and Amanda. Abby continued on in the woods, intent on finding Ryan. She heard a man yell out and honed in on that direction and came toward them from the opposite side from Mark. She had just found a tree to hide behind when she saw Mark and then heard the shot. She kept her eyes on the other two men and saw them turn towards Mark, raising their rifles. She threw one knife without putting much thought behind it. She intended to even the odds in Mark's favor. As she threw the knife, Mark was firing off a shot. Both men fell to the ground. Mark just stood there for a few moments, wondering what the hell had happened. There was no possible way he could have hit two men facing him with one bullet. Abby stepped out from behind the tree. *What she was doing out here? She didn't even have her pellet gun.*

This whole encounter had lasted maybe ten minutes total. Abby reached down for Ryan to see if he was hurt. The man was lying on part of him, holding him down. Ryan saw her and reached out to her; she dragged him out from under the man's body. She'd been closer to them than Mark. Ryan hugged her real tight and grinned, then his face screwed up into a grimace and he held his side. It was obvious that he wasn't seriously injured.

Mark reached them and grabbed Ryan. He willingly went to him and hugged him, too. He looked up at Mark. "I told them you'd come for me and kill them, but they wouldn't listen to me. I told them you'd chew them up and spit them out."

Mark started to laugh. "You betcha. No one messes with my kids and lives." He didn't even realize what he'd said. Ryan's grin got bigger. Mark said to Abby, "What are you doing out here?" He was looking at the two men lying dead on the ground. One was lying in a large puddle of blood. He let go of Ryan and bent down to look closer and saw the knife sticking out of the man's back. He had a puzzled look on his face. He looked all around them, but didn't see anyone else. He could hear someone coming from the direction of the cabin, so it had to be Eric, Lisa or Maria. His money was on Eric. He looked up at Abby and realized that she had to have been the one to throw the knife. He was just about to ask her how she did that when Eric reached them.

Eric saw Abby and said, "What are you doing out here?"

Abby didn't say anything. She reached out for Ryan. "We need to get him inside and make sure he is all right." She was motioning towards the bodies with her head.

Eric finally understood what she meant. "Yes, that's a good idea." He turned to Ryan and hugged him. "Are you all right?"

Ryan was still grinning. "I told them Mark would kill them and they didn't believe me."

Eric smiled and said, "Of course he would. We can't have people running around and kidnapping our children and getting away with it now, can we?"

If Ryan's grin got any bigger, it was going to split his face. He hugged Eric tightly, too. "I told them Mark was a hero."

Eric said, "Yes he is. Now you'd better get back inside and let Amanda know you are all right. She's real worried about you."

Ryan had been trying to hide the pain he was feeling in his side. Abby rolled her eyes. *Men!* Even the young ones thought they had to be tough around other men. But let anyone try to treat them or clean out a wound and they turned into a quivering jellyfish. She urged Ryan forward. They'd leave the men to clean up this mess.

Abby had her arm around Ryan as they slowly made their way back to the cabin. He chatted happily about his ordeal. She hoped Mark and Eric would be smart and burn the bodies. With men, you could never tell if they were going to do the smart thing or not. Most of the time, men let that macho crap get in the way of good sense.

The men came in after it was dark outside. Eric had come in earlier, bringing Chris inside. He told them they were going to be busy for a while and to stay inside and keep everything locked up. The women agreed. They knew he was worried about them and protecting them came naturally. They had learned a hell of a lot about security since all of this started. Abby put the other knife back into the wooden block when no one was looking. She had meant to bring the other one back with her, but the men hadn't given her an opportunity to grab it. She took another knife out of a drawer and placed it in the empty slot.

The men burned the bodies. They didn't talk about it, but it had to have been horrible. The women understood this and didn't really say much about it except to say they were sorry it had to be done. Lisa told Eric and Mark they were there if they wanted to talk about it. Both men said no, they didn't really want to talk.

Mark and Eric had emptied out the men's pockets and brought their backpacks and guns back with them. They brought the guns inside and left everything else in the garage. They'd quickly gone through them, looking for bullets and shells. They would go through them more thoroughly tomorrow and see what else they found.

The only part of this that was a good thing, besides ridding the world of some scumbags that would terrify and kidnap children, was that they now had five more rifles and two pistols. They had a Ruger 10-22 semi-automatic with two, thirty shot magazines and three hundred sixteen rounds for it, a .270 bolt action with a BSA scope that held five shots with thirty-seven rounds for it, an AK-47 with two thirty round magazines and one hundred eighty-six rounds for it, an H & R single shot 12 gauge shotgun with seven shells of buckshot, three slugs and seventeen shells of various bird shot, an old 45-70 lever action that was a real mule kicker with only twenty-three rounds for it, a Hi Point .45 pistol with forty-three bullets and a SIG 9 mm with two clips for it and thirty-six rounds. Mark and Eric put all the rifles in the closet in their bedroom so the children wouldn't be able to touch them and get hurt. Mark had taken the .45 and strapped it on, Eric had taken the SIG. Later that night, Mark stood alone in the dark bedroom and walked over to the window. He looked outside at the darkness and thought to himself, *At least now they'd be able to teach the women to really shoot and maybe it would make a difference in the future.* He sure hoped so, because they were going to need all the help they could get.

Chapter 18

The Mothman Warning

"Everything you can imagine is real."

Pablo Picasso

They had all settled into a routine to get as much done as possible before the snow arrived. Joe was kicking himself for not buying that log splitter he had talked about. They sure could have used it now. At least they had a metal wedge; that helped some. It was slow going, but they'd made a nice dent in the pile of logs. The wood was vital; not just for heating the house, but for cooking and hot water, too. Both Joe and Preston had wood burning hot water heaters.

They'd all been picking apples and other fall fruits for the last three days and had not spent as much time chopping wood as Joe would have liked. He sighed. It was a pain in the butt to chop wood in the snow. He was trying his best to get it all done. He felt they had enough to get them through January now. He continued to swing the ax. He looked over at the pile of logs and judged that when they had half the pile chopped, it would be enough for the whole winter. They were halfway done. Now, as long as nothing else happened, they could spend all their time chopping. They should be able to get it all done before the snow came. He smiled to himself. It would be nice to get this out of the way.

Michael was working just as hard as the men. He was in constant motion, either loading the wheelbarrow up or stacking the wood. It was his job to keep the wood box on the back porch filled for the kitchen cook stove. He never complained about his workload. At night, he was still bouncing around with energy; it made all the adults feel old as they watched him.

He was doing well on his watches, too. He moved from side to side every five to ten minutes. He had a keen eye and spotted a lot of animals. He had fun recording their nighttime activities. The hardest part of watch duty was being the tower in radio conversations. His call sign was one five. He remembered that most of the time, but he would answer the radio and say, 'barn here' or 'barn out.' He forgot to call it the tower. A few times he'd gotten confused which place was Bravo Team and which was Delta Team, but, that was understandable for a boy his age. Over all, he did really well being the "Eye in the sky," as Amy called it. All the adults would take turns checking on him when he was on watch. They liked to read his entries in the logbook, too. It always made them smile and laugh.

It was 8:15 pm and Michael was on watch. It was Preston's turn to check on him. He climbed the stairs and peeked around to see what he was doing. Michael was intently watching something out of the window with the night vision. Preston quietly walked over to the logbook and picked it up to read. It started out in Michael's handwriting with 6:00 pm, with the heading, 'Michael's watch started at 6:00 pm.'

6:10 pm: Saw something flying over big oak trees down past smaller ones on the left.

6:21 pm: Saw coyote walking down trail on right by downed stump, going towards trailer side of our property.

6:47 pm: Saw a raccoon coming down trail towards barn on left side. He stopped on trail, stood up, and looked around twice. He went back to where he came from.

7:06 pm: Raccoon came back again, went past barn. He stood up and looked around for a while. He kept going down the trail this time.

7:29 pm: Saw two deer in field behind barn. They were eating something on the ground.

7:42 pm: The two deer left field, going towards back of property by tree with missing branch.

7:50 pm: One of the deer left and went down trail by Jane's tree stand.

8:01 pm: Saw three deer in field by trailer. The three deer were eating something on ground.

8:07 pm: Other two deer left and went down trail on back of our property by those big bushes.

Preston laid the logbook down. Michael was still looking out the same window. Preston asked, "What are you watching?"

"A rabbit was hopping down the trail and stopped to sniff at things. I was watching him to see what he was sniffing at. I think it was the raccoon he smelled that came down earlier. He turned back the other way and didn't follow the raccoon."

Preston smiled. "Maybe he found a better scent to follow. How's everything going?"

Michael said, "Fine. Its fun watching all the animals and what they do."

"You are remembering to look for people, too, aren't you?"

"Of course I look for people, but Joe told me the animals will let me know if someone is coming their way. So, I pay attention to what they do, too. If they get spooked over something, I pay close attention to all the windows to see what it was."

Preston said, "Good thinking. Do you need anything?"

"No. I'm fine," Michael said. "I gotta go make my rounds now." He turned away and went to the next window and looked out. Preston smiled and walked down the stairs. Michael really enjoyed being on watch. Amy had been right to include him. It was teaching him a lot all at the same time.

In the mornings and in the afternoon, Amy, Joan and Michael practiced shooting. Joan already knew how to shoot, but hadn't done so in a long time, with the exception of her situation with Randy. She was practicing with a rifle in the mornings and a pistol in the afternoons. She was a really good shot. Amy picked up shooting the .22 really fast. Preston had a 22-250 rifle for her to use as an all around rifle. Both rifles had night vision scopes on them. In the daytime, they both used a 22-250 that had daytime scopes. Joan would carry the Marlin .22 semi-automatic she'd taken from Randy and Joe had loaned her a Browning .22 pistol to use. Michael was learning to shoot a .22 rifle. He was doing well. He could hit a target, and with practice he'd get even better. Michael was carrying it around with him all day now. Joe felt more secure with everyone armed and practicing. The new watch schedule was working out really well. Getting a good night's sleep was a real bonus and he liked having time alone with Jane again.

Amy was doing her hour of practicing with the bow. Her arms didn't hurt anymore. She was getting real good at hitting targets. Preston kept teasing her that they'd turn her into "Robin Hood" yet. He shot an apple off of a tree branch to prove it could be done. Amy was very impressed and was striving to do that herself. Jane laughed and told Amy that she and Joe could do that, too. Joe said she took to learning these things like a duck takes to water. Joe had taken to calling her G.I. Amy. Jane laughed the first time she heard that.

Jane, laughing, said, "Oh God, help us now. We have a G.I. Joe and a G.I. Amy. Enemies, you'd better watch out now."

Preston still went around reminding everyone, "My girlfriend got three deer and didn't even have to be outside or go hunting to do it." Joe kept telling him to shut up.

Joan was still healing. Her face now looked like someone had poured some paint and smeared it around. Her split skin was healing with no infection. That was what worried Jane the most. Joan's side still bothered her. Jane had taped her up because she suspected that some of her ribs were fractured. She didn't let it slow her down, though. Now that she understood it wasn't safe to try to leave, she really pitched in and was a big help around the homestead. She'd shared some of her knowledge about how to run a farm and showed them a few things that would save time and supplies, too. She had shared a few recipes for canning spaghetti sauce and ketchup. Jane had her write down a lot of other recipes she remembered. She also showed them how to make lard from animal fats. They were busy now making apple cider, applesauce, pie and cobbler filling and apple butter. They dehydrated a lot of apple slices to add to oatmeal, biscuits and muffins. Joan had shown them how to bake the apple peelings spiced with brown sugar, cinnamon and nutmeg in a little water with a dab of butter. She'd taken over most of the cooking for meals and the house cleaning until she healed and could get around better. At night before going to bed, she would knead some bread dough and let it rise overnight to bake first thing in the morning. The aroma of fresh baking bread was the first thing to greet everyone in the morning.

They had butchered the three deer and the pig. Joe and Preston thought they were great teachers because Amy picked up on how to do it really fast. She didn't want to burst their bubble, so she just didn't say anything about watching *Buckshot's Preparing Game for the Table* DVD a few times. They spent a whole day grinding up all the leftover pieces into venison burger. They used some of the leftover pieces from the pig to add for some fat. Amy made a large pot of spaghetti with the venison burger. Michael had three helpings and the men had two large helpings each. Everyone was eating more because they were doing hard, manual labor and their appetites had increased.

Michael loved being on watch. He saw the interesting things that animals did at night. He figured by the time he was grown up, he'd know the habits of all the animals around here. He set his thermos of hot chocolate on the desk. He'd brought his second piece of apple pie with him for later. He was still stuffed from dinner. He got the logbook out and wrote the time. He had settled into a routine. This night started out the same as the others he'd done.

It was 8:12 pm. He knew this because he had just looked at the watch he borrowed from Joe. He was watching a raccoon on the trail behind the barn, when all of a sudden he could hear the beat of very large wings and some whooshing sounds. It was getting closer. His heart started to pound really hard. It was an eerie sound and fear rushed through every cell in his body. He looked up at the roof because the sound was coming from up high, but he couldn't tell which direction it was coming from exactly. It sounded just like that movie he had seen about the Mothman. He thought, *Oh my God, the Mothman is here. The Mothman is real and it is here.* It landed on the roof with a thump and another eerie sound. He thought, *Oh no, it's not the Mothman, it's aliens!* He'd seen that movie, too. He heard more eerie sounds and scraping. He rolled over onto the floor with the rifle pointed up at the roof. He was ready to fill the roof with holes. He was shaking so hard the rifle was pointing all over the place. His heart was thumping in his chest and the rifle was bobbing up and down and around. He was waiting for the aliens to make a move so he'd know where to shoot.

There was a weird rustling sound coming from above, accompanied by a few thumps. He could hear scratching. *How many of them were up there?* It sounded like a lot. His hands were sweating, making it harder to hold on to the rifle. He gripped it harder, but his small hands kept slipping on the metal. He swallowed nervously, getting even more frightened as time went by and the aliens hadn't made a move. He wondered, *What are they doing up there on the roof? What if they're waiting for the adults to come outside?* How was he going to warn them? He couldn't hold the rifle and call on the radio at the same time. What was he going to do? Then he heard it take off with a weird screeching sound; it was the Mothman.

He quickly got up and looked out the window and something black and huge blocked out the moon, making the whole window go dark. He looked down and saw the shadow; it was the Mothman for sure. He could see the huge wingspan now. This shadow was about six or seven feet long. He looked farther out at the ground and saw a barn owl grab a mouse. He thought that owl better hurry up and get away or the Mothman might get him. Who knew what the Mothman ate? The owl flew off with the mouse. He waited but didn't hear another sound. What was the Mothman doing? He looked cautiously out all the windows and couldn't see anything. He looked up at the roof, waiting for more sounds that would tell him the Mothman was still up there. After ten minutes of no sounds coming from the roof, decided that the Mothman wasn't up there anymore. *He must have left and I missed it because I was watching the barn owl grab the mouse.*

He picked up the logbook and turned on the little blue light. He chewed on the pen for a minute, thinking of how to word this. He wrote, '8:12 pm: Barn owl screeched and grabbed a mouse on the ground by big tree on trail to back of property. Didn't see or hear anything else. It wasn't the Mothman, either.' There, that covered everything. He put the logbook down and turned the little light off. He went back over to the window and looked out. He'd just pretend nothing happened.

At ten minutes to 10:00 pm, Preston walked Amy over to the barn for her shift. He would stay awhile to keep her company, then he'd go take a nap for a couple of hours to be alert for his watch shift. They climbed the stairs. They silently entered the watch room; Michael was at a window, looking out.

"Oh, it's you," Michael said.

"You were expecting someone else?" Amy asked.

"Michael, why are you scared?" Preston was concerned.

Michael looked at them. "I'm not scared. I'm not a little kid. Nothing scares me."

Preston and Amy exchanged a puzzled look. "Anything happen tonight?"

Michael hurriedly said, "No. Nothing happened at all. Didn't see anything." Preston was really puzzled now. Michael usually told everyone several times about every little thing he saw when he was on watch. It was usually a chore to get him to shut up. Something definitely scared him shitless but, what? What could have happened to scare him like this? His mind raced, trying to think. He had no clue what it could be.

Michael walked over to the log book and looked at the watch and then wrote, '9:57 pm: Michael's watch is over.' Michael said, "If anyone dangerous shows up, just fill them full of lead, like Joe says."

"Okay," Amy agreed. Amy and Preston shard a look and then she said she left her flashlight and would walk Michael over to the house so she could get it. When Amy got back she had a big smile on her face.

Preston said, "What's so funny? Were you able to get Michael to tell you what scared him so badly?"

"Yes, Michael told me what terrified him."

Preston waited for a few minutes and when Amy didn't say anything he said, "Okay, what was it?"

"I can't tell you. It's a secret. Michael made me promise not to tell you or the other adults."

Preston blinked at her a few times with a puzzled look on his face. "Aren't you an adult? Why would he tell you and not us?"

Amy shrugged her shoulders. "I don't know why he told me. But he feels no one would believe him."

Preston nodded. "I thought it was something like that. Come and read what he wrote in the log book."

Amy turned on the little blue light and read it. She looked up at Preston with a thoughtful expression. Preston said, "He obviously thought he saw a Mothman. What is a Mothman, by the way?"

Amy raised an eyebrow at him and shook her head. She said in a mournful tone, "I have got to tell you, Preston, your lack of knowledge of movies is truly astounding."

He sighed. "So, how do we deal with this?"

"I don't know for sure. I'm not a mother. Maybe we should talk to Joan about this." She was thoughtful for a few moments. "I think I've figured out what happened to make him think he heard and saw the Mothman, though. In the log, he said a barn owl got a mouse. If the barn owl was on the roof and flew off after the mouse, the shadow would look really big. The wingspan could be what made him think he saw the Mothman and there would have been the sound of flapping wings to accompany it. I bet that's what happened and his imagination got a little carried away."

"That sounds like a reasonable explanation."

"It will be really hard to convince him that he didn't see the Mothman, though. I don't know how to handle that part."

He said, "I'll show Joan the log book and let her decide how to handle this. She's the one who's experienced with children, and Michael is her son. I'm sure she would want to know about this. If it were my child, I'd want someone to tell me if something scared him."

She smiled, leaned over and kissed him. "The key part is how do we convince him that he really didn't see the Mothman? Because I can tell you with one hundred percent certainty that he whole-heartedly believes it."

He said, "I don't know. That will have to be up to Joan."

The next afternoon they were inside having lunch at the table. Every afternoon and evening, they turned the radio on for two hours. Usually it was on between 12:00 pm and 2:00 pm, and then again from 6:00 pm to 8:00 pm. The radio automatically scanned for a channel to lock onto. They set the wind-up timer so they wouldn't forget to turn it off and run the batteries down. While they were eating, static and some weird screeching sounds came out of the speakers, making everyone jump in surprise and turn toward the radio. More static and screeching came out of the speakers. Joe jumped up and began pushing the scan button to see if he could find out if anything was really coming through.

The speakers blared, "This is an emergency broadcast. Everyone stay tuned for an emergency broadcast. Bleep, bleep, bleep. This is an emergency broadcast. Everyone stay tuned for an emergency broadcast. The President of the United States of America will speak to the nation in one minute. Bleep, bleep, bleep. This is an emergency broadcast..." Everyone looked at each other as they waited to hear what the President had to say.

Finally they heard the President's voice. He said, "This is the President of the United States of America. I have declared martial law across the nation. All military personnel are to report to the nearest military base or station in your area. All military personnel active duty, reserve or retired are to report to the nearest military base or station. All police and security personnel are to report to their stations and resume their duties to protect and serve their towns and cities. We cannot have anarchy rule here in America.

"The United States was hit with a high altitude nuclear blast that took out our electrical grid across the nation. This caused the collapse of the stock market and the banking system. We are working hard to restore power to the electrical grid and bring America out of the darkness. The electrical power will soon be on across our nation once again, but first we must restore order. All military personnel active, reserve and retired report immediately to the nearest base or station in your area. All police and security personnel report immediately to your stations and restore order. That is all. God Bless America."

Joe and Preston burst out laughing. Joe said sarcastically, "We'll be right there, Mr. President."

Preston said, "Don't wait up for us." They continued to laugh hardily.

"What is the matter with you two?" Joan said. "This is great news. Soon everything will be back to normal again." The men burst out laughing again.

Joan's face flushed red and she said with tight lips, "What in the hell is so funny?"

Preston said, "You don't understand. They would need roughly one hundred million transformers alone to fix the electrical grid. That's not even including the other components that will be needed. Even if we still had the industrial base here in America to build them, which we don't anymore, the industrial plant would need power to run. Even if they could somehow find or make that much power to make the transformers, they would be able to make maybe one million a year at best. That means it would take one hundred years to restore power here in America." The men continued to chuckle and shake their heads.

"You think this is funny?" Joan demanded.

Joe sobered immediately. "No. This isn't funny, but what else can we do? He was lying. The government has lost all control here in America. We are free at last. It's a wonderful time to be alive. The future is so much brighter without all the corruption that was in our government. We should be throwing a party to celebrate."

Joan said, "I don't understand you two. We must have the government to save us from all this chaos we're living in now. They have to fix everything and make it like it was before."

The men started laughing again. Preston said, "Think a moment. How long has it been since the lights went out? Are we okay? Are we surviving without the government's help? Has anyone given us anything with which to survive with? Has the government given any of us any food? Water? Shelter? Power? Did they even bother to tell us what had happened until now? No, the government hasn't given us one single thing. We have to provide everything for ourselves. Without a tax base, those parasite liars of politicians will have to get off their butts and learn to survive just like the rest of us."

Joan said, "Then what will happen to us if we don't have a government to save us?"

"We will establish a government in time," said Joe. "But first, we have to learn how to survive ourselves. Then we can pick up the pieces and make it better than it was before. Hopefully, we'll have learned some valuable lessons in governing ourselves by then. At least, I hope so, anyway."

Amy said, "All through history, it is a proven fact that when a government becomes corrupt and self-serving and forgets the people they are supposed to be looking after, they all fall down one way or another and can't put themselves together again. Just like Humpty Dumpty. Our whole government was supported by taxes. Think about that for a moment. Every single person that was a politician, or employed by the government, or a civil servant, was paid from our taxes. Do you have any idea how many people we're talking about? Well, we got to the point where there were more of them and retired people on Social Security than there were people working regular jobs to pay for them. That's why the deficit was so high. That and a lot of useless liberal rights programs from the Democrats. Then we had the communist ideas filtering into our government. Demographics showed how those ideas affected us as a nation. And we all know how well those ideas worked in Russia. It was only a matter of time before the house of cards was blown down by a strong wind. In our case it was an EMP. What caused it doesn't really matter. What matters is it was inevitable. Now, we are faced with the challenge of surviving. That's the only thing that really does matter, that and keeping our humanity; not turning into some sick, demented person like others we've seen. Those are the only things that truly matter now. The future can take care of itself, but we have to survive right now, just to get there. And believing what the President of the United States said is not a way to do that. He's just trying to hold onto power that is no longer his to hold. He lost that right when he abandoned the people of this country to save his own ass and left the rest of us to survive on our own. I shudder just thinking what will happen to those men's families that will be defenseless if they do report for duty. They won't have anyone there to protect them. We all know what it's like out there with no law and order."

"That was well said Amy," said Preston.

"Yes, you stated what has happened to our country really well." Joe was in agreement.

"So," said Joan, "what you are saying is that we're on our own now."

"Yes. That's it in a nut shell." Amy reached for Preston's hand.

Jane said, "And we are doing just fine. We'll continue to be fine, too. We are all committed to do our part to survive."

Joan sighed. "I will do whatever I can to help us all survive, too."

Joe smiled. "That's the spirit to have. See, the future is looking brighter every single day that we survive."

Michael said, "I'll do my part to help, too."

Joe patted him on the shoulder. "We're counting on you, Michael, because the future is for the next generation to look after. I hope you guys do a lot better than we did." All the adults looked thoughtful. Joe was right. The future is always for the next generation to do something worthwhile with.

The next day, Amy, Preston and Joe were taking a break inside the house getting something cold to drink. They had all worked up a good sweat. They had just sat down and relaxed their muscles when the FRS crackled with a call from Jane over at the barn. Jane said she was up in the loft cleaning and looked out the window and saw a large crowd of people heading their way.

Joe, Preston and Amy stood up. Joe said, "Okay. You two take your places in the tower. Send Jane over here."

"We do this just like we planned, right?" asked Preston. Joe nodded. Preston and Amy ran to the back porch and grabbed their Load Bearing Vest. They ran over to the barn and met Jane on her way to the house. "We do this just as we planned." Jane nodded, still trotting to the house. Joan and Michael had went to the trailer to do some cleaning. They heard Joe on the radio telling Joan and Michael what was happening and to stay there and defend the trailer.

The loft was fortified for a long siege. Now that they had the cot in there, they could stay for a relatively long time in comfort. They had a fifty-five gallon drum of filtered water and a five-gallon bucket with a fitted toilet seat on it that they used for a toilet when on watch. There was a one-burner cook stove and shelves were stocked with food and coffee. The outside of the barn had been sealed with metal, even the soffits and roof were metal. The house was protected with metal, and the paint they used was fire resistant. They had tried to prepare for as many situations as they could think of.

Everyone was all set. Joe and Jane were at the house and would defend it; Joan and Michael were at the trailer and would defend that. Everyone was set for a long siege, if necessary. Preston and Amy kept close watch on the windows for the mob of people coming their way, giving everyone an update on how many and where they were. It didn't look good. There were twenty-five to thirty people coming and they all were carrying rifles. That asshole, Danny boy, was leading them.

Preston said vehemently, "That son of a bitch. We should have just killed them all and rid the earth of those scumbags."

"Well, it looks like fate gave us another chance to rectify that situation," Amy answered.

"It's a chance I will personally make sure is not wasted. When the shooting starts, he'll be the first to die. I'll make sure of that."

"They all look angry," Amy said. "I wonder what he told them that made them mad at us?"

"You can bet on it being a bunch of lies. I don't think he's ever told the truth in his life."

The mob stopped at the gate. One man started to climb over the top and Preston placed a shot a few inches in front of him that made the man change his mind. The man dropped to the ground on the outside of the gate.

Preston yelled, "I have no idea what you people want, but I highly recommend that you all move on before a whole lot of you end up dying."

A man in the back held up a rope with a hangman's noose on it. "We've come here to get the woman that shot Randy in cold blood and hang her for it. We've already had a trial and heard testimony from Danny and his family, proving her guilty of cold-blooded murder. She shot him in the back of the head."

Preston got even angrier. "Did you hear the testimony about her being kidnapped, beaten and raped? And her son had been thrown into the root cellar while this was going on? Did they tell you that Danny helped with the kidnapping and mistreatment of the woman? Did they happen to tell you about that, too?"

Danny boy spoke up. "No, they didn't hear those lies you made up. They heard about you shooting at my wife and we're here to teach you all a lesson and to get justice for Randy."

Preston laughed out loud. "You are nothing but a little bug on my windshield, Danny boy, and you will get squished if you don't leave right now. You are a punk to think you could teach me anything. Anyone coming onto this property is going to end up dead. Do you all understand that?"

The mob milled closer together and started talking among themselves. Preston got on the radio to Joe. "We need to end this real fast before it gets out of hand down there. I figure if we pick a target and drop them, the rest will break off and leave. I'm taking Danny boy out."

"Okay," Joe said, "I'll take out the guy with the rope."

Danny yelled out, "Listen up, Army boy. You surrender right now and we'll let you live." All of a sudden there were thirty rifles pointed up at the barn.

Preston bent down behind the sandbags to steady his aim at the shooting hole. He looked over at Amy, who was safely situated and had her 22-250 ready to fire. "As soon as they start shooting, just pick a target and shoot. Keep doing this until there are no more targets. Do you understand?" Amy looked intently at him and nodded her head. "Are you going to be all right with this?" Amy didn't answer for a few moments thinking things over. Then she nodded. Preston gave her a small nod back, then turned back to the window. He yelled out, "Whenever you're ready to die, go right ahead and try, Danny boy, because you will be the first. You other men are fools for listening to a liar like him."

Thirty guns opened up on the barn. Preston squeezed off two shots and ducked down for cover. Amy had hesitated for a few moments, then shot once and ducked down, too, working the bolt on her rifle. He popped back up and saw the men were already over the fence and running for the barn. He thought, *What a bunch of dumb asses.* His AR-15 started singing and he dropped one, but the lead man was really hauling ass and he missed him. He could hear Joe and Jane firing, too. He heard some of the bullets punch through the metal, splintering the wood behind it. The man he missed made it to the front of the barn and was out of sight. He couldn't lean over to shoot him or he would be exposed for return fire from the others. Another man was running pretty fast for the barn, too. He aimed at the man's feet and the man ran right into the bullet. He fell over on the ground. He quickly sprayed bullets at the men and they started jumping down in a ditch for cover. They had nowhere else to go. Amy's shots took more time between them since she was using a bolt-action rifle. He looked over at Amy and she had a hard, intense look on her face. He picked up his radio as Amy kept firing at the ditch to keep the men pinned down. "Joe, one got past me in front of the barn." He heard several more bullets hit the structure. He dropped his clip, grabbed a fresh one off the vest, and slammed it in. "Okay, reload now." He started firing and Amy leaned down behind the sandbags and reloaded. She crouched, ready to fire again.

The radio crackled and Joe said, "He's down. You are cleared in front." Amy started to fire again. He looked and saw a few of the men get up and run back the way they had come. He thought, *I didn't think you had the stomach for serious fighting. Most people don't.*

He picked up the binoculars and counted how many were down. There were five dead in the yard, one was hanging over the gate, Danny was lying in the driveway next to the man with the rope, and one was down in the ditch. You could just barely see the man's feet. Nine people had died so far. He yelled out at the rest of the men, "This all happened because you believed a backstabbing liar. You were giving your support to a rapist. You had all better leave before you die, too. Because I promise you this, we will not stop nor will we give up. We will kill you." A few more ran off, not having the stomach to continue with this attack. He could see the rest of them talking down there but couldn't hear what was being said.

The radio crackled and Joan said, "Four are sneaking off, going the back way. They're heading for the trailer."

Preston picked up his radio. "Joan, you have to shoot them before they can get to you. They're here to hang you for killing Randy. They believed the lies Danny and his family told them about what happened."

Joan said, "What, are you crazy?"

"Danny and his family made up lies about what really happened, and they are here to teach us a lesson and hang you for Randy's murder."

Joan said faintly with a shaky uncertain voice, "Oh God."

Michael was worried about his mother and what these men would do to her. He heard the radio conversation and decided to open up with Amy's twenty-gauge shotgun that was loaded with number three buckshot. Amy had left it in the trailer when she switched to carrying the 22-250. The men were about twenty yards away from the trailer now. He fired five quick shots. He hit two seriously and they fell to the ground. The other two ran off.

Joan saw Preston's bandoleer lying on the couch where the shotgun had been. She walked over to Michael, took the shotgun, reloaded it, and handed it back with a pat on his shoulder. She said, "Just aim like you were doing at anyone that comes close. You heard what Preston said, they're here to hurt us." Michael nodded seriously and aimed out the shooting hole again.

The men in the ditch, hearing those shots in the back, started firing again. Some were aiming at the barn and some were aiming at the house. Amy returned fire at the men in the ditch and Preston ducked down behind the sandbags and called Joan on the radio. "Are you two okay?"

Joan replied, "Two bad guys are down. Two ran off. We're taking fire back here."

"Okay, keep them away from the trailer. Don't let them get in. Stay behind the sandbags. You see any part of them, you shoot. Do you understand?"

"Yes." Preston got hit on the side of his face with a splinter. Little pieces of wood were flying about all over the place. Amy had splinters stuck in her hair and some were on her clothes. The blood dripping down his chin onto his shirt went unnoticed. Amy sucked in a quick breath and almost yelped because something just struck with a hard, painful, burning jab into the side of her leg. She hoped it wasn't a bullet but didn't have time to worry about it now. She tried to concentrate on her training, but she could feel something warm running down on her leg. She realized she was bleeding. She shook her head and thought, *I don't have time for this. Concentrate on what you learned.* She spotted a man in the ditch peeking out and said in her head, *remember your training. Brass, breath, relax, aim, slack and squeeze. Do this over and over till there are no more targets.* She squeezed the trigger and the man flinched, then crawled out of sight.

Preston was shooting at the ditch when something hit him in the forehead and almost knocked him down. It felt like someone was holding a hot poker to his forehead. Blood was running down into his eyes, making it difficult to see anything. He ducked down and put his hand up to feel what happened and felt a piece of metal sticking into his forehead. He started to pull it out and it ripped more skin open; the blood really started running down, making it almost impossible to see. It burned like a son of a bitch. He ripped it out of his forehead and threw it across the loft. It had been a four-inch piece of metal. He could hear the .22 popping in the back from the trailer. He could hear Joe's AR-15 firing away and a much louder blast from Jane's 22-250 in between the loud blasts from Amy's 22-250. He felt sorry for any fool those women got into their sights. Especially Jane, she was deadly accurate with that rifle.

Amy ducked down to reload. She asked, "You hurt bad?"

"No, I just can't see right now." She quickly looked at him and saw all the blood running into his eyes and the huge four or five inch gash in his forehead. She quickly pulled a bandana out of her pocket and threw it at him. "Wipe your eyes, then wrap that up with the bandana."

"Yes, ma'am."

Amy smiled. "And don't you forget it either, Mister." Preston chuckled. Amy started firing again. Joe was the one that made her carry around bandanas. Sometimes when she was practicing, she would perspire and it would run into her eyes and cause her to blink at the wrong moment. He told her that's what bandanas were for. So, she had raided Preston's drawers until she found a few and had used them ever since.

The return shooting had slowed down. Most of the men out there had shotguns, some had .22s and a few had deer rifles. Joe called on the radio for a status report.

Joan called in first. "We have two back here, but it looks like they're backing off. We have two down. We're okay."

Preston said into the radio, "I got a piece of metal in my forehead. It's bleeding like a sieve. Amy is fine, though."

Joe said, "We're good over here."

Joe called out from the second story of the house, "Are you people stupid or what? Go home. We don't want anymore killing."

A few minutes later a white t-shirt was raised up out of the ditch. It was attached to the barrel of a .22 rifle. A voice called out, "Okay. We're leaving. Don't shoot."

Joe called out, "Take your wounded with you." Several men stood up and staggered out of sight, holding onto some men as they made their way back home.

Amy dropped down next to Preston. "Thank God that's over."

Preston had tied the bandana over the cut after wiping his face of as much blood as he could. He looked like he had smeared red paint all over his face and the front of his shirt. He said, "It ain't over yet."

Amy looked at him. "What?"

He looked deep into her eyes. "Now we have to go out there and make sure they're all dead and not just faking it."

Amy got a little pale and then straightened her shoulders and softly whispered, "Oh."

He reached out and took her hand and looked in her eyes. "Listen. If even one of them is alive out there, they can kill you or any one of us walking to the house. Do you want to take that chance, not with just your own life, but with everyone else's?"

Amy looked down and thought for a few moments and then looked back up at Preston. There was misery in her eyes and she sighed. "No. I will not take that chance. You all mean way too much to me to care about what happens to a bunch of morons that believed anything Danny would say. They had to have known what kind of a person he was, and they believed him anyway, without even trying to find the truth. If that's what it takes, then that's what I'll do. I took an oath to you and Joe that I would do whatever it took to protect us, and I will do it. I won't like it, but I will do it." He touched her face and left a red streak down her cheek.

The radio crackled and Joe said, "Clean up time. Make sure they're all dead."

Joan was the first one out the door at the trailer. Michael ran past her and said, "Mom, I will protect you."

He turned back to look at her. One of the men lying on the ground had been waiting for this moment. He lifted up his arm holding the 9mm he had in his hand, pointing it at Joan. Joan saw this and swung the .22 Marlin at him. They both shot at the same time. Joan was shot in the lower right side of her stomach. The bullet Joan fired went into the man's chest, but he hardly felt it and fired again at Joan. He hit her dead center in the chest. She fell back onto the ground. Michael stared in disbelief at what had just happened. He swung the twenty-gauge shotgun and shot the man almost at point blank range in the face and neck.

Joe walked out to check the downed men on the ground. Jane was on the porch, covering him with her 22-250. They were all dead. Everyone at the farmstead had all been shooting soft points, and at the range they were shooting, the bullets had left devastation and quick death to each one that had been hit. Just to be sure, though, Joe carried a .22 pistol and shot them all in the head. Preston and Amy were doing the same thing on the other side of the yard. Joe and Preston were working towards each other. Preston was doing the shooting and Amy was covering him from in front of the barn. When they had shot the last body lying in the ditch, Joe called an all clear for the barn and house.

Jane said, "Preston get your ass over here and let me take care of that wound right now."

"No. Take care of Amy first."

Jane looked over at Amy. Amy started limping towards them. She had blood on the side of her leg and a tear in her pants. She said, "I'm fine for now. You take care of Preston first."

Jane turned to Preston. "In the house, now." Preston looked between Jane and Amy and turned and started walking to the house. Both women had used the same tone. He was not feeling up to an argument at the moment with both of them ganging up on him. Jane started towards the house, too.

Joe said to Amy, "Do you feel up to going with me to check on Joan and Michael or do you need to stay here and be doctored, too?"

"I'm fine. Are they all right?"

"I don't know. I heard a few .22 shots from back there and then a shotgun blast and they aren't answering the radio."

He lifted his hand and said into the radio, "Joan, come in. Joan, are you there?" Nothing. No one answered. Joe and Amy looked at each other and then they started to jog to the trailer.

"It probably isn't anything to worry about,' Joe said. "They probably just forgot their radios inside the trailer." Joe thought to himself that they had to get everyone up to speed a lot sooner than they had been doing. Civilians always got things wrong or forgot things. He sighed. Amy winced every time her foot hit the ground, making her leg jar and she could feel something warm run down her leg again. She paid it no mind. Her worry over Joan and Michael greatly outweighed the pain in her leg. They came out of the trail and stopped dead in their tracks. There were three bodies lying on the ground. Michael was standing over one man holding the shotgun, looking over at his mother lying on the ground. Joan was staring straight up and was clearly dead. She had one bullet hole in her chest and one in her stomach. The man Michael was standing over had clearly shot her. Amy limped over to Michael and grabbed him, pushing the shotgun out of the way. She gently took it out of his hands and flipped the safety on.

Michael looked up at her with tear-filled eyes. "The Mothman tried to warn me about this. I just wasn't smart enough to figure out what he was warning me about. Now my mom's dead. I should have known what to do to save her. I tried."

Amy hugged him to her. "Michael, it isn't your fault that your mom died. It is that man's fault for shooting her. No one else is to blame but that man lying dead on the ground. You killed him, Michael. You got justice done by doing that. If you hadn't shot him, he would have shot all of us if he could. That's why those men came here today. They wanted to hang your mother and teach us a lesson. Each and every one of them came here armed with a rifle and a lot of ammo. They had hatred in their hearts and intended to kill us. I'm so sorry your mom died. We all tried to save her, Michael. That's what this attack was about. Come with me to the house. Come on." She nudged Michael gently with her hand on his back.

She looked over at Joe and saw the sadness on his face. He said, "Wait a minute." They stopped and turned to him. He reached out and grabbed the shotgun from Amy and walked into the trailer. He came back out carrying Michael's .22. He handed it to Michael. "Stay armed at all times. It isn't safe out here." Michael nodded. Amy nodded to Joe as they shuffled back to the house.

She didn't know how to handle this sort of situation, but she knew she had to make Michael understand that it was not his fault. He needed to put the blame where it truly lay, and that was with the man who had done this and the others that had come there to kill them. She kept her arm around Michael, comforting him the best she could.

When they came out of the trail that led to the house, Michael saw all the bodies lying about. His eyes got big. He looked up at Amy. "How many were there?"

Amy said, "I don't know for sure, but it was somewhere around thirty or forty men.

"How many did you kill?"

She sighed. "I don't know for sure but, I think it was two."

He nodded his head and continued to look around as they walked to the house. When they were almost to the porch he said, "I'm glad."

Amy stopped and looked hard at Michael. She steered him to the porch steps and directed him to sit down. She sat down next to him and put her arm around him. "Michael, dealing out death is never a good thing. You should never feel glad that it had to come to an end like this. I know right now you're feeling good that these men died. That's not a good thing, Michael. They didn't give us a choice but to shoot back at them. Preston tried to stop them because he knew how this was going to end." She looked at him. "Not that your mother would die, exactly, but that a lot of people would die needlessly because they listened to lies from someone else. He tried to stop this from happening. Every one of those men out there had families, Michael. Tonight there will be a lot of crying and heartbreak because they will never be coming home again. Some of these men had children, too. There are children out there right now crying because their fathers will never come home again. They feel as you do right now over the loss of your mother. Think about all of that, too, as you think about how good this makes you feel. Can you do that for me, Michael? Can you think about those children and the wives that are now alone and have no one to protect or provide for them? The way I see it, everyone lost today. There are no such things as winners in a situation like this."

They sat in silence for a few minutes and then Michael said, "I don't want those other kids feeling like I do."

She hugged him. "Remember this always, okay? Now listen real close to what I'm going to say now, okay?"

"Okay."

"Those men didn't give us a choice. They brought the fight to us today. We have no control over what other people do. We only have control over what we do. Do you understand what I am saying?"

"I think so. They came here and made us kill them because they came here to kill us."

"Yes. That's it exactly." She hugged him. "Michael, I want you to know that I love you very much. From this moment on, all of us adopt you. You are a member of our family. You are not alone. You are one of us, okay?"

"Okay."

Amy and Michael went into the house. "I have to check on Preston, he was hurt pretty badly today." Michael started to cry again. She hugged him. "He'll be all right. He only got hurt. He's tough."

Michael just clung to her and cried. "I don't know what to do now. What should I do?"

She looked at him. "What do you feel like doing right now?"

"I don't know," Michael said, "I don't know."

"That's okay, too. We'll just stay right here and be okay together, even if we don't know what to do."

He hugged her tight. "I'm scared. I don't know what to do."

A strong pair of arms wrapped around both of them, holding them tightly. Preston said, "I'm so sorry, Michael. We tried to stop them from doing this. I'm just so damn sorry." Michael just cried harder. Preston rocked both of them for a while. "Amy, Jane needs to look at your leg."

"Okay, in awhile. I'm busy at the moment."

"No way. You made me go get stitched up. Now it's your turn. Don't be such a wimp about it. I went peacefully to my doom so you can, too."

She looked up at him and his forehead was all taped up. "Are you all right?"

"Yeah, I have a hell of a headache, though." She shook her head at him. He motioned with his head for her to go.

She thought about this for a few minutes and then decided to leave and let Preston handle this for a while. She needed to talk to Jane about this and get some advice about what to do and what she should say to him at a time like this. She had no clue. She hugged Michael and told him she had to go get patched up, too. He looked at her and she showed him her leg with the small tear in her pants and the huge spot of semi-dried blood that went down her leg. He looked scared and she smiled. "I'll be fine. You behave while I'm gone, okay?" He nodded.

She turned and left the room. Joe was standing in the hall looking pretty down. She socked his arm and said, "Cheer up, it could have been much worse today, you know. What if we'd all been shot? So, look on the bright side."

He said, "I just feel so bad about what Michael is going through right now."

She sighed. "I know. Me too. But how do we help him through this? That's what I want to know. I have no experience in this area at all."

He looked at her. "Didn't you lose your parents?"

"Yes, I did. They died when I was a child. My grandfather and great uncle raised me. So I do know what it felt like."

"Let that be your guide."

She looked at him. "Wow. That's pretty profound, coming from you."

He narrowed his eyes at her. "You must still be high from the adrenaline rush from the battle. You're like jumping all over the place."

Jane peeked out the bathroom door and said in a no-nonsense voice, "Get in here and let me look at your leg." Amy meekly turned and went into the bathroom with Jane.

Jane told her to take off the pants. They could mend them later. Jane had her hop up on the counter and stretch her leg out so she could get a good look at the wound. Jane washed it out. You could clearly see a groove where a bullet traveled along the side of her thigh for about three inches. It was still sort of bleeding. Both women were amazed that it had been a bullet and not a splinter. Jane sprayed some stuff on it and then put a bandage on it. Amy put her pants back on again. Amy thought that it hurt worse now after Jane had poked and prodded it.

Jane asked, "How is Michael doing?" Amy filled her in on everything and the conversations she had with Michael. "The world is a different place now than it was. I personally feel that you handled it very well. Only time will tell, though. We are all here for Michael. We'll just make sure that he knows that."

Amy said, "I think it would be best if he stayed here with you and Joe. I told him we all adopted him, but I think you and Joe should be his primary parents now. Preston and I will help, of course, but we have a new relationship and aren't stable like you and Joe are. Do you understand what I mean?"

Jane smiled. "I do understand what you mean and thanks. We always wanted to be parents. I could never get pregnant, though. We were just starting to talk about adopting now that Joe was around all the time."

"Well, I guess it was a good thing that you two didn't get a baby yet. Can you imagine what that would be like now?" Jane nodded. Amy said, "Is Preston all right?"

Jane smiled. "It's a good thing it hit his head and not somewhere else. I told him it's a good thing he has such a hard head." She didn't mention that now they needed to worry about infection.

Amy asked, "What are we going to do about a funeral? Michael will be expecting one. Should we have a showing of her body or just bury her? I don't know how to go about doing this."

"It's cool outside, but not cool enough to preserve a body," said Jane. "We have to bury her today if we can. We'll let him have a few minutes alone with her if he wants, and then we bury her."

"Okay, just tell me who does what and I'll do it."

Jane said, "We'll have to dig a grave for Joan. We need to talk to the men and decide who will do what."

"Okay." They both left the bathroom. Jane had straightened everything up as they talked.

Joe was sitting in the den, looking out the window. When he saw them he said, "We have to dig a grave for Joan." Both women exchanged a look. "I think you two should stay here with Michael and let Preston and I get everything cleaned up and the grave dug. Then we'll have Joan's funeral. We do this armed to the teeth in case any of them decide to come back or are lurking around somewhere. You two protect Michael. Then Preston and I will take the men's bodies down the road a couple of miles and let the families come get them to bury them themselves."

Amy said, "Okay. I'll go relieve Preston and you two can tell him the plan." She turned around and went down the hallway to the living room. Michael and Preston were sitting on the couch talking and Preston had his hand on Michael's shoulder. "Joe needs to talk to you."

Preston said, "Are you okay?"

"Yes, I'm fine. It's just a scratch, nothing to worry about." He kissed her and went down the hall. Amy sat down on the couch and turned to Michael.

Michael asked, "When will we be burying my mom?"

"Later today."

Michael looked at her. "Why are we doing it today?"

"Because we don't have anywhere to keep your mom until the funeral."

Michael nodded his head and started to cry again. Amy held him and just let him cry. She remembered how her grandfather and uncle would just hold her and let her cry. How comforted she felt because they never told her to stop or anything like that. They were just there for her.

She would let him decide what he wanted to do. If he wanted to talk, she would do that, too. Jane came into the living room and sat on the couch on the other side of Michael. She patted his arm in comfort. After an hour, Jane got up and went into the kitchen. She came back with cups of hot chocolate for the three of them. They drank in silence. Jane was holding Michael and murmuring soothing things to him. He would cry and then be silent for a while. Sometimes he would talk about his mother. Both women just tried to be as comforting as possible and let him lead them in conversation. It was a little over two hours later when the men came in and Jane got up and went into the kitchen with them. Amy stayed and talked with Michael.

After a few minutes, they all came into the living room and Preston walked over to Michael. "Michael, we have dug a grave for your mother and it's time to bury her." Michael sobbed a little at that news, then nodded his head and stood up. Amy hugged him.

Joe came over and hugged him. "I'm so very sorry, Michael. We tried hard today to save her."

Michael nodded. "I know that. I saw the bodies out there. I just wish I would have shot that man on the ground before he could shoot my mom."

Joe nodded at Michael. "Whenever we lose someone we love, we always have regrets. We always say I wish I would have done this different or done that different. It doesn't matter what it was. We just always regret that we didn't do something different that would have changed things so that person would have lived. Unfortunately, we just don't know enough at the time it happens to change things for the better. We only know these things after they've already happened. I'm sorry for your loss, Michael. We are here for you. You are part of our family now. I'm glad you're here with us."

Michael looked up at him. "I'm glad to be here, too. I just wish today didn't happen." Joe put his arm around Michael. "I know. I wish that, too." They all got ready to go outside. The adults armed themselves to the teeth. Joe had refilled all the tactical vests with ammo. None of them were feeling very trusting toward outsiders. They went outside. The men had moved all the bodies out the front gate to be moved after the funeral. The men guided them over to the far back of the property and beyond. Not too far from a really nice hardwood tree, they had dug a grave. They had placed Joan's body beside the grave and only left her head uncovered from a tarp.

Michael cried really hard when he saw his mom there. He ran over and sat down next to her and touched her face. The men had closed her eyes. The adults gave him some time to be with his mother. He talked to her quietly for several minutes and then stood up. Jane and Amy came over and hugged him and turned him around a bit in the process. The men completely covered her with the tarp and tied a rope around her shoulders that also supported the head and a rope around her legs so they could lower her into the grave. They stepped back and Jane opened her Bible and began reading out loud. When she was finished, she stepped back again. The men lowered her body into the grave. Jane was standing behind Michael, holding his shoulders. The men picked up the shovels and started to fill in the grave. Michael turned around and sobbed against Jane, holding her tight. The women were crying, too. It was tearing them up inside seeing Michael so grief-stricken. They were going to miss Joan, too, but not anywhere near the depth that Michael would miss her. It took awhile to fill the grave in. When the men finished, Preston walked over and placed a cross they made out of two by fours at the head of the grave.

They all walked slowly back to the farmhouse. Joe and Preston didn't go inside because they still had the other bodies to deal with. The men said they'd be back later. Michael asked where they were going.

Joe said they were taking the men's bodies down the road so the families could come and get them to have a funeral, too. Michael nodded and walked inside the house. The women followed him in. They went into the kitchen. Jane made Michael some more hot chocolate. Amy and Jane started dinner. The men had to be starving by this time. They had all missed lunch and it would be dark outside soon. It was past dinnertime, too. Michael sat at the table looking really sad and alone. The women would stop and give him a hug every now and again; most of the time it was just so they felt better, too. It was really starting to sink in that Joan was gone. They had all been standing in this very kitchen laughing just this morning. It seemed unreal. The whole day just seemed like a nightmare. So much had happened once again.

The men had gotten the bikes and Joe put a frame they had made with five two by fours across them so they could stack the bodies on it to take them down the road. It was going to take two trips. They stayed alert in case someone wanted revenge for a friend or family member. Joe didn't relax until they got back from the second trip and had the gate locked up tight once again. Both men were very tired and hungry. They were hoping the women had put something on for dinner. If not, it would be understandable. They could scrounge around and make something if the women were too busy with Michael. Right now, Michael came first. None of them had ever had children and didn't have very much experience with them, but they knew this was going to be hard for him and he would probably need a lot of attention.

Michael just stayed seated at the table, staring down at his hands, while the women worked in the kitchen. He felt so lost and alone and weird. He kept thinking about the Mothman and the warning he had tried to give him about those men. If he could have only understood what that warning message had been about, then his mom would still be alive. He just wanted this day to get over with. Joe and Preston came into the house after radioing in to Jane to let her know they were coming. She went and let them in the door because she had dropped down the steel plate sealing the door against intruders. The smell hit the men and their mouths watered.

Jane said, "Dinner will be ready shortly. Go wash up; Preston, don't get that bandage wet."

Preston walked behind Joe to the bathroom and called out, "Yes, Mom," then stopped dead and realized that if Michael heard what he had said it might upset him. He shook his head at how careless he was.

They sat down to eat and Michael said he wasn't hungry. Amy and Jane tried to get him to eat a little, and he did eat some, but not very much. The men cleaned up. There wasn't even one little morsel left anywhere. No one knew what to say. Michael finally got up and said he was going to go read his book. His mother had him reading some of the classics. It was part of his scholastic studies she wanted him to do. Jane said she would come and check on him in a little while. He walked out of the kitchen. The adults just sat there looking sad and not knowing what to say or do to help ease his hurt.

Amy finally said, "One thing I do know for sure. He killed a man today. That has to affect him a lot, too. We'll need to talk to him about that and help him through it." The others nodded and thought, *how do you help a child get over killing someone?* It didn't matter that it was in self-defense. It was not an easy thing to live with.

Amy reached out and hugged Jane. "I'm sorry you had to go through all of this today. It's not easy."

Jane hugged her back. "I'm okay with it. I've seen death before. I've never caused it before, but death isn't new to me. I'm just pissed as hell that anyone would even listen to one word that Danny had to say. Everyone knows what a liar he is and anything he says can't be trusted. These people know that, too, but they went ahead and used their anger for everything else that happened and directed it at us; especially Joan. They were really going to hang her. I'm so mad right now that if one of you suggested we go hunt every one of them down and deliver justice to them, I would seriously consider it." Everyone looked a bit shocked.

Amy said, "I feel in some ways that I'm to blame for all of this."

Jane looked puzzled. "How could you be blamed for any of this?"

Amy sighed. "If I hadn't interfered and suggested we let Danny live, none of this would have happened. I am also the one responsible for Joan being in the trailer cleaning. If she would have been here, she wouldn't have died."

Joe said, "Amy, you can't blame yourself for Danny. We all agreed he deserved a second chance because of his wife and children. We are all equally to blame for that decision. And the reason Joan was in the trailer was a good reason, too. Joan felt needed and helpful. It was all she could do until she healed. She just told me the other night that she really liked how we didn't try to keep her from doing things and helping out. You're just going through what I was explaining to Michael. I call it the 'If I had only known or suspected syndrome.' Everyone thinks they could have, should have done something different. It isn't really true. There's no way you could have possibly known that those men would pick today to come after Joan."

Preston said, "Joe is right, you know. If we had a crystal ball, we could probably avoid everything bad in our lives. But since we don't know things ahead of time, there is no way we can know these things. The facts don't come out until afterwards."

Jane said, "Don't blame yourself for any of this, Amy. If there is any blame, then it should go to Joe and I and possibly Preston. We're the ones that knew about Danny and what he was like and we still agreed that we should let him live for his children. Danny didn't understand what a gift we gave him and his family. They totally threw it out the window. Danny thought if he brought enough men with him, he could take all of us out. He didn't understand the difference between a poacher like him and military combat trained men like Joe and Preston, or how they have trained us, either. He thought like a civilian that he and thirty or forty men would take us out. Well, they sure found out different. The others around here will think a third and fourth time before trying something like that again."

Joe said, "I still say we made the right decision at that time. We couldn't possibly have known he would be believed by anyone, let alone by all those men. They all knew Danny."

"I agree," said Preston.

The women looked thoughtful. "Amy, you need to get some rest, and Preston should rest, also. You both were wounded today. Hey, I almost forgot. Amy was the first one to be shot here, too."

Preston said, "What? When were you shot? Where were you shot?"

Amy held her hand up. "It's nothing. It is just a flesh wound."

Preston looked at Jane and she nodded. He looked back at Amy and said, "Your leg wound?" Amy nodded her head. "How did a bullet get through?"

Joe said, "We'll have to go look over every inch of the loft tomorrow and find out how this happened."

Preston said with an outraged edge to his voice, "Damn right we will. We're trusting those walls and sandbags to protect us from bullets when we are up there."

Preston and Amy walked slowly and quietly over to the trailer, being alert for trouble of any kind. When they came out of the trail and could see the trailer, they both stopped and looked around for a few minutes assessing the area. When Preston felt that the area was clear and no one was around, they stepped out from the trail.

They had just taken a second step when two men stepped out of the brush. There was one man on each side of them. The man on the right said, "Don't even move a muscle. Drop those guns. Don't try anything stupid. You're not so safe now up in the barn, are you? One of you killed my brother today."

Joe and Jane sat at the table for a while, talking quietly. Joe was holding Jane close. He knew that she talked pretty tough and was pretty tough, too, but the act of killing someone is not an easy thing. He knew it affected her. She always had such a big heart and hated anyone to be in pain or discomfort of any kind.

She sighed. "I had better go check on Michael. It isn't good for him being alone right now."

Joe said, "I know. But maybe he needs to be alone and figure out what he is feeling so he can deal with it. We'll help him in any way we can."

Jane smiled at him and kissed him. "You'll be a good father for him, Joe." Joe looked pleased. Jane stood up. "I'm going to go talk to Michael for awhile if he wants some company. If he wants to be alone, I'll just let him be. But we need to talk to him about his killing that man today. I think the sooner, the better." Joe nodded. Jane turned and walked out of the kitchen down the hallway.

    ***

Michael was lying on his bed. He'd been trying to read the book his mom wanted him to read, but he couldn't remember anything he had just read. His mind kept going back to the scene of his mother dying and him killing the man that shot her. It just kept playing over and over in his head. He was all mixed up. He wasn't sure what he felt about anything. He kept seeing the look in the man's eyes, when he knew he was going to die. Michael closed his eyes and started to cry again. He felt so many things and wasn't sure how to sort them all out. Then he faintly heard some sounds coming from outside. The sound came closer to the house; he heard the flapping of wings. He stood up and walked over to the only window that wasn't sealed up and looked outside. He bent down quickly. Something was out there. He crawled along the floor to the lamp and turned it off. Joe had always told him to turn the light off if he thought something was outside, so he could see without the reflection in the glass interfering. He grabbed the .22 rifle and leaned up against the bed. He could faintly see some shadows out there. His heart was pounding fast; he could hear the thumps in his ears. He kept the rifle pointed at the window. He was trying to get his courage up to look out the window again. He was shaking all over, making it hard to hold the rifle steady. He kept seeing something out there blocking the moon. It seemed to be coming closer to the house. The flapping was getting louder. He was crying, not knowing what he should do. Something thumped against the house and scared him really bad. Then something came up close to the window and he pulled the trigger on the .22, shooting it over and over again. Glass was flying everywhere.

Chapter 19

HellHounds

"Don't let the same dog bite you twice."

Chuck Berry

The firewood in Junior's arms hadn't even had time to hit the ground before the Rottweiler was on him. In the next instant, Junior was on the ground, gasping for a breath and fighting for his life. He heard Gayle scream. He barely managed to bring his left arm up to protect his throat in time. The SKS had been knocked off his shoulder. The impact with the ground had knocked the breath out of him. The face of the Rottweiler was inches in front of his as he tried to hold it away with his left arm in the dog's mouth. The dog was trying to get past his arm and rip his throat out. He couldn't seem to get a breath. The slobber from the dog's mouth was dripping onto his face and chest as he fought. All he could hear was the dog's deep growl. The dog had a hold of his left arm, trying to bite through the padding. Thank God, he still had the duct-taped towels on the sleeves of his coat. He didn't know how long they'd hold up, but so far they were working really well. The strength of the dog was incredible. He was shaking Junior like he was a rag doll.

Junior worked his right arm free and punched the dog as hard as he could on the nose. The dog winced in pain, but still hung on, shaking him all over the place. This had taken place in a matter of seconds. Junior swung his right arm again to hit the dog on the nose, but the dog shook him at the wrong moment and he was not able to get his arm to swing around and connect with the dog. He started to wonder if the dog was going to break his arm.

Gayle yelled, "Oh my God, more are coming." Gayle ran over to Junior and put the SKS by the Rottweiler's ribs, almost at point blank range, and pulled the trigger. There was no noticeable effect. The dog and Junior were moving all over the place, and she had to make sure she didn't shoot Junior in the process of killing the dog. She pulled the trigger again, and again and again. The last shot broke the dog's pelvic bone and he finally let go, falling over on the ground, yelping in pain.

The rest of the dogs, smelling the blood, surged forward. Junior jumped up and they both ran for the door. Just as Junior was swinging the door, a large black lab rushed inside before it slammed shut. The dog lunged at Gayle and knocked her to the ground, going for her neck. Junior grabbed a piece of firewood and swung it down like a sledgehammer on the dog's head. The dog yelped in surprise and pain, jumping off to the side. It started circling them, growling real low in its chest. Gayle was trying to get the SKS up to shoot it, but it was caught on her coat somehow. The dog leaped for Junior. He cracked the dog on the head so hard he lost his grip on the piece of firewood and it rolled away. The dog dropped to the floor, shaking its head, and then came in at him low, trying to bite his legs. Gayle finally managed to work the SKS loose and bring the rifle up and shoot the dog in the spine. It fell over, whining and yelping in pain, trying to use its front legs to pull its body forward. Junior ran over, grabbed the .22, and shot him twice in the head to end its suffering. The rest of the pack outside was in a frenzy, barking and scratching at the door like they were possessed. The smell of cordite was thick in the air, and their ears were ringing. It was a nightmare, with hellhounds at their door. The scratching at the door finally stopped, but not the howling and growling.

He said with a dry laugh, "These hellhounds would make a great true life movie for the Lifetime channel."

Gayle shuddered. "I agree with you. It seems that no matter how many we kill, more keep showing up. How's your arm?"

He pulled her close and hugged her. "It's a bit sore, but it will be fine. I thought that dog was going to break my arm the way it was shaking me around. The padding held up really well. We should pad you up to protect you from any more dog bites."

"That's a good idea," she said. "What are we going to do with the dead dog? It stinks really bad. It smells like it's been rolling in rotting fish." She put her hand over her mouth.

"I know it does. Just don't touch it. Who knows what it's been rolling in? We'll throw something over it. If we throw it outside, it will just be more food for the pack and keep them around longer. We'll worry about it tomorrow. Clint will be back soon." He took a deep breath, coughing a little from the smell. "They're acting like they've done this before. I know I keep saying that, but each time we encounter them, they act the same way. Like it's a practiced move. With the way they trapped me in that house, and the way they've been acting here, it makes me think they've trapped people inside before, and waited for them to come outside. Eventually people always have to go outside for something, like we needed to go out for firewood. It just seems like they know what they're doing. They have no natural fear. Most people wouldn't understand the danger until it was too late, because people don't have a natural fear of dogs, either. Just as you had no fear when you saw them when you were looking for me." Gayle nodded in agreement. "We have enough firewood now that we can wait until Clint gets back before we have to go outside again."

Gayle said, "I sure hope Clint is all right and doesn't get attacked by those hellhounds out there."

"Don't worry about Clint. He's one man you can be sure will be safe out there. He can take care of himself."

Gayle missed her mother. She found herself tearing up and crying over the silliest things when she would think of her. Junior would just hold her and let her cry it out. She raised the steel plate over the window to look outside and saw it was snowing, which reminded her of her mother taking off in a blizzard. It was like everywhere she turned, she had a reminder of her mother. It was getting a little easier, but it felt so wrong not to have had a funeral for her. It was like it was still hanging over her head, and she couldn't put it into perspective because she had no closure. There was no grave she could visit or anything. It just felt so wrong.

They had settled into a routine of sorts. It was great living with Junior, and it seemed they fell more in love every day. Their lovemaking was passionate and satisfying. She had never believed that love was real. Her mother had even told her that romance writers made most of the stuff up in their books. She had emphasized that real relationships were not like that. She had changed her tune some when she had started a relationship with George, though. She said he made her feel young, desirable, and passionate, and he filled all the empty spots inside of her. That's how she felt about Junior. He was always surprising her with things he'd say and the depth of his feeling. He didn't try to impress her, he was just being himself. She really loved who he was on the inside. She chuckled to herself and thought, *he is such a hottie, too.* Her heart would start to beat faster and her knees would get a bit weak every time he walked into the room. It was just like in the romance novels. Sometimes when he smiled at her, she got butterflies in her stomach. Even when she wasn't looking, she always knew when he walked into the room. It was like something inside of her recognized him even if she didn't see him. He said she affected him the same way. He got a kick out of how he could make her tremble just being near her. Well, if they ever found a minister or priest or someone who could marry them, she was doing it. She wanted to be with him forever. She was ready to be a wife to him and take him to be her husband. She just wished her mother could have understood a little better about their relationship and gave them time to figure it out. She sighed. Everything always seemed to come back to her mother in some way or another.

He started teaching her how to cook. She was now using recipes and they were coming out just right. She had always felt that she couldn't cook; it just seemed that no matter what she did, she couldn't cook like her mother. Well, she found out differently now. She could cook after all, and she enjoyed it. She hadn't made anything hard yet, but she was working up to it and felt confident. It changed her perspective about a lot of things. She didn't feel like such a failure anymore. She had found out that there were many things she could learn to do, like trapping, snaring, tanning animal hides and working the hides to make them soft. It was hard work, but she kept thinking about how beautiful and silky it would be when it was finished. She had started working on his coat again for Christmas. It was coming out wonderfully. She couldn't wait to see him in it. She was also going to make him a fur hat to wear that covered his ears and could be rolled down around his neck and throat to keep him warm from the wind. When Clint got back, she would measure him, too, and make him a coat and hat. Then she'd have to tackle making gloves. Their gloves wouldn't last forever and she had the patterns to make them. She looked forward to the challenge.

On the fourth day after Clint had gone for his stuff, they were still waiting for him. They were both going a little stir-crazy, being locked up inside, even if they were together. The dead dog was stinking worse every day and the walls were closing in on them. They were trapped inside with a pack of hungry hellhounds outside.

Junior said, "Clint must have been delayed by something."

Gayle had enough of waiting. "I can't take the smell anymore. The metal ash pan for the wood stove is over flowing. We need to clean this place up. I just can't take it anymore." It had stopped snowing, and was around twenty degrees outside, going down to around ten or twelve degrees at night.

"Well, we haven't seen them for awhile. Maybe they've moved on. We can toss the dog out and empty the ash pan." They put their outside clothing on and Gayle carried the SKS. He grabbed the twelve gauge Remington 870 and loaded it with double aught buckshot. "Enough of this playing around stuff. This should bring them down and keep them there."

They went outside and Gayle stayed at the door with the SKS at the ready for any danger. He walked out about twenty feet and looked all around for dogs, making sure to check the roof this time. He half expected to see a flying dog coming at him again. So far, they hadn't seen anything moving. He walked back to the house, grabbed the dead dog, and dragged it outside. He dragged it over to a spot where he would be able to see it and have a clear shot at the area from the shooting hole in the loft when the dogs came back. It felt down right eerie out here now, waiting to be attacked. It was completely silent. He quickly came in, and grabbed the ash pan to empty it. When he came back, he whispered to her, "I'm going to grab an armful of wood since we're out here." She shook her head no at him, but he ignored her. He quietly loaded up his arms and walked back to the door quickly, keeping his eyes glued on the roof. That was one lesson he would not soon forget. He walked in and locked everything back up.

They both sighed in relief. She said, "Good. They're gone for now."

"We'll know for sure tomorrow if the bait dog has been hit or not." They set about cleaning the place up and getting rid of the smell of the dead dog. Just being able to go outside safely had greatly lifted their spirits.

He didn't say anything to her, but he was getting a little bit anxious about Clint being gone for so long. They had cleaned out his old room and had everything ready for his return. It had been a little hard, and felt really strange moving his dad's clothes into his old room for Clint to use. They had spent the rest of the day arranging their things in his dad's old bedroom.

She hadn't said anything to him about her arm, but it was really hurting now. She had taken over caring for it, and it was swollen, red and puffy in spots. She didn't know what to do. She just kept cleaning it and putting new bandages on it. She hoped she hadn't gotten some horrible disease. She just ignored it most of the time.

****

Clint had reached his camp with no other incidents. He got some sleep, and then got up and started to take his camp apart and get everything packed up. He took his time, making sure he didn't leave anything behind. He started out in the afternoon, heading back to Junior's place. He hadn't gone far when he came across some fresh human tracks in the snow. It looked like six or seven people were traveling together. They were too close for comfort. He decided to follow them and see what they were up to. He buried his stuff and just took his normal pack with him. Not many people could survive these types of conditions for long. The tracks were heading off to the northwest. He started tracking them. He knew that Junior and Gayle were expecting him, but they would just have to wait and handle things by themselves for awhile until he found out what these people were up to.

****

The next day, Junior and Gayle checked the bait dog and it hadn't been touched. *Good,* he thought, *now we can set some snares.* The cold must have driven the pack off. But the question was for how long? He explained to Gayle again about the cycles coyotes follow. The dogs should be doing something similar. The problem with that was most of the time it was a six-day cycle, but it could be as long as eight days. There was just no way to know for sure. They went outside and looked around, there were no tracks in the snow. She asked him if maybe the dogs had moved on permanently and he smiled. "That would be nice, but I doubt it. They'll be back. That has been their pattern, and they'll stick with it. It has obviously produced food for them in the past, so they'll keep at it until either it doesn't work anymore, or they're dead."

He dragged the dead dog farther off, to a thicket of small alder trees. He then walked around, trampling the snow down on four different paths. The dogs had already hit this spot and eaten the muskrat guts he had left in the bait pile. He brought three dozen camlock snares with him to set up to catch the dogs. On the trails, he put a stick every ten feet to get the dogs used to ducking down to go under it and hung four snares per trail. They would duck down and walk right into the snare and die. He backtracked and set up a snare in every naturally narrowed down spot, too. Before he knew it, he was on his last dozen snares. It was eerily quiet. There were no squirrels chattering in the sun, nor were there any chickadees flying around the bait pile. It was really strange. It had been a few days since the dog pack had moved on, but everything around them still was acting like the hellhounds were nearby. They walked a circle around the house and set out the last dozen snares. Junior smiled. "This should even up the odds a little in our favor."

They went back inside after grabbing a few more days of firewood. No more taking chances of running low. They were keeping at least seven days' worth of wood inside. He was feeling much better now. If they could catch at least ten dogs every time the pack came through, the odds would change in their favor quickly.

Gayle smiled. "I have a really good feeling we're going to make it now." They made lunch. They checked the snares every day. So far, the dogs hadn't been back. They caught a lone coyote that came through the area, though. Gayle was excited about that. The fur was beautiful. She still had visions of making them all really warm things to wear. She would start spending a lot of time at it just as soon as her arm started to feel better. Her arm was getting to be a real pain in the butt. It kept throbbing and breaking her concentration.

****

Clint was still following the people. They weren't traveling very fast. It looked like there were three women and the rest were men. They had rifles and a few supplies. He wondered where they were going. They had gotten lost a few times and had to back track. He speculated that whomever it was leading them hadn't been here in a few years. Also, in winter everything looked different. One also had to take into account that the roads hadn't been plowed, either, and it all looked the same out there. He was glad Junior had given him so much food to take with him. He was rationing it to make it last as long as possible. He had no idea how far these people were going. A few times it had snowed, and they made a crude shelter under the trees and holed up until the storm was over. He had done the same. He was going to follow them for at least twenty miles if they didn't stop somewhere before that. Then he'd head back to Junior and Gayle's place. By then he'd know if they were just passing through or had a place up here to stay. That's what he really wanted to know. In situations like they were in now, it was best to know who, how many and where your neighbors were. He didn't like surprises.

****

Junior and Gayle talked for a while after doing their evening chore of breaking in the hides. This was also the night they had to grind flour for bread. Junior was telling her that they needed other people up here around them so they could set up some kind of a trading system after surviving this winter. That would be real nice. They both agreed that God made the best material for staying warm. She told him they could make coats, hats, gloves and boot liners to trade. He smiled and agreed. He also mentioned that people would want the pelts for blankets and other things. They had a lot that they could trade for other necessary things. They went to bed, feeling a little better than they had been. He still hadn't said anything to her, but he was getting worried about Clint. He should have been back days ago. He kept trying to imagine what could have delayed him but couldn't come up with anything.

The next day they went outside to check the snares. They cautiously peered around; it looked clear of dogs. Still there were no tracks in the snow. They were walking to the trail and he was just thinking about animal cycles when the pack appeared. They were like a well-trained army in the way they surrounded them. He thought, *Damn, I'm carrying the shotgun.* He wanted to kill that St. Bernard more than anything, but that damn alpha never came in close enough. He was one smart dog. He was like a ghost. He would appear and vanish without a sound. Junior and Gayle stood there waiting to see what was going to happen with all the snares set out. The pack ran into a few problems right away as they circled around them. They heard the first dog yelp in surprise at being caught in a snare and then it started to fight and quickly died. The professional camlock grade snare stopped it in its tracks. He motioned for Gayle to start back to camp and he followed. He was listening with every fiber of his body for the sounds he wanted to hear: more dogs getting caught in the snares. He heard another yelp, and then another and another. The snares were saving their lives.

They were halfway back to the house when the attack happened. Five dogs were racing towards them, kicking up a cloud of snow behind them. They shared an intense look as they waited for the dogs. He took out the first one at twenty-five yards. The copper-plated double aught buckshot ripped right through the skull and chest, plowing it into the ground. The clack-clack as the pump worked sounded really loud. The next dog was shot at fifteen yards. A dense pattern hit it full in the chest. It died before it hit the ground. He could hear Gayle shooting, too; blam, blam, blam from the SKS. He worked the pump action again instinctively, without thought. The next dog was too close, about seven yards away, and when he shot it, the spread was about five inches, tearing straight through the skull. The other dogs swung out wide. He could still hear Gayle shooting. He worked the pump and stepped to her right to look, and there was four more dogs coming at them. He picked the closest one out, about eight feet, and took half of its skull off. Before he could work the pump again, the next dog lunged at him. He instinctively cracked it with an upper cut with the stock of the shotgun. It fell off to the side. He quickly worked the pump action and shot another dog at almost point blank range.

Gayle yelled out, dropping to the ground, "I'm out. Cover me." They had worked out how to do this ahead of time so they would be prepared and be able to respond better. No more fumbling around. They were realizing how important it was to work out how to do things beforehand than trying to do them on the fly. He worked the pump action and swung around over her head, firing his last shot at the closest dog, dropping it to the ground.

"I'm empty. It's your turn to cover me, now." He heard the stripper clip fly off as she cocked back the lever and let the bolt slam a fresh round into the chamber.

"I got it," she yelled, coming up swinging a full three hundred sixty degrees around them both. There were no more dogs charging at them.

Junior had dropped down fast, grabbing shells out of the fifteen on the sling load. He put the first shell in and racked it, then quickly fed in four more into the tube. He stood up. They were ready now to retreat to the house. Nine dogs lay dead or wounded on the battlefield. They looked around for more, but didn't see anything moving. They made their way back to the house. They reached the door, and Junior turned around and looked all around them, studying the landscape for any movement. Out of the corner of his eye, he spotted that big bastard St. Bernard taking off. He thought, *I will kill you. Just you wait and see. I will make it my life's mission.* By the time he turned his head around to look, it was long gone. All he could see was the snow settling back to the ground. He slammed the door shut and locked everything back up. They both sighed in relief. Then they grinned at each other.

Junior laughed. "All that practicing paid off. It worked just great."

She joined in. "It worked just like you said it would. I feel much better and more in control now that we have the reloading part worked out."

"We'll go out tomorrow and see how many got caught in the snares."

"I heard a lot of them out there fighting the snares. I think it will be at least six or so. I just hope they aren't smart enough to start avoiding them now that they know what they are."

"I doubt it, they blend right into the brush on the trail and they can't see them. So, they won't be able to avoid them. We'll just have to remember to move them around and not set them at the same place twice. We'll confuse them; they won't be able to figure out where the snares are and it'll make them think twice about coming around here."

She smiled at him with bright, happy eyes. "We are an awesome team. I swear that is the only time in my life I felt really and truly alive in every cell of my body. It was a fight to the death. It was either kill or be killed. Did you see those vicious, starving hellhounds trying to rip us apart and kill us? We stood our ground and won the battle. Oh, what a great day today was."

He laughed at her enthusiasm."Tomorrow will be even better. We'll see how many dogs the snares caught." They hugged and kissed.

They were high on adrenaline from winning the battle and made passionate love. Afterwards, they lay talking about things. They were so happy to have finally won a battle with those hellhounds. It made them believe they could find ways to survive. The future wasn't quite so dark and hopeless. They both had started to doubt. It put the spring back into their step and made them smile again. They had survived and it was only going to get better each day as more dogs died. Junior thanked God his dad had the foresight to have so many camlock snares for the end of the world. It had made a huge difference in living and dying.

****

Outside as the dogs got caught in the snares they would yelp, causing the other dogs to come see what happened. As they did this, the next snare on the trail would catch a dog and kill it, too. It was working better than either of them could have imagined. The snares were really and truly evening up the odds.

****

Clint watched the group approach a cabin. The leader of their group went up the steps and pulled a key out of his pocket and unlocked the door. They all went inside. Well, at least these people weren't breaking in or stealing anything from someone else. They belonged here. Knowing that made a big difference in determining their intentions. He made himself comfortable and watched for a while. He had already walked all around it to see how many doors and windows they had. He saw two of the men come outside and go around to the back and return with their arms full of firewood. After awhile, he saw smoke coming out of the chimney. He could see them inside, preparing a meal. They had lit a few lanterns. The sky was darkening again. It looked like it would start snowing any minute. The people in this group had treated each other very well from what he had observed. They seemed like decent people, but time would tell. He would come back every now and again and keep an eye on them. He'd followed them for about eighteen miles. He was going to watch them for another hour or so, and then head back to the trail where he had buried his stuff. Then he'd go straight to Junior and Gayle's. He hoped those two had listened to him about one of them providing cover when they went outside. He would be greatly disappointed if he came back and found them dead and eaten by those dogs.

****

The next day Junior and Gayle waited for full light to go outside. They stood outside the door, studying the area. When Junior thought it was clear, they both cautiously started out to check the snares, keeping alert to any movement around them. It was hard for her to contain her glee at how many dogs they had killed with the snares. They had set out thirty-six snares and killed twenty-seven dogs. He was really disappointed that they hadn't caught the alpha male. That damn St. Bernard was just too smart. It had avoided getting caught. He was so thankful to have finally evened the odds in their favor. If they wouldn't have had any snares to set out, they would have sooner or later made a fatal mistake and been killed by those hellhounds. He explained to her that they had to burn all the dogs' bodies. Who knew what kinds of diseases they had. He dragged all the dead dogs to one area. He grabbed a few tires to layer in with the dead bodies to make them burn hotter. He added a layer of wood and branches between the dogs to make the fire burn longer. Gayle said she would help him. She had no sympathy for any of them; they had killed her mother.

She was on top of the world. Her heart was uplifted and she had a new confidence. They were winning against the hellhounds. They didn't know how many were left in the pack, but it couldn't be very many. They had moved the snare sets that hadn't caught anything and set out two dozen more. It was hard work for Junior, dragging the dead bodies around to the pile. She kept alert for more dogs. Junior had worked up a sweat. The more time that went by and no dogs showed up, the more confident they felt. They started to drop their guard and not be so vigilant. They were heading back to the pile.

He was dragging two dead dogs, one with each hand and she said, "I feel so good. It's great to be alive. People that have never had to fight for their lives and experience all the terror and struggles that we have can not possibly know or understand what we are feeling right now with our hard won victory." He grunted and smiled at her. Damn those dogs were heavy. Every once in awhile a dog would get caught on something and he would have to free it before they could move on.

The St. Bernard was silently waiting for them on the trail. The St. Bernard could hear them coming closer. The Alpha was between them and the pile of his dead dogs. The St. Bernard stood there all alone, its whole focus on the human man. As its pack had died, it had gone around to each of them to see what had killed them. The same smell was on all of the things that killed them. The St. Bernard had smelled this scent before. It had been this human's scent on the snares that killed its pack. The St. Bernard was mad, ferocious and deadly. This brought the struggle down to the bare bones of survival in the animal kingdom. Who was the true Alpha here? The St. Bernard heard them getting closer and took off flying towards them. The St. Bernard jumped up and lunged at the human.

Junior heard the St. Bernard coming down the trail. He instinctively knew it was the Alpha male. He quickly dropped the two dead dogs he was dragging and tried to yank the shotgun off his shoulder. Before he could do it, he was knocked to the ground and the shotgun went flying off, no doubt now full of snow. The battle had begun; it would only end when one of them were dead. It was a very practiced move by this Alpha dog. Knock a person to the ground and then rip out their throat, breaking their neck in the process. This dog was two hundred pounds of pure muscle. Junior had been caught completely off guard. He raised his left arm up to protect his neck as he fell. It was becoming a familiar gesture on his part. The dog tried to bite his arm and he reached up and grabbed the dog's windpipe in an iron grip with his right hand. The dog instinctively knew he was in trouble and tried to retreat, but Junior hung on tightly for his life. The adrenaline was making him incredibly strong at this moment. Junior's sole focus was on this dog, in total crystal clear clarity. The dog started to shake wildly from side to side, freaking out because it couldn't get a breath. Junior finally lost his grip when the dog lurched to the side with his huge head shaking wildly about. The dog actually pulled him up into a sitting position before he lost his grip. The dog was heaving. Just at that moment, he saw the SKS rifle almost at point blank range next to the dog's head. He heard the shot and saw the bullet rip right through the skull in front of the ear, exiting with a large blast out the other side. That shot dropped the hellhound in its tracks. The dog fell over and didn't even twitch.

He looked up at Gayle standing there smiling. She said, "It is over now and we won. That huge bastard is dead and won't be forming any more packs ever again."

"Thank you. If you hadn't been here, I would be dead. I could never have fought that huge beast off by myself."

"You're welcome. Thank God we had the snares or this whole thing would have turned out very different." He got up from the ground and stood on shaky legs for a while. "There is no way to drag these two dogs past him. He's blocking the whole trail. I guess I'll have to drag him over to the pile first. We'll have to come back for the other two."

"Okay. Well, let's get moving. Do you want me to help you drag the dogs?"

"No. I got it. Just keep looking around for any other danger." She nodded, greatly relieved, because her arm was hurting badly. They started off together down the trail. When they had all the dogs gathered together into the pile, he poured some gasoline on them to get the fire going. She lit the match. They stayed there and watched them burn. The wood and branches caught fire. Soon, it was too hot to stand close. Junior took his coat off because he was sweating. He used a shovel to push things back into the pile. They waited until there was hardly anything left before going home.

When they got inside she said, "Come on, lets get washed up and then we'll cook something to eat." She wasn't feeling very well at all.

"That sounds good. I'm starving." He had locked the door tight. He walked over and picked her up and swung her around in circles, laughing. "We did it. We really did it!" She laughed a little but he was making her feel really sick. She was afraid she would throw up any second when he finally put her back down. She clung onto him for a few minutes, waiting for her stomach to settle back down. That was strange. She loved the roller coaster and twirl-a-whirl rides and they had never made her sick before.

"I need to go change the bandage on my arm," she said. "Can you start cooking? I'll only be a few minutes, then I'll help."

He kissed her. "How is your arm?"

"It's sore. I think I have been using it too much lately; it isn't healed yet."

He looked concerned. "I'll cook and you rest your arm, okay? You just relax. I'll take care of everything else."

She smiled at him. "Thanks. I appreciate it. I'm feeling a little sick today." Then she brightened up. "But I'm totally happy. We got that big damn Alpha male. I told you we could outsmart a dumb dog." He laughed and went into the kitchen.

She went into the bathroom and closed the door. Her arm was really throbbing and hurting. She unwound the gauze bandage and had to keep pulling on it hard; the punctures had started to seep pus and gunk, it had dried, making it difficult to remove. She washed it with soap and water. She could feel some hard, puffy lumps under the skin by some of the punctures. They were red and swollen and hurt like hell. She put some ointment on them and wrapped her arm up again. She washed her hands really good. She took two Ibuprofen because her head was pounding so hard. She was feeling sick to her stomach again and was a little dizzy. She straightened everything up and left the bathroom.

She joined Junior in the kitchen and sat down at the table. He said, "What's wrong?" She didn't look good.

"I have a headache. I took something for it. My stomach is a little upset, too. I think I've just been doing too much lately or something."

He kissed her. "After you eat, maybe you should lie down and take a nap."

"I don't think I can eat anything right now. I think I'll just drink a glass of Tang and go lie down." He poured her a glass. "Thanks." She sipped it; she felt a little better. When she was done, she got up and put her glass by the sink. He tucked her in for a nap. He kissed her and shut the door so she could rest. He hoped she wasn't coming down with anything. It wasn't like they could go to the doctor. But this was the flu and cold season, so she might have a virus of some sort. Rest and drinking liquids would be the best thing for her. That was what the doctor had told him when he had the flu. He finished cooking and sat down to eat. He was starving. It had been hard work dragging all those dogs. He yawned. He decided to take a nap, too. He straightened the kitchen up and went into the living room. He would just lay down in his recliner and take his nap there so he wouldn't disturb Gayle's rest. He settled down and soon fell asleep.

It was several hours later before he woke up. He looked at the time and couldn't believe he'd slept so long. It was way past dinnertime. He went into the bedroom to check on Gayle. She was still asleep. He felt her forehead and she felt warm. He went and got two Ibuprofen tablets and another glass of Tang and brought it back to the bedroom. He woke her up and had her take the tablets and drink the whole glass of Tang. He let her go back to sleep. She needed the rest. He went back into the living room and decided he'd better get dinner going. He was hungry again. He smiled, thinking of what his dad would have had to say about that. He was letting the spaghetti sauce simmer for a while, so went into the living room and started reading his book on bridges. He heard a noise at the door. His heart leaped into his throat, thinking that someone had found them and was trying to get in. He grabbed the shotgun and went up to the loft and looked out the shooting hole.

Clint looked up at him. "I'm glad you're being cautious about who's out here." Junior smiled, relieved that he was back. He ran down to the door, unlocked it, and let Clint inside.

"I'm so glad you're back," Junior said. "I was getting worried about you. What held you up?"

Clint was taking off his large pack; it was covered with several smaller packs and bags. "I was delayed because I ran into some human tracks. I followed them to see who else is out there." Junior looked alarmed. "It was a group of seven people. They went to a cabin quite a ways from here. We'll keep our eye on them to see what they are up to from time to time. But I think they just came out here to survive away from the city." He took his coat, hat and gloves off and hung them up on the hooks by the door.

"Sit down and I'll get you a cup of coffee."

"Thanks. I could sure go for a cup of coffee right now. I ran out a few days ago."

Junior went into the kitchen and came back with the coffee pot and two cups. Clint had taken his pack into his room. He returned and sat down with a sigh. "It is sure good to sit in a comfortable chair again." Junior handed him a cup of coffee. "Thanks. I didn't run into any dogs on my way here. That was unusual. They've pretty much stayed between my camp and your house. They must have moved on. But they'll be back. So, what have you and Gayle been up to?"

Junior smiled real big. "We took care of the dog problem while you were gone."

Clint raised an eyebrow at him. "How?"

"We used professional grade snares made from aircraft cable and caught and killed them, that's how."

"I'm impressed."

Junior was feeling good, because praise from someone like Clint meant a lot. He said, "We burned all their bodies. Who knew what kind of diseases they had."

"Good thinking."

"Gayle helped me, too. She had no compassion for those hellhounds that killed her mother."

Clint said, "Hellhounds. I like that name. They did kind of act like that. Where is Gayle?"

"She wasn't feeling very good," said Junior. "I think she has the flu. She's resting right now. Are you hungry?"

"Yes, I am. I ran out of food this afternoon."

Junior grinned. "I'm making spaghetti. I better go check on it right now. It should be done in about ten minutes."

He went into the kitchen and Clint followed him. Junior set about cutting some bread slices for garlic bread.

Clint set the table. He asked, "Should I set a place for Gayle?"

Junior shook his head. "I don't think she'll be up to eating spaghetti. I'll heat her up some soup later if she wakes up. I just gave her some Ibuprofen tablets and a glass of Tang about an hour ago." They sat down and ate. Clint wanted a play by play of how they had handled the dog problem. As Junior was telling him, Gayle came into the kitchen. She had woken up and felt a little better. She heard them talking, so she decided to join them in the kitchen.

Junior asked if she'd like some soup, and she shook her head. "My stomach still isn't up to any food yet." He poured her a glass of Tang. They both told Clint what they'd done while he was gone. He was impressed how they'd learned to reload like that on their own. Hell, the whole way they had handled everything was impressive. They had been lucky, too. If that St. Bernard had gotten a hold of his neck, it would have been all over. That dog would have snapped his neck like a stick.

Clint noticed how glassy-eyed Gayle was. He knew it was from fever. He noticed that she didn't use her injured arm. It should have been almost healed by now. That was not a good sign.

Junior asked him if he wanted another helping of spaghetti.

"Sure. You're a good cook." When they finished eating, they went into the living room.

Junior said, "I'm going to go out and check the burn pile."

"I'll go with you and take a look around," said Clint. Gayle followed them into the living room and walked them to the door. Junior had just reached for his coat when she fainted. Clint caught her before she hit the ground. She was burning up. He picked her up and laid her down on the couch. Junior looked scared to death. "Turn that light this way so I can get a look at her arm."

Junior stood there, trying to think why he'd want to look at her arm at a time like this. "Why?"

Clint had his hand on her bandaged arm. "She doesn't have the flu. Her arm is infected. I can feel the heat through the bandage." Junior got real scared. How could they treat an infection? He started to shake with fear for Gayle. He couldn't lose her, too. He just couldn't.

Clint said in a firmer voice, "Junior, I need the light turned this way. Do it now." Junior snapped into action and turned the light shade upward to shine the light on her arm. Clint pulled out his knife and cut the bandage open along her arm. It smelled bad. The bandage wouldn't come off. It was stuck to the wounds. He could see some red lines going up her arm, heading towards her heart. "Get something large her arm will fit into and fill it with warm water. We're going to have to soak this bandage off. I'll be right back." Clint got up and went into his room. He came back out carrying a military surgical field manual. He looked some things up and read about how to treat the wound. Junior came in carrying a large roasting pan with warm water in it. Clint pushed the coffee table on an angle with the couch so Junior could set the pan down. Clint placed her arm in the water to soak. He returned to his reading.

Gayle woke up and started thrashing around. Clint dropped the book and held her down so she wouldn't fall off the couch. He told Junior to bring three tablets of Ibuprofen and a small glass filled with only a couple inches of Tang and to grab a couple of towels. Junior ran to the kitchen. Gayle settled down some and tried to ask what was wrong. Clint told her that her arm was badly infected. She nodded. This wasn't news to her She'd already known that, she just didn't know what to do about it. Junior came back into the living room.

"Get behind her and help hold her shoulders and head up so she can take these," said Clint. Junior climbed over the table and got behind her on the couch, pulling her against him. He could feel how hot she was. He was scared. Clint got her to swallow the tablets and drink the Tang. Clint wrapped a towel around her arm.

Clint laid her arm on the coffee table, unwrapped it, and took the bandage off. It was red, swollen and badly abscessed. There was foul smelling pus coming out of some of the puncture wounds. Gayle was sweating and shivering with chills. She started drifting in and out of consciousness.

Clint and Junior shared a look. "Lay her back down and come over here." When Junior got over beside him Clint said, "How much whiskey is left?"

"Not much."

"I was afraid you were going to say that. Let me think a minute." He paused. "Do you have a pressure cooker?"

Junior said, "Yes, my dad has two of them for canning meat." Clint picked the book back up to read something. "All right, take this pan, rinse it out, and refill it with warm water. Put one capful of bleach in it, stir it up, and then bring it back here."

Junior grabbed the pan and hurried into the kitchen. Clint continued to read. Junior came back. Clint placed her arm in the pan to soak. He stood up. "Get the pressure cooker ready and find a small towel. Where are your medical supplies?"

"They're in the big cupboard in the bathroom. Is she going to be all right?" Clint hesitated a few moments. "I don't know. We'll do what we can. Right now we have to drain those wounds and clean them out." Junior's eyes filled with tears. He turned away.

"Go get the pressure cooker and I'll get some supplies," said Clint. Junior wiped his eyes with his hand and went into the kitchen. Clint looked at Gayle; she was resting more comfortably than before. He felt her head, the fever was dropping a bit. He went into the bathroom and looked in the cupboard. He grabbed several things and took them into the kitchen. Junior was just standing there looking at the pressure cooker. There was a small towel laid on the counter next to it. "Do you have a stainless steel knife without a plastic or wooden handle?"

Junior thought. "I don't think so."

"Did your dad have a scalpel?"

"I don't know."

Clint sighed. "Okay we'll have to use one of my knives." He went to his room and came back after a few minutes with a knife, it was all stainless steel with holes for fingers. He washed the knife well with soap and water. He wrapped it up in the small towel and placed it in the pressure cooker. He added some water, closed it up tight, placed it on the stove, and turned the burner on. When it started to make noise, he turned it down until there were just thirteen pounds of pressure, and then turned the timer on for thirty minutes. "When the timer goes off, the knife will be sterilized." Junior nodded.

They cleaned off the table and washed it down with bleach water. Clint said, "Do you have a couple of clean blankets?"

"Yes, in the hall closet."

"Go get them." Clint checked on Gayle while Junior fetched the blankets. She looked the same. "We'll need a couple of clean towels, too." Junior brought some to the kitchen. The timer went off. Clint turned the burner off and waited until it was safe to open it. "Go take off Gayle's shirt. Be careful of her arm. Cover her front with one of the towels." Junior nodded, grabbed a towel and went into the living room. Clint was waiting for his knife to cool down.

Junior came back and Clint said, "I'm going to make a soft spot on the table where we can lay her down so I can clean out the abscesses." Junior nodded. Clint spread the two blankets out on half of the table. He then placed a large absorbent pad he found in the bathroom cupboard where her arm would rest. He asked Junior if he had a large paper bag. Junior went into the pantry and came back with a paper shopping bag. Clint opened it up and placed it under the table where he would be standing. He looked at Junior. "Let's carry her in." He explained how he wanted to place her on the table. Clint wrapped her arm in a towel and placed it on her stomach. Clint placed a flat sheet sheet under her and showed Junior how to carry her using the sheet. They placed her on the table.

Gayle woke up on her ride to the kitchen. She thrashed around, not understanding what was going on. Junior reassured her and explained what they were doing. She closed her eyes and settled down. When they had her in the position Clint wanted, they laid her down on the table. She woke up again.

"Junior, get the whiskey and a glass." Clint looked at her. "This is going to hurt. It will hurt really bad. I want you to drink as much whiskey as you can." She nodded a little. Junior raised her up and helped her to drink several mouthfuls. Clint nodded and Junior laid her back down. They waited a few minutes and then Clint said, "Do it again." Gayle turned her face away and fought taking a drink. Finally, Junior was able to get her to drink the glass. They waited a few more minutes and then Clint scrubbed his hands and arms with antimicrobial soap he had found in the bathroom. He made sure to clean his fingernails really well with the soap. He instructed Junior to do the same.

Clint had already placed all the gauze pads and other things he was going to be using on the table. He explained to Junior how he needed to hold her arm still. Gayle would yell and scream and try to get away from the pain. Junior took a deep breath, nodded, and placed his body cross-wise over her. He grabbed her arm with both of his hands to hold her steady. Clint had Junior wear his coat for protection in case she tried to bite him in reaction to the pain. They didn't need any more wounds to care for. Clint warned Junior that she would probably cry and beg them to stop. It was a long, hard process. He had to cut open each infected spot and scrape all the gunk and dead skin out. She cried and screamed and tried to stop them, just as Clint had warned. Junior was crying almost as hard as Gayle by the time they finished. It hadn't been easy for Clint, either. It was hard knowing he was hurting her so much, but it had to be done. Sweat kept dripping down into his eyes while he cleaned out the wounds. He stopped a few times so she could catch her breath, and Junior helped her to blow her nose. He explained how they'd have to keep the wounds open and let them heal from the inside out and not let them close up. All of them sighed with relief when it was over.

Clint hadn't said anything, but he was more worried about the red lines going up her arm than about the actual wounds. He let everyone have a few minutes to collect themselves before he rinsed all the wounds out, packed them with antibacterial ointment, and wrapped them up with gauze. He had her take some more fever reducer and drink the last of the whiskey. She finally passed out cold. Clint washed the rest of her arm in bleach water and checked under her armpit for swollen lymph glands. Yup, the glands under her armpit were swollen. This infection was bad.

They got her settled into bed and then walked back into the living room. Junior blew his nose. "I hope to hell I never have to do that again. I don't think I'd live through it."

"You did real well, Junior," Clint said. "I hated hurting her, but it had to be done."

Junior nodded and sighed. "I wish we had more whiskey because I sure as hell could use a few drinks." Clint nodded.

Junior went into the kitchen and put some coffee on. Clint cleaned everything up. He took the paper bag full of dirty gauze pads and threw it in the fire. He washed his hands again. They each grabbed a cup of coffee and went into the living room. Neither man wanted to be in the kitchen right now with their memories so fresh.

Clint said, "She's really sick. The infection is spreading up her arm, heading for her heart. We have to get her antibiotics or she'll die." Junior looked like someone had just punched him in the stomach. "I'll go out tomorrow and search the houses for antibiotics. I'll be back as soon as I can. It may take awhile to find enough, she needs to take them for two weeks." Junior didn't know what to say. He felt like the world was falling in on him again. "Don't give up hope," Clint said. "I won't come back until I have enough antibiotics for her to get well. I promise you that." Junior clung to that as if he was a drowning man holding on to a life preserver. All he could think of was that he couldn't lose her, too. He just couldn't.

Clint looked at him. "Pull yourself together, Junior. She needs you to be strong now and be there to take care of her. You can't fall apart, this isn't over yet. You remember what I said about keeping the wounds open and draining?" Junior nodded. "Well, remember that every four hours she has to have some fever reducer, too. If that doesn't work, you have to put her in the bathtub and fill it with cold water. You might have to bring some snow in and put it in the bathtub to cool her down. I'm going to go take a shower and get some sleep. I'll be out of here before the sun rises to get her antibiotics."

Junior took a deep breath and stood up, too. He faced Clint. "Thank you, Clint. I wouldn't have known what to do for her."

Clint looked at him. "You're welcome."

Junior had tears running down his face. "I really mean it. She would have died for sure, because I wouldn't have known what to do, like you did. I wouldn't want to live without her. I couldn't live here by myself again without her." Clint reached out and patted Junior's shoulder.

He had to be back within forty-eight hours or it might be too late to save her. He didn't know how fast that infection was traveling up her arm, but it wouldn't take long to get to her heart. He didn't say anything to Junior. He didn't want to bring him down ant more than he already was. They ate and talked of other things. He had one more cup of coffee and then he went to bed after checking on Gayle. She was the same, and her arm wasn't bleeding everywhere. So, that part was okay. As he drifted off to sleep, he wondered how many houses he was going to have to check to find enough antibiotics.

He was up again at 4:00 am. He gathered up a small pack and his rifle, then he left. Junior didn't wake up this time, so he made sure the outside door was locked. He had eaten another plate of cold spaghetti for breakfast. It didn't taste as good as when it was hot, but it wasn't bad, either. He filled the thermos with hot coffee. It was great having coffee again. He started towards town because there were more houses that way. He was going to check all the unoccupied houses he could find. People rarely took all of the antibiotics that a doctor prescribed for them. It was stupid, but people did it all the time and wondered why their infections always came back. Every time he saw a mailbox, he went down the side road until he found the house. So far he hadn't found any occupied houses. He had found ten amoxicillin. His book had said Gayle needed seven hundred and fifty milligrams a day. So he had three and a half days worth. He kept walking. He came over a rise and found a spot that had five mailboxes together. He was more careful because they might have banded together to survive. They wouldn't be friendly to a lone man.

He stopped and looked at the first house; it looked abandoned. No footprints around it. He watched it for a half an hour, and there was no movement in any of the windows. He silently tested the back door; it was unlocked. He opened it, stepped inside, and shut the door. He stood still and listened. After ten minutes, there still weren't any sounds. He stepped out into the living room. There was dust everywhere. He looked in the bathroom and found a bottle of amoxicillin. He went into the kitchen and found another bottle with amoxicillin tablets. He went into the bedrooms and looked at the nightstands. He had found one bottle there at one of the other houses. He looked in the drawers and found another bottle that had some amoxicillin in it. He quickly went back outside. He stood in the brush and counted the pills. Six were in one bottle, five were in another bottle and three were in the last one. That made fourteen. That was seven days worth. Well, he was halfway there. He went to the next house and watched it for a while. There were no tracks here, either. He waited and watched. The back door was locked. He jimmied the handle and the door popped open. It was a very old lock. He stepped inside and closed the door. Dust was everywhere. He looked around the whole house, but couldn't find any antibiotics. He left out the back door. He kept going down the road checking all the houses. He found one more that had four amoxicillin tablets. He went back to the road. At least the houses were closer to each other. That was a bonus. But the danger became greater, too. The more houses, the more chances of running into people.

****

Junior woke up because he could feel the heat coming off Gayle. She was burning up with fever. He went and filled the bathtub up with cold water, got three Ibuprofen tablets and a glass of Tang, then came back into the bedroom. He woke her up and got her to take the tablets and drink some of the Tang. He went back and turned the bathtub off. He stripped her of clothes and carried her into the bathroom.

She tried to fight him when he was putting her into the water. They both ended up soaking wet. She glared at him from the tub. Her teeth were chattering. She kept saying, "I'm freezing."

"I know, but you're burning up with fever. We have to get your fever down."

"Let me out of here." He felt so bad for making her do this. After twenty-five minutes, she felt cooler and he helped her out of the tub. He got her back in to bed. He told her how sorry he was for hurting her. She didn't say anything. The Ibuprofen was working; her eyes were a little clearer and she said it didn't hurt nearly as bad as what they had done to her last night. "Where's Clint?" He told her. "When I see him, I'm going to give him a black eye."

Junior was shocked. "Why would you do that?"

"Pay back is a bitch." Junior was speechless. She looked him in the eye. "Don't get too close or I'll sock you in the eye, too." She scooted down and closed her eyes for a nap. She wasn't happy with either one of them.

Junior walked out of the bedroom and shut the door so she could sleep. He was upset that she was mad at him. They'd only done what had to be done for her health. It wasn't like either one of them had liked hurting her. Maybe the fever was making her weird. He locked and secured the door outside. He didn't know what time Clint had left, but when he woke up it was only 6:00 am. It was now 8:30 am. He sure hoped Clint would find enough antibiotics to heal her. He didn't think that she realized how sick she was. He noticed the red lines had moved higher on her arm. He started cleaning the kitchen and got some food cooking. He was going to try to keep busy and not think about those lines going up her arm.

****

Clint found a lone house with three more antibiotic tablets. He kept going. He found a little road that dead-ended not too far with several houses. He watched the area for a while and didn't see any movement. It was kind of eerie, because there were a couple of swing sets out back and they were moving with the wind. It looked like a kid had just jumped off and would be back in just a moment, at least until you looked closer at it. The seats had snow on them. He watched the first house for a while. He slowly walked around, watching the whole area. He waited an hour, watching everything from up on a rise. There were no footprints and no movement. He slowly made his way and checked the houses. He found a lot of antibiotics. There must have been a lot of children on this little street. He had enough now. He threw all the bottles into his pack and left. It was almost dark. As he headed back to Junior and Gayle's place, he found a spot to stop and eat a few sandwiches Junior had made him. He had a cup of coffee. He hoped she hadn't taken a turn for the worse. He hurried his steps as fast as he could in the deep snow. He walked in the tracks he had already made whenever possible. He didn't want anyone following his tracks back there.

****

Junior had to put Gayle in the tub twice more. She still wasn't speaking to him. He knew that she thought he was being mean to her, and it hurt him that she could think that about him. It was about 9:00 pm now and he had just got her settled down in bed again. He had found her thrashing all around the bed in some kind of delirium, having nightmares of the dogs coming after her. He didn't know what more he could do. He made sure she took the Ibuprofen on time, but twice today she had thrown it back up again. Her temperature had spiked before he could get more into her, so he had to put her into the bathtub with cold water. The lines were really climbing up her arm now. He felt so helpless. He wanted to just rip that infection right out of her somehow. He paced and kept an eye on her. He went in and put a temp strip on her forehead. It said she had a 102.2 temperature. He knew high temperatures were dangerous. He was pacing when he heard something at the front door. He raced up to the loft and looked out; it was Clint. He yelled, "I'll be right down to open the door." He kept thinking, *Thank God he's back*. He opened up the door in record time and locked everything back up.

Clint had taken off his outer clothes and grabbed his pack. He took several bottles out, counted them, and then put most of them into one container. He put the rest back in a bottle and set it aside. He had three pills still in his hand. He handed one to Junior and said, "Make sure she takes this right now."

Junior grabbed it, ran into the kitchen for a glass of Tang, and took it into the bedroom. He woke her up and got her to swallow it and drink some of the Tang. He made sure she was able to settle back down again. He touched her; she was warm, but not hot like last time.

He walked into the living room. "Thank you. I know that probably wasn't easy. But I thank you for getting her medicine."

"I want her to get well, too."

Junior laughed. "She told me that as soon as she sees you, she's giving you a black eye."

Clint laughed. "I'll stand still and let her hit me if it will make her feel better."

Junior smiled. "She told me not to get too close, either or she was going to sock me in the eye, too." They both laughed. "Sit down and I'll bring you a cup of coffee. I just made a pot before you got back." He went into the kitchen and Clint sat down with a sigh and rested. Junior came back with a cup for both of them. He sat down. "How long until the medicine starts to work?"

Clint said, "I don't know. But we should know in the next couple of days if it's working or not."

Junior looked alarmed. "What do you mean?"

Clint said, "This should work. But sometimes the infection is too bad and things don't always work like they should. We'll have to wait and see. Have you been changing the bandage and making sure the wounds stay open?"

"Yes, I've changed it four times today. Twice because she splashed it with water when I had to put her in the bathtub because her fever was so high." Clint nodded at Junior. Junior thought he looked tired. The poor man had been on the go for a long time. "Are you hungry? I made a big pot of stew for dinner."

"Yes, I'm starved." Junior grinned and got up to reheat some stew. It was the least he could do.

The next two days were pretty rough on all of them. Gayle was sick to her stomach and she sometimes threw the pills back up. So they'd have to give her another one. They had to put her in the tub several times for her fever. The lines stopped climbing up her arm and were slowly disappearing a little at a time. On the third day, her head was a little clearer and she was able to keep some crackers and broth down. Her sleep seemed more natural. Her temperature hovered around 101 degrees. On the fourth day, she woke up feeling a lot better. Junior made her some broth to sip and she ate a few crackers. She was still pretty weak, but a lot better than she had been. She wanted to get up and go lie down on the couch, maybe watch a movie. Her fever had broken in the middle of the night. She told both of them that as soon as she was feeling better, she was socking them in the eye.

Clint said, "All right." Junior was outraged that she wanted to hit him. She laughed at both of them and said she was only kidding, but told them if they ever did anything like that to her again they'd better never go to sleep again, because she would kill them. The men exchanged a look. Clint laughed. "I would expect nothing less than that from you."

She looked quite satisfied. Then Gayle and Junior argued over which movie to watch. Clint stayed out of it. Finally Gayle said, "Clint, which movie do you want to see?"

Clint promptly said, "Tombstone." Both of them looked at him like he had two heads. That hadn't been one of the choices at all.

Gayle finally said, "Well, okay. I like that movie, too." So, Junior put it in the DVD player.

That night they sat around the table talking after dinner. They started talking about the dogs again. She said, "I wonder how many people went through the same thing?

"You mean how many times had the same attack plan worked for them?"

"Yes."

"There is no way to know for sure," said Junior. "But I would estimate that it took them awhile to establish the attack plan that worked so well."

Gayle nodded. "But my real question is where did all those dogs come from?"

"They came from people." He gestured with his hands all around. "When people could no longer feed them, they just let them go free out in the woods. They think that the dogs will have a better chance at survival out there hunting their food rather than staying there and starving to death. Instead of killing them and putting them out of their misery, they just let them go. Most of them just starve to death anyway, or get killed by coyotes. They've been domesticated and don't know how to live out in the wild and hunt for food. The ones that don't starve to death form packs with other dogs. They all revert back to their true nature. They are unafraid of humans. In fact, they think humans will give them food. When this doesn't happen, they go a little crazy from starvation and have no other choice but to attack. That's what happened to the ones that attacked us. Because the people who owned those dogs didn't take responsibility for them and put them down. My question is, how many more packs are out there?"

She looked shocked. "There are more packs of them out there we'll have to face? How many?"

Junior said, "I don't know for sure, but there were like ninety million dogs in America. Who knows for sure? I bet this isn't the last pack we have to face. We'll leave the snares set out to catch as many as we can when they do hit us."

Clint said, "That's a good idea. There is no way to know when a pack will come through and attack."

She looked sad. "I wonder how many people are out there right now, facing these packs without guns or snares to protect them?"

"There's no way of knowing for sure, but I can tell you one thing, when this is over, there won't be one idiot animal lover or anti-gun nut left alive in this country," said Junior. They all nodded in agreement.

The weather turned colder and stormy. Junior was pacing around inside, worrying about all the dog packs. He just knew that the cold was going to kill a lot of people that weren't prepared for the winter and it would give plenty of food to the dog packs. This was going to be bad, real bad. Spring was going to be a very dangerous time. He rubbed his face and paced some more.

Clint finally said, "Maybe if you talk to us about what's bothering you, it will give you more clarity in which to work out your problem." He told them all his thoughts on the danger of the dog packs and how dangerous springtime was going to be. Clint agreed with him.

Gayle went up to him and hugged him. "That's something we'll have to figure out when spring gets here. Right now, let's just be happy to have survived that huge pack and celebrate life." She looked around at the two men. "Let's for once, just this one time, be thankful for what we have, and not what we don't have or what we can't control. Or what our fears are for the future. Let's enjoy right now. We're all together. We have many things for which to be thankful. Let's have a party."

Both men laughed. "What?"

It was comical how they both had the same look on their faces. She started to laugh, too. She said, "Tomorrow is party day. We're going to dance and sing and eat and be merry together, just like a family should be. I'm going to make each of us a list of things to do to get ready." She left the room. Both men looked at each other in bewilderment. Junior shrugged his shoulders and Clint started to laugh. Nope, nothing these kids did would surprise him now. Well, he guessed they were having a party tomorrow.

They spent the morning fixing the food for the day. Gayle handed the men their lists when they were done. At the top of each list was written:

1.) No talking about anything other than the party, books, movies, food, our little family and silly things.
2.) A prize will go to the one who can tell the most jokes and make the other two laugh like a hyena.
3.) You are required to dance several times with the one and only girl here. (Ha Ha)
4.) Pick one movie to watch.
5.) Pick out a few songs to play today.
6.) Have fun. Be happy.
7.) You have one hour to compete your mission, gentlemen. Don't waste one second of it.

The men read their lists and started laughing. She said, "I'm going to go shower and get ready for the party. I suggest you do the same." She turned around and headed for the bathroom. The men had showered that morning, so they just changed clothes into something a little nicer. They went through the movies and picked one each, and then they went through all the CDs to pick out songs. They were having a good time. When Gayle came out of the bathroom she had a dress on, high heels, her hair was fixed just so and she had makeup on.

Junior gave her a wolf whistle; she blushed and bowed. "May I have this dance?"

She smiled. "Yes, you may." Clint put a dreamy blues number on and they danced and smiled at each other. She danced with Clint next. They stuffed themselves with food and cake, watched movies and laughed. Clint went into his bedroom and took a bottle of very good wine out of his pack. He had grabbed several bottles of alcohol when he was out looking for antibiotics. He came back into the living room and poured them all a glass.

Gayle said, "To us. The three Musketeers." She touched glasses with them. They all smiled at each other and then they took a drink from their glasses to seal the deal. They were now closer than any family could be.

Chapter 20

Mutant Roman Zombies

*"All the world's a stage, And all the men and women merely players; They have their exits and their entrances, And one man in his time plays many parts, His acts being seven ages." **As You Like It,** Act 2, Scene 7, 139-143 (Seven Ages: As a man goes through all the stages of his life. From infancy through old man. About seventy years.)*

William Shakespeare

Lisa woke up and looked at the clock. It read 6:45 am. She sighed and wished she could snuggle under the down-filled comforter and go back to sleep. She yawned and sat up, being careful not to disturb Maria. This was her morning to get up by 7:00 am to look after the children. They all took turns getting up early in the morning with them. They weren't taking any more chances of a repeat of Amanda's pancake experiment. These children woke up with the chickens, no matter what time they went to bed. She reached over and turned off the alarm so it wouldn't wake Maria. She shivered in the chill air. Whichever adult got up first went straight down to the basement and put more wood in the furnace. It heated the house up nicely. They turned off the heat vents that went to the unused rooms, so the rest of them heated up quickly. She pulled her clothes on, put on thick socks and slipped on her tennis shoes. She left the room and quickly went downstairs to the kitchen. As she passed by the coffee pot, she flipped it on. One rule in this house was to make sure the coffee pot was clean, filled with water, and fresh coffee grounds added so it was ready for morning. She also turned a burner on low under the teapot to heat water. Abby like to drink teas and was an early riser. Abby had stopped drinking coffee all together. Once in the basement, she opened the furnace and pulled down on the large handle that made the ashes fall into the bottom ash pan, then added three pieces of wood. She turned the damper down again and went back upstairs. Mark said this place was very well insulated and that the furnace was efficient. They only put wood in three times a day; early in the morning, in the afternoon and again around 9:00 or 10:00 pm at night. The whole house stayed toasty warm. Mark said when the snow started, they'd probably have to use more wood. The men had been chopping wood as fast as they could. Who knew how much it was going to take for a whole winter? None of them had used wood heat before, so it was hard to know how much to have on hand.

She grabbed a cup, filled it with coffee, and sat down at the table. Today Mark and Eric were going to clean the weapons they got from those assholes that had kidnapped Ryan. The men wanted the weapons in top shape; then they were going to teach the women, Chris and Ryan how to shoot and load each weapon. Mark wanted them all up to speed as soon as possible. Then they all could respond to a threat when it came along. If there was one thing you could be sure of in this crazy world, was that something else dangerous would show up. Lisa looked forward to learning to shoot a real rifle. Then the next time she faced down some asshole, she would have a real weapon to kill them with.

Ryan came into the kitchen, yawned, and sat down at the table. Lisa reached over and ruffled his hair. "And how are you on this bright early morning?"

Ryan shook his head, looking up at her with sleepy looking eyes. "Cut it out. I'm not even awake yet and you're already pestering me with questions." Yup, he'd been hanging around Mark way too much. He had even picked up his grumpy attitude. The women had been discussing this very thing the day before.

She smiled, wiggling her eyebrows at him. "And just think this is the first of many, many questions that I will ask you today."

He groaned and laid his head down on his arms on the table. Lisa laughed loudly at him. Chris and Amanda walked into the kitchen. Amanda had taken to carrying around the black teddy bear she found in a closet ever since Ryan was kidnapped and she'd been chased by those men. She also had disturbing dreams about being chased and would wake everyone with her terrified screams. The encounter they had with the men at the blockade into Redding hadn't affected her at all. She just talked about them being mean. Those assholes that had chased her and kidnapped Ryan had scared her to death. Amanda was rubbing her eyes and the teddy bear was still held in one of her hands and was flopping all around. She looked so cute. Lisa reached out and pulled her into her lap for a morning hug. Chris, thinking he was a grown up now, tried to be like Eric and had started drinking coffee. You could tell he didn't like it, but so far he had stuck with it. Lisa rolled her eyes. *Guys, who could understand them?*

Chris said, "When's breakfast? I'm starving." *God, when wasn't this kid hungry?* He ate like a horse and always wanted more. At the rate he was going, he would grow up to be seven feet tall and weigh at least three hundred pounds. It looked like he had grown a couple of inches just since he'd arrived. They had to let the hem out in his pants to make them long enough. She sighed. Who would have ever thought they would have three growing children to look after? If her old friends could see her now they'd have a big laugh.

She put her hand up in the air. "I will deal with breakfast after I have another cup of coffee and not one minute before."

Ryan groaned again. "We always have to wait for you to drink coffee first. What I want to know is why? Why do we have to wait for you all the time?"

Lisa looked at him, raised an eyebrow, and was just about to let Ryan have a piece of her mind when a voice said behind her, "Because when it's Lisa's turn to get up with you, she is in charge of when breakfast gets cooked and served. That's why."

They didn't know it, but Abby was in the bathroom throwing up at that very moment. Lisa got down a teapot and measured out two tablespoons of Abby's concoction she had mixed for her tea. She put it in the metal basket that hung down into the teapot, and then filled it with hot water to steep.

Those scumbags hadn't taken care of their weapons. Mark was totally disgusted with their condition. He had seen other people's guns in bad shape, but this was just unacceptable. Not many people kept their guns in top shape as he and Eric did. They both looked at their guns as tools to keep them alive and wanted them ready to meet any challenges they might face. If the gun was not cared for, it might jam or break down at the wrong moment. It was a wonder those assholes lived as long as they had with their guns in this bad of shape. Mark and Eric both agreed that they wouldn't trust shooting them in the condition they were in.

Mark and Eric sat there and contemplated how they could clean them. They had torn the place apart looking for a gun cleaning kit. Mark muttered, "Of course we would pick the only place up here without a gun cleaning kit." Eric smiled and thought it sure felt like that at times. It seemed that the odds were always against them these days. They only carried a small cleaning kit for their own guns. They didn't have enough oil or Hoppes number nine to even make it through one cleaning for all of these guns and it would take a few cleanings to get them in working condition. They looked in the tool room down in the basement and didn't find anything. They went out to the garage and Mark found a can of WD-40, a quart of automatic transmission fluid and a quart of 5/30 weight motor oil. The oil was a little on the heavy side, but was synthetic and would not get super thick in the cold like regular oil would. It would have to do.

They went back down to the basement. Mark sprayed each of them on the outside with the WD-40 first, to remove all the dirt and rust. He and Eric used a rag to wipe them down. The WD-40 did a pretty fair job. Next they put some oil on a rag and wiped them down again. Eric took out his pocket gun cleaning kit, which was a modified German gun cleaning kit he bought at the Army/Navy surplus store. He had removed the brush and replaced it with a twelve-gauge brush to use with his shotgun. He used this on the single shot twelve gauge. He couldn't believe the amount of dirt, gunpowder and bits of leaves and dirt that came out of the barrel. "Those morons must have thought guns last forever or something," said Eric. He used the last of his small half ounce bottle of Hoppes just getting the barrel clean.

Mark had a .30 caliber brush and it would work great on the AK-47, but it was too small for the 45-70 and too big for the .270 barrel. Neither one of them had a brush for a .22. Mark sighed. Both men were frustrated as hell. They had all the gun cleaning supplies they would ever need at their retreat.

Mark thought the slotted jag on his gun cleaning kit would have to be used. But it wouldn't work on the .22 or the .270.

Eric said in frustration, "What I wouldn't give for a universal gun cleaning kit right now."

Mark chuckled. "You mean like the ones we bought and stored up at the retreat? The same ones that are sitting right next to several quarts of Hoppes and the gun oil?"

Eric laughed. "Yeah. Hey, I have an idea. Call up your dad and have him mail them down to us." They both laughed loudly.

Lisa walked into the room just then. "What's so funny?"

They both laughed harder. Mark said, "Your boyfriend here thinks he's a comedian. He said I should call my dad up and have him mail us a gun cleaning kit we have at the retreat."

Lisa was taken aback at Mark's reference to Eric. She said stiffly, "Eric is not my boyfriend."

Mark laughed. "Come on, admit it. You two are the perfect pair. He's an all right guy for a lughead who thinks he's funny."

Lisa was stunned speechless. Was it that obvious? Could everyone see how she felt about Eric? What? She had a 'deer in the headlights' look on her face.

Eric smiled at her. "Don't mind him. He's just joking around." She turned and ran from the room, all the way up the stairs to her room. She sat on the bed to think. She was very confused. Was Eric saying he doesn't like her? Or was he just trying to act cool in front of his friend? Or was he just trying not to put any pressure on her? This was all just too much. She lay down on the bed and hugged her pillow to her chest. Tears started rolling down her cheeks.

Eric turned to Mark with a worried look on his face. "You shouldn't have said that."

Mark made a face at Eric and spread his arms out. "Come on. Everyone can tell you two are attracted to each other. I meant it when I said you two are the perfect pair."

"I know that, but she's not ready yet for something like that. You can't forget what these women have been through, Mark. She'll let me know when she's ready."

Mark brushed everything Eric said aside. "Let's figure this out." Eric was still staring at the doorway with a wistful look on his face.

Abby and Maria came upstairs to talked to her. They helped her sort out her feelings and fears. They were a great help in helping her to figure out what she wanted and what she was going to do to get it. Lisa marched down the stairs and into the room where the men were messing around with the guns and walked right up to Eric, sitting by the workbench.

He was working on one of the guns. Eric turned to her to see what she needed and Lisa reached out, grabbed his head, pulled him quickly forward, and kissed him. Mark sat in his seat watching and his mouth dropped opened in surprise. It was a long kiss. When the kiss was over and they were staring into each other's eyes, Mark started laughing. They both turned and looked at him. "I knew it. I told you that you two were the perfect pair." Lisa straightened up, turned, and walked out of the room with her head held high. Eric just stared after her with a stunned look on his face.

He turned to Mark and shook his head. "Can you ever not say the wrong thing?"

Mark said innocently, "What? What are you taking about?" Eric sighed, shook his head, and went back to what he was doing.

Lisa went into the kitchen with a spring in her step. She had kissed Eric and it had been wonderful. She wasn't upset at all. It hadn't made her scream or cry or anything. See? She could be normal if she wanted to. She wasn't letting those assholes that had attacked and tortured them affect how she would live her life. Abby had been right. She was smiling.

The men muttered in frustration as they worked. Mark said, "Okay, hand me the fishing line you found. We'll feed that through the barrels and then tie a piece of rag to it and pull it slowly back out again until it's clean. It's the only thing I can think of." Eric handed him the fishing line and they got to work. It was a very slow process. They used Eric's towel from his pack as the rags. They cut it up into strips. It had several holes in it, anyway. They had used it for a lot of things and it definitely looked pretty ragged. When dinnertime rolled around, they still weren't done. The guns were starting to look better, but it was going to take more work before the men would be even a little bit satisfied. Ryan came and got them for dinner.

After dinner, they went right back to work. The 10-22 was a real pain in the ass to clean. It took a long time just to get it into halfway decent shape. When they took it apart, the slide was packed with burnt powder and crud. Mark said, "I bet it would jam every other shot." Eric nodded in agreement. They finally finished all the rifles; they were at least in working order now and not dangerous to fire.

Eric said, "We will have to clean them again before too long."

"Yeah. Those assholes are a disgrace to gun owners everywhere," replied Mark. The two pistols were in just as bad of shape. The automatic transmission fluid worked fairly well stripping and cleaning the gunk out of them.

"Those assholes could have at least packed some oil to keep the rust off." Eric glared at the weapons.

Mark said, "I guess they figured they would find a miracle oil well out here somewhere to keep their guns free of rust." They finally stopped working and set them aside with a sigh.

Eric looked up at the clock and saw it was 11:15 pm. He stretched his shoulders and arms and rotated his head a little to work out the kinks and stiffness. He had never worked so hard cleaning weapons in his life and hoped to God he never had to do it again. His hands were sore from pulling on the fishing line. Well, at least they'd be able to use the weapons. He yawned.

Mark said, "Well, they're halfway clean." They looked over at the stack of weapons. They had a Ruger 10-22 semi-automatic, a .270 bolt action that held five shots, an AK-47, an H & R single shot 12 gauge shotgun, an old 45-70 lever action, a Hi Point .45 and a SIG 9mm. They put all the ammo into separate piles for each gun. They had two thirty-shot magazines and three hundred sixteen rounds for the Ruger 10-22 semi-automatic, thirty-seven rounds for the .270 bolt action that holds five shots, two thirty round magazines and one hundred eighty six rounds for the AK-47, various shells for the H & R single shot 12 gauge shotgun, twenty-three rounds for the 45-70 lever action, forty-three bullets for the Hi Point .45 pistol, two clips and thirty-six bullets for the SIG 9mm. It was not nearly enough, but it was better than they had before.

Mark sighed. Eric said, "I'm going to go get my Leopold Boone and Crockett scope and put it on the .270. I'll have to sight it in."

"Good idea," said Mark. Eric went upstairs and got it. The women were in the large reading area at the top of the stairs talking and working with the computer. Maria was using this area for the children as a school room. Eric and Mark had brought up a round wooden table Maria had found in the basement that had four padded matching chairs. She said it would be suitable for Chris and Ryan to use. They had found a cute red and yellow plastic children's picnic table with molded seats in the garage and Maria and the women had moved it up here for Amanda.

Lisa saw Eric and smiled at him. He said, "We're just about done cleaning the guns. Tomorrow we start training you to handle them."

"Good. I want a real rifle, so next time I can stop someone myself and not have to rely on you or Mark to kill someone for me. Especially when I have to protect the children."

Eric looked at her seriously. "We'll get all of you up to speed with the weapons as soon as possible."

Lisa smiled. "I appreciate it, Eric." He nodded and went back down to the basement.

Eric attached the scope and then took the .270 out to the garage to sight the scope in. Because of the shortage of bullets, he would have to bore sight it in. Even then, it would take three shots to get it zeroed in just right. He removed the bolt out of the rifle. He placed a small flashlight where the bolt would be. A small beam of light came out of the barrel and showed clearly on the garage wall. He used a vise to hold the rifle in place. He used the adjustment screws and got the target lined up straight with the beam of light on the wall to zero it in. That worked great. He sighed and sat there for a moment, thinking. He felt a bit overwhelmed. That had worked, but what about everything else they had to deal with? Now what? Two single guys with three women and three children and no clue what they are doing or how to survive. He pushed all his doubts out of his mind. He couldn't let the others see he was worried or stressing over the coming winter.

All in all, the women spent over five hours that day learning all the safety procedures and proper care of the rifles. The woman were allowed 5 shots at the targets and did very well. They needed practice loading and unloading to build their speed up, but Eric was satisfied with how well they were learning. He had started Chris and Ryan out with the pellet rifles. They had plenty of pellets. They were doing pretty good. Ryan had a good eye.

Eric was worried about Mark. He was stressing way too much. But, with the world as it was, who wasn't stressing out? Not only did they have to worry about surviving, they were on constant alert for invaders. The windows stayed covered up tight, and that wasn't just for security reasons. It kept the heat inside with them. This place had good insulated shades, blinds and window coverings. He also decided to carry around a rifle. They'd been very lucky so far and most of the battles had been close-in fighting, where the shotgun was supreme, but for any shots needing distance, he would need a real rifle.

That evening after dinner, Mark told Eric he needed to talk to him privately. They went into their bedroom and sat down. Mark explained to him what he'd been thinking about all day, and how he was feeling a little resentful about Eric leaving all the hard things up to him to have to tell the women and children about rationing things and not wasting anything. It was making him feel like the bad guy. Eric nodded and thought about what Mark said. He could see Mark's point of view. He turned to Mark. "You're right. I'm sorry. I didn't even realize I was leaving all of the heavy-handed things for you to do. You're just so good at them we all took you for granted, I guess. I'll do better."

Mark said, "Thanks. I'm tired of being the bad guy here."

Eric smiled. "But Mark, you make such a good bad guy."

Eric got up and patted his shoulder in comfort. He knew Mark always felt intensely about things. Sometimes, when one learns things about oneself that one don't like, it has a tendency to shake the foundation of what one believes. He needed some time to think. Ever since the EMP, it had been one thing after another with no time to just think about things. Mark had been reacting almost constantly and had always been on the defensive side of things. He just needed to put everything into perspective. He knew his friend very well. They had been through a lot together.

Mark seemed calmer and a little more approachable now after Eric had talked to him. Everyone was given work to do every day to prepare for winter. They trained with the guns every day, too. They loaded and unloaded them over and over again. They practiced cleaning them and how to clear a jam. Eric thought, *Damn if he had any idea .22 ammo would be so valuable now he would have bought cases of it back when you could buy it for ten dollars for five hundred and fifty rounds. Oh well, twenty-twenty hindsight.*

Mark and Eric did the patrols and training. One part was learning to walk in the woods. Another was reading a compass and learning how to follow directions and find spots using only a compass. Mark and Eric had worked out how they could work in teams and learn to use what they had learned in a real way. Mark went out early one morning and left some markers for them to bring back, proving they had really followed the directions using the compass. They would go four miles and find the spot, pick up what Mark had left there, and then go to the next place and so on. It would roughly be a four mile square. So, they would walk sixteen miles and bring back the four markers with them. They would go in pairs with each of them carrying a gun. They would stop and build a fire and cook their lunch and dinner. They would find water to drink. They would learn to sneak through the area. It was a lot harder than most people would think. It should take each two person team eight to ten hours to do this. Lisa and Maria were the first team. Chris and Abby would go next. Lisa loved shooting the 10-22. It was a fun gun to shoot and light to carry. She felt confident now about any confrontations they might run into. Mark had Lisa carry his 30-30 to get familiar with it and Maria carried the .22.

They headed out at first light. The morning air was crisp and there was a heavy frost on the ground that crunched under their feet. Walking on pavement and sidewalks was easy compared to walking in the woods. Pavement and sidewalks were straight and even. There was nothing truly level or flat in the woods. Eric had stressed to take their time and not rush. They should check the compass reading every few minutes to stay on course. They walked like they had before on their trek up north, five paces apart. It was easier than they thought it would be because they had been through so much and were battle-hardened warriors now. They moved silently through the woods with a purpose. Lisa was thinking about what Mark and Eric had said about the women having to take over if something happened to the men. She didn't like to think about that. But Mark stressed that they needed to know how to move through the woods and brush and not be afraid. The woods and forests were a friend to them and they had to unlock the secrets of making it a friend so they would feel comfortable. They found the first spot around 10:00 am. The sun had broken through the clouds, warming the day up a little. They found a spring flowing out of the hill; they filled their canteens and took a long drink, then refilled them again before leaving. Mark had left a red rag tied around a branch on a tree. They put it in their pack. They headed east on the first part of their journey; now they turned ninety degrees and headed south. As they walked, Maria said, "I'd always been afraid of the forest before. Now it seems like a friend that will help hide me from bad things. This isn't so hard now."

Lisa smiled. "Yes, it does seem more of a friend. But, we can't ever forget that there's danger out here, too. Let's push on a little faster so we can stop and have lunch. I want us to get there about 1:00 pm."

Maria said, "Okay, that's a good idea."

One pm rolled around and they still hadn't found the next spot. Lisa was getting worried; they should have spotted it by now. Had they made a mistake somewhere? Had they passed the marker and not spotted it? They came up to the top of a rise and stopped to looked around and take a compass reading. Down in the small gully below she saw a small single tree off by itself near some rocks with a red rag tied around it. *Thank God,* she thought. She had started to think they were hopelessly lost. She turned to Maria and gave her the thumbs up signal that they had found the right spot and pointed to the rag.

Maria said, "That's a nice looking dog. I wonder if it's lost out here. We should take it home for the children to play with." Lisa turned and looked over where Maria pointed; there was a black and white spotted English setter. It was approaching them; it looked like it had missed a few meals. Its tail was wagging a friendly greeting.

Before Lisa could comment on this, she saw more dogs out of the corner of her eye. She turned and looked at them. "Well, it looks like we have several here to pick from. Maybe we should pick that good looking collie over there. I've heard they're friendly and good with children." She saw something out of the corner of her other eye and turned and looked; more dogs. She turned around; more dogs were coming from the back. She got a weird feeling. These dogs were acting kind of strange. All of a sudden she had a strange, tingling sensation all over her body with the urge to run. She said in a very calm but firm voice, "Something is not right."

Maria looked around and said, "The dogs are surrounding us. I don't like it." She was edging slowly over to a nearby tree. "Get closer to that tree over there in case we have to climb up to get away from the dogs." Lisa turned to look at her and then slowly edged over to the closest tree. Maria said in a scared high pitched voice, "A lot more dogs are coming over the rise behind us, too."

The women started moving a little faster. That cute, friendly English setter changed in a blink of an eye into a growling, snarling deadly threat. He charged Lisa. She'd taken the gun off her shoulder a few moments before; she quickly raised it up and shot the dog. She hit it in the back, he dropped howling and squealing in pain. At that very moment, the woods exploded with dogs. The tree Lisa was near was five or six feet away from the tree Maria was in. She would never make it to Maria's tree. She yelled out, "Catch!" She threw the 30-30 at Maria. There wasn't time for her to sling it back on her shoulder and the .22 wouldn't stop these dogs. It wasn't a big enough caliber. Mark and Eric had showed them the difference in knock down power between the different calibers. If she didn't make it to the tree before they attacked her, she wanted Maria to have the larger caliber rifle to kill these dogs. Lisa watched the rifle sail through the air; it fell short of Maria by about a foot and fell towards the ground, hitting a large rock. The homemade pine stock split on the rock, then it fell the rest of the way. There was no time to grab it. Lisa jumped, grabbed a branch, and pulled herself up. As she was pulling herself up, a dog grabbed the back of her boot and tugged, trying to pull her back down. She started to swing around with the dog hanging onto her boot. She thought her arms were going to come out of their sockets. She kept saying to herself, *Don't let go. Just don't let go of the branch.* She was trying to use her other boot to kick the dog, finally succeeded in kicking it in the head and pushing down with her leg on the dog's head. It yelped and let go. Lisa quickly grabbed another branch and pulled herself higher in the tree. The dogs were attacking. They were jumping around, snarling and barking, trying to climb the tree, tearing gouges into the tree trunk with their claws. She climbed even higher, shaking with reaction and disbelief at what had happened.

Maria said, "My God, what are we going to do now?"

Lisa screamed out with frustration and fear. "Survive. That's what we're going to do." They sat down on branches where they could see each other and the dogs. The dogs were acting like some demented, nightmarish creatures. They sat there watching the dogs trying to get up the tree. Lisa kept thinking, *What the hell is going on? Why are they acting like this?* There were twenty-five to thirty dogs. They were a mix of all different kinds. One of the dogs was sniffing at the rifle lying on the ground and started to drag it off. Two other dogs came over and grabbed different parts of the rifle; they played tug of war over it. This caused the homemade pine stock to split the rest of the way. Both women heard the loud crack of the wood. Lisa looked at Maria. "Shoot a couple of them."

"Mark is going to be so pissed at you for breaking his rifle again."

"I didn't break it. You didn't catch it. It wouldn't have broken if you would've caught it."

"That's because you didn't throw it far enough."

"I had thirty dogs on my heels, so I did the best that I could."

Maria aimed at a dog, took a shot and missed. She aimed at another dog, fired and missed that on too. She said, "They're jumping around and moving so much I can't hit them."

Okay, stop. Don't waste anymore bullets. Let me think a minute." *Now what do we do?* She tried to remember what Mark had said about larger animals and hitting them with the .22. He'd said to hit them in the head. "Maria, aim for their heads. Mark said that's the only way we can kill them with the .22."

Maria tried to aim for the head of a dog, and wasn't able to. "I tried to aim at their heads, but they won't stay still long enough for me to shoot them."

"Okay. So, get comfortable and stay calm. Make every shot count. Shoot when I tell you to." Lisa looked over all the dogs and saw a German Shepherd standing out a little further from the other dogs. It wasn't moving around a lot. She pointed. "See that dog over there by itself? Aim at the head." Maria aimed and missed again. "Calm down and aim," Lisa said, "and don't jerk the trigger. Try aiming a little lower." The dog Maria shot at had ran off. Maria picked another dog, aimed and fired. The shot went too low and kicked up a little dirt into the air. "Just calm down and aim for the middle of the pack. You're bound to hit something."

Maria picked a big black lab and shot it in the side. The black lab yelped in surprise, then howled in pain and ran off. Maria asked, "How come that dog didn't fall over and die like in the movies?"

Lisa chuckled. "That's just fantasy. Mark said that never happens unless you hit them in the head. That rifle is for hunting small game or practicing or scaring someone. It doesn't just blow them away like they show in the movies." Lisa looked around. "Shoot that hound that keeps trying to climb the tree."

Maria aimed almost straight down the tree and fired. Just as she fired, the hound jumped up with an open mouth, howling like mad. The bullet ripped right through the lower jaw straight into its throat. The dog fell over; the rest of the dogs stopped and looked at its death throes. It got eerily quiet as the dogs waited. The women had no idea what the dogs were waiting for.

"Quick, shoot some more." Maria aimed and hit the next dog in the head; it dropped like it had been pole axed straight to the ground. The rest of the dogs ran off. Lisa wondered aloud, "Is it over?"

Maria said, "I don't know, but we should stay up here and watch to see if they come back or not. What was the matter with them?"

"I don't know, but they were acting like they were killer attack dogs or something." They sat in their trees and thought about this for awhile. Lisa's mouth was dry, so she took a drink from her canteen.

Maria was worried. "We have to get back to the cabin. It will be getting dark and then the dogs will have the advantage; they can see in the dark. We have to warn the others. What if the kids were outside and they attack?"

Lisa's heart jumped into her throat at the thought of the children facing down these dogs. What in the hell could they do to stop this from happening? Lisa heard a strange sound coming closer. It sounded a bit like train wheels rolling, but smaller, faster wheels with a whooshing, whirling type sound added in. "What in God's name is that sound?"

Maria looked around with a confused look. "A weird dog call or something?" Whatever it was came closer. It would stop for about ten seconds and then start up again. The closer it got, the higher pitched it was. They kept looking around, but couldn't see anything. After a few more minutes, it stopped. Lisa counted to ten and it started up again. Lisa was looking at Maria and saw her eyes go wide. Maria said, "You're never going to believe this one. Not in a million years."

Lisa said, "What?" Believe what?"

Maria staring up higher at the trees. "Tarzan is coming."

"What? Did you hit your head or something?" Just then Lisa saw a large shadow cross in front of the sun and felt something hit up high in her tree. She looked up and saw a guy. At least she thought it was a guy in the higher part of the tree. Her mouth dropped opened. "What the hell?"

A voice called down to her, "Are you okay down there?" Lisa and Maria exchanged a shocked look. Lisa was blinking up at the guy in amazement. The voice called down again. "Are you two okay?"

Maria answered with awe and confusion. "Are you Tarzan?" They heard the guy bust out laughing. The women again exchanged a look. Lisa had a fleeting thought they must have walked onto a movie set somehow.

The voice said, "That's a good one. I'll have to remember that one. Yeah, well I guess you could call me Tarzan and I have come here to save you. But I don't wear a loin cloth and swing on vines." The women looked at each other again. "I'm going to go over to the other tree and bring your friend over to this tree, then we can talk and I'll explain, okay?"

Lisa asked, "Are those your dogs? If so, call them off and we'll be on our way."

The voice said, "Now, if those were my dogs why would I be here to save you?"

The women shared a quick glance at each other. Maria tilted her head as if to say, he has a point. "How many are in your group?" Lisa asked.

"Group? What group? Oh, you mean how many people am I with?"

"Yes, how many men do you have?"

"We're just a small group of young families. We have twenty-one people. We mean you no harm."

Lisa said, "We've had problems with groups before. Thanks, anyway. We'll be on our way now." Lisa turned to Maria. "We're climbing down and leaving." Maria and Lisa started climbing down. Lisa was faster and got to the last branch first and jumped down. Before she could even straighten up, the dogs were running back over the rise. She grabbed the branch again and quickly climbed back up. The dogs surrounded them, snarling, growling and howling.

Lisa looked down at the dogs. *This can't really be happening. This has to be some kind of a weird dream or something.* She shook her head to clear it and looked down. The dogs were still there, fighting each other to get up the tree. The women looked at each other again. Lisa looked up the tree. "All right. We'll do this your way."

The voice said, "I thought you'd see it my way. I'm going to go over to the other tree and get your friend. I'll be right back." Lisa heard the weird sound again for a few seconds and then the voice said to Maria, "Climb up here." Maria looked at Lisa and then back up where the voice was coming from, sighed, and started to climb. "You'll need to climb on my back and hold tight so you don't fall. Okay?"

Lisa could hear the uncertainty in Maria's voice. "Okay." Lisa started climbing higher in her own tree. She wanted to keep an eye on what was going on with Maria.

The two of them were already in her tree by the time she climbed up. They were standing on a little platform waiting for her. Lisa looked him over. He looked like a surfer dude hanging out at the beach. She climbed up on the platform. He extended his hand. "Hi. I'm Clark."

Lisa shook his hand. "I'm Lisa."

Maria did the same. "I'm Maria."

Lisa was looking curiously at the contraption he was holding. She asked, "Did this thing make the weird sound we heard?"

Clark chuckled. "Yes. It runs on cables. We have them strung up all over the place up here. We use the cable to travel above the forest. We are the tree people."

Maria said, "Tree people."

Lisa laughed. "You live in the trees?"

Clark smiled. "Yes."

"How does this thing work?"

"We use this two wheel contraption. You put the harness on and clip yourself to it. You hold on like this, then swing your body out and your weight will take you across to the next tree. You unhook from that cable and then re-hook onto the next one and so on. We've built small platforms to land on. It's easy once you get the hang of it. It's a totally safe way to travel."

Lisa looked intently at him. "Does your group have guns?"

Clark looked at her for a few moments and then smiled. "Of course. Why?"

Lisa said, "Then why haven't you killed those dogs down there?"

"They just showed up two days ago. They hadn't bothered us. So, why would we kill them?"

Lisa looked at him for a few moments. "Well, maybe you should because they are a threat to people, don't you think?"

Clark shrugged his shoulders. "We live up here. Most things that go on down there don't concern us up here." Lisa and Maria shared a look and then turned back to Clark. He said, "Come on with me to our tree houses and you can rest. Then we can take you nearer to where you're going when it's safer."

Lisa didn't like that idea at all. Maria said, "How are we going to do that?"

Clark reached over and unhooked a bag that was clipped to the side of his harness. He opened it up and pulled out two of the wheel things and two harnesses. He smiled at them. "With these." The women smiled.

They reached the main tree house. The women had a lot of fun getting there. It was like riding a roller coaster, but better because they were in control. Clark showed them around the main tree house. It was large and broken up into sections. He said they cooked their meals and ate there. It also had a large area in the back where they held meetings. He showed them the average small tree house. Each house had a sleeping area with hammocks strung up to sleep in, a sitting area with plastic chairs and tables and a small room with a door that closed.

Maria looked around "Where do you go to the bathroom?"

Clark laughed. "Everyone asks that question." He pointed to the closed door. "We use plastic buckets with toilet seats on them. We put a plastic bag in the bucket and each day we replace the bags with a fresh bag. We climb down and bury it. We sprinkle lime on it, then put rocks and dirt on top it."

Maria said, "Wow."

There were several children that were peeking out of several of the tree houses, looking at them with curious eyes. Clark led them back to the main tree house.

Lisa looked around. "We have to get word back to our place and let them know about the dogs and that we're okay."

Clark smiled. "It's already been taken care of. We sent our best mountain bike rider to tell everyone at your cabin what happened to the two of you. She'll be back before it gets dark."

Lisa looked up at him and with narrowed, suspicious eyes. "How did you know we were staying in a cabin?" She was reaching slowly down to her leg where she had a knife. Abby had been teaching her and Maria how to use a knife for defense.

"We've watched you guys before at your cabin. You left with a bunch of supplies, and then you came back. Why did you come back?"

Lisa stopped reaching for the knife and sat straight up. "There was a bunch of jerks running a road block right before Redding. They weren't letting anyone use the road to go through town."

Maria said, "They threatened to shoot us if we didn't turn around. We had no choice but to come back here."

Clark nodded. Just then an older man came into the tree house and smiled at them. "Hello, I'm Jeff. You are welcome to stay here with us. Are you hungry?"

Lisa and Maria exchanged a look and Lisa said, "Thank you for the offer, but we have to get back to our place."

Jeff said, "It's not safe to leave until we get a report back from Kathy. She's the one taking the message to the cabin to let them know where you are and that you are safe. She'll be back before dark." Lisa and Maria looked at each other.

Some of the tree people moved over to some other trees, bypassing the area where the dogs were. Kathy was the only one who climbed down, where they had some hidden storage containers buried into the side of a mountain. The others pulled the rope ladder back up and hooked it into place. She got her mountain bike out, listening for the dogs. She didn't hear anything and signaled up that she was leaving. She jumped on her bike and took off. Kathy was having a great time being on pavement again. She loved riding her bike up and down the mountains. It was a way to be alone and the scenery was beautiful up here. She loved all the pine trees. She wondered about the two guys at the cabin. She hoped they were nice. She kicked up the speed of the bike. She had two more miles to go before she got to the road leading to the cabin. She wondered what was up with the dogs. She had been one of several of the tree people that had seen the attack on the two women. She shivered at the thought of running into those dogs. All of a sudden, a dog came running out of the forest right in front of her. Fear gave her the fortitude to build up more speed on the bike. She leaned forward over the handle bars and pedaled like the hounds of hell were coming after her. She sped by the dog. It lunged and missed her. It started barking and racing after her. She turned around and looked; more dogs were coming out of the forest. Her heartbeat increased rapidly and another fear ran through her. She gained some ground on them, but they were right behind her, keeping up. She had hoped that they'd give up and leave her alone. She looked behind again. Damn, there were nine or ten dogs on her tail and they just kept coming. There was one skinny dog that was faster than the others and was outdistancing the pack. This dog was gaining on her. She pedaled as fast as she could. She saw the road coming up. *Great, just great,* she thought, *I'm going to have to slow down to turn and that one dog had almost caught up with me.* She was carrying a Glock 9mm that held sixteen rounds. That was enough to take care of these dogs. She was debating if she should stop and climb a tree and just kill them all. Then she remembered that the one woman had been firing a rifle at the dogs and it only killed a few. What if she got stuck in a tree just like the two women did? They didn't have any cables that ran all the way out here. She would be stuck up in the tree until someone came along and killed all the dogs so she could climb down. Then another thought hit her. What if she did that and even more dogs showed up? That's what happened to the two women.

No, she wasn't stopping until she got to the cabin. Hopefully, they'd help her kill them. Her heart was beating wildly in her chest and her lungs were burning with each breath. Her legs were getting tired of the constant pedaling. She thought, *Legs don't fail me now.* As she slowed down, that damn skinny dog was right beside her on the road jumping at her and biting at her legs. Fear sent a shock through her body as she realized that the dog was trying to knock her off the bike. She already had several rips in her pant legs from the dog. It lunged at her and grabbed a hold of her jeans in back and tugged. She stiffened her legs and held on. The dog finally let go when she turned the bike a little; it hit the back wheel and almost made her crash. She straightened the bike out and raced around the corner, trying to build her speed up again. This was a dirt road, not pavement. She was having difficulty getting up to high speed. The dog was back again. They sounded like a pack of vicious wild animals. She saw the driveway up ahead and gave a quick look behind her and saw the rest of the pack was catching up. Oh God, would she make it? She whipped off the road and onto the driveway and pedaled as fast as she could. The skinny dog jumped up to bite her, just as it lunged, her right knee was coming up from pumping the pedals and it hit him in the jaw, making it yelp and drop away from her.

She sucked in a breath. That hurt like hell. She looked ahead and saw she was a hundred yards from the door. Then she was fifty yards. The skinny dog was back alongside her. At ten yards from the door, she slammed on the brakes and jumped off the bike. The dog jumped at her and grabbed onto the ripped part of her jeans, almost knocking her to the ground. She heard her jeans ripping as the dog tugged. She grabbed the Glock, turned her arm, and shot it in the head, right next to the ear. It dropped away from her. She ran to the door and tried the handle. It was locked. She started pounding on the door screaming, "Please let me in. Oh God, please let me in!" She turned around; the other dogs were almost to her now. She held the Glock straight out in front of her and tried to steady her aim by leaning on the door. Her hands were shaking so hard she wasn't sure she could hit anything. A huge beast lunged for her throat, and before she could squeeze the trigger, she felt the door give and felt herself being yanked inside, then the door slammed shut. As she slid across the tile, they heard the thumps as the dogs hit the door.

Before she came to a stop, a woman kicked the Glock out of her hand and was leaning over her holding a knife to her throat. This happened so fast she wasn't sure if she even had time to blink or to take a breath. The woman said, "Who the hell are you? Why are those dogs chasing you?" The dogs were jumping and throwing their bodies against the door, trying to get it to open. They sounded like something out of a nightmare, snarling, growling, barking and howling.

Mark and Eric were down in the basement stacking firewood. They had a window open and they used that as a way to throw the firewood into the basement from outside. It saved them walking down the basement stairs carrying the firewood inside from the garage. This way they split it outside, then just threw it into the basement, saving a lot of extra work and time. They both heard the shot outside and raced up the stairs to see what was going on. They could hear loud thumps coming from the door. Then they heard all the dogs.

Mark raced through the kitchen yelling out, "Abby, what in the hell is going on?" Both men stopped dead in their tracks seeing Abby leaning over a woman holding a knife to her throat. Kathy looked behind the woman and saw the two men she was sent to deliver the message to standing there, aiming pistols at her. She saw movement out of the corner of her eye and saw two teenage boys standing on the stairs; they had two rifles aimed at her, too.

A cute little girl flew down the stairs, running to the woman standing over her. The little girl held onto the woman's leg, peeking around it. "Where's Lisa and Maria?" she asked.

Mark said, "Abby, you can let her go. We all have her covered."

Abby quickly took a step back, bringing the little girl with her, but staying close and ready. She pushed the little girl over towards a chair and said, "Get on the other side of the chair and stay there." She walked over and picked up the woman's 9mm.

Kathy tried to get a breath and talk at the same time and it made her choke because her throat was so dry. It took a minute until she was able to talk. Fear was closing her throat and she couldn't get a word out. She finally was able to haltingly croak out, "I'm bringing you a message from the two women."

A shock of fear raced through Eric's body and he rushed forward, grabbing the woman's hair at the top of her head with one hand and held the pistol to the woman's temple with the other he said in a very menacing intense voice right into her face, "You'd better not have harmed even one hair on their heads. Tell me right now if they are all right or I'll blow your brains out all over this floor right now." The last thought Kathy had before the darkness claimed her was that these people were truly one hundred percent insane. The woman's eyes opened wider in fright and she just slumped like a rag doll in Eric's hand. Eric thought for one confused moment that he had pulled the trigger and killed her. No, that isn't what happened. There was no blood or brains. He thought in total amazement, *Have I scared her to death?*

Abby said, "Help me get her on the couch. Then we'll tie her up."

Eric looked confused. If he killed her, why tie her up? Then it hit him. She must have fainted. He let out a breath of relief. They couldn't let anything happen to her until they could find out where Lisa and Maria were. Eric put his pistol away and helped Abby carry her over to the couch. They threw her down; she didn't do anything but flop around. Well, at least now they were pretty sure she wasn't faking it. No one was that good an actress.

Mark was looking out the window. There were fifteen or more dogs outside in the front, snarling, and scratching at the door. Some were throwing their bodies against the door. What the hell was going on? These dogs were acting like they were demented. Then he remembered they had the window open in the basement. He quickly turned around and said, "Eric, the basement." Eric looked at him for a second and then it registered. Both men raced for the basement and Mark called out to Abby, "Guard the woman. We have to go close the window."

Abby only heard about half of what he said, but she knew what he meant. Abby said to Chris and Ryan, "I'm going to go into the kitchen for a second to get a chair to help hold the door. Watch her." Both boys nodded. Abby quickly went into the kitchen, grabbed a chair, and ran back and shoved it under the door handle, making sure it was tight against the door. She went back over to the couch.

Just as Mark and Eric got down the basement stairs, two dogs jumped at them. They both shot twice and the dogs fell straight to the floor and didn't move. They raced forward; two more came around the side of the wood stove. They both shot again and the dogs fell dead. Mark went around the wood stove on one side and Eric took the other side. They both heard each other shoot again. The window was on Mark's side of the wood stove. He looked up and two more dogs were on their bellies, trying to crawl through the window. He aimed and hit one and the other one backed off. Eric came around the wood stove at that moment and Mark yelled, "Cover me." He raced to the window, almost tripping on a piece of firewood. He reached up and pulled the stick away from the window. They had used the stick to hold the window open. The window slammed down into place and Mark quickly turned the lock. He picked up a piece of plywood and shoved it up tight against the window. It didn't quite fit, but was good enough. Both men just stood there for a few moments, breathing in deeply to calm themselves. That was close. That was just too damn close. They went back upstairs after making sure all the dogs in the basement were really dead.

When they got into the living room, the woman was lying on the couch with a blanket over her. Eric noticed her torn jeans were lying on the floor a ways away from her with her shoes and socks beside them. He looked at Abby, wondering what she was doing. Abby said, "She's hurt. I looked her over and it's not too bad. Just a few bruises and scrapes." The woman was just starting to open her eyes. She looked at them with terror. Abby handed Mark the Glock 9mm that she had kicked out of the woman's hand. She'd been using it to guard her. He popped the clip out, then cleared the chamber and set the 9mm down out of the woman's reach. The woman just watched them.

Mark looked at the woman, and in a calm, gentle voice said, "Where are Lisa and Maria?"

The woman said in a terrified shaky voice, "They're safe. We rescued them from the dogs."

"Are those your dogs?"

"If those were my dogs, why would they attack me?"

Mark said again in a calm gentle voice, "Where are Lisa and Maria?"

The woman said, "They are being treated as honored guests. I was sent to give you the message that they were safe. I was to warn you about the dogs. The dogs treed them and we rescued them. They are being treated a whole lot better than I am, that's for sure." She burst into tears.

Abby made a move with her head for them to move off and talk. Abby said, "She is absolutely terrified. I don't think she's a threat. I've been watching her eyes and body language while you questioned her and I don't think she meant us any harm. All she had on her besides the pistol was a pocket knife." Mark looked intently at Abby and then nodded his head.

Mark walked back over to the woman. "Why did you come here armed?" The woman said between sniffs, "With the world as it is, and the now the dogs acting like this, we don't go anywhere down here on the ground unarmed. It isn't safe out there anymore." Mark stood there and looked at her intently, trying to figure out what she meant by, 'Down here on the ground.'

He turned to Eric and Abby. "Untie her." Abby stepped forward and pulled a knife out a cut through the plastic strip she had wrapped around her wrists. The woman rubbed circulation back into her hands. Abby pulled the blanket up a little and cut the plastic strip that was around her ankles and then covered her back up and stepped back. Mark told Chris and Ryan to put the rifles away. Through all of this, Amanda had stayed back and watched from behind the chair she was hiding behind. Mark said, "My name is Mark, this is Abby, and that's Eric over there. What's your name?"

"Kathy."

"We should apologize for our behavior. We've seen how people are now, and it's not good to trust just anyone. Now Kathy, will you please tell us about Lisa and Maria?" He was trying hard to remain calm. They had scared this poor woman so badly that she'd fainted. He wasn't sure how he should feel about that, but, they had reason to be cautious.

Kathy took a deep breath. They were acting normal now. Should she trust them not to go insane again? She took another deep breath and then reached for the coffee cup the blonde man had set there. She could still see the red marks on her wrists that the plastic had left. Her hands was shaking. "We are the tree people. Our families have been coming up here for around thirty years. It started out as a Robinson Crusoe thing with a few of our parents and grandparents. They had a blast making tree houses and staying up here for vacations and holidays. Then it turned into a kind of club when people found out what they had done and wanted to join and make a tree house. Some of us had come up for hunting season when the changes happened. There are twenty-one of us. Our older members stayed home this year. We don't know what happened to them. We keep expecting them to show up here, but so far no one has shown up." Tears welled up in her eyes and spilled down her cheeks. She used a tissue from the box on the coffee table to wipe them away., "We've run cables all over the forest and we travel on the cables with a pulley that clips to a harness. It is totally safe. We've been watching you guys ever since you showed up here. We saw you leave and then come back. We thought that was strange. Anyway, a few days ago, these dogs showed up and we didn't think anything about it. We live and travel above ground, so what goes on down here really doesn't have anything to do with us. We saw the two women take off into the woods and we followed them from a distance to see what they were up to. The two women climbed trees to get away from the dogs after they attacked them. They killed a few of them, but it wasn't easy. The dogs were trying to climb the trees to get to them. Our leader is Jeff. He was with us when we saw what happened. He sent Clark with a couple of harnesses so he could bring them to the main tree house where they would be safe. He asked me to get my mountain bike out of storage and let you all know that the women were safe and warn you about the dogs. We bypassed the dogs, I got my bike, and hit the road to bring you the message. The dogs jumped out of the woods at me on my way here. You know the rest." She took another sip of coffee and waited to hear what they would say.

Eric felt really bad about treating this poor woman like he had, but he'd been scared at the time thinking someone had hurt Lisa and Maria. He looked at Kathy. "I want to apologize for treating you so badly and scaring you. I was scared someone had kidnapped them again and were torturing them."

Kathy's eyes got big. They had actually been kidnapped and tortured before. Wow. She asked Abby, "Can I have my pants back now?"

Abby smiled at her. "Sure. Come with me." She walked over and picked up Kathy's pants, shoes and socks. Kathy stood up and wrapped the blanket around her. "Come this way." She followed Abby down the hall to the downstairs bathroom.

Eric and Mark looked at each other. Mark said, "Don't, Eric. We didn't know. We did the best we could in the situation. There was no way to know she was friendly. She had a loaded pistol in her hand."

Just then the women came back into the room. Kathy was still wearing the blanket but had put her socks and shoes on. Abby said, "We have to sew these before she can wear them." The men nodded. Abby went to get the sewing kit.

Mark said, "I'm sorry we overreacted, but we have children to protect. We take that job seriously. Not long ago, Ryan over there," he pointed to Ryan, "was kidnapped right out of this yard and held at gunpoint."

"I heard some of our people talking about something like that, but I never got any details. I did see and smell the fire, though."

Amanda had waited long enough to find out where Lisa and Maria were at. She had been hiding behind the chair, just as Abby had told her. She ran up to Abby, grabbed her leg, and peeked around it at Kathy. "Is Lisa okay? Is Maria okay?" Tears welled up in her eyes and started running down her cheeks. "They should be here with me, but that mean old Mark sent them away and now they're never coming back." She turned and ran for the stairs, crying loudly. "Just like my real mommy. She left and never came back. Lisa and Maria are never coming back." She raced up the stairs, stumbling.

Kathy called out to the child, "They're fine. They will be back." The little girl was long gone by this time. They heard a door slam upstairs. The adults looked at one another. Abby handed Kathy the sewing kit and said, "You start sewing on that side; I'll start on this end. We'll get done a lot faster that way."

Kathy had been watching them throughout the child's outburst. That must be Eric's daughter. Either Lisa or Maria must be her stepmother. Mark must be married to the other one, because both of them reacted like their spouses had been in danger. The kid standing by Mark must be his son, because he had darker hair and looked a little like Mark. The older boy must be Eric's son, he was blond like Eric, and so was the little girl. Both those boys were worried and were trying not to show it. Oh well, there were no single men here. She sighed, then thought maybe that was a good thing. The tree people had some single women and it would have been a contest for the women trying to outdo each other to get a boyfriend. Boy, some of their single men were going to be greatly disappointed to find out these women were taken, too. They had been speculating for awhile now. The guys thought the women were pretty and admired them for learning to shoot. She smiled and started to sew up her pants.

Eric decided he would go with Kathy to their camp. The dogs had left about an hour ago. Eric was carrying the AK-47. Kathy said they only had a couple of miles to go to get to the prearranged meeting place. Someone would be there in the lookout. Then they'd be traveling from tree to tree. They'd bring her bike with them. She came the long way around before, because her bike had been in storage. She made better time riding the whole way on the bike than carrying the bike with her from tree to tree. She was riding the bike while Eric walked alongside her. They started to hear a distant clanking sound, a little like metal hitting on metal. They looked at each other in puzzlement. It was getting closer whatever it was. Eric whispered to her, "We have to get off the road. Something isn't right."

Kathy jumped off the bike and they walked into the woods. Eric found a spot with a downed tree and some branches up on a rise. He quickly arranged them so they could hide the bike and still see the road clearly. The sound was coming closer. They started to hear other noises; a clop-clop like sounds and something was creaking like leather. They looked at each other and then back at the road. It took about fifteen minutes of waiting before all was revealed.

They were stunned speechless. Eric shut his eyes and looked again, thinking he couldn't have seen what he thought. The scene still looked the same. There were seven men on horseback, traveling down the road towards Redding. That wasn't what made Eric shut his eyes and look again. What made him do that was all seven men were dressed like Roman soldiers. They all wore long red capes that billowed out behind them in the wind. They had metal helmets, metal breast plates, metal shields, swords, crossbows, long pikes and were wearing leather clothes and gauntlets. They looked like they just stepped out of a time warp or a movie set. Eric thought, *Only in California could this happen. Yup, only in California. Nobody was going to believe this.* He was seeing it and didn't believe it himself. He whispered, "Mutant Roman Zombies."

Chapter 21

Survival Snaring Made Easy

"He can best avoid a snare who knows how to set one."

Publilius Syrus

A barn owl landed in the oak tree near Michael's bedroom window. A sparrow had been nesting in the tree and flew off, racing for its life. The owl took off in hot pursuit to capture its evening meal. As the owl closed the distance between them, the sparrow, in a panic to get away, took a hard right turn and smacked into the side of the house with a loud thump, falling onto the porch roof. The owl set its wings to swoop in and pick up the unconscious sparrow. The owl flew past a couple of windows and landed on the porch roof. Its sharp claws made scratching sounds on the shingles as it walked closer to the sparrow. It bent its head down and picked up the sparrow in its beak. All of a sudden, there were loud noises and glass was flying all over the place. The owl took off, leaving behind the sparrow and its evening meal. In its thoughts was the equivalent of *crazy humans.*

Michael was leaning against the end of bed, looking at the window, crying. He whimpered in misery, "Leave me alone. No more death. Don't warn me of no more death. I can't stand it. Go away. Just leave me alone. Please, just leave me alone." He sobbed so hard he couldn't seem to get a breath into his lungs. His vision blurred from the tears. He sank down and sat on the floor. He was shaking like a leaf. The moon was full and shone brightly up in the sky, making the shadows seem darker and larger than normal.

Jane had just entered the hallway when she heard the shots; they sounded like they were coming from Michael's room. Her heart leaped into her throat and she raced down the hallway, drawing her 9mm pistol out of the holster on her hip. Joe raced down the hallway right behind her holding his AR-15 in his hands. She was surprised he had moved so fast. They got to Michael's bedroom door and exchanged a look. Joe stepped to the right side of the door while Jane took the left side and got down on one knee. They hugged the wall, staying out of the way of the door. They both held their weapons tightly, determined and ready to face whatever or whoever was in Michael's room. Joe reached his hand over and flung the door wide open. Both of them quickly peeked around the doorway into the room as their hearts thumped loudly in their ears with fear for Michael. Jane prayed silently, 'Please let him be all right.'

Preston and Amy exchanged a look. The man on the right said, "I said drop those guns right now." He gestured with his rifle. Preston and Amy dropped their weapons. "Step back." Preston and Amy took a step back. The man on the right gestured to his friend to take care of the rifles. The man on the left picked up each gun and threw them into the bushes out of sight. "Turn around and start walking." Preston and Amy did as they were told. "We're going over to the house. When we get there, you're going to get us all inside. Then we'll take care of business."

Preston was pissed. They had just cleaned those guns after dinner while they talked about the events of the day; now they would be filled with dirt and leaves. These guys were morons. How stupid could they be? They hadn't patted them down for more guns, nor had they made them take off all the other weapons they had on them, like knives. Well, that was good. Now, he would watch them and be ready to make a move at the first opportunity. They were amateurs, no doubt about it. They weren't trained and wouldn't know how to get what they wanted. They probably thought they had it all figured out in some vague plan. If they had the guns, then they were in total control of everything. They mistakenly thought they were the ones with all the power. Well, it would be the last mistake they made, either way this turned out. If they got lucky and took him out, he was going to make sure he took them both with him. He would do his best to make sure they didn't harm Amy. He hoped Amy would be ready to move when the time came. He knew she paid very close attention to everything Joe and he had told her about different situations, so he was pretty confident that she wouldn't stand there and be a target. She wasn't the type to be a bystander. She'd do something. He was watching the guy on his side out of the corner of his eye. The guy on his side was next to him but back a little ways. He would have to take him out first. The moron was walking too close to him. Just like he thought. These two were definitely amateurs and morons. Preston almost felt like laughing out loud. Since Preston and Amy had complied, they were dropping their guard around them. They were watching the house more intently than the two of them. That was a big mistake. Too bad they wouldn't live long enough to learn from it.

Amy knew that Preston wouldn't lead these two guys to the house and get them inside so they could hurt Michael, Jane and Joe. He'd make some sort of a move long before they got there. She tried to keep her eye on the guy walking behind her and slightly off to the right and keep watch on Preston for when he made a move. Her mind was racing at top speed, going through different scenarios so she could help Preston. She watched the guy on her right more intently and noticed that he didn't always keep his rifle trained on her. The rifle was pointed vaguely in her direction most of the time. Amy had excellent night vision and saw this clearly. She also noticed that the guy held his rifle loosely in his hands. That was not very smart. Joe and Preston had showed her over and over again what could happen if you didn't keep a firm grip on your weapon and keep control of the situation. They had showed her how easily things could go south. She had found herself lying on the ground with her own weapon pointed at her many times during training. She decided on a plan of action. She thought through it again and hoped like hell it worked. She slowly inched her left hand over to one of the pockets on her pants. She reached inside and pulled out the container, keeping it cupped in her hand out of sight. She worked it around until it was facing the right way. She just held it in her left hand and waited for Preston to make his move.

The quiet of the night was shattered. It sounded like a major battle was going on. Multiple shots were fired and the sound of breaking glass was heard coming from the direction of the house. The man on Preston's side stopped and looked intently in the direction of the house, turning his gun from Preston to the house. Preston thought, *nice going, Joe.* He turned to the man on his left and let out a primal warrior yell, pulling out his razor sharp knife from the sheath on his belt. With his left hand, he grabbed the rifle and yanked down on the barrel. The man grabbed the rifle with both hands and tried to pull it back up, giving out a startled little yelp. He left his throat wide open. The knife sliced across the man's throat in a wicked quick flash, cutting all the way through to his spine. Blood spurted out in streams in time with the man's pulse, covering everything between the two men and beyond. Preston whipped around to handle the other guy and saw he was on his knees on the ground, whimpering and rubbing his face. Amy was standing there holding the man's rifle on him, ready to fire if he gave her any trouble.

When the gunshots started, Amy was watching the man on her right. All of his attention was on what was happening at the house. She stepped back and knocked the gun down with her right hand. She swung her left hand up to the man's face and pushed down on the top of the container, making sure to keep it away from her face as she did this. The man immediately dropped the gun and put his hands over his eyes and fell down to his knees, whimpering and cussing. Amy quickly reached down and grabbed the rifle and stepped back, aiming it one handed at him. She slipped the container back into her pocket and held the rifle up, covering him. She gave Preston a quick glance and saw he was standing there looking at her and the other guy was on the ground and blood was everywhere. She looked back at the man just as he lunged toward her; she pulled the trigger twice, hitting him in the chest at almost point blank range. He fell to the ground.

Before either Preston or Amy was able to say anything, they both felt their radios vibrate on their belts. They looked at each other and then both reached for the radios. They set them to vibrate mode when they wanted to remain silent so they didn't to give their positions away. Preston answered his first. "This is Delta one." Amy flipped the answer button and then clicked it back over to vibrate. She would be able to hear what was said on Preston's radio. They had changed their call signs because Michael was having a hard time remembering who was who. Joe was Bravo one and Jane was Bravo two. Preston was Delta one and Amy was Delta two. Michael was still one five.

Preston said. "That was great timing Joe, thanks. How did you know?"

"How did I know what? Explain." Preston did.

"Need any help?" Joe's voice crackled through the radio.

Preston smiled. "Negative, Bravo Team. We handled it."

"When's your ETA?"

"Four minutes, Delta one out."

"Bravo one out."

Preston looked at Amy. "Are you all right?"

"Of course."

He shook his head at her. "Nice going. Did you hit him with your pepper spray?"

"Yup, I did. It worked just like they said, too. The guy at the military surplus store said I should buy the police grade because it worked better to bring an attacker down. He was right."

He laughed. "You never used it before?"

She shook her head no. "I could never get anyone to attack me so I could try it out."

He really laughed at her now. He stepped over the body on the ground and pulled her close. "Yup, you're the one for me." He kissed her. He was very relieved she was okay.

She smiled at him and then sobered up. "I really didn't want to have to kill him, but he decided my course of action the moment he went for the rifle."

Preston looked at her. "Sometimes we just don't have much of a chance to change the outcome no matter how hard we try. It always comes down to you or him."

He just held her for a few moments and then she said, "We had better go see what they were shooting at. You need a shower. You have blood all over your back."

She raised one eyebrow. "This is advice coming from a lunatic ax murderer covered in blood?"

He looked down at himself. "Knife killer babe, not ax murderer." He put his hands up in a pleading manner. "It was self-defense, your honor. Honest."

She smiled and tilted her head to one side, evaluating him and then raised one eyebrow. "Likely story. That's what they all say."

He laughed. "We'll head over as soon as we find our rifles." He picked up the two rifles and he patted the bodies down for more weapons. Not finding any, they walked back along the trail and found the spot where their rifles had been tossed into the bushes. They pulled their flashlights out and started looking. Amy found her rifle just about the time Preston found his. He got pissed all over again.

There was dirt and leaves stuck to it. He brushed it off, muttering about incompetent people, making Amy laugh. They smiled as they walked over to the house. They both knew this could have ended with them being injured or killed. They were glad to be alive and unharmed.

When they almost reached the kitchen door, Preston called on the radio, "Delta one and two at the back door."

Joe said, "Roger that."

Joe and Jane were already sitting at the table waiting for them. Amy sighed and said, "Is this day ever going to end? Or are we going to be stuck replaying over and over like the movie, *Groundhog Day*? Except we just keep killing people over and over again." Jane looked at her strangely.

Joe chuckled. "That's an interesting perspective. I sure hope to hell it isn't something like that. We'd run out of bullets for sure then."

Amy said, "Not necessarily. We could always keep killing them with their own guns and use up their ammo instead of ours."

Joe and Preston laughed. "That's the way to think," said Joe.

Preston said, "She's my girlfriend and she got three deer in one day and didn't even waste one bullet or arrow, either."

After a few minutes Jane said, "Now, would you mind telling me why you two looked like some mad scientists conducting bloody experiments?" They told had what happened to them.

"You got lucky," said Joe.

Preston said, "I know."

"You two are staying here tonight," Jane said. "It may not be safe out there. We can all do a sweep of the property tomorrow and make sure no one is left. I'm glad you two are okay."

Amy said, "The guy at the military surplus store that sold me the pepper spray talked me into buying it to use until I could afford a gun and learn how to shoot. He told me it wasn't safe for anyone to be walking around without anything to defend themselves with. I wish I could tell him someday that he was right and to thank him for his advice."

They sat in silence for a few minutes, lost in their own thoughts. Preston said, "We should talk to Michael about what happened. He was really so scared he was shooting at shadows? I'm not sure what we should say, but we should help him through this somehow."

Joe nodded. "I need your help fixing that window tonight, too."

"No problem."

Jane stood up. "I'll go get Michael."

Amy followed her. "I'll come, too, and talk to him." The women went down the hall to Jane and Joe's bedroom. Jane opened the door and Michael was lying on the bed. He sat up. "I'm in trouble, aren't I? I swear the Mothman was out there again. I know you don't believe me, but it's true."

Amy sat on the bed next to him and hugged him. "Michael, it's okay. We'll talk about this. But first, I want you to remember just one thing, okay?"

He looked at her. "Okay. What?"

"You probably saved Preston's and my life tonight. Sometimes things happen for a reason. We may not understand why until later, and sometimes we never figure it out, but this time it saved our lives. I want to thank you for that."

He looked at her with a puzzled expression. "Maybe the Mothman was trying to tell me that you and Preston was in trouble and he scared me on purpose so I could help you both."

Amy hugged him. "Maybe."

When they were back in the kitchen after the men and Michael went to fix his window. Jane looked hard at Amy. "Are you really all right?"

Amy sighed. "This has been a real nightmare of a day. I really didn't want to kill that man tonight. I would have let him go home to his family. There has been enough killing today. But he didn't give me a choice. I'm confused. I just don't understand why he didn't take the gift I was trying to give him."

Jane reached over and rubbed Amy's back in sympathy. "We may never be able to figure out why he did what he did. Maybe he was judging your actions like he would his own. They both came here intending to kill us. He might not have recognized that you weren't going to kill him. There hadn't been enough time for you to make your intentions clear and he forced the issued. You can't blame yourself for this."

Amy sighed again. "It's not so much that I blame myself as it is an inability to understand why he would force me to kill him. I guess the issue I'm trying to deal with is what the hell is the matter with people? Isn't the world crazy enough? Why do they have to bring this on themselves?"

"No one seems to be thinking things through anymore. Everyone is just reacting. They aren't considering their actions or how others may react. I think people are still in shock."

Amy said with a hard voice, "I wish they would get their heads on straight and realize that we're not just some stupid people that they can do whatever they want to. There will be consequences. Didn't what happened today prove that to them already?" Jane didn't say anything, she just continued to rub Amy's back to comfort her. There really wasn't anything she could say.

Preston and Amy slept in the bedroom Joan's had been using. Amy lay in bed with Preston's arms around her, thinking about how horrible this day had been.

Preston finally said, "I feel the wheels turning in your head. You're thinking too much. You need sleep. Think about it tomorrow when your emotions are more under control."

"I can't help it. I keep thinking, is this what life is going to be like?"

Preston kissed her temple. "Yeah, this is pretty much what life will be like. But, remember, each situation will be different, and we'll face them one at a time together. You aren't alone anymore, Amy. I wish I could make the world a better place for you, but I can't. I wish we didn't have to face more days like today."

Amy snuggled closer. "It helps that you understand what I'm feeling; you don't make me feel bad for it. I'm so glad I have you, Preston. I wouldn't have made it this far without you."

"I'm the lucky one," he said. "I have you; don't underestimate yourself. You are a survivor. You are a warrior at heart. You learn very fast and apply what you learn to everything."

Amy sighed contentedly. "Thank you. You always make me laugh and smile. Don't ever stop." Preston promised.

In the morning after breakfast, Joe had them out doing a sweep through the whole property to make sure no one was still around. Michael reluctantly carried the .22 rifle. He went with Joe and Jane. They searched everything; no one was around. Michael spent a few minutes at his mother's grave site and then they returned to the house. Preston and Amy stopped at the trailer to get the wood stove burning and make sure none of the pipes had frozen. They all met back at the house. Joe said he was moving the motion detectors out a little farther and putting the last few out, too, so they could cover the area more thoroughly. The men said they were going to do that then move the two bodies over with the others from the day before, so family could come and collect them. Amy said she'd go with them to provide another rifle in case things got out of hand. They weren't going to take any more chances. Those people had proven twice now that they couldn't be trusted.

Joe and Preston got the bikes from the barn and loaded the two bodies on the boards. Amy walked ahead of them and off to the left, so everyone would have a clear area to fire if necessary. They didn't encounter anyone. On the way back, Amy walked behind them, backwards, most of the way.

Joe said, "I hope this doesn't turn into a never-ending feud like the Hatfields and the McCoys."

Preston didn't say anything for a minute. "We should have listened to Joan; she said they all needed to be killed. Then Danny boy wouldn't have been alive to rile everyone else up. By not listening, we caused her death and everything else that happened since then."

Joe shook his head. "We didn't know anyone would believe him. We made the best decision we could at the time."

Preston's face got tight and he clenched his jaws in determination. He turned to look at Joe with cold, steely eyes. "But we know better for next time. Believe me, this chaos is far from over."

Amy said softly but clearly, "We'll be ready." Joe sighed.

They returned to the house. The men went out to chop wood. Jane had spent the time talking to Michael about shooting the man that killed his mother. She told Amy when she came into the kitchen. Amy went to talk to Michael and see how he was doing too. Amy walked into the living room. Michael was sitting in a chair, staring out the window. "What are you looking at?"

"Just watching to make sure no one else comes to hurt us."

Amy patted his shoulder. "I doubt anyone will come back today. They have a lot of bodies to deal with out there. I think they're learning not to mess with us, because when they do, we give them back a lot of bodies."

Michael looked up at her. "Why do they hate us and keep trying to hurt us?"

Amy sighed and thought for a moment. "I really don't know. At first it was because they believed what Dan said about us. Now I think they just hate us and blame us for everything bad in their lives."

"Do you think they'll be back?"

"I hope not. But these people aren't in their right minds. They still don't understand that we live in a different world now. We need to work together to get through this, but they haven't figured that out yet."

Michael said, "I don't want to have to kill anyone again."

Amy hugged him. "That choice isn't up to us. The choice belongs to them.."

Michael sighed "I miss my mom."

"I know. I do, too. But, if she was here, she would be on us for sitting around talking and looking out the window when there is a lot of work to get done before the snow comes. You know what she'd say."

Michael smiled. "Daylight is a-wasting."

Amy laughed. "Yup. That's exactly what she'd say and make us feel like bums for sitting around."

Michael stood up. "I better go stack the wood. I don't want her to think I'm a lazy bum."

Amy smiled. "It's okay to take a break now and then. But we better get busy, because Thanksgiving is almost here and the snow won't be far behind. Joe wants all the wood done before the snow starts."

Michael said, "I won't forget." He went to get this coat, hat and gloves.

Amy stood there for a while, looking out the window. Jane walked in. "Are you okay? Michael went out to stack wood. Do you think he should be doing that right now?"

Amy said, "I think it will be the best thing for him. If he sits around, he'll probably just brood. That won't accomplish anything except to make him feel worse. He was sitting here keeping watch."

Jane sighed and shook her head. "This world is just so screwed up. We have children watching out for people who want to hurt us and knowing the reality of what they can do."

Amy looked at her seriously. "We have no choice. Those out there made sure of that. If you need to blow off steam about it, get mad at them. They brought the fight to us. We tried to be merciful and look where it got us. Joan is dead. I tried to let that man go last night, and he forced the issue and caused his own death. They're all stark raving mad. The whole world has gone crazy. I think the sooner we accept that reality, the better off we'll be."

Jane looked startled. "We can't let that make us like them."

"No, that isn't what I mean. I mean they're reacting crazily to everything that happens. We need to accept that fact and be ready for whatever crazy thing they do, because they will do something else. Count on it. Until they can think straight and realize we all need each other to survive. Until that times comes, I don't think we can get through to them."

Jane looked out the window with a worried expression. "You're probably right."

"But life goes on no matter what. Don't let this depress you. We'll do the very best we can. But nothing will ever be the same again. We have to accept that reality. And the fact that everything that happens also affects the children and the way they think."

"You're right. What they do out there does affect all of us, including the children."

About 2:00 pm Amy brought the men some coffee and Michael a glass of lemonade. The men sat on a stump and took a break. "Jane sent me down to the basement to bring up more coffee beans," Amy said. "Wow, do you have a lot of coffee beans stored. I asked Jane why you have so many and she said to ask you. So, how come you have so much coffee?"

Preston burst out laughing and Joe got a very embarrassed look on his face. Preston finally managed between chuckles, "You want to tell her or do you want me to?"

Joe shook his head. "Go ahead, Mr. Big Mouth. I'm surprised you haven't told her already."

Preston kept chuckling. "Well, you see Mr. Wheeler and Dealer here who always says that 'I can get anything we need' ran into a bit of a problem. We had an Army buddy that was selling green coffee beans. Joe told him I wanted the best price I could get on them. Well, the best price was for a pallet full. Joe thought it was a pallet of five hundred pounds. That the pallet was ten bags, weighing fifty pounds each. So, Joe here orders a full pallet." He had to stop because he was laughing so hard.

Amy and Michael said, "What's so funny about that?"

He finally got himself under control and pointed to Joe. "You will have to finish telling them."

Joe looked even more embarrassed. "Well, ahh, the pallet showed up when Mr. Big Mouth was up for a visit. It was a semi-truck with a lift gate to unload the bags of coffee beans."

Preston, chuckling, said, "Go on. Tell them the rest of the story."

"It wasn't that funny."

"Yes it was." Preston turned back to Amy. "He was going around bragging to everyone that he got fifty pound bags of coffee beans for one hundred dollars each. He told everyone that he had five hundred pounds of Columbian Supreme coffee beans coming. But, that wasn't what he really ordered. He ordered a pallet and got a semi-truck full of twenty-five hundred pounds of coffee beans for a total of five thousand dollars."

"Shut up Preston. Jane was ready to shoot me over that one."

You couldn't pay that," Amy said.

"No, I couldn't. So, I called up my Army friend and said, 'I told you I only wanted ten bags.' My friend said, 'That isn't what you told me. You said you wanted 10, and they ship per pallet, and that is what you got: 10 pallets.'"

"Anyways, Mr. Wheeler and Dealer here agreed to buy twenty bags so we have a half ton of coffee beans." Preston started laughing again.

"Your boyfriend agreed to buy half of them, and it saved me from getting shot by Jane."

Preston smiled. "If you could only have seen the look on Jane's face when it happened. It was really something. I don't think I've ever seen her so mad before."

Joe smiled, too. "She could have fried eggs just by looking at them that day." They both started laughing.

Michael looked at the men with a puzzled expression "That's like what, a million cups of coffee?" Everyone laughed.

Preston gasped out, "It's just twenty-seven years' worth." Preston was holding his side.

Joe said gruffly, "Enough of this. Its time to get back to work."

Amy gathered up the cups and glass and went back inside the house. She told Jane she'd found out about the semi-truck full of coffee beans.

Jane burst out laughing. "I thought for sure I'd end up divorced or in jail for murder that day. Lucky for Joe, Preston agreed to pay for half."

Later in the afternoon, Jane asked Amy, "Can you get those snares of yours and set them up for a raccoon? When I was in the barn a little while ago, I saw some scratches on the chicken coop. This happened before, and it took us awhile to shoot the raccoon responsible. They run along the beams in the barn."

"Sure. We can take care of that problem right now. I'll run over to the trailer and get what I need. I'll use the medium-sized snares. While I'm gone, can you get a can of tuna and empty it? Just leave a little in the bottom of the can. We'll use that as bait." When she got back, both women went over to the chicken coop and looked around. Amy saw the digging in the dirt and the scratches where the raccoon had tried to get in. She saw the beams and realized how easy it would be for the raccoons to climb down. They got a ladder and Amy climbed up and looked for the best place to put the two medium snares. She explained to Jane what she was doing and why. It felt really good to share her knowledge. She set one snare in the center of the beam on the left side of the ladder. She used rebar wire to hold the snare at the correct height. She nailed it to the bottom of the beam with a couple of sixteen-penny nails and bent them over. This would hold the snare swivel. She made a six inch loop just wide enough to cover the beam so the raccoon couldn't get around it. She turned to the right side and set another snare the same way. Amy said, "That should work. Now we'll put the bait out." Jane handed her the empty can of tuna fish and she placed it in the middle between the two snares. The can of tuna still had some pieces and juice in the bottom. Amy climbed down and they put the ladder away.

As they walked back to the house Jane said, "I think it's better to handle the raccoon problem this way. If we tell the two trigger-happy men about it, half the barn will be shot up. Did you notice the patches on the walls?"

"Yes."

"That's what happened last time. It sounded like world war three."

Amy laughed. "We'll check the snares in the morning. We don't have to tell them anything. We'll just surprise them if we catch one."

Before they all sat down to dinner, they had a long talk with Michael about the last couple of days. They had noticed his reluctance to shoot the .22 at practice that afternoon. He did fine once he got going, but to hesitate in a battle would leave him vulnerable and none of them wanted to lose Michael. They also talked to him about killing the man that shot his mother again. The adults realized that this was going to take some time for Michael to come to terms with. He was still very confused and missed his mother a lot. They told him to come and talk to them whenever he needed to. They weren't sure how to handle this situation. It wasn't like there was a book that explained how to help a child deal with this. They just did the best they could. They moved the conversation on to talk about the watches. They were starting the watches again that night after dinner. Michael insisted on taking his watch so he wouldn't be a lazy bum. They all agreed to let him; he was very set on doing his best for their safety. He was told that if he saw any kind of trouble, to just radio immediately and they would be there to help. Michael would take the first watch until 10:00 pm, then Jane would have the 10:00 pm to 2:00 am shift. Joe would take the 2:00 am to 6:00 am shift. They'd do this for one week, and then they would switch with Amy taking the 10:00 pm to 2:00 am shift and Preston taking the 2:00 am to 6:00 am shift. Whoever was not on the watch schedule that week would trade off with Michael, taking a 6:00 pm to 10:00 pm shift every third day to give him some time off. They were all happy with that schedule because it wouldn't leave anyone overtired. They were all pretty sure that this wasn't over yet. Plus, it kept Michael busy.

Early the next morning, Jane went into the barn to feed the chickens, and swinging from the beam was a huge raccoon. She ran back to the house. "We got a raccoon! It's huge! It really worked! Those snares are awesome."

Amy smiled excitedly. "That's great."

Jane warned her, "We have to be quiet about this. We can't let the men know until after we skin it. They'll just interfere with our learning to do this right. Michael will have a raccoon hat now, just like Davy Crockett."

"All right. We can do this on our own. I brought another book I got off eBay by that same Buckshot guy that wrote that book I gave you to read. I read about how to do it last night." She pulled the book out of a pocket on her pants leg. "This one is called *Buckshot's Modern Trapping Guide*. I marked the place you need to read. I'll get the kitchen cleaned up while you read and then we can do this." Jane picked up the book and turned to the page Amy indicated with a bookmark and started to read.

After Jane finished reading the part about skinning the raccoon, they talked about it for a while, and then headed excitedly over to the barn. It was hard to keep their steps looking normal because both of them wanted to get started. When they got to the barn, Amy and Jane looked around, making sure they hadn't attracted any unwanted attention. When Amy saw how big the raccoon was, she jumped in excitement and the women high fived each other and laughed. Jane said, "We make a great team. Thank God you're here. I would've killed Sharon by now for sure."

Amy said dryly, "It crossed my mind a few times, too." They both laughed. They looked at the raccoon and ran over the details of what needed to be done. "I only saw it being done on my *Buckshot's Animal Skinning* DVD. I haven't actually done it yet."

Jane smiled. "Well, after today, we'll both know how." They both smiled excitedly. They dragged the raccoon down from the snare. Amy used some strong twine on the back feet to hold it up on a four by four in the barn. She tied about twenty knots on each leg; it was a hell of a workout. The raccoon's legs were tapered, and it kept slipping to the ground. It was hard work getting that heavy thing up there so they could skin it. When they finally got it so it stayed like it was supposed to, Jane handed Amy her Mora Survival Knife.

Seeing the Mora Survival Knife in Jane's hand reminded Amy about the time when she had showed it to Preston. He looked at the sheath it came in and without even looking at the knife, he asked, "How much did you pay for it?" She told him it had cost her under twenty dollars. He had said, "Its junk. I'll give you one of mine to use. That wouldn't hold a good edge. It's a cheap piece of junk made with inferior steel."

Amy looked back at him indignantly. "How can you say that when you haven't even looked at it or tried it, or even found out what company made it?"

Preston had looked at her. "Amy, any knife worth having costs a lot more than twenty dollars."

She looked at him for a minute. "Bet me."

"No. That would be a sucker bet and not fair to you."

She rolled her eyes over his arrogance and attitude. "I'm serious. Bet me."

He looked at her and sighed. He shook his head. "Why are you being stubborn about this? I do know a bit more about knives than you."

"I bet you one week of watches that my knife is just as good as your knife, and will hold just as good or better edge than yours does."

He shook his head. "Amy, why are you doing this?"

"Come on Mr. Big Shot; I know about knives, bet me." He didn't say anything, just looked at her like she was being childish and foolish. "Fine. I'll have Joe try it out if you're too chicken to give my poor cheap knife a try."

"I can tell you right now that Joe won't even touch that cheap, inferior piece of junk. He's even fussier about his knives than I am."

"We'll see about that. I know for a fact that he'll take me up on my challenge. He isn't a chicken like you."

He looked deep into her eyes. "Amy, I will not take advantage of you. Agreeing to this challenge of yours will do just that. I can't do it to you. I care about you a lot." He reached out and kissed her. She sighed. When he put it like that, how could she possibly stay mad at him?

Later that day when she had showed it to Joe, he had said, "Wow, that's a Mora knife. I served with this guy that had a Mora knife. His uncle had used it in World War II. He gave it to him to use in the service, too, because it had served him well and stood up to the challenge. It was a really good knife. A lot of times when the rest of us were sitting around sharpening our knives at night, my buddy would be playing cards or resting, watching us like we were morons. We asked him once why he wasn't sharpening his knife and he'd say he didn't need to, because his knife still had a good, sharp edge. His uncle had paid two dollars for it back then. How much did you pay for this one?"

Amy said, "It cost me under twenty dollars."

"You should have bought ten or more. They hold up real nice. They can take a beating and stay sharp. I would have bought a lot of them if I found someone selling them. Where did you get it?"

Amy said, "From that Buckshot guy's website where I got the snares, DVDs and other equipment. He was selling them."

Joe sighed. "I wish I'd known. That sheath has a clasp on it to keep it from falling out or snagging on branches and brush and it will keep anyone from just grabbing your knife out of the sheath. That's always a good thing." During this conversation, Preston's mouth had hung open in shock.

Amy turned to him and said smugly, "See, I tried to tell you that my knife was good, but you wouldn't listen. I researched this before I bought it. This knife was made in Mora, Sweden and they've been making knives and swords for over three hundred years. They've been doing this since the1600s. They have their own secret steel formula, too. I'd say they were pretty experienced after all this time. If it was junk as you said, they would have been out of business centuries ago." Preston hadn't known what to say. Amy smiled and took the knife from Jane.

Amy turned to the raccoon and made a slice along the back leg. Then she did the same to the other leg. She pulled down on the skin; that part was kind of easy, but it was hard to keep a good grip because it was so greasy. It had a lot of fat between the flesh and its skin, making it hard to hold onto. Then the pelt got stuck and wouldn't pull down any farther. Amy looked and looked and couldn't find what the problem was. All she could see was thick white fat everywhere. She looked over at Jane."It's stuck. What should I do now?"

Jane looked inside the book and read a little. "You should cut it in the middle. That should be okay to do without ruining the hide." Amy did that and pulled the skin down a little more.

"Now I have to cut around the butt hole. Oh, this is sick." Jane laughed and agreed. When Amy had finished pulling the skin about halfway down the tail, she said, "Hand me the two screw drivers."

Jane smiled. "Why? Does it have a loose screw you need to fix?"

Amy laughed. "No, that's silly. It will help me get the skin off the tail."

Jane handed her the two screwdrivers. "When you said we needed two of them, I grabbed a Phillips head and a flat head. I wasn't sure which kind to use. When I read about this part in the book, I wasn't really sure what you're supposed to do with them."

Amy took them from Jane. "That's why I got *Buckshot's Skinning DVD*. In the DVD, he shows you what he was talking about in the book. Now, I understand how to do this even though I've never done it before."

Preston walked over to the barn to get a file for sharpening the ax and glanced into the main part of the barn. He saw what the women were doing. He ran back and got Joe and Michael so they could watch, too. This was going to be more fun than watching a comedy routine. The men and Michael crowded around the back window to watch the show.

Amy slipped the two screwdrivers in place on the tail. "You pull up on the tailbone as I pull down and the tailbone will pop out. Ready?"

"Okay. Are you sure about this?"

"Yes. I saw that guy do it on the DVD. It looked easy enough."

"Well, okay." Jane grabbed the tailbone and Amy held a screwdriver in each hand, one on each side of the tailbone.

"Ready?"

"Yes." The two women pulled as hard as they could. The guys could see their faces turning red with the effort, but nothing was happening. Jane's hand slipped off the tail because of all the greasy fat. "Hold on a moment," said Jane. "I need to put gloves on so I can hold it better." She grabbed a pair of leather gloves. "Okay, let's try it again." It looked like they were playing a game of tug of war with the raccoon. The men and Michael couldn't see exactly what they were doing because Jane was standing in the way but they could clearly see both of their faces and how hard they were straining and pulling on the raccoon.

Joe said, "What in God's name are they doing?"

Preston chuckled happily. "I have no idea, but it's funny. Just look at them struggling and straining and wiggling around." Amy leaned back as far as she could with all of her weight, pulling as hard as she could with the screwdrivers against the skin on the tail. Jane was straining for all she was worth, when all of a sudden the tail popped out, free of the skin.

What happened next was like watching a cartoon. Jane was hanging on to the tail so tight that when it popped free of the skin, it swung straight at her and smashed her in the face with a hard wallop, spilling several pieces of white thick fat into her face and hair. She let go of it quickly and pushed it away from her. It swung straight over to Amy's side.

When the tailbone had popped out of the skin, Amy had fallen straight back on her butt with a hard plop on the ground. Her mouth opened in stunned surprised at her abrupt fall onto her backside. Just then, the raccoon swung straight at her and a piece of the white fat and fur flew into her mouth. She jumped up, spitting and screaming, "Oh my God, that tastes horrible!" She kept spitting and making faces as she jumped around in reaction to the disgusting taste in her mouth. The raccoon swung back towards Jane, and before she could grab it so it wouldn't hit her again, it smacked Amy on the side of the head and it knocked her off balance, sending her back down to the ground on her hands and knees.

The guys were laughing so hard they had tears running down their faces. Michael kept saying, "Do it again." They were pounding on the side of the barn wall in uncontrollable laughter. Amy stood up again. Jane and Amy looked over at the wall to see what was making all that noise and the raccoon swung around again and hit Amy in the back of the head this time. It wasn't swinging hard enough to make her fall again, but it left a lot of greasy fat globs in the back of her hair. The guys quickly jumped to the side of the window so the women couldn't see them. Amy ran over to the window and they took off running.

Joe said with a wide grin, "We better get back to work so they don't find out we watched that scene in there."

Amy looked out the window and couldn't see anything. She shrugged her shoulders and walked back to Jane and the raccoon. They finished skinning the rest of the raccoon. The men kept busting out laughing remembering what they had seen through the window. A little over an hour later, the men walked over to the barn and went inside. They burst out laughing really hard at the sight that met their eyes. Both women had chunks of white greasy fat stuck everywhere. It was all over their hair, face, hands and clothing.

Preston said, "Is this a new Skin So Soft™ product you're trying out or are you trying to making it from scratch?" The women had just finished getting the hide off. Both women had fire in their eyes.

Amy stomped over to Preston and tossed the raccoon hide at him. "All right, Mr. Know It All. You can flesh all the fat off this hide for that statement. We'll see how you like it then." She stomped off in a huff.

Jane looked like she had been through a battle as she marched up to Joe and Preston and said in a very tight voice, "You two had better figure this out real quick. Amy wants to make a coonskin hat for Michael, so you had better not screw this hide up." She turned around and marched over to Amy and they both stomped out of the barn. The men, seeing the fury in their eyes, waited until the door was closed before bursting out in hearty laughter once again.

Their sides were aching and they had tears in their eyes. Every time one of them would try to get control and stop laughing, the other one would mention something and it would start them both up again. It took a long time, but after a while, they finally managed to stop laughing and only chuckled every once in awhile.

Preston said, "Now, how are we going to do this?"

Joe smiled. "I seen this done once. You know that one-handed grass cutter you bought with the fifteen inch curved blade?" Preston nodded his head. "We can cut the handle off it and mount a wooden handle on each end so it looks like a draw knife. Then we'll use a half post to place the hide on and use the cutter blade to scrape the fat off." They set to work. They spent all afternoon making the handles for the cutter blade. Michael came in and joined them in the barn when he was done stacking wood. The men gave him the job of planing and sanding the half post.

While they were doing this, Jane came out and handed a bowl to Joe. He took the bowl in confusion. Jane said, "Save all the fat. I'll use it to make soap." She turned around and looked at the hide sitting on a bench. She shook her head and walked out of the barn.

When they were all done with the various chores to get the equipment ready, Joe picked up the hide and brought it over to the half post they had made into a skinning beam. He laid the pelt down flat and started to scrape the fat off. It was hard work. Both men couldn't believe the amount of fat that kept coming off that hide. Joe said, "They have a lot of fat on them. They are like little bears." It wasn't easy finding just the right amount of pressure to push on the cutting blade to scrape the hide. You couldn't push down too hard or you would cut a hole in the hide. He had already nicked the hide in a couple of places trying out the amount of pressure you needed to do it just right. It looked a lot easier than it was. When they could get a patch of fat going in the right direction, they could chase it all the way down to the end of the hide without too much trouble.

Preston was in charge of putting all the fat into the bowl and not letting any of it fall on the ground. It took well over an hour before it was done. Preston commented to Joe, "There is definitely a learning curve to this, but now that we're set up for it, each one should get a little easier to do." Joe agreed with him. His arms and back were tired from using the cutting blade and having to bend over the hide to flesh it. He straightened up with a wince. That was damn hard work. He had a new respect for all the old timers that had done this for a living. He thought about how many hides the Mountain Men in the past had fleshed and it made him think about them in a completely different way. He couldn't imagine doing twenty or more at one time. Mountain Men had dealt in hundreds of pelts at one time. He shook his head. It was amazing they survived. The men walked over to the house and asked the ladies to come outside. Joe held the fleshed raccoon skin up so the ladies could see it. The women had showered and looked much better. At least now they didn't look like they'd done battle in a fat factory. The women looked the pelt over and noticed the holes in the skin.

Joe said, "I did my best. It was the first time I ever fleshed an animal, you know." Both women looked at him. "Well, you didn't do too bad," Amy said, "and you're right, it was the first time you did this. But after this is tanned, it might not be good enough to make Michael a coonskin hat out of. We'll have to catch another raccoon and try it again, just to be sure."

Both Joe and Jane sighed at the thought of having to do this again. Jane said, "You did a good job for your first time, Joe." She patted his arm, reassuring him.

Preston stepped up and handed Jane the full bowl of fat. "Here you go. That's over five pounds of fat."

Jane smiled. "Thanks. I'll render the fat down tomorrow and get it ready to make a tray of soap. Come on. Dinner will be done in about an hour. We heated water for you two to take a shower." They had grease and white specks on them, too.

They all sat down for dinner. Michael was a little more like his old self, asking Amy and Jane questions about skinning the raccoon. He seemed really interested in the details. The women asked if he'd like to learn the next time they skinned something. He got a little excited about that. Before he realized it, he'd eaten everything on his plate and got seconds. The adults noticed this right away and were greatly relieved that his appetite was getting back to normal. He had worked hard today. Jane started teaching him how to stack the wood in the kitchen stove to keep the fire going for cooking. He was a fast learner. Jane and Amy had a long discussion while they were making dinner about his education. Amy suggested they might make a run into town sometime to see if they could find some school books, and maybe hit the library, if it was still standing, and get more books. He needed reading material as well as books for learning higher math and other subjects.

After Michael went up to the loft for his watch, the women approached the men about this. They weren't happy to hear they wanted to go into town. Jane said, "We do realize that the town people aren't happy with us, but Michael's education is very important. Joan felt strongly about this, too; you both know that." The men went into the den and discussed this while the women cleaned up the kitchen.

Everyone got a cup of coffee and sat down at the table. Joe said, "I'm sorry, but we just can't take a chance of going into town for anything right now. We agree that Michael's education is very important. But it wouldn't be a smart move to leave right now. Preston and I will help you educate him. We have a lot of books here, and we can keep him busy all winter learning things. We all have a lot of different skills, so we can teach him enough to keep his mind and body active. In the spring, we can reopen this discussion about getting schoolbooks. But as it stands right now, we just can't do it."

The women were a bit disappointed, but understood their reasoning. Amy said, "We thought it couldn't hurt to bring this up for discussion, because neither Jane nor I know the first thing about educating a child. I've never really given it much thought, either, and that isn't a good thing. People should've brought this subject up more when they were advising how to prepare for the end of the world. I know a lot of people home school their children, and have the materials to educate them, but what about the rest of us? How could we have even imagined we'd end up with concerns about educating a child? I, personally, never considered how important it is that we not lose basic skills like math, English, science, geography and history. We need to teach all the children about government, our constitution, and what it was supposed to mean. They need to know what went wrong so we don't repeat this again. Now we have a child to educate. What if we end up with more children to educate in the future?"

"I understand," said Preston. "Joe and I never considered this, either. In all of our preparedness discussions, we never once thought about this. We'll just have to do our best until we can get more guidance on how to do this. You're both right. We don't want to lose basic skills and end up in some kind of a dark age."

Jane said, "Okay. We'll bring this up again in the spring and see what we can do about a formal education for Michael. In the meantime, we'll just teach him what we can." They all nodded.

The men had to get rid of the raccoon carcass. They were going to leave it out a ways from the property for the other animals to eat. Amy had cut off the back legs to make a meal with. They weren't sure how to cook it, but she wanted to try and see if she could come up with a decent recipe so they could expand their meat choices. The men went out the back door. The women talked about spending a few hours in the afternoon going over some basic skills with Michael, and having him write book reports and essays in the evening before bed. Kind of like homework assignments. It would at least keep him from forgetting the skills he already had learned in school. They decided to look through the books they had and decide which ones they should use. They wanted to get started on this as soon as possible. They made a list of possible subjects and materials they could use, and then figured out how to make some sort of organized schedule.

Jane said, "I have a couple sets of encyclopedias we can use for geography and things." Amy was glad to hear that, she didn't remember a lot of details about some countries. But they were going to concentrate on the United States as much as possible, because that's what they knew the most about.

Joe and Preston walked quietly out to the barn and got the raccoon carcass. They both carried their AR-15s and had their .45s in a holster. They went up and talked with Michael for awhile and made sure he knew they were going out in the woods. They asked him to keep watch for intruders out their way and warn them by radio if he saw anything. These days it wasn't a question of if they would run into anyone out in the woods, it was more of a question of how many. With everything that had been happening, they weren't taking any chances. Both men knew the encounter with the townspeople was far from over. Soon their grief wouldn't be the strongest emotion guiding them. It would turn into anger and then they'd probably come back for revenge. What both men were concerned with was the sneak attacks. Those men that had come to hang Joan had found out what a direct confrontation had brought them; people would now change tactics. The two men that had ambushed Preston and Amy had figured out that a direct approach wouldn't work, so they used a sneak attack to accomplish what they wanted. They both stayed alert for any sounds and movement. Preston was a bit jumpy; he kept stopping and looking around with his night vision goggles. He'd been ambushed once and didn't want to repeat the experience. Joe had been teasing him about it, too, which didn't help. It was embarrassing enough without Joe making a big deal about it every time he turned around.

They were just about at the spot they had decided to leave the carcass when both of their radios started to vibrate on their belts. Both men went to reach for their radios when Preston saw two guys standing by a tree. A voice called out, "If you're throwing that animal away, can we please have it to eat?"

Preston stood still for a moment in stunned surprise. Joe and Preston turned their rifles towards them quickly. Joe could barely make them out in the dark under the tree. One of the men held his hand up and said, "Whoa, Mister. We didn't mean any harm. My friend was just asking a question."

Joe, being overly cautious, asked, "How many are there in your party?" The man just blinked at them.

"Answer quick now," said Preston. "How many are you traveling with?" Joe and Preston kept alert for any others that might be around. These two could just be a decoy.

The man said, "Ahh, um, what do you mean traveling with and what party? What do you mean?"

"Be very sure of your answers, because both of your lives depend on it," said Joe.

Both strangers looked confused. The taller one said, "Sorry to have bothered you. We don't want any trouble. We'll just be on our way." Both men headed away from Joe and Preston, going down the trail. Both men kept glancing back as they quickened their pace to get away. They looked like they expected Joe and Preston to turn into psychos any second. Joe and Preston shared a look. They trailed after the guys, looking around for any more people in the darkened woods. After about five minutes when they didn't see anyone else or hear anything out of the ordinary, Joe gestured with his head and Preston nodded. They quickened their pace and got in front of the two men.

They stepped out onto the trail in front of the two guys. Both men jumped in surprise. Joe said, "You two can have the raccoon carcass." He set it down on the grass by the trail and stepped back.

"Where are you guys from?" asked Preston.

The shorter man said, "We're from the Twin Cities."

"How did you get out here?"

The taller man said, "We walked. We thought it would be a lot safer out here."

"What's it like in the Twin Cities?" asked Joe.

"A nightmare," the smaller man said. "Your worst nightmare. It's like everybody went nuts. People tried to get out of the city. The gangs hunted them down. There was robbing, raping and murder everywhere you looked. All the people who were unarmed or pacifists changed their minds in a hurry, I can tell you that. They sure wished that they owned a gun. The cities have turned into a big turf war between rival gangs. When we got out of there, the gangs were trying to control all the supplies in the cities. There were a lot of huge firefights with innocent people just trying to get food. They were mowed down. Dead bodies were all over the place. At night there were bonfires and the screams of people being tortured and raped by the gangs. Then they'd be murdered." The man shuddered. The other man looked sick to his stomach. Joe and Preston shook their heads in sorrow. They weren't surprised, just sickened.

Preston said, "Where are your wives and families?"

"I'm divorced and don't have any kids," said the taller man.

"I never got married," said the other.

"We used to come pheasant hunting around here. We decided to try to make it out here. It's a lot better than the craziness we left."

Joe said, "What about the government? Didn't they send any help to the cities?"

The smaller man laughed bitterly. "Are you kidding me? They sent soldiers to protect the food and to hell with the people in the cities. They were just as bad as the gangs. When we left, the soldiers and the gangs were fighting each other to get control of all the food. Who knows who will win? Neither side cares about the people. The soldiers didn't even try to stop the gangs from robbing, raping, or murdering anyone. You guys are so lucky to be out here. Do you know what happened?"

Joe said, "Ya, Homeland Security said it was a big nuke that took out our electrical grid and all electronic things were fried."

The taller man said, "Oh, that explains it."

Joe thought for a minute. "What did you guys do before this happened?"

The taller one said, "I was a machinist. Give me a lathe and I can make anything you need."

The shorter one said, "I worked construction. I was a foreman. I worked my way up the ladder learning all the different areas."

Preston looked at Joe, knowing what he was thinking. He nodded. Joe turned to the two men and said, "How much food do you two have to get through the winter?"

The taller man said, "Not much."

Joe shook his head in understanding. "Meet me here tomorrow around noon. We'll talk again." Joe and Preston disappeared into the woods in a blink of an eye. The two men stood there for a few minutes, in stunned disbelief. They kept looking around, expecting the men to pop back out at them. Joe and Preston watched them for a while and smiled at their reaction to their vanishing act. The two men finally turned around and headed off towards their camp. Joe and Preston followed along. At least, they thought they'd be heading back to where they camped. Either way, they wanted to know what they were up to. Turned out they did take the raccoon back to their camp. Joe and Preston observed them for about forty minutes as the men set their camp back up, cut the raccoon up into pieces, and cooked it over the fire. They ate hungrily. Joe and Preston left them to it.

When Joe and Preston got close to the barn, they called on the radio to let Michael know they were there. Michael sounded upset. "Where did you go? We've all been really worried because you two didn't answer your radios." Joe and Preston exchanged looks.

Amy's voice came out of the radio. "Are you both all right?"

Joe said, "That's affirmative, Delta Two. We'll be right there." The two men looked at each other and smiled. It was nice to know they had been missed and worried over. They went up to the loft to check on Michael and reassure him that they were fine. When they got up there, Amy was there, too.

She glared at them. "You had better have a very good reason for scaring us like that. If Jane or I did something like that, you two would have had a fit, so don't say 'we knew what we were doing and you shouldn't worry' because that won't be good enough. You both told Jane and me that we should always answer the radio, no matter what, just so everyone knows that we're okay. You said we all follow the same orders and rules. You both were out of communication for over an hour and a half. So, what happened to following those rules, gentlemen?"

Both men looked a bit sheepish. They had just turned off the radios and not given them another thought when they had vibrated. Amy stood there with her arms crossed, tapping her toe, waiting for a good explanation for their behavior. Neither man said a word. She marched to the door and then looked back. "That's what I thought." They heard her stomp down the stairs.

The two men looked at each other. Joe said conversationally, "Wow. She has a fiery temper. I think you're in trouble."

"She is beautiful when she's mad, isn't she?" Both men smiled.

Michael said, "Where did you and those other two guys go?"

"They escaped out of the city," said Joe. "It was really bad there. We're considering helping them to survive the winter."

Michael said, "You trust them?"

"No. We don't," said Preston. "They haven't earned our trust. We'll test them and see what they're made of before considering anything." Michael nodded.

Joe said, "We have to go talk to the women. We'll fill you in on anything that's decided, okay?"

"Okay."

Preston said, "Did anything else happen while we were gone?"

"No. Just Jane and Amy worrying about you."

The two men nodded and then Joe said, "We'll see you when your shift is over."

The men walked over to the house. "Jane is likely to shoot you over this."

Joe smiled. "Yeah, she has a fiery temper, too." Both men laughed quietly as they walked in the back door.

Jane and Amy were standing in the middle of the kitchen, looking at them. Jane said, "I don't see any wounds or blood. No, that couldn't be the reason you two didn't let us know what you were doing." She looked more intently at them. "Well, your fingers don't appear to be broken, either, although that situation might change drastically very soon. That couldn't be the reason you didn't tell us you were okay. So, if it wasn't any of those reasons, do you think that maybe you could fill us in on and why you didn't answer the radio and let us know what you two were doing?"

Joe calmly told them everything that happened. Jane was still shooting daggers. "And because of this, you couldn't call the tower or the house and let us know you were all right? You couldn't let us know about the two intruders? Amy and I had to hear about it from Michael. Do you know that you two had ten more minutes to return or Amy and I were going out to search for you?" Only then did the men notice that the women had tactical vests and equipment lying around. Joe and Preston exchanged an astonished look.

Preston said, "We're the ones experienced in these kinds of situations. We would let you know if we ran into trouble. We had everything under control."

"Right," said Jane. "Only you two can break the rules whenever you please. Is that it?"

Joe hastily broke in with, "Okay, we're sorry we didn't let you know what we were doing. We were concentrating on these two men at the time, and not the radios. We'll talk about that later. Right now we have a decision to make."

Jane said, "What is there to decide?"

"We need more people. We've talked about this before. We especially need help right now with the townspeople. We need more guns and more people to man the watches. Two more people would be a great help. They could also help chop wood and help us get ready for winter."

Preston said, "That's true, but they'll have to prove themselves first. We can't just let anyone in here. They have to be worthy. We'll be giving up our supplies to feed them." Joe nodded.

They all remained thoughtful for a while. Joe finally spoke. "I wish we could have found more people before this happened who understood. Then we would have had full fire teams already set up here."

Preston nodded. "Well, I guess we need to think about the negative side now."

"Well, Amy is young, attractive, and single," Joe pointed out. "That would cause trouble with you, Preston, if they made a play for her."

Preston said heatedly, "Amy is mine and they had better understand that right off the bat."

Amy raised her eyebrow, but didn't say anything. She wasn't feeling very kindly towards him at the moment. She was still mad over the radio incident and their arrogant attitude.

"Worst case scenario is that they wait for their chance to kill Preston and me to take over this retreat and you women."

Both women looked amused. Amy said, "That might be on their minds, but it would never happen for two reasons. First, Jane and I would kill them with our bare hands if necessary, and two, you two are too good to be taken unaware like that. They wouldn't live through the attempt." Joe and Preston looked amused now.

Preston said, "We need to make it clear to them they have to pass our tests before they'll even be considered for membership in our group. They will be part of our well-oiled machine or they're out. What should their first test be?"

Joe said, "Let's keep in mind that a full ticket to get into our group is one year's worth of food for everyone in their party and family, battle rifles for each member with one thousand rounds of ammo, a .22 rifle with five thousand rounds, and medical supplies. And of course they'll need clothing for all kinds of weather. Check them out tomorrow and see what you think of those two."

"All right."

The next day Preston and Amy got ready to meet the two men. Amy was going to provide cover from a distance with her rifle in case of trouble. They would never know she was there. They both wore camo face paint and fatigues. As they were dressing, Amy asked how come she had been accepted into the group and didn't have to be put through any tests like these two guys.

Preston looked at her. "I vouched for you. I brought you here. Besides, you've already proven that it was a very wise choice. You filled the freezers with enough meat for the whole winter and then some." Amy smiled at him.

"How will putting these two guys through tests make them prove themselves worthy of joining our group?"

Preston turned and looked at her seriously. "Inviting people to be here with us takes a lot of trust. They have to earn the right to be one of us. Trust, honor and duty are not just catchy phrases. Warlord gangs are forming all over now. For some reason, man is inherently evil and there is always some egomaniac that wants to control everyone else. They hate freedom and can't leave well enough alone. This spring we could very well be facing huge numbers of organized gangs. When that time comes we'll have to stand tall and fight. We won't have a choice. This isn't a game and there is no reset button. This is real life. We only get one try to survive or not. Those are our only choices. We already lost one person because we didn't train her properly. We won't make that mistake again. This is about training them and hardening them up for the coming challenges. Also, it will build loyalty. We helped them and trained them; no one else did. We'll push them hard during the day training them and make them stand watches at night. If they don't quit or get asked to leave for some reason, you'll have two more in your training sessions." Amy nodded in understanding.

They both walked quietly into the woods. Preston had already explained what he wanted Amy to do and how they would handle the situation. He explained what to look for and how to respond. They both had turned their radios to an unused channel so they wouldn't interfere with the other radios at the farmstead. Preston was going to lock down the send button on his radio so Amy could listen to what was being said. She had an ear set plugged into her radio so the other men wouldn't know what was being said was broadcast to someone else. They had tested this out earlier to make sure it worked. There were no telltale echoes or other noises to give this secret away. Preston and Amy walked separately in the woods about fifty yards apart; Amy stayed behind Preston off to the left, covering his back, as they scouted around to make sure the two men were alone. Amy had been working on this very thing in her training and had passed the tests that Joe and Preston had given her. She had learned to be one with the trees and bushes and loved this part of her training. She had learned to walk quietly and be very quiet and still so she could hide in plain sight. It was an awesome feeling to have mastered this skill. When they got close to the meeting spot, Amy found the tree stand and climbed up. She would be able to see the meeting and keep Preston in sight at all times. She quietly set up to observe them. She was using a bi-pod on the rifle for steadier shot placement. Plus, she would keep watch for any others that might approach the area. She watched Preston's approach through the Leopold Scope on the 22-250. He looked quite impressive and scary all at the same time, all decked out in camo clothes and face paint, holding his AR-15, with his .45 strapped to his side and the L.B.E. vest he was wearing. She was just as impressively decked out so she would blend into the woods. She had her hair tucked up inside a camo hat so she totally blended into her surroundings. Preston was sneaking along the side of the trail and would pop out and surprise the men again. She couldn't wait to see the look on the men's faces.

Preston stepped out of the woods onto the animal trail by the tree, startling the hell out of the two men. They jumped in surprise. Preston walked aggressively up to the two men and barked out orders like a drill sergeant. He demanded, "You two. What are your names?"

The taller one with dark brown hair said, "John. My name is John."

The shorter one, who had light brown long hair in a ponytail, said, "My name is Steve."

Preston said in a harsh drill sergeant voice, "John and Steve, you have a once in a lifetime opportunity. We have room for two more people at our farmstead. If you want to join us, we have some rules that will have to be observed. Do you understand what I've just said?"

Both men looked uncertain and a little scared but answered, "Yes."

Preston barked out, "You two will have to pass some tests to prove yourselves worthy of our time and attention. Do you understand?"

"Yes."

"If you prove worthy of our time and attention and learn what we teach you, you might be asked to join our homestead. Is that understood?"

Both men were now getting used to the way Preston was questioning them. "Yes."

"We promise you nothing but some food and a roof over your heads."

Before Preston could say anything else, both men yelled out, "Yes."

"Yes, what?"

John looked puzzled. Steve said in a questioning tone, "Yes, sir?"

Preston almost burst out laughing. "Do you understand we will provide some food and a roof over your heads and nothing else?"

"Yes."

"If you two thought you could come out here and be backpack survivalists, you are dead wrong. You'll both be dead before the end of January."

John said, "Why?"

And at the same time Steve, looking confused, said, "What's a backpack survivalist?"

Preston barked out at John, "Explain to your friend what a backpack survivalist is."

John did so and then asked Preston again, "Why do you think we would be dead by the end of January?"

"It is very simple. You haven't been surviving very well out here if you are already low on food in November. As the snow starts to fall and the temperature drops, you'll have to increase your calorie intake to stay warm and healthy. By January, you'll have to double your calorie intake to stay warm. You'd have to kill all the deer around here just to feed yourselves. But the deer, after being hunted so much, would simply turn nocturnal and you'd never see them to be able to hunt. Then you'd starve. You'd become desperate and probably attack our homestead for food because you'd be out of your minds with hunger and not thinking clearly. That'll only make you dead. Do you understand what I have just said?"

Both men thought about it for a few minutes then John said, "I see your point." He swallowed. "We've seen what desperate people do. Some people still tried to get food, even though they knew they'd be shot down anyway."

Steve said softly, "They were out of their minds with hunger. They would beg and when that didn't work, they'd still try to get to the food in the warehouses and get shot down."

Preston barked out, "You two had better think long and hard about this, because make no mistake, you will be shot if you attacked us in any way whatsoever. Do you understand what I just said?"

Both men looked uneasy. "Yes."

"None of us here wants to see that happen. But on the other hand, we will not hesitate to kill you if it becomes necessary. Did I make myself clear on these issues?"

"Yes."

Preston said not quite so harshly, "If you can't agree with any of this, it would be better if you two just cleared out right now and saved us all a lot of time and effort. Think about your answer before saying anything, because I will expect a promise and an oath from each of you, regardless of your choice."

John said hesitantly, "What kind of tests are you talking about?"

"First, I'll have to see your camp and equipment. Second, you'll need to tell me how much you two have eaten in the last week. Then I'll be able to judge what shape you're in and what test to give you first."

John and Steve looked at each other and shrugged their shoulders, realizing that they would gain nothing by refusing to show this man their camp and what little food and equipment they had. John said, "Our camp is this way." He pointed off to the northwest.

"Lead the way." John and Steve set off and Preston followed, keeping his eyes on the men.

He was confident that Amy would handle any others that might be around so he could concentrate. When they entered the camp, the men went over to their small nylon tent that had a tarp over it and showed Preston what food they had left; a small bag of rice that was a third full, and a container of oatmeal that had very little left. They next showed him their camping equipment, two hunting-style knives, one pocketknife and their shotguns. They had forty shells of different kinds. That was it.

Preston closed his eyes and thought, *this is pitiful, just plain pitiful.* Preston said in his best drill sergeant voice, "How much have you eaten this week?"

The men shrugged their shoulders, looking embarrassed. John said, "We've been rationing everything to make it last as long as possible. We've been hunting for deer, but haven't had any luck yet. Last night we ate really well. We cooked up the raccoon you gave us. We've been making a watery rice soup once a day. That's it." He looked down at the ground, waiting for the man's judgment.

Steve looked Preston in the eyes and said earnestly, "We will work really hard for food. We don't expect any handouts. We aren't that kind of people." Preston kind of liked this Steve guy. He at least understood the value of working for what you get and didn't expect or want a hand out. The rest remained to be seen.

Preston said firmly but not harshly, "Okay, your first test will be to break down this camp and move. Do you know where the farmstead is?"

John looked at him and nodded. "I think so. Is it the one that has that big red barn in the back?"

"Yes, it is."

Steve said, "We saw it one day from a distance when we were hunting. We stayed away, because we don't want any trouble from anyone."

"That was good thinking. Now break down your camp and leave no trace that this was ever a campsite or that anyone has been here. Don't take the same trail you were on when you saw the farmstead from a distance. Take a more direct approach. Once you are close to the farmstead, pick a location in the back where no one can see you from the road or trails. Make sure the location won't flood. Once you have the campsite set up, you are to make a hidey-hole. This hidey-hole will be like a covered foxhole that will blend into the surrounding area; it should look natural and not be seen by anyone because it blends into the surroundings. You'll both stand guard duty at night for six hours. One of you will take the shift from dark till midnight, and the other will take midnight till sun up. We will check up on you from time to time. If you fail to accomplish this task, you will be asked to leave this area and move on and not come back. Do you understand what to do?"

Both men looked at him kind of strangely but didn't say anything. Preston reached around and pulled off his small backpack and opened it up. He took out four MREs and tossed them on the ground. "Here is lunch and dinner. If you feel that you can't do what I've asked, then just move on and don't ever come back."

Preston turned to leave and John said, "That's kind of extreme, don't you think?"

Preston looked them both in the eyes. "In case you haven't noticed, the world is very extreme right now. There are those that train and learn to survive, and then there are those that die. I prefer to train, don't you?"

Chapter 22

Gray Wolves The Unknown Battles

"'Wolves In Russia' unmasks the Disneyesque view of wolves propagandized in the U.S."
By Will N. Graves, Published May 10th, 2007

Gayle was in the bedroom working on Junior's coat for Christmas. She went through the patterns that George Sr. had and decided to make Junior a capote-style coat like the mountain men had worn. Junior really admired the mountain men, so she decided she could make a change in the design of the pattern she'd been following. She didn't have enough time to make him a separate hat so the capote coat would help because it had a hood. She decided to use the beaver pelts for the coat, sleeves and hood. She would use raccoon fur for the cuffs and trim and use two buttons at the neck so it could be closed tight to keep the wind and snow out. She was also going to use buttons to close the coat instead of a waist tie like the pattern called for. With that settled, she set about using the leather punch to poke holes in the leather to make it easier to use on the old sewing machine. It was coming along nicely. She had measured him for height because the coat was going to come down just past his knees. It would be warm and probably last him for the rest of his life.

She needed something to line the coat with. She thought about using a wool blanket, but decided it would be too heavy and impractical. Then she remembered the three bolts of flannel cloth they'd found under the bed in the bedroom. It would be perfect. There was a dark navy color, a medium brown color and a dark forest green color to choose from. She decided on the dark green for Junior's and the medium brown for Clint's. With that, decided she got to work. It was almost Thanksgiving and she wanted to get it done so she'd have plenty of time to make Clint's coat, too. She laughed as she worked, thinking how Junior and Clint were speculating about what she was making. She'd overheard them talking; they thought she was making a shirt or pants or something like that. They were going to be really surprised on Christmas morning. She smiled as she worked.

Now that her arm didn't hurt so much anymore, she was able to spend several hours every day sewing on the coat. Junior and Clint were taking turns cooking while she was doing this. Plus, Junior and Clint had some projects of their own going on in the garage that they said was a secret, so she couldn't come out to the garage anymore unless she asked first. Who knew what they were doing out there? Clint said he'd start training them as soon as her arm healed up totally. She was excited about that, too. With the hellhounds taken care of, it was a little safer to go outside. She looked forward to being outside and learning to be able to take care of herself and not have to rely on Clint or Junior to save her. She liked the feeling when they had practiced reloading and covering each other when Clint was gone. It made her feel confident that maybe, just maybe, they would survive this insane world.

She looked over at the clock; it was almost dinnertime. She put the coat away in a box under the bed and straightened up to stretch the kinks out of her muscles. After dinner, they devoted time to relax. They played board games, cards, watched a movie, or just sat around talking, enjoying the companionship. Then they all worked the tanned hides for an hour or two. It is something she really looked forward to. She did the dishes every night because the men had been doing the cooking. It was only fair. They had settled into being a small group with common goals. Gayle and Junior kept trying to win the game *Risk*. Clint would use strategies that would take over their territories every time they played. They were determined to win against him and would discuss strategies to out-think him. It was fun. But the one game she was good at that surprised the guys was *Battleship*. She would win almost all the time. Junior's game was *Monopoly*. They all had competitions going to see who could outsmart the others.

The weather had settled down for a few days and Junior and Clint decided now would be the best time to go and get Marion's bones and put them into a wooden box they could bury in the spring. They got the snowshoes out and everything ready to go, then Junior came into the house and called Gayle out to the living room to talk.

Gayle came out of the bedroom. "What is it?" J

Junior took a deep breath. "Clint and I are going to go and get your mother and bring her back here in a wooden box. We'll bury her in the spring."

"Oh." She sat down on the couch and looked at him.

"We want to do this before the snow gets any deeper. We'll be gone all day. I left some soup on the stove you can heat up for lunch. I just wanted you to know that I hadn't forgotten I had promised to do this."

Gayle said softly, "Thank you. I do appreciate it."

"Are you all right with this?"

Gayle thought for a moment. "Yes, I am. I'm just a little surprised. But thank you for doing this."

He nodded. "You're welcome. Will you be all right here by yourself all day?"

She smiled at him. "Yes, I'll be fine. I'll be sewing, anyway. I'll keep an ear out for when you return to let you back inside." They walked over to the door and she stepped outside with him and waved to Clint. He was waiting on the trail. Gayle turned to Junior. "Did you pack enough food?"

"Yes, I packed three days' worth, just in case something happens to delay us. So, don't worry if we aren't back by dinnertime. We're planning on being back by then, but you never know." Gayle nodded in understanding.

Junior said, "We brought in a week's worth of wood so you won't have to worry about that. You shouldn't use your arm yet to carry things." They looked at each other for a few moments, then he kissed her., "We'll try to be back by dinnertime." He and Clint walked down the trail. Junior was pulling a wooden sled with wooden sides on it. There was a wooden box on the sled. She watched them until they were out of sight, then went back in and locked up tight. She got some coffee and thought about her mother for a while.

Clint and Junior walked briskly down the trail. It was a beautiful winter day. The sun was shining and the sky was crystal clear blue with just a few wispy clouds. They both wore sunglasses because of the reflection of the sun on the snow. Clint had mentioned that he wanted to stop at all the abandoned houses on their way and bring back anything that could be useful. Junior agreed it was a good idea. Clint wanted to grab all the medical supplies and medicine that he could find. Gayle's injury had shown him how important it was to be prepared. Gayle had mentioned that they should bring back all the paper, pens, and pencils they could find. What they had wouldn't last forever. Both men agreed it would be a good thing.

They had found quite a bit of copy paper for printers, several notebooks, and assorted stationary, along with various pens and pencils. Clint had taken off a large hand-cranked pencil sharpener from a wall with his Gerber Multitool to sharpen the pencils. They put them all into a canvas bag Junior had brought from the garage. Clint was collecting as many band-aids and other medical supplies and putting them in his backpack. He also kept an eye out for tools. One could never have too many tools. It made Junior smile, because his dad had a similar outlook.

Now came the hard part. They had to look for Marion's bones. They arrived at the place where Marion had died. They used shovels to dig into the snow. When they found a bone, they would examine it to make sure it was human before placing it in the box. The bones they weren't sure of went into the box, too. They had dug up a good-sized area. Both men knew there would be bones scattered around that they wouldn't be able to find. At least this would give Gayle the closure she was looking for. Junior wasn't going to mention that the dogs had reduced Marion to bare bones, either. There were just some things that she didn't need to know. Clint found her skull off to one side and placed it in the box. Junior uncovered the double barrel shotgun and placed it in the sled to bring back home. Junior said it was enough when they hadn't found another bone in awhile. They had gotten most of them. They refilled the holes with snow. Both men were silent on the way back to the house. It was almost dark when they arrived. Junior placed the box of bones outside by the garage and placed the sled in the garage. They had filled their backpacks that day. Junior knocked on the door; after a couple of minutes, they saw her look out the hole in the loft to make sure it was them. Junior waved. Gayle smiled at them. She opened the door and they went inside.

Junior handed her his backpack after taking out the food. "Here, this is for you." Gayle took the heavy pack and opened it up. "Wow. That's a lot of paper."

Junior grinned. "We brought what we could."

Clint handed her some more paper, then a small bag that was filled with pens and several unopened packages of pencils. She was about to ask if they had a pencil sharpener, but Clint was already handing her a large one. She smiled. "You read my mind."

He smiled back. "I thought this would come in handy."

"Thanks. This will do very nicely."

"I have another bag for you, too," Junior said. "Hang on." He went back to the door and brought her another bag. "I hope these fit. I did the best I could. I know you don't have a lot of clothes here, so I thought I'd see what I could get for you."

She looked in the bag and laughed. "Thanks." She pulled out a nice fleece bathrobe in light blue and some matching slippers. There was a new ski jacket in red and white in her size. Some nice warm socks and five warm fleece pullover tops in various colors. They had also grabbed several pairs of sweat pants. Junior had checked her size out last night. The clothes were a bit dusty, so she started a load of laundry.

When she came inside later she seemed fine and more settled than she had been. They played some cards and went to bed. The next morning, Junior was going through his Dad's desk, making room for some of the paper they had brought back, when he found a how-to manual with diagrams for the different systems in the house. Good old Dad had thought to write it out in case something happened to him. He studied it intensely. "Clint, come here and see what I found in my dad's desk." His dad had all the details of the whole house broken down into the different systems. The water pump was explained; the length of black plastic pipe in the well to the strainer to the check valve, halfway at fourteen feet below the check valve was a strainer to help keep dirt out of the pipe. The check valve helped keep the whole system primed. Next was the twelve volt pump that supplied the water from the holding tank; this was your water pressure for your house. Extra pipe, strainer, check valve, twelve volt pump and a rebuild kit for the pump.

Solar system was explained. The panels, the diodes in the panels, the charge controller, the golf cart batteries, the inverter that changed it to one ten current; but the house was set up both twelve volt and one ten current. The idea being you lose energy in the inverter so you ran as much as you could on twelve volts. A twelve volt fluorescent light worked awesome for lighting and the twelve volt pump that supplied the water for the house. A diesel generator was on standby to charge the batteries during the winter. The idea was; run it for one hour to charge the batteries and do your load of laundry. At the same time, get what you needed out of the freezer, etcetera. Brilliant set up with five 100 watt solar panels that supplied most of the power. Enough diesel was stored to run the generator for two years. Junior thought his dad had been really thinking to put this all together so well. The wood stove and the hot water system was listed with spare stovepipes. Also, stored was furnace cement gasket for the doors and other things they'd need to keep the systems running smoothly.

The manual showed the cabin was designed to be bulletproof. The pipe above the door was for spraying lye on people trying to break in. Junior thought, *I sure wish would have known about sooner. Like when the hellhounds were outside trying to get in.* The manual had a section on reloading. It had a list of everything. There was a step by step how-to with a complete break down of all the guns and cleaning supplies. Junior was fascinated by the details. Inspect the brass, re-size, trim, clean the pocket, new primer, powder, seating the bullet, measuring to keep it into spec. A big warning about following the powder charts and not to max out the powder over the limit or you cause gun failure, brass failures and jams. A complete list of trapping and snaring methods, with step by step directions covering all the animals in the area. It also had a list of reference books to read, like *Buckshot's Survival Trapping Guide* and DVDs to watch on trapping and snaring. Hunting was broken down into respecting the animals and only taking them in the fall and winter months. Leave them time to have their babies and replace the ones you took in the fall. A complete break down with maps covering fishing spots, trapping spots, beaver dams and hunting spots. Notes on how the deer act during the rut, how many does you should keep around, etcetera. A complete list of wild plants with pictures to ID them and a map of where they were. This covered everything from when to harvest to how to cook and prepare. Also, wild plants for medical purposes with the same details of the ones he found and how to prepare them. Salt was the weak spot living so far from the oceans, so two hundred pounds of iodized salt was stored, also a lot of canning salt. Junior was so thankful for having such an awesome dad to have provided for him so well. This was a man he never really appreciated until this very moment. *Thank God, for those with ears to hear,* he thought.

December came in with a storm. It snowed for three days straight. Three feet of snow was on the ground. For those people unlucky enough not have a wood stove, the struggle for survival became unbearable. It was hard work struggling through the snow cutting firewood with an ax, then hauling it back to their living space. Hard work like that required five thousand calories a day to keep the body warm and fit. With the food shortage and the brutal cold, it was losing battle for many people. Some just gave up and froze to death. Others moved into the basement and tried rigging up a wood stove to the chimney. Most were jury-rigged and the basement filled up with smoke. The knowledge of using only seasoned, dry wood was lost, and some folks struggled hard to try and make a fire with green firewood.

People were dying in droves. Some groups that had wood stoves and fuel tried to help as many people as they could, but their own survival was at stake, too. Their stores of food would not last long if they took in too many people. Some folks only let children in and the parents had to fend for themselves. It was time for hard decisions to be made all across America.

Junior and Gayle decided to go for a walk and do a little recon and see what and who was around them. After the brutal dog attacks, they were not too inclined to travel very far from home. A nice warm spell was happening; it refroze at night making a hard crust on top. Using snowshoes, they would be able to cover the ground quickly. They decided to do a six mile circle around the place. That should give a good feel for what's going on around them. They headed out with Gail carrying the SKS and Junior carrying the 12 gauge loaded with the first two shots of number six bird shot in case they jumped a snowshoe hare. Fresh meat really sounded great. They had no problem staying on top of the snow; it was a beautiful day outside. The black cap chickadees were out and the red squirrels were running around.

They walked out to the road first and checked for human traffic. No human tracks were seen, but a lone deer had traveled the road with coyote and wolf tracks following it. Junior pointed out a lot wolf tracks. It looked like a large pack. Junior said, "We need to start thinning them out. Every wolf we kill is forty to fifty more deer for us. Our survival is much more important than huge predators."

Junior decided he was not going to shoot any rabbits, even if they saw one. *Why advertise we are alive and well?* They walked back to a beaver dam and a small stream his dad had listed. He wanted to check to see how the area was fairing this winter. When they made it back to the stream, they saw human footsteps and a bloody trail. The trail was old and had been made sometime after last week's storm. Wolf tracks were following the human trail like sharks following a blood trail in water.

Gayle stopped and looked at Junior, her SKS in hand ready to shoot. She asked, "Dog pack?"

"Nope. Not a wild dog pack. Those are wolf tracks. Looks like a pack of ten or more."
Gayle was scared. "Should we head back?"

Junior thought about it for a few moments. He decided it was time to change out the number six bird shot. It wouldn't do much against a full grown hungry wolf. He wanted double aught buckshot. "We better follow this trail. This person might need our help." Gayle nodded in agreement.

They followed the trail to a lean-to, or what was left of a lean-to. There were broken human bones scattered around, a bloody AR-15 with a broken stock and a bloody knife. Junior thought, *It must have been a fierce battle.* "This person was surrounded by hungry wolves. They probably attacked at night. No doubt the wolves could see, but this poor person was defending themself shooting at shadows in the dark." Twenty-three empty brass casings shone in the sunlight. Junior picked up the the AR-15 and examined it. It had jammed. It looked like a double feed. The poor guy must have tried to use it like a club, then had to use his knife as a last ditch effort to save himself. There were five half-eaten wolf carcasses laying around. It must have been one hungry pack of wolves to attack like this.

As Junior was trying to piece together the events of the fight, Gayle was searching through what was left of the lean-to. She called out, "I found a journal."

Off in the distance, they heard a lone wolf howl. It hit Junior like a ton of bricks. "We have to go right now."

Gayle looked up, scared at the sound of his voice. "Why?"

"The wolves will be coming back to feed and we're the new threat; they'll attack us. Plus, they're now human killers and will look at us as a food source. Come on, let's beeline back home as quickly as we can. The wolves can run on top of the snow much faster then we can walk."

Gayle shoved the journal in a coat pocket. They headed out. "How far do you think we have to go?"

"About three miles. If we hurry and nothing goes wrong, we should be there in an hour or so."

It was too late. A lone wolf was already trailing them. As soon as the wolf spotted them, he let out a howl to tell his pack mates. Junior yelled, "Shoot him!" One hundred yards behind them was too far to shoot for the buckshot in the 12 gauge. Gayle spun around and fired three quick shots at the wolf. It turned and disappeared in the brush. "Come on, let go. Hurry." They heard a wolf howl on their right and another answered on their left. *Damn, we're in trouble,* Junior thought. Stupid, moronic people that wanted the wolf packs back in the lower forty-eight states had made surviving the end of the world much harder.

They headed out at a fast walk, keeping an eye out all around them for any movement in the woods. Junior didn't know a lot about wolves, but knew enough that they were in trouble.

We have to get to the open hill by the oak trees, Junior thought, *then we could see them coming. We have to get out of this swamp.* A mile later they broke through the cedar swamp. They could sense the pack was all around them, but they didn't see any of them. *They must still be full from eating that guy. But we're leaving a trail for them to follow us right to the cabin. Too late now to worry about that.* There were two miles to go. "Gayle, we're going to make it. We can see them coming now. My guess is they follow people back and attack at night. Once in the cabin, we'll be safe. If they get too close to the camp, the snares will quickly even the odds in our favor." They stopped.

"This truly is the end of the world. We have to fight crazy people, dog packs and now wolves. What's next, African lions?"

Junior laughed. "Maybe, if they escaped from the Zoo."

Cayle smacked his arm. "That is so not funny."

They saw quick glimpses of the wolves. They were smart, staying about two hundred yards away on either side. *They're waiting for darkness,* Junior thought. Without a camp, the only choice would be trying to survive in a tree. With the frigid cold, one would freeze to death pretty fast.

They made it back to home with no real problems. Once they were safely locked inside, they sat down at the table to read the journal. Clint joined them. They told him what happened. "Tell us what the journal says," said Junior.

Gayle started reading. "The bones we found was a guy named Scott Bailey. He was from Green Bay. He had set up a camp in early October after arriving here on foot. His ideas were sound. He hunted small game with a .22 Ruger Mark11 with a seven inch barrel. His AR -15 was his only other gun. He tried dead falls and homemade snares. From his journal, the dead falls were next to useless. His wire snares caught red squirrels, but the little squirrels were just barely bigger then a chipmunk. It took four to make a meal. He had one four pound sack of rice that was used up in October. The only thing that helped through November was the bouillon cubes he had brought. He had spotted our place and thought about coming and asking for help, but was afraid he would be shot on sight.

The last week of November started the battle with the wolves. He managed to shoot a small deer. When he was gutting it, the wolf pack appeared. Having read the popular propaganda on wolves the animal rights groups had put out, he believed they would not attack him. The smell of fresh blood brought the wolves in. He gutted the deer, leaving behind the heart and liver that he truly wanted to save for himself, but was hoping would satisfy the wolves, along with the rest of the gut pile. He dragged the deer back to his camp. The wolves quickly cleaned up the gut pile and followed him. He skinned the deer out and hung the meat up in the trees. He kept a big fire that night and could see the pack of eleven wolves. Their glowing red eyes were watching him. It was eerie. They would leave and howl in the distance. He didn't get any sleep that night. He checked his trap line of homemade snares in the morning. The wolves had cleaned out all his catches of red squirrels. The light wire was easily snapped in the powerful wolf jaws. Not only did he lose the caught animal, but the snare itself was ruined. The long winter nights were hard to get through. He dreaded each night as it approached. The wolves came back, testing him and his defenses.

He came to realize his only choice was to fight them. He had to kill this pack off for his very survival. That night when the wolves came in, he started his battle. He was able to only kill one wolf before the rest disappeared. Shooting at night was very hard. He wasted too much ammo trying to get a second wolf. He thought he might have wounded one. The wolves did not return for the next three nights and he thought he'd driven them off for good. With no other food except the deer, his meat supply was going quickly. He figured with luck he might be able to stretch through December. He again talked about coming to our place.

Junior interrupted. "I sure wish he would have. We would have helped him."

Gayle said, "I know." She continued reading. "He was out cutting firewood and the ax glanced off the tree, hitting him in the right leg, leaving a nasty wound. He made it back to camp. The wolves followed his blood trail. They circled him and waited for him to fall asleep, then they attacked. He fought them off the first night by killing another one. Silent ghost killers, he called them. His wound got infected. He could no longer walk. He tried to cut out the infection and cauterize the wound. That was his last entry."

Junior said, "It makes sense. The wolves would sense his weakness and they would wait and watch him get weaker and weaker by the day. Then they charged. He must have had one last adrenaline rush and fought like the devil himself. Who knows? If his gun hadn't jammed, he might have survived. We would have found him in time. Just three days earlier." Junior shook his head. "We have to kill this pack just like the dogs. They have a taste for human blood now. Who knows how many they've killed or found dead and ate this winter? There are five left in the pack now and they must all die, especially before the female can have pups. That's all we need, a wolf den near us."

Gayle said, "I wish he would have came up and maybe left a note to meet."

"Too late now. We have to get this damn wolf pack cleaned out now." He thought, *Well, the snares worked on the dogs, so they should work on the wolves, too.* He figured the kill snares; the seven foot long camlock should work. He told Gayle and Clint about how utterly stupid people were about the woods and how the wolves were destructive by nature. He remembered his dad talking about a pack of wolves that killed one hundred twenty sheep in a single night in Dillon, Montana. He also mentioned that ranchers in Michigan state had been driven out of business by the wolves. The profit margin was too thin raising cattle to allow wolves to eat for free. The MIDNR did the usual thing and tried to blame every other animal except the wolves. His Dad had books on wolves and did lot of research. He said the wolves were wiped out for the health and safety of the public. He had found all kinds of cases of wolves killing people. He read some references out of the books to Gayle and Clint.

Iowa Citizen, The 12-09-1892 The 3-year-old child of Peter Lyons was killed and partially devoured by wolves near Kingfisher.

Manitoba Daily Free Press 1-13-1891 woman and child attacked, 1 child died.

An Invasion by Wolves. WICHITA, Kansas. Jan. 12.— Wolves are invading the western border counties of Kansas in great packs in search of food, A short distance from Liberal this morning, Mrs. Jarvey and her child were attacked by a pack of wolves a few steps from their home, and while the woman escaped with slight injuries, the child was carried some distance and mangled so horribly that it cannot recover. The men about the place finally beat off the savage beasts.

Bismarck Daily Tribune 10-31-1891 1 child October 30th Mr. Jenson's 4-year-old son died and his daughter injured. The wolves had attacked several people along the road. But on Oct 30th a dreaded day for the parents, they heard the terrifying screams of their young children. The father, armed with a shotgun, raced to help. He was too late. His 4-year-old son was torn to pieces and dead. The pack was now working on his 6-year-old daughter; he was able to drive them off, saving her. She had several scratches and bites on her arms from fighting off the vicious wolves.

Janesville Gazette, The 11-19-1891 3 documented wolf killed children.

St Paul, Minnesota Three children killed and ate by wolves. These are the large vicious gray wolves from Northern Minnesota. The pack was seen fighting over the remains of the 3 children. The children had wandered into the woods by the Twin Cities. No one knows the final terror these poor children felt as the savage beast ripped the life out of them. Men, taking a shortcut, found the wolves and left to get help. Upon returning with a number of armed men, the beasts would not leave until two were shot. Once driven off, the grisly scene of the three partial eaten children were found. A huge hunting party was formed to drive the beast away.

Waterloo Courier 02-27-1889 A Sad Fate 2 children killed and eaten in Minnesota.

Feb. 21. —The Tribune's special from White Earth, Minn., that news from a creditable source reached there that a few days since, in sparsely settled country around Aitken, two white children returning home late in the afternoon from school were attacked and completely devoured by ravenous timber wolves, a few scattered bones and shreds of clothing remaining as horrible testimony of the children's fate.

Waterloo Courier 6-26-1889 2 boys devoured by wolves

Devoured by Wolves, KANSAS CITY. Mo., June IS.—Two children, aged 10 and 11

Indiana Democrat, The 11-24-1887 2 children killed.

Two children, while returning home from school near High Prairie, Minnesota, last Friday, were attacked by wolves and before assistance could reach them they were devoured. The wolves attacked some men in the same vicinity and it was only after a long fight were they able to escape.

St Joseph Herald Saturday, January 15, 1870 Saint Joseph, Michigan 1 child A lost child which had strayed from his home in Elysian, Waseca county, Minn., was afterward found to have been killed and partially eaten by wolves.

1864 Marion County, Arkansas. 3 dead a woman and 2 children - Their awful doom and destruction can never be accurately described, but never let us imagine the heart rending shrieks and dying moans of the unfortunate family. This mixed with the noise made by the wolves snapping and snarling was certainly awful. The story was told by those who discovered their remains that the evidence on the ground showed that the woman made a desperate effort to defend herself and her children. She had fought the wolves over the space of half an acre. Stones, clubs and chunks of dead wood that she had used in resisting the attack lay scattered on the downtrodden grass. They were the only weapons of defense and she made desperate use of them to the finish. Probably she had beaten them back and kept them at bay for some time before the ravenous beasts finally overcome her and gloated in the blood of the helpless human creatures. Their fate was simply awful. Who can imagine the consternation and terror of these poor beings when they were attacked by the vicious and hungry pack, and with loud screams and hard struggles were forced to yield their lives in such a horrible manner. Their destruction is sad to reflect upon.

Racine Weekly Journal 2-11 1857 Ravenous wolves. Two children left home to visit a neighbor two miles away.

They were never heard of again. It is believed the wolves ate them.

Junior's dad's research of wolves had found out all kinds of things, like the Native Americans had hunted, trapped and poisoned wolves in their dens. Some tribes believed it was a delicacy to eat wolf pups. They would kill the mother, then pull the pups out to eat. Certain tribes used poison to protect their sacred burial grounds; other tribes trapped the wolves for the fur. The Eskimo found that wolf fur was the perfect hood trim to protect the lungs during sub-zero weather. They believe the Great Spirit provides for the people through the animals.

After reading all this they were convinced it was time to clean these wolves out for good. At least in their area. It would take most of the winter before they caught the last five in the human killing pack. Skill was needed and the wolves quickly learned to spot the snares after one of the pack was caught.

Chapter 23

Trading With Junk Silver

"All government, indeed every human benefit and enjoyment, every virtue and every prudent act, is founded on compromise and barter."

Edmund Burke

Kathy looked at Eric, waiting for him to explain. Eric just motioned to stay silent. They watched the Roman soldiers ride past and out of sight. Kathy went to say something, but some instinct warned Eric that they had to be quiet. Very quiet. He motioned for her again to stay silent. Eric listened and heard the horses stop. He leaned over and whispered in Kathy's ear, "Stay here and be silent. I'm going to sneak over and see what they're up to. I'll be back." Kathy tried to grab him to have him explain, but he was already silently moving out of sight among the trees. She sighed and settled down to wait.

Eric slowly made his way among the trees to get closer to the Roman soldiers. He hid behind a tree and watched the men talking as they sat on the horses. He couldn't make out what they were saying. He saw the man up front say something and then he pulled an object out from under his cape and put it to his mouth. He wondered if the man was eating something. Then he heard a lot of noise in the brush and several dogs ran through the woods towards the men. The dogs stopped and wagged their tails, as if they were waiting for something. Two other men opened large leather bags and threw items towards the dogs, who grabbed them and hungrily ate them. It took a few moments for Eric to register that what the men had thrown to the dogs were human arms and legs. Shivers of revulsion ran through Eric. *Oh my God, that's just down right evil,* he thought. It registered that the man had to have used a dog whistle to call the dogs. After several minutes, the two men closed the bags. Then the Romans continued down the road. The dogs ran back into the woods ahead of them. Eric was in shock. These men had trained the dogs to what? Tree people? Kathy said that had happened to Lisa and Maria. *No, that's not quite right. Oh my God, they trained the dogs to kill and eat people.* Thank God Lisa and Maria was smart enough to climb trees to get away.

Eric silently made his way back to Kathy. He wasn't sure how to tell her what he'd seen. He finally decided not to mention it to her. The whole thing made him sick. The Roman soldiers had moved on; if they kept going, Eric wouldn't tell anyone but Mark about what he'd seen. No use in grossing everyone out.

Kathy whispered, "What were they doing?"

"Nothing. They stopped briefly and then went on. Let's get going." This time Eric had them walking on the side of the road so they could get into the trees fast if it became necessary.

They reached the meeting spot. They stood there for a few moments, then Kathy said, "I'm going to hook my bike up so it can be raised first." She grabbed one of the two hooks that had been quietly lowered from the trees. Eric was startled; he hadn't heard or seen anything until he saw Kathy reaching upward. She clipped the hook closed around the handlebars, and then put the other hook under the seat. The bike started to rise into the tree. After a few moments, a rope ladder unwound from above. Kathy motioned for him to climb up. Eric grabbed it and started to climb and Kathy held the rope steady for him. He wasn't as experienced at climbing the rope ladders as the rest of them were and needed a steadying hand.

Eric reached a platform and three armed men were waiting for them. They weren't pointing their rifles at him, but were ready if there was any trouble. Kathy quickly came up the ladder and joined them. She pulled the rope ladder up and secured it on a hook. She turned to Eric. "This is Bill, Jim and Brandon. Guys, this is Eric." The men all nodded at each other.

Bill said, "Did you have any trouble?"

Kathy glanced at Eric. "We'll talk about it later."

Brandon eyed her. "What happened to your jeans?"

"The dogs attacked me," said Kathy. "I'll tell everyone about it when we're gathered together." The guys nodded.

Jim said to Eric, "We travel by pulleys and wear a harness and go from tree to tree by cables." He demonstrated the technique for Eric. When he got back to the tree, he said, "It's safe to use. Just follow us and do what we do, okay?" Eric nodded his head. Jim handed him a harness and Eric tightened it snugly. Jim took off again and Eric watched what he did. Bill handed him a pulley contraption and motioned for him to go ahead. It was fun.

A while later they reached a large platform that had many wooden walkways leading off in different directions. He followed Jim and Brandon, and when they crossed over to a different walkway, he could see some of the tree houses that they lived in. It was pretty great, actually. He was gawking all around, wondering how they did everything. As they walked by some of the houses, he could see inside and noticed the hammocks and plastic chairs, tables and things inside. The windows had a one-piece shutter that swung down and latched into place on the frame of the tree house. The shutters had a window in the middle of them to let the light inside. Most had curtains on them and he couldn't see inside. The tree houses were varied in size. They walked by a large building that was stretched between several trees.

Jim turned. "That's our main tree house." It was closed up tight and he couldn't see inside. They kept walking. They came to a large platform that had three rope ladders; one was in the middle and the others were on the ends of the platform going in different directions. Jim grabbed the one in the middle and let it fall to the ground. He climbed down. Eric was confused. He thought they were going to meet Lisa and Maria in the tree houses. He noticed they were close to the mountain. It would provide some shelter from the wind and weather. Eric noticed a small waterfall on the left side of the mountain. He saw a steam ran down the mountain between the rocks. You couldn't see it until you were up here, because the rocks hid it from sight. *That must be where they get their water*, Eric thought.

Brandon said, "Go ahead, climb down."

Eric looked at Brandon. "Where are Lisa and Maria?"

Brandon smiled. "In our winter place. The tree houses are only used in the warmer months, once it turns cold we move to our winter place."

"Where is that?"

"Not too far. Go ahead and climb down; we'll show you." Eric looked around one last time and thought it couldn't be too far because they were almost touching the mountain right here. He climbed down. Jim held the rope at the bottom to keep it steady. The others quickly followed. Brandon grabbed the rope and pulled on another piece of rope that was swinging freely on the side; the rope ladder lifted back up into the tree. He climbed on a branch, secured the rope, and tied it to a stake that was nailed into the tree. *You'd never see it. You had to know where it was. That was amazing.*

Jim said, "Follow me."

They were going around several large boulders and rocks that had fallen off the mountain. All of a sudden, Jim disappeared. It startled Eric. He looked around and couldn't see him anywhere. Brandon smiled. "Look." He pointed to a large bunch of rocks of various sizes that had very large boulders in the back next to the mountain. Eric was still puzzled. Brandon walked in front of him and then stepped around a very large boulder and disappeared.

Eric walked over and peered around the boulder; Jim and Brandon were waiting for him. He shook his head. "It doesn't look like there was enough room to walk back here from the front. It actually looks like the rocks are up against the mountain."

Jim laughed. "Exactly. This is our winter home." Eric looked around and didn't see anything but rocks. Jim waved him forward. Jim bent over and picked up a rock and knocked on the side of the mountain with it. Eric wondered if Jim had lost his mind. A peephole opened up in the rock, then closed, startling Eric. Then an area about the size of a door opened up in the side of a mountain. Jim stepped inside and they followed right behind. Eric looked around in total amazement. There were about twenty-five to thirty small log cabins built along one side of the cavern of various sizes. Some looked to be about ten feet by twelve feet. It looked like a little community.

There was a large barrel-type wood stove on the other side with pipes running up into the rock overhead and across to the cabins. In the middle was an area of wooden tables and chairs; behind that was a play area for children. It had a wooden jungle gym with some swings and tunnels and a slide. On the left side of the wood stove was a large kitchen area. On the other side were four small rooms with doors. It was really warm in here. Eric took his hat and gloves off, looking around, trying to spot Lisa and Maria. Lisa and Maria turned to see the new arrival. So many people had come to introduce themselves that there was no way to remember everyone's names. And the single men had let it be known that they were interested. Lisa wasn't sure what she felt about the tree people watching them at the cabin. That must be why sometimes she felt as if they were being watched. It kind of gave her a creepy feeling.

When she saw Eric, she jumped up and ran over to him and hugged him. She whispered in his ear, "Pretend I'm your girlfriend. There are single guys here, and by the way they're acting, I expect them to get down on bended knee and ask for our hands in marriage. I told them you were my boyfriend."

Eric looked at her. He kissed her softly and said loud enough that everyone could hear, "I'm so glad you're all right. I've been so worried about you." He hugged her tight and then left his arm around her waist and turned to Maria. "I'm glad you're all right, too. Mark has been worried sick about you." Maria smiled in appreciation. The men here were nice, but they came on kind of strong. They all acted like they'd known them for a long time. It was a bit disconcerting at how familiar they acted. She wasn't sure if she should categorize them as peeping toms or not, since they'd been watching the cabin. Not that they could have seen anything like a normal peeping tom. They always kept the shutters, blinds, and heavy, insulated curtains shut. It was the thought of them watching what they did outside that gave her an uneasy feeling.

Jeff introduced himself and asked Eric to have a seat. He had someone bring Eric a cup of fresh coffee. Eric sat next to Lisa with Maria across the table from the tree people. Jeff sat down at the table and Kathy joined them. More people came into the room now that the word had spread that Eric and Kathy had arrived. Jeff asked Kathy about her journey to the cabin and she told them everything that happened. Eric looked a little uncomfortable, but still felt a bit justified in his actions. Everyone looked at Eric, waiting for an explanation.

Eric explained his side. Jeff nodded his head in understanding, even though he thought they overreacted over one lone female. Eric said, "You haven't seen the things we have. You don't understand how bad things are. I can't even express how awful and dangerous it is out there. And now we have these dog packs to deal with." He sighed and looked sad. Lisa squeezed his arm in understanding. Maria nodded; she understood what it was like out there. These tree people had been isolated.

Jeff said, "I have been looking for an opportunity to meet all of you. Maybe we could establish some kind of a barter system. Do you have enough supplies to get through the winter?"

Eric said cautiously, "We're doing all right."

Jeff nodded and thought Eric was going to be difficult to put at ease; understandable with some of the things he'd been through. Lisa and Maria had been very reserved at first, too. He decided to change tactics. "Eric, would you like a tour of our little community here?"

Eric smiled. "I'd really like to see how you manage to live in a cave."

Jeff grinned. "Okay. Come with me and I'll show you around." Eric joined him. Lisa and Maria exchanged a look. Both of them knew what Jeff was up to. He had made it quite plain that they all needed each other. Jeff wanted to get to know everyone in the area and start some kind of barter or trade system so everyone would be able to survive. He was worried about all of the people in his group and their survivability. He told both women that if they all didn't work together, none of them would be able to survive very long, but if they worked toward a common community goal, it might increase everyone's chances. The women were undecided. The question deserved a lot of thought and discussion first before they could decide. Lisa wondered what the benefits and drawbacks were.

As Jeff showed Eric around the cave, he explained some of his ideas. Eric listened intently to what he said and what he didn't. Jeff showed how they were set up in the cave. They had solar panels for electricity with battery storage for power. They used the wood stove to heat the cave, cook with and to make hot water. Above the large wood stove was a thirty gallon water tank. How they heated the water was really ingenious. They ran a six-inch vent pipe through the end of the water tank. It was welded with a quarter inch thick pipe on the top and bottom. All the heat that would normally be lost going up the vent was being used to heat the water in the tank. The four rooms on the left side of the stove had toilets, sinks and shower stalls. They had a septic system set up so the toilets could be flushed. They had cold running water, but not hot. To take a shower you used a five gallon bucket and filled it half with hot water from the tank and then half with cold water. They had a hose that clamped on the bottom with a sprayer handle on it. The filled bucket fit on a bracket on top of the shower stall. The whole place was pretty amazing.

Jeff said, "Let's go get some coffee and sit down."

"Thanks. I could use another cup. It's snowing outside," said Eric. He sighed and followed Jeff back to the big room. They sat down with Lisa and Maria. A woman brought them a cup of coffee and they thanked to her. Lisa and Maria waited to see what Eric and Jeff had worked out.

Jeff said, "Do you think we could work out a trade?"

Eric looked at him. "What are you trading?"

"What do you need the most?"

Without a hesitation Eric said, "A universal gun cleaning kit."

Jeff nodded. "We could trade one."

"We are talking about a complete universal kit, right?" Jeff nodded. "What do you want for it?"

Jeff answered right away. "Ammo."

"Sorry, we don't have any spare ammo to trade."

"Okay. Do you have any gold or silver?"

"Yes, we do. All our silver is pre-1964. How much are you asking?"

"One silver dollar and two dimes." Jeff held Eric's gaze.

Eric looked at him. "Is there anything you need here that we might trade with?"

"We can use some fluorescent light bulbs."

"We could spare some. How about one dime and one fluorescent light bulb for the gun cleaning kit?"

Jeff countered with, "One silver dollar and four light bulbs."

"How about one dime and two light bulbs?"

"The gun cleaning kit is much more valuable than that. Three silver quarters and three light bulbs."

Eric looked at Jeff for a few moments. "One dime and three light bulbs."

Jeff studied Eric for a while. "Two silver quarters and four light bulbs."

Eric said, "Make that one quarter and three light bulbs and it will be a deal."

Jeff smiled. "Sold. You have yourself a deal."

Eric was very relieved. They needed that gun cleaning kit very badly. He made sure to keep a poker face and not give any signs of how important this deal was. He smiled at Jeff. "Do you have any extra Hoppe's number nine and gun oil I can trade for?"

"Yes. I think we could spare some."

Eric said, "Can you spare two, two-ounce bottles of each?" Jeff looked around at the group and several people nodded that they had some spare bottles.

"Yes, we can spare a few bottles of each."

"I offer one nickel for each bottle."

Jeff laughed. "They're worth a lot more than that, Eric. How about two quarters and three light bulbs for each of them?"

"Two nickels."

"Two quarters and two light bulbs."

"One dime and one nickel."

"Two quarters and one light bulb."

Eric thought for a moment. "One dime, one nickel and one light bulb."

Jeff looked intently at him. "One quarter, one dime and two light bulbs."

Eric said, "Two dimes."

Jeff sighed. "One quarter and two light bulbs." Eric said, "Two dimes and one bulb. That is my final offer."

"Okay. Sold."

Eric smiled. "You drive a hard bargain."

Jeff smiled back. "I do my best." Eric laughed. Jeff said, "Is there anything else you need?"

Eric looked around and then said, "I could use some aircraft cable, but what you use in the trees is too thick."

Jeff smiled. "We have some three-thirty-second seven by nineteen aircraft cable. Would that be small enough?"

Eric said, "How much cable are you offering?"

"One thousand feet."

Eric almost choked. He contained himself and showed no reaction. "What are you asking for that?"

"Three dollars, three quarters, two dimes and ten light bulbs."

Eric raised his eyebrow. "One quarter and one light bulb."

"Eric, that is a ridiculous offer. The cable is worth a lot more than that. Okay, Two dollars, three quarters and eight light bulbs."

"Three quarters and three light bulbs."

"Two dollars, two quarters and seven light bulbs."

Eric shook his head. "I don't need the cable that badly. My final offer is one dollar, two quarters and six light bulbs."

Jeff studied Eric for a few moments. "Sold."

Eric smiled and extended his hand. "Deal."

Jeff shook his hand. "Deal." Both men thought they got the better end of the deal. Eric thought Mark would probably do a jig when he found out the deal he made.

Jeff said, "It was nice to meet you, Eric. I hope we can do business again. We have a cabin prepared for the three of you. In the morning after breakfast, we'll take you and the trade items back to the meeting place Kathy took you to and wait until you return to make the trade. Is that agreed?"

"Yes. Thank you."

"I have some things that need my attention. Dessert is about to be served. Enjoy it and we'll talk in the morning." Jeff got up, walked over to a cabin at the end, went inside, and shut the door.

Eric looked at Lisa and Maria; they smiled back. Lisa said, "I'm going to ask if they need any help."

Maria said, "I will, too." They approached two women who were serving up cake from two large pans.

Lisa said, "Is there anything we can do to help?"

A woman with brown hair, whose name Lisa couldn't remember, smiled at them. "I'm Nancy. I know it's a lot of names to try to keep track of. You're all our guests here, so sit down and enjoy being waited on. I'm sure it doesn't happen much anymore."

Lisa and Maria both nodded their heads. Lisa said, "That's for sure. These days we consider ourselves lucky to have coffee that we didn't make." Lisa sighed. "But on the other hand, we are very thankful to have coffee at all, and food to eat." Nancy nodded in understanding.

Nancy turned to the other woman standing next to her. "This is Ellen."

Maria said, "Are you sure we can't help you with anything? I feel like a slug just sitting around while you're all working."

Ellen said, "Enjoy it. Next time you visit we may put you all to work for your supper." Nancy and Ellen laughed.

Lisa and Maria said, "We wouldn't mind."

"Sometime when the weather is nicer, I would like to bring the children here to meet your children. I think it would be good for them," said Maria.

Ellen said, "I would like to meet them, too. They sound like terrific children."

Lisa and Maria beamed with pride. They might not have given birth to them, but they both felt all the maternal feelings for each one just the same. Lisa said, "You'll have to come visit us, too. It would be nice to have friends visit again." Ellen and Nancy agreed. Lisa picked up two plates and Maria picked up one. "It was nice talking to you both. Thanks for the cake."

Maria said, "Thank you." They went back over to the table. Eric was in conversation with two men at another nearby table. Lisa placed the cake down. Another woman brought a metal coffee pot over and refilled their cups. All three of them thanked her. She nodded back. As they enjoyed their cake and coffee, they started yawning. They'd been up very early this morning and had been through one hell of a day. They were pretty much dead on their feet.

Clark appeared at their table. "I'll show you which cabin we prepared for you. Follow me." They stood up and followed him to a cabin two down from the one Jeff had entered. Clark showed them inside. It was neat and clean; there a pitcher of water on the table and three cups beside it. It was nice and cozy. There were several blankets on each built-in bunk for them to be warm and comfortable.

Clark stuck his hand out to Eric. "I'm Clark."

Eric shook his hand. "Nice to meet you."

"Likewise. I'll be back in the morning about 7:00 am. I'll see you at breakfast. If you need anything, just open the door and ask for what you need from anyone out there. There will be several people on watch." He left, shutting the door.

The three of them stood there for a few minutes and looked around. Maria finally said, "Mark is going to be very happy with the trade, Eric."

Eric smiled and laughed. "I know. I can't wait to see the look on his face when he sees what we got."

Lisa said, "He'll probably be so shocked he'll have a heart attack."

Eric motioned for them to not say anything else. Both women understood immediately.

Maria said, "How are the children?" Eric explained that Amanda had demanding that he go and get Lisa and Maria right then and not wait for morning. The women laughed.

Lisa smiled. "I miss them, too." Maria nodded. Lisa looked around and noticed there were only two bunks; one double and one single. They all sat down at the table.

Lisa said, "I'm going to go to the bathroom. I should have gone before we were escorted to the cabin, like Maria did." She opened the door, took a deep breath, and walked outside.

Maria smiled at Eric. "I'm really tired. I'm going to bed."

They had provided some cotton pajamas for the women to sleep in. There was a curtained off dressing area and Maria grabbed the pajamas and went behind it. She came out a few minutes later and climbed into the bunk and was asleep almost before her head hit the pillow.

Eric wasn't paying any attention to Maria. He was lost in his own thoughts about the trade he'd made. He was overjoyed with getting the gun cleaning kit, Hoppe's number nine, the gun oil and the aircraft cable. Now he could stock the freezer up with deer meat. It was a big relief that something was going their way at last. Mark was going to shit bricks over this. Eric smiled just thinking of the expression that would be on Mark's face. Lisa came back inside, shut the door, and locked it. She turned around and noticed right off that Maria was in bed. The sight made her almost run out of the cabin again. What the hell had Maria been thinking to climb into the single bunk to sleep? She sighed and sat down at the table. Eric was looking down at the table, resting his head on his hands, lost in his own thoughts. Lisa poured herself some water to drink. She was a little nervous now with the sleeping arrangements. It's not that Lisa had never slept by Eric before. On the way up here, most of the time there wasn't much room where they'd bed down for the day, and they all would be almost touching when they slept. But this was different. This was a real bed. Eric looked up at her and noticed the worried expression on her face. He looked around to see what caused it and saw Maria sleeping in the single bunk. He thought, *that's what she is worried about.*

He reached over, grabbed her hand, and held it. He looked her in the eyes. "Don't worry, I won't be sleeping in a bed tonight. That bunk is all yours." The tension went right out of her. With those words, she knew everything was all right. She looked at him and then felt bad for any stray thoughts she had about the sleeping situation. This was Eric, who she trusted as no other man.

She smiled at him. "It's all right. It's not like I haven't slept next to you before. You don't snore half as loud as Mark does."

He smiled at her and relaxed. "Mark swears he doesn't snore."

Lisa laughed. "Well, he's never had to spend any time next to him trying to sleep over the racket he makes, either. Maybe we could make a recording and prove it."

Eric laughed. "I'd like to do that. The look on his face as he denies that it's him snoring on the tape would be priceless, don't you think?"

She laughed. "I can see him stiffing up and getting that look on his face. The one where he thinks everyone has gone completely crazy except him. And saying something like, 'don't you all have better things to spend your time on? If not, I have a list of jobs that needs to be done.'" Eric knew the look she was talking about and they both laughed hard. Mark was his best friend, and they weren't laughing at him, just sharing a moment.

Lisa yawned. "I'm going to bed. I can hardly keep my eyes open any longer. It has been a very weird, Twilight Zone day."

Eric smiled. "Yes, it has been a very weird day all around." Lisa grabbed the pajamas and put them on the table. She said with a twinkle in her eyes, "I'm wearing my own thermal underwear to bed. You can wear these if you want."

Eric looked at her and then raised an eyebrow. "I would look down right goofy in them. They wouldn't fit, anyway." Lisa went over to the dressing area and took her outer clothes off, leaving her thermals on. She went over to the double bunk and climbed into it, scooting over to the back. She turned on her side and faced Eric.

Eric wasn't sure how to handle this situation. He didn't want to move too fast or put any pressure on Lisa. He wasn't sure if he should join her in the bunk or not. He knew nothing sexual would happen. That isn't what he was worried about. He didn't want to take advantage of her. He'd decided a long time ago to let her make any moves. She would let him know when she was ready.

Lisa said, "Aren't you tired? You look tired to me." She lifted the covers up, smiling with a mischievous look on her face. "Come on, Eric. Come to bed. It's okay. I promise I won't bite or take advantage of you. You can trust me."

Eric stood up. "Well, with an invitation and promise like that, how could I possibly refuse?" He went into the dressing area and removed his outer clothes and came out in his thermals. He turned the light off and climbed into bed. She scooted over closer to him and put her head on his shoulder. He wrapped his arms around her and kissed her on the temple. "Goodnight, sweetheart."

She snuggled down in the covers. "Goodnight, handsome. I'm glad you're here." She knew Eric would guard over her and Maria and keep them safe from any harm.

It was wonderful being held in his arms. She put her arm across his chest and her fingers brushed across the AK-47 lying on his other side. Eric lay awake, enjoying the feel of Lisa in his arms. He was tired but didn't want to miss out on enjoying holding her close. He had wanted this for a long time. He smiled, thinking that she trusted him enough to lay in his arms as she slept. Things were moving along nicely. This had happened a lot sooner than he thought it would. He was lying on the SIG that he had placed under the mattress as he climbed into bed. He reached down with his free hand and grabbed it and pushed it under his pillow. There, that was better. That was the last thought he had before sleep claimed him.

****

Unbeknown to all of them, they had been under observation. There was a man that lived in an underground bomb shelter that had been built in the fifties. No one knew this place was there. It was a totally self-sufficient bomb shelter made into a survival retreat. He had bought this particular property because of the bomb shelter over ten years ago, before he retired from the Merchant Marines. He needed a secure place to put all of the things he'd bought over the years in foreign countries. He was a very serious-minded survivor. He had seen the world over several times and knew how fragile society was, pieced together like tinker toys. He had seen different rulers come into power and economies collapse and the chaos it brought. He felt it was only a matter of time before this happened in America. He'd started buying up whatever he could find on the black market around the world. He set his property up to last a lifetime with food and a well and every single thing you could think of that may possibly be needed. He set up remote cameras all over the place to keep his eye on what happened up on top and who came close to his property and the surrounding areas. He had watched the tree people ever since he bought the place. They hadn't gotten along very well when they first met. He knew where they lived and where their winter cave was, too. He had watched the people who had taken over the Anderson place from a distance . They seemed like all right folks. He had seen the children when they had been wandering around the forest.

He had gone out and made odd noises to herd the children over to the people at the Anderson place.

It had worked, too. The people had taken the children in and let them stay with them. That had been a test to see what kind of people they were. After all, Tim Anderson had told him that if he and his family didn't make it up here, that the place would then belong to him. So, he was taking care of the children and providing for them in a way. Tim Anderson had been the real estate agent that sold him the property. Tim was the only one that knew he was up here and that there was a bomb shelter. It wasn't even on any blue prints

He had seen the dogs attack those two women. He had gone out and was going to help them because he thought the tree people would have all been in their winter cave already. But they had reached the women first. It was just as well, because he wanted to remain hidden. He didn't do too well around young people and children. They were always asking questions and talked non-stop. They would chatter on about the dumbest things. He liked the quiet of his own thoughts. He had watched that young woman from the tree people ride her bike over to the Anderson place. He was already out, so he kept an eye on them. He saw what happened at the door with the dogs and heard the shots that were fired in the basement. They had been plain stupid for leaving that window open during a dog attack. Well, experience is the best teacher. He bet they wouldn't do that again. He was up in a tree on the road that led to the Anderson place keeping an eye on things when those crazy men in the Roman soldier getup came by. He also had seen what they had fed the dogs. Those dogs had to go. They were human flesh-eaters now. He climbed down the tree, keeping them in his sights and saw where they had made camp for the night. He was going to come back later and bring some meat with strychnine on it and kill those dogs.

****

After getting the children ready for bed, Abby sat down with a sigh. She was feeling a bit queasy. Mark was sitting in the living room reading a how-to book he had found in the reading area upstairs. "Are you all right?"

Abby said, "I've never gotten all three of them ready for bed by myself before. It's a lot harder than it looks."

"You just rest now. I'll go check up on them in a little while."

"I can't just sit here and rest. I have to go read a story to Amanda, and then I have to clean the kitchen and do the laundry and several other things yet."

Those kids sure make a lot of work."

Abby smiled. "But it's worth it. When they look up at you with trusting eyes and hug you, there just isn't anything else like it in the world."

Mark said, "Okay. I'll clean the kitchen and then I'll read a story to Amanda. How hard could that be?"

Abby smiled. "Are you sure you want to do that?"

"Come on. You women and Eric do it all the time. I'm capable of reading a story to a child. I am educated, you know."

Abby laughed. "I didn't mean it like that. I just meant that sometimes Amanda can be a little difficult to put to bed so that she stays there like she should."

"Piece of cake. I can handle one five-year-old. You just need a firm hand with her. As soon as she understands that I won't put up with all that nonsense, she'll settle right down and go to sleep."

Abby chuckled. "Good luck with that. I'll go start the laundry and leave you to the dishes and your firm hand thing." She chuckled all the way down to the basement. Boy, did he have an experience coming.

Abby finished up everything and sat down with a cup of tea. It was 11:00 pm. Mark still hadn't come back from upstairs. She wondered how it was going. She heard someone coming down the stairs and thought, *Finally*.

Chris walked up to Abby. "Can you please come up there and make them shut up so I can get some sleep?"

Abby set her cup down on the saucer. "What are they doing?"

Chris sighed. "Mark is telling Amanda war stories. Every time he stops, she starts whining and crying so he just keeps on telling more. Ryan and I can't get any sleep because he's doing all the sound effects from helicopters and airplanes and missiles and stuff. Please save us."

Abby laughed and muttered to herself, "A firm hand, huh?" She followed Chris upstairs and went into the children's room; there was Mark standing in the middle of the room with his arms out to the sides, flying around the room pretending to be an airplane with all the sound effects. Chris climbed up into his bunk.

Mark turned and looked at Abby. "What? I'm just telling her a story. She likes it." Amanda nodded at Abby in agreement.

Abby said, "No doubt. You do sound quite entertaining."

"I'm almost done with the battle of Midway. Give me a few more minutes."

Abby crossed her arms in front of her. "I don't think so. You can finish this story another time. The children need their rest, Mark. That's the whole purpose of putting them to bed."

He looked disappointed and started to protest, but then noticed the look on her face and changed his mind. He leaned down to Amanda. "I'm sorry. I'll finish this another time. You have to go to sleep now." He turned and walked out of the room and went down the stairs.

Chris and Ryan thanked Abby. Chris said, "He was like an insane jack in the box that just kept popping back up with another sound effect every time Amanda so much as yawned. What was the matter with him?"

"He just likes war stories, I guess." She walked over to Amanda. "You know you're supposed to go to sleep when you go to bed. You only get one story, too."

Amanda said sleepily, "I liked his stories. They were funny. He makes a good rabbit, too."

"Rabbit?"

Chris said, "Don't ask. Okay? You don't want to know. Take my word for it."

"All right, I won't. Goodnight, children." She turned off the light and went downstairs.

She picked up her cup, went into the kitchen, and put it in the microwave to heat it. She came back and sat down. "Amanda said you make a good rabbit."

Mark looked over the top of his book at her "I don't want to talk about it."

"What happened to the firm hand thing?"

"I guess I got a bit carried away. But she liked my stories."

"I didn't know you had such a theatrical side. You're quite talented."

"Okay, okay. So, I caved. Every time I tried to quit, she would start crying and she said Eric tells her stories."

"Eric tells her fairy tales and stories about princes and princesses. He does not tell her actual war stories. Do you want her to have worse nightmares than she's been having imagining that bombs are going to be dropped on top of us by airplanes or that helicopters will come and shoot missiles at us or use their machine guns?"

Mark said sheepishly, "I didn't think of that. I'll admit it. It's a lot harder than I thought it was to get them to go to sleep. She was a tough audience, too."

Abby laughed. "All five-year-olds are pretty hard to please."

Mark glared at her. "Rub it in, why don't you?"

Abby just continued to laugh. She knew that most of his tough talk was just that. He was a very decent human being on the inside. He just had a bit of a difficult time conveying his thoughts and ideas to others. When he was out of his comfort zone or confronted with new ideas or situations, he would put up a big gruff smoke screen until he could get a handle on things. That was just Mark's way of dealing with things.

****

A little after 2:00 am in the morning, the man that lived in the converted bomb shelter made his way through the snowstorm to the Roman's camp. When he was close, he climbed up in a tree and got comfortable. He could see the soldiers sleeping under a few low-branched trees. The dogs were asleep all around them, keeping them safe. He threw small pieces of meat at the dogs to eat. He made sure each dog ate several pieces. The dogs walked all around, sniffing at the ground, trying to find where he was. After awhile they gave up and lay back down and went to sleep. The man waited until they were all in a deep sleep and then climbed down and made his way back home. He hadn't done anything to the men because he didn't know if they had killed the people they had been feeding to the dogs or just found bodies and were using the meat to feed the dogs. Tomorrow when they woke up and found the dead dogs, he'd find out what their reaction would be. It would tell him a lot about what kind of men they really were. He hoped for their sakes they behaved themselves. They were in his territory now, and he was judge and jury of his kingdom. He would not put up with any nonsense.

****

Eric, Lisa and Maria were up and dressed and sitting at the table waiting for Clark to come get them for breakfast long before 7:00 am rolled around. All three of them were uneasy being away from Mark, Abby and the children. Clark finally showed up and led them out to breakfast, saying it was ready. They were having dehydrated ham and scrambled eggs. Eric was impressed. This cave must be well-stocked. Kathy came over and joined them for breakfast. Eric was antsy to get going. He wanted to show Mark the gun cleaning kit in the worst way. He kept imagining the look on his face.

When they were finished, Jeff came over and said with a worried look on his face. "We have a bit of a problem."

Eric instantly went on red alert. "What kind of a problem?"

Jeff said, "The snow turned into slush and froze on the cables overnight. We can't use the cables to get the three of you back to your cabin. It's too dangerous to try to use the cables with ice on them."

"You mean we have to walk back to the cabin?"

"Yes. And the sky is darkening again, so we think another snowstorm is on the way."

"How long will it take to get to the cabin from here?"

"It's an all day walk. You should arrive just before dark."

"Well, I guess we'd better get going then."

Jeff nodded. "You still want to do the trade right now?"

Eric said, "Yes, I do. Can you spare a few members of your group to bring the trade items? They can spend the night with us and return in the morning. That way they won't have to travel in the dark in a snowstorm."

"Sure. I'll send four with you. That way if those dogs show up, you all can take care of them."

"Yes, those dogs must die." Jeff gave him a puzzled look. He turned around and picked four people to go with them and carry the trade items back and forth. They gathered up their things and they left. It was not easy walking in the snow. Sometimes they would fall through to the ground. The top layer was slippery with ice. They would just get back up and brush the snow off and keep going. It was going to be an incredibly long day.

Mark, Abby and the children finished breakfast. The children cheered because they thought with Maria being gone, they wouldn't have any schoolwork today. Maria had been a teacher before the world went dark. Abby quickly squashed that idea by telling them that Maria already had the lessons made up and Abby would be taking her place today. The two boys grumbled.

Amanda told Abby, "I like you for a teacher. You help me with the numbers."

Abby gave her a hug. "Thank you." She herded the children upstairs and got them started, then came back down and cleaned the kitchen.

Mark said, "I'll be down in the basement. I'm going to name all the tools on your inventory list."

Abby smiled. "Maria will be happy about that. She's been fretting over not knowing the names of the tools. She wants that done so if we need a certain tool we can look on the list and see if we have it and where it's supposed to be."

"I know. She's a great organizer and this will be really useful." He went down to the basement and Abby went upstairs to teach the children. She was going to show Amanda how to make a line of several snowflakes connected together out of folded paper today as an art project. Maybe later on she could teach her how to make some origami figures to hang in the children's bedroom and playroom.

****

The Roman soldiers woke up to the sound of the dogs in their death throes. They made a quick sweep around to see who had been around in the night. They didn't find any tracks or indications that anyone had been around. This angered the man in charge. He ordered the men to their horses so they could look for whoever had done this. They started an intensive search of all the roads leading off the highway looking for someone to blame. At mid-morning, they found a large log cabin that had smoke coming out of the chimney. The leader decided whoever was inside had to be responsible for killing the dogs, because they hadn't found any other people around. He gathered the men around him and explained how he wanted to handle the situation.

****

Mark, Abby and the children just finished lunch when they heard noises coming from outside. Mark looked out the front window and did a double take. He turned to Abby and said, "You're not going to believe this."

Abby walked over. "Believe what?" She looked out the window and gave a startled gasp. She looked at Mark. "There are Roman soldiers out there. What in the world are they doing here?"

"I have a bad feeling about this. Send the children upstairs right now. I'm going to go outside and see what they want."

"That may not be smart. They have swords and spears."

Mark said as he walked over to the door, "And I have a gun." He opened the door and stepped outside. He left the door open a little way so Abby could hear what was being said. If he needed to make a fast retreat, he wouldn't have to waste time opening the door to get inside.

Abby turned to the children. "Get upstairs right now. Chris, go into my bedroom and get the .22 and take it with you into your bedroom. Stay in your room and shut the door. Don't come out until I or Mark tells you to." Chris was about to protest but Abby said, "No arguments, Chris. Your brother and sister's safety may rest in your hands. Go now." Chris, looking worried, turned and hurried his brother and sister upstairs. Abby turned around and looked out the corner of the window at the Roman soldiers.

The Roman soldiers were marching up the driveway. Mark said, "What do you want?"

The leader said, "We've come to kill you for killing our dogs."

"You should have taken better care of them and not let them roam around attacking people." Mark thought they were talking about the dogs they had killed yesterday when they had followed Kathy to the cabin.

The leader said, "No one kills our property and lives." He gave the attack command to the men. They rushed toward Mark.

Mark took aim with the .45 and fired twice at the man in the lead. The bullets made a ping, ping metallic sound and bounced off the metal armor. Mark thought, *Oh shit.* He turned and ran back into the house, slamming the door and locking it. He turned and said fiercely, "Go upstairs and get me the 45-70 and all the ammo. Hurry."

The Roman soldiers were at the door, using axes or something similar. Others were trying to kick the door open. A spear came right through the metal door and just missed Mark by about a half an inch. He moved away from the door.

As Abby ran upstairs, she saw the spear come through the door. She ran into Mark and Eric's bedroom and grabbed the 45-70 and the shells and ran out into the hallway. Chris was looking out their bedroom door at her. Abby ran by the door to the stairs. "Get back inside and protect Ryan and Amanda."

She ran down the stairs as fast as her feet would carry her. Just as she reached the level where Mark was standing, the door was kicked opened. She handed the rifle to Mark. Two Roman soldiers stepped inside with swords raised. Mark took aim and fired at the one in the lead. He fell over. The other one just kept on coming. He aimed and fired. The Roman soldier fell down to the floor dead, like his companion. Mark was waiting for more to come through the door. He was panicking because shooting the rifle inside had destroyed his ability to hear what was going on outside the cabin. He slowly crept over to the window to peek out the corner of the blind to see what they were doing. They were retreating.

He turned to Abby and yelled, "We have to fix the door right now. They'll be back. This isn't over."

Abby yelled back, "How do we fix the door?"

He pulled the front door as closed he could get it. It wouldn't latch. Mark handed her the 45-70 and yelled, "I'm going to go get something for the door." He ran out into the garage and looked around frantically. *The plywood, where is the plywood?* He ran over to the wall where some boards were stacked up against the wall. *There it is.* He grabbed it and pulled it inside, locking the door again. He ran down the stairs to the basement and grabbed a hammer and put a handful of nails in his pocket. He ran back upstairs, grabbed the sheet of plywood, and ran into the living room. He dragged the plywood over to the front door. Abby helped hold it in place as Mark started hammering nails into what was left of the door frame. It wouldn't hold through any kind of an assault, but it was better than letting the snow pile up inside.

Mark said, "Cover me while I get rid of these bodies." Mark grabbed one body and dragged it out the back door. He dropped it in the snow. He went back in, grabbed the other body, and dragged it outside and over to the ravine, where they had dumped the dogs' carcasses. He went back and dragged the other body over and rolled it down the ravine, too. Abby stood just outside the door to cover him with the 45-70. They went quickly back inside and locked up. Mark went over to the window and looked out. It was clear, from what he could see. They just stood there and looked at each other. They were probably not going to live through the next encounter with those Roman soldiers.

Mark said, "We're going to have to send the kids out the back way and have them go find the tree people. They can't stay here. It is much too dangerous."

Abby knew what he meant. She said sadly, "All right. I'll go get them ready." She went upstairs. Mark stood at the window and watched for the soldiers. It was only going to be a matter of time.

Abby quickly explained to the children that they were going to have to leave. None of them wanted to. They were all scared to death. Abby explained as much as she could as she got them ready to go out in the snowstorm. She came downstairs and made up a bag to take with them. She put enough food for a few days because they wouldn't be able to carry any more than that. She kissed and hugged each of them. Mark talked to Chris for a few minutes alone. Ryan quietly moved closer to hear. Tears welled up in his eyes. Mark and Abby thought they were going to die. They would defend the cabin so that Eric, Lisa, Maria and the children had some place to come back to. They would do the best they could and hold them off for as long as they could. Mark squeezed both boys' shoulders and gave them a reassuring pat. He kissed Amanda on the cheek and told her to be good and not to say one word when they were out there. He cautioned them about the dogs and about making sounds. He led them outside and pointed them in the right direction. He told Chris to take a compass reading every few feet. Mark and Abby stood there and watched them until they were out of sight. They both went back into the cabin and locked the door.

Abby had tears running down her face. She wiped them away with the sleeve of her shirt. Mark looked at her. "We'll do our best to make sure we survive." She nodded her head and picked up the 22-250. They walked into the living room and Mark sat by the window where he could look outside and keep watch.

"Since we probably won't survive, I have something to tell you. I haven't told anyone yet. I was waiting for a while before I told everyone. But now I want to share it with at least one person before I die."

Mark looked at her. "What are you talking about? What haven't you told anyone?"

Abby looked him square in the eyes. "I'm pregnant."

"What?" Then he stared hard at her for a few moments., "From when you were held captive?" Abby nodded her head yes. "Damn, I'm sorry."

Abby smiled. "I'm not. I mean, I'm sorry for the way it came about, of course, but I'm not sorry that I'm having a baby. I was looking forward to it. I may not know who the biological father is, but he or she would still grow up with two very wonderful father role models. You and Eric are the best. I want to also take this time and thank you again for rescuing us from those animals. I appreciate everything you've done for us."

Mark wasn't sure what to say. He thought for a few minutes. "You're welcome, Abby. You've done some saving yourself. You saved my life. You've learned pretty fast how to do things. I'm glad we were able to rescue you. If you're happy about the baby, then I am, too."

Abby smiled. "Thank you, Mark. I appreciate it. I wasn't sure how you were going to take it that we'd have another mouth to feed soon."

Mark laughed. "Well, at least this one won't eat much for the first few years." Abby smiled and laughed with him. Then they settled down and waited for whatever came next.

****

Chris, Ryan and Amanda were not making very good time. Amanda kept getting stuck in the snow. Chris would have to stop and get her out before they could go on. Amanda was crying now and softly calling for Eric. Chris kept whispering to her that they would find the tree people and then Eric, Lisa and Maria would be there, too. Finally, Amanda fell down for the hundredth time and wouldn't get back up again. Chris tried everything, but all Amanda would do was lay there and cry. Chris was exasperated with her and didn't know what to do. He was trying to get to the tree people so he could tell them about the Roman soldiers so they could come help Mark and Abby. Maybe then they wouldn't die. Now Amanda wouldn't even get up.

Chris pulled Ryan aside. "Ryan, you're going to have to look after her. I'm going to leave you here under the trees with the bag of food. Amanda is slowing us down too much. I have to get to the tree people and ask them to help Mark and Abby. Then maybe they won't die."

"Do you think you can get to them in time?"

Chris swallowed hard. "I'm going to try my best."

Ryan said, "I'm scared."

"I'm scared, too. But I have to try and get help for Mark and Abby. Just watch her and don't let her wander off anywhere. Protect her." Ryan was carrying his pellet rifle and nodded. "I'll be back as soon as I can." Chris turned around and started jogging and sliding on the snow. Soon he was out of sight. Ryan turned around and got Amanda up and explained to her that they were going to wait right there for Chris to come back. Ryan cleared a spot for them to sit under some trees. The snow was really coming down now. He hoped Chris didn't get lost in the storm. Amanda was still softly calling for Eric and Lisa. Ryan told her to be quiet because the bad people were out here somewhere and they might hear her. He gave her a sandwich to eat. He sat next to her and worried. He kept thinking, *please God, don't let them die.* He silently said a few prayers for added insurance so God would know how important this was. They sat there and waited.

****

The man in the underground retreat watched the kids. They were pretty close to his retreat. The picture kept fading in and out because of the snow. He had lost the signals from the cameras near the Anderson place. They must be covered in snow. He would have to go out tomorrow and wipe them off and clear out around them so he could see again. Why are those two kids sitting under the trees? That's what he wanted to know. Where did the other one go off to? He would like to know that, too. Finally, after about twenty minutes he lost those pictures, too. The snow was interfering with the wireless signal. He sighed. Why aren't those people at the Anderson place out looking for these kids? Did the kids run away? Or had something else happened? Well, he'd better go keep his eye on them because the big cats in this area would be out hunting soon and these kids wouldn't stand a chance against a cougar. He got his outside clothes on and then put on a snow ghillie suit so he would blend in to the background and not be seen. He left his retreat.

He set up by a small group of trees and kept his eyes on the kids and the surrounding area. Those kids were so cold; they were huddled together and shivering. Now what was he supposed to do? He sat and thought about it. He heard a cougar scream not too far away. The boy under the trees pulled his pellet gun up and looked around. He thought with disgust that little thing wouldn't stop a charging cougar. Well, there was nothing else he could do. He had looked at this problem from all angles and just kept coming up with unknowns. He was going to have to go get them and bring them to his retreat and warm them up and find out why they were out here in the snowstorm. Dang blasted kids anyway. He sighed and made his way over to the children.

The little girl looked up and saw him coming; she jumped up screaming, trying to walk backwards in the snow. Ryan looked all around and then saw him coming, too. He jumped up and grabbed Amanda's hand and they started running away. The little girl was still screaming. *What in the hell is the matter with them?* he wondered. He took off after them. *Couldn't they see he was trying to help?* The little girl was running as fast as she could and looking back over her shoulder, screaming in a high pitched voice. The boy was half dragging her as he ran away. The little girl was screaming something about a snow monster. *What snow monster?* He stopped and looked all around and didn't see anything. He shrugged and just kept after them. They would get tired sooner or later and stop and let him help. The little girl was saying, "Don't let the snow monster get me!" Finally they were slowing down. *Took them long enough.* Those kids had a lot of energy, that was for sure. They must have run a quarter of a mile. He was impressed.

The little girl fell down and screamed, "Don't let the snow monster get me!" The boy stopped and turned around and aimed at him and shot him with a pellet. He pumped the pellet gun and just kept shooting.

The man finally got close enough and reached out and took the pellet gun from him. "Why do you keep shooting me with this thing?"

The boy said, "Stay away from my sister."

"I'm not going to hurt you."

The boy kicked him in the shin. "Stay away from us. You'll have to get through me to get my sister. Go away and leave us alone."

The little girl screamed again. "Don't eat my brother!" She was scooting away from him in the snow. She screamed at him, "Go away, snow monster!"

The man was confused. "I'm not a snow monster."

The little girl nodded. "Yes, you are."

Ryan kicked him again and stood between him and his sister. "Stay away from her."

"I came to rescue you from the snowstorm."

"Stay away from us." The man reached up to knock off the snow that had settled on his goggles and realized how he must look to the children. He pulled his goggles up. "I'm not a snow monster."

The little girl and boy exchanged a look and the little girl said, "I thought you were a snow monster. You looked like one."

He laughed. "Come with me and I'll see to it you get home. Are you lost out here in the woods?"

Ryan said, "No we aren't lost."

"Come on. It's really coming down now. Let's get you both inside." The little girl was having a hard time walking in the deep snow. He reached out and picked her up. They would make better time if he carried her.

She touched his whiskers. "You really are a man and not a snow monster."

He chuckled. "That's what I was trying to tell you."

She looked seriously at him. "But you looked like one before."

He just shook his head at her. They reached his retreat and he got them inside where it was warm. Both children stared around with big eyes. There were all kinds of stuff stacked inside crates. One whole wall was nothing but guns, very big guns. Boxes of ammo were stacked under them on shelves.

Ryan said, "Wow."

The man said, "Don't touch anything. You'd hurt yourself. Just sit down over there in those chairs. But first, take off those snow things and I'll hang them up to dry." Ryan helped Amanda and then he took his outer clothes off and handed the pile to the man.

Amanda saw all the monitors. "What are you watching?"

"Nothing now. The storm knocked out my reception."

Ryan was looking at all the big guns. He thought if Mark had one of those and a lot of ammo, he'd be able to kill those Roman soldiers. He turned and looked at the man and said, "Can we borrow one of those big guns and some ammo?"

The man looked up at him. "No. I don't loan my stuff out to anyone."

Ryan said, "Some Roman soldiers came to our cabin and attacked us. We need one of those big guns to kill them."

"Roman soldiers came to your cabin?"

"Yes."

"Tell me everything. Don't leave one thing out."

Ryan told him everything that happened. Amanda started to cry when she heard Ryan say that Mark and Abby thought they were going to die. "Please. Can you go save them from the Roman soldiers?"

Amanda continued to cry really hard. She looked up at the man with tear-filled eyes and begged. "Please save Mark and Abby. Mark and Eric are heroes. They saved Lisa and Maria from some bad men that captured them. Please? Please save them?"

Ryan was almost crying. "They took us in when our mother didn't come back from looking for food. Please, Mister, can you help them?"

Amanda climbed up on the man's lap. "Abby, Maria and Lisa are our mothers now and Mark and Eric are our daddies. Please save them for us, please, Mister?"

The man sighed deeply. "All right. I'll go save them. But you kids have to stay here and don't touch anything. Do you promise? Because I'll know if you so much as touch one little thing."

Both Ryan and Amanda promised they wouldn't touch anything. The man got up and put his outer stuff on. He looked like a snow monster once again, but not quite as scary as before. He didn't have real snow all over him this time and he hadn't pulled the goggles down over his eyes. He went over and picked his rifle up, then he walked over to the steps that led to the outside. He turned and looked at the children and said, "Remember, you promised not to touch anything. See that you don't." He turned and went up the stairs.

The children sat there for a few minutes and then Ryan got up and walked over to the guns and ammo.

Amanda said, "Ryan, we aren't supposed to touch anything."

Ryan said, "I'm not touching. I'm just looking around at all this great stuff." The crates had weird letters on them. He did notice some big things of gunpowder. It said thirty pounds on the containers. His eyes got big just thinking about what Mark could do with all that gunpowder. He went back and stared at the guns again. He knew Mark would be happy if he had some of these. He wished he knew what they were. He recognized some of them from movies. He sat down and just stared.

Amanda said, "Ryan, I have to go to the bathroom." Ryan looked around and there were two doors that were closed. He went over to one and it was locked. He tried the other one and it opened into a very small bathroom. He called Amanda over. When she was done, they went back and sat down. Ryan was getting hungry. It had been a long time since the Romans showed up after lunch. He went over to the bag he'd been carrying and grabbed a sandwich. Amanda lay down on the chair and looked around for a while, then fell asleep. Ryan just kept looking at all the guns and ammo and wishing he could get some for Mark.

****

The man walked briskly past the cabin. He couldn't see anyone around. Hopefully he wasn't too late. He studied the cabin for a while and then saw movement inside by the door. They must be trying to fix it. As soon as he heard the boy talk about the Roman soldiers, he knew he'd have to come and finish what he started. He gave them a chance to leave peacefully and they threw it away. He walked on and set up on a hill under some trees for cover and to keep the snow off of him as much as possible. It might be a long wait. He was watching the road that led to the cabin from the main road. They'd have to come by him before they reached the cabin. Well, these men in Roman soldier gear had shown their true colors. He set up his FAL .308 semi-automatic and checked the twenty shot magazine. He was ready. He adjusted the bipod legs and leveled it out a little more. There, that was better. He lay on his stomach, keeping his eyes on the road. He would see what these men in Roman soldier gear did when and if they came back. If they attacked the cabin again, they would die. This Mark character had killed two of them, so that meant there was five left. He was impressed with how detailed the boy had been about the first bullets just bouncing off the armor. The boy had said that they had watched out the side of the window and saw everything. The boy had seen the two dead bodies lying inside the front room when they were leaving.

The man had been up on the hill waiting for about an hour and a half when he heard the horses. He watched them go past him. They were carrying lit torches that sputtered when the snow hit them. They stopped and tied the horses to a fence post down a ways from the cabin. The snowstorm was letting up some and it wasn't snowing as hard as it had been. Maybe they had waited for that to happen before coming back. The Roman soldiers went down the driveway a little and then started to shoot flaming arrows at the cabin. The man rolled his eyes a bit. How stupid could you be? Shooting flaming arrows in a snowstorm. He thought, *Well, they showed what they had come to do.* He aimed at one and fired. He found another target and did the same. He kept going until all five of them were down. They'd scattered after the second shot. He could see where they went from his perch on the hill. He waited to see if any of them moved. They didn't. After fifteen minutes, he got up and packed his things up. He reached down and picked up his brass and headed back to his retreat.

****

Mark and Abby were getting jumpy waiting for the soldiers to come back. Mark paced around the room. Abby made them a couple of sandwiches and they took turns eating and keeping watch. The waiting was getting on his nerves. Abby didn't say anything. She just watched him pace back and forth occasionally. Finally after a couple of hours he said, "Maybe they aren't coming back."

Abby looked at him. "I think they'll be back. They were pretty mad about the dogs."

"Yeah. But they lost two guys. Maybe they decided not to come back and lose more men."

"Time will tell."

Mark gave her a half smile. "A lot of good you are. You're supposed to agree with me."

"I'll agree with you when I think you're right."

Mark glanced out the window. "They're back. They have lit torches with them. Are they going to try to burn us out in a snowstorm? That's stupid."

Abby glanced out the window. "They're lighting arrows with the torches." They both heard a thump as an arrow struck the house.

Mark said incredibly, "Holy shit, they really are trying to burn us out." He was just about to tell Abby he was going to go upstairs and shoot from up there when they heard several really loud shots fired. The men in the Roman soldier gear fell over and stayed where they fell. "Who's shooting?"

"I have no idea."

"Stay here. I'm going to go take a look. Cover me from upstairs, okay?"

"Okay." She went up the stairs as he put on his outer clothes.

Abby closed the bedroom door and opened the window up just enough to see where to shoot. She watched Mark creep around out the end of the driveway. After several minutes, he came back towards the house. She hadn't seen anything moving out there. She closed the window and went downstairs. Mark came in and said with a mystified look on his face, "They're all dead." They left their horses tied up on the road. It looks like we have seven horses now. What do we do with horses, for God's sake?"

Abby laughed "Horses. What's next, a couple of pigs and some cows?"

"I don't know anything about horses."

"Who shot them?"

"I don't know. But whoever it was used a big gun. The bullets went right through that armor."

"Did you look everywhere?"

"Of course," said Mark. "You know, this is supposed to be an isolated cabin in the middle of nowhere. It sure seems that a lot of people know where this place is. Every time we turn around someone else shows up. Now, we have a mysterious shooter, too." He shook his head.

"Hey, we're still alive. We survived once again. At least this shooter helped us. That's a nice change, don't you think?"

Mark laughed. "Yeah. It's a nice change."

Abby said, "I hope the children are all right."

"I'm sure they are."

****

Chris finally found the tree people. Or he should have said, they found him. They had some men set up to watch the area and they spotted him walking in the snow. A man climbed down almost on top of him and scared him half to death. He quickly told them what had happened. Chris said, "Will you help Mark and Abby at the cabin?"

The man said, "We can't. One of us has to stay here. The other one will have to go with you and get your brother and sister before they freeze to death. There are cougars around here, too. These mountains are very treacherous. The snow will cover up many dangers until it's too late. You should have kept them with you."

Chris said, "Where are Eric, Lisa and Maria?"

The man said, "They're on their way back to your cabin now. They had to walk because the cable has ice on it and it's too dangerous."

Chris said, "Oh." He didn't understand what he was talking about.

The man said, "I'm going to go talk to my friend and then we'll go get your brother and sister." He climbed back up into the tree and Chris waited. The man climbed back down after a few minutes. "Come on. Let's go find your siblings before anything happens to them." Chris led the way.

****

The man entered his underground retreat. Ryan was standing and looking at guns again. Amanda sat in the chair and was counting the crates. The man looked around. "Did you touch anything?"

Ryan said, "No. I was just looking. Oh, Amanda had to use your bathroom." Amanda sat quietly to see if she was going to get in trouble for touching the bathroom.

The man said, "That's okay."

Amanda climbed down out of the chair. "Did you save Mark and Abby?"

"Yes, the Roman soldiers are all dead now."

Amanda said, "Mark and Abby are okay?"

"I assume so. A man came outside and looked around and he was okay. I didn't see the woman."

"Thank you for saving them, Mister." She went over and hugged his legs. He didn't quite know what to say.

Ryan asked, "What's your name?"

"My name is Bert Gunner."

"I'm Ryan and this is my sister, Amanda."

"Well, it's about time to get you two home. I'll get your coats and stuff and then we can leave."

Amanda clapped her hands. "Thank you. I want to go home."

Ryan smiled. "Thank you for helping us, Mr. Gunner." Bert unclasped their outer clothes from his clothesline over the wood stove and felt them. They were dry. He gave them to the kids and Ryan helped Amanda get everything on. When they were done, Bert led them outside. He told Amanda she could ride on his back and to hold on to his neck. They'd get there faster that way.

****

Chris and the man, who said his name was Ken, looked everywhere and couldn't find Ryan or Amanda. Chris was frantic. The snow had covered all the tracks, so they didn't even know what direction they'd gone.

Ken said, "We need more help to search for them. We're closer to the cabin than where I live, so let's go to the cabin and let them know your brother and sister are missing. Then we'll have to come back and search with flashlights as best we can." Chris was so upset. He didn't know what to do. He just followed Ken and each step made him more miserable. Where could they have gone? It was almost full dark now. How was he going to find them? Ken was right, he should never have left them.

****

Eric, Lisa, Maria and the four others were almost to the cabin. It had been pure hell walking through the snowstorm. It had finally let up and was just snowing occasionally now. It would sure be good to get home. He was still looking forward to seeing Mark's face when he saw the gun cleaning kit. They only had a few more miles to go. When they came out of the trees and walked down the trail, they saw the horses tied up on the road. Eric had everyone stop. He looked around and didn't see anyone. Then he looked closer at the ground and saw a lot of blood and drag marks in the snow. *What was going on? What had happened?* He had them follow him cautiously up to the cabin. He saw the front door.

Lisa whispered to Eric, "What the hell happened here?"

"I think Mark and Abby ran into some Roman soldiers."

Lisa blinked at him a few times. "I couldn't have heard you right. Could you say that again?" Eric did. "Roman soldiers. Real Roman soldiers."

"That's what they looked like." They crept around the back and knocked gently on the door.

After a few minutes, they saw the blind move a little and Mark said, "Who's out there?"

Eric said, "It's us. Who else would it be?" Mark opened the door and Abby was standing behind him with the 22-250 pointed at them. "There are seven horses tied to a fence post out on the road."

Mark said, "I know. I don't know what to do with them." He stepped back and everyone came inside.

Everyone took off their outside clothes and hung them up in the mud room. Eric introduced Bill, Alan, Brandon and Clark. Abby bustled around and got everyone some hot coffee. "Nice to meet you all," she said. "We haven't had dinner yet. I'll fix us something to eat in a little while. We've had a bit of an exciting day."

Lisa said, "What happened to the front door?" Mark and Abby told them everything that had happened.

Eric said, shaking his head, "I leave you for one lousy night and look what happens." Everyone gave a half-hearted laugh and the women got up and started preparing dinner. It was going to be a long, stressful night. Everyone was worrying about the children, but had kept their thoughts to themselves. Voicing their concerns wouldn't change anything. All the adults knew how dangerous a situation it was. They all hoped the children had arrived at a place where the tree people would see them.

There was another knock on the back door. Mark and Eric jumped up with their pistols drawn and went to the back door. Mark said, "Who's out there?"

"It's me, Chris, and one of the tree people." Mark and Eric exchanged a surprised look and Eric opened the door. Chris was standing there with another man a little behind him. Mark and Eric immediately aimed their pistols at him. Before they had a chance to say anything, Clark stood up and said in a surprised tone, "Well, I see the children found you, Ken."

Mark said, "Clark, do you know this man?"

Clark said, "Yes. He's one of ours." Mark motioned for them to enter the house.

After they stepped into the mud room, Mark and Eric poked their heads out and looked all around and didn't see Ryan or Amanda. Mark turned back around and faced Chris. "Chris, where is Ryan and Amanda?" Chris burst into tears, hanging his head down, and haltingly explained everything that happened. Abby walked over to Chris and led him to a chair and sat him down. He was so scared and upset he was shaking and swaying on his feet. She patted his shoulder. Everyone sat in stunned disbelief as they absorbed the information.

Lisa started pacing around the kitchen. She then stopped and looked at Chris. "Chris, what in the hell were you thinking leaving them alone in a snowstorm?" Chris just sat there, staring at the table, and didn't try to answer her. What more could he say? Lisa turned to Mark. "We have to go look for them right now. They're in danger out there."

Maria said, "Oh dear God, let them be all right." Chris slipped down farther in his chair wrapped up in deep misery. He felt more tears forming. He blinked, trying to keep them from rolling down his face. *What if they died because I left them out there because they were too slow?*

Mark took a deep breath. "Okay, everyone calm down. Eric and Lisa, go get every flashlight you can find."

Abby said softly, "We shouldn't have sent them off in a snowstorm. What in the hell were we thinking?"

Mark turned to Chris. "Do you remember the exact spot you left them?"

Chris mumbled, "Yes. I tied one of those red rags we were using as bandanas on the branch of the tree they were under." The red rag was still there, but Ryan and Amanda were not. Chris was looking at the table and refused to look up and see everyone's disappointed faces.

Mark said, "Chris, look at me." Chris shook his head no. "Chris, look at me." Chris still couldn't do it. "If you had the guts to leave your brother and sister under a tree in a snowstorm so you could get help faster, then you have the guts to look at me when I'm talking to you." Chris hesitantly looked up. "That was good thinking. Tying the rag on the tree is a sure fire way to find it again. We told you to look after Ryan and Amanda. You shouldn't have left them out there alone. We hope they've just wandered off and it's not something else. You're coming with us to help look for them. Get ready." He turned to Eric just as he walked into the room carrying a few flashlights. Before either one of them could say anything, there was another knock on the back door.

Amanda said, "Open up. It's me and Ryan."

Mark and Eric were at the back door so fast they almost gave everyone whiplash. Eric opened the door and there was Amanda and Ryan, just standing there. Eric peeked around the door frame and didn't see anyone else.

Ryan said, "We're alone." Eric practically yanked them inside. Amanda looked at Eric and then looked around and found Lisa. She clapped her hands, knocking snow everywhere from her coat and mittens. "Eric promised to bring you home to me." She ran across the kitchen straight to Lisa and jumped into her arms, hugging her tight.

Mark grabbed Ryan and looked him all over for any sign of injuries or anything wrong, then hugged him tight. He said in a shaky, unsteady voice, "Where have you been?"

After a few minutes, Ryan struggled to get out of the bear hug Mark had him in. "Can I sit down? It's been a long walk." Everyone chuckled. Mark reluctantly let him go. Chris was very glad to see his brother and sister and to know they were all right. Amanda was hugging Maria now. Ryan sat down and told them everything that happened. Amanda interrupted a few times to mention something Mr. Gunner said or did. She kept telling them he was a good snow monster.

Clark said, "Wait a minute. What did you say the man said his name was?"

Ryan said, "Bert Gunner."

Clark started to laugh. "That guy has a wicked sense of humor. He was giving you a false name. What he probably really said was Burt Gummer, not Gunner. That was a character on those *Tremor* movies. Remember the wacko that had all the guns and explosives and stuff?" He turned to Bill. "You remember the one I'm talking about?"

Bill said, "Yeah, I do. But there are people out there with the real last name of Gunner, you know. It could just be one of those things where they have a similar sounding name is all."

Clark said, "How many could be out there and have all the same stuff as the character in the movies? Huh? Answer me that one."

Bill said, "It could happen." Clark shook his head at Bill in disbelief. Ryan continued to tell them about the wall of guns, the thirty pound containers of gunpowder, all the ammo and all the crates with weird lettering on them.

Clark threw his hands up in the air. "There. I rest my case." Mark questioned Ryan some more about where this underground place was. Ryan wasn't sure. Everything was covered with snow and it looked just like a lot of other places out there. Mark was disappointed. He'd like to meet this man.

The women went back to preparing dinner with much lighter hearts. They were so very thankful the children had made it through this without a scratch. Their family was once again together as they should be. Jim, Brandon and Alan said they would go take care of the horses. Eric went upstairs and got one silver dollar, three quarters and eight dimes out of his bag. He went into the unused rooms and unscrewed eleven light bulbs. He wrapped them carefully in old rags. He put them into a plastic shopping bag. He went into the living room and he signaled to Clark.

Clark saw what he was holding, so he brought his bag with him into the living room. Eric handed him the silver coins and Clark looked them over and nodded in satisfaction. He looked at the light bulbs and smiled at Eric. "Okay. Your stuff is in here. I need that bag back, though." Eric told him he would take it upstairs and empty it and bring it right back. He went upstairs. He laid all the stuff out on Mark's bed. He brought the empty bag back down and handed it to Clark. Clark placed the silver and the light bulbs inside and zipped it up. Eric walked into the kitchen and signaled to Mark to come with him. Mark got up and followed Eric out of the kitchen.

Eric headed for the stairs. Mark whispered, "What's this all about?"

"You'll see." They got to their room and Eric opened the door. He turned to Mark. "I bought you a few presents."

Mark looked at him strangely. "How could you buy something?"

Eric said, "With my silver and some light bulbs." He stepped aside and shut the door as soon as Mark entered the room.

Mark looked around and then noticed the things on his bed. As soon as he realized what it was, he turned to Eric with a big grin on his face. "This is great." He walked over and examined the gun cleaning kit thoroughly; the Hoppe's number nine and the gun oil. He was rubbing each item reverently. He patted Eric on the back. "You did good. You did real good. A real gun cleaning kit again." Mark was practically bursting at the seams he was so happy. He looked over at what else was on the bed and noticed the cable. "Is that what I think it is?"

"Yes, it is. Now we can stock the freezer up with venison for this winter."

Mark said, "I almost did as well as you, today. We have seven horses now." Mark and Eric laughed heartily at their bounty. Mark wondered idly who had shot the Roman soldiers and left the horses there for them. Weird and wonderful things were happening. Today had been a day filled with miracles instead of just bad shit happening. Maybe their luck was finally changing.

Chapter 24

Thanksgiving Dinner

Benjamin Martin: *'Aim small, miss small'*

The Patriot

The next morning Joe had Amy go out in the woods and find a concealed place where she could watch the two new guys. They didn't have a clue she was even there. They were digging the hidey hole with metal pots from their mess kits; they obviously didn't have a shovel. It would take both of them months at the rate they were going. Well, at least they were doing what Preston had told them to. She shook her head. What morons they were. How could they possibly make the area look natural when they had a big pile of fresh dug earth sitting right there next to it? Now they'd have to move the dirt twice, because that pile stuck out like a sore thumb. They could have put the dug up dirt on a blanket or a shirt or something and then scattered it around. She shook her head again. Well, she could just imagine what Joe and Preston would have to say about this.

She sat and watched them for an hour, then it was time to leave them their breakfast. She had a small sack filled with a package of freeze-dried scrambled eggs and ham that served two people, half a loaf of bread, a container of water and two instant packages of coffee, creamer and sugar for them. She wondered if they had anything clean left to cook with. Well, that wasn't her problem. She silently made her way closer. She picked up a rock and threw it over on the other side of their camp; they turned to see what was there. She slipped the sack next to the mound of dirt and quickly left. Yup, they were proving to be real morons. Joe and Preston were going to make mincemeat out of them. She smiled as she walked back to the house. Now, they both had two other people to pick on besides her. The way they looked, she was going to run circles around them. She smiled wider.

Amy was in the mudroom taking off her outer clothes when Michael walked in. She asked, "How are you feeling today?"

"All right, I guess." Amy rolled her eyes at his evasive answer.

When she was finished, she looked over at Michael. He was standing there with his hands in his pockets, rocking back and forth on his feet. She had seen many teenagers doing the same as they stood around on the street. She looked at his face and knew something was on his mind. "What's up?"

Michael looked at her seriously and then looked away again. Amy thought, *Wow this must be something really important to bother him this much.* She waited for him to speak.

He finally looked at her. "We shouldn't trust those two men."

"Why?" Michael shrugged his shoulders in reply. "Why don't you trust them?" Michael still didn't say anything. "Michael, look at me. Now, tell me why you don't trust those two men?"

Michael looked at her with a very earnest expression. He took a deep breath. "How do we know we can trust them? What if they're spies from that group that attacked us? What if they're just here to get inside and make us trust them? Once they're on the inside, they

355

could shoot us in the back or something. Or they could let the rest of their group in here to kill us when we least expect it."

Amy thought over what he said. He had some valid points. "Why do you think that about them?"

Michael said, "Because they showed up here right after the attack. We fought the group off the first time. They killed my mom, but they didn't win and weren't able to kill us all. Then those two captured you and Preston and that didn't work, either. Now these two men show up. It seems like they could all be connected, don't you think?"

Amy thought through his reasoning. She couldn't find one reason to disagree with him. She looked him steadily in the eyes. "That's very good thinking, Michael. Why didn't you say something this morning at breakfast when we were talking about them?"

Michael looked down at the floor and then back up. "Because I thought you'd think I'm just a kid and don't know anything. That maybe I'm just paranoid since my mom died or something."

Amy hugged him. "Michael, you are a part of our group. You have a say in what goes on around here just like the rest of us. If you're concerned about something, please bring it up and we'll discuss it. You're a valuable member of our group; we'll listen to what you have to say." Michael looked a little more confident now. "You brought up some very good points. I'm going to go talk to Joe and Preston about this because you're right. How do we know who they are? Or what they claim to be?" Michael looked relieved that Amy had listened and understood what he meant.

Joe and Preston were out back chopping wood. Amy walked over to a stump and sat down. Before she could say anything, Joe said, "Report." She told them what she had seen.

"At least they're doing what I told them to do," Preston said. Amy didn't mention how they were doing their tasks. Preston would see that for himself soon enough.

Amy didn't leave when she had given her report, so Joe knew she had something else on her mind. Joe said, "Out with it."

"Did either one of you verify what they told you?"

"Verify? How could we verify anything now?" asked Joe.

Preston gave her a thoughtful look. "No, we didn't."

She nodded and said, "Don't you think you should at least look at their IDs and verify they are who they claim to be?"

Joe said, "Why? It doesn't matter who they are. They could make up names they always wanted and go by that. Who cares?"

Preston said, "Why are you feeling uneasy about them? Did they do something to make you suspicious?"

Amy shook her head. "No. They didn't do anything to make me think they are anything but what they claim to be. Michael came and talked to me. He's very suspicious of them."

Preston said, "Why?" She told them what Michael had said. Both men stopped chopping wood and thought about it. Joe and Preston exchanged a long look.

Joe shook his head and said, "Out of the mouths of babes."

Preston said, "He's right to be suspicious. We'd better go and have a talk with them because he's right. We took their word that they are who they claim to be."

Joe turned to Amy. "Go and find a spot in the woods that will conceal you but give you a full view of their camp about fifty yards out on the west side. Keep your scope on them and watch what they do and how they act when we talk to them. Be ready for trouble if they aren't who they claim to be." She nodded, then made her way silently over to their camp.

She found a good brush pile for concealment. She got comfortable and rested her 22-250 rifle on a branch for a nice steady aim at both of them. She watched them finish their breakfast. Joe and Preston popped out of the woods. Both men in the camp were startled by their abrupt entrance.

Steve said, "Thank you for breakfast." Preston nodded.

"Yeah, thanks," said John.

Joe said, "We need to see both of your driver's licenses."

Steve said with a puzzled expression on his face, "Why? Are we driving somewhere?"

"What are you, a cop?" asked John.

Joe smiled. "Just call me Sheriff and this is my deputy."

"Is that what you want us to call you?" asked Steve. "You never told us your names."

Joe said, "We'll talk after we see both of your IDs. We just had a nasty shootout and a lot of people died. That makes a lot of enemies. We lost one of our own, too. We need to know where you both came from. You don't have to comply. You're free to go at any time. The world out there is a cold, hard place right now and being kind is sometimes mistaken for weakness. We wouldn't want any misconceptions of our actions, now, would we? We have to go chop wood right now. Gather up your IDs and anything else that you have to prove you are who you say you are and meet us over there." Joe and Preston turned and left.

They almost walked right by Amy. She smiled at them, then turned and watched the two men. They just stood there, uncertain, for a few minutes. Amy moved in closer to hear what they were saying.

Steve said, "Well, I guess with the world as it is, you have to be down right careful about who you let in."

"They were in a shootout, he said, and a lot of people died," said John. "That means they killed a lot of people, Steve. He said only one of theirs died. Maybe we should rethink joining them. What if they're some paramilitary nutcases or something, like we used to hear about on the news?"

"I don't know about you, but I like eating," said Steve. "They've kept their word about that. I don't see that we have any other choice right now. You can also look at it that they're better prepared than whoever they went up against, and are much better shots, too. I'm going to go get my ID and show them. You can do what you want." He turned around and went into the tent. John stood there for a few moments, undecided about what he wanted to do. He turned and went into the tent, too. Amy watched them. They came out and headed towards the farmstead. Amy let them get a head start and then she slowly followed.

Michael was loading up the wheelbarrow with split wood when Joe and Preston returned. Preston said, "That was good thinking, Michael, about verifying where they came from and who they are. You have really listened and learned well about security." Michael stood taller and looked a little surer about his place among them.

Joe walked up to Michael and patted his shoulder. "Good job, Michael. You're thinking and using your brain for our survival. That's what all of us need to do. Now, listen very closely. There's only one of three things that will happen when and if they show up. One, they show us their IDs and that's that. Two, they split and don't come back. Or three, they come to take us out." He shrugged his shoulders. "We'll find out soon enough. Now Michael, I need you to tell Jane what's happening and get your .22 and be ready in case there's any trouble."

Michael's eyes got larger and fear ran through his body. He nodded. "Yes, sir." He turned to go inside.

Preston said, "Don't worry, Michael. I don't think there will be a shootout. We're just being cautious and ready, just in case." Michael still looked upset, but more determined. Joe and Preston started chopping wood as if they didn't have any concerns about anything at all.

John and Steve reached the barn and hesitated. Steve finally walked around the side toward the sound of chopping wood. Amy kept them in sight. They still didn't realize they were being followed. Amy looked up and saw Jane at the window with her 22-250, ready for whatever might happen. Michael was beside her with his .22. She nodded to Jane and

Jane nodded back. She bent down by some bales of hay they use for bow practice. She kept her eyes on the men, watching their body posture and every little thing they did with their hands. She also looked around and made sure they were alone and that she hadn't been followed. She knew Jane would watch them like a hawk, so she could make sure no one else showed up to join the party. The two men hadn't looked up, so they didn't even see Jane or Michael at the window.

Joe and Preston saw them coming and set down their axes. They spread apart; two warriors, ready to strike if necessary. They appeared to be calm and relaxed, but anyone with any training would have noticed the controlled readiness of these two men. Appearances can be very deceptive.

Joe said, "Put your wallets on the stump over there and back away. Keep your hands out where we can see them."

John looked crossly at Steve as if to say, *See? What did I tell you?* They put their wallets on the stump and backed away. John looked at Joe. "What in the hell is going on? Did you guys get paranoid overnight or what?"

Joe said, "Nope. It's just better to be safe than dead."

Preston stepped over to the stump and picked up the wallets. He asked each of them their addresses and birthdays, and so on. He looked all through the wallets and at the pictures. He pulled out one from each wallet and asked who they were. The names and dates were written on the back. They answered all the questions right. Well, they at least knew that they hadn't stolen the wallets from someone who looked like them.

John, with an angry look and tightness in his voice, said, "So now what? You know we are who we say we are and we're from where we said we were. What do you want to know now? What type blood we have?"

Joe said calmly, "That won't be necessary at this time." John just looked disgruntled about the whole thing.

Preston said, "Would you two like a cup of coffee?"

"Yes, thank you," said Steve.

John hissed, "Sure, why not?" Preston smiled. He kind of liked them and their different attitudes. They were a bit rough around the edges, but they'd take care of that with training. He couldn't wait to train them. G. I. Amy was going to run circles around them and make them try harder than they ever had at anything. Can't let a girl do better than they can. Right? He laughed all the way into the house to get coffee. Jane and Michael were in the kitchen. Preston got them all a cup of coffee and Jane helped him bring it outside. Joe introduced his wife to them as G. I. Jane and they all shook hands. Joe and Preston told them their names. Joe brought his radio out and called Amy to come have some coffee. Steve and John were a little startled when Amy stood up from behind the bales of hay. John just kept staring at her. She was all decked out in camo, with full-face paint and a camo hat. She walked over to them with her rifle hung on a sling over her shoulder. Preston introduced her as G. I. Amy. She rolled her eyes.

Steve said, "You both were in the Army?"

"No. But we are now," said Amy. Joe and Preston laughed. Michael came outside and was introduced. When they had finished their coffee, Joe and Preston walked back to the other men's camp to talk.

Joe wasn't the least bit happy how they'd been digging the hidey hole. He explained to them what they were doing this for and how to do it better. Preston informed them they had just joined the Army. John said there was no way he joining any Army.

Preston said, "It's either that, or hit the highway. There's no other way to train you to be what you need to be and to learn what you need to know."

"All right. We'll give it a try." Steve stepped forward.

John hesitated and then said, "What are we going to have to do?"

Preston said casually, "You had better do your very best and learn as fast as you can, because we never know when we'll be faced with another mob of people intent on killing us. It's for your protection to learn as much as fast as you can. So, John, are you in or are you out?" John and Steve's bodies stiffened with tension.

John said, "I'll give it a try."

Preston said cheerfully, "That's the spirit." Joe and Preston explained this was no game and that all of their lives were on the line. Joe said for John to come to the barn with him and he'd give them shovels to dig with. He told the men to finish up the hidey hole and to report for training at 6:00 am sharp. John walked back to the barn with them. Joe gave him two shovels, two pairs of gloves and six MREs to eat. Joe showed him the faucet in the garage where they could get water. John said they didn't have a watch or an alarm to wake them. Preston said he'd bring his wind up alarm clock and let them use it. John left and seemed to be in a better frame of mind, but both Joe and Preston knew he was still debating if he wanted to stay here and train or not. Preston was going to remind them to stand their watches and not to fall asleep, because they would be checking on them. The penalty would be separating the chicken feces from the hay and putting it into the compost pile. That would take a lot of time and effort and would mean no sleep, because the watches still needed to be done along with the training everyday.

Preston went back to the house. Jane said they should start including the men at meal times and not waste anymore MREs. Joe and Preston agreed they would eat what everyone ate, but they weren't allowed in the house yet, so their meals would be served in the barn. Preston said that after a few weeks, if they worked out and passed all the tests, they would move them into the trailer. The trailer would be inspected daily. They had to earn the trust that would be placed in them. Jane smiled, because she'd been trying to talk Preston and Amy into moving into the house with her, Joe and Michael. Amy smiled and thought about how much easier it would be to all live in the house together. Preston said he'd make it very plain that they had to take care of the trailer and treat everything in there as if it was gold. Preston then asked Joe to help him move all the supplies out of the trailer and put them down in the basement. They left to clear out the trailer. Amy came along to get her and Preston's personal things. Preston and Joe were managing everything by using dollies to transport all of the supplies.

The next morning at 5:45, Joe, Preston and Amy were out in the yard waiting on John and Steve to show up. Preston and Joe had taken turns all night long checking on them for the watches. So far, they had been doing okay. At least neither one had fallen asleep. At 5:55, they showed up. Joe and Preston was impressed that they were not only on time, but a little early, too. Joe and Preston took turns explaining to them about the mini boot camp they would be going through. This was to get them into shape physically and to learn to react automatically when situations arise. When a firefight starts, the pressure can make some people freak out so they can't handle it. Shooting a gun does not make one a warrior. A well-trained person is more able to overcome the natural fear and be able to react as they were trained. That's what training was all about. How to react to each situation.

Getting in shape physically was very important. A strong body equaled faster reflexes and quicker response time. One bullet taking out a bad guy comes down to milliseconds in reaction time. If everyone was to survive the next attack, everyone had to be trained how to react with deadly force. They had assembled packs for the two men and Amy to carry. They had them take them apart to see what they'd be carrying. It was a kit to survive for three days. They started the physical training by doing exercises. Then they had them run for three miles around the farm. Amy found out that she was a lot stronger and could endure more than she had ever thought. She had already been doing these exercises and running, so she was way ahead of the two men. The guys worked harder just trying to keep up. She was the perfect trainee, too. She never complained about what they wanted her to do. She was the spark that kept them going. If a girl or woman could do it, then so could they.

When they were cooling down from their run, Preston explained what the difference between a soldier and a warrior was. It all came down to one thing: his or her willingness to fight to the end. Fighting was not always the solution to every problem. Because they were a very small group, everyone had to use their heads because each and every one of them was vital to the well-being and ability for the others to continue to exist. They had to work as one unit. From this moment on, there was no more I in anything. It was always the group that was important.

Preston had them doing exercises and running until they could run five miles with ease. He had them climbing up the sides of a hill, jumping over holes, climbing trees and other strenuous activities. As they mastered that, he moved them on to learning to crawl on their stomachs. He showed them how to move and use the terrain to help hide them and keep anyone from knowing they were there. Next, they learned how to use the camo face paint and totally conceal themselves. Through all of this, Amy excelled. It was as if she was born to do this. The days went by really fast. They were always doing something. Amy showed the men how to on sew buttons and to mend tears in their clothes. John had torn a really big gash in his pants when they were practicing crawling around in the brush. Amy gave them pointers and helped them practice and perfect each thing they were taught. John accused her of already having been trained, and that was why she was so good. Amy laughed explained that until she got together with Preston, she had been a web site designer and a nine to five type of woman.

John didn't believe it. Steve commented that he understood why they called her G. I. Amy. Both men were having a lot of trouble with the concept of using the natural terrain to move and conceal themselves. When they were done with training for the day, they approached Preston.

Preston stood there with a stern look on his face and shaking head. "You two looked like a pair of monkeys out there. You're going to have to practice a lot more. I could see every single move you made without binoculars. You both are too busy trying to make it where you're going and not paying attention to the lay of the land. This isn't a race. The purpose of this training is to get where you're going and not be seen. You pick the easiest paths to follow and skip the deep terrain that could conceal you. Are you both doing this on purpose? If that's the case, then we'll be at this until next spring at the rate you're going. We won't stop until you can do this right. Do I make myself clear?" They both looked exhausted and said yes, they understood. "Good. Now, go do it again and do it right this time."

Amy was excused because she had done it perfectly several times now. She went off to do other chores while Preston worked with the two men. They had weapons training in the afternoon. He told them to practice the advice Benjamin Martin had given to his son in the movie 'Patriot'. He'd told him, 'Aim small, miss small.' It was damn good advice too. John was a good shot, but Steve was really becoming an excellent shot. Steve was as good as Jane with the 22-250 and she was very good. They both were learning to take the rifles apart and clean them and put them back together again. Michael practiced shooting with them, too. He was improving quickly. Joe was happy with all their shooting abilities. So far, the men had done everything asked of them and they didn't complain to anyone but each other. The weather had turned cold. It would soon be snowing.

Tomorrow was a big day for the men. It was Thanksgiving Day and they were invited to have dinner in the house with all of them at the table. They would each stand watch the rest of the time, trading off sleep or watch duty among them for the whole day. They were coming along pretty well. Joe said that training Amy had spoiled him and Preston. She took to everything like a duck takes to water and they had forgotten how hard it was to teach these things to ordinary people.

John and Steve treated Amy really well. When they had free time, they helped her as much as they could with her chores or anything else she was doing. Preston noticed that they stayed close to her wherever she was. Amy was the only unattached female around. She was also very pretty. Joe worried this might cause problems in the future. Preston decided the best way to handle this was to let Amy take care of it. He wanted to tell John and Steve to keep away from her, but that wouldn't be right if he wanted them all to become one unit. It also wouldn't be right for him to interfere with the bonding between the three of them from training together, either. He did his best to stake his claim whenever the situation arose, though. He would kiss her and put his arm around her whenever he could to show those two she was taken. He wasn't worried about them trying to force her or anything like that. He was confident that she could take them if that ever happened. She carried two knives on her just for that kind of situation. He and Joe had showed her some self-defense moves and had her practice with the knives. She still carried her pepper spray, too. She'd been through a battle and taken a few lives, and he knew she wouldn't hesitate to do so again if it became necessary. It was just kind of hard watching them pay her so much attention. He hadn't noticed any change in the way she treated them back, though. She just thought they were kind of sweet.

Joe was spending his time in the evenings going through the Army manuals, reading up on how to make improvised weapons. He thought that using the culvert that allows water to run under the driveway and entrance to the property would be a perfect place to set up a four-inch buckshot gun. He had saved all the old pipes he could find for years just for this purpose. The ones with the caps on the ends would be perfect. He would cut the pipe to be three foot long. They could be loaded just like an old cannon. Use some gunpowder and wrap up a pound of rocks and old mails and bolts in a cloth. This would form a seal to allow the powder to form pressure to shoot out. But how to rig it to fire remotely and how to protect the powder from collecting moisture as the seasons changed? This was going to take some experimenting to get it to work just right. When the townspeople had first attacked and they had shot back, most had jumped down in the ditch for cover. This was useful information for forming their defenses. So, if they came under attack again, whoever it was would most likely use the ditch for cover. Well, if he could figure out how to rig the three-foot buckshot pipe, it would make a huge difference in their defenses. He had squibs and a remote control firing system, but it was fried from the EMP. He was going to have to think about this and come up with a solution. What could he use instead? Then it hit him. What about using a .22 tracer round fired into the powder charge? Would that work? It was going to take some testing and experimenting, and he wanted to think about it some more and see if he could come up with something else as a back up. That EMP had really ruined a lot of things he'd planned on using for their defense. Oh well, no use crying over spilled milk. He couldn't change the situation, so he had to think of a way to go around it. They all needed to put their thinking caps on and work out solutions, not just sit around worrying.

John asked Preston if they could move into the trailer at the back of the property. He said it was getting really cold and they weren't getting very much sleep. Preston explained to both of them that if he let them move into his trailer, he would expect it to be taken care of as if everything inside was worth its weight in gold, because if a faucet broke, there wasn't a hardware store anymore to go get a new one. Also, it would be inspected every day to make sure they took care of it. Both men agreed. He told them that if they pass all the tests in the next seven days, he'd let them move into the trailer. Both men smiled at that news. They made up their minds that whatever they had to go through was worth it not to sleep on the ground and to have heat and a bathroom again.

They all sat down for Thanksgiving dinner. They had three wild turkeys that Joe had hunted earlier in the year. Jane and Amy had roasted one in the oven and it smelled heavenly. Everyone had pitched in to help make the big dinner and they were serving all the trimmings. John and Steve were a bit nervous because this would be their first time eating inside. Amy had remarked to Preston and Joe that they all needed to start including those two in the meals and evening socializing so they would form an attachment to all of them there and feel like they were a part of it. Jane agreed. Michael liked John and Steve, and was a little more comfortable around them now. He thought they must be okay because the Mothman hadn't shown up to warn him.

After dinner they all played Monopoly and laughed and talked. Joe gave everyone a beer to make a toast with. They even let Michael have a sip in a glass for the toast. Jane smiled because she was sure he wouldn't like it and not want any more in the future. Joe held up his bottle to make the toast. "To new beginnings and new friends."

Chapter 25

Christmas & Giving Thanks

"Look not mournfully into the past, it comes not back again. Wisely improve the present, it is thine. Go forth to meet the shadowy future without fear and with a manly heart."

Henry Wadsworth Longfellow

Clint and Junior went out and checked the snares to see if they had caught any more of the wolves. They had caught two yesterday. Junior had spent the rest of the day showing Clint how to skin the hide properly and put it on the stretcher to dry. Clint helped them at night working the hides they had already tanned to get them ready for use. So, he already knew some of what he needed to know. He had hunted animals and gutted them, which made him pick up what Junior was teaching him really fast. Plus, Junior had him watch *Buckshot's Animal Skinning DVD* so he would know how to properly skin an animal. But doing it and watching it was two completely different things. Junior also had him read the two *Buckshot Trapping Books* that his dad had. Clint understood about predators and keeping their numbers down to allow the other animals a chance to repopulate the area.

The snares were empty today. There were five wolves left after the fight they had with Tim, so that meant that there was still three more. Junior said, "They're getting a little shy about coming close to the snares. They're also starting to realize that coming closer to our place is killing their pack members. We'll have to move them and set out some bait to draw them to the snares. We can do this today after lunch. My dad has homemade predator bait we can use."

After lunch they set out to move the snares. Both of them were heavily armed and on constant watch. They had heard the wolf pack howling last night, so they knew they were around here somewhere.

The next two days produced nothing in the snares and Junior was considering moving them again. He finally decided to just leave them for a few more days and see if they were still around. They hadn't heard them howl the last few nights. Maybe they had moved on. Well, they'd just have to wait and see. He and Clint stayed away from the snares and only looked at them using binoculars so they wouldn't leave any signs that anyone had been there. The next day they caught one more wolf. Junior let Clint skin and put it on the stretcher. He did a really good job. Now there were just one more wolf. None of them were inclined to want to go outside for any length of time with the wolf still out there. Wolves were nothing but lean, mean, killing machines. Wolves kill for sport, not just for food. They'll kill several animals in one night and only eat small parts of them. Junior was explaining all of this to Clint and Gayle. Gayle said she wasn't going outside until they were all caught. She still vividly remembered the nightmare with the dogs. Wolves were bigger, meaner and lot scarier.

It snowed for two days straight and neither Clint nor Junior felt like checking the snares in a snowstorm. It's dangerous to come face to face with wolves, and they didn't want the added danger of the storm weighing against them, so they just decided to wait the storm out. If they caught the wolf, it was dead and not going anywhere, so it wasn't like they needed to go out right now. On the third day, they went out and checked the snares. They had caught the last one. Junior studied the tracks intently to make sure there wasn't another around in the fresh snow. He did this just to be sure. They took turns dragging the dead wolf back to the garage.

Clint wanted to skin this one, too. Clint said, "It was really great that your dad had the foresight to put up ten dozen of these camlock snares. They've really cleaned up the feral dogs, and now the wolves."

Junior smiled. "Yes, that was my dad. He really believed in preparation. He also got ten camlock repair kits from that Buckshot guy so we can replace the twisted up cable and ends on the ones we've used. That is really being prepared, as far as I'm concerned."

Gayle was glad there was no more wolves left. Everything she learned about wolves made her skin crawl. She couldn't understand how people could possibly think they were mystical or anything good. She had heard of farmers complaining about the amount of livestock they would maim and kill and then just eat a portion of the animal. They were very bad news in a survival situation like this. She hoped there were still a lot of other animals left around here. First the dogs were cleaning out the small game animals and now the wolves were hunting here, too. She shivered just thinking about it. She remembered the bones of that poor man, Tim. He had fought them off as best he could. She still wished he would've come up to the house. They would have helped him. Junior and Clint believed the last wolf in the area was dead because there have been no new tracks for three days now. They hadn't heard a wolf howl, either. That was a scary sound. Hearing that howl and knowing what went with it gave her a sick feeling in her stomach.

Gayle sighed and laid down Junior's capote coat. She had been using a leather punch on it. She flexed her fingers and stretched the kinks out of all her muscles. She had been working on the coat for a few hours; it was hard work punching all the holes into the leather. She was getting the coat ready to attach the fur trim on the hood and sleeves. She was going to use a sewing awl to sew the fur trim on. She was anticipating the look on both their faces when they saw what she'd made them. She could hardly wait until Christmas. They had turned out really professional looking. She was very proud of what she had created out of the furs. The design was her own creation, too, she thought with a smile. Clint told her earlier that he wanted to talk to her after dinner. He said he had a project for her. She looked over at the clock and saw it was almost dinnertime now. She put the coat away in the box under the bed. She got up and went into the bathroom to wash up. It was Clint's turn to cook tonight and her turn to wash the dishes. That way everyone got to have one whole night off from the kitchen.

She walked into the kitchen and Junior grabbed her and kissed her. "What were you doing? Are you going to give us a hint?"

She smiled and laughed. "No. Not even one hint. You have to wait until Christmas morning to know what it is."

Junior said, "Aw, come on. Give us just one little bitty hint."

She smiled and shook her head. "Not even one little bitty hint are you getting, Mister, and quit pestering me about it."

Junior pouted. "The least you could do is let us open our gift up on Christmas Eve. My dad and I always opened our presents on Christmas Eve. It's not fair that you're going to make me wait until Christmas day to open mine."

She looked sternly at him, tapping her foot. "You always opened your Christmas presents with your dad on Christmas Eve because you were with him then. You opened up your other presents with your mom on Christmas Day. You aren't fooling me for one second with that puppy dog look, either."

Junior sighed. "Well, it was worth a chance to try to get you to change your mind. What difference would a few hours make, anyway?"

She glared at him. "My point exactly."

Junior looked puzzled for a moment, then got a sheepish look on his face."Wow, now I'm even supplying you with ammunition and logic to use against me."

Clint had listened to this whole conversation. Not that he had a choice, because he was in the kitchen cooking. He said to Junior, "You better quit while your semi-ahead in this conversation."

Junior sighed and hung his head. "Everybody's a critic tonight."

She said, "You are not fooling either of us with that look."

Junior threw his hands up in the air and walked out of the kitchen; Gayle and Clint's laughter followed him. They could hear Junior muttering to himself about everyone being against him as he walked away. Clint called out, "Don't go too far, dinner's almost done."

Junior said, "Yeah, yeah, I hear you."

After dinner, they sat around the table enjoying a cup of coffee. Clint said, "What I wanted to ask you, Gayle, was if you would sew something for me?"

She looked at him with a puzzled expression., "Sure, I'll sew something for you. What do you need?"

"When I was out looking for your medicine, I grabbed some white sheets. I want you to make two snow camo suits that have a pair of pants and poncho for you and Junior. They'll need to fit over your outside clothes. Do you think you can sew that?"

She thought for a moment and wondered if he really thought that she couldn't sew very well. Then she remembered that he hadn't seen anything she had made. She smiled. "Clint, come with me for a few minutes and I'll show you something." She stood up. "Junior, you stay here."

Junior said, "That's not fair. Your going to show him my present, aren't you?"

Clint gave him a steeling look. "Life is never fair. Anyone who tells you different is either dreaming or lying."Junior sighed.

He followed Gayle out of the kitchen and into the bedroom. She closed the door and pulled the box out from under the bed. She set it on the bed. She pulled the coat out and the fir trim she had cut to attach to the hood and sleeves. She handed it to Clint. "This is how good I can sew."

Clint took the heavy coat from her and looked over all the seams under the flannel lining. He looked at her and said, "This is a wonderful coat. He'll be really happy when he gets to open it on Christmas morning." They shared a smile.

She took the coat and put it back in the box. She turned to Clint. "Thank you. My mother made sure I could sew and do embroidery. She started teaching me when I was a little girl. I really like to sew and make things."

Clint said, "I don't have a pattern for you to follow to make the snow camo suits."

She smiled. "Sure you do. You have a snow camo suit and I can use that to make a pattern for Junior and myself."

Clint looked a bit worried. "Will you have to destroy my camo suit to do it?"

She laughed. "No. I won't even have to take it apart." Clint looked relieved at that. They went out and joined Junior in the kitchen.

Junior said, "You saw my Christmas present, didn't you? Maybe she should show me something she sewed, too, so I know she isn't destroying the furs."

Clint said, "She sews really well. She didn't destroy anything. You'll like it." Junior started to say something then changed his mind and remained silent. Clint thought, *well, at least he is learning to think first before just saying whatever pops into his mind.*

Gayle said, "I'll make the snow camo suits. I'll start on the pattern as soon as I get the dishes done." She used old newspapers taped together to make the patterns. She measured

Junior with his insulated suit and coat on and made sure the pattern was plenty big for movement but not too big that the material would move when the wind was blowing or snag on bushes or branches. Clint answered all of her questions about the snow camo suit as she was measuring Junior. She wanted to know about the requirements necessary. She used three white sheets. One was for the two pairs of white pants. The other two were made into long ponchos to wear over the top. She had both sets done in two days. While she'd been making the suits, Clint showed Junior how to make snap caps. He explained to Junior how he'd been making them for a long time and he used them for training when it was too dangerous to use real bullets. He used a once fired brass and he didn't put a primer or any powder in it. He said to put a new bullet on it so it would feed correctly in the rifle. This protected the firing pin. They made up a lot of them. Junior thought it was really cool. Gayle brought the snow camo clothing she'd made and showed Clint. He looked it over and told her she had done an excellent job.

Clint told her, "Now, look over my suit really well and smear these two colors on them so yours look just like mine." He handed them each a container of shoe polish. Gayle got black and Junior got the brown color. They looked at Clint's snowsuit really closely and then went into the kitchen and used the table to spread their suits out and they applied the polish to the material. Gayle got the idea of using string to make small lines along the areas so that it didn't look so rounded and more natural for outside. Like leaves and sticks or something similar. It took them a few hours, but they were satisfied with the results. Now it was time for Clint to approve of their work. Junior called Clint in to look at them. He studied them for a while and then made a few suggestions to improve the suits. They did as he suggested and he said they were ready to use. He informed them that now their training was going to start, since the wolves were gone and it would be safe. Both Gayle and Junior looked a bit startled.

Junior said, "You want us to train now? Right now, in the middle of winter?"

"It is the best time to teach you," said Clint. "We can't have you sitting around getting soft and out of shape—who knows what we may face when spring gets here." Gayle and Junior exchanged bewildered looks. Clint smiled in satisfaction. Now was payback for all the bickering he had to put up with. "Starting tomorrow morning at 6:00 am, you had better be ready for your first lesson. That means you'd better eat before then or you'll miss breakfast altogether, because we aren't stopping until lunchtime. Then we'll have afternoon training, too."

Junior said, "But what about all the other chores that we have to do around here? When will we do them?"

Clint smiled. "You'll do them in the evening, after training. This will be your last night of leisure, so don't waste one second." Gayle and Junior exchanged another look.

Gayle looked hard at Clint. "Yes, sir."

Junior looked at Gayle kind of weird, then looked at Clint. After a few moments of thought, he said, "What are we supposed to call you when you're training us?"

Without hesitation, Clint said, "Sir."

Junior nodded. "Yes, sir."

Clint said, "Now enjoy yourselves. It will be awhile before you have any time to waste in the future."

They all met in the kitchen at 5:15 the next morning. Junior made hot cereal to eat. Gayle made some sandwiches for lunch and put them in the refrigerator. She took out a small container of muskrat soup to go with it from the freezer to defrost. Clint said they would wait and do the lunch dishes with the breakfast dishes and save time, soap and power. Not that they really needed to, but it couldn't hurt to start that kind of training, too. They had to conserve their supplies for who knew how long and the sooner they started doing so, the better it would be in the long run. Clint led them outside and they did an hour of exercises. Then he had them running for an hour. It was not easy in the snow. Gayle kept tripping because she didn't have long legs like Junior. He had them tromping around in the snow and studying the terrain around the house. Clint showed them how to walk and stop and listen every few feet. He explained how to spot unnatural things in the terrain. He had them practice and see what they could find that wasn't natural. He had gone out the night before and placed some things out, and even used snow to make unnatural shapes. He wiped his snowshoe prints out with brush so they couldn't follow them to the objects. He was having fun. Junior and Gayle thought they were in shape because of all the trapping they did. They found out they were wrong.

Clint called them in to lunch and to give their reports on what they found. Junior did a lot better at spotting things than Gayle. He had a lot more practice looking for animal tracks and signs than Gayle. They ate lunch. It was more like devouring than eating. They were starved. In the afternoon, he had them dry firing weapons at targets and mentally counting the shots to know when to reload. He then had them take apart their weapons to clean them and learn how to field strip them. He told them they would be using the snap caps for all of their training from now on because real ammo was too precious to waste. They would use real ammo when they practiced to improve their accuracy. He had Junior show Gayle how to make them correctly and told them at night they would need to make up more for the next day's training. He had them make up little gun cleaning kits that fit in their pockets. He wanted them to get used to always having it in a pocket. The rest of the afternoon was spent on hand signals. He showed them the basic ones. 1. See something. 2. How many? 3. Human or animal? 4. Check it out. 5. Cover me. 6. Advance forward. 7. Retreat. 8. Drop down. 9. Crawl. 10. Be still. 11. Be silent and listen.

Everyday they got a little better. Slowly Clint added more for them to do. He would use blankets and backpacks for rocks and brush, as if they were outside, and had them practice concealing themselves and blending in with the environment. The hardest thing to learn was to be still and silent. Movement would attract the eyes of anyone around, and it could make sounds, too. When he thought they were good enough, he had them go outside and practice what they had learned about firing, concealing themselves and using hand signals. Then he had them cover each other as they moved from position to position. He told them they would work on firing accuracy later. Now, they were learning to be team members and the basics.

Then he had them practice defensive shooting. He had them defend the garage from invaders. He made them practice and practice and practice. They needed to know what to look for, and how to react to someone trying to take over the garage. After they got that halfway down, he switched to learning how to shoot aggressively and take something over. They used the garage for that, too. Most of the time Junior and Gayle didn't even know what day it was, they were so tired and busy. Their days were filled with training and chores; at night they slept like the dead, only to jump up when the alarm went off to do it again. Clint still made them do their share of cooking and washing the dishes, too. He didn't cut them any slack. Junior was getting pretty fed up with running or hiding by the house and seeing Clint in the window, watching them while drinking a cup of coffee.

That night when he and Gayle went to bed, he said, "I've had enough of this shit. I'm sleeping in tomorrow morning and he can kiss my ass as far as I'm concerned."

Gayle looked at him. "We asked for this. Remember when you talked me into doing this? Well, thanks a lot." She plopped completely clothed on the bed and moaned.

"I didn't talk you into doing this. You volunteered all on your own."

"I'm too tired to argue. I'm too tired to get undressed. I'm just plain tired. Every bone and muscle in my body is aching and screaming at me to hold still. But I have to move to breathe, and it hurts, too. I don't remember enlisting in boot camp. That's what this is, isn't it?"

"I think this is worse. We have to live with him twenty-four hours a day. He's always standing there with that look on his face that makes me want to punch him. If he says, 'Do it again, better this time,' one more time I'm going to punch him in the nose."

Gayle looked at him. "Have you watched him? He doesn't even breathe hard when he runs with us outside in the mornings. Are you sure he's human and not a machine? I'm having serious doubts. No one could do what he does and not even breathe hard. Every single day he leaves us in the dust."

Junior started talking about how he wasn't going to put up with this treatment anymore and started ranting and raving about what a lunatic Clint was turning out to be.

Gayle looked at him. "If you feel that way, then just go out there and tell him that. He's like a super soldier and I'm not brave enough to do it. He could snap me in half without breaking a sweat. The way I feel right now, he could blow hard and knock me over as easily as that." She snapped her fingers.

Junior was debating what to say to Clint. He was trying out different things out loud and asking for her opinion on them. Gayle fell asleep fully clothed and didn't hear anything else. He finally realized that she'd fallen asleep. He stopped mid-rant and stared at her. How could she fall asleep when he was talking? He sighed in disgust. He got undressed, climbed into bed, and turned off the light. He hoped she got a crick in her neck. It would serve her right for falling asleep when he was talking. He didn't set the alarm clock on purpose. That was his last thought before sleep overtook him.

The next morning, Junior woke up and looked at the alarm clock. It read 6:45. He shut his eyes and thought, *it's too early to get up*. All of a sudden he remembered that he hadn't set the alarm for training. He panicked. *Oh shit*. He jumped out of bed.

Gayle sat up quickly. "What? What's the matter?" She turned and saw what time it was and she jumped off the bed. "Shit, we're in trouble for sure now." Both of them raced out of the bedroom into the kitchen. No Clint. He wasn't in the living room, either. His room looked just like it always did. Perfect. They looked at each other in puzzlement.

Junior said, "He must be outside waiting for us." Neither of them really had their eyes open yet nor were they thinking on all cylinders. They hurried into their outside clothes and went outside. No Clint. They looked everywhere and he wasn't to be found. Junior even looked in the garage. They stood there looking around. "Maybe he's on the run around the house. I'll go one way and you go the other; we'll meet up that way."

"Okay." They met in the middle of the run. Neither one had seen any new tracks in the snow. "I didn't see any new tracks just my own."

Junior said, "Me either."

"Where could he have gone? Do you think we pissed him off so much he left?"

"I don't know. I hope not." They jogged back to the house. They went inside and sat down at the table.

Junior got up and felt the coffee pot. It was barely warm. He turned the burner on under it. Neither one of them said anything. When the coffee was hot, Junior got them both a cup and placed them on the table. He sat down and put his head in his hands. He felt really bad about not getting up and at least talking to Clint about needing a morning off.

Gayle jumped up and left the kitchen. She came back in a few minutes later. "He didn't leave for good, anyway. Most of his stuff is still here. I don't know exactly what he took with him, but he'll be back. I hope. But his backpack is gone."

Junior looked up at her. "He might not be back. Is his stuff here or just the stuff we gave him?"

Gayle said, looking a little lost, "I don't know. I forget what he brought with him." She sat down and drank a little of her coffee. "We let him down, Junior. He offered to train us to fight and we let him down because we were too tired."

He looked up and she had tears running down her face. Now he really felt bad. It was all his fault because he hadn't been grown up enough to talk to him the night before. What if he left for good? What would they do then? He reached out and took her hand. "I'm sorry. I didn't mean to cause all of this. I was just so tired and fed up with everything."

She squeezed his fingers and then wiped the tears away. She sniffed and said, "I feel really bad. He's been so good about everything. He didn't even complain when we would get bitchy with each other and argue. He always cleaned up after himself and was always willing to lend a hand to help. I hope he comes back and lets me apologize for acting this way. He got me medicine when I needed it so I wouldn't die. I really owe him." Tears were rolling down her face again.

Junior said, "I feel bad, too. I owe him for saving your life. I wouldn't have known what to do to help you get better."

Gayle sniffed again. "I really like him. I don't want to lose him, too." Junior didn't say anything for a while and they just sat there, lost in their own miserable thoughts about Clint. "I'm going to make something to eat. Then I'm going out and doing my exercises. I can at least do that. I can also practice firing and cleaning the guns. I just wish I wasn't so darn sore."

Junior said, "Me too. I'm sore everywhere. I thought I was in shape with hauling all the traps around and from running the trap line. Boy, did he show me just how out of shape I am." They both chuckled. Junior got up and helped prepare breakfast. Then they went outside and did their exercises and ran the course. They came inside and practiced firing and cleaning the guns.

Gayle announced, "I'm going to clean the house. I can't just sit around all day. I hope he comes back soon." She went into the kitchen and started washing down everything in sight. She straightened out the cupboards and mopped the floor. Junior came into the kitchen to make lunch. She went to clean the bathroom. She was worried sick that Clint would think they were weak, unworthy worms for not getting up after only two weeks' training. She kept praying, *please let him come back and be all right.*

Junior came and got her when lunch was ready. They sat down to eat. He said, "It just doesn't feel the same."

"I know. I miss him, too. He's part of our family now. I just hope he realizes that. I couldn't stand it if he left for good. We've lost too many people already." Junior nodded.

The house was sparkling clean, and everything that could be washed or dusted had been. Gayle had taken to pacing the living room by late afternoon. She kept asking, "Where could he have gone?" Junior was at the point where he'd shrug his shoulders because she'd asked the same question over and over. "I'm going to go work in the bedroom. I can't stand here and pace a moment longer." She went into the bedroom and closed the door. She pulled out the box and set to work finishing Junior's coat. She only had the trim left on Clint's coat, too. She sure hoped he came back so she could give it to him. She started to cry again. She wiped away the tears and set to work on the coat. She'd been working for four straight hours and finished all the trim on Junior's coat. Now, she only had to sew the buttons on and it would be finished. She could smell that Junior was cooking something for dinner. It smelt like a roast of some kind. Her stomach rumbled. She hadn't eaten much lunch. As the day wore on and Clint didn't come back, she started to think that he wasn't going to. She felt miserable. She put the coat away and went out to the living room. Now her fingers were sore along with the rest of her body. Sewing by hand, even with a sewing awl, was hard to do for four straight hours. It was dark outside and Clint wasn't back. She sat down on the couch.

Junior came into the room. "I thought you weren't ever coming out."

She looked up at him. "Clint isn't coming back, is he?"

"I don't know. I hope he does." He sat next to her on the couch and pulled her close. They sat like that, just holding each other and thinking about Clint. After a few minutes, they heard some noise at the front door.

Gayle jumped up. "Clint. He's back. Thank God."

"Wait. Don't go near the door. Let me go look outside and make sure it is Clint, first." Gayle waited in the middle of the living room for Junior to go look out the hole and see who it was. He came back into the room and smiled. "It's Clint." They rushed to the door and hurriedly opened it up to let him inside.

Gayle said, "Thank God you're all right."

"Are you mad at us?" asked Junior.

Clint took off his backpack and then his outer clothes. "I guess it's time for us to have a talk."

Junior said, "I want to say up front that I'm sorry for not setting the alarm and getting up for training. It was all my fault."

Gayle said earnestly, "I was worried about you. I thought you weren't ever coming back. I'm so glad you did. Please don't be mad at us. We're just stupid kids. We won't do it again."

Clint looked at both of them. "I've been pushing you both like you have no choice in the matter. I was training you as I was trained. I had no choice because I joined the military. This is how I've always trained people. But, I forgot I'm just a guest here."

Gayle went up to him and hugged him. "That isn't true, Clint. You're not a guest here. You're part of our family. This is your home, too. I know you haven't exactly been my favorite person lately."

Clint and Junior both laughed. Junior walked over to Gayle and Clint. "I want to apologize to you for not coming out and talking to you like a man should. I acted like a spoiled kid and just refused to set the alarm. I feel really bad to have treated you that way. I'm sorry."

Clint said, "I'm the one trying to apologize and explain. I'm sorry for pushing you so hard."

Gayle started to laugh. "Listen to us. We're all standing here apologizing to each other when all we had to do was talk this through. Okay, so we were all wrong. Now, let's sit down and work this out so we can train and not get killed in the process. Okay? My aches and pains have aches and pains."

Junior laughed. "I agree with you."

"Sit down and I'll get us all some coffee." The two men sat down and Gayle went into the kitchen.

"Clint, I want you to know that you are not a guest here. You have just as much of a say about things as we do. You are a part of us now and not a guest. Gayle was crying a few times today, thinking that you hated us. She was worried that you wouldn't come back. I was worried that you wouldn't come back, either."

Clint looked at him and opened his mouth to say something when Gayle came back in with coffee and cups. He took his cup from her. "Thank you. I had to get away today and think about things. I thought about how I was training you and what I could do different to make it a little easier. I realized that we have more time than I'm used to. I don't need to drive you so hard. We have four to six months, depending on the weather. Most courses are only for six to eight weeks. There's a lot of difference in those two time frames."

Gayle said, "We went out and did our exercises. We ran the full length of our run one and half times. We also practiced shooting and cleaning the weapons today. I want you to know that I do appreciate what you're teaching us. I'm learning a lot. I'm learning things that I could never have even imagined. I've learned to push myself more than I thought I could have endured."

"I am learning things, too," said Junior. "I like what you're teaching us. I do like getting into shape. I thought I was in reasonably good physical shape before from the trap line, but you showed me that I'm not. I still huff and puff running the course. So, that's good for us. We just need to go a little slower."

Clint said, "So, how do you want to be trained?"

Junior looked at Gayle, then back at Clint. "We want to learn all the things you've taught, but just for a few hours a day so we have time to do other things, too, and not just fall over when its time to sleep."

Gayle nodded. "Maybe three hours a day would be good. We'll still do the exercises and running because you've shown us how out of shape we really are. So, we won't count that time as part of the three hours. Is that doable?"

Clint looked at Junior and Junior said, "That sounds good to me."

"Okay. We'll do it that way."

Gayle said, "But we should take all day Christmas Eve and Christmas Day off, so we can cook up a storm and celebrate and relax."

Clint smiled. "That sounds like a plan to me. We should concentrate for a while on the normal chores and be thankful for all we have. We're a lot luckier than most people out there." Junior and Gayle nodded.

Junior said to Clint, "I'm making a beaver roast for dinner. Are you hungry?"

"I'm starved."

Junior smiled. "Dinner will be ready in about a half hour." He got up to finish making dinner.

As soon as he left the room, Gayle said, "Come on. I want to show you something." She got up and led the way to her bedroom. She shut the door. She pulled the box out and showed the coat to Clint. "I only have to put the buttons on and then it's finished. 'What do you think?"

He looked the coat over and handed it back to her. "It's really nice. You did a great job. He's a lucky guy to have someone as talented as you to make him things. It'll really be warm, too."

Gayle was happy he liked it, because he was getting one, too. She smiled. "Thank you for the compliments. I worked hard on it."

Clint smiled. "It shows." Gayle put the coat away and they left the bedroom.

Junior saw them and said, "She showed you my present again, didn't she?"

Gayle growled. "Will you get off the Christmas present kick? You're not getting a hint, so all you can do is wait until Christmas morning."

Junior said, "You're no fun. You're supposed to give me really wild hints so I could never guess."

She walked by him. "You wish."

Junior said to Clint, "Darn it. I can't even make her mad enough to give me a hint."

She yelled back to him, "Christmas is in one week. You'll last until then. I promise you won't die of curiosity." Clint just shook his head at the two of them. Everything was back to normal as far as he could tell.

The next day they all went out together to pick a Christmas tree. Junior carried the ax. After looking around for two hours, they finally all agreed on one tree. Junior chopped it down and Clint's job was to drag it back to the house. They brought a tarp to wrap around the tree and make it easier to slide it back to the house. Gayle had them stand it up in the shower so it would dry out and not drip water on everything. They rearranged all the furniture to put the tree up as far from the wood stove as possible. Gayle wasn't taking any chances of a house fire. They searched all through the garage and other storage areas and finally found the Christmas decorations. The next day the tree was dry, so they put it in the tree stand and added some water. They made eggnog with powdered eggs and some rum that Clint had grabbed from one of the houses. That night they decorated the tree and put a pretty multi-colored star on top. Gayle put some Christmas songs on the CD player and they sang along with most of them. They found several rolls of Christmas wrapping paper, bows and name tags in with the decorations. They all grabbed some to wrap their presents. There were even several rolls of clear tape in the box. Junior's dad had thought of everything.

On Christmas Eve day, they spent the day cooking and baking. They got everything ready for Christmas dinner so all they had to do was cook the goose that Junior's dad had in the freezer and warm everything else up. Gayle made her first pie. It was an apple pie, of course. The smell was driving Junior crazy. He kept pestering her to make two of them so they could eat one now and still have one for Christmas dinner. She made one. He said he'd need to test it to make sure she did everything right. She told him too bad. They'd all taste it together. She forced him to leave the kitchen. He pouted for a while and then cheered up when she presented him with an apple tart she had made for dessert for Christmas Eve dinner. She let him taste it, then they all went and got their presents to put under the tree. Each of them had two gifts. They had decided to watch *Scrooged*, starring Bill Murray, on Christmas Eve. They laughed through the whole movie.

Christmas morning Gayle was awakened at 7:00 by Junior bouncing on the bed. "It's Christmas morning, I get to open my present, so get up or I'm opening it without you."

Gayle opened one eye and looked at him. "Go ahead. But you should consider whether I booby-trapped it or not first." She turned over and went back to sleep. She woke up again at 9:00 and decided to get up and see if Junior liked his coat or not. She came out to the living room and the presents were still under the tree. She was puzzled for a moment. He must have believed her. She laughed and went into the kitchen. Junior and Clint were sitting at the table, talking. She smiled. "Merry Christmas."

Junior said, "I thought you were going to sleep the whole day away."

She looked up at the clock. "It's a quarter past nine in the morning on a holiday. How is that sleeping the whole day?" She went over and poured a cup of coffee. She stood by the counter and took a sip.

"It's because I've been waiting forever to open that present and you wouldn't even give me a hint."

"You want a hint now?"

Junior shook his head. "No. It's too late now. In a little while I'll know what it is. I don't need any hints."

"Suit yourself. How come you didn't open it already?"

Junior looked at her. "Because you told me you booby-trapped it and Clint said you two had been talking about making bombs and explosives the other day."

She looked at Clint and he smiled at her. She laughed. "That's true. We did talk a little about it."

"I've waited this long to find out what it is and I didn't want to take the chance of damaging it before I even got to see it. You've been so uncooperative about that present so far, so I didn't want to take the chance that you'd be that mean."

"It's not yours until I hand it to you."

"See? See how mean you are?" She laughed again.

Clint said, "Well, shall we go open the presents up? I'm a bit anxious to see mine, too. It's been a long while since I had any Christmas presents."

They all went into the living room and Gayle turned the tree lights on. It was Christmas day and in her house they always had the tree lit up all day in celebration. She reached down and grabbed Junior's present and walked over to him sitting on the couch. She bent down and kissed him. "Merry Christmas." She handed him the box.

He looked at the box and shook it. "Is something going to pop out at me?"

She laughed. "Well, there's only one way to know for sure." He ripped the paper off the box. The box was taped up really well. He had to use his knife to cut the tape off. He opened the box and looked inside. He didn't say anything at first. He reached in and pulled the coat out. It was a long coat, so he had to stand up to get it all the way out of the box. He looked it over. "This is so cool. You made me a capote coat. That's the design, isn't it?"

"Yes. My own variation of it."

He rubbed it inside and out. "You used flannel on the inside. It will really be warm." He tried it on and it fit him perfectly. He buttoned the coat and the sleeves and pulled the hood up and saw how she'd made it so he could close it to keep the wind out. He took it off. "Thank you. This is a very nice gift. It's really warm, too. I was starting to sweat." He kissed and hugged her with an amazed happy look on his face. He was still running his hands over the coat in awe.

She walked back over to the tree and grabbed Clint's present. She walked over to him and kissed him on the cheek. "Merry Christmas."

He took the gift. "Thank you." He slowly opened the paper and then he had to slit his box open, too. He looked inside and laughed. He looked up at Gayle. "Thank you. No one has ever handmade me anything like this before. This is really great." He pulled his coat out of the box and tried it on. It fit perfectly, too. He was smiling as he took it off. He looked at Junior. "I was starting to sweat wearing it, too. It's very comfortable and warm."

Junior smiled. "We both got a great gift. It looked good on you, too." They compared coats and saw the different colored flannel lining so they could tell them apart. They both smiled at each other, happy with their gifts. Junior got up and took his presents out from under the tree and handed one box to Gayle, kissing her. "Merry Christmas."

She slowly opened her box and took a wooden box out. It had a top that opened and four small little drawers that opened on the front. She smiled at Junior. "Thank you. This is beautiful. I don't have much jewelry to put in it, but I can put other things in here, too." Junior beamed at her.

He turned to Clint and handed him a long thin package. Clint said, "Thank you." He unwrapped the little package and saw a very nice expensive hunting knife. He smiled at Junior. "You can never have too many knives." Junior was happy that Clint liked his dad's knife. He had spent a long time making sure it was oiled and very sharp.

Clint went over to the tree and handed a box to Gayle, saying, "Merry Christmas."

She took it and opened it up. It was a small neck knife, with its own sheath and lanyard. Clint had burned her name in the leather of the sheath. She smiled up at him. "Thank you. This is very nice. Now, I have a knife of my own to use. Will you teach me some good moves for it?"

"Sure." He walked over and handed a heavy package to Junior. Junior opened up the box and it was a very nice aged whiskey.

"Thanks. We need it." They all laughed.

When they all sat down for Christmas dinner, Clint said, "Is it alright if I say grace" Junior and Gayle nodded their heads.

"Thank you, God, for all the good things you have brought into our life. I thank you for helping us through the bad parts, too. I am thankful that you directed me to this place and to meet Gayle and Junior. I thank you for providing us with all of these things that we have when so many people are out there suffering. I ask that you help them in any way you can. And if Junior's father is near by, please tell him that he raised a great son and I'll teach him what I can and that I say thank you for all his foresight in preparing for hard times. If Gayle's mother is around, please let her know that she raised a wonderful woman and that I'll look out for her as much as she'll let me. In Jesus' name, Amen."

Junior and Gayle both smiled and looked a bit misty-eyed. They both said, "Amen."

Gayle reached out on both sides for their hands. Junior held her right hand and Clint held her left. Gayle had tears in her eyes as she said, "Merry Christmas to my family."

Clint and Junior said, "Merry Christmas."

Chapter 26

Just One Big Happy Family

"Be not afraid of greatness: some are born great, some achieve greatness, and some have greatness thrust upon them."

William Shakespeare

Clark said, "We used to bring our horses up here with us to ride. Where's Mark?"

Eric looked up. "Behind you."

Clark turned around and looked thoughtfully at Mark. "Can we talk?"

"Talk? Isn't that what you've been doing?" said Mark.

Clark laughed. "I mean can we talk about another trade?"

Mark looked intently at him. "No, you can't have the horses. Is that what you were going to ask? That you would take them off our hands because you all know how to care for them and we don't?"

Clark looked at Eric and smiled. "I thought you were a tough negotiator."

Eric laughed. "You haven't seen anything yet. He makes every penny scream for mercy before he lets go of it for anything, no matter how important the item might be." Clark looked impressed.

"You're damn right I make every penny scream," said Mark. "Pennies are very valuable. Metal that has been already smelted is easier to work with than using raw ore. Pennies that were minted before 1983 have real copper in them. Copper is useful to have around. It can be used for so many different things, like generators for instance. It will also be a key ingredient to reestablishing communications. Even the newer pennies are valuable because they have zinc in them. Zinc is used to make an anti-corrosion coating on steel, that's called galvanizing. You can make precision components for die casting with it. It is also used in construction materials. And the most important thing zinc is used for is to make brass. Need I say more?" Clark looked fascinated with what Mark said.

Jim said, "How come you know so much about metal?"

Mark smiled. "Eric and I are engineers. We studied all about metals in college." Jim nodded at Mark with a thoughtful look on his face.

Clark said, "So, how are you going to care for the horses?"

Mark said, "I'm sure there is a book or two about horses upstairs. The library here is very extensive. I guess we'll just have to read them and figure out what to do from there. It'll probably be a lot of trial and error at first, but I'm sure we'll figure it out."

Clark looked disappointed. He very much wanted to get a hold of some of those horses for his own group. Jim and Brandon looked disappointed, too. But Clark was far from discouraged. He'd keep trying to make a trade. It isn't easy to care for horses without grazing land. The tree people had a lot of grazing land. Land that Mark and Eric didn't know about. He made up his mind right there and then to wear Mark down.

Eric wondered at first what Mark was up to. Then he realized Mark was employing his normal tactics of making the other person think he really didn't need what they were offering. Mark said you had to be in a position of equality in a deal, or the other person could and probably would walk all over you. The other side would have the advantage because they'd know ahead of time that you really needed whatever they were offering. Mark was showing Clark they really didn't need anyone else to care for the horses because they could learn to do that themselves. So, if Clark wanted some of those horses, he'd have to offer fairly for them. Clark seemed to really want the horses. Eric smiled. This was going to be interesting.

They all went into the living room to be more comfortable. The children joined them when they were done getting ready for bed. Amanda entertained them all with her stories of what had happened since her mother hadn't come back. She asked the men if they had seen her mother. They said they hadn't seen her, but would keep an eye out for her from now on. That made Amanda happy. She explained to them that now they had three mothers and two fathers. The men really got a kick out of Amanda and the dramatic way she talked. Ken said she was going to grow up to be an actress. They all laughed. Everyone who lives in California knows at least one person who's an actor or is studying to be one. It was a common joke.

Clark got Mark off by himself to talk about the horses. Eric smiled. Mark's strategy had worked. It usually did. He was a very good negotiator. Where Mark had worked, everyone always fought over getting him on their team for a project because he always laid out exactly what would be needed and usually got all that he asked for. They all knew he'd do what he said and in what time frame. He was usually the team leader. The only thing he'd really disliked about being team leader was doing all the reports for the weekly progress meetings. He'd talked about it a lot with Eric. Eric had smiled and nodded his head as Mark complained. Eric knew Mark really loved doing it and being the guy in charge, even if he did hate the paperwork. Eric shook his head. That was all in the past now. That way of life went the way of the dinosaurs. Now everything came down to survival. Who would have ever thought they'd be cut off from all their supplies? Or that a gun cleaning kit would have been so hard to obtain? Eric realized right at that moment that they'd lived in a sheltered world of their own making. Mark and he had always talked about survival and what was needed to prepare. They even thought they had it mostly figured out. But not all people had lived as they had or thought as they had. He thought about all they'd been through since the EMP. They'd prepared as best they could for the end of the world. They had at least some supplies with them from their BOBs. How in the hell are the other people out there coping? He sighed.

Lisa came over and put her arm around his waist. She leaned in and whispered into his ear, "We have a slight problem with the sleeping arrangements."

Eric looked at her and whispered back, "What problem?"

"Maria and I told them that you and Mark were our boyfriends. We did that to keep the men away, because they were looking at us as potential girlfriends. They're expecting us to sleep with those arrangements in mind. We hadn't considered a situation like this when we told them. I won't mind sleeping next to you again, but I don't know if Maria is ready to share a bed with Mark yet. Any suggestions?"

Eric looked at her for a few moments. "Have you mentioned this to Maria yet?"

Lisa shook her head. "I thought I'd run this by you first and see if you had any suggestions or a solution."

Eric smiled. He was pleased that Lisa came to him first. This was a good start to their future relationship. "Talk to her and find out how she feels. Then we can come up with a plan of action. It wouldn't be fair for you and I to make that decision for her. We'll also have to ask Mark."

Lisa smiled, leaned in, and kissed him. "Good thinking. Okay, I'll go talk to her and see if she's come to the same conclusions." She turned and walked over to Maria.

Lisa explained the problem and told her that it would be okay because Mark liked her. "Why do you think he likes me?"

"Because he watches you when he thinks no one else will notice," said Lisa. He always smiles at you and says thank you when you do something for him. Abby and I just get a thanks when we do something for him."

Maria said, "Really? I haven't noticed that."

"He also jumps up to do whatever you need when you're doing something. Even Abby has mentioned that to me."

Maria smiled. "I hope you're right. I really like and trust him."

Lisa smiled. "All right! Now go get him. Use your feminine wiles if necessary."

Maria laughed. "He probably wouldn't even notice if I did."

Lisa hugged her. "Well, there's only one way to find out." Maria chuckled as she walked away.

Maria walked into the living room and looked around for Mark. He was still over talking to Clark.

Maria walked over slowly. Just as she reached them, they reached out and shook hands to agree on a deal. She sat on the loveseat next to Mark. Both were smiling, so they must have come to a fair agreement. There had been no doubt in her mind that Mark would make a deal over the horses. They had no way to care for them. Mark was just evening the odds earlier. It had been a good tactic. Clark had been eager to make a deal for the horses. Either Clark wasn't as good of a negotiator as Mark, or the tree people really needed the horses.

She said, "I see you've both come to an agreement."

Clark sighed "Yes, we finally did. He's a very tough negotiator; way out of my league. He got the better end of the deal."

Mark laughed. "Don't believe him. He's not just some surfer dude that used to hang out at the beach all day. His looks are very deceiving. He's no amateur at negotiating. He was a lawyer in the old world. He got just what he knew he'd be able to get."

Clark looked intently at Mark and then smiled. He looked at Maria. "That's not true. I only got half of what I wanted."

Mark said, "But you settled for exactly what you knew you'd get. We have to deal with reality. Not hope and dreams. If we're going to be trading in the future, we have to be fair to both sides or it won't work."

"I know," said Clark. "We're hoping to expand trading with others in the community around here in the spring."

Mark nodded., "Exactly. Those that will survive until then will be a lot smarter than they were before. The first few years will show exactly what we're all made of."

Clark nodded. "With a lot of luck and planning we all just might make it." It was Mark's turn to nod.

Maria turned to Mark. "Can I talk to you?"

Mark looked at her questioningly. "Sure. What do we need to talk about?"

Maria blushed a little. "I need to talk to you privately." She turned to Clark. "Would you please excuse us?"

Clark looked at both of them and said, "Sure thing." He got up and walked over to the other side of the room where everyone else was.

Maria swallowed loudly, and then said in a low miserable voice, "When we were with the tree people, we said that Eric was Lisa's boyfriend and that you were my boyfriend. We did that because of the way the men looked at us and treated us."

Mark said in a deep intense voice, "I see. How did those men treat and look at you?"

Maria sighed. "They were looking at us like we were a prize they needed to possess. Like we were the last women on earth or something. It was really creepy."

Mark looked away for a few moments, thinking. He turned back to her. "For all they knew, you women might have been the last women on earth. But that's no excuse to upset you both. Did they do anything wrong or try to touch you in any way?"

"No. It was the way they talked about watching us from up in the trees. They acted like they knew us or something. It was really creepy. We'd never seen them before and they tried to act like we've been friends for a long time. It was scary and disconcerting. Anyway, the only way Lisa and I got them to keep their distance was to tell them we already had boyfriends. I'm sorry, I didn't mean to put you in this position by lying."

Mark smiled., "That's okay. If it was the only way they'd leave you alone, I don't mind at all."

Lisa got up and went into the kitchen to put more coffee on. Abby followed her. Abby whispered, "What happened tonight with Mark and Maria? Did you see how they had their arms around each other?" Lisa smiled and pulled her into the mud room and filled her in on everything that happened. "Wow. You guys really told the tree people that Eric and Mark were your boyfriends?"

"Yes, just to make the men back off. Abby, do like Mark in a romantic way?"

Abby looked shocked that Lisa would even ask that. "No. There's no chemistry between us at all."

"I just asked because you looked worried about what I said."

"I am worried about this situation. Mark really likes Maria a lot, but he's scared of approaching her because of what we went through. I hope Maria really likes him, too, or he'll be deeply hurt by all of this. It'd be like giving candy to a child and then snatching it back. Have you seen the look on his face when you and Eric are messing around?" Lisa shook her head no. "He looks so wistful sometimes when he looks at the two of you. I think he wants to be a couple with Maria, but doesn't have a clue how to go about it. And from what you said happened tonight, it is clear that Maria doesn't know how to interpret what Mark says from what he means."

Lisa said, "Like you and Eric do. You two explain a lot about what Mark means when he says things that confuse the hell out of us."

Abby smiled and said, "Yes, he does need an interpreter, doesn't he?"

Lisa laughed and then sobered up. "Maria told me tonight that she likes Mark, but isn't sure if she's ready for a relationship yet."

Abby sighed and rubbed her temples. She was getting a headache. It was probably a hormonal headache from being pregnant. She'd have to tell everyone else about the baby soon. "Well, all we can do is be supportive to both of them and help them as much as we can."

The next morning everyone was up bright and early. It had stopped snowing. Maria, Lisa and Abby made a huge breakfast. Brandon and Jim went out and saddled up the horses to ride back to their cave. They seemed really happy to have the horses. It sure beat walking everywhere. Everyone shook hands.

Clark said, "I'll be back with Jeff, our leader, in a few days. It will depend on the weather, which day it will be. Is that all right with you?"

Mark said, "That'll be fine." They had agreed that Jeff and Mark should meet. Mark had said that he wouldn't be leaving the cabin to go anywhere, so Jeff would have to come to the cabin. Mark didn't like leaving anyone else in charge of security just yet. Everyone needed more experience and training before he'd be comfortable. Clark understood because of the attacks that had happened already.

After lunch, the adults were sitting in the living room and talking about the deal with the horses and about the tree people in general. Eric shared his observations of how they had everything set up. As the talk died down, Abby cleared her throat. She looked at Mark and he nodded.

She said, "I have some news to share." Everyone looked at her curiously. "I wanted to tell you that I'm pregnant." Everyone was completely silent.

Eric looked accusingly at Mark. "A baby, huh?"

Lisa jumped up and glared at Mark. "How could you do this after what we've been through?"

Mark stuttered out, "What?"

Eric said, "Oh my God, Mark. What in the hell were you thinking?" Maria had been on her way over to Abby to give her hug. She stopped, turned around, and looked at Mark. Mark was still stuttering, not knowing what they meant. She turned back and walked over to Abby and hugged her.

Abby had tears in her eyes and said loudly, "Will you two knock it off? Mark had nothing to do with this."

That stopped Eric and Lisa in their tracks. They all turned and looked at her in stunned silence. Abby said, "It happened when we were with those animals." Maria hugged her tighter. She had figured it happened from when they'd been held captive.

Lisa rushed over and hugged both Maria and Abby. Lisa whispered, "I'm so sorry."

Abby straightened up. "I'm not. I'm sorry for the way it happened, but I want this baby very much."

Maria smiled through her tears. "Congratulations. We'll love it and help you raise your child. We're a family." Abby's tears ran down her face in relief.

Mark looked intently at Eric and said sarcastically, "Thanks for thinking I'd be the better choice for taking advantage of Abby than what really happened."

Eric sighed and looked a bit embarrassed. "All right. I'm sorry for saying that. I'm also sorry for accusing you. This just took me by surprise is all. I'm not thinking right." Mark didn't say anything. Eric thought about what he just said and then it hit him. His breath hissed out in a rush as he looked at Mark with a stunned look. "Oh my God, this means that Lisa and Maria could be pregnant. What in the hell will we do if they're pregnant, too? Damn, this is bad."

Mark glared at Eric and said in a harsh voice, "Stop it. When we rescued those women, we took responsibility for them. We will deal with whatever comes up as it comes up."

The snow was a Godsend, because it would keep most people inside and they wouldn't be out causing trouble for others. But the snow and cold weather was a very hard reality to those unfortunate people who had not found good shelter with a heat source. People's calorie intake dramatically increases as their bodies try to produce heat to keep warm. The myth that a person could survive without food for thirty days was being proved in this cold weather. A person's body will cannibalize itself in its fight to provide energy for movement and heat. The first thing that will happen is the person starts to lose weight, because their body is using up all their body fat for fuel in its desperate fight to provide nutrition. This makes most people feel colder, because fat is what insulates them from the cold. Their thinking processes starts to break down rapidly. They feel very tired and weak, and they lose control of their muscles. Their stomach starts to swell and their bones become sharply outlined through their skin. When they reach this point in their starvation process, they will either fall down and not be able to get back up again, or they will not be able to get up at all. Their fight for survival is over. Mark was thinking about all of this as he looked out the window watching the snow fall. Another storm had moved in early this morning.

Mark had been thinking along these lines ever since Abby had shared her secret of being pregnant with him. Especially since Lisa was with Eric now, and he and Maria had become a couple. They hadn't talked about birth control. What would they do if all three women became pregnant in the future? What could they do for birth control? He didn't know anything about it except that women can take pills to prevent getting pregnant, and of course, to use rubbers. They didn't have any birth control pills for the women to take and they didn't have any rubbers, either. He rubbed his face with his hands in frustration. That's another thing that was up at the retreat. They had stored a lot of rubbers because he and Eric had read a few articles about what would they do to prevent pregnancy in a survival situation. You didn't want to take a chance of getting a woman pregnant every time you had sex, right? You had to be careful or you'd end up with a lot of extra little mouths to feed. He sighed deeply.

The reality of the situation that the world was in would be pretty clear to everyone by this time. Men that loved their families would learn street smarts pretty quickly. They'd have to hone their brain power and mental alertness. They'd have to have the fortitude to toughen their mental and physical strength to face each situation and have the determination to survive no matter what. They'd do this for their families because they needed him to stay alive to protect and provide for them. He thought about what the cities must be like. The desperation the men must be feeling right now as reality hit them that it wasn't going to get better and no one was going to help. Mark shuddered. What would he be willing to do to make sure that Chris, Ryan, Amanda, Maria, Abby and Lisa had food to eat? How far would he go to make sure they did have food? Dark scary thoughts were flying through his mind as Eric walked up behind him and looked out the window, too.

Eric said in a concerned voice, "What in the hell happened now? What's wrong?" Eric knew him too well. There was no way to hide what he was thinking from him.

He turned and looked at Eric. His face was so tight and stretched it almost looked like he was in pain. Eric had never seen him so tightly coiled. It must be something really bad and important to have him react this way. Mark said in a deep, serious, controlled voice, "We have to start standing watches twenty-four hours each and every day. The only reason Abby and I are still alive because those wanna-be Roman Soldiers didn't have guns. If they had real guns, we both would be dead you would have walked right into a trap. No more playing at surviving and running around with our heads up our asses. We have to get dead serious right now. It's our job to protect the women and children that share this cabin with us. The snow out there means anyone that's left out there that doesn't have shelter, heat and food will come and try to take it away from us. If we get attacked by a group with real equipment and real weapons, with even a small amount of training, we'll be history in nothing flat if we don't train everyone how to defend this cabin. Eric, it is our responsibility to teach them what they need to know. We haven't been doing a very good job so far. We've already been attacked here twice and the real serious business of surviving is yet to come. What do you think would happen if we got attacked by a group of desperate, starving people that aren't in their right minds? Remember, they haven't got anything to lose and we have everything to lose."

Eric looked at him with a sober expression. "Holy shit. You're right. We have to start training right now."

Mark said, "Think about this for awhile. Let's say we never found this cabin. Let's also say we still have the children after being turned back from Redding. We've used up all the snare cable, so we can't set out any snares for food. We're all starving. We don't have shelter from the snow or any heat for the women or children. What would you do to provide them with food, shelter and heat? How far would you go to do it? What lines would you cross to provide them with what they need? How desperate would you be?"

Eric continued to stare at Mark. He finally said, "I'm beginning to hate that EMP. Before I was saddened and disappointed that the world had ended. Especially since we had to walk to get here. But now ... now it's like we're in an alternate universe fighting every day for our lives with unknown obstacles and hidden enemies around every corner. Like that video game that was popular back a few years ago. The only reality we have is who'll come next to try to take what we have. It's not just our lives we'll lose if we screw up. How did two single guys end up like this?"

Mark gave a bitter laugh. "Hey, that's my line."

Chapter 27

High Emotions Bring Trouble

"Failure is blindness to the strategic element in events; success is readiness for instant action when the opportune moment arrives."

Newell D. Hillis

Preston and Joe walked into the kitchen and poured a cup of coffee after checking that the coffee was still hot. They sat down at the table with a sigh. Joe said, "How in the hell did you get so many supplies jammed into that little trailer?"

Preston said, "Well, it didn't happen overnight. It's been a few years of accumulation for the end of the world. I found stuff I forgot I'd bought."

Joe chuckled. "I know. You were acting like a kid on Christmas morning as you were going through the boxes. That's what took so long. Well, at least it's all moved over here now."

"I sure hope we don't ever have to move any of it again."

Joe glared at Preston. "If you want it moved again, I ain't helping you. Once is enough."

Amy walked into the kitchen carrying their backpacks. She set them both down by the table with a sigh "I need coffee." She grabbed the cup she'd used earlier in the day, filled it up, and sat down at the table. She looked at Preston. "You had that stuff packed very well. I never would have guessed how much was in that room. I'll finish marking the boxes later with a list of contents. I'm giving my hand a rest. I think I have just as much permanent ink on me as on the boxes." Her hands had black spots and slashes all over them, some were on her clothes, too. She also had a few black smudges and streaks on her face that were going to take a few days to wear off. The ones on her clothes were hardly noticeable because she was wearing woodland camo pants and shirt. It kind of blended right in.

Preston said, "Well, at least it is done and over with."

Amy said, "After I rest a few minutes, I'll go over and straighten everything up in the trailer. I'm taking Steve and John with me to help. I'm going to show them how to wash the clothes, when to take a shower, that kind of thing, so they don't run into any problems trying to do everything at the same time. They're sure going to be happy to get to sleep in a real bed. They'll be moving in this afternoon."

Joe said, "I can relate to that. It'll be nice not to have to hear John complain about how hard the ground is every day."

Amy chuckled. "Well, he has a good point. The ground is hard. I don't think he knows you've heard him complain about it, though."

Joe smiled. "I know. I eavesdrop on them every chance I get. It's a good way to learn things. So far, they seem to be what they say they are."

Preston nodded. "When I'm training them, I push them extra hard to see if it will piss them off enough to show their true colors. John's the only one that has come close to taking a punch at me so far. Steve just does his best to do what we say. He's come close to collapsing a few times, but he just keeps on trying. John has more attitude than Steve."

Joe grinned. "Yeah, I know. You should hear him talk about us. Most of the time he swears that G. I. Amy is not human; she has to be a machine. They're in awe of her. He thinks you're worse than Attila the Hun could ever have been. They like Jane and are a bit scared of her. They've seen her practicing at the range we set up. And they talk about me being the guy in charge like a general, issuing orders that everyone has to obey or else. They both like Michael and think he's a great kid."

Amy smiled. "What's not to like about Michael? He's a great kid." Both men agreed with her. Amy stood up, "Well, break time is over. I'll be over at the trailer with Steve and John. There will be just enough time for them to get settled in before dinner." Starting tonight, both Steve and John would be joining them in the farmhouse for meals. So far they'd done really well and earned those privileges. Joe and Preston were still a bit leery.

Steve and John had worked hard to be a part of the group. Their training was coming along. Amy never complained, so she set the standard by which each man measured himself. They never complained to anyone else, just among themselves at night when they thought no one else was around. They didn't want to appear weak in front of Amy in any way, so they learned things fast. Their biggest problem stemmed from the concepts. They had never thought about defense or offense before in a 'do it right or die' kind of way before. They were coming along, though. They were also learning to think outside the box. Until they got the hang of watches and Joe and Preston trusted them enough to let them stand watches in the evening, they were having to patrol around the property during the day in between their training and other chores. With Steve and John's help they had all the firewood cut and stacked that they were going to need. Joe had a few extra cords cut, too, just in case it was a really bad winter or a longer one than they expected. Both had happened before. It was better to be prepared. Springtime would bring its own sets of dangers without having to worry about firewood, too.

Preston had sent John to the east side of the property to patrol and sent Steve south. He had Michael patrol north. He took the west. He found a good spot by the road to sit and observe the whole area. It was much better to sit quietly and let people come to them, thinking they hadn't been spotted yet. It would be a big mistake on their part to try to take them on at the homestead. But on the other hand, it would be a mistake they would only make once. He was sure their reputation in town would precede them. Earlier today he had checked down the road to make sure no one was hanging around where they had dropped the bodies off. There were some fresh signs that people had been there recently, but they were gone by the time he got there. The townspeople had dragged off all the bodies. The snow was late this year. He looked around at the sky and noticed the clouds were darkening and had that heavy look of snow clouds. It was going to snow either today or tonight. The snow would make it easier to spot if intruders came on the property. But the hazard with that was that you left footprints, too, and it would alert anyone that there were people around here. They were going to have to talk about how to conceal their footprints, maybe using snowshoes and some pine brush or something like that.

The radio on his belt crackled and a voice said, "Holy shit." Preston winced. Those damn fools still needed to get their radio comm down right. Then he heard, "Ahh… Battlestations. Ahhhh… Red Alert. Ahhh, Holy shit. There are twenty or more of them coming this way."

Preston grabbed the radio off his belt and said forcefully, "Shut up and return to base." *Damn*, Preston thought. That was John on the radio. He was going to have to drill it into his head until he got the radio comms down right. There was no sense in giving any intelligence out to the group that was coming if they were able to monitor the radios. Well, it looked like they were going to find out how well Steve and John had paid attention to their training.

Everyone should be in the yard in a few minutes awaiting orders. Joe was already coming out of the house.

Joe pointed to John. "You take the back foxhole and make sure no one is sneaking up behind us. People, we do this just like we trained." John ran off. He turned to Steve. "You take the foxhole under the old car. You know where it is. If trouble starts and they use the ditch for cover, your job is to cut them down." Steve turned and ran off. Amy was just running out of the house, putting her gear on. He turned to her. "You go up in the loft. Preston will join you there." She nodded and ran off to the barn.

Michael had followed Amy out of the house and ran up to Joe. Joe put his hand up. "Get back inside. You go to the second floor and watch all over and make sure you watch the back really well for anyone sneaking up on us. I want radio silence unless it's a sneak attack and the rest of us can't see it. Do you understand?"

Michael said, "Yes sir."

Joe said, "Go." Michael turned and ran back to the house. As Joe turned around, Preston came running up. Joe pointed at the barn and waved for him to keep going without saying a word. Joe walked inside and grabbed his AR-15 and his vest with ten thirty-round clips. He only loaded them with twenty-five rounds to keep the springs from wearing out too fast.

Jane came running up from the basement and said one word, "Where?" She had her trusted 22-250 with her.

Joe said, "Second floor. I want you to take out the most dangerous shooters first. The semi-automatics, shotguns, and handguns, in that order if you can. If they rush us, just kill the lead person as fast as you can and anyone else." She nodded and ran upstairs. Everyone was now in place.

The waiting was the hardest part. Facing the unknown is very unsettling because your brain keeps going around in circles with questions like; who's coming? What do they want? Were they just traveling through? Or are they a looting party? Also, to consider was how much training do they have?

Well, in the long run it doesn't really matter, Joe thought. Kill the leader is the first thing to do. Looters don't have military discipline. When they see their friends dying all around them, they tend to wise up real fast and move on. It would be better for them to find softer, easier targets. They'd find out real fast that this retreat was filled with battle-hardened, well-trained, and organized people who would reduce the number in their group very quickly.

As Joe sat there and waited, he thought about how he wished he'd worked out the buckshot cannon he wanted to make before this encounter. Well, it was too late now. At least he had one trick up his sleeve. He did have homemade claymore mines. Years ago he had bought a Lee two cavity .38 caliber mold and had collected lead wheel weights.

In the winter one of his pastimes was to melt the lead wheel weights and make buckshot. He had about thirty-five pounds of buckshot already made up and another two hundred pounds of wheel weights to make more. Both he and Preston had loaded up with exploding targets. He had built a "V" plate to direct the buckshot out in front with a top plate slanting forward. The idea was to blast all the buckshot out forward in a spread action. He had originally planned to use squibs to fire them off, but he could rig it up to use the exploding targets instead. He'd modify the back with a two inch round hole. He'd use a three pound coffee can to set the exploding target inside. He'd load the rest of the three pound coffee can with his homemade buckshot. On the backside of the can, he had painted a glow in the dark target so even in the dark they'd be able to set off his homemade claymore mines. He lined all of this up just right in the three pound coffee can. Some buckshot would come out the two-inch hole, so you had to be careful not to be too close before setting it off. He had set one of his homemade claymore mines on the other side of the front gate. This would cover the driveway out to the road. It was still untested, but he was sure it would work just as he wanted it to. It was the best idea he could come up with since the last attack.

He was watching the ragtag bunch of people coming down the road about a hundred yards out with binoculars from behind the sandbags. Some of the people had shopping carts, backpacks, luggage with wheels, golf cart bags with two wheels, but one thing they all had were guns. *Damn,* Joe thought. There was no way to hide the wood smoke from the house or Preston's trailer. Everyone coming by would know that at least two people and probably more was living here. He studied the group of people closely, looking at their equipment. One thing he hadn't seen was any radio gear. He grabbed his radio and said quietly, "Only answer yes or no. Does anyone see any scouts?" Everyone replied no. Well, that at least was on their side. They must be refugees passing through. They must be heading south for a warmer climate. It looked like they should have started their trek a lot earlier. He glanced up at the clouds and thought; they aren't going to make it to a warmer place before the snow starts to fall. He expected snowflakes to start coming down any second. These people had to be nuts to be traveling now when a snowstorm would likely kill most of them, especially the children. How could they drag their children outside to face the elements like this?

He shook his head at their stupidity. Maybe they ran out of food wherever they'd been and decided to head south to see if they could find any down there? But why wait until they would run into bad weather? It didn't make any sense unless something else drove them out of their homes. As the people who were walking in front of the group came even with the driveway, one person called out, "Do you have any food? Can you spare some for us?"

Joe said, "No. I'm sorry, but we only have enough for us. Just keep moving along."

A woman called out, "What about our children? Surely you could spare some food for them. We haven't eaten in days and it is going to start snowing." Joe replied with the same answer. The woman's body slumped and she looked at the ground with a defeated look. Joe swallowed hard. He felt really bad. But his first priority was his own group. They had planned and prepared and these people hadn't. A little girl and boy stared at him with pleading, hungry eyes. His throat was very dry and he swallowed loudly again. How could he possibly allow these children to starve to death when they had so much food? Then he imagined what Jane and Amy and Michael would look like in the spring if he gave their food away to these strangers. It strengthened his resolve and he just stared right back at the refugees. He was responsible for his family and group, not these people. Not even the children. He felt miserable denying the children food, but that was the way it was out in the world. He cared a lot more about Jane, Amy and Michael than he could ever care for any of these people. He said again, "Sorry. Just keep moving on down the road. I can't help you."

One man took a few steps closer down the driveway holding his Mini 14 and said, "How about we just kill you and take all of your food?"

Joe was still aiming his AR-15 at them. He steadied his aim. "Listen, Mister, and listen very carefully. I don't want to kill you. But I will not hesitate if I have to. You need to understand something right now. If one shot is fired, if it is your fault or my fault doesn't really matter, you will be the first one to die. Do you understand me?"

The man said, "Well, maybe it would be better to die quickly than to starve to death slowly." But the man lowered his rifle down to his side.

Joe replied, "That's your decision to make. But I would just as soon not to be the one to arrange the meeting between you and your maker. Now move along down the road."

The man got a little braver and took a step forward. "We have ten guns and we can rush you and take you out. One man can't win against that many guns."

Joe said, "I never said I was the only one pointing a gun at you. If that's what you think, you're a fool. If even one shot is fired, all hell will break loose and the decision if you live or die will be answered."

A woman inched her way up closer to the man and tapped him on the shoulder. He turned around and looked at her. She said, "Come on. We have to get going. They're not going to help. We'll just leave them to their fate."

The guy smiled and laughed. "You're right, Jenny. What's coming behind us is going to wipe out your little place here and everyone in there with you. They take no prisoners." He walked back to his group.

Joe thought at warp speed. He needed intelligence, but didn't want to lose the upper hand. He called out, "What's coming behind you?"

The guy turned around and looked at Joe. "Give us some food and we'll tell you." Joe thought about that for a second. He needed that intel really bad. But, he also couldn't give away the fact that they did have a little extra food they could spare.

Joe called out, "Let me check and see if we have any food we can spare." Information was very valuable. He needed that intel right now.

He pulled out his radio and before he could say a word Jane whispered, "I have some food ready for them. I'll bring it out right now." The door opened and Jane walked slowly over to Joe.

He whispered to her, "What are you giving them?"

"One pound of rice, six bouillon cubes, two cups of oatmeal and three slightly bruised apples." He nodded his head as she handed him the plastic shopping bag. She turned and went back into the house.

When she was safe inside, Joe called out, "Okay, here's the deal. I have one pound of rice, six bouillon cubes for flavoring, two cups of oatmeal and three apples. That's all the food we can afford to spare."

The man shook his head. "That's not enough to feed us. Give us at least five pounds of rice."

Joe said, "This isn't the welfare office. If you don't want the food, then just keep moving on down the road. There are more people coming down the road right behind you that will think this is a feast. I'll make the deal with them and learn the same information."

The man standing in the driveway was considering what to do. The same woman that had approached him before did so again. She whispered in his ear, "For the children's sake, take the deal."

He whispered back, "They have more food. We need more than that for a filling meal. They can afford to give us a little more."

The woman whispered, "Take the damn deal right now. The children are hungry."

The man whispered back, "No. I know what I'm doing."

The woman pushed the man aside in anger and frustration and took a few steps closer to Joe. "Thank you for your generosity. We'll gladly accept the deal for the children's sake."

Joe said, "Yes, ma'am. You and only you can come over the gate and tell me what's going on. Then I'll give you the bag of food."

The man in the driveway shook his head. "Jenny, no. Don't trust him."

She turned and looked at him and said in a harsh voice, "The children need food today. They're very hungry. I'm getting them some. So, knock it off and stay here so I can feed the kids." She turned and walked up to the gate. She had a bit of trouble climbing the gate, but finally made it over. She slowly walked closer to the porch.

When she was thirty feet away, Joe said from behind the sand bags, "That's close enough. Now tell me what's chasing after you."

Jenny stopped and took a deep breath. "It's some kind of gang. We don't know what they are called. There's about fifty of them or more. They have a lot of guns. They have some older trucks that still work and they have trailers they are towing behind them. They come into an area and take over a house, and then they go on a raiding spree. They steal from the weak and kill everyone."

Joe said, "Where are you from?"

Jenny said, "A little town north of here, about two hours south of the Twin Cities. We've been on the run for ten days now. We don't know if they're coming this way or not, but if they do, they'll kill all of you and take whatever you have. You don't stand a chance. Not unless you have an army hidden around here somewhere. They don't ask or demand anything. They just kill and take what they want."

Joe said, "Where are you headed now?"

The woman said, "South Oklahoma or maybe Texas. Somewhere the winters aren't this hard."

Joe tossed her the bag. "I'm sorry we don't have more."

Jenny caught the bag, and with tears in her eyes, she said, "Thank you. My children will have something to eat today."

Joe said, "I have a few more questions. What else have you heard?"

"Not much. Just that the U. S. was hit with an EMP. Nothing electrical will work. We heard the President over the radio and he said they're fixing everything. But the lights didn't come back on and we never received any help whatsoever. We heard that the bigger cities are a war zone. Some cities have soldiers and they've tried to restore order and are fighting it out with the gangs. Who knows who will win? Gangs have taken over most of the towns and cities and they freely roam the streets. No one is safe. The gangs are getting larger every day and they get more brutal every day too. We've heard that every night you can hear the screams from the unfortunate people they've captured that would make your hair stand out straight in shock. Barbaric is what people are saying." She paused for a few moments. "Oh yeah, about three days ago we passed a church. We stopped to spend the night there. It looked deserted and safe. It was full of dead people and children. There was one crazy woman there. She kept saying that they had prayed and prayed for the rapture but it never came. The preacher got tired of waiting for the rapture and had everyone drink poisoned kool-aid to help them reach heaven. She couldn't bring herself to do it. She was going crazy trying to dig graves and give them Christian burials. She said this was her punishment because she hadn't believed enough to join them. She asked us to pray for her lost soul. We offered to help, but she wouldn't let us."

Joe said, "I figured there would be a lot of religious nuts waiting for the rapture. I thought after it didn't happen, people would wise up and leave their pastor and church behind to their false teachings. I never thought they'd commit suicide with them."

Jenny nodded her head in agreement. "Remember Jim Jones?"

Joe said sadly, "Yeah. I do."

She said, "Maybe most of these people didn't have anywhere to go or any food left to eat. They must have been really desperate and disillusioned. Do you think we have a chance to make it to Oklahoma before winter sets in too bad?"

Joe said, "I really don't know. All you can do is try." She nodded in acknowledgment. "Is there anything else we should know about the gang that is coming?"

She looked thoughtful for a few moments then said, "They send teenage girls into the houses first to find out how many people are there and what they have inside for food, guns, and ammunition."

"How do you know this?"

"A friend of ours was able to escape out the back. She told us that's how they knew what was in her house. She'd been there with two other friends. They were just trying to survive. She let two teenage girls into her house to get them off the streets." She sighed and paused. She looked down at the ground and then looked Joe in the eyes. "She made it out and her two friends didn't. We're traveling on the back roads and staying off the main highways. We're hoping they're staying on the main roads and highways. We hope to bypass them, or at least to stay out of sight."

Joe said, "Thanks for the information."

Jenny said, "Are you sure you can't spare any more food?"

Joe said, "I'm sorry. I don't even know if we have enough until spring ourselves."

Jenny nodded her head ."Thank you. At least my children will eat today."

She walked back to the gate and climbed over it. When she got to the man, he turned and followed her back to the rest of the refugees. They continued their journey to safety. When they had passed by the house, he heard some shouting and arguing going on. He moved to the other sand bags so he could see what was going on. A man and two women were trying to take the bag of food from Jenny. She held the bag of food tightly to her chest shaking her head no. The man that had talked to Joe aimed his gun at the three of them and yelled for them to back off or he was going to shoot them. The three backed off. The man ordered them to start walking way ahead of them so he could keep his eye on them. Jenny had pulled an apple out of the bag and was cutting it up into three pieces. She handed a piece to each of her children. They quickly ate them. She hugged each child and they moved on down the road. Joe sighed and went back to the other sand bags, so he could watch the road for more refugees. He waited for an hour and no one else showed up. He pulled out his radio and said, "Michael, take the watch up in the tower. Go relieve Preston and Amy. The rest of you, meet me in the house."

Everyone arrived at the house within minutes of each other. They had heard most of it, because Joe had left his radio turned on. Joe briefed them on everything Jenny had said just to be sure they knew everything.

Steve said, "I thought you were Christians. Why didn't you give them more food for the children? They were starving."

Preston said in a steely voice, "It's not our concern to be the provider of free food. Every single person in America had plenty of chances to prepare for situations like this. Everywhere you turned, people were saying to get prepared. Even the government said to prepare. They didn't listen. They chose not to do it. Instead, they blew their money on vacations and things like that. It's their fault they have no food to feed their children. It's not our responsibility to have to feed the children of the world. It may look like we have a lot of food, but the plain truth is that with taking you two into our group, it's stretching us pretty thin as it is. We don't know if we have enough food to last us until the produce from the garden is ready to feed us next year." He paused to let that sink into their heads. "Joe and Jane have worked the soil here and cleared the land to insure we can plant enough to feed us through next winter. But it's going to take all of us working together to make it. Doing the harvest by hand is very hard, serious work. We'll also have to protect the crops from looters that will try to steal our food. The food that we worked long hard hours to produce."

Joe said, "All those people out there starving now laughed at us when we warned them to prepare for a situation like this. They believed we were safe here in America. They didn't want to hear about it and called us right wing nutcases and worse. Lots of people out there warned everyone to get more self-sufficient and store food, drill a well, plant a garden and get solar and wind power. Now, they're paying the price for their arrogance and placing their faith in an uncaring government to protect them."

Amy said, "It's very sad. It's become a cold, cruel world out there. Now we have to live by the rules of survival of the fittest and the best prepared." She thought for a few minutes. "I have compassion for those poor misguided people. but it's not our responsibility to feed the world, or even the children of the world. It's the responsibility of those children's parents to ensure they have food and shelter. Our concern is to ensure our own survival first. We prepared and they didn't. I know it sounds cold, cruel, and very selfish, but what do you think will happen if we run out of food? What if the crops fail next year? What will we eat then? If we have a good crop next year, then we can figure out how much extra we have and we can trade with others so they can have some, too. But in order to do that, we have to survive first." Steve looked shocked. He'd never really thought about it except that everyone needed food, and now they were starving out there, just like he and John had been doing before joining them here at the farmstead.

Jane said, "I'd like to read you something I found in a U.S. history book about the first Thanksgiving in America. William Bradford, in his own writings, which I quote in my book, *See, I Told You So,* describes their first experiment. "For the young men that were able and fit for labor and service did repine that they should spend their time and strength to work for other men's wives and children, without recompense. The strong, or men of parts, had no more division of food, clothes, etcetera, than he that was weak and not able to do a quarter the other could; this was thought injustice. The aged and graver men to be ranked and equalized in labor, and food, clothes, etcetera, with the meaner and younger sort, thought it some indignant and disrespect unto them. And for men's wives to be commanded to do service for other men, as dressing their meat, washing their clothes, etcetera, they deemed it a kind of slavery, neither could husbands brook it."

"The experience that was had in this common course and condition, tried sundry years, and that amongst the Godly and sober men, may well convince of the vanity and conceit of Plato's and other ancients;—that the taking away of property, and bringing into a common wealth, would make them happy and flourishing; as if they were wiser than God. For this community (so far as it was) was found to breed confusion and discontent, and retard much employment that would have been to their benefit and comfort." Having had enough of this failed system, and to avoid further devastation, another system was tried, free enterprise, or "Capitalism." Instead of working for the "common good," each citizen was responsible for their own survival, had private property, and enjoyed the fruit of their individual labor: The product of this experiment was also written in Bradford's diaries: "And so assigned to every family a parcel of land, according to the proportion of their number for that end ... This had a very good success; for it made all hands very industrious, so as much more corn was planted than otherwise would have been by any means the Governor or any other could use, and saved him a great deal of trouble, and gave far better content. The women now went willingly into the field, and took their little ones with them to set corn, which before would allege weakness, and inability; whom to have compelled would have been thought great tyranny and oppression."

"By this time harvest was come, and instead of famine, now God gave them plenty, and the face of things was changed, to the rejoicing of the hearts of many, for which they blessed God. And the effect of their planting was well seen, for all had, one way or other, pretty well to bring the year about, and some of the abler sort and more industrious had to spare, and sell to others, so as any general want or famine hath not been amongst them since to this day."

Jane said, "So you see, Steve and John, you might think you're working for us for free, but in fact, we're doing a Capitalist system. You owe us rent and for the food and supplies we have provided for you. You, in turn, agreed to work for us to grow food, defend the property, chop firewood, etcetera. But, you will be given your own plot of land to produce more food for your own storage or to sell and trade with. The seeds we provide you with will be replaced by you. We have heirloom seeds that are not hybrid plants. You dry them and save some for the next year's harvest. You then save some extra for your own planting the following year and so on."

Preston said, "We also understand at some time you may want to add a girlfriend to your camp. Now, this causes a lot of problems. A single woman could play you two off against each other and disturb the whole place, so she would have to be approved by all of us first before this will be allowed. And of course, remember that you are free to go out on your own at anytime if you don't like our rules. But if you both find girlfriends, then we would need separate housing for that couple, which in turn brings on a whole set of new problems. In the Army we had what's called a six-month rule. New guys would bend over backwards for six months, then in the next two months, you would see the real person come out. You see, you two are still on probation until we see the real you. So far, you're working out quite nicely."

John looked stunned. "You people have really thought all this out, haven't you?"

Preston said, "Of course we have. We're not amateurs. We both retired from the military." Steve and John shared an intense look.

Joe said, "We can discuss this more at a later time. Right now we have a real issue of fifty or more gang members probably headed this way. We know how they operate. They have trucks that run and that gives them a little advantage, but not as much as they think it does. We can send out a raiding party of our own. First priority is to take out their wheels. Then we can even the playing field. We'll send out a two person team to sabotage their trucks. That will put them on foot. The two person team will have to be sneaky and very quiet."

Steve said, "We can pour sugar into the gas tanks."

Joe smiled. "*Mythbusters* proved that doesn't work. But what does work every time is maple syrup. You pour a pint of it into the oil. Once the engine starts, the valves on the crankshaft get crystallized by the melted syrup and they stick open. This kills the engine. It takes a major rebuild on the engine before the truck will work again."

Preston said, "I'll go."

"Me too," said Amy. Steve and John both volunteered, too.

Joe said, "Preston needs to be one, and I think Amy should go, too, because they work as a great team. Use the bikes. Find them and take out their vehicles and then return."

Preston said, "How far out should we look for them?"

Joe said, "Take three days worth of supplies and do a thirty mile circle."

Preston nodded. "When?"

Joe said, "As soon as you two are ready. Jane will make a meal while you two pack." Preston and Amy both nodded their heads.

Amy looked at Jane. "Can I borrow your 22-250? The stock on mine needs some work and yours is exactly like the one I've been using with the same kind of scope and everything. Preston hasn't been able to fix mine yet."

Jane looked hard at her. "Only if you promise to return it even if you're dead." Everyone laughed.

Amy smiled. "I promise to stay alive and return it. That sounds like a much better option to me." They left to get ready. Jane started cooking. Amy came into the kitchen and gathered some supplies for their trip. Jane lent her some really thick thermal underwear to stay warm on the trip. As they pedaled down the road, it started to snow tiny snowflakes. Just a dusting, Preston hoped. When they neared the highway. They got off the bikes and walked cautiously up to look out on the interstate.

They took cover in some brush. They both took out a pair of binoculars and scanned both ways. There were more straggling refugees heading south. *To the promised land*, Preston thought. They watched for over an hour. The groups passing by were as small as one or two, and the largest they had seen was eleven or twelve people. They were all either pushing a cart that held their belongings or dragging it behind them. Preston shook his head. These people were the new homeless. "I wonder whatever happened to Sharon?"

Amy said, "I haven't thought about her in months. For all we know, she could be in one of these groups we're watching."

"Could be. I wish she'd listened. But she was so blind to the truth. It was easier for her to stay a sheeple than to open her eyes and really see. I feel bad about leaving her behind."

Amy patted his arm. "It was her decision. She left and gave us no choice."

They watched the interstate for twenty more minutes. "It's too dangerous to travel in the daytime. Let's bring the bikes up here. We will head out after dark." They brought the bikes up next to them and resumed watching. Every once in a while, there would be a lull in refugees, and ten to twenty minutes would go by without seeing anyone. When it was four o'clock in the afternoon, it started to get dark. It was still snowing lightly every once in awhile. Preston and Amy had a cup of coffee. It was about ten after four when five women and one armed man came hurrying over the hill. They were pushing two shopping carts and glancing back over their shoulders.

Preston and Amy shared a look. They both got ready because they could faintly hear a vehicle coming closer. "Trouble is coming our way and traveling fast." Amy nodded. She had found a sturdy branch to set her rifle on to steady her aim. The six people hurrying down the highway were just about even with them when an old Ford pickup with a snowplow formed into a "V" came flying over the hill. There were two guys in the cab and four guys in the back. The women started screaming and abandoned the shopping carts. They took off running in all directions. The man yelled something they couldn't hear and took cover behind an abandoned car and one woman joined him there. The woman pulled out a pistol from under her coat. The man had what looked like a 30-30 rifle. Preston wasn't sure he only had a glimpse of it as he ducked behind the car.

Amy whispered, "Are we going to help them?"

Preston whispered back, "If we can. Our first priority is to take the vehicles out, period." Another truck came flying over the hill, right behind the first one. "This is the scouting party. Reinforcements are probably not too far behind. We can't take a chance of giving away our position."

The truck raced for the car the two were hiding behind. The two people started shooting, but it was too little and way too late. Their bullets were bouncing off the raised plow. The truck smashed into the car, flattening the woman and sending the man flying off to smash down hard on the highway. They didn't move. The four guys in the back jumped out and took off laughing after the other running women.

Amy said, "We have to help those women." She remembered what had happened to Joan and didn't want to be responsible for the same thing happening to these women.

Preston said, "No. If we try to help them, we'll just get run over like those other two. Our job is to take out these two trucks and that's what we're going to do." Amy was breathing a little hard from the anger and disgust she felt. She glared at Preston but he didn't see the look because he was watching the men. She turned to see what they were doing. She knew the women didn't stand a chance because they were too far from any real concealment and it didn't look like they had any weapons.

One of the guys grabbed a woman by her hair and slammed her down hard to the blacktop. The guy was laughing and yelled out to his friends, "I got my entertainment for tonight." The other three guys were quickly closing the gap between them and the three other women. They were running and screaming at the top of their lungs, trying to get away from them.

All the women were caught now and Preston whispered, "These are some evil dudes, for sure." The men were dragging the women back to the truck. The women were screaming and fighting the men, but to no avail. The men didn't even flinch as the women hit them and scratched them. One guy stopped and pulled up on the woman's coat, pulling it up over her head and threw it off to the side. He then ripped her top down the front. He pulled a pocketknife out and cut her bra in half. He laughed and yelled, "Nice tits. You're going to put a show on tonight to get us in the mood." Amy had had enough. She wasn't going to leave these men alive if she could help it.

Preston heard a shot ring out and the man that had slammed the woman to the blacktop flew back beside a car with his brains splattered everywhere. He lifelessly fell to the blacktop. Amy quickly worked the bolt and another shot rang out, hitting another guy in the shoulder, knocking him to the ground. Preston was surprised and then he got pissed. "Shit." He opened up with his AR-15. Amy hadn't given him a choice. His mission was to disable the vehicles, so he took aim trying to hit the alternator or the radiator. He alternated between the two places, hoping this worked. Amy shot one more man just as they took cover. Two of the women got away and ran off down the side of the highway, and then they jumped into a ditch.

Preston switched magazines to armor piercing rounds. He said to Amy, "Keep those idiots occupied and their heads down." Amy quickly shot at the area around the truck, making the two guys inside duck down. She reloaded and shot at the ones inside the truck. The other truck was getting close. The guys in this truck were firing their rifles, but they weren't hitting anything important. Preston stood up and shot at the engine several times. He sent his last ten rounds at the driver. The second truck didn't have a snowplow on it. Steam started coming out from under the hood. The truck veered off to the side and crashed into another abandoned truck on the highway, bringing it to a screeching halt. The guys in the back flew out all over the place and lay still on the highway, injured or dead. The two in the cab flew into the windshield.

Preston slammed in another magazine and said in a deep, angry voice, "Time to go." One of the women got away and made it over to him. She said, "You've got to help my friends. Please help my friends." A third truck was on the way towards them now, having just come over the hill.

Preston said, "Sorry, we can't help you. We're out of here." He took aim and emptied a magazine into the engine of the oncoming truck, then hurried back to Amy. The men that had fallen out of the truck and were still alive had moved to cover. Amy was still firing at them. The men started firing back all at once. Preston and the woman barely made it back to Amy. Lead was flying everywhere, making branches snap and you could hear bullets ricocheting. Preston and Amy grabbed their bikes and took off pushing them. Preston said, "Head towards the road so we can start to pedal." The woman ran alongside them. She said, "What about my friends?"

Preston looked at her. "Sorry. We can't help your friends. You have a choice to make. Come with us or go back to your friends."

They reached the road. Amy jumped on her bike and Preston got on his. They could hear some of them coming after them. Just then a shot rang out and it ricocheted off the road a few inches from the front tire on Preston's bike. Preston told the woman get on the back of his bike right now or he'd leave her standing there to face those men. She climbed on and they took off. They pedaled as hard as they could and started gaining some speed. The men were still shooting. Bullets were flying all over the place. They had a bend in the road coming up.

Preston was trying his hardest to get around it and out of sight and range of the bullets. He was muttering, "Shit, we're leading them right back to the homestead." There was just enough snow to show the tire marks. Amy was in the lead. Just as they got close to the bend, he saw Amy jerk, but kept on going. The woman behind him on the bike at the same time cried out, "Shit!"

Preston said, "What?"

The woman said, "I got hit."

"How bad?"

"I don't know. It's in my back and it burns."

Yup, that's a bullet. They got around the bend and he said, "How much pain are you in?" The woman said," It's not too bad. It just burns a lot."

Amy seemed to be fine. He must have been mistaken thinking she was hurt. They went about ten miles and Preston said, "Let's pull over."

Amy pulled over to the side and he rode up next to her. He looked at her with dark angry eyes. "You really screwed up, Amy. You weren't thinking like a trained soldier, but like an emotional woman. You have now put our whole retreat in jeopardy. Those guys are going to follow us right back to the farmstead. If they weren't going to turn down the road here, they will now. They'll send their whole gang after us."

Amy said heatedly, "I was not going to let them treat those women that way and do nothing. Remember what happened to Joan? I won't sit idly by and let that happen right in front of my eyes, Preston. I don't care how mad you get. I won't do it. You even said they were evil." Preston didn't say anything.

He walked around in back of the woman and looked at her back. On her right side was a tear in her coat. He lifted the coat and looked at the groove the bullet had made. It was still dripping blood. He pulled out a dressing from his pack and taped it to the wound.

The woman asked, "How bad is it?"

"It's not too deep. The bullet just grazed along your side and left behind a deep groove. That'll hold it until we can take care of it properly." He turned to Amy. "Take the woman back to the retreat and tell everyone how you screwed up because you didn't do what we were ordered to do. Also, tell them to get ready for the fight of their lives." He took his bike and walked off into the woods. He watched as Amy and the woman rode away. Preston was mad at himself. He forgot sometimes that Amy wasn't a full trained soldier. He should have anticipated that something like this might happen after what had happened with Joan. He sighed and looked around.

It would be full dark soon. It was time to set up an ambush. He'd need to get on his way back to the retreat soon. It was almost too dark to see when he spotted two men walking down the middle of the road like they didn't have a care in the world. Preston shook his head. *What dumb asses. They aren't used to facing real soldiers. They used their guns and greater numbers to overwhelm small bands of people. Well, assholes, you're about to find out what coming against a trained warrior is really like.* These two must be the scouts. They were not very well trained. Time to send a message to the rest of them. When they were about fifty yards out, he shot the first one in the head and double tapped the other one in the chest. He waited and watched for more of them to show up. After ten minutes, no one else showed, so he went out and stripped them of their weapons and ammo. It was time to head to the retreat. On the ride home, he went over how many they'd already taken out. It would all depend on their true numbers, but they had between forty-five and fifty more guns to go through. What a mess.

Amy and the woman neared the farmstead. Amy stiffly pulled out her radio and said, "One back with a passenger. Road is clear."

Joe's voice came out of the radio. "Roger." He met her at the gate and opened it for her. The two of them walked through and then Joe secured the gate. Amy leaned the bike up on the other side of the house and met the two of them up on the porch. "Who is this?"

Amy said, "I don't know her name. Let's talk inside." He nodded. He was worried because she came back alone. Amy didn't look so good, either.

They went into the house and Jane greeted her. "Where's Preston?"

Joe turned and looked at Amy. "He stayed behind. Preston said I have to tell you that I screwed up really bad."

Joe said, "Screwed up how?" Steve and John came into the living room and heard what she said. Amy told them everything that happened. Joe turned to the woman. "What's your name?"

The woman said, "Vicki. My name is Vicki Smith."

Jane said, "Let me look at that wound." She led the dirty woman off to the bathroom after giving Amy a reassuring pat on her arm that made Amy flinch. Jane hadn't seen the flinch.

Joe turned back to Amy. "Now they'll all be on their way here to even the score."

Amy looked at the floor and nodded her head miserably. Then she looked back up at Joe and said with a defiant look in her eyes, "I'd do it again, too. Those women needed help. We were only able to get one out, but it was better than not to do anything at all."

Joe looked at her long and hard. He finally said, "Is her life worth more than any of our lives here at the farm?"

Amy looked crushed and tears filled her eyes. She closed her eyes and whispered, "No."

Joe said, "When you decided to help them, you also decided that they were worth more than any of us here. By not sticking to the plan, you've brought them right to our door."

Tears ran down her face and she whispered miserably, "I see." She was getting unsteady on her feet and swaying a little. The men had never seen her cry before. Steve and John didn't know what to say or do.

Joe just looked at her and she looked back. He could see she was pale and sweating. "Take off your coat, Amy. You're getting too warm. We have plans to make." Amy just stood there and then she tried to undo her coat, but her left arm wasn't working very well and it was hard to unzip her coat with one hand. She fumbled around and finally got it unzipped. She slipped the coat off her right arm and gently eased it off her left arm. "Are you hurt?"

Amy nodded. He stepped behind her and saw the bullet hole in the upper part of her left arm. Blood was dripping down her back and arm. "Holy shit." He turned to Steve. "Go get Jane." He led Amy over to the couch and had her lay down on her stomach with her hurt arm towards the coffee table. Jane came running into the living room and sat down on the coffee table. She had brought a small bag with her. She reached into the bag and took the scissors out and cut Amy's shirt.

"Preston's going to be mad at me for ruining his shirt, too."

Jane said, "Why didn't you say something before? My God, Amy, you have a bullet hole in your arm."

"I deserved to get yelled at first because I've put all of you into jeopardy."

Jane shook her head. She cleaned out the wound some. "Joe, can you get her to the table in the kitchen? I'm going to have to sew both sides of this up after I debrie it some more." Joe came over and helped Amy up, trying to move her left arm as little as possible. Jane laid a blanket on the kitchen table with an old plastic shower curtain on top of it with a sheet over the top of that. Joe helped Amy to climb up and lay down. Jane arranged her how she wanted her. She told Amy, "I'll be back in a few minutes. I have to go check on Vicki and get some more supplies." She squeezed Amy's good arm as she walked away.

Amy wasn't sure how she felt about getting shot, except it was not something she wanted to ever happen again. This hurt a lot worse than when her leg had been grazed by a bullet when she'd been up in the loft. She turned to Joe, who was sitting at the table next to her with a concerned look on his face. "I messed up, Joe. I really messed up bad."

Joe looked her seriously in the eyes. "Yes, you did. If we survive this, then we can say it is a learning experience. If not, well, then it won't matter." Jane came in and brought a tall floor lamp with her. She took the shade off and positioned it next to Amy's arm to see better. She went to the sink and washed up. Joe stood up. "We'll be out preparing a welcoming for when the gang gets here."

About forty minutes later, Michael radioed Joe. "Someone is coming down the road on a bike."

Joe said, "Roger.'" He put his radio away and started to walk towards the front gate. Preston was already over the gate and on his way to the barn to put his bike away. Joe had just taken Amy's bike out to the barn to put it away.

Preston said, "Where is everyone?"

"Set up just like before." Preston nodded and hurried to the barn to put his bike away and came back out to Joe. The place looked dark and eerie. "How many are left?"

"We took out between three and seven people. So, there are still forty-five to fifty guns to go."

Joe said, "How long do you think it'll take them to make it here?"

"There's no way of knowing how far back they were from the scouts. We did take out three trucks, for sure though. We just didn't take them out the way we planned."

Joe nodded. "We have some surprises for them, too."

"They're not used to having anyone experienced fighting back. In fact, I doubt they're used to anyone really fighting back at all. They just overwhelm them with their numbers."

Joe nodded. "I left the best for last. You and I will take some of my homemade surprises and set up an ambush. We'll set out as many as we can and then race back here and set one up out front by the gate."

Preston said, "It sounds like a plan."

They were done by about seven-thirty that night. They had set up an ambush by an abandoned car two miles from their homestead. Joe's surprises were homemade claymore mines. The one out front was set up so Joe had a clear shot at it from one hundred yards. It was set underneath the car. Joe was carrying his .270 with a Leopold scope. The claymore mine was covered with a white cloth so it blended in with the snowy road. He had a target painted on it with glow in the dark paint and it showed up very bright in his scope. The way he had it set up you could only see it from the side facing the house. The plan was when the gang made it to that car out front, he'd shoot the target and make the claymore blow up. Preston would be pouring lead into them and he would snipe at them, too. It was a quick plan, but it just might work.

Joe and Preston were both in snow camo, and blended right in with the terrain. Joe set up his Harris bi-pod and used his mitten on the backside to raise the gun to the correct level. He slowly squeezed the trigger a little and he was dead on. He relaxed his grip. About twenty minutes later they watched a dark figure walk down the road. About a hundred yards back was the main part of the gang. Joe signaled to Preston to let the scout pass by the car. The car itself would cover the glow in the dark paint unless he bent down and looked under the car from the back at the right angle. He signaled to Preston to kill the scout when he shot the target. They were old friends and had served together in combat, so it seemed sometimes they could almost read each other's minds and had no trouble understanding what each other meant, wanted, or needed. They both blended into the moonlight night as if they weren't there at all. The scout slowly passed by the car. *So far, so good*, Preston thought. The rest of the gang spread out, filling up the whole road. Joe smiled and thought, *this is just perfect*. They were getting closer. Fifty yards. Then they were forty yards out. Joe's breathing was increasing and he had to consciously slow it back down. The scout was about forty-five yards from where Joe lay on the ground. Joe waited patiently with the target in his sights.

The scout suddenly stopped and held up his arm for them to stop. The scout was looking right at Joe and could see the outline of the rifle raised up off the ground by the bi-pod. Preston saw the exact second when it registered in the scout's mind what he was looking at. He shot him in the head. This made all the others come running down the road to see what happened. When they were about twenty-five yards out from the homemade claymore, Joe squeezed off his shot at the target. A very loud kaboom rang out, sending hot lead in every direction. Almost at the same time, the screams started. It looked just like in the movies when cannon shot hits the front lines of troops. Eighteen died instantly and nine more were injured. They stumbled or crawled off to the ditch, looking for cover. At the time of the kaboom, Preston started mowing down the stunned ones, standing there in shock. Someone started shooting at Preston, so Joe aimed and dropped him right where he was standing. It was time to retreat. He signaled to Preston. They hit five more with gunshots as they retreated. They ran back over the small hill and dropped down to watch how the gang would react. Joe and Preston counted them as they came over the small hill. There were twelve left out of fifty or so gang members.

Joe whispered to his best friend, "What do you think? Will they back off now?"

Preston smiled at him. "If they were smart, that's exactly what they'd do. When you lose three quarters of your men in one engagement, that's a clue to go elsewhere." The gang members had stopped firing wildly. Joe and Preston watched and waited to see what they were going to do. The ones left standing took off running. A few minutes later, they heard an argument break out. Two of them were shouting in each other's faces, and then one of them shot the other, ending the argument. They all started to walk back the way they'd come. Some of their wounded comrades called out, asking for help. A few that were slightly injured were helped up, and the rest were left for dead. They waited there for over an hour and there were no other signs that anyone was around except for a few moans of the dying men.

Joe said, "We'll wait until it's light out, then we'll do a recon and collect their guns, ammo and supplies. We got lucky that they were stupid enough to walk into an ambush." They got the bikes from where they'd hid them and started riding home. This had worked out even better than they'd hoped.

Preston said, "What size explosive target was that?"

Joe laughed. "Two and a half pounds."

"Your metal plate system worked great, too. It looked like a cannon with grapeshot taking out an army."

"Yeah, we got lucky. We'll pick up what's left in the morning. It did look pretty impressive, though, didn't it?"

Preston laughed. "Yes, it sure did. It looked like it was raining fire for a few seconds. They never knew what hit them."

When they reached the farmstead, they lowered the bikes over the gate and then climbed over themselves. Jane stepped out from behind the sandbags. Vicki was right beside her.

Joe asked, "Are Steve and John still in the foxholes?"

Jane nodded. "Amy and Michael are still up in the tower."

Joe nodded. Jane could tell what they had to say was good news by the way they were acting. He pulled out his radio. "Steve, John, meet us in the house. Amy, Michael, you stay up in the tower. We hope it's over, but we won't drop our guard in case it isn't really over." They all acknowledged their orders. On the way into the house Joe said, "Those bikes sure have come in handy. That was a very good idea you had."

Preston smiled. "Thanks. I thought so, too." They walked into the kitchen through the mud room after taking off their outside clothes. Preston did a double take at Vicki. Wow, did she look different cleaned up.

Vicki was the first to start asking questions. "Are you guys in the Army or something?"

Preston laughed. "We're retired Army. Now we're a militia, sort of."

"Good. Now we need to rescue my friends."

Joe looked at her. "Your friends are probably dead by now. We're not doing anything until morning. It's too dangerous out there right now. We have a lot of dead and wounded out there we have to clean up before we can do anything else. Then we'll talk about going and looking for your friends."

Vicki said, "I don't understand. Why can't you Army guys go right now?"

Jane said, "We lost a very good friend to a wounded enemy. We'll wait until daylight. We're not taking any chances in the dark."

Vicki looked sad. "Oh. "Thank you for saving me back there and letting me come with you." Preston was still a little pissed about how all that had turned out and just nodded at her.

Jane said, "Sit down." They complied. Steve and John were looking at Vicki, trying to make it look like they weren't doing it.

Preston smiled. "That homemade claymore mine worked rather well. It saved our asses out there. Without it, we'd still be in a firefight right now." They told them what had happened. Jane poured Vicki a cup of broth. She hadn't eaten in awhile and Jane wanted to start her out with clear liquids and work up to heavy foods. Right now, regular food would just make her sick and she'd probably just throw it right back up. Earlier, Jane had gotten another one of their spare rooms ready for her to sleep in. She showed Vicki where her room was so she could get some sleep. Joe said they should all get some rest right here in the house, so they could be ready if any gang members showed up before daylight. Steve slept on the couch in the den and John took the couch in the living room. Jane got them blankets to use. Preston took a large padded chair and relaxed in it, keeping watch out the window. He had a clear view down the hallway where Vicki was sleeping. They still didn't know if they could trust her or not.

Jane said to Joe in the kitchen, "How long are you going to leave Amy up in the tower?"

"This is part of her punishment. She doesn't know what happened tonight. We'll let her stew, wondering how it went and if anyone was hurt because of what she did. He rubbed his face with his hands. "Life is never easy; problems are always complicated with even more complicated solutions. Now, we have another mouth to feed."

"Just remember she was shot, too."

"I know." Jane reached for his hand and they took some comfort from each other.

Jane said, "Go get some rest. Tomorrow is going to be a long day. I'll take a nap later."

"No."

Jane rolled her eyes. "I promise I'll wake you at the first sign of anything. Now go and don't argue with me. I mean it, Joe."

He looked at her. "Okay, but wake me up before daylight."

"I will." Joe kissed her and walked out of the kitchen to get some rest.

Jane woke Joe before daylight. He went in and woke John. He pulled him aside. "Today, when we do the clean up, I want you to stay here and keep an eye out for any trouble. Michael will be up in the tower. I also want you to watch Vicki very closely. Keep her near you the whole time we're gone. We don't know anything about her yet. Remember how that gang worked. They sent females in first. I'm not saying that's the case here, but just watch her as a precaution."

John said seriously, "I'll watch her every move." Joe nodded at John and then went to get some coffee. Preston came into the kitchen and grabbed a cup of coffee, too. They drank it in companionable silence.

Jane came in. "Breakfast is ready. I'm going to make up plates for Michael and Amy and take it over to them. You can just help yourselves."

Joe and Preston said, "Okay." Jane took the food over to the tower.

Jane had just got done putting a new bandage on Amy's arm. "It's looking good, but just to be sure, you're staying on antibiotics for two weeks." She handed Amy a pill to take. Amy took it with a swallow of water. Jane had brought Amy a clean shirt. She had already put it on, along with a spare coat that Jane had lent her without bullet holes. Amy didn't look too good. She was pale and looked really tired. Jane said, "Don't forget to take three to four ibuprofen every four to six hours for the pain, either."

Amy nodded. "I just took some about an hour ago."

"Good."

It was decided that Amy would come with them as part of her punishment so she could see what the outcome of helping Vicki had been. Joe and Preston rode the bikes. Amy rode behind Joe because she wasn't in any shape to walk. John and Steve walked down to the site of the ambush. None of the others were prepared for the slaughter around them. Branches and twigs were blown all over the place. The bodies looked like they'd been butchered. It had stopped snowing last night and they could see everything in vivid color in the bright sunlight. There was blood scattered everywhere.

Joe said, "We'll shoot the ones that are still warm in the head. We'll use two teams: Preston and Steve. John, you're with me. One shoots and the other one covers. Got it?" They nodded. Amy you watch both ways and let us know if anyone comes.

The men started dragging bodies. When they were done, Steve and John spread out a large tarp and collected all the guns, equipment and backpacks they'd taken off the bodies and put them on the tarp. They'd already checked all the bodies for ammo and knives and other useful things before dragging them into the pile. When they were done, Preston and Joe rode back with Amy to the farmstead. John and Steve dragged the tarp full of guns behind them. When they got to the farmstead John and Steve hauled the tarp inside the barn.

Vicki asked them to please go check if her friends were alright. Joe and Preston reluctantly agreed. Amy wanted to go to see this through to the end. Joe agreed. Joe told John to watch Vicki while they were gone, like before. Steve went with them. Riding the bikes back to the highway the four watched for signs of anyone being alive. Preston and Steve headed down to check for survivors. They found the other three women with their throats slit.

When they returned, Preston grabbed Amy and held her as tightly as he could without hurting her left arm. She said, "We really didn't make a difference, did we?"

Preston looked at her. "Yes, Amy, you did make a difference. You saved Vicki's life. If you hadn't, then she'd be over there dead with her friends right now."

"How bad was it?"

"They all had their throats slit."

"What about the van?"

Preston said, "A woman was inside. She'd been raped several times, then they slit her throat."

Amy said, "Bastards."

Joe said, "That's how these types work. Then they don't have to feed them or give them water. They just go find more women later and do it all over again."

Steve said venomously, gesturing at the dead gang members, "Bastards. They're scum. If those killers weren't dead already, I'd kill them."

Joe nodded his head and looked at Steve. "The whole world is full of them."

Steve said, "How could they act like this?"

"They were already like this before the EMP. Probably not killers yet, but already on their way." Joe paused. "The EMP didn't change people. Whatever you were like before is the kind of person you'll stay unless something drastic or traumatic happens to change your point of view. But you're right, Steve. This kind is just scum." They got the bikes and started pedaling back to the house.

When they got back Amy said, "I should be the one to tell her." The three men looked at her. "I started all this, so I'll tell her about her friends."

Joe said, "That isn't necessary, Amy."

Amy nodded. "Yes, it is. I saved her, so I should be the one to tell her about her friends." Amy sat down next to Vicki. Jane was standing by the stove, watching. Amy took her hand. "I'm sorry, Vicki, but none of your friends made it."

Vicki started to cry. "What happened to them?"

Amy looked at her. "They cut their throats. I'm so sorry." Vicki cried great wracking sobs. Amy tried to hug her, but didn't do a very good job of it with her hurt arm and Vicki's wound. Jane gathered Vicki into her arms and held her tight. John was on the other side of the kitchen, where he could watch Vicki. He looked a bit misty-eyed, too. All of them looked sad and angry.

John said, "I hate the world we live in now." He turned away and faced the window. No one said anything. Awhile later, Jane led Vicki out of the kitchen and down the hall.

Steve said, "I'll go relieve Michael so he can get some rest." Joe nodded. "John, relieve him in six hours. Get some rest now until your watch." John nodded and walked into the mud room to get his things. Steve went out the door with him.

Preston said, "Amy hasn't had any real rest. I'm going to put her to bed so she can heal."

Joe nodded. "Get some rest, too. I'll make sure Michael eats and gets to bed." He patted Preston on the shoulder and walked out of the kitchen. Amy had tears in her eyes. She was at the end of her emotional endurance. Preston gave her a pain pill Jane had given him for her. He helped her up and held her tight as he led her down the hall to their room. He got Amy undressed and into some warm, clean thermals and tucked her into bed.

She grabbed him. "Are you going to leave me?"

Preston said, "No. I'm going to climb in bed and hold you. I won't leave you alone." He got undressed and held her gently so he didn't hurt her arm.

Amy laid her head on his shoulder. "The world we live in is so screwed up."

"Yes, it is."

Amy's voice sounded soft and lost sounding. "I don't think I'm going to make it. I don't like this new world very much."

Preston held her closer. "You're doing fine, babe. You're doing just fine."

"Preston, you have to promise me something."

"All right. What?"

"If I'm ever taken by a gang or by anyone, you have to promise me you'll kill me and not let me go through what those women did."

Preston said, "What?"

Amy grabbed him tighter and got right in his face. "You have to promise you'll do that for me. That I won't ever have to go through anything like that." Preston just stared at her and couldn't say anything. Amy shook him and said fiercely with tears rolling down her face, "You have to promise me, Preston."

"All right, all right. I promise."

Amy relaxed her grip on him and laid back down. "Thank you."

Preston lay there thinking, long after Amy's breathing evened out, staring at the ceiling. He loved her and there was no way in hell he could ever hurt her. He would protect her to the end and beyond if he had anything to say about it. He told her silently, "I'm sorry, babe, but that's one thing I could never do."

Chapter 28

A Pregnant Pause

"Adapt yourself to the life you have been given; and truly love the people with whom destiny has surrounded you."

Marcus Aurelius

Gayle stood looking out the window at the piled up snow. She watched Clint and Junior as they shoveled in front of the outside door. Then they made a path to the garage and cleared the snow between the two structures. It had snowed a lot in January and now that it was February, the snow just kept on coming down almost daily. She rubbed her hands up and down her arms for warmth. It was bitter cold out there. The snowdrifts were so high that it hid the areas they shoveled from sight if anyone was stupid enough to be outside in this kind of weather. Clint had called off all outside training for a while. She smiled, thinking how Clint had said it was now time to act like a bear and hibernate. It was too dangerous to be outside in this bitter cold. He had them doing exercises in the living room. He also had them cleaning the guns over and over again, practicing hand signals, and how to hide in plain sight. He started teaching them about improvised weapons and IEDs (Improvised Explosive Devices). It was a competition to see who could be the fastest and best at whatever they were doing. The bet was for cooking and washing dishes, and the one that had the most losses in the day had to do the chores. They laughed and argued about it a lot. They would tease each other about being a loser. She smiled just thinking about it. They took Sundays off as a day to clean and rest up for the coming week. Who'd have ever thought that the world could end like it did and they'd still be able to joke around and have fun learning new skills? She shook her head in amazement that they were so happy and cozy here.

She went back into the kitchen to finish the morning dishes. She swallowed hard, trying to keep from throwing up. She must have picked up a flu bug. This past week she had felt tired and sick to her stomach a lot. Clint said that was no excuse. She smiled a little, thinking about how she'd told him she felt like she was going to throw up, and he had her do the exercises anyway. She threw up all over his pants and boots. After that, he got a big pan from the kitchen and set it next to her so she could throw up in it if she felt the need. He was a hard teacher. Once they got over the shock of how different he was when he was their instructor instead of their friend, she and Junior really liked it. He was making them into dangerous people. It was just hard at first, separating the two personalities from each other. During training they called him sir, the rest of the time they used his name. They had learned a lot and he told them they were just beginning. If someone a year ago would have said she'd be doing this, she'd have laughed and thought they were nuts and lost all touch with reality.

Clint said, "Grab the ash pan and empty it; I'll grab another load of firewood." Junior nodded and stepped inside to grab the ash pan. They tried not to talk very much when they were outside, because it hurt when the bitter cold air hit their lungs. It made their teeth ache, too. Junior opened the stove up and gently grabbed the ash pan, trying not to get the ashes everywhere. Gayle ran by him on the way to the bathroom. She had her hand over her mouth, so she was going to throw up. It was becoming a familiar sight. He shook his head. She needed rest and refused to stay in bed. She said by noon or so she'd feel a bit better. Women, who could understand them? He thought for sure that after living together he'd get an understanding of what they were about. Well, so far that hadn't happened. Clint told him that he'd probably never completely understand Gayle. Women were a lot different than men. He could hear her in the bathroom. He went and emptied the ash pan.

Clint and Junior walked into the house and locked everything securely. They hung up their outer clothing so they'd dry. When it was snowing, they took turns going up on the roof and cleaning off the solar panels. It was a routine now. They had settled into a regular routine for everything. They kept busy so they didn't get too bored. Cabin fever still set in, though, at times. Clint was the hardest hit. He wasn't used to being caged up in a house all winter long. It was hard sometimes to get used to people constantly being around; he was used to being alone. It wasn't that he didn't like or care for Gayle and Junior, it was just a lot different. The way they argued and bickered over every little thing got on his nerves sometimes. He knew they were just having fun, but it was irritating. He was set in his ways. He spent a lot of his free time on Sundays alone in his room or going for a long walk to check the area outside.

That's what he was going to do after lunch today. It would have to be a short walk, because it was so cold, but it would at least get him outside for a while. He'd remember to bring his shades with him this time. Last time he'd forgotten and got a very bad headache from the glare of the sun on the snow. He'd been using Junior's dad's cross-country skis to check around the whole area. It gave him a lot of exercise and he really enjoyed it. He went into his room to read before lunch. He sighed as he settled in the chair in his room, deep in thought. He laid the book on his lap.

What he needed to do was find a woman to be a companion and lover. He chuckled. Like that was ever going to happen. He hadn't found a woman that would stay around when the world was still fine.. How in the world would he find one now? He shook his head. It was Gayle's fault. She'd been filling his head with nonsense telling him he'd find the perfect woman All he had to do was wait. She kept telling him she had a strong feeling. He smiled, it would be nice, but he knew deep down that it wasn't going to happen. He sighed, and thinking about women brought him to the subject of babies. Gayle said she had the flu, but he'd noticed the last few days she seemed to feel better in the afternoons and evening. Some evenings she didn't have any flu symptoms at all. He'd asked them in the beginning if there was a chance of her getting pregnant, and she'd said no, that they were using a preventative and she was very careful. But he wondered.

Well, there was only one way to know for sure, and that was if she stopped having periods. He'd heard other guys talk about it over the years. He didn't know very much about it, but one thing they all agreed on was that for morning sickness, slowly eating a few crackers before getting up in the morning could help with the queasy stomach. Alcohol, cigarettes and drugs would be out of the question during the pregnancy. A few guys had said also that they shouldn't drink coffee, but herbal teas. He didn't think any of that would be a problem for her. He'd seen her eating a piece of toast and sipping a cup of herbal tea when she didn't feel well. Oh boy, what if she was pregnant? What would it be like to have a baby around? He'd only seen babies from a distance when his buddies met their families on base after a mission. All he knew was they cried a lot, they drank formula and they needed a lot of diapers. He sat deep in thought, tapping his fingers on his thighs as he contemplated how to get a pregnancy test. Well, they could try the crackers in the morning and if that took care of it then that would be a pretty good sign that she was pregnant plus, if she stopped having her periods. With that worked out, he picked up his book and started reading.

After lunch, Clint sat down with Gayle at the kitchen table so they could talk. Clint said, "Gayle, I know that we talked about this before, but I'm going to ask you, anyway. Could you be pregnant?"

Gayle jerked back in shock. "No way."

"Are you absolutely sure?"

"Yes, I'm…" She stopped mid-sentence and sat there with a serious look on her face. "There was only one time I forgot to use anything. It was when I was sick with the infection. I didn't even realize it until the next morning. But it was only one time."

Clint said, "That's all it takes, Gayle."

"But I'd know if I was pregnant. I'm not."

Clint got a bit red in the face. "When was your last period?"

Gayle blushed. "I'm not talking about that with you."

" Believe me I don't like to talk about this, either, but it has to be done."

Gayle said more firmly, "I'm not talking about it with you."

She started to get up; Clint reached out and pulled her back down to sit in the chair. "Gayle, grow up. Now use your head. I'm not asking because I'm nosy or curious. I'm not a pervert, either. I'm asking because if you are, we need to know right now for your training. We don't want to do anything that could make you lose the baby if you are pregnant."

Gayle looked at him for a long time. "Let me go look at my pocket calendar. I always mark it down in there. I'll be right back."

She got up and went into the other room. Clint studied the table, waiting for her. He had a feeling she was going to come back and say her period was very late.

She came back in the room with a scared look on her face, holding her pocket calendar. She slumped down in the chair. She started to talk several times before she finally was able to make a sound. "I haven't had a period for the last two months. I hadn't even realized it. So much has happened and I never even realized I'd missed them. Oh God, I'm pregnant." She looked up at Clint with a look of panic. Tears welled in her eyes. "My mother was right. Dammit, my mother was right. Oh God, what do I do now?"

She covered her face with her hands and her shoulders shook as she cried. Clint reached out and patted her arm. "Gayle, why are you crying?"

Gayle pulled her hands down in shock and looked at him like he was a foreign substance she'd never seen before. She finally choked out, "How can you ask me that? The world ended, and now I'm pregnant."

Clint chuckled. "Well, that is how we re-populate the planet, you know." She just stared at him like he was mindless. "Gayle, it isn't the end. You and Junior are going to have a baby. Didn't you want children with Junior?"

Gayle nodded. "Yes, I did, but way, way sometime in the future."

Clint looked at her seriously. "Well, the future is here now." He reached out and held her hand. "I'm sorry you're not happy about this."

"It's just a shock. I'm flying right along and then wham, I get hit with this. I haven't even thought about this at all."

"When are you going to tell Junior?"

She looked up at him with scared eyes. "What if he won't want me now? What if he kicks me out?"

Clint smiled. "Junior will want you. He loves you."

She said, "Yeah, but that was before I got pregnant. Guys get weird when their girlfriend gets pregnant."

"I bet he'll be happy."

Gayle looked uncertain. "I don't know."

Clint said, "You're building a mountain out of a molehill. He loves you and will love your children, too." She sat there, looking scared, and rubbing her arms with her hands. Clint sighed. "Gayle, get a hold of yourself. Now go tell Junior. He needs to know right now."

She stared at him for a few minutes and then she swallowed. "All right. I'll go tell him."

She walked into the living room where Junior was lying on the couch with earplugs in his ears, listening to his IPOD and reading a book. She sat down on the coffee table and tapped his book.

Junior looked up at her and said loudly, "What?" She motioned for him to turn it off. He pulled the earplugs out of his ears. "What is it?"

She said softly, "I need to talk to you in the bedroom."

Junior looked at her questioningly. "Okay." He laid everything down on the couch and they walked into the bedroom. She closed the door.

Gayle told Junior to sit down, that she had something to tell him. Junior sat on the bed and looked at her. She turned away and sighed. She turned back around. "You know when you have news about something but you don't know how the person is going to take it, and you get nervous and a little scared?"

"Yeah, I do. So, what do you have to say that's making you nervous and scared?"

Gayle sighed. "I love you. I want you to know that first."

Junior laughed. "You are acting like you smashed my truck into a wall and are afraid to tell me. Just tell me. What have you done?"

Gayle looked indignant at him. "It's something we both did, so you can't put all the blame on me."

Junior looked at her seriously. "Okay. I take half the blame of whatever it is."

Gayle smiled a little. "We're pregnant."

Junior blinked at her a few times. "What did you say?"

"You got me pregnant."

"Are you sure?"

Gayle said, "Yes, I'm sure. I haven't had a period for the last two months."

"Pregnant, as in a baby?" Gayle hesitantly nodded her head, expecting the worst. Junior broke into a huge grin. "I'm going to be a father." He grabbed her and danced around the bedroom. "We're pregnant. We're having a baby."

Then he noticed the look on Gayle's face and stopped, standing still. "What's the matter? Don't you want to have my baby?"

"No, it's not that. I just didn't want to get pregnant yet. Not for years in the future."

Junior looked hurt. "You don't think I'll be a good father, do you?"

"I think you'll make a terrific dad. I'm just not so certain about having a child now."

Junior grinned. "Well, it happened, so we have to deal with it, and I'm happy." He reached down and patted Gayle's stomach and talked seriously to the baby. "Little one, this may not be a good time to have you, but we love you and don't worry, we'll take good care of you and protect you, no matter what."

Gayle burst into happy tears, smiling at what Junior said. Junior wrapped her happily into his arms and rocked her. "Everything will be fine, don't you worry about anything. Everything will be just fine." They stayed that way for a few minutes. "Oh wow, come on, we have to tell Clint our happy news." He dragged her out of the bedroom and into the kitchen before she could tell him that Clint already knew.

Clint was standing at the counter, getting things ready to put in the slow cooker for dinner. Junior said, "Guess what, Clint?"

Clint turned and looked at him, glancing at Gayle behind him. She shrugged her shoulders. "What?"

Junior had a huge smile on his face. "We're having a baby. You are going to be a Godfather."

Clint smiled and patted his shoulder. "Congratulations to both of you." He stared at them for a few seconds. "What does a Godfather do? I take it's not like a mafia Godfather." Both Junior and Gayle laughed hard. Junior explained it to him. "Okay, I got it now. And I accept. Your child will be safe with me."

A few days later, when Clint got back from his afternoon walk, he called out that he was turning on Crazy Larry. Gayle and Junior hurried into the living room. Clint turned on Junior's dad's ham radio. It was the only way they got any kind of updates on what was going on in the world. He'd found this person accidentally one afternoon when he was flipping through the channels. The man was in northern Minnesota and he called himself Crazy Larry. He said some of the ham radios still worked and others would call him and give reports on what was going on in their part of the country.

Music was just ending and Crazy Larry said, "Today is February 6th, 2016. The weather here in the north is freezing cold and the damn wind is howling outside, blowing the snow everywhere and packing it down good and tight. Don't go outside unless you're covered up real good or your uncovered parts will freeze and fall off." Clint smiled and thought, *now that's the way to give a weather report.*

Crazy Larry continued, "For the newcomers just starting to listen who don't know what happened, here it is: We were hit with an EMP bomb. Everything electrical that wasn't shielded doesn't work anymore. The world went nuts and they sent those bombs everywhere so the whole world is pretty much in the dark. Overseas, some places aren't even there anymore. So, we're all pretty much in the dark together, worldwide. After five months in the dark here in our country, most of the druggies and welfare scum have died off, or been killed or starved to death. I say good riddance to bad rubbish.

"There is a major exodus all across the country. People are heading down south for the winter and have caused major problems in some areas. I have reports from all over stating that it's like locusts have stripped everything bare within five miles of any major highway.

"Diseases are cropping up all over the country. The bubonic plague is in Denver. They think it came from the prairie dogs passing it to the rats and they in turn passed it on to the dogs that people are eating. Some reports state that ninety percent of the population will be dead come spring. New York City has reported they have cholera and dysentery problems. They expect fifty percent of the population will not see spring. Chicago has completely burned to the ground and ash has covered other major areas, causing problems. L A and Detroit have been taken over by gangs and no one knows what is happening there. Reports state people go in but they never come back out.

"And now we come to a very horrible thing that I must report to you all. I've been getting many reports of cannibals forming gangs to feed off the weak and the helpless. Folks, this is happening all over. Most of them have settled in to wait out the winter now that it is bitter cold outside. But in the south, these gangs have as many as a hundred or more in them. Some of these gangs are working together and are a constant threat. So, be prepared to run into these gangs if you are traveling. These gangs are completely crazy. I have reports that they're doing sacrifices to gods and are conducting scary and bloody rituals in some places. So people, think twice and maybe even three times before you decide to leave wherever you are to go somewhere else. You just might end up as dinner for these crazy people.

"I have more reports than I know what to do with on crazy religions and messiahs that have sprang up all over the country. Some are fanatical and dangerous. Some of them gather up anyone that comes by and you join their religion whether you want to or not. So, be warned if you're traveling. On the other hand, some of you that are staying put, be on the watch for some of these religious groups that are roving all over the country and taking what you have for the good of all, they say. If you protest or resist, they kill you and take your stuff anyway. Be on the look out for these crazy groups.

"We all know food is in crisis mode everywhere. The major part of the wheat harvest never came in. What was harvested has not been distributed because there was no way to get it to the grain mills or to the population centers. Ranchers all across the U. S. are just keeping a small herd on the family farm to start again when things get better. They let most of the livestock go wild or they killed it, cooked it, and gave it to starving people. There is plenty of food in a few small areas and none in most places. The ones with some livestock herds left are losing their animals to the bitter cold and frozen water. It's estimated that they'll lose at least fifty percent of their herds. This, folks, means even less food in the future.

"I am still getting reports of a lot of wild dog packs roaming all over the place. The bitter cold outside has brought the human death toll to immeasurable numbers. These wild dog packs are feeding on the human remains. Come spring, they'll be even more dangerous because they'll be experienced in hunting humans. I have a lot of reports of huge wild dog packs terrorizing some cities and towns. My advice is if you see a dog, kill it and get to shelter real fast so you don't become Fido's dinner.

"I also have reports from some states that the wolves are getting completely out of control. They are attacking and killing people. The wolf pack moves into an area and they pretty much wipe out all the game and then they hunt humans. Those of you living in forested areas, be on alert. But, I also need to mention that I've had some reports of wolves going into the cities and eating dead bodies there, too. So, even if you're in a city or town, wolves are a danger, so beware. Wolves are expert killers, so kill any you see. They are lean, mean, killing machines.

"It has been brought to my attention recently that there are some small communities in mountain regions that have some things that still work. A geologist contacted me and explained his theory. He thinks it was the high ore content in the rocks surrounding them that stopped the EMP pulse wave from penetrating through. Who knows if he is right or not? His guess sounds as good and logical as any other. We may not figure it out for years yet.

"I have more reports than I know what to do with about gangs. Gangs have formed everywhere, folks. Most have taken over sections of highways or towns as their base and source of revenue. They are violent and vicious. I also have reports of some gangs that have stolen older vehicles that still run. Be on the lookout for them. They send in girls or women asking for shelter. These women sneak out and give all the information so the gang has intel before they strike. Some gangs are using children, too. They're wiping out everything in their paths. Be very careful of who you allow into your home or town.

"I have reports of military soldiers that came into the towns and cities to restore order on the President's say so. Most are not distributing confiscated goods and foods to the people. Some places, the soldiers have taken off and refused to do what their higher ups ordered them to do. A lot of military bases and stations that still have military personnel have a closed-door policy. Don't head for them expecting them to help you or to let you inside, because it is not going to happen. Also, some towns and cities have closed their borders. They're not letting anyone inside. They're not helping any outsiders, either, so don't go begging for a handout, because you just might get shot.

"I have a report from a doctor that asked me to please tell all you folks to burn any dead body you come across. The rodents, animals, and insects that are feeding off of them are spreading diseases. Also, I was asked to tell everyone to not drink any contaminated water. Filter all water before drinking, or boil it. The diseases that are contacted from drinking contaminated water are becoming a pandemic worldwide. Dead bodies are contaminating the water, too. Be safe and boil it or filter it before drinking.

"Folks, it is truly horrible and shameful what our country has turned into. Reading some of these reports makes me think we're living in a South American banana republic. What we used hear about on the news is our everyday reality now. It's a fight to survive the chaos. Only the strong and the smart will survive. Be back tomorrow, right here, same time. This is Crazy Larry signing off." They heard the National Anthem playing over the radio.

Gayle stood up with tears running down her face and her eyes looking wild. She cried out, "Oh my God. Oh my God." Both Junior and Clint were broken out of their thoughts by her outburst and they quickly looked at her. Gayle choked out, "The world has gone insane. And I'm pregnant. What kind of a cruel mother would bring a child into this hell of a world?" She ran out of the room, sobbing loudly.

Clint and Junior shared a surprised look. Clint said, "Remember, she'll be really emotional until the baby is born. I've heard it's from their hormones."

"Do you know when the baby will be born?"

Clint said, "Sometime in August or September, I think."

Junior looked down the hall. "That's a long ways away."

"And each day it seems longer than the day before." Junior nodded. Gayle's moods had been going all over the place lately. They never knew what was going to upset her or when she'd take offense at something. It was making both men a bit jumpy and hesitant to say anything.

Junior sighed and got up. "I better go calm her down. This isn't good for the baby." Clint nodded in agreement. Junior headed down the hall. That night they sat down and talked about the sad shape the world was in. It was decided that Gayle wouldn't listen to Crazy Larry's news anymore. Junior would keep her company when Clint listened to Crazy Larry. If Crazy Larry reported anything really important, Clint promised Gayle he'd tell her. So, when Clint and Junior went outside to get firewood or to patrol, Clint would fill Junior in on what Crazy Larry had reported. The only thing new was that they were now adding sawdust to all the available flour to make it stretch farther and diseases were still spreading like wildfire all over the country.

Junior asked, "Clint, is it safe for people to be eating sawdust?"

Clint said the Soviets had done the same thing. There was no nutritional value in the sawdust, but it did help fill empty stomachs. Clint went on to say, "Your dad was really smart about where he picked to make his self-sufficient house. Up north here, all the lazy people and addicts will die off this winter. Many believe the myth of being able to survive for thirty days on just water alone. That can be done, but not when you're dealing with very cold weather. When it's cold outside, your body burns a lot of calories just to stay warm. If you have no calorie intake, then your body will cannibalize itself and use the fat to produce heat. When the fat is all gone, you'll die. How long it takes depends on how fat you are. Also, another good thing is there isn't a large population close by. Just a bunch of small towns and some farms spread out over a wide area. That's why I chose this place, too. Most of the diseases will pass us by up here because of the low population. Another reason I picked this areas is because there's plenty of water and game animals. That's very important when considering a survival situation."

Junior nodded. "I love it up here." They finished up and went inside.

Clint still had Gayle doing some exercises, just not anything really strenuous. They still trained in the afternoons, then Gayle would take a nap. Clint had her increase the amount of protein she ate every day so she would stay healthy. They weren't going to take any chances because they wanted a healthy baby. He had her increase the amount of vitamins she took every day, too. That was one thing that Junior's dad had stocked a lot of, vitamins and minerals. He started teaching them strategy and psychology on how to beat your enemy and how to effectively use it against an enemy. Gayle really took to this part of the training because she had already studied some psychology.

About a week later, Gayle took her nap early so Junior was able to listen to Crazy Larry's report with Clint. They kept the volume turned down and Junior had turned on his CD player in the bedroom with some soothing music. He told her it was good for the baby. She just smiled at him when he talked liked that. Junior put a fresh pot of coffee on and they sat down. Right now Crazy Larry was playing some Patriotic music. His report would start in a few minutes.

Crazy Larry said, "Today is February 13th, 2016. I have some really important news to report today. I already told you folks about all the crazy religions that have sprouted up all over the place because these nutcases have claimed that God talked to them. Well, now I've been getting a lot of reports that these crazy nutcases are now forming actual armies to cleanse the land of harmful, wicked people. These religious groups are fighting each other for control. Larger groups are taking over some of the smaller religious groups and forming huge armies. It has been reported that these armies are on the march. They're going from place to place, wiping out whole areas where people refuse to believe and change their wicked ways. They're leaving behind death and devastation wherever they go. They give you a choice of changing your ways and joining or death. People are joining these groups in huge numbers because they're desperate for food. That's the one thing they promise everyone: food. They have food and will feed you if you join. No one knows how they've gotten so much food. I'm waiting for some reliable reports on where they got all this food. Just understand that these armies are on the move and they are fanatical in nature. I'm awaiting some reports on what they're preaching to the people. A few people have contacted me and said they were going to go undercover and find out what's really going on with these armies. I haven't heard back from any of them yet. I'll keep you posted as this situation unfolds. Just believe me when I tell you, folks, that they are deadly serious. They've wiped out whole areas and burned down what's left. They're killing anyone who doesn't join them and believe their teaching. I am sad to report that means women, children and babies, too." Crazy Larry cleared his throat and then went on with his news...

When the report was over, Clint and Junior sat deep in thought. Finally Junior said, "How long will this insanity last, do you think?"

"Historically speaking, it will be a very short time. Somewhere between three to five years before some sort of order is set up. The question you should be asking is what kind of order will be set up. That's the important part. Our country is now so desperate that it would be easy for some dictator to take over and establish complete control of the country. That's something I don't intend to let happen. We'll have to play this out by ear and see what's happening. We don't know if we can really rely on what Crazy Larry tells us, either. He hasn't said anything about foreign troops or any kind of an invasion. He could be giving out disinformation, too. See, that's the real problem. We just don't really know. We'll have to wait and see what develops." Junior looked thoughtful.

Clint broke into his thoughts with the question, "Junior, how much food do we have? How long do you think it will last?"

"I'm guessing here, but I think we have about eighteen months' worth if we stretch it out."

"Then what will we do?"

Junior was thoughtful for a few minutes. "We have a lot of stuff we can barter with farmers for things and food items we need. We have a lot of those small sewing kits; nail clippers, soap and shampoo; things like that, and the furs."

Clint said, "You know fur mittens and hats will be in hot demand around here and probably the number one trade items."

"What will we trade for?"

"Whatever we need. Wheat for flour, beans, corn meal, and maybe even fresh butter."

Junior smiled. "That sounds good. We have enough seeds for a few years for a really large garden. Plus, we can save the seeds for the next year or maybe use some of them to trade, too."

"In the spring we'll do a recon of the area and find out who made it. We can make some friends and set up trade with the people around here. Maybe even set up a mutual defense agreement."

Junior smiled. "Yeah, we have a lot of possibilities for the future."

"Your dad prepared really well and we could probably stretch everything out to last for two years or so and stay out of sight, but humans being what they are, that isn't a very real possibility. We'll have to deal with warlords, cannibals and religious nuts that want to control everyone. It will be imperative that we make contact with people and form pacts and agreements for mutual safety. We'll then be able to stand up and fight for our freedom."

Later in the day when they were training Clint said, "Today's training session will be on vital information. All information reported needs to be done quickly, completely and accurately. You both are going to learn to use the SALUTE report format for reporting and recording information. SALUTE is an easy way to remember what to report. S stands for size. How many enemies do you see? A stands for activity. What are they doing? L stands for location. Where are they? Which direction are they traveling? Do you know which direction they came from? U stands for uniform. That means to identify who they are. Are they a trained army? Are they a foreign army? Are they civilians or refugees? T stands for time and date. E stands for equipment. What equipment do they have? What kind of guns do they have? Do they have machine guns? What kind of packs are they carrying? When you go out on patrol or do recon, this is the information you will need to report accurately. All of this is vital information." Clint brought out a book. "We are now rangers and you both need to learn the rules." He gestured with the book and said, "This book was written in 1759 by Major Robert Rogers. It is named *Standing Orders Rogers Rangers.*" This book contains vital information for all soldiers. What you will learn form this book is that not much has changed." Gayle took the book and opened it up so she and Junior started reading it.

Standing Orders Rogers Rangers

1. Don't forget nothing.
2. Have your musket clean as a whistle, hatchet scoured, sixty rounds powder and ball, and be ready to march at a minute's warning.
3. When you're on the march act the way you would if you was sneaking up on a deer. See the enemy first.
4. Tell the truth about what you see and what you do. There is an army depending on us for correct information. You can lie all you please when you tell other folks about the Rangers, but don't never lie to a Ranger or an officer.
5. Don't never take a chance you don't have to.
6. When you're on the march we march single file, far enough apart so one shot can't go through two men.
7. If we strike swamps, or soft ground, we spread out abreast, so it's hard to track us.
8. When we march, we keep moving till dark, so as to give the enemy the least possible chance at us.
9. When we camp, half the party stays awake while the other half sleeps.
10. If we take prisoners, we keep'em separate till we have had time to examine them, so they can't cook up a story between'em.
11. Don't march home the same way. Take a different route so you won't be ambushed.
12. No matter whether we travel in big parties or little ones, each party has to keep a scout 20 yards ahead, 20 yards on each flank, and 20 yards in the rear so the main body can't be surprised and wiped out.
13. Every night you'll be told where to meet if surrounded by a superior force.
14. Don't sit down to eat without posting sentries.
15. Don't sleep beyond dawn. Dawn's when the French and Indians attack.

16. Don't cross a river by a regular ford.
17. If somebody's trailing you, make a circle, come back onto your own tracks, and ambush the folks that aim to ambush you.
18. Don't stand up when the enemy's coming against you. Kneel down, lie down, hide behind a tree
19. Let the enemy come till he's almost close enough to touch, then let him have it and jump out and finish him up with your hatchet.
20. Don't Drop Your Guard.

Chapter 29

Don't Drop Your Guard

"Everywhere man blames nature and fate, yet his fate is mostly but the echo of his character and passions, his mistakes and weaknesses."

Democtitus

Eric rubbed his face harshly, leaving behind red areas. He said, "I need a few more drinks."

"I need a few, too," said Mark. "Come on. We'll go into the den. It's snowing pretty heavy out there, so I don't think we'll get attacked right now." He paused for a second and with a thoughtful expression on his face said, "Although those Roman guys did attack when it was snowing."

Eric glared at him. "You're not helping, you know."

Mark grinned at him. "Welcome to my world."

Eric sighed. "I know. I'm sorry about not helping more. I don't know what to do to help is more like it. It's not like we've ever been in this kind of position before."

"Let's go into the den and have a long talk. We haven't done that in a long time. I think it would help to get us back on track and come up with some ideas." Eric nodded. They walked out of the mudroom. The women were upstairs helping Maria teach the children.

Mark said, "I'll go up and tell Maria what we're doing. I'll let them know not to disturb us unless it's a real emergency."

"Okay. I'll go open the vents to let some heat in there and I'll start a small fire in the fireplace to warm the room up in the meantime."

Mark went up the stairs and Eric walked down the hall to the den. Mondays, Wednesdays and Fridays were language days for one hour in the mornings. Lisa was teaching Chris French, Abby was teaching Ryan Japanese and Maria was teaching Amanda Spanish. They were sitting in three groups a little ways apart from each other with notebooks open in front of them. Mark walked over to Maria and Amanda. She looked up and smiled at him. Mark leaned down and gave her a kiss. "Eric and I will be in the den. We need some time to figure out some things. Please keep everyone from coming in and bothering us unless it's an emergency. Okay?"

"Okay." He looked around. Everyone was looking at him, so he told them the same thing. He went back downstairs.

The three women looked intently at each other. They could tell something was going on. Maria shrugged her shoulders as if to say *we'll find out what's going on when they tell us*.

Ryan said, "What's going on?"

"Nothing important. Go back to your lessons," said Maria. She looked down at the book she was using to teach Amanda Spanish, pointed to a picture and said, "House."

Amanda said, "Casa."

Maria smiled. "Very good."

She pointed to a picture of water and Amanda said, "Agua." Amanda was learning Spanish at a rapid pace.

Mark walked into the den and sat down in a comfortable chair and put his feet up on a footstool in front of the fireplace. Eric handed him a highball glass with a double shot in it. It was chilled from being in the cold room and didn't need any ice. It went down very smooth. They sat in silence for a while, gathering their thoughts. This was like old times. Except the scotch was much better than they ever bought and the room was a lot more glamorous then anything they had owned. It was nice to just sit and think in companionable silence like they used to.

Mark broke the quiet with a question, "What do you want to start with?"

"How to secure this place to make it harder for someone to break in."

Mark nodded. He'd figured that's what Eric would want to talk about first. It wasn't going to be an easy thing to do because the cabin was so large and had a lot of rooms. It might not be easy, but it was far from being impossible, either. They'd talk until they came up with a plan of action. The women and children depended on them.

When it was lunchtime, Abby made some sandwiches and put them on a tray with two bowls of homemade soup. She walked down the hall to the den and knocked once on the door. She set the tray on the floor and went back to the kitchen. Everything was ready for lunch. She could hear the children stomping down the stairs. She smiled, thinking that in a few years her child would be going up and down the stairs, too. That is, if they survived that long.

Every time they turned around, someone was trying to either kill them or take what they had and most likely would do both. She grimaced and realized that this was indeed just like the old Wild West. No one would be safe going around unarmed and no woman was truly safe unless they had others to protect her. In the world they lived in now there was no such thing as equality for men and women. Now the rules were fight or get run over, chewed up and spit out. There was no safe place unless you made it so by using force. She wished the world were a better place to raise her child in than what they faced right now. But when you really thought about it, the world they'd left behind had been just as bad and just as unsafe. The package had just had a pretty wrapping paper on it called civilization. But inside the box it had been rotten to the core. Most people believed in the illusion of the pretty wrapping paper. But as soon as the illusion was shattered by the EMP, they threw off the wrapping paper and showed their true selves.

They no longer needed the pretty paper to mask their inner selves or their bad intentions. Humans had not changed or evolved since time began. There are good humans, bad ones and evil ones. It had always been that way and it didn't look like it would ever change. We are what we are and there was no way to change the basic genetic code to make us more peaceful and considerate to others. If it hadn't happened in all this time for thousands of years, it was a pretty safe bet that it would never happen. She sighed. Reality was a real bitch. But at least in that other world you could at least obtain the things you needed if you worked hard and earned the money for them. What she wouldn't give for a baby store or a clothing store to buy some maternity clothes or even a grocery store. She sighed again. It was no use thinking and wishing for things like that now. Wishing and hoping never accomplished anything. The only thing that produced results was to work hard for what you wanted.

She was thankful that Mark and Eric had rescued them and that they were the kind of men they were. It was really hard to find good men, even in the old world. Men who had honor and decency were rare. Not once had either one of them tried to take advantage of the women in any way. They had provided them with the things they needed as much as they could and had shared what little they had themselves. They never once asked for any kind of payment or favors. They did the best they could. They had never played favorites, either. They had treated them all the same way. They still did even now that Maria and Mark were together and Eric and Lisa were together as couples. They never made her feel out of place or not wanted. Everyone included her in whatever they were doing. They had truly incorporated the women into their little two-person group just as they all had done with the children. Those two men were the best of what men should be. She was very glad they would be the role models for a father to her child. She couldn't have picked out better men even if she'd spent a few hundred years looking. They had an honorable code of justice they lived by, just as her father and grandfather had.

That phrase was almost an oxymoron in the old world, too. There just weren't very many people like them. Lisa and Maria were great, too. She'd never really had the time before to cultivate very many friends and had never had any close female friends that weren't relatives. She loved them like sisters. Her child was rather lucky to have them as aunts. She was sure that if something happened to her, they'd care for her child as if it was their own. On that she had no doubts, whatsoever. They had given their word.

Mark and Eric heard the knock on the door. Eric opened the door and saw the tray of food on the floor. He brought it in to the room and set it down on a table. Mark smiled. They had taken him at his word. It made him feel good that they had understood that some times he and Eric just needed to talk and reconnect and get their heads pointed in the right direction.

They had already covered what they'd do to reinforce the downstairs and the basement windows to make it difficult for anyone to get inside. Then they covered what they were going to do about the watches. Then they talked about getting more meat for the freezer and so on. Now, they were moving on to future things. With some luck, they just might have a future. Eric had calmed down and was more like himself. His panic attack was over. They needed to focus on action. They were working out a plan to stay busy. They needed projects and goals to stay on track. Making everything up on the fly was getting really old.

When they were done eating, Mark said, "I wish we could meet this Bert guy that Ryan and Amanda talk about. If only half the things they said are true about what they saw at his place, he could be the answer to saving us."

Eric looked thoughtful. "Well, he already saved you and Abby once when he killed those Roman soldiers."

"I know. He appeared and disappeared like a phantom. I'd really like the chance to thank him in person."

"I'd like to meet him, too."

"Do you have anything else you want to discuss?" Mark asked.

"No, we covered everything that I was hyper over."

Mark smiled. "Okay, we can go out and join the others. I bet the kids have been pestering the women with questions on why we're holed up."

"I won't bet against you on that one."

They gathered everything up to take to the kitchen. Mark made sure the fire was pretty much out in the fireplace and he closed the heat vents again. Later that night, when Mark and Eric were coming upstairs after re-enforcing the basement windows, Mark said, "You know, Clark was right. Come springtime, we're all going to have to come together as a community. Everyone that makes it until then will be real survivalists. We're going to need to get some livestock, crops growing and just like an old time town, we'll need to set up trades with other growing communities near us."

Eric smiled and then started laughing real hard. As they passed by Lisa in the kitchen she asked, "What's so funny?"

Mark looked kind of frustrated. "Yeah, what's so funny, Eric?"

Eric winked at her. "Mark here was just telling me we have to rebuild civilization on our own. I find that pretty funny. First, we have men kidnap Ryan, then we have killer dogs attack us, then Roman soldiers try to wipe us out, a mysterious man kills the Roman soldiers and disappears after saving Ryan and Amanda, we now own horses and run into tree people, we have three women and three children to protect and provide for. We're just two right wing nutcase survivalists and now we're talking about rebuilding civilization." He burst out laughing again. "Ahh, which survival manual is that covered under?"

Mark finally saw the irony in what Eric had said and started laughing, too. Lisa giggled and then out right laughed. "Just two single guys without a care in the world. Now it's like you're married with instant families, and the only other thing you have to do is rebuild civilization in our part of the world. Could you guys please hurry it up and have it done before Christmas? I really could use some new clothes and would like to get my nails done. I also need to do some Christmas shopping." All three of them roared with laughter as they walked into the living room to sit down.

Abby and the children were watching a Disney movie that was almost over. The three of them were still chuckling. Amanda climbed up on Eric's lap and asked, "Is Mark telling war stories?" She smiled up at him. "He does a really good airplane and machine guns, too." The movie ended.

Chris and Ryan, laughing, said almost at the same time, "Not if you're trying to sleep." Everyone laughed at the boys and they rolled their eyes at each other, which made the adults laugh harder.

Maria looked at Mark. "How come you sent Eric and didn't come rescue me yourself?" Mark grinned and said, "'Cause Eric always saves you and Lisa. Amanda made sure of that." He winked at Amanda. "Besides, I had to tell stories to Amanda."

Abby laughed harder than the others. "That's because he said he'd put the children to bed and that all they needed was a firm hand to make them understand that it was bedtime and that he wouldn't put up with any nonsense." Eric and Lisa practically rolled on the floor.

Mark rolled his eyes. "You'll never let me live that one down, will you?"

Abby's eyes sparkled gleefully. "Not in this lifetime."

Mark sighed. "It's bedtime. Ryan and Amanda, upstairs."

Amanda looked up at him. "Are you going to finish telling me about the boat battle?" Ryan groaned.

Eric scooped up Amanda in his arms. "Not tonight, sweetheart. You and Ryan are going straight to bed."

Ryan said, "It's not fair. Chris is a kid, too."

Eric looked intently at him. "Not anymore. In another two years, you'll be able to stay up just like he does. Now it's bedtime. Let's go." Amanda kissed all the adults, then Eric hauled her upstairs after Ryan.

Lisa was waiting by the stairs when he came down. She grabbed him and kissed him hard. "Thank you for coming to rescue me again."

"I'll always come to rescue you."

She smiled. "You say the sweetest things to me." They smiled at each other and then walked with their arms around each other back into the living room.

Mark said, "We need to have watches from now on. Starting tomorrow night, Chris will take the 8:00 pm to midnight watch. Abby will take the midnight to 4:00 am watch. I'll take the 4:00 am to daylight watch. We'll do this for one week. Then we'll trade off with Maria having the 8:00 to midnight, Lisa will have the midnight to 4:00 am and Eric will take the 4:00 am to daylight watch. This last attack happened during daylight. Large forces will use the early morning hours to attack. That's when people are usually at their weakest point. Midnight to 4:00 am will be the time for the sneak thieves. One or two people will sneak in to steal food and test our security measures. Any questions?" They all shook their heads. "During the day, attacks will come from desperate people. We have to make sure to use the snow to our advantage. No more walking out to the road for a look around. We don't want any tracks in the snow leading to the cabin. Since we can't use the front door any more, it makes it a lot simpler to keep all of our tracks in the back. The wood smoke is against us. It shows anyone passing by that people are living here. There isn't anything we can do about that. I know it sounds cold hearted, but we have to let everyone go on by us. We have just enough food if we ration it out right to survive. We desperately need three to four more deer to put in the freezer. Eric will be taking Chris and Ryan out tomorrow to show them how to set snares. The really great thing about using snares is that they're silent. There will be no gunshots to advertise that we're hunting for meat." They talked about a few other matters then called it a night.

A few days later, they had four deer butchered and in the freezer. Mark relaxed a little now. They hadn't seen anyone or any tracks but their own in the snow. Mark and Eric took turns emptying the ashes from the wood stove outside in the back down a small incline. It was pretty much hidden from sight unless you looked right down at the pile of ashes. Plus the wind was blowing around and scattering them. Mark and Eric both felt better now that they had set up the watches. Ryan had been hurt because they hadn't included him in any of the watches. Maria talked to Mark about it, so he set Ryan up with watching from dinnertime until 8:00 pm, when Chris would relieve him. They had boarded up the windows downstairs and in the basement. They used whatever they could find that was sturdy enough; extra tables and pieces of wood that were in the garage and basement. They even used a few metal shelves they'd taken off the walls down in the basement and used screws to hold them in place. Mark and Eric had cut twelve-inch square holes in whatever they had used to board up the windows so they could shoot out of them if they had to.

Eric had even made a few hinges after they used up all the available ones for the square shooting holes. Everyone stayed pretty busy.

It was a few weeks before Clark made it back with Jeff, so he could talk with Mark. They stayed for a few hours and then headed back to their winter cave after a meal of venison steaks. Mark liked what he'd seen and heard from Jeff so far, anyway. He didn't have a very trusting nature to begin with, and now that it seemed he couldn't really trust anyone, it made him even more cautious. They talked a little about spring and what would need to be done to prepare for next winter. They were all in agreement about forming a community for trade and safety. The news that Clark and Jeff brought with them was that they got an old ham radio going. They could listen, but they couldn't send out messages. They shared what they'd heard on the radio from someone named "Crazy Larry." The adults were glad they were in the north, holed up in a scarcely populated area. It seemed the world had gone completely crazy. The adults talked about the crazy religious fanatics after the children went to bed that night.

Before they knew it, Christmas was fast approaching. The days had started to blend together as routine. Nothing new happened and they felt more and more secure as each day passed quietly. No one was allowed outside except for Mark and Eric, and that was just to empty the ash pan when it was needed. They made sure to use the tracks they had already made in the snow. There was a large metal bucket in the basement that they used to empty the ashes into from the wood stove. When it was full, they went outside to empty it. They only needed to do this two to three times a week. One thing all the adults soon learned was that they were grateful for the cabin being as large as it was. They could get away from each other when they needed to and have a bit of privacy. Mark had cleared an area for all of them to exercise every day. He made it so they could all stay in shape and not be slugs come springtime. It also helped with their mental attitudes. None of them were used to being housebound all the time.

Two men were watching the cabin. They were getting frustrated with how little the people in this cabin came outside. The man on the left asked, "How come they don't go outside for walks or to hunt?" Their food supply was getting real desperate. They only had a little rice and a few grains of salt left. The other man answered, "We have about two days' worth of food left. We either have to make our move or move on. We can't afford to waste our energy waiting for them to make a mistake."

The next morning, Mark went outside to empty the metal bucket. He was thinking about the book he'd just read on gardens. It said that pot ash was good for them. If he hadn't dropped his guard due to not seeing anyone out there for so long, he might have noticed the new tracks in the snow. When he did notice the tracks, he wasn't thinking clearly and immediately thought he needed to have a long talk with whoever had been outside to make them. He had been perfectly clear that no one was to be outside. He stood looking at the tracks and suddenly realized that they were man-sized tracks. As soon as he realized that, he dropped the metal bucket and reached for the Sig. He heard a foot crunch in the snow behind him and turned just in time to see the club aiming for his head. He didn't have time to block and it hit him with a solid crack. He felt pain and then blackness as he fell down in the snow. The other man quickly grabbed him and pulled his coat off, duct taping his hands together behind his back. The man tore off a strip of tape and put it over his mouth and then dropped him back down to the snow.

The two men were well-versed in their actions. The man that had hit Mark put his coat on and grabbed the metal bucket, placing his K-bar knife under the bottom. He would enter the house wearing Mark's coat and hat. Once inside, kill any threat was the plan. He would use the knife if he could and the other man would cover him with a P-32, a very small easy to hide handgun. The last house they'd hit had been pretty simple. An old couple had lived there. He'd taken the man outside and killed him, and then he'd gone back into the house and slit the old lady's throat. They were living off the last of the food they'd taken from there. But now they needed more. Hopefully this place was stocked better then that old couple's place had been. They entered through the back door and walked through the mudroom into the kitchen. A dark-haired lady was standing in front of the stove, just about to add something to a boiling pot of water. She turned her head just in time to see a knife flash before her face in the fist of a man. He had one dirty finger outstretched and put it to his mouth and whispered, "Shhhhhh."

Mark had drilled it into the women and children's heads: Never, ever comply with any intruder's demands. Maria screamed like bloody murder at the top of her lungs, saying, "Intruders, intruders!"

The man took a step closer and thought, *Damn, she's a good looking woman. Too bad she screamed.* Before he could even finish his thought, boiling water was flying at his face. Maria was determined not to go down without a fight. She would do whatever it took to warn the others.

At the same time, Lisa was just stumbling down the stairs, still half asleep, for her first cup of coffee. When she heard Maria scream, she was instantly shocked wide-awake and alert. She heard the word 'intruders' and raced for the 12-gauge shotgun hidden down on the first floor. She grabbed it and checked the shells. Buckshot was exactly what she needed. She flipped the safety off the shotgun, running towards the kitchen. She met up with Eric on the other side of the living room. They heard a shot from the kitchen. They both exchanged a worried look. Eric used hand signals to tell her to come in after him. He raced through the kitchen doorway and leaned down and slid on his right side across the floor. He already had grabbed his 9mm; it was in his hand as he saw Maria on the floor, lying in a puddle of blood. He didn't wait to see any more and looked around for targets. Death was coming to whoever had done this.

He saw a man bent down on his knees on the floor next to Maria, was with his hands and face red, screaming in pain. The man's partner was behind him with a gun in his hand, turning towards Eric. Eric opened up on the man by Maria just as Lisa burst through the doorway into the kitchen with the 12 gauge, looking to deal out death to whoever had attacked.

Abby heard Maria screaming 'intruders' and raced out of her bedroom with her beloved knives, ready to kill whoever crossed her path. She was just in time to grab Chris by the collar and shove him back into the children's bedroom. She looked at him sternly. "You and Ryan stay here and protect Amanda." Chris had the .22 rifle in his hands and Ryan was holding his pellet gun. "All of you stay inside this room until I tell you different." She closed the door and raced for the stairs. A gun battle erupted in the kitchen. Her sharp hearing heard the 9mm open up and another gun she wasn't familiar with, and then she heard the deafening roar of the 12 gauge. She thought, *What in the hell is going on?* She instinctively tightened her grip on the knives she was holding and calmed her breathing, focusing on killing anyone that came for the children. She found a darkened corner and slid into it to wait, out of sight of anyone coming up the stairs. She heard the rack of another shell being readied to fire from the shotgun as the empty shell bounced and rolled along the floor. Abby wondered, *Is that Eric's 12 gauge or a bad guy's?* She was so focused on the kitchen that she could swear she heard Eric breathing roughly. Then she heard Eric yell out, "Abby, we need you NOW!"

She took off flying down the stairs and raced into the kitchen. Eric was holding a guy up a little off the floor with his fist twisted around the man's coat at the neck, almost face to face. He was saying in a strange, threatening voice they had never heard from him before, "Where is Mark? I swear to God we will patch you up and torture you for days if you don't answer me right now."

Lisa was standing with the 12 gauge pointed at the back door, ready to kill anyone who would dare to come through. Maria was lying on the floor in a puddle of blood next to a man, also lying on the floor. Her heart rate rapidly increased and her chest felt heavy, thinking that Maria was probably dead.

Maria was lying next to the man that had been holding the gun. Eric had put two shots into him before he was able to get his aim right. The man had shot twice over Eric's head, missing him completely as he fell to the floor. The other man then stood up, screaming, as Lisa came through the door into the kitchen. She shot the guy before she even had time to think about it, seeing Maria lying on the floor in a puddle of blood. The 12 gauge from ten feet away was devastating. The guy was slammed back into the wall and slid down to the floor, leaving a bloody mess on the wall with a one-inch hole ripped through the center of his chest.

Abby took all this in at a quick glance. She yelled at Eric, trying to get his attention, "Eric, stop it." Eric ignored her and dropped the man back to the floor. He reached down and picked up the handgun. He stepped on the man's right hand with his left foot and bent down, pointing the barrel at his trigger finger and said again in that scary voice, "You have two seconds to answer me before I shoot off your finger. Where is Mark?"

The man blinked up at him weakly. "He's... He's outside... by the wood pile."

Eric screamed at him, "Alive?"

The man was fading fast and his eyes were getting glassy. He whispered, "I don't... know. Maybe." Eric ground his heel into the man's wrist, making him scream and wriggle around.

Eric yelled, "How many are outside?" The man didn't answer him and Eric pressed harder with his foot making the man whimper. "Tell me how many more are outside?"

The man coughed and blood ran out of the side of his mouth down onto his cheek. He faintly whispered, "No one else... just us." Eric reached down and shot him under the chin with his own gun, spraying blood and tissue in an arc of red mist towards the wall where his partner already lay dead.

Abby was over on the other side of Maria, examining her. She looked up at Eric, standing over the man he had just killed, still pointing the gun down at him. "Maria is alive."

Eric didn't even look at her. "That's good, but this isn't over yet. We don't know if he was lying or not." He shoved the gun he was holding at her. "Watch the door. If I don't call out it's us coming, you shoot first and ask questions later, if you can." He turned to Lisa. "Let's go." Neither one of them was dressed to be outside in the bitter cold, but they had to end this now and find Mark. They spread out, each taking cover on opposite sides of the back door. Eric whispered, "Stay here until I'm out, then follow. If you see anyone else, retreat back inside and protect the children." Lisa nodded once in acknowledgment. As soon as he was outside, the bone-chilling cold hit him hard, making it hard to breathe. He quickly looked around for tracks in the snow. The only new ones were two sets heading into the cabin. He quickly scanned the area. No movement anywhere and no one was shooting at him.

He called out, "Mark, where are you?" He waited; there was no answer. Lisa stepped outside, standing in the snow out in front of the door with only a pair of socks on her feet. The snow was melting into them, freezing her feet. She thought, *Good, it will keep me sharp and alert.* Eric followed the new tracks back towards the woodpile and saw Mark lying in the snow without a coat. His arms were behind him, bound together, and there was tape over his mouth. A breath hitched in Eric's chest at the sight of him lying there so still, making his heart race with fear. He slowly approached the woodpile to make sure no one was hiding behind it. He peered around the side and it was clear. He raced over to Mark, holstered his gun, and pulled his knife out of the sheath. He bent down and cut the tape from his hands and arms. He then reached up and rolled him over, making Mark moan. Eric brightened up immediately thinking, *At least he's alive.* He pulled the tape off his mouth, making a loud tearing sound. Mark moaned again. He shook his shoulder. "Mark, can you hear me? Wake up." He reached down, grabbed him under the arms, and started dragging him towards the back door. When he got near it, he said, "Get the door and tell Abby that Mark is hurt. Make sure she knows it's you so you don't get shot."

Lisa called out to Abby. She opened the door and Eric dragged Mark inside to the kitchen, away from the bodies lying there. Mark started fighting him and Eric yelled, "Mark, it's me. Get it together. You're in the kitchen and are safe." Mark tried to open his eyes, but couldn't focus on anything. All he could see was a big blur. He tried to get his tongue out to wet his lips, but nothing was working right yet. He grunted and Eric said, "It's all right. The men are dead. You're safe now." Mark tried to nod to let Eric know he heard him. He wasn't sure if he was nodding his head or not.

Abby had wrapped Maria's head with a towel and she moved her out of the puddle of blood to examine her more closely. She looked over at Mark. "Maria has a head wound, too. The bullet glanced off her skull and ran along the side of her head, knocking her out. Head wounds bleed a lot. When she wakes up, I'll know more." She thought to herself, *if she wakes up. It depends on if she has any chipped bones in her skull.* They couldn't take an x-ray to know for sure. She sighed. Eric nodded, so she guessed he had heard the report of Maria's bullet wound. She looked around at the kitchen. The two bad guys were dead, that was for sure. Eric had a cold, dark side to him that they hadn't seen before. But now they were one big family and they had to turn cold and hard in order to survive. He would be as cold and vicious as he needed to be to protect them. She smiled a little, thinking they were very lucky to have been rescued by these two men.

Eric looked around. "Lisa, go upstairs and check on the kids. Tell them that Mark and Maria were hurt. Tell them to stay up there until we come and get them. Put on a dry pair of socks and come back down here and help clean this mess up." He turned and looked at her. "Okay?" Lisa reached out and rubbed his arm, then nodded. She turned and went into the living room. Eric looked at Abby. "Where do you want Maria?"

Abby said, "Put her on the kitchen table so I can examine her fully and make sure that's her only wound." He picked Maria up in his arms and laid her gently on the table.

Mark was mumbling. "I'm sorry. I'm so sorry. Dropped my guard. Wasn't thinking right."

Eric said, "Relax Mark. We got this under control."

"I want Maria. I want to see Maria." Eric helped Mark into a chair and leaned him towards the table so he wouldn't fall. Mark grabbed Maria's hand. As soon as Eric was sure he wasn't going to fall over, he turned around and surveyed the mess.

It was time to get the kitchen cleaned up. Eric grabbed an arm and a leg and started dragging the body to the back door. It was time to get these scumbags out. He checked around outside and it was still clear, so he dragged the body out about twenty feet and went back inside and grabbed the other one and dragged it out. He left them in the snow, stained red from their blood. He went back inside and locked the door up tight with the extra barricade they had made so it would be more secure. Eric sighed. *Damn, will we ever be able to relax again? Will Mark be okay? And Maria, is she going to live? You always have to be on guard. You just never know when some scumbags and assholes will come and try to kill you and take what you have.*

He walked over to Abby. "What's the verdict?"

Abby looked up at him. "There are no other serious injuries. She has several bruises and bumps, but I think that was from her fall to the floor. As for her head injury, it is too early to tell. We have to wait for her to wake up." She pulled Eric into the living room out of hearing range from Mark. Lisa came down the stairs and joined them. Abby whispered, "If, and this is a very large if, if the bullet didn't chip a piece of bone into her brain or cause too much swelling on the inside of her skull, she should wake up in a few hours. Mark is blaming himself, but all we can do is wait and see if she wakes up or not." Abby sighed deeply. Lisa had tears in her eyes. Eric reached out, grabbed both of them, and gave them a big hug.

When he stepped back, he noticed the calendar up on the wall that Amanda had made; a calendar that Maria had helped her make to count the days until Christmas. A huge lump formed in his throat and he blinked his eyes hard. He looked at Abby, and she and Lisa were looking at the calendar, too.

Lisa said in a tight, thick voice, "It's two days until Christmas."

Eric thought, *What a shitty way to spend Christmas.* He sighed again. "What about Mark? Will he be okay?"

Abby gave him a small smile. "With his thick head, I'm sure he'll be fine. I think he has a concussion, because his eyes aren't dilated right."

Eric said, "Where should we put them?"

"Nowhere right now. I want Maria to stay on the table until she wakes up. When she wakes, we'll move them into their room and care for them until they're well."

"Okay. That's a plan. We'd better get the kitchen cleaned up before the children see it. Both women nodded and walked back into the kitchen.

Just as they were gathering up some rags to begin cleaning the mess, a loud male voice yelled from outside in the back of the cabin, "You're surrounded. Come out with your hands up, unarmed."

Eric rolled his eyes and said disgustedly, "What now?"

Chapter 30

Frozen Pipe

"The ultimate measure of a man is not where he stands in moments of comfort, but where he stands at times of challenge and controversy."

Martin Luther King, Jr.

Preston looked at the clock. It was 3:10 am and it was almost time for his watch. He lay there and looked at the ceiling for a while. They still made sure that either he or Joe had the last watch until way after daylight. That's when the organized attacks would take place. They had changed the watch times to accommodate the later day breaks in winter. Well, he might as well get up and take a shower. If he went back to sleep now, it would just make him groggy when the alarm went off. He reached over Amy and turned off the alarm. She just snuggled down deeper under the covers without waking up. He smiled at her. She looked so cute all covered up except for her nose sticking out. He got up and gathered clean clothes to put on. When he was done with his shower, he walked into the kitchen and stoked up the fire in the wood stove so he could heat up the coffee. He'd put some in a thermos to take with him. He grabbed his lunch that Amy had made last night before bed. He drank a cup of coffee, then filled the thermos up. He bundled up in his good winter clothing and headed over to the barn. It was bitter cold outside, just what you would expect for the middle of January in the Great White North. He chuckled. He had run into a guy in the Army that came from the Upper Peninsula of Michigan and that's what he used to call where he'd grown up. It was really fitting, because they're only separated from Canada by Lake Superior up there. He'd mentioned it to Joe a few years ago, and it had kind of caught on.

The wind seemed especially bone chilling this morning. They'd been talking last night about how this winter seemed to be a lot colder than normal. It probably wasn't, but it did seem that way. Well, he'd read the log Michael had written earlier. It was always fun to read. That kid saw more animals then all of the rest of them put together. He walked up the stairs to the loft and peeked around at Steve, who was on watch. Steve was sitting at the table, writing in the logbook with the little blue light reflecting off his face and his breaths blowing eerie shapes in front of him. It made him look like it was a scene out of a horror movie. He smiled at his fanciful thoughts this morning. What in the world was wrong with him? It must be the boredom of deep winter getting to him. None of them were used to being closed up like this or even stuck at the farm and not able to go anywhere else. Steve looked up and noticed Preston standing there.

Preston said, "Anything happening?"

"No. It's as quiet as a church mouse out there. Just normal, freezing wind, it snowed a little, then stopped, nothing is moving out there." Steve was ready to get out of this cold and into a warm bed. He was sleepy and his feet were freezing. He had done extra jumping jacks just to keep his feet warm.

Preston said, "Did you do your exercises?'

"Yes. I did extra jumping jacks, too, just to keep my feet warm."

"Good. We all have to keep in shape, or come spring we'll all be huffing and puffing just walking around. You wouldn't like what I'd have to put you through to get you in shape fast, either."

Steve sighed. *Yeah, right. He just loves to see us keel over from exhaustion no matter what.* "Later today I'll go down in the basement for a real workout.

Preston said, "That's the way to go. You'll thank me this summer when you're working your ass off."

Steve said, "So, what do you think?"

"About what?"

"Our chances of surviving to the end of this chaos."

"I don't know for sure, but we're better off than ninety percent of those left alive. The chaos will last three to five more years. Some type of order will be established by then. We'll need to learn to trade at first, then we can set up a monetary system. The first thing that will need to be done is get the electrical power plants back up and running. Then we can start making new parts for things that were blown out by the EMP. We'll need machinists like John, who can make just about anything we may need. We'll also need construction workers and foremen like you to help rebuild and make things livable again. Then we can get some old cars going and make parts to fix the newer ones. It'll be a long time before everything is normal again. Maybe not even in our lifetime. It wasn't built easily the first time, and we'll be starting out just about from scratch again. I'm guessing here, but before it's all over, America will be down to about twenty percent of our population; say about sixty million will survive, maybe less. It's hard to say."

Steve looked worried and a little sick at how few would really survive. He sighed. "So, what's next? What will we have to face between now and then?"

Preston said, "Well, as Amy would say, we first have to live through facing the little zombies. They're the thugs, thieves, rapists and murderers. Then slowly one leader will pull them together to form a larger, more organized gang, like the one we just faced. Those Amy would call the big zombies. Now remember, this will be happening all over America. There will be many of these larger, more organized gangs everywhere. There will be a lot of fighting between these rival organizations. Then the next step will be the Warlords. These will be the most dangerous. They'll try to control huge areas with well-armed soldiers that will be collecting taxes from everyone for protection from the outside forces that want to take them over. These will be the worst. Then you have the religions and cults that have formed. You'll have large groups of Eco Nazis and environmental groups that want to remake America into some kind of a communist dream of utopia. That was already going on before the EMP. Just like the communists, they'll have to kill off those that won't join them in a massive purge. All of these groups think they are the rightful rulers of America. Also, keep in mind that all of these groups will kill you if you don't join them or do what they say. This is when we'll have to pay attention and act to restore our Republic or we'll be overrun. It's called communism and share the wealth. They want to take everything that people have worked hard for and give it to those less deserving and those that didn't work, not even for one minute, to provide anything themselves. Then, on top of all this, we'll be having invading armies coming from different countries to grab our resources and land. If that happens, it may take another five years or more to drive them off our land. There will be no fast way to get us back to normal. Like I said, it may not even happen in our lifetimes even if by some miracle we last that long to try to do something about it."

Steve was absolutely stunned. He stood there with his mouth hanging open, trying to decide what he wanted to comment on first. Finally, shaking his head, he tried to say something, but his throat was too dry. He coughed and swallowed and was finally able to get out, "I had no idea."

"That's a normal reaction. Just remember, every great super power throughout history has fallen from one thing or another. Usually it's from arrogance and they forget the needs of the common man. But the average person in each of those governments and countries thought that it could never happen to them, either. Just as everyone here in America thought the same thing. I'm sure you were one of those people, too."

Steve said, "I was. I just never gave it any thought at all, really. In the civilized world we lived in, who would have thought that this could become a reality?"

Preston looked at him intently. "It's because Joe and I have been in other countries that were experiencing these things that we know what we're talking about. Saying we in America were safe from any of them happening was nothing but propaganda. It was bound to happen here sooner or later, especially with our unstable debt-ridden government not listening to what the people wanted. They became arrogant and stopped listening to what the people really wanted and used the arrogant communist way of saying they knew what's best for us."

Steve looked really upset and asked in a soft voice, "Do you think we'll make it?"

Preston studied him for a few moments. "We'll do our best for America. We took an oath to that effect." Steve nodded. "Go on inside, warm up, and get some sleep." Steve nodded again, gathered up his things, and left Preston in silence.

Preston sighed. It was hard whenever you got hit with reality right between the eyes. Reality has a way of biting you in the ass when you least expect it. He turned and did a round of looking out the windows for movement. He remembered some of the long talks that Joe, Jane, Amy and he had shared about this same subject. They were all pretty much in agreement. He smiled remembering Amy said that they all had to live so they could be part of rebuilding our government to make sure they got it right this time. He didn't know about that, but he and Joe were willing to do their best to make it happen. He opened the log and recorded the time and that there wasn't any movement outside. He turned on the little blue light to read Michael's entries. He always had something worth reading.

Michael wrote; 8:15 pm: A rabbit crossed the yard heading east. Used regular hop.

8:51 pm: Harry the mouse came to visit me. He's eating the seeds in the hay bales.

9:20 pm: Lone coyote howled. Sounded like it came from the northeast side of property.

10:00 pm: Temperature outside has dropped. It's getting real cold. Have to keep using the scraper on the windows to see out. Ice is building up in places.

10:30 pm: No movement from anything.

11:15 pm: The barn is making cracking noises from the cold. Sometimes it almost sounds like a gunshot.

11:45 pm: An owl flew down to the ground and then flew away with something small in its claws like a mouse. I hope Harry the mouse is okay and wasn't dinner for the owl.

12:00 am: Michael's watch is over. Then Steve signed on for his watch. Preston closed the logbook and placed it on the desk, chuckling.

At 6:00 am, Preston had just finished his exercises. He was bored. There was nothing outside to see. It had started snowing again. He grabbed his lunch and ate the rest. He sighed and wished Amy was here to keep him company. She hadn't been coming to visit him too often since it had gotten so cold. He'd just gotten used to them being together for their watches. It had been real nice. He sighed again and did his rounds, looking out of the windows. He paid special attention to the stumps and lumps outside. A good lookout person has identified every single stump and lump in the area. That way if there are any new lumps, even if it is perfect and blended into the surroundings by some kind of camo, it will still stick out to the person on watch as a danger. All was normal outside. He walked around to warm up some. It would be really nice to be curled up in bed next to Amy's warm body right about now. He did fifty more push-ups. He kept reminding himself that they had to stay in top shape even in winter.

At 7:15, Amy came up for a surprise visit. He was very glad to see her this morning. Her left arm was still a little stiff, but it was healing nicely from the gunshot wound. Preston kissed her. "Am I glad to see you."

She smiled at him. "Bored, huh?"

He laughed. "Yeah, I am. I almost wish something else would happen just to break up the boredom. But, I really don't mean it in a bad way. Just something that would be a little exciting for awhile."

Amy studied him for a few moments then rolled her eyes. "You just had to tempt fate, didn't you? Just remember, I'll remind you of this when you're bitching about it when it does happen. This future event will be all on your head because you were bored."

Preston laughed at her. "Well, it'll be better than just sitting around all the time." They shared a smile. Amy poured him some fresh hot coffee from the thermos she brought. She pulled a wrapped bundle out from her pocket and handed it to him. It was still steaming. He opened it up and looked at a piece of coffee cake.

He leaned over and kissed her, and then ate it as fast as he could before it got cold. "Thank you. That hit the spot. Have you been baking this morning?"

She looked at him. "No, I haven't been baking. Vicki made it. She got up real early. She said she couldn't sleep so she decided to bake. She baked a whole bunch of things.

Amy kissed him hard, and then hugged him. Jane showed up for her watch and Amy stayed to talk with her.

As Preston walked back to the house, it felt just as cold now as it did at 3:40 am when he'd walked over to the barn. When he walked inside, the heat felt overwhelming at first. He took off all his outer clothes. The smells were making his mouth water. He walked into the kitchen and Vicki was standing at the stove.

She turned and looked at him. "Your breakfast will be ready in a minute."

He said, "Wow, it sure smells good in here." He looked around and there was baked goods all over the place. Coffee cake, a cake, muffins, tarts and he could see several cookie sheets of rolls rising.

Vicki walked over to him. "I made apple pancakes. You can have maple syrup with them or a special sauce I made with apples."

"Thank you." He took the plate piled high with the pancakes and sat at the table. He decided to try the special sauce and see what it was like. He took a bite and almost moaned in enjoyment. He quickly ate everything on his plate. He got up and grabbed a cup of coffee. He was so full he felt like falling asleep right there at the table. Vicki was doing something to one of the cookie sheets full of rolls.

Joe and Michael walked into the kitchen. Vicki went over to the oven and opened the top warmer of the wood stove and pulled out two plates piled high with pancakes. She handed a plate to Michael and one to Joe. Both said, "Wow, everything smells so good." Vicki explained about the special sauce she'd made and they both tried it. Preston watched them wolf everything down. Joe noticed one of the big bags of Jane's special flour on the floor by the cupboards. He sighed. Jane was going to have a fit about this.

Vicki walked over to the sink and turned the water faucet on and nothing came out. She tried the other faucet and nothing came out from there, either. She turned to the men. "No water is coming out of the faucet."

Joe looked at her. "Where did you get the water for cooking?"

"I used the water we stored in the pantry that's filtered. It's better for baking and cooking."

"Have you turned the faucet on at all this morning?"

Vicki looked like she was going to run and hide. She gripped the counter and said softly, "No, I haven't."

Joe jumped up. "Shit, the pipe is frozen."

He looked at Preston. "Come on. We have to get that pipe unfrozen right now before it breaks." Preston and Joe ran out of the kitchen to the basement door and flew down the stairs. Michael followed behind them. When they got downstairs, they ran to the back wall, where the water pipe that carried water to the house from the well was. They could see some ice built up on the pipe.

Preston groaned and thought, *so much for relaxing today.* He turned to Michael. "Get Amy down here. She's in the loft with Jane." Michael nodded and ran up the stairs to his radio. "Has this happened before?"

"Yeah." Joe was still looking at the pipe, trying to figure out what to do about it.

Preston said, "Well, what did you do about it?" Joe turned and glared at him, then reached out and grabbed the plug hanging there. "I would plug in the heat tape. The solar panels don't produce enough for that." They could hear the back door open and Amy walking across the floor. Then they heard footsteps walk to the basement door and start down the stairs.

Vicki was behind Amy and Michael. Amy walked up to Preston. "What's wrong?"

Before he could say anything, Joe yelled out, "Michael, get back here. I'm going to need your help." Michael had been on his way upstairs to tell the others about the pipe when he heard Joe swear. He stopped and turned on the stairs to see what Joe was swearing about. He stood next to Amy and Preston.

Preston said to Amy, "With Joe and plumbing, this could take two to three days to fix."

Joe said, "Michael, come here."

Preston looked at Amy. "Told ya, two to three days." Michael looked at Preston. Preston winked at him. "Well, we could leave Michael down here and he could rub the pipe all day and that should unthaw the pipe."

Joe whipped around and said in an irritated voice, "Will you get serious for once?"

Michael quickly moved close to Joe to be ready to help. Preston rolled his eyes. "Kind of grouchy this morning." Preston sighed. "Well, I guess we could heat up some rocks or something and place them on the copper pipe. We could just keep rotating them with fresh hot ones. It should take about three to four hours, but we should be able to clear this up."

Joe said, "Sure if the rocks weren't buried under the snow and they aren't frozen to the ground."

"Michael, why don't you go upstairs and try the kitchen faucet again and see if it's working?" said Preston.

Michael looked up at Joe, and then at Preston and shrugged his shoulders. "Okay." He turned and ran up the stairs.

Preston asked Joe, "What's wrong with you? You're acting like a defeatist."

Joe said angrily, "We have all these people depending on us. We need water. If the pipe cracks, we can't just drive down to the hardware store and replace it. This is serious. This is deadly serious and you're joking around like some clown."

Preston sighed. "Joe, calm down. We'll get this fixed. Let's go check the garage for some stuff. We'll get everyone else working on heating up something on the wood stove to rotate on the pipe to unfreeze it." Preston thought a moment. "What about your propane torch? Do you have fuel for it?"

"Yes, I have fuel for it. I use it to solder with."

"Let's go get it and use it on the pipe."

Preston turned to everyone else. "Find something solid that can be heated up and placed on the pipe. We'll be right back." They walked into the kitchen and Michael was still turning the faucets on and off.

Preston and Joe shared a smile. Joe said, "That's good enough, Michael. Go get John and Steve and tell them we have a frozen water pipe." Michael nodded and raced down the hallway. They got their outside clothes on and went out to the garage. They stood there looking around for a minute, then Joe headed to where he left the propane torch. He reached out to grab it when he noticed the stack of firebricks he'd gotten for the wood stove. He smacked himself on the forehead. "I forgot all about getting these fire bricks. I bought them for the wood stove and never got around to using them. We can heat them up and have everyone rotate them. I'll use the torch and you get everyone on rotation detail." Preston grabbed an armful of bricks and Joe grabbed the torch and an extra tank of fuel.

Soon everyone was working on heating the bricks and carrying them over to the pipe, laying them on top of it for a couple of minutes, then rotating that one for a new one. Joe started using the propane torch on the pipe from the wall to about three feet and then back again. He kept doing this over and over again. Everyone else was setting at least four bricks on the pipe at a time. After three hours, the propane tank on the torch ran out. Joe was getting really stressed by this time. The water still hadn't thawed. Joe looked like he was going to either keel over or blow his top.

Preston said, "Go take a break. I'll use the torch and make sure they keep the bricks rotating. Go on. We can manage this." Joe nodded and walked upstairs. He filled up a thermos with hot coffee and took it and a couple of apple tarts over to see Jane. Preston put the new fuel tank on the torch and repeated what Joe had done.

Two minutes was the routine for those heating bricks. They would heat the brick for two minutes, wearing thick leather gloves, then carry them down two at a time to the pipe. They would spread them out for two minutes, then the next person would be there to lay more heated bricks on the pipe. It was a real workout going up and down the basement stairs, but this needed to be done. All the brick heaters were sweating and down to t-shirts by this time because they kept the fire in the wood stove going really hot. Michael's job was to fill some one liter plastic bottles with the filtered water and lay them in a pan of snow to cool them and have that ready for everyone to drink. Joe came back after about fifteen minutes. He'd been thinking that at least he'd gotten an adapter so that he could refill the propane cylinders from the two one hundred pound propane tanks they had. After talking to Jane, he felt a little better. He took over from Preston with the torch. Preston went back to carrying bricks.

Everyone completely lost track of time. It was about 2:15 that afternoon when he said, "Quiet. Everyone stop." Everyone froze in place and hardly breathed. They all strained their ears but didn't hear anything. He waved everyone back to work and he kept heating the pipe. A minute later, he heard something again and before he could say anything, they all could hear the water running full blast in the kitchen sink. Everyone cheered and jumped up and down. Joe sank down to the floor in relief.

He was thinking over and over again, *Thank God.* He finally stood up. "From now on until it warms up, we'll run the water for two minutes after all the night shifts. That will keep new water flowing through the pipe and make it take longer for the water to freeze." Everyone just sat down and rested where they were. They'd been doing aerobic exercises since breakfast almost continuously for over six hours. Everyone slowly got up and made their way upstairs.

Michael was going to take over the watch for the rest of them so they could get some rest. Amy told Michael this watch could be a long one. Preston told him to call him if anything happened. Amy told him to call her and wake her up in six hours if she wasn't awake by then. He nodded and went to get Joe and Jane so they could eat and Jane could warm up. He'd taken a pack with him filled with some books, food and things to occupy himself.

Joe and Jane came inside. Jane went straight for the wood stove and stood close to get warm. Amy dished them up some stew, cut another loaf of bread, and heated the loaf up in the oven so it would be warm and steaming when they dug in. Amy stood, rubbing her arm and shoulder. It ached really badly. She had overworked it carrying the bricks for so many hours. Jane came over and checked the wounds. They hadn't opened up and weren't bleeding at least. Jane squeezed her arm in sympathy and motioned for her to follow. They went into Jane's bedroom. She went to the closet and brought down a large container. She grabbed a pill bottle from inside and opened it. She shook out two tablets. She closed it back up and placed it back in the container. She handed the pills to Amy and said, "Take these right before you lay down. They'll deal with the pain right now. You can't get any rest if you're tossing and turning in pain."

Amy took the pills and hugged her friend. "Thank you. You need to take your husband to bed after you eat. He was really stressed out about the frozen pipe. He needs to relax and just rest, even if he can't sleep. Maybe some soothing music would help."

Jane yawned. "I will. I'm sleepy now that I'm warming up. Thanks for making lunch and handling everything in here."

Amy said, "Thank you for staying on watch all this time, freezing your ass off." They smiled at each other. Jane put the container back up on a shelf. They both walked back into the kitchen.

The next two months went by with nothing much happening. Joe and Preston had kept up everyone's training. Vicki was doing pretty well for her size. She worked out down in the basement with weights every day. She was building up some serious muscle. Now that it wasn't below freezing all the time, Preston and Joe had them all outdoors running and doing all kinds of things. Vicki was even getting good at breaking down all the guns to clean them; she could clear a jam and she pretty much kept up with everyone else. She didn't do as much as everyone else did, but insisted on training. She was getting to be a pretty good shot. She'd taken over as the official cook and baker. This took a lot of her time. She also cleaned house. The other women helped with laundry and few of the harder things. They had found that doing all of these chores in the evening worked out a lot better for them. Vicki did the prep for all the meals for the next day and that cleared her more time to train during the day.

John and Steve were tripping over each other trying to get Vicki's attention. Amy was relieved. It had been nice being there center of attention for a while, but it had grown old very fast. They were always trying to carry things for her. They still did this a little, but now Vicki had most of their attention. She just hoped there wasn't going to be any fights or hurt feelings when Vicki made her choice. Amy's money was on Steve. Preston said John was going to win because he tried harder. Amy told him Vicki would pick Steve because he always had something nice to say to her and would make her laugh. Well, time would tell. She was young and could take her time. Today Joe had all of them out in the fields moving rocks that the cold and ice had brought to the surface. He told them after they readied the fields for planting, there would be even more rocks to move out before planting would begin. His advice was to get used to moving rocks. After dark Steve would ask Vicki to go for a walk.

A few weeks later, Preston asked Amy to camp out with him in a tent. She was excited. They packed up and walked out several miles and found a perfect spot by a stream. Amy set out three yo yo automatic fishing reels so they could have fresh fish to eat for breakfast the next morning. They got the tent set up in the brush and used his camo netting over it to blend into the surroundings. Without their fire you'd never know they were there. They had set up the fire pit under some tall trees so it would break up the smoke and not be so easy to spot. It would still be easily smelled if anyone was close, but they weren't too worried about it. They had brought plenty of ammo with them so they felt pretty secure that they'd be able to take care of themselves and just disappear into the woods.

That night after dinner, when they were sitting around the campfire, Preston got down on his knees in front of Amy and took her hands. "Amy, I love you more than I thought could ever be possible. Would you marry me?"

Amy looked at him in surprise. "I love you more than anything else, too. Yes, I will marry you."

He said, "We are bound to run into a preacher someday that can marry us. Until then, I want you to know that I think of myself as your husband." He reached inside his camo jacket and pulled out an old gold twenty-dollar piece that had a hole drilled through it with a leather lanyard on it. He put it over her head and settled it down between her breasts. "In the metal market, that gold piece is worth about twelve hundred dollars. When things get more settled, we'll cash that in and have a ring made out if it for you. Until then you wear this and keep it close to your heart."

Amy had tears running down her face. She grabbed him and kissed him passionately. She looked deep into his eyes. "I'll think of myself as your wife from now on. I'll always wear this close to my heart. Thank you." He kissed her back and they lay down on the ground, looking up at the beautiful night sky, holding each other tight.

Chapter 31

Spring Beaver Trapping & Smelt Run

"Courage is grace under pressure."

Ernest Hemmingway

Clint looked out the front window at the melting snow as he sipped his morning coffee. The view before him looked wild and mysterious in the predawn light. For the last week, the snow level had been rapidly dropping in the April sunshine. As he scanned the area, he could even see some bare spots. Now was the time to be very cautious outside. It was hard to imagine there were so many dangers outside when looking at the scene before him. It looked untouched by civilization. He mentally counted the dangers. He decided to start with human dangers first. Let's see, there would be people who want what they have; starving people who want food, sick people who could contaminate them with horrible diseases, cannibals that want to eat them, gangs that want to kill them, hunting parties sent by warlords to gather supplies would kill anyone who resisted. Environmental nutcases that worshiped the earth would kill anyone who wouldn't live a green veggie life, religious nuts cleansing the earth of wicked people, which includes anyone who didn't agree with them, and then there were the plain psychopaths that enjoy killing. Then there were the natural elements. Springtime is a dangerous time in the wild. It's easy to slip and break a bone, avalanches could bury a person in a snowy grave, unseen holes covered with snow could cause injury or death, a misstep on ice hidden by snow over a stream, lake or pond could mean a plunge into the icy water and drowning, a freak snowstorm could hit unexpectedly, causing a person to get lost and die, footprints left in the melting soft snow could lead others right to you, wild dogs, wolves, etcetera. He smiled and chuckled. It was good to be alive. What would life be like without a little excitement now and then and a few challenges? Boring. Just plain boring. He grinned. Soon they could be outside more. He really, really looked forward to it. He didn't like being cooped up inside. He was looking forward to seeing all the fresh new growth. He had never just been able to observe and absorb all the changes springtime brought day after day. It had always seemed to him that one day you just woke up and noticed everything was green and all the trees had new buds on them. This time he'd be able to see it up close and personal in all of the stages of nature's glory.

He headed into the kitchen for more coffee. Junior was sitting at the table, drinking a cup of coffee. He'd turned on the burner under the teakettle so he could make Gayle a pot of green tea. His dad had stored a lot of it. He had a cup set out and a few crackers he'd take in to Gayle so she could eat them before getting up. The crackers were kind of stale, but they weren't bad if you drank something with them. She was doing better with the morning sickness now that she was about four months along.

"Good Morning."

Junior looked up at him, blurry eyed. "Good morning. How much snow has melted?"

Clint smiled. "There are bare spots of ground showing."

Junior grinned. "Thank God. Now we can get out of here and do some things outside."

Clint grinned right back at him. "My thoughts exactly." The last couple of months they had all been reading Junior's dad's journal over and over again and reading the other books he had on gardens and such. They also watched all of the *Buckshot Wilderness Survival* DVDs that showed how to do things like smoke fresh meat, make maple syrup, catch fish, and what plants to look for food substitutes and other helpful things. They had a lot of work ahead of them to prepare for next winter.

Junior said, "We can also put out some snares to get beaver for fresh meat and fur."

"I look forward to it. I've been reading the trapping books and watching the DVDs, so I have a better understanding of what to do. But there's nothing like hands on experience."

"You'll catch on really fast. Even Gayle did last fall; she turned into a pretty good trapper."

"How is she this morning?"

Junior grinned. "She was complaining that my son was keeping her up at night, moving around and kicking her, keeping her from getting any good sleep. It's so new a sensation that it wakes her right up. She's a light sleeper, so that doesn't help, either. She was just getting used to me moving around at night. She calls the baby my son when things like this happen, and when the baby is good and we're just talking, she says it's her daughter."

Clint laughed. "She better be careful with that. Fate might be listening and she could have twins. A son and a daughter."

Junior laughed. "Oh wow. I didn't even think of that. She'll have a cow when I tell her. I can't wait to see the look on her face."

Clint grinned. "Be careful, though. She doesn't have much of a sense of humor anymore. She's so touchy about some things."

"I know. Her mood got really bad the other night. I was talking about what I missed from the old world, and said I really wish we could go to the store and buy some Rocky Road ice cream. She screeched at me, saying now I'd done it. She's been craving ice cream ever since. I do feel bad about her cravings. But there's no way to satisfy them now."

"I know. I feel bad about that, too. She seems to really be suffering from them. Nothing else will do as a substitute. She kind of acts like a drug addict needing a fix."

Junior laughed and agreed. "Well, at least we lucked out with the peanut butter. My dad stored a lot of peanut butter, thank God."

Clint laughed with him. Gayle put peanut butter on the damnedest things. Sometimes when she was eating, she would get up and grab a jar of peanut butter and eat a couple of spoonfuls between bites of her meal. Clint gave up thinking she was weird about peanut butter when she put it on the powdered scrambled eggs Junior had fixed her one afternoon. She moaned in ecstasy as she ate them. She even spread it on top of fried potatoes. He shook his head, remembering. But the one combination that really got him was when she was eating spaghetti. She would take a bite of spaghetti, then eat a spoonful of peanut butter, alternating between the two. He shuddered just remembering it. She kept saying it was really good and to try it. She pestered Junior so much he finally tried it. All he would say about it was it was an experience that he didn't want to ever repeat.

The teakettle started to whistle and Junior turned the burner off. He poured the hot water into the teapot and then added some green tea. He left it to steep and poured himself and Clint some more coffee.

Clint said, "Today, if the weather holds, we should go out on a tour of the area and see what and who is around here."

Junior grinned. "That sounds like a plan. I've been thinking that we should look around for useful things, too. I want to bring the large sled and some rope. If we go by some abandoned houses, I want to look and see if we can find some baby stuff and maybe some maternity clothes for Gayle. She's complaining that all she can wear is my sweat pants now that her jeans don't fit anymore. I noticed some boxes in a couple of houses that looked like baby clothes when we were looking for paper and pens. And those houses also had baby furniture in them I think."

Clint said, "If we can, we'll check and see what we can find for the baby."

Junior grabbed a tray and put the teapot, crackers, a cup and the ever ready jar of peanut butter with a spoon already in it on the tray. He grinned at Clint. "Let's leave as soon as I can get her settled. I'm looking forward to getting out of here."

"I'll grab us some supplies and thermoses. I'll be ready as soon as you are." Junior nodded and took the tray to Gayle.

Junior set the tray on the nightstand. Gayle yawned and stretched, then yelped and hopped out of bed, rubbing her leg because she got a cramp. She'd been getting them more and more lately. He was worried that she wasn't getting the right kind of vitamins and that may be causing the cramps. They didn't have a doctor he could ask, or even another woman that might know about stuff like this. He hoped the baby was all right. He worried about things like that, but had never said anything to her about it because he didn't want her to worry. He noticed lately that he'd been praying a lot more than normal. He didn't know what else to do. He had left it up to God to guide them. Gayle sat down on the bed and rubbed her calf.

Junior said, "Are you all right?"

"Yeah, I'm fine, except for the cramp in my leg. I have to go to the bathroom." She limped out of the room. Junior waited for her to return. She walked back in after a few minutes and climbed back in bed. She looked up at him. "Stop worrying. It's only a cramp. You worry too much about everything."

"I love you and our child. It's only natural that I worry about the two of you. What kind of a man would I be if I didn't worry about you both?"

She reached up and pulled him close for a kiss. She looked into his eyes. "You wouldn't be you if you didn't worry. I'm sorry if I sounded a bit upset. I'm not. The cramp just really hurt. I love you."

She kissed him again and then let go of him, leaning back against the headboard. Junior poured her a cup of tea and handed it to her. He then handed her a cracker so she could slowly eat it. She nibbled on it and took a sip of tea. "I feel fine this morning. My stomach isn't upset at all. Maybe this morning sickness stuff is over."

"Well, I hope it's over so you feel better ,but we should continue with the tea and crackers for a few days just to be sure."

Gayle nodded. "That's probably a good idea. But I sure hope this lasts. I hate being sick like that."

Junior sat down on the bed next to her. "The snow has melted enough that Clint and I are going to scout around and see what's happening around us. We might be gone overnight. That'll depend on what we see and how far we decide to go. We'll make sure everything is done first and you're set, so you don't have to go outside. Please promise me you won't go outside while we're gone."

Gayle looked at him. "I promise. But I hope you aren't gone overnight."

Junior held her hand. "I'll try to get us back, but be prepared in case it doesn't happen."

Gayle grinned. "Okay. I'll keep the home fires burning." Junior grinned back at her.

A half-hour later, Clint and Junior were ready to leave. Gayle walked them outside and then she went back inside and they waited to leave until they heard her tightening the bolts. Junior went to the garage and got the sleds and some nylon rope, then they headed out. They talked quietly. Mostly Clint just wanted to get a feel for what was happening around them. He headed out, going northwest. He planned on making a full circle and a few crisscrosses if they found anything interesting to investigate. Junior was really enjoying being outdoors. The sun was shining, birds were chirping and flying about and squirrels were running around from tree to tree, scolding them as they went past.

The only thing that was missing was having his dad with him. It was still hard at times to accept that his dad was gone. As he looked around, he realized this would be his first spring without him around to guide him. It seemed like a lot more time had passed than just six months since his dad had died. So much had happened. He sighed. Soon they'd be burying Marion next to his father. He sighed again. So much death had touched him since the world had ended. Then his heart lifted as he thought that soon he would be out showing his son or daughter all the things that his dad taught him. He'd keep his dad's teaching alive in his children. They'd know all about their grandfather and what a wonderful man and father he'd been. As he envisioned what he would do and say to his own children, his steps grew lighter and so did his heart.

Gayle got up from her nap late in the afternoon and felt better than she had since she realized that she was pregnant. She also became aware that she was really hungry. She grabbed a bowl of stew from the slow cooker and ate some peanut butter with it. All of a sudden she felt energized. She decided to start the wheat grinding a little earlier than normal. She wanted to bake. She wasn't sure what she wanted to make yet, but would decide that later. She was tired of being sick and cared for. She was going to do some cleaning and baking as a surprise for Junior and Clint. She doubted they'd be back tonight. Junior had been cooped up inside for so long she just knew that he'd need to stay outside for a while, and so prepared herself to spending the night alone. He deserved it. He'd taken care of her through all of her morning and afternoon sickness. He never made her feel bad for being under the weather. He always listened to her patiently, even when she knew she was being unreasonable. She just felt so weird sometimes. One minute she'd be laughing and the next she'd either be angry or crying. She had no idea pregnant women went through so much. It's a wonder the human race continued on, in spite of pregnant women.

She really wished she had another woman to talk to and ask about what to expect. She was scared of giving birth. She kept worrying that something was going to go wrong or that something was wrong with her or the baby. Was all of this normal? She got so frustrated sometimes with all they were reading; there wasn't one thing on childbirth. It was hard to explain to Junior and Clint. They were men and couldn't quite grasp her meaning sometimes. They kept telling her that women had been giving birth since the beginning and that it was a natural thing that happened and not to worry. She sure wished her mother was around. She sighed and started grinding up the wheat. No use going down that road. She felt good and wanted to think good thoughts and not worry about the future.

Late the next afternoon, Gayle jumped in surprise when she heard banging on the outside door. She ran to the door to open it up and then remembered she'd better go up to the loft area and look out to make sure it was Junior and Clint. She went up there and peeked out cautiously; there was Junior, standing there smiling at her. She yelled down, "I'll get the door." She hurried down and started undoing the bolts. She'd noticed a couple of sleds with tarps over them with rope strung across to make everything secure. *I wonder what they brought back.* She was excited. As soon as she got the door undone, she slipped her coat on.

Junior grinned. "We brought you back some presents." Gayle laughed in excitement and stepped towards the sleds.

Clint said, "Stop. Be careful and don't slip on that patch of ice."

Gayle looked down and saw she almost stepped right on a big patch of ice. "Thanks for telling me."

Clint grinned. "I have to look out for my godchild, and you, too, of course."

She laughed. "Gee, thanks for including me in that show of concern."

He laughed. "You're welcome."

Gayle rolled her eyes. "So, what did you bring home?"

Junior said, "Is the coffee hot?"

"No. I'll need to put a fresh pot on," said Gayle.

Junior said, "Would you please put one on? We'll unload the sleds while you do that." He leaned over and kissed her and she smiled.

"Sure. I'm excited to see what you guys brought home and what my presents are." She went back inside the house and got a pot of coffee going. Junior and Clint unloaded the sleds into the living room. Gayle set the table so it would be ready for dinner. She turned down the burner under the coffee pot when it started to perk. She looked up at the clock to time it for three minutes. As she waited, she could hear Junior and Clint going in and out. She couldn't wait to see everything. When the coffee was done, she filled two mugs and walked into the living room.

She met Junior at the doorway. He had been on his way into the kitchen. She handed him a mug and he said, "Thanks." He took a sip. "This is great coffee."

She smiled and said, "Thanks." He reached out and took the other mug out of her hand. "I'll take this to Clint. Go ahead and see what we brought." He couldn't wait to see how surprised she was going to be over all the baby stuff they brought home.

He turned around just as she squealed, "Oh my God." She was looking at a folded up baby crib that was leaning against the couch. The mattress for it was right next to it. They brought a bassinet, a changing table and all sorts of things for a baby. There were a lot of boxes stacked up by the chairs. Clint was standing there watching her reaction, just as Junior was doing. Junior set both coffee mugs down on an end table. Gayle turned to Clint and whispered, "Thank you." She had tears running down her face. She stumbled over to him and hugged him. "Thank you so much." Then she turned to Junior and almost knocked him down, she hugged him so tight. She kissed him saying over and over again, "Thank you." She then laid her head on his shoulder and cried for a few minutes. Junior was kind of worried that maybe she didn't like what they brought. He hugged her tight and rubbed her back. It was hard to know if she was upset or not with the way her moods changed so quickly. She leaned back and looked at him, smiling, and her eyes were shining. He grinned. What a relief. He was getting worried that maybe he hadn't done something right.

She turned and looked at all the stuff. "Thank you both. Now our baby won't have to sleep in a dresser drawer." Junior was startled by what she said. He had never had any intentions of letting his child sleep in a dresser drawer or anything like that. Gayle walked over and ran her hands over all the baby furniture, smiling.

Junior said, "Look in the boxes. We're not sure about all of the clothes in them. You know the sizes and things."

Clint said, "Gayle, sit down and I'll put each box in front of you and you can go through them and see if you want what's in them."

She smiled at him. "Okay." She sat down and Clint placed the first one in front of her. She squealed again in delight as she opened it. The boxes had maternity and baby clothes in it. She hurriedly pulled out all the clothes and looked at them.

Later that night as Junior and Gayle lay in bed, Gayle rubbed the side of Junior's face with her hand. "You are the best almost husband in the world."

Junior kissed her hand. "Thank you. I try hard to be a good almost husband and I'll try just as hard to be a good dad, too." As Gayle drifted off to sleep, visions of all the maternity clothes and baby clothes swam through her mind. She smiled and imagined all of the stories she would tell her child about his or her father and godfather as sleep claimed her.

Junior lay there holding her close and tried not to think about all the dead bodies they'd found as they looked for baby stuff and checked around. The dead children really tore at his heart. It made him want to run back here and make sure Gayle and his child were all right. He could tell that it had affected Clint, too, because he had turned to Junior and said, "Gayle and the baby are fine." He hadn't sounded so very sure himself. It was almost like he was trying to convince himself, too. It had been hard just seeing all that death. They had heard how bad it was from "Crazy Larry" on the ham radio, but seeing just a small part of it was hell. He couldn't even imagine how bad it must be in the cities. What had taken them so long was they had dragged the dead bodies to one house at the end of the street that stood off by itself and set it on fire to burn the bodies. He had never been so glad to see someone as he had been to see Gayle, looking out the watch hole in the loft at them when they got home. Seeing her smile made him relax and know that everything was fine and she and the baby were safe. He kissed the top of her head and just let himself enjoy holding her, knowing that everything was all right at least for this moment. The future? Who knows? The odds were against them surviving. He intended on beating those odds.

The next day they went out to the garage and made some things they were going to need to tap the maple trees for syrup. They had watched *Buckshot's Wilderness Survival DVD Volume 2* and paid close attention to how to do it. They went out and tapped the trees. It was great to be outdoors and enjoy the beauty surrounding them. They set up an old fifty-five gallon wood stove outside with a tank above that fed into a stainless steel boiling pot to make the maple syrup in. It took a lot of work, but they finally were done making maple syrup. They had boiled down eighty gallons of sap into two gallons of syrup. On and off while they had been doing this, Junior had Clint read in his dad's journal about trapping and snaring the spring beaver.

Clint told Junior, "Your dad said there's a spot down by the beaver dens that the two-year-old beavers will take over when they're kicked out of their parents' den to make room for the new babies that will be born. He stated that trapping them will give us fresh meat and fur, but to leave the mom and dad's area alone to provide more beaver each year to trap. This is truly a sustainable resource. Your dad, Junior, was an amazing man. I have hunted most of my life and I don't know half of what he knew about this."

Junior smiled at Clint. "Trappers are the number one woodsmen of all the different sportsmen. They see so much more than hunters do in the woods. They study and learn all the animals. They are modern day mountain men."

Clint said, "I believe it."

"Every year we'll learn more and more about the habits of the different animals. Our skills trapping and snaring them will improve, too. I really feel we have the best chance of surviving this mess. We'll always have food and fur for warmth."

Clint smiled. "I can't wait to learn more. You know, I'd been getting really bored with everything I'd been doing. I retired because I wanted to do something different. This is like a gift straight from God for me. I would rather be outside in the woods than anywhere else. I'm learning a new skill that will round out all my other skills and make me a better survivor."

Junior laughed and nodded. "I'll remind you of this when we're dragging beaver out of the frozen pond in the middle of a snowstorm. Let's grab a dozen snares and some twenty-four inch rebar stakes and go set them out." They put on snowshoes and headed out.

When they got there, the stream was open and flowing. The snow was still deep in spots and the snowshoes were working great to get them around faster than trying to walk on top of the snow and falling through every other step. They went down the ridge about a mile, and it was just like his dad had described in his journal. They set out six snares on the stream, and then crossed over the hill. Another creek was feeding into the main stream and they set up the last six snares there. Some of the snares were set up in naturally narrowed spots, and in others they made fake mud piles and used Buckshot's Beaver Blaster Lure. Junior had picked this up when watching *Buckshot's Survival Snaring DVD*.

Junior stood back and looked the area over. He turned to Clint. "Tomorrow we better bring a sled with us to carry the beaver back."

Clint, being new to trapping and snaring, asked, "How many do you think we'll get tomorrow? Like ten or twelve?"

Junior laughed. "It is not quite that easy. But, if we're lucky, we should have two or three. According to my dad's journal, we can safely take four from each stream."

"I meant to ask you about that. Why only four?"

"Because that way we'll let some of the two-year-old beavers pass through and set up dens farther down, so we continue to have food and fur in the future."

"That's good thinking."

Junior grinned. "Come on, we'll head for home now. Rest up tonight, because tomorrow we'll be very busy skinning and tacking the beaver pelts on boards to dry." They turned and headed home.

The next day, they headed out bright and early. Clint was all wound up and excited to see how many beaver they'd caught. Junior kept telling him to slow down, because he was dragging the sled they'd use to haul the beaver home on. They checked the first two snares; they were empty. Clint was disappointed. The next set was in a narrowed down part of the stream; it was knocked over and empty.

Clint looked at it and asked, "What happened?"

Junior shrugged his shoulders. "Who knows? Maybe a muskrat knocked it over." The next set they checked was a fake mud pie set they had made and used Buckshot's Beaver Blaster Lure on. Waiting for them was a two-year-old beaver that was about twenty-five pounds. The beaver was still alive. Clint raced up, all excited, and Junior said, "Wait. Slow down." It was too late. The beaver was out in the water, faster than you could blink and flipped about a hundred gallons of water at Clint when he reached down for the snare cable. A beaver's tail and their powerful back feet can throw one hell of a lot of water at a guy. Clint looked up at Junior as icy water dripped off his face and clothes. Junior busted out laughing. "I tried to warn you."

Clint said with sarcasm and faked humility, "Next time I'll listen to your young wisdom." Clint unzipped his coat and wiped his face off with his inside dry shirt. "What do we do with the beaver now?"

Junior pulled the .22 Bucksmark pistol and shot the beaver in the head. "You do that first, then you reach for the snare cable." He showed him how to drag it out of the water and cut the snare wire before he placed it on the sled. "These are the best tasting beaver and they're easier to skin than the bigger ones." They moved down to the next snare set. It was empty. Junior turned to Clint. "Do you want to head back home with this beaver and change into dry clothes?"

Clint shook his head. "No. Its over forty degrees out here, and as long as we keep moving, I'll be fine." They headed over the hill to the next stream and Clint was more careful this time. Nothing like icy cold water to dampen your excitement.

Over on this side they did a little better. The first mud pie set near the main stream held a good fifty-pound beaver. *It's a male*, thought Junior, *no doubt protecting his territory from the new scent they had left there with the lure.* The beaver lure was made to cause a territorial response from the beaver that lived here. Clint shot this one and placed it on the sled and they headed upstream to check the other snare sets. The next snare had another two-year-old in it. Junior was thinking that they'd done good getting three beaver, totaling over a hundred pounds. That was a lot of meat. The next snare was empty; they walked on by. The last set was missing. There were bear tracks leading up over another hill. The bear must have killed the beaver and pulled up the rebar stake when he carried off the dead beaver to high ground. Fresh blood was shining, standing out crystal clear in the sunlight on the snow.

Clint unslung his AR-15 and whispered to Junior, "What should we do?"

Junior whispered back, "It's better to just let the bear have it. But, you might want to take a look and see if we scared the bear off. Maybe he dropped the beaver if he ran away. We can then recover the snare parts and the rebar stake."

Clint nodded. "You stay here." He bent down and took off his snowshoes.

Junior leaned towards him. "If you have to shoot it, aim for the head, hopefully for the eyes. That mouse gun you're carrying doesn't have the knock down power for a bear."

Clint nodded. "I know."

Clint's hands were sweating. He wished he had a 30-06 instead of his AR-15. He took a step and then paused, straining his ears to hear the slightest of sounds. He did this all the way up the hill. When he nearly reached the top, he slowly and carefully made his way through the brush. *God, it's really thick here.* When he was almost at the top, he peeked out of the thick bushes and didn't see anything. He slowly moved a little forward. He heard a sound and froze in place. With all his senses on high alert, he strained his ears for any sign of the bear. His breaths increased along with his heart rate. He took five more slow, careful steps and just passed by a trunk of a fallen tree. On the other side was a low spot and Mr. Bear was watching him closely as he approached. The old male was not sharing his meal with anyone.

With his next step he heard a warning, "Woof." He quickly spun towards the threat. The black bear looked huge up close. Clint froze for a second, and then slowly backed off. He thought, *It's all yours, big guy.* There's nothing quite like facing a hungry spring bear. You know he's really, really hungry and grumpy after sleeping most of the winter. Your adrenaline races through your body faster than you can blink. Your face feels flushed and your heart beats hard and fast against your ribs. Clint had felt this same feeling many times before. Everything is narrowed down to this time and place that you see and feel in total clarity. Every detail is stuck in your mind. This is what's meant by being alive, truly one hundred percent alive at the moment. He slowly took another step back. His AR-15 felt like a BB gun in his hands compared to the huge beast he faced. He looked like he weighed about four hundred pounds. The bear was totally on alert, watching him intently. He kept slowly backing up as the bear stood guard over his meal. When he reached the top, he moved a little faster, backing away. When the bear was out of sight, he turned and ran the rest of the way to Junior. Clint said, "Time to go. It's a big bear. I mean a really big, hungry bear."

Junior thought, *it must be a big bear if Clint is backing down.* They quickly made sure they had everything and turned around and headed for home.

Gayle was in the living room, watching out the window, when she saw Clint and Junior walking on the trail towards the house. She went to the door and unlocked the bolts. Gayle saw the look on Junior's face. "Oh my God, what happened?"

Clint said, " Big bear. Yeah, it weighed at least a thousand pounds. We thought it was better to let the bear win and keep the beaver."

Junior laughed. "More like four hundred pounds. We have to go take care of the three beaver we caught. We'll be eating good tonight. We'll tell you all about it later." He kissed Gayle.

She said, "I'm glad you're both all right. I'll start lunch." They went out to the garage. Junior quickly skinned the beavers. Clint watched close to learn how to do it.

Junior gutted them and then cut the meat up. He showed Clint how to use the fleshing beam to flesh the beaver hides of fat and pieces of meat. Clint was rubbing his hands through the beaver fur. "This is super thick fur. It's beautiful."

Junior smiled. "Of course it is. God created it." Junior left Clint to finishing fleshing and went into the house to wash and store the meat. He and Gayle wrapped some of it up in freezer paper and put it in the freezer for later. He kept the back strap out to cook for dinner tonight. Beaver back strap tasted better than deer back strap. Just thinking about it made his mouth water.

He went back out to the garage to help Clint. When the hides were fleshed right, Junior showed Clint how to roll them up so they could carry them into the house so they wouldn't get dirty. They brought them into the house and tacked them out on plywood boards that his dad had made. They'd have to make up a fresh batch of acorn tanning solution.

Clint was still running his hands on the fur, admiring the softness. He looked up at Junior. "I'm going to ask Gayle if she'll make me a hat out of this one for next winter. It will match my new coat."

Junior smiled at him. "Everyone starts to like the feel and look of fur after they're around it for any length of time. It's truly a bounty from God."

Clint nodded and smiled. Over a week's time, they took ten beaver total from five different streams and creeks. They had restocked the freezer and that would take them until the fall, along with the fish they'd catch during spring and summer. Then they'd again restock the freezer with meat for the winter. Clint understood the renewable resource that beaver were. They left plenty of them alive so they'd be able to come back and do the same thing year after year and always have fresh meat and fur in the springtime.

Gayle was feeling fine now and the morning sickness was finally gone. It greatly improved her moods, too. She was busy doing spring cleaning and arranging everything for the baby. She sang and hummed as she worked. She smiled a lot, too. It really lightened the atmosphere of the house. She also got her sense of humor back and both men didn't have to walk around on eggshells anymore. The next afternoon, Junior took Gayle on a picnic to a spot that wasn't very far from the house. It was a place that Clint would be able to see and hear them if they ran into trouble. Junior and Gayle had checked the snares earlier in the day, resetting them all around the house to protect them from wild dogs and wolves. They had decided to leave them out all the time, because you just never knew when wolves or dogs would show up. It was much better to be safe than sorry. Gayle sat on a stump with a cushion on it that Junior had brought for her. It was wonderful being outside in the sunlight and seeing the birds flying and the squirrels running around chattering at each other. It was easy to forget that the world was in such a mess sitting in this peaceful, beautiful place. It was so warm in the sunlight that Gayle had to unzip her coat. She was enjoying the time alone with Junior.

The next morning, Junior and Clint were heading out to the place to catch smelt. They would be gone for six to seven days. It would take them two days to reach the area. They planned on spending three days catching as close to a hundred pounds of smelt as they could get, and cleaning and drying them to carry home. How long they were gone would depend on if they ran into trouble or not, or maybe they'd need to take another route home because they ran into people along the way. She was disappointed that she had to stay home. Clint and Junior explained all the reasons why she had to stay. She understood them, but was downhearted about being left behind. Both men made sure to do everything so Gayle didn't have to go outside. Junior had even brought in an old metal washtub he'd found when moving some stuff around in the garage for her to empty the wood stove ashes into so she didn't even have to go outside to do that either, although now that it was warmer, they only kept a low-grade fire going in the wood stove at night.

She had decided to spend her time altering some of the maternity clothes they had brought her that were too big and to use some of the baby clothes as patterns to make more baby clothes from. There hadn't been very many newborn clothes in the boxes they brought back. Junior had also grabbed her some books they'd found on pregnancy and child development. She would read those at night and learn everything she could. She'd stay busy, and hopefully the time would pass quickly.

Early the next morning, Gayle fixed them breakfast when it was still dark outside, while the men went through their packs one more time to make sure they had everything they would need. Gayle told Clint to be on the watch for the woman that was the right one for him. She had dreamed about it that night. Clint laughed and shrugged it off as a pregnant woman's fantasy. Clint and Junior left just as the sky was lightening. They had their packs half-filled with food and equipment and some five gallon buckets, and of course, the nets. They brought plenty of ammo in case they ran into trouble. That was a lesson Junior had learned the hard way and one he'd never forget. It was a good thing they'd spent some time on reloading this past winter. Both men were excited and anxious to get going. They walked with a spring in their steps, just happy to be outside in God's country. When they stopped for lunch, Junior pulled out the map he had marked the route on and studied it for a few minutes. Junior had used the map he kept in the glove compartment of his truck. Clint sat down next to him and looked at the map, too. Junior pointed out the small creek they would see first that ran into another creek, that ran into the main stream where it flowed into Lake Superior. He pointed last to the mouth of the main stream and said, "That's where we're heading. The smelt will run up that stream, according to my dad."

Clint said, "I can't wait for fresh fish to eat."

Junior smiled and nodded. "I love smelt."

"I have never fished with a net before. It sounds like fun to haul all those smelt from the stream in one. I don't think I've ever seen as many in one place as your dad described in his journal."

Junior looked at him. "I remember when I was ten and my dad took me on a smelt run. We had a ball. There were people all along the stream bank and they had campfires going. We all waited for the run to start. I asked my dad how we were going to get any smelt with all those people there. He laughed and told me to just wait and see how many of them would be in the stream." He paused and took a sip of coffee. "Boy, he wasn't kidding. There were so many smelt that there were more of them almost than water. Everyone was hauling in filled nets. We had a great time. We cooked up a bunch over the fire in butter. I've been hooked on smelt ever since." Clint was excited. They packed everything up and eagerly headed out with a bounce in their steps and hearts light as the springtime air.

That night they made camp after it had gotten too dark to see. They tried to go as far as they could before setting up camp. They were trying to time it so they would get to the stream before setting up camp on the second day. They didn't know when the run would start. The journal just said the end of April. They might have to wait for a few days. The only thing that worried them was that they could miss the run. They both had visions of frying pans filled with smelt browning in them and couldn't stand the thought of missing out. They both kept waking up all night, afraid that they had overslept. They had eaten and had the camp packed up and ready to go as soon as the sky started to brighten on the horizon. They hurried down the game trail they'd found the day before that was headed in the right direction. They were men on a mission. They really pushed themselves that day and when it was starting to get dark, they reached the creek that fed into the main stream they were looking for. Both men grinned at each other.

They only had four to five miles to go and they'd be right where they needed to be. They pushed on and found a spot to camp that had thick brush all around it on high ground, giving them a clear view of the stream and the surrounding area. The mouth of the river was up farther, but they decided to make their camp in this spot and wait to scout around in the morning to see if they could find a closer spot to make their permanent camp. They were excited but tired. They ate a cold dinner and then went right to sleep.

Clint was up before the sun the next morning. He let Junior sleep in. He decided to scout around and see if anyone was around. So far they'd not run into anyone. Later that morning, after the sun came up, Junior awakened to the smell of bacon frying. His dad had some canned bacon that he'd bought for the end of the world and they brought a can to use for this trip. He quickly untangled himself from his sleeping bag and went outside the small tent. Clint was cooking breakfast. Junior quickly used the bushes and then joined him at the campfire, yawning.

Clint handed him a cup of coffee. Junior mumbled his thanks. Clint said, "Breakfast will be done in a few minutes." Junior nodded his head and took a sip of coffee. After they ate, they took turns going down to the stream and splashing water on their face and hands to wash up. That sure woke him all the way up. The water was so cold it burned when it touched his skin. They packed the camp up so they wouldn't leave any of their stuff unattended that anyone could steal. It also made their presence less obvious.

They cautiously headed out, keeping alert for any signs of others. Clint kept a special look out for bears. He didn't want to meet up with another hungry bear anytime soon. They had about four or five miles to go to the mouth of the river. They took their time to be careful and not leave any footprints or signs for others to follow. They had gone about three to four miles when they heard two different rifle shots up ahead. Clint and Junior looked at each other. Then they heard a few more shots and then they heard several wolves howling, growling, and yipping. They took off their packs and stashed everything but their guns and ammo. It was time to move fast. They both broke into a hard run, checking their rifles to make sure they were ready to use as they ran through the thick brush.

Both men remembered how wolves had killed and eaten Tim. Clint stopped and motioned to Junior. There stood three wolves. Junior and Clint aimed at the barely seen wolves and fired a couple of shots. Clint hit the one on the left. Junior hit the one on the right. They yelped and jumped. Blood was running down their sides. The wolves disappeared into the thick brush. Clint and Junior cautiously crept closer to see who had been shooting earlier. They came to a small clearing, a few hundred yards up from the mouth of the river. A woman and young boy were surrounded by eleven wolves. They were standing close to their campfire, facing outward towards the wolves. The woman had a High Point 9mm carbine with a laser and flashlight on it and a 9mm in a holster on her hip. The boy had a Ruger 10-22. They both were clearly scared to death.

Clint and Junior started shooting at the wolves to clear a path to the woman and boy. Making sure that the woman and boy were not in the line of fire, they shot two wolves, which dropped down dead in front of the men as they made their way closer. The other wolves turned around, growling and snapping their jaws. They continued to move forward over the dead wolves. Clint angled to the left and Junior angled to the right, going around the campfire to the sides where the woman and boy were. They kept shooting at the wolves, covering each other as they changed magazines. The woman and boy started shooting at the wolves in the middle, being careful not to shoot in the men's directions. Four wolves were dead on the ground and several more were wounded and bleeding. After a few intense moments, the wolves turned and disappeared into the brush. They all stayed as they had been, looking around, waiting and ready, to see if they would come back.

After a few minutes, Clint said, "I don't think they'll be back for awhile."

The woman aimed her rifle at Clint and said in a clear commanding voice, "What do you want?"

Clint and Junior exchanged a look. Clint looked back at her. "We don't want anything. We'll be on our way now."

He turned to leave and the woman said, "Hey, wait a minute." The woman stared at him intently for a few seconds. "Thanks for helping us." Clint nodded his head once and didn't say anything. She sighed and moved her finger off the trigger and lowered the rifle. Robbie did the same with his rifle.

Junior said, "I'm going to go and make sure they have left the area." Clint nodded and Junior disappeared into the brush. Clint looked around and then at the woman and sighed. The boy was watching him apprehensively, too. He asked, "Is it all right if I sit down?" The woman nodded. He sat down by the fire, within reaching distance of the woman and boy.

He wanted to stay close so he'd be able to protect them if the wolves showed up again. He said, "My name is Clint." He was trying to put them at ease. He knew his size intimidated a lot of people.

The woman looked deeply into his eyes like she was searching for something, almost like she could see his very soul. He felt a shiver run down his spine. She held her hand out for a handshake. "I'm Katlin." Clint very carefully reached out and gently shook her trembling hand.

The boy was watching their every move like a hawk with a thoughtful expression on his face. He looked Clint fully in the eyes. "My name is Robbie." He reached out his small hand for a handshake, too.

Clint carefully shook that small hand, too, and nodded at Robbie. He said, "When was the last time you both ate?"

Katlin said, "Last night I made a kind of rice soup. I'm trying to make what I have last as long as possible. I was just about to make some more when the wolves showed up."

Clint said, "I'll be right back. I have to go get my pack. We have some food we can share with you."

He found Junior on the way. "Let's get our gear." They quickly their way over to where they had stashed the packs and headed back to Katlin and Robbie. When they arrived Clint looked at Katlin. "Is it all right if we sit down by your fire?"

The woman gave him a long look. "Sure, make yourself at home." Clint smiled at her sense of humor.

He took off his pack and put it down on the ground in the same place he'd sat before. He pulled his pack closer and said, "Thank you. We don't have much, but we can share some food with you." He reached inside his pack and pulled out a thermos. He then reached back inside and brought out two stainless steel coffee mugs. He opened the thermos and poured some coffee into one of the cups.

As he was doing this, Katlin jumped up, spilling the boy off her lap and yelled excitedly, "Is that real coffee I smell?" She had an eager, excited look on her face. He nodded and handed the cup to her. She almost ripped it out of his hands and before he could say anything, she was taking a big gulp of it.

He said, "Careful, it's hot."

At the same time, Katlin opened her mouth and fanned her hand in front of it to cool her tongue. She grinned at him. "It was worth burning my tongue. Thank you, thank you, thank you." She sighed in pleasure and took another long drink from the cup.

Clint chuckled and knew exactly how she felt. He smiled at her. "You're welcome. I know exactly how you feel."

He then brought out a clean frying pan from his pack and made them some powdered whole eggs and heated up some canned bacon. The woman and boy's eyes got wide as they watched him cook. He felt weird with them watching his every move. Junior handed a cup of hot chocolate he'd made to Robbie.

Robbie carefully took the cup from him. "Thank you."

"You're welcome."

When Clint was done cooking, he handed a plate to both of them, piled high with eggs and bacon and a slice of homemade buttered bread. Robbie looked up at his mother and she shook her head no. Clint was puzzled and said, "What's wrong?"

She said, "You eat it first."

"I'm not hungry. I already ate." Katlin shook her head no. Clint said, "Don't you like eggs and bacon?"

Katlin hesitated a moment. "Will you and Junior eat a mouthful of each thing first?"

Clint looked puzzled and he and Junior exchanged a surprised look. Clint was thinking she hadn't been acting like she was crazy before. Junior said curiously, "Why do we need to take a bite of everything?"

"Please bear with me on this. Its important or I wouldn't ask you to do it."

Clint and he exchanged another look. Junior shrugged his shoulders as if to say, *who can understand women?* Clint reached down and picked a piece of bacon off one of the plates and broke it in half, handing a piece to Junior. They both ate the piece of bacon as they closely watched Katlin for her reaction. Clint reached into his pack and pulled out a spork and took a bite of the eggs off each plate.

Katlin let out a relieved sigh. "Good. You're not Rainbow Warriors sitting us up to die."

Clint and Junior exchanged a puzzled look. Clint turned back to Katlin. "What's a Rainbow Warrior?"

At the same time, Junior said, "What?"

Katlin said, "Robbie and I are from Green Bay. Not long after the world came to a screeching halt, these Rainbow Warriors came to town and took over the whole city. They forced everyone to convert to vegetarianism or die. Some of us made plans to escape. Most of us didn't make it and died. Robbie and I barely got away. My family owns a cabin on Lake Superior. We made our way to the cabin. Our food was just about gone when, last week, five men came and tried to beat down the cabin door because I wouldn't let them inside. They were vile men, issuing threats and taunts. Robbie and I escaped out a back window and made our way to our boat. This is where we ran out of gas two days ago I had planned on leaving shortly anyway, and had already prepared some things and placed them on the boat in preparation to leave." She gestured around. "This is all we have now."

Clint and Junior shared a knowing look. Clint thought, *Well, at least that part of what "Crazy Larry" had said was true.* He said, "Is it all right if you both eat now?"

Katlin smiled. "Yes, please." Clint handed them both a plate again and they both reached out eagerly. Robbie dug right in, eating very fast. The woman looked at Clint, and then looked away and blinked the tears out of her eyes. "Thank you. What do you want in payment?"

Clint looked at her. "Only some information." The woman looked at him long and hard, trying to decide if he was lying or not. "I only want some information about those Rainbow Warriors and what you've seen on the way. Now eat before it gets completely cold." The woman looked at him for a few more seconds, then nodded and dug into the food.

When they were done, not one crumb of food was left. Katlin said, "Thank you. It was very good. I'm grateful. It's been awhile since we had such good food to eat."

Clint said, "You're welcome."

Katlin studied Clint and Junior for a moment. "Why are you two here?"

Clint and Junior glanced at each other. Junior slightly nodded his head. Clint said, "We came here to catch smelt. Every year the smelt run up this stream. We could use some help. You can have some for yourself and Robbie."

Katlin said, "All right. We could sure use the food."

Junior brightened right up. "Can we make our camp here by yours? It's close to the stream, but far enough away not to let others know that we're here."

Katlin looked at him thoughtfully. "Sure, why not? It's a big place and I don't own it, anyway. What I really would like to know is, what insane idiot decided that re-introducing the wolves was a good thing?" Clint and Junior looked at each other for a few moments. Clint said, "It was obviously some bureaucrat that sat behind a desk and never had to live with them, or I should say co-exist as they call it."

Junior said, "We found someone that the wolves attacked and ate." He explained about finding Tim and his journal. Kaitlin shook her head sadly. "As if we didn't have enough problems without having to fight off wolves every time we turn around." The men agreed with her and explained about the wild dog problem too. Kaitlin was horrified to hear all they had been through.

Later they built a couple wood smokers to smoke the smelt that afternoon. Robbie helped them. Junior explained to him why they were doing it and what it was for. He helped him gather maple twigs for the wood smoke. He explained not to ever use oak or pine. Katlin became interested, too, and offered to help when they needed an extra pair of hands, which turned out to be quite often. Junior explained that they didn't know exactly when the run would start and they needed to watch the stream in teams and be ready at a moment's notice. All of them got caught up in the excitement. They ate and rested in shifts and waited in anticipation of having all the smelt they wanted to eat at one time. Robbie fell asleep about 10:30 that night, and Clint helped Katlin get him into his sleeping bag.

Katlin looked at Clint as they went back to sit by the fire. "It seems my partner is out for the count."

"It does look that way." They sat down on stumps in comfortable silence, listening to the night noises.

About a half hour later, Junior ran into the camp area. "The smelt are running. Grab the buckets and nets. Come on." He grabbed a few buckets, his net and took off running and laughing. Clint and Katlin stood up and looked at each other.

Robbie poked his head out of their tent. "Is it time?"

Clint said, "Yes, the smelt are running. Come on." Robbie crawled out of the tent and ran in the direction of the stream when his mother voice stopped him.

"Where do you think you're going without your boots and coat?"

Robbie rolled his eyes. "But Mom, the smelt are running right now."

"They'll still be running after you get your coat and boots on." He sighed and stomped back over to the tent and reached inside to get his coat and boots.

Clint tried to hide his smile from Robbie. He said out of the corner of his mouth, "How do you keep from laughing when he does things like that?"

She looked at him, smiling. "Years of practice. Toughen up, soldier."

He laughed. "Yes ma'am."

When Robbie was ready, they all grabbed buckets and Clint grabbed his net. They took off running to the stream. Katlin said, "Robbie, be careful. Don't fall in."

Robbie didn't pay her any attention. His eyes were open in amazement. The stream was filled with smelt. He jumped up and down and yelled, "Yeah!" and pumped his arm up and down like he was watching a game and doing a victory dance. Everyone laughed and joined in. Clint let Robbie wear his headlamp so he could see what he was doing. He helped Robbie lift up the net to empty into the buckets. He also made sure to keep him from falling head first into the freezing water. They were all laughing and carrying on like it was a huge party. Katlin even grabbed a bucket and was scooping up some fish. After a few hours, they decided that Katlin would stay at the camp with a lantern to cut and gut them and get them ready for drying.

Every few hours or so, more smelt would swim by and finally they filled up the buckets. They worked until almost sunup getting the smelt ready to be dried. Katlin had saved a quarter of a bucket full to cook for breakfast. They were all starving. Junior brought out the two frying pans and the powdered butter and started cooking. Everyone ate until they could hardly move. Then Junior started the fires for the smokers and told everyone to go ahead and get some sleep. He would wake Clint up in a few hours and they'd do this in shifts. Robbie's eyes were drooping and he kept trying to wake himself up, denying it when he was asked if he was tired. Katlin dragged him off to get some sleep.

When Katlin woke up, she hurried out to help. Robbie was already up and zipping around doing stuff for Junior. She yawned and Clint handed her a cup of coffee. She took it and said without thinking, "Bless you."

As they worked that day, Junior got an idea. He needed to think about it some more before he said anything, but he'd decided they were going to bring Katlin and Robbie back with them. This must be the woman that Gayle told Clint to look for. Besides, they couldn't leave them here to fend for themselves. They wouldn't stand a chance and he liked Katlin and Robbie. He wouldn't leave them here to who knows what kind of fate. She could be a great help. He just hadn't figured out how exactly yet. He thought Clint and she made a good couple. He had seen how they laughed and joked around last night as they worked. Clint seemed to really like Robbie and Robbie seemed to like Clint, too. Now, how to convince both of them? Yup, this needed some more thought.

He was trying to carve a piece off one of the branches to make it fit better on the smoker and wasn't paying attention; he sliced open his hand. He looked down and thought, *Oh great. That looks bad.*

Katlin immediately examined it and said, "Robbie, get my bag."

Clint said, "How bad is it?"

Katlin said, "It's bad enough. Take a pot and fill it half full of filtered or treated water and bring it to a boil so I can wash my hands." She was holding the cut closed with her shirt. She started to worry about that because her shirt wasn't very clean. She pulled Junior over to their sitting area. Robbie ran up with her bag. She opened it up and flipped a few sections up to reach something. It was a full emergency medical hospital kit.

She grabbed a large bandage and pressed it on the cut, holding it by the sterile wrapper. "Keep pressure on this while I wash up." Clint brought the water over to her and she used a little of it to wash her hands thoroughly with germicidal soap. She then used some Betadine and washed the cut out really well. She grabbed a suture kit and readied it. She braced his hand on his thigh after she placed a sterile pad down. She looked up at him. "This is going to hurt some." Junior nodded and braced himself. She put on sterile gloves, then stitched his hand up. Clint was amazed at the neat, small stitches she was making. In no time, she was done. She bandaged him up and told him to watch for signs of infection, and if that happened he should try to find some antibiotics to take. She named a few different kinds he should look for. Junior thanked her. "Keep that hand up today. It will throb if you hang it down. Change the bandage daily. You won't have to remove the stitches. I'm sorry, but you might infect that cut worse than it is if you get it wet. You're done with smelting. We'll have to do it for you." She washed the rest of the blood off his hand and then washed herself with the rest of the water. She handed the bag back to Robbie and he took it back to their tent.

She leaned back and stretched. "That wasn't so bad, now, was it? It was only eleven stitches."

"Where did you learn to do that?"

She smiled and said with twinkling eyes, "At medical school." Junior's eyebrows shot upward in surprise. She laughed and then bowed. "Dr. Ziegler, at your service."

Junior said, "Holy Shit." Then he blushed. "Sorry. Excuse my language. You just surprised me. Wow, you're a doctor."

She laughed again. "Yes, I am."

Junior said urgently, "I need you to come home with us. My soon-to-be wife is pregnant and needs a doctor." Katlin looked at him and didn't say anything. Junior went to say more, then thought better of it and just looked at her.

Clint had been just as surprised as Junior and said worriedly. "Do you have a safe place to go?"

Katlin looked up at him. "No. No, we don't."

She stood up and walked over to Robbie and then they headed down to the stream. Junior around and said, "Clint, we have to convince her to come with us. We can't leave her and Robbie out here all alone. They wouldn't make it. I like them. You've got to do something. Anything. Just convince her to come home with us. She's a good person. She's a doctor. We need her." Junior looked at Clint imploringly. He could see they both were attracted to each other and Gayle had said to be on the outlook for the one Clint was meant to be with.

Clint said, "I don't know. I'm not very good at this sort of thing."

Junior said, "Do whatever it takes to convince her to come home with us."

Clint looked thoughtful. "Well, I'll do my best."

Clint talked with her. She listened intently to everything he had to say and to the things he didn't say but meant. He asked her and Robbie to come back with him to Junior and Gayle's house. She realized he meant it personally, as in him and her as well as her being a doctor. She finally said with eyes twinkling with mischief, "I don't know. That's a hard decision to make about someone who hasn't even kissed me yet." Clint looked a bit startled and it almost made her laugh. He stepped towards her and pulled her close, then kissed her hard and long. She knew after the kiss that she would definitely give her and him a chance, but was cautious because all of this was happening so fast. She also realized that courtship rituals had drastically changed along with the world too. Under the circumstances there wasn't time for any long courtships. Time would tell if this was meant to be or not. She left it in God's capable hands.

A while later after they talked for awhile longer, they walked back to the camp. Clint had his arm around her. Junior smiled and thought, *Thank you God*. He wasn't sure he could have lived with himself if they would've had to leave her and Robbie to fend for themselves. He couldn't wait for Gayle to meet them. She was going to be so happy. She had complained to him about not having another woman to talk to. He had told her to pray about it and see what happens. That's what his dad used to tell him about things that were out of his control. Well, here was the answer. It also looked like it was an answer to Clint's prayers, too. All of this felt so very right. Katlin and Robbie just kind of fit in with them. It wasn't like they were strangers at all.

Katlin was telling Robbie they were going to eat and then take a nap to be ready for tonight's smelt run tonight. They wanted to be well rested so they could work very hard, because they had to make up for Junior being hurt. Robbie was taking all of this in and believing every single word.

Clint smiled. "You're going to have to be faster tonight because Junior says the run will be over soon, maybe even by tonight. We need to get as many smelt as possible in that time." Robbie smiled and said he'd work really hard and fast tonight. Clint said, "That's good enough for me. Come help me make lunch for everyone." There was a lot of laughing and teasing going on. Junior was very satisfied how well they were all getting along. He felt this was the right thing to do. This was meant to happen, just as Gayle had said.

Junior sat with his hand up, and was very thankful that it was his left hand that was injured, not his shooting hand. Later that night, Junior was down at the stream watching for the run with Robbie. They had checked all the drying fish and packed it away to make room for the fish they'd get tonight. Robbie was fascinated with the headlamp. He thought they were the greatest invention. Junior kept him busy with thinking up uses for it. It was really late and Junior was just about to give up and say the run was over when Robbie squealed that the smelt were running. Clint and Katlin came running down to the stream, laughing, carrying buckets and the nets and immediately started scooping up as many as they could. Clint kept his eye on Robbie and grabbed him a few times to keep him from falling into the water. They filled up the buckets and and all the pots and containers that they had. Then the stream cleared up. They waited a couple more hours and they didn't see any more smelt. Junior said, "I think the run is over."

Robbie groaned. "Can we come back and do this next year?"

"You betcha. We'll be back every year we can."

Katlin and Clint lugged all the smelt up to camp and they set to work cleaning them. Katlin told Robbie to go change out of his wet clothes. After he changed, he helped Junior get the fire going to smoke them. Junior hoped his child was a son. He thought how wonderful it would be to do things like this together just as his dad and he had done. It was well past daylight when they finished. Clint fried them up some smelt to eat that they had saved just for that purpose. They all were starved. Katlin took the dishes down to the stream to wash them and Robbie came to be the lookout for bears, wolves or intruders. Clint told him his job was very important and that he had to be on alert, looking around all the time. Robbie took his job seriously and kept watch just as Clint had said.

Clint had everyone go to sleep and he'd stay on watch and keep the fires going to smoke the fish. Junior would relieve him later. They couldn't go until the fish were completely dry anyways.

Later that afternoon they were packed up and ready to go. Robbie was excited that they were going to live with Junior and Clint. Katlin and Clint had talked to him about it. Junior promised to teach him how to trap and snare. He was excited to learn all about the animals and couldn't wait to get to the house. Junior kept Robbie entertained with stories to give Clint and Katlin some time to talk and get to know each other better.

That night after they made camp, Katlin told them all she knew about the Rainbow Warriors. She said, "They plan on taking over the whole state." They had an army of over a thousand soldiers. They had military weapons and a big gun that horses pulled around. Some of them rode horses, too. They're coming this way. They kill anyone who stands in their way or won't become a vegan." Clint thought that maybe the big gun was a 105 artillery gun. What Clint wanted to know was when were they coming. Katlin told them that she was pretty sure they were coming this way soon. At least that's the plan she overheard. She doubted that they'd change it. She told them that the top guy in charge was an idiot and very mean and sadistic. He loved to torture and humiliate people. He would torture people until they made up stuff about anyone they knew just to satisfy their torturer. She wouldn't go into details, but they got the picture. Clint said they did the same thing in the Spanish Inquisition and most of the stuff confessed to was made up so they would stop torturing them.

Clint sat there thinking. He finally told himself, *Welcome to the war front. Well, if they wanted a war, he would give them a war and make them fight hard for every single thing, but he would make them pay for all of it in blood. Their blood.* Junior and he exchanged an intense look. Junior kind of had an idea Clint was over there figuring ways to make them pay and beg for their mothers. Clint was very good at what he did.

The next day, Junior and he talked about it for a while on and off. Clint said they needed to round everybody up in their area and get them organized to fight a resistance. They'd have to train them fast. He explained a little of what he had in mind to Katlin and asked her medical opinion. He planned to use psychological warfare on them. Katlin told him that the lead guy was very unstable. He was a nutcase waiting to happen. Clint smiled. He knew several ways to drive him over the bend into complete madness and he planned on using every one of them against these so-called soldiers.

He explained to Katlin about him being a S.E.R.E. Instructor and a little of what he could do. Junior filled her in even more about his training. She turned to Clint, laughing, and said earnestly, "Oh boy, I can't wait to see this. Those assholes deserve whatever you dish out to them and then some. Not one of them deserves any mercy."

That made Clint wonder what she'd seen and endured when she'd been in Green Bay. She was a doctor and swore to heal and not to harm, so it must have been very bad indeed. He figured when she was ready to talk about it, she would. He wouldn't ask her about it unless it became absolutely necessary. He told her he'd do his best. She was quite satisfied with that.

By mid-morning of the next day, they arrived at the house. Katlin had to look hard to find the house at all, the way it was tucked up against the hill. If they hadn't shown her, she never would have noticed it was there. Gayle looked out of the loft and said she'd get the door. She was very curious about the woman and boy. She unlocked the bolts and opened the door.

Junior went inside, grabbed Gayle, and gave her a big kiss and hug. "We've brought you a doctor and a woman to talk to."

Gayle laughed. "Well, shouldn't you invite her in?"

Junior turned and said, "Come on in and meet Gayle."

Katlin looked at Clint and he smiled. He already told her she would really like Gayle. Robbie stood beside Clint and looked uncertain about going inside. Clint put his arm around his shoulder. "Come on. We'll go inside together. You'll like Gayle. She's really nice. Remember, she's the one that made the chocolate chip cookies you ate."

Robbie straightened up and then walked inside, confident that Clint was right behind him. Clint followed and closed and bolted the door. Junior introduced everyone. Katlin said, looking all around, "Excuse me for staring at everything, but you have lights that work."

Junior grinned. "Yeah, we have electricity."

Katlin looked stunned. She turned to Clint. "You didn't tell me that." Clint shrugged. Katlin looked at Gayle. "They obviously didn't think that piece of information was important enough to share."

Gayle laughed. "What can you expect? They're men." Both women laughed. "Come on and sit down and rest."

Katlin said, "We're dirty. I wouldn't want to sit on anything."

Gayle nodded in understanding. "All right, come with me." Katlin looked at her curiously. Gayle smiled. "Come on. You won't regret it." Katlin took off her pack and followed her down the hall. Gayle went into the bathroom and Katlin looked around. Gayle said, "The faucets have hot and cold running water."

Katlin squealed, "Oh my God."

Gayle said, "Do you have any clean clothes?" Katlin shook her head no. "Okay. You're a little bigger than me and taller. Well, when I'm not pregnant, anyway. I do have a pair of sweat pants and some other things you can borrow if you'd like to take a shower or bath. We can wash your dirty clothes later."

"You mean like right now?"

Gayle laughed. "Right this minute."

"Oh yeah. I can handle that."

Gayle went to the linen closet. "Clean towels are right in here. Help yourself to anything you need. New razors are in this drawer, here." She pointed at the sink cabinet.

Katlin felt very overwhelmed all of a sudden and tears of gratitude sprung up into her eyes. "Thank you so very much."

"My pleasure. Later tonight you can give yourself a manicure. I brought my kit with me."

Katlin giggled and said in amazement. "Civilization. Oh my God. I found civilization."

Gayle laughed with her. "I'll be right back with some clean clothes in just a minute." She retrieved some clothes and underwear for Katlin and brought them back to the bathroom. She knocked on the door and said, "Katlin, it's me. I have your clean clothes."

"Come in." Gayle walked in and laid the folded clothes on the counter. Katlin was sitting on the closed commode, taking off her boots.

"We'll be right outside if you need anything. Just put your dirty things in the hamper over there and we'll wash them later tonight with your other clothes."

"A bath. A real bath and clean clothes."

"I know how you feel. Take your time and enjoy yourself." Katlin was mumbling about first coffee and now this. Gayle smiled at her, then left her to it. She quietly shut the bathroom door.

Gayle walked into the kitchen and Robbie was sitting at the table, eating a cookie and drinking a cup of hot chocolate. She saw how Clint was looking at the boy. She walked up to Clint and hugged him and whispered, "I told you to have faith and it would happen."

Clint gave her a big smile. "How did you know?"

Gayle shrugged her shoulders. "I'm not sure on the how. I just knew this was going to happen because you deserved it. I felt that deep in my heart. You're a good man."

"Thank you. I don't know how you did it, but thank you."

"Thank the man upstairs. He's the one that's in charge of these things, you know."

Clint said, "I'll do that." Gayle nodded and then stepped back.

Junior saw Gayle standing there and went over and kissed her. Gayle wrinkled her nose. "Wow, you smell like fish and swamp water." Junior and Clint laughed. Gayle said, "What happened to your hand?" Junior told her. "Well, its a good thing it wasn't any worse or she would have had to take off your whole hand."

Junior looked horrified. "That's not funny."

Gayle laughed. "Well, next time when you have a really sharp instrument in your hand, maybe you should pay more attention to what you're doing with it."

Junior scowled at her. "How do you know that I wasn't paying attention to what I was doing?"

Gayle said smugly, "Elementary, my dear Watson. I've seen you use a knife many times and you're very experienced with using one. So, the only thing that could have caused that to happen was your mind had wandered off somewhere and you weren't paying attention. It doesn't take a genius to figure that one out."

"You think you are so smart, don't you?"

"Correction. I know I'm smart. So, what were you saying?"

Junior gave up. "Nothing. I wasn't saying anything at all." Clint and Gayle laughed. Junior rolled his eyes at them.

Robbie said, "Can I please have another cookie?"

Gayle said, "Of course you can, my dear young man."

Robbie looked at Clint and whispered. "She talks funny." Clint and Junior laughed. Junior turned to Gayle, laughing. "See what happens when you read too much Sherlock Holmes?"

(Found this on the internet doing research)

First of all, some background. I am an experienced adventurer. I have been on over 30 Arctic expeditions and have taken 16 wilderness trips to Alaska. While I admit wolves have never attacked me, I am a firm believer that any hungry, wild animal will attack and kill anything. To not believe this is naive. I will start with a conversation that happened to me around a campfire many years ago in the Arctic. A member of our party (on his first trip to the arctic) hearing a pack of wolves howl at night said:

"Isn't that wonderful. And to think they are wild and harmless." To which our Indian guide said. "Who told you that?" "It's true," said our first-timer. "There's has never been a documented case of a wolf attacking a human being." "That's because there's usually nothing left," said our guide. "You come up here and spend the winter trapping with me and you'll think differently. Last year, I was running my trap lines, pulling a sled of pelts with my snowmobile. The snow was soft and deep and I couldn't run fast. Suddenly, a pack of nine wolves surrounded me. I shot the Alpha male, then five more before they backed off. "This has happened to me many times. Do you think they would not have attacked me if I didn't have the gun? If you do, you are a fool." Our fellow adventurer was stunned. Our guide added: "Many members of my tribe have been attacked and killed by wolves. It is a horrible thing."

For those who still doubt, please read the following information researched by T. R. Mader: It has been widely discussed whether a healthy wild wolf has ever attacked a human on this continent. In fact, many say such attacks have never occurred in North America. History states otherwise. Although attacks on humans are uncommon, they have occurred on this continent, both in the early years of settlement and more recently.

Chapter 32

Strange Meeting

"Every man's life ends the same way. It is only the details of how he lived and how he died that distinguish one man from another."

Ernest Hemmingway

When Mark and Maria were hurt by the intruders, Clark and several other tree people had been coming over to invite them for Christmas dinner. They heard the shots and hurried over to the cabin as fast as they could through the deep snow. When they got there, they saw the two dead guys lying in the snow. One had on Mark's coat; they thought it was Mark and Eric dead outside, and the women and children were being held hostage. Clark had yelled for them to come outside and give themselves up. Eric thought the intruder had lied to him and more people were outside. Eric yelled back that they'd best be on their way or they would die, too.

After a few minutes, Clark said, "Eric, is that you?"

Lisa whispered to Eric, "That sounds like Clark."

Eric yelled out, "Is that you, Clark?"

Clark yelled back, "Yes. We came by for a visit."

Lisa whispered, "Ask him what kind of people they are. That way we can know for sure."

"What kind of people are you?"

Clark laughed. "Tree people." They all sighed in relief. Eric went to the door and let them inside. The tree people looked around at all the blood and saw Maria lying on the table, knocked out, with her head wrapped in a bloody towel. Mark was holding her hand, leaning on the table so he wouldn't fall over. He had a large lump on his head that had split open and bled. He looked like he was drunk and ready to pass out himself. Using his best surfer voice, Clark said, "Dudes, you had a party and didn't like, invite us. That's way not cool with us being like, neighbors and all." They all broke out laughing.

Alan had walked over to Abby, introduced himself and asked what he could do to help. They couldn't go for Christmas dinner with two of them so seriously injured. Clark, Alan, Brandon and Kathy had stayed with them, sending the others back to the winter cave to let everyone know what happened. They helped by taking watches and caring for Mark and Maria. She remembered how Eric, Lisa and she had cried that night together in relief when Maria finally woke up with a splitting headache. Not too long after that, Mark passed out.

Over the winter, Jeff had agreed to come see them or send a few others once a month so they could have a community meeting. They had settled a lot of things and done a lot of planning at these meetings for the springtime and beyond. Last month in March, when Jeff and a few other tree people came for the meeting, it had been agreed that Maria would start teaching all the children because she was more than qualified to do it. She would train two of their people to be teacher's aides to conduct lessons when she wasn't there. She'd write up all the lessons and keep track of the grades. The tree people had a midwife, a doctor and a nurse. What they didn't have was someone with general medical knowledge that wasn't conventional. Abby agreed to come stay with them and teach their medical people about herbs and homeopathic medicine. In exchange for doing this, the tree people agreed to share some of their food and some of their seeds to plant. That would help get them through to the fall harvest. Plus, Mark and Eric had agreed to come learn how to plow a field with horses and share in the all the farming work. They would grow their own food and hopefully have some left over to trade with others around in the community. Abby was moving over to the cave until her baby was born. It was due June 23rd. That way, Abby would be there in case there were any problems with her pregnancy.

Since Mark and Eric were engineers, they had come up with a plan on how to irrigate the fields. The tree people had a small valley, completely closed in on all sides by mountains, on the other side of their winter home cave that had a large, deep stream running through it. The tree people brought a detailed map of the area where they planned on planting crops. The tree people had also built a frontier town in the valley. It was almost completely done and they had planned on opening it up to tourists. But the world had ended before they could. They had a lot of old time equipment, including plows. All of this equipment would now be used for their survival. That's why Clark and the others had been so excited about the horses. They had all agreed to work together for mutual survival and protection. The tree people were working on the plans that Mark and Eric drew up for irrigation ditches and getting ready for spring planting time.

Abby and Lisa were sitting at the table. The tree people would arrive later. Abby had found a great little book called *Drying Foods*. She was taking it with her to share with the tree people and they were all going to learn the methods now before the harvest was in so they would know what to do. She opened it up and starting reading it again.

'Drying or dehydration, the oldest method of food preservation, is particularly successful in the hot, dry climates found in much of New Mexico. Quite simply, drying reduces moisture necessary for bacterial growth that eventually causes deterioration. Successful dehydration depends upon a slow steady heat supply to assure that food is dried from the inside to the outside. Drying is also an inexact art. Size of pieces, relative moisture, and the method selected all affect the time required to dehydrate a food adequately.'

She closed the book when the back door opened up and Mark came inside holding Amanda, who had tears running down her face. She was holding her left hand outwards. Mark said, "Amanda ran her hand along a log and got a splinter in her thumb." Mark and Amanda had been waiting outside for the tree people. Abby got up and brought the first aid kit back to the table.

Amanda said in a teary voice, "It hurts, Mommy." Amanda had been calling Lisa Mommy for awhile now.

Lisa reached up and took her out of Mark's arms and said soothingly, "I know, sweetie," hugging her tightly. Lisa sat down and put Amanda on her lap. "Let's take a look at it." Amanda showed her the splinter in her thumb. "Wow. That's a bad one. Abby will take care of it and make it all better."

Abby took the tweezers and pulled the splinter out. She then rubbed some light green herbal ointment on it she had made and put a cartoon band aid on top. She looked at Amanda seriously. "It will stop hurting in a minute. It's all better now."

Amanda smiled, admiring the colorful band aid. "Thank you."

Abby smiled. "Does it still hurt?"

Amanda shook her head. "No. It's all better." Amanda turned and looked at Mark. "Can I please go back outside with you to wait?"

"Only if you promise not to get anymore splinters."

"I promise." She jumped down off Lisa's lap and ran to the back door. The adults laughed.

Mark walked over to the door and opened it up. "You wait until I look around. I'll tell you when you can come out."

Amanda said, "Okay."

"Do you remember the rules?"

"If any strangers come or we hear some guns shooting, I run into the cabin and lock the door and tell the adults."

"Good girl. It's important for you to remember this even if you're scared."

"I will." Mark pulled his rifle off his shoulder and walked cautiously outside and looked around. He then called out to Amanda, "Okay, come on outside now and walk to me. No running." Amanda stepped out and closed the door. Lisa and Abby shared a smile. Over the winter they had all gotten a lot closer as a group. They all had learned to trust each other completely. The children had learned to trust them, too. Even Ryan had come around and was not as suspicious as he had been before. He finally realized that the adults did love him and really had all of their best interests at heart. He had stopped complaining so much about things the adults did.

Abby stood in her bedroom and looked around to make sure she had packed everything she was going to need. She reached down and closed the pack. She was as ready as she was going to be. She patted her stomach to settle down the 'Little Warrior' inside of her. She felt sure she was having a son. The baby was always kicking and tumbling around in there. She smiled, remembering when her baby had gotten the nickname, 'Little Warrior.'

They all had been watching a movie and she'd been lying on the couch with her stomach prominently showing. Mark moved over by her and said, "That baby is always moving around and kicking. I think you have a little warrior in training inside there." Everyone had laughed, and ever since, the nickname stuck. She picked the pack up and walked downstairs with it. She went into the kitchen and set it down on a shelf by the back door.

Lisa was sitting at the table, grinding up roasted dandelion roots to add to their coffee supply to make it stretch farther. Abby's grandfather had showed her that trick when she was young and learning how to make dandelion tea. Lisa said, "Hey, how you feeling?"

She sat down at the table. "I feel fine."

Lisa looked at her. "Don't worry. They're nice people. You'll like them and they'll like you, too. You already know some of them."

Abby hesitated and then said, "I hope so. I'm just going to miss all of you."

Lisa smiled. "We'll miss you and the 'Little Warrior,' too." She felt tears fill her eyes. She blinked them away. Lisa reached out and patted her arm. "It's not like we're sending you off forever or anything. You did agree to this."

She nodded. "I know. It's just hard to leave all of you. You're my family now."

Lisa stopped what she was doing and pushed everything over to the side of the table. She turned back and faced Abby. "That's right, and don't ever forget that. We are family. All of us here love you like a sister. In fact I can't see how a blood sister could be any closer than you are to us. We go way deeper than just sharing some blood." Lisa leaned towards her and hugged her tight.

Both women were thinking the same thing. When you said goodbye to someone, you might never see them again. The world they lived in was a very dangerous and uncertain place. Lisa leaned back and looked at her. "We'll be by for visits. Plus, we'll be taking turns staying there and working, too. Besides, you won't be alone. Maria's going with you and you'll see her every week. She'll bring you all the gossip and news we have." Abby looked a little better and sat up straighter in her chair. "I'm just worried about all of you. I couldn't bear to lose any of you, so you'd better stay alert."

Lisa smiled. "I don't think you have anything to worry about on that subject. Maria will be gone two days a week. You should be feeling sorry for us here. We'll have an irritated Mark to deal with when she's gone."

Abby chuckled. "You're right. You all have my sympathy and condolences." They both laughed and shared a smile and hugged again.

After a few minutes, Lisa leaned back and looked at her. "Besides, it will give you time to get to know Alan." Abby blushed and looked down at the table. Lisa laughed. "He really likes you. When he's here, he can't keep his eyes off you. He's totally crazy about you."

Abby said, "I have no idea why. It's not that I'm very attractive. I'm starting to look like I have half of a basketball under my shirt. My back aches and my feet swell when I stand too long."

Lisa smiled. "Now, be honest. You like him, too, don't you?"

Abby hesitated a few moments. "Yes, I do. But, I don't think this can go anywhere."

Lisa said, "Why not?"

"Because I can't see him accepting my baby. I've seen the way he looks a my stomach sometimes when he thinks no one is watching."

Lisa let out a surprised gasp. "What do you mean? How does he look at your stomach?"

"Like he isn't sure what's in there. I don't know exactly how to describe it."

Lisa laughed. "Well, next time he does that, ask point blank what he means by those looks. It may be something totally different than you think. You might just be overly sensitive about it." They shared an intense deep look, filled with meaning.

Abby understood what Lisa was getting at. She might be overly sensitive because of who fathered her baby. She sighed. "You may be right about that. My emotions are all over the place these days like a roller coaster."

Lisa squeezed her hand, smiling. "I have to get back to grinding these up before our fearless leader comes back inside and sees me slacking off." They both smiled. Abby leaned back and thought about how they'd met Alan while she waited.

Amanda opened up the back door, stuck her head inside, and said, "The tree people are here," then closed the door.

Maria was just walking into the kitchen. She had a small bag and a briefcase with her that she took to the back door and set them down next to Abby's pack. She asked Abby, "Are you all set?"

"Yes. I'm as ready as I'm going to get."

Lisa and Maria shared a concerned look. Maria walked over and hugged Abby. She looked her in the eyes. "If you feel the least bit uncomfortable, you tell them to bring you home, okay? We'll work something else out about the herbal medicine. This is your home and we are your family."

Abby nodded her head. "Thank you. I'll be all right. I don't know what's wrong with me this morning."

Maria smiled. "Alan will be there. He'll make sure you're well looked after."

"Yeah, Alan."

Maria wrinkled her forehead in confusion. "Don't you like Alan?"

Abby sighed. "Just forget it. I'm just in a weird mood this morning, I guess."

The back door opened up and everyone came inside. Alan walked straight over to Abby. "Hi. How are you feeling today?"

Abby looked at him. "I feel fine. Thanks for asking." Alan smiled like she had just given him a great reward or something. Everyone knew that Alan liked Abby, but they weren't too sure if she liked him back in the same way. Abby had kept him at a polite distance and didn't treat him any different than she did the other tree people. Mark had told Maria that they'd just have to wait and see if he could win her heart or not. Ryan walked into the kitchen with his backpack ready to go. He was going to learn herbal medicine, too, and be a helper to Abby. He already had helped her pick a lot of herbs and moss and things like that. He was also going to learn about gardening. Ryan was going to spend his mornings with Abby learning herbal medicine and the afternoons and evenings he'd be working in the big communal garden. Abby would also be working in the garden. Her group was in charge of gathering herbs to use for seasonings and medicines as well as saving seeds and plant clippings to grow the herbs next year, too. Abby and a few other women were in a group and they were in charge of preserving foods. They planned on experimenting all summer to find the ways that worked best. Everyone from both groups had multiple job titles. There was a lot of work to prepare for next winter and not much time to do it in.

There was a knock on the back door. Mark went and let Eric and Chris inside. They were back from scouting around the area. Eric shook his head, indicating that they hadn't seen anyone or any sign of anyone.

Abby stood up and walked into the mudroom to get her pack. Eric grabbed her and gave her a big hug and whispered in her ear, "You need us for anything at all, send a message with one of the tree people and we'll be there as fast as lightning."

Abby hugged him back hard, smiling. "Thanks, Eric. I really needed that."

Eric smiled. "Anytime."

Mark looked hard at her and then said, "You sure you want to do this? You don't have to if you don't want to."

Abby hugged him. "Yes, I'm sure about this. We have to teach as many people as we can what skills we have. We also have to learn new skills, too. It's important to everyone's future."

Mark said protectively, "But still, if you don't want to go, you don't have to."

Abby smiled and hugged him again. "I'm really sure. I'll be fine."

Brandon said, "We'll take good care of her."

Lisa said, "She needs a few hours to rest in the afternoons. Make sure she does. She always tries to do too much. Don't let her over do it."

Maria said, "I'll talk to a few of the other women and have them keep an eye on her, too."

Abby said, irritated, "Hello, I'm standing right here. I'm not a child, you know. I can take care of myself. I don't need others to do it for me." Everyone stopped talking and stared at her. She blushed and looked down.

Lisa went over and hugged her. "We know that, silly. We're just reassuring ourselves that you'll be all right when we aren't around." Abby hugged her back really hard and wished she didn't have to go. She stepped back and turned to Chris and hugged him.

Amanda was standing next to Eric, so she went over to her and bent down and hugged her. Amanda said, "I don't want you to go."

Abby said, "I have to. I'll see you soon. You all will be coming for visits. I'll miss you." She hugged her again and then stood up and turned to Brandon. "I'm ready."

She went over to pick up her pack, but Alan grabbed it first. "I'll carry it for you."

Abby looked at him and said with an edge to her voice, "I can handle it."

Alan hesitated, unsure if she was mad at him or not. "I know nothing about any of this, but you're already off balance with your stomach expanding. Carrying the pack will make you even more off balance and more likely to fall or stumble and hurt yourself. I'm just thinking of the safety of you and your baby." Abby sighed and let him carry the pack.

Mark was kissing Maria goodbye. Lisa was hugging Ryan and giving him last minute instructions to behave himself. Ryan was squirming around, wanting to go. He was excited. He was going on an adventure to a cave and an old time frontier town. When all the goodbyes were finally over, the tree people, Maria, Abby and Ryan took off through the woods. They would be using the cables to get back to the cave.

Mark, Eric, Lisa, Chris and Amanda watched them go. When they were out of sight, Mark said, "All right, everyone, back to work." They all went inside to their various jobs and didn't say anything. Tomorrow, when the tree people brought Maria back, they were bringing five guys to be security trained by Mark. Both groups picked Mark to be the head of security. One of his jobs was to train all of the tree people's security team, which would provide security for both places. He would assign who went where and for how long. When he was busy doing some of his other jobs, he would leave some of the security people at the cabin to keep it safe from intruders. He was also the one in charge of sending out teams to scour the community for survivors. He would also relieve Eric, plow the fields, and was in the Mr. Fixit group. Both groups would be rotating people around to do the many jobs that needed to be done. Eric would soon be going over and learning to plow with a horse. Lisa was on the planting team and would be going with him to plant and make up plans of what would be planted where. They had a long growing season and would able to get in two crops of vegetables. She was also on what they called the welcome committee. They would be sending out teams to scour the whole community for survivors to set up trade with. They wanted a woman who could handle herself to be available to talk to other women out there who might not trust men. So after the planting was done, all summer and fall she would be in and out, going on the scouting trips in between her other jobs. Plus, she was on the entertainment committee, too, having been a singer in the old world. She had been hired by the tree people to give music lessons on the piano and guitar over the winter months. Eric was to help train the security details, too, plow the fields, he was on the watering committee, and he was in the Mr. Fixit group, too. He would also help out part time with the welcoming committee. Chris was learning all about how to care for the horses and take care of the manure for the fields and garden. He was also teaching two other boys how to snare. They were in charge of protecting the fields and gardens from animals. Amanda was on the weeding detail for the garden and on general clean up duty, which was putting things away in their proper place after being used, tools etcetera. Maria's other jobs were inventory, supplies and organizing everything. She made up the lists of who would do what jobs. She was in charge of sending people out to look for specific items that were needed. Clothing, soaps, school books, etcetera, and to keep track of what they had, how much, and where it was stored. She was in charge of issuing supplies to everyone and whatever was needed for the various jobs. Everyone had to work hard at many different jobs to prepare for next winter.

Later in the afternoon, when Mark was outside scouting around, he was on his way back to the cabin when a man stepped out from behind a tree, startling him. The man said, "Are you one of Amanda's adopted dads?"

Mark looked the old guy over. "Yes, I am. You must be Bert."

Bert said, "Yes. I have a deal to make with you."

"Okay. Can we go to the cabin and make it there? We shouldn't stand around in the open like this."

"Good idea." Mark led the way and the two walked silently towards the cabin. Mark led him around to the back door. He knocked on the door and said, "It's me."

Lisa opened up the door and brought the shotgun up, looking at Bert. "Put your hands up where I can see them."

"Lisa, lower the shotgun. This is Bert."

"As in Amanda and Ryan's Bert? The snow monster?"

"Yes."

Lisa lowered the shotgun. "Please come in." She stepped aside to let them to pass and then locked the door and joined them in the kitchen.

Bert was looking around, noticing the bullet holes."Been a hard winter, huh?"

Mark said, "We had our share of trouble, if that's what you're asking."

Bert turned and looked at him. "I told myself if you all survived until spring, I'd come and see you. What would you have done if the Andersons had showed up wanting their cabin back?"

Mark said, "I have no idea. I would probably have negotiated some kind of a deal for our mutual survival. They have Redding closed off. They aren't letting anyone through their city. We couldn't get to our retreat farther north, and were stuck down here."

Lisa had put a pot of coffee on a little earlier and it was just now making noises announcing it was done. Lisa said, "Bert, would you like a cup of coffee?"

Bert looked at her. "Sure." Lisa poured them all a cup and brought them over to the table.

"Please take a seat and get comfortable." Bert sat down at the table, took his pack off, and sat it on the floor by his chair. Lisa handed him a mug of coffee. "I'm Lisa. Thank you for saving the children and killing those Roman soldiers that were attacking Mark and Abby."

Bert looked at her. "That little girl, Amanda, made me promise to save them from the bad men."

Mark said, "I would like to thank you for your help, too."

Before anyone could say anything else, Amanda came flying into the kitchen. "Mr. Gunner is here. Hi, Mr. Gunner." She ran over to him and climbed up on his lap. "I missed you." She turned to Lisa. "He's a good snow monster. You don't have to be afraid of him." Everyone laughed.

Bert said, "Here she goes with that snow monster stuff again."

"How have you been, Mr. Gunner?"

"Fine." He didn't quite know what to do with the little girl on his lap. He looked at her like she was a strange and foreign thing.

Mark said, "Amanda, are you done cleaning your room?"

Amanda nodded her head. "Yes. It's all cleaned up now. I even made my bed."

"Is the play room cleaned up, too?"

Amanda said, "Ryan didn't put away the games he played like he was supposed to."

"I'll yell at him next time I see him about it." That seemed to satisfy her. "Will you please go and clean that up, too?"

Amanda sighed. "Okay. But Ryan is the one that made the mess." Lisa and Mark laughed. Amanda looked at Bert. "I have to go clean up my brother's mess. I'll be back." She got down from his lap and ran out of the room.

Mark said to Bert, "She likes you."

Bert cleared his throat. "I don't know how to talk to a little girl."

"I didn't either. She grows on you. You said something about a deal. What kind of a deal are you wanting?"

Bert reached down inside his pack and brought out a one pound vacuum packed foil wrapped container of one hundred percent Columbian coffee. "I figured you were all pretty low on coffee about now."

Mark said, "You're right about that."

Bert took a sip of his coffee. "What have you added to it that makes it taste like this?"

Lisa said, "We have ground up dandelion roots and mixed it in with the coffee to make it stretch farther."

"It's not bad. I brought you a pound of coffee." He shoved it over to Mark. "The deal I have is this." He reached inside his pack and brought out a can and set it on the table. "There are non-hybrid vegetable seeds inside. That means you can save the seeds and plant them next year. You do this every year."

Mark just looked at him for a few minutes. "What you want for them and the coffee?"

"The coffee is yours. I brought it for you."

"Thank you. What about the seeds?"

Bert said, "The deal is you can use my seeds and plant a garden. I'll take some of the produce and you can have the rest to eat for your people and the children. We'll both save the seeds to plant a garden for the next year."

That's very generous of you. Why are you doing this?"

Bert said, "I would make the same deal with the Andersons. They didn't make it up here. You did."

"Do you know Jeff and the tree people?"

"We've met." He said it like he hadn't been impressed.

Mark said, "We worked out a deal with them to use their valley for growing food. Is it okay if we add this to our garden? We'll make sure that you get all the produce you want from the entire plot."

"I don't care how you grow them, just that you do."

"Okay. You have yourself a deal."

He stuck his hand out for a handshake and Bert shook his hand. "Okay then." He drank the rest of his coffee and stood up.

Mark said, "So, you have to be going?"

"Yes."

"Come back anytime. You are welcome here."

They could hear Amanda coming down the stairs. She flew into the kitchen. "Mr. Gunner, you can't leave yet."

Bert looked at her. "Why not?"

"We didn't get to talk."

He said, "Don't have the time right now."

Amanda said, "You will come back and see me, won't you, Mr. Gunner?"

Bert looked at her. "Sure. I'll be out and around."

She ran over to him and hugged his legs. "Be careful outside. There are bad people out there sometimes."

Bert patted her head. "I'm always careful. Don't you worry about that."

Lisa walked over and picked Amanda up in her arms. Mark walked Bert to the door. "I would really like to talk you sometime about what Ryan told us you have. Maybe we could work our some kind of a trade for some ammo or something."

Bert said, "We'll see."

Mark said, "We'll get your seeds planted real soon. How should we get in touch with you?"

"I'll be around. I'll stop by from time to time."

Mark opened up the door. "Thank you, Mr. Gunner. It's been a pleasure to do business with you." Bert nodded his head once and then walked outside. Mark closed the door and turned around.

Amanda said, "I like Mr. Gunner. Isn't he nice?"

Lisa said, "Yes, honey. He's real nice." She put Amanda down. "Go finish your drawing. Maria will be back tomorrow and she'll want to see it."

Amanda said, "Okay, Mommy." She ran out of the kitchen and they heard her going up the stairs.

Lisa looked at Mark. "What an odd man Mr. Gunner is."

"I think he's a recluse. He seems uncomfortable around people. I wish he could have stayed longer so Eric could meet him. He should be back anytime now."

"I half expected him and Chris to show up when he was here." Eric and Chris were out scouting around for intruders on the south side of the property. Mark had taken the north side. They were all staying on alert because they could hear rifle shots every once in awhile outside. It sounded like people were out hunting for food. Lisa said, "Well, it was very nice of him to bring us a pound of one hundred percent Columbian coffee. That stuff wasn't cheap in the old world."

"Look at the package. Most of the writing is in Spanish, I think. He probably ordered it in bulk and not from the good old U. S. of A., either."

Lisa said thoughtfully, "Ryan did say he had a lot of crates and boxes that had foreign writing on them. It looks like some of the writing on that package might be in Portuguese."

"Well, he's certainly an interesting character. We need to really get to know him. He could be the answer to our prayers for defense. He probably has the right equipment."

"He sure didn't think much of Jeff or the tree people."

"I wonder why," said Mark. "It sounded like they didn't get along very well."

"Well, if Clark went into his surfer boy act, I could understand why. Those two would be worlds apart."

He said, "Well, I'll ask Jeff about it. I'll ask Mr. Gunner about it, too. I hope we haven't made a mistake getting involved with the tree people."

Lisa said, "With the world ended, I don't think we have made a mistake grouping together so that we all can survive. I think it was a smart move on your part to have gotten us as much as you have in that deal. They have to deal with us fairly. Using their equipment and land and only giving them ten percent was more than fair. Besides, they wouldn't want us as enemies."

He looked at her in surprise. "What do you mean?"

She looked at him like he'd asked a very stupid question. "Mark, you would pay them back a hundred fold if they messed with us. They know that. We know that. They don't want to mess with us."

He smiled. "You think you know Eric and I so well you could predict that?"

"I know that. Neither of you take too kindly to anyone that isn't as honorable as you are."

He said, "Thanks. That's a nice compliment. I think." She laughed and walked out of the kitchen to go check on Amanda.

A few days later it was time for Eric and Lisa to join the work forces. They decided to leave the night before and give themselves a night to be alone together. There hadn't been very many times they had a whole night to just relax and enjoy themselves. They were walking to the tree that the tree people used to watch them from. They had shown Mark and Eric which tree it was. There was a wooden box there that they kept the harnesses and pulleys to use on the cables. Both of them were looking forward to using the cables. It was a fun and fast way to travel through the forest. They'd be at the cave in hardly no time at all. It had been awhile since they had any time just to themselves and looked forward to it. Jeff had assigned them a cabin in the frontier village to stay in. He told them they could work out a deal later if they wanted to own that cabin, but for now they could stay in there when they were at the cave to work. They reached the tree they were looking for and climbed up after making sure no one was around. They each put a harness on and grabbed a pulley and then grinned at each other. Eric took off and Lisa waited for ten seconds and then took off after him. When they arrived at an intersection where cables went different ways, they looked closely at the platforms for what color was on the last board facing outward. Jeff had made sure they were marked so they wouldn't go the wrong way and get lost. They were following the color green. So far it had been a pretty straight shot.

About halfway to the cave, they came up on a platform and Jeff was standing there waiting for them. He waited until both of them were on the platform before whispering, "Take the harnesses off and leave them here. Come with me. You two will love seeing this." Eric and Lisa exchange a puzzled look. Jeff motioned for them to follow him down a walkway. They went down a ways and then he crossed over to another platform and they followed him, wondering what was going on.

They came to a sheltered wooden area in the trees; several other tree people were there. Jeff nodded his head and Jim whispered, "They'll be here in a few minutes." Two men turned and went over to another platform and a few more moved up higher in the tree and were lost to sight. The sky was just starting to darken for the night and everything had that surreal twilight look to it.

Jeff leaned over and whispered, "Sit down on the boards and get comfortable. You both are in for a treat. Watch closely." Lisa and Eric sat down on the boards and hung their feet off the platform. They were up so high no one could see them through the branches.

Three men were walking slowly through the woods. They all had rifles. Eric and Lisa exchanged a look and then turned back to watch whatever was going to happen. As one of the men came close to a tree, all of a sudden there was a wild animal type yell that raised the hair on Lisa's arms. She jumped and looked around. Jim was playing a tape recorder next to a speaker. The three men walking in the woods gasped, stood in place and looked all around them wildly for the source of the cry. Then Lisa saw a bigfoot appear around the side of a tree, being lowered by pulleys. She nudged Eric and pointed and he smiled and nodded and then turned back to see what the men were going to do. The man that was a little ahead of the other two saw something moving out of the corner of his eye and swung around, bringing up his rifle ready to fire. All three men turned and looked in shock at the creature that had appeared in their midst. Lisa saw another bigfoot appear behind a tree just beyond the men. She giggled and wrapped her hands in front of her mouth to keep from laughing out loud. As they stared at the creature, the mouth opened and it roared again. All three of them dropped their rifles and ran full out until they were lost from sight. Lisa leaned back, laughing so hard she thought she might fall off the platform. All of them were laughing as quietly as they could. The look on those men's faces was priceless. She doubted she'd ever forget it. Eric finally recovered enough to ask them how long they'd been doing that.

Jeff said, "Our parents started doing it to keep people away from this area several years ago. It works like a charm."

Lisa asked, "Where did you get all the bigfoot costumes?"

Jeff said, "We only have one; we got it from an auction at a movie studio in Burbank."

Lisa looked puzzled. "You only have one?"

Jeff smiled. "Yes, just the one."

Lisa looked at Eric and then back at Jeff. "But I saw two of them."

Jeff said, "That isn't possible. We only have the one costume."

Eric looked at Lisa and asked, "Where did you see the two of them? Point out where they were."

Lisa pointed to the one tree in front of them and off to the right. Jeff nodded. "That's the one." Lisa then pointed at a tree over farther and behind that tree. "Back there is where I saw the other one."

Jeff said, "Ain't possible."

"I know what I saw."

"You must have just seen a shadow or something and thought it was another bigfoot."

Lisa shook her head. "It was looking right at us and the three guys. I saw eyes and a mouth and a lot of long hair all over its face. It didn't look exactly like the other one, but close."

Jeff went to say something and Eric held his hand up. "There's a good way to solve this. You got any flashlights with you?"

Jim stepped forward. "We have a few here."

Eric said, "Well, then come on, let's climb down and go look."

Jeff looked like he wanted to protest, but then he shook his head. "Okay, let's go. I'll prove it to you." They grabbed their flashlights and they climbed down the tree.

Eric said, "Walk behind us so we don't make any footprints. We'll step only on leaves and brush." Jim handed him a flashlight and they set off. When they got close to the area, Eric said, "Do you see the tree where the bigfoot was?"

Lisa looked around, and then up at the tree they had been in, and turned around and said, "It's right over here."

Eric said, "Don't walk straight to it. Come to it from the side so you don't mess up any footprints that might be there." Jeff rolled his eyes, thinking this was a wild goose chase. A couple of the other guys bent down and picked up the three rifles laying on the ground and then hurried up to the rest of the group. When they came near to the tree, Eric said, "Stop. Jim, come up here with your flashlight and shine it on the ground on the right and I'll shine mine on left and we'll see if there is any sign of something being here or not.

They pointed the flashlights to the ground and Lisa said, "Yeah, right there is where I saw it." Her voice trailed off when she saw what the flashlights clearly showed. Both flashlights showed a large footprint right where Lisa said she'd seen the bigfoot. Eric turned the flashlight up farther and they could make out large footprints going off in that direction showing clearly in the leaves and pine needles and the soft dirt. It had been something very large and heavy to make indents like that in the ground.

Everyone looked at each other and Jeff said, "That's not possible. Bigfoot isn't real."

Jim looked at Jeff. "Well, tell that to whatever made those footprints."

Eric said, "Let's get back up in the tree. We can discuss it there." They all moved quickly back to the tree, making sure to leave no prints or signs for anyone to follow. They all climbed back up.

Jeff sat down and said in a stunned voice, "That isn't possible. We made it all up."

Eric said, "There have been bigfoot stories up here for hundreds of years. Even the Indians had legends of them. There was a guy at my work that claimed to have heard the cry of bigfoot when he was out camping with a few of his buddies." Eric turned to Jim. "Where did you get that recording from?"

Jim said, "We downloaded it off one of those bigfoot sites on the internet."

Eric said, "It must be a real bigfoot cry and one in the area must have come to see what was happening." Everyone looked a bit unsettled and spooked.

Jim said, "Let's head for the cave. There are just as many bad bigfoot stories as there are good ones. Let's get out of here in case it shows up with some buddies." Everyone stood up. Jim led the way and they all followed behind him over the platforms and walkways. He led them back to where Eric and Lisa had met Jeff. Everyone got their harnesses on. Jim went first and the rest of them followed at the count of ten.

When they were safely in the cave, Jeff said, "Lisa, I owe you an apology. I still can't believe it, but I'm sorry to have doubted your word."

Lisa smiled. "That's okay. I'm still kind of stunned about the whole thing, too."

Jeff said, "Come on, let's all get some coffee and sit down." Everyone walked over to the area where they had the big coffee urns and poured a cup, then walked over to a table and sat down.

Tim said, "I don't know about the rest of you, but that scared the hell out of me." Everyone nodded in agreement.

Jim said, "Lisa tell us exactly what you saw. Take your time and remember every detail. It might be very important."

Lisa took a sip of coffee. "Well, we were watching the three guys. I noticed movement behind them back in the trees, and looked hard at it because I thought there might be more people back there in the shadows and I wanted to warn you guys if there were. As I watched, this bigfoot peeked out from behind the tree. I thought it was you guys doing it to cut off the three guys retreat. Like you were herding them back the way they came from or something. Then you opened up the other fake bigfoot's mouth and let out that terrible cry again that scared those guys half to death. They turned and ran off. I was laughing so hard. When I looked again, both bigfoots were gone."

Jim said, "What was its actions? What was it doing? I mean, did it look like it was angry or upset or what? What was your impression?"

Lisa thought for a minute. "It looked like it was curious and wanted to know what was happening. At the time, I thought it was another costume and it was either on pulleys or one of you guys were wearing it and wanted to watch the three guys get scared. I didn't pay it a whole lot of attention. I thought it was part of the show."

Jim said, "Tomorrow I'm going to go back and take some casts of the footprints." Several of the others said they'd go with him. A few other tree people wandering over and asked what was going on. Jim told them. No one wanted to believe it. Jim said he'd show them the footprints in the morning.

Eric reached out and pulled Lisa closer to him. "Are you all right?"

She looked at him and said, "Yeah. I'm okay. It was just weird, you know?"

Eric nodded. "Yeah, it was weird all right. I noticed when we went back up in the tree that where you were sitting at had a clear view of the tree and beyond. That view was blocked from the rest of us by trees on each side. We wouldn't have seen it even if we had been looking in that direction." Lisa got goosebumps at hearing that. Eric hugged her. "You're okay. It must have seen you, too, and didn't feel threatened by you."

Eric turned and asked Jeff, "When you scare people with the bigfoot act, do they usually drop their rifles like those three did?"

Jeff laughed. "Yeah, they mostly do. Some shoot at bigfoot and miss by a mile because they're shaking so hard and others just turn around and run for their lives. Since the world ended, we've been picking up the rifles." Eric looked around. Brandon and Tim were taking the rifles apart, cleaning them.

Just about then, Abby walked in and saw them. She came towards them, smiling, holding a basket filled with herbs she'd picked out in the valley. She sat the basket down on another table and then walked over and sat down next to Lisa. She couldn't wait to show them the frontier town and see their reaction. They weren't going to believe it.

Lisa hugged her. "You okay?"

Abby smiled. "I'm fine."

Alan came walking in from the same direction. carrying a basket of herbs, too. He set it down next to Abby's basket. He smiled at Eric and Lisa. "Everything okay?"

Eric said, "Yes, everything is fine."

He looked at Abby. "I'll get your tea. Rest and visit with your friends."

"Thank you." He nodded and went over to the cooking area.

Lisa asked, "How's it going with Alan?"

Abby smiled, blushing, and looked down at the table. "I saw him looking at my stomach weird again and I did as you said. I asked him why he was looking at my stomach so weird?"

"Well, what did he say?"

Abby smiled, looking up at her. "He said that I was such a tiny thing he couldn't figure out how I could fit a baby inside there. He also said that he thinks that's why the baby is always turning around and kicking, because its trying to get out of that cramped space."

Lisa laughed. "I told you. I figured it was something like that, not what you thought it might be. So, do you feel better about Alan now?"

Abby blushed again. "I do." They sat in silence for a few minutes and then Abby said, "Did you know that they have a minister here?"

Lisa said, "No, I didn't know that."

Abby said, "He's conducting a kind of unity church service tomorrow morning. Come on and I'll introduce you to him." Lisa looked at her, deciding if she wanted to meet him or not. She hadn't gone to church much in the old world. Abby saw the look on her face. "Lisa, remember when we were talking about how our prayers had been answered when Mark and Eric showed up and saved us?"

Lisa said, "Yes, I remember."

"Remember when Maria told us about how she prayed for all of us to be safe and to reunite once again when we all got separated on the way up here? And about how we all agreed it was a miracle that we found each other the way we did?"

"I do remember."

"Well, maybe its time we properly thank the big guy upstairs for all that He has done for us by going to a church service, since we're lucky to have a minister here and share in fellowship with one another."

Lisa said, "You're right. We have so very much to be thankful for. Okay, introduce me to this wonder of God." Abby smiled at her attempt at a joke.

Lisa followed Abby across the room to a bench where a man was sitting writing in a notebook with a Bible open in front of him. Abby waited for him to finish writing and look at them. He smiled when he saw Abby. He said, "Is there something I can help you with, Abby?"

"No. I just wanted to introduce you to my friend. Reverend Blackstone, this is Lisa. Lisa, this is Reverend Blackstone of the tree people."

Lisa stuck out her hand for a handshake and the Reverend said, "Call me Bob. Everybody does."

Lisa said, "Pleased to meet you, Bob."

"Likewise. Are you coming to church services tomorrow morning before work?"

Lisa said, "I'm considering it."

Bob smiled. "Fair enough. We would be pleased to have you."

"Thank you."

"Bob, she has an excellent singing voice. She had a band in the old world."

Bob looked at Lisa. "So, you're the one that's going to give music lessons. Would you consider singing in a choir?"

Lisa was thoughtful for a few moments. "I wouldn't mind, but we'd have to find the time for practice in between all our other jobs."

Bob laughed. "We'll just have to approach Maria with the task of figuring out a time when we can all practice. She is a whiz at time management, among other things."

Lisa laughed. "I know; I live with her. She's a miracle worker at organizing everything."

Bob smiled. "She does manage to get things done and make it look effortless. But we all know better."

Abby said, "We will let you get back to your task. I just wanted the two of you to meet."

Bob said, "We met before when the dogs attacked her and Maria. But she probably doesn't remember."

Lisa said, "I'm sorry. I don't remember. There were so many names and faces and we were still in shock from the attack."

Bob said, "Well, I'll look forward to seeing you tomorrow morning at the church service."

Lisa didn't say anything, and she and Abby went back over to Eric.

Eric leaned over to whisper in Lisa's ear, "Is everything all right?"

Lisa said, "Yes. I just met the Reverend Blackstone."

"They have a Reverend here?"

Lisa nodded. "They're having a unity church service tomorrow morning. We're invited."

"Are you going?"

Lisa looked at him, searching his face for a clue to how he wanted her to answer. She decided on honesty. "I'm considering it. He asked me to be in a choir."

"I'll go. We have a lot to be thankful for."

"Yes, we do. That's what Abby said."

Eric said, "Are you going to be in the choir?"

"Only if we can find time to practice. We have so many other things to do that are much more important than singing in a choir right now." Eric nodded his head and didn't say anything, because it was true. There was so much work to be done.

Eric reached out and pulled her close. "So much for coming here a night early and having it to ourselves, huh?"

Lisa smiled. "The night is still young."

Eric raised his eyebrow. He turned to Jeff. "We're going to call it a night. We'll see you in the morning."

Jeff said, "I almost forgot to mention it with the bigfoot thing happening. Dinner will be ready in about an hour, plus we're having church services tomorrow and you're welcome to attend."

"Thank you. I'll see you there. Ahh, where?"

Jeff smiled really big. "At the church in the frontier town in the valley, of course."

Eric smiled back. "Of course." The tree people had kept the valley secret. They also didn't mention they had an old time town built there, complete with houses, cabins and everything. They'd only recently told them about it. They had boarded the horses in the livery stables in the frontier town that had a pasture connected to it. None of Mark's group had visited over the winter. This was the first time they'd see it.

Abby leaned over. "I'm your guide tonight. You don't mind if I hang around with you, do you? I've missed you a lot."

"We missed you, too," Lisa said. "We'll need someone to show us which cabin is ours, too." Abby smiled, then drank the last of her tea from the mug that had been waiting for her. "Let's put our mugs in the wash basin and then I'll show you where it is." They all took their mugs over to the basin and then followed Abby down to the back of the cave that veered off to the right. One would never know that the cave didn't end right there, because they had a lot of stuff stored back here and it looked like it was up against the cave wall. The children's playground area was in front of the stored stuff, too. There was a softly lit hallway that led to a metal door that opened up on the other side of the cave.

Abby opened up the door and walked outside, waiting to see their reaction. They both stopped and looked around in wonder. There was a path lighted by solar street lamps that led to the town. It was a real old time town. "Come on, I'll show you the town. We'll walk through it to the living area." She closed the door and started down the path. Eric and Lisa were looking everywhere at once. It looked just like they had seen in the movies, with the wooden walkways and everything. There was a general store, a jail, a saloon, a shoe maker, a hotel, a restaurant, a haberdasher, a barber, a lawyer's office, a doctor's office, a laundry, an apothecary, a post office, an old time theater where plays and operas were put on, a bank, a blacksmith, a veterinary office, a glass house where they make things of glass and clay, and a court house. At the end of the street, all alone, facing the town, was a beautiful white church with a spire and bell tower. They could see everything clearly in the solar lights. Plus, some of the buildings had lights on inside. They walked around the path to the side of the church and there was a fenced in graveyard back a ways down the road. The path led around a hanging tree, complete with a rope dangling down with a noose tied on it. Out farther was a large park area with a playground for children. Next to it was a one room schoolhouse. Turn the other way and there were several streets of old time log cabins with porches and decks. They had fenced-in yards with grass. Eric also noticed the solar panels they had. There were a few windmills at the end of the streets and a few other places, too.

Abby said, "These cabins were built for the workers from the town and their families to live in. The owners of the businesses and the others have houses farther out where they live. The guests and tourists would be staying in the hotel along with the hotel staff."

Lisa said, "My god, this place is wonderful."

"I knew I should have taken that blacksmith course."

Lisa said, "Why?"

"Because then we could make horseshoes, plows and other things that we'll need."

"Reverend Bob is the blacksmith here. He's a real blacksmith and they'd planned on putting on demonstrations of him making things for the tourists. If you want, you can probably apprentice with him to learn blacksmithing."

Lisa laughed. "Bob Blackstone is the blacksmith."

Abby gestured out farther down the road, leading deeper into the valley. "The real farms are down the road quite a ways, a few miles apart, actually. They were going to conduct tours of the farm houses and buildings and show how to plow a field with a horse and things like that. Oh yeah, they have some cattle and sheep, too, out that way in the pastures. They also have a few chicken coops that supplies fresh eggs every day. And out over that way is where the orchard is." She gestured the other way. She smiled at them. "I came in the daytime and got a buggy ride all around and a tour of everything." Eric and Lisa stood there in stunned silence. They didn't know what to think or to say.

Abby said, "Come on. I'll show you which cabin is yours. It's right next to mine." She led them to a cabin that had a number two on it and then opened up the door with a key she took out of her pocket. She walked inside and flipped a wall switch and wall lanterns came on. It was made up to look like a normal house with a couch, a couple of chairs, end tables and carpeting. It had a fireplace with a wood stove inserted for heating. Next to it was a dining area with a table and chairs, and off that was a kitchen that looked old fashioned with a wood cook stove. Abby showed them down the hall off the living room that led to three bedrooms and a bathroom. Then down a couple steps on the right, you went into a family room that opened out onto a deck in the back.

Lisa asked, "Does the bathroom work?"

"Yes, it does. But if you want hot water, you have to go outside and light a wood burning hot water tank and wait until it is ready to take a shower or to wash dishes or anything. We'll show you how to do it tomorrow. It's really a great set up here." Eric was looking everything over and didn't know what to say. "Ryan is staying with me. Right now he is with Jeannie and Phil and their two children. They're gathering up all the manure to spread in the fields to be plowed under for the crops. There's coffee and a coffee maker in one of the cupboards in the kitchen, along with some canned and dried food that they thought you might like. You don't have to cook. Just go to the hotel at mealtime and eat there. The mealtimes are posted outside of the hotel. There are more people here than we knew. They were already staying in the valley when we met the tree people. They were going to make the tree house a tour, too. They also have some vehicles that work here."

Before she could say anything else a voice said, "Abby, this is Jeannie. Where are you?"

Abby reached down and took a radio out of her pocket. "I'm showing Eric and Lisa their cabin. What do you need?"

Jeannie said, "We're done for the night. Do you want us to drop off Ryan at your cabin, the main cave, or take him with us to the hotel? It is almost dinnertime and we're heading over to the hotel."

Abby asked Eric and Lisa, "Should I tell her we'll meet them at the hotel for dinner?"

Eric and Lisa looked at each other and then shrugged in confusion. Abby said into the radio, "Meet us at the hotel. We're on our way." She walked over to a cupboard in the dining room and brought out two radios and handed them out. "Carry this at all times so we can get in touch with you if need be. Also, if you need something, you can just talk into the radio and someone will tell you where to go or who to see. You charge them every night in a charger on the nightstands in the bedroom." They took the radios and clipped them onto their jeans. She handed each of them a key on a little key ring. "This will open the front and back door." Abby looked at them. "They have a lot of clothes and other things in the general store. Even baby things. The hotel has a gift shop and a jewelry shop. I can't afford to buy anything yet, but at least it's available. Jeff told me in my spare time I can make home remedies and other herbal things like shampoo and stuff and sell them at the apothecary's. So I might be able to get the things the "Little Warrior" is going to need after all. Also, the position of bank manager is open because the person who was the manager and owner never made it up here. I can make a regular salary that way, too. But that's for the future."

Lisa asked, "What do they use for money?"

"They have a lot of silver and gold coins because that's what was used in the frontier towns, but they aren't using them yet. They haven't set up a monetary system because they don't know how. That was the bank manager's job. Jeff said I could have that job if I wanted, because I'm more than qualified for it. But right now they are using script."

"What is that?"

"Basically, it's just a piece of paper that is given out worth however much is written on it. And you can redeem them for goods around town. That hasn't been working so well for them, because there is no standard to go by."

Lisa said, "What's a standard? You've lost me."

"It's like saying a one dollar script is worth a hamburger. Kind of like that, but more complicated. And everything is priced according to the standard. Like a wool blanket would be worth twenty one dollar scripts, or four five dollar scripts, etcetera."

Lisa nodded. "I understand now. It's kind of like what a dollar would buy."

Abby smiled. "Not really. With a dollar you have to include inflation and deflation of what a dollar's worth. In reality, a dollar could only be worth, say, a quarter of buying power. That's a totally different thing. But to make this simple, we'll agree it's kind of like that. We'll be making a standard here by metal content and weight. It'll be easier that way and something we can use as a standard to be measured by. Different metals are worth different prices."

Eric said, "That would be an ideal standard to make. Then everyone can use the same system and everyone will understand."

Abby said, "Come on. Let's go over to the hotel and eat. I'm starved."

Later, after meeting everyone at the hotel and eating, they walked back to the cabins. Ryan had talked nonstop about everything he'd seen and done. Eric and Lisa were kind of overloaded with information. They went inside their cabin and sat down. Lisa said, "Maria had to have seen this, too. Why didn't she tell us about it?"

Abby said, "We talked about it a lot that first night here. We decided it would be best if you saw it and experienced it all just as we did, without prior knowledge."

Eric said, "Well, it sure is a shock."

"But a good one. We didn't want to spoil it for you. What I can't wait to see is Mark's expression when he first sees everything."

Eric said doubtfully, "Mark doesn't like surprises."

Abby said, "Well, he's going to get a shock no matter what we do or say about this. So, Maria and I decided to let him experience everything with no preconceived ideas."

"Do you think this is too good to be true?"

Abby said, "I think this is a good place. From what I've seen, the people here try to get along and work for the community's benefit. With the world like it is, this is pretty much paradise from their point of view. It is from my point of view, too. At least they're trying to make it a nice place for everyone to live and they make sure there's enough to go around. Abby stood up. "I'm going to take a bath and relax. My back is killing me."

Lisa said, "Do you need me to give you a back rub?"

"No. You don't need to bother with it. I'll be fine after soaking in a tub of hot water. Thanks for offering, though." They all stood up and walked to the door. Abby opened it up, motioning for Ryan to go outside first.

Across the street, Alan was leaning against the light post, waiting for Abby. Lisa saw this and said in a low voice, "Is he waiting for you?"

Abby blushed. "Probably. We've been spending most evenings together talking."

Eric said, "You could have invited him to come over. He didn't have to wait outside."

Abby looked at him. "He knew I wanted to talk to you two alone. We had a lot to discuss." She hugged both of them. "See you in the morning. Church starts at 9:00 am." She turned and walked over to Alan. Ryan said goodnight; he jumped off the porch and ran down the street ahead of Abby and Alan. Eric and Lisa went back inside the cabin.

Eric shut the door. "What a night."

Lisa said, "I agree. First bigfoot, then a minister and now all this."

"Want me to put a pot of coffee on?"

Lisa smiled. "Sure. It's probably real coffee too without the dandelion roots."

"Exactly." He went into the kitchen and found the coffee pot and everything he would need. Lisa took her boots off and then grabbed both their packs and took them into the bedroom. There was a beautiful quilt that looked handmade on the bed. She ran her hand over the top of it as she walked out of the room. "The coffee's going."

Lisa said, "Imagine that," as she sat on the couch next to Eric. Eric put his arm around her and she laid her head on his shoulder. She said after a few moments, "Half of me wants to jump up and down and yell yippee and the other half wants to know what's the catch?"

"Exactly. We really need to think about this before committing ourselves to anything." They spent a lot of time going over the pros and cons of living in the valley before going to bed.

It was over three weeks later before Mark got a chance to see the frontier town. Eric came back to their cabin to take over the training. Mark had everything written down in a notebook that he was to teach the security guys. Mark left in the afternoon with Maria. It was time for her two day visit to the tree people. Eric wished he could be a fly on the wall when they presented him with their proposal of making him sheriff. He'd have to wait until Mark came back to talk to him about it. He sighed. It had been hard to keep the secret from him and he wasn't going to be happy to know they'd kept the secret from him, either. Oh well, that was life. He had a long talk with Maria about it and they agreed to let the tree people approach him with their offer before saying anything about it. He turned around and started the men walking in the woods. Amanda was with him and learning about walking in the woods, too. She was getting pretty good at it. Mark thought they should include the children in all aspects of the training that they could handle. It would make it easier to train them later as they grew up.

Mark got back and said he understood why no one had said anything. He said that Abby was coming for a visit tomorrow so they could all discuss this proposal then. For two days they went over all the details of the benefits of being in that community versus going it alone. They decided to take the offer. They'd be a part of the community, but they were still a group and would always be a group, no matter what happened in the future. Abby had some news to share with them now that they decided to take the offer. Alan had proposed marriage. She told him she'd have to think about it. She wanted to wait until everything had been decided before answering him.

The deal Mark had worked out with Jeff was they'd keep this cabin, too. They needed a place outside the valley to train and to have as a first warning if they were being invaded. They'd always maintain some people here as a lookout for the rest of the community and not just for the valley. They'd also use this as a place to get away from the community to remember what the rest of the world was like. They decided that, at first, they would still use this cabin as their real home and continue on with the plans they'd made for the summer and fall. This would, for the time being, be their base of operations. It was also decided that Ryan would live with Mark and Maria when they were in the valley. Amanda would live with Eric and Lisa, and Chris would live with Abby until she got married, then he would live with Eric and Lisa. It wasn't really a big deal because they all lived right next door to each other and would probably be in and out of each other's places every day.

Maria was offered the position of being head of education and supplies. As a group, they decided to semi-join the tree people. Mark would be sheriff and head of security starting as soon as he gave them their decision, and Maria would be head of education and supplies. Mark went back to the valley with Maria and Abby to deliver their decision. After that, things went back to normal and they all got busy with their jobs. Bert stopped in several times and talked to Mark. Eric was getting a complex about never being there when he showed up. Everyone else had met him, even Abby had on one of her rare visits back to their cabin. He started to feel like Bert didn't like him for some reason. Mark told him it was probably just a chance thing.

A few days later when Mark was conducting a training session, Chris came running up to them, carrying his .22. Chris and Maria were on watch in a foxhole by the highway. Chris said, "Five people are walking down the highway in military clothing carrying rifles. Maria's in the foxhole watching them."

Mark pointed to three men. "You three come with me." He pointed to two more. "Inside, upstairs, cover the cabin, front and back." He pointed to the rest of the men. "Disappear into the woods and cover the cabin and the road. Be ready for trouble. NOW MOVE IT." The men knew where to go to defend the cabin. They'd already trained for this. Mark turned to Chris. "Chris, at the sound of any shots, you take off for the cave and tell everyone what happened. You stay inside the cabin and be ready to leave if necessary."

Chris said, "But I want to fight with you."

Mark said, "Chris, if something happens to us, they need to be warned."

Chris looked at him. "No. I'll fight with you; not run off like a scared girl."

Mark grabbed Chris's arm and shook him. "Listen to me and listen to me good. You will need to tell Eric what happened. If you don't, he or any of the others would come back here and walk into a trap and die. Is that what you want?"

Chris hung his head. "No."

Mark said, "Now promise me that if you hear shots, you will go warn Eric and the others."

"I promise."

"Now get into the cabin. I don't have any more time to waste on this nonsense." Chris ran into the cabin and slammed the door. They all took off jogging down the road. Mark turned and pointed at two men. "You two cover the road from the north." He turned to the last man. "Cover us from the south side of the road and keep the foxhole in sight at all times. Provide cover fire if needed." The man nodded and turned off into the woods. They were all heavily armed. Mark had the 45-70 and the men had AR-15s that the tree people had bought for security in the valley. They all had pistols in holsters on their hips.

Mark reached the foxhole they had dug to watch the highway. He slowed down, then lay down on the ground and slowly and quietly crawled over. Maria smiled at him, lowering the binoculars. "You are never going to believe this one."

Mark asked, "Believe what?" As he brought his pair of binoculars up to his eyes, looking at the people walking up the road, she said excitedly, "There are eight people coming this way. Two women, three men, two children and one baby. One of the women is Channon; she's carrying a baby."

Maria went to call out to the people coming and Mark tapped her arm. "Don't say anything. We have to find out if she's a captive again or if these are her friends from Chuck's group or what. Keep your gun pointed at them and let me do the talking." When they were about twenty yards out, Mark yelled, "Channon, is that you?"

All of them scattered into the woods, taking cover, pointing their guns at where the voice came from. Mark and Maria could hear them whispering to each other. Channon called out in amazement, "Mark, is that you? It can't really be you."

Mark yelled out, "Channon, are you with friends?" He watched the men for their reaction. Channon quickly said, "We're friends. What are you doing here?"

Mark said, "Everyone relax and lower your weapons." He watched the men closely to see what they were going to do. Channon nodded to her friends and they lowered their weapons. Mark took a deep breath and relaxed. He whispered to Maria, "Stay here and keep alert. We have to make sure this isn't a trap." Mark said, "Channon, please walk up here, towards my voice."

An African American man yelled out, "Channon is my wife and I go with her. I don't know you or trust you."

Mark said, "Okay, come with her, but shoulder your weapon first and come up here slowly. Don't make any sudden moves. We might get the wrong idea." Channon and the man slowly walked towards them. Mark looked at the man and he looked vaguely familiar. He was trying to figure out where he'd seen the man before. When they got close to the foxhole, they could clearly see each other.

Channon raced over and hugged Mark. He hugged her back, one armed. Channon said, "This is my husband, Lonnie, and he's carrying my daughter, Hope. What are you doing here? Is this your retreat?"

Lonnie said, "I remember you from last fall. You let Channon stay with us."

Mark relaxed and signaled back to everyone that all was well. "I remember you, too. Tell your friends to come up and join us." Lonnie turned and signaled to his friends to come up. When everyone got there, Mark said, "Come on. We'll go to our cabin and talk." Maria jumped out of the foxhole and Channon squealed at seeing her. They both hugged each other, asking questions and talking a mile a minute. Mark and Lonnie shared an exasperated look. Channon took Hope out of her carrying pouch and turned back to Maria to show her the baby. Mark signaled to the man covering the foxhole to take over the watch. Mark led the way and said to Lonnie, "Come on up to the cabin and tell us why you're so far from your base." As they walked, Mark signaled to the other men he had hidden in the woods to meet at the cabin.

Mark was sure they'd hear an interesting story. No one left a group like Chuck's unless they were kicked out or because they didn't see eye to eye. Especially with the world in the condition it was in right now. Whichever it was it would at least be interesting. After a little while, Lonnie said as they were walking, shaking his head and looking down at the ground, "The base is gone. We're what's left of our fighting force."

Mark felt a shock run through his whole body. "What?"

Lonnie looked around nervously and said, "We'll tell you everything, but first, let's get everyone off the road."

Mark nodded, his mind racing, trying to figure out what could have happened to Chuck's group. A deep fear filled him. This was not good. No, this wasn't good at all. He was sure it was going to be bad. Very bad. He took a seat in a chair and said, "First things first. What happened?"

Lonnie said, "Some whacked out group called Rainbow Warriors, about five thousand strong, hit us. They have two 105mm artillery guns. They come into an area and tell people to covert to being a veg head or die. They swear they're on a mission from Mother Gaia to cleanse the earth of evil people that eat animals."

Mark closed his eyes and thought, *only in California. This could only happen in California. This almost makes the Roman soldiers seem normal. This is just great.* Why did the name Rainbow Warriors sound familiar? Where had he heard it before?

He opened his eyes. "Where are they now?"

Lonnie said, "They're back about two and a half to three weeks behind us. They travel slow because they go down each side road for about twenty miles killing all the animals eaters that won't convert. They meet back up on the main highway and then head north to the next road."

"How come we aren't seeing more refugees?"

"I don't know. Maybe everyone else is heading south instead of north. We didn't have a choice. It was either head north or get overrun by them again. Channon said we should head north, that she had a feeling coming this way would be safer. I don't see how it could be with them hot on our tail. Now we're stuck on the highway having to go through the pass with no alternatives to go anywhere else." He hesitated for a moment. "Not that I know where we should go anyway, to be safe."

Mark said, "How many of your group made it out?"

Lonnie looked sadly at him and said, "As far as we know, you're looking at them."

"Out of how many?"

"We had about a hundred and fifty people. Most were noncombatants; women and children. We had a good plan, but those 105mm's are murder. They kept them hidden in the back under cover. We didn't even know they had them until after we launched our attack. They cut right through us like we were nothing. They sent in clean up crews for survivors and the wounded. We grabbed what we could and got out of there. We had to clear a path as we made our way. We used a lot of our ammo up doing it, too."

Eric was learning to plow the old-fashioned way. He was sweating like a stuffed pig and his shoulders and back ached. This was brutal hard work that seemed to take forever to accomplish much of anything. He laid the plow down and walked over to the stream to get a drink of cool water. He picked up the metal cup he had left there earlier, bent down, and dipped it in the stream. He brought it up to his lips and drank it all. He reached down again, filling the cup, and then poured it over his head. He then refilled the cup and sat down in the shade.

The bush next to him gently shook and a male voice whispered, "Don't be alarmed. I am a friend. Name's Bert." Eric was holding the metal cup and had just taken a drink when he saw the bush barely move out of the corner of his right eye and heard the low voice of a man. Without conscious thought, his right hand shot out to grab or punch at the bush, throwing water out of the cup in a high arc. Eric wasn't sure of what he was going to do, but before he could connect with the bush, it moved out of range. He jumped up so fast he got a head rush. He turned, facing the bush in a fighting crouch, hands out in front of him with his heart pounding and thumping in his chest. He could hear the blood rushing through his veins at warp speed. The man in the bush whispered a firm harsh command, "Sit down and quit looking at the bush like that before someone sees you and gets suspicious."

Eric blinked and his brain started working again, catching up to his instinctive reaction to whatever this was. A Threat? A Leprechaun? God? Then he relaxed as it dawned on him who this had to be. He said, "The snow monster, Bert." He sat back down on the ground. His whole body was shaking from the large dose of adrenaline that had flooded his body. He said, "What the hell, Bert? You almost gave me a heart attack. There are easier ways of introducing yourself. What if I'd been armed?"

Bert chuckled and said in an amused tone, "But they wouldn't have been nearly as much fun as doing it this way."

Eric slowly smiled, shaking his head, and then sobered up and said sincerely, "I want to thank you for all that you've done for us. All of us want to thank you. If you hadn't have taken out those crazy Roman soldiers they would have killed my best friend, Mark and a wonderful woman named Abby. She's pregnant." Eric paused and sighed deeply. "And also for saving Ryan and Amanda in the snowstorm. We are deeply in debt to you. What can I do for you?"

Bert said, "You are one of Amanda's and that boy's adopted dads, right?"

"Yes, I am. My name is Eric."

Bert peered out of the side of the bush and pushed back his face covering so Eric would recognize him. Then he covered his face back up and disappeared back into the bush. "I thought you were, but wanted to make sure. I told myself if you clowns all made it to spring, you'd be worthy of my time and help."

"We're always looking for help from others, so that we might all work together and have a better chance of surviving this chaos." Eric wasn't sure what this was all about. Did Bert want or need something from them? It sure didn't sound like he liked the tree people very much. "Does Jeff know about you?"

Bert said, "We have met before. I have a shortwave radio. I have some news to tell you. You have five people Mark welcomed and brought to the cabin." Eric looked startled and wondered who they could be. Bert went on, "But that isn't the news I came here to tell you. You need to go to the others at the cabin right now. An army of five thousand is on the highway, heading up here right now. They're killing anyone that doesn't swear an oath to Gaia and that they will never harm or eat any animals. This army goes down twenty miles on any side road, spreading their terror. They march back to the highway and move on to the other side. Then they head north to the next road, and so on. You need to move everyone and everything you can to the cave. They have scouting parties out all over the place. They'll be here within two weeks."

Eric looked at him. "What are you, crazy?" Eric was thinking, *talk about paranoid*. Bert was obviously nuts.

Bert laughed. "Yes, I am. But that's beside the point. I came to warn you so you could prepare. It's up to you what you do about this. I would just hate to see that cute little girl die a gruesome death. You haven't heard the reports of how crazy things are out there. I have. I'm going to brief everyone here. You do whatever you want."

Chapter 33

Survival Of The Fittest

Shallow men believe in luck. Strong men believe in cause and effect
Ralph Emerson

Preston looked out of the loft window at the falling rain. It was 6:00 am. Half of his watch was over. He stared at the muddy ground and thought about how they had to get the crops planted soon. He watched the sun rise and brighten the horizon. In the winter it was such a pain in the butt to get up in the freezing cold and stand his watch. It seemed every day it was harder to leave Amy snuggled down warm in the blankets and quilt. He wanted nothing more than to be able to stay snuggled by her side in the warmth. But the world had changed and it was survival of the fittest and smartest. It would be just plain stupid to ignore your duty to stand watch and stay in a nice warm bed, no matter how much you wanted to do so. His mother had not raised a stupid boy. He smiled and realized that they had survived their first winter. He wondered how many other people had been lucky enough to make it.

He looked out all the windows, then glanced at his watch again. It was almost 6:30 am. Amy would be along any minute now with fresh brewed coffee for him. This was their alone time. They could talk, dream and plan a future together. Most of it was pure B. S. but it kept them entertained and focused on the future. He shook his head at how much time he had wasted on Sharon, trying to please her, when Amy was right next door. Amy was practical, strong and shot straight from the hip, just like him. What you saw was what you got. No games or manipulation. Just straight forward talking without a lot of double meanings or questionable statements. She could hold her own in just about any argument or debate. He was damned proud of her and very glad they had found each other. He heard Amy climbing the stairs to the loft and smiled in anticipation.

There she was, his G. I. Amy in her combat vest, carrying her trusty 22-250 slung over her shoulder, always ready for whatever was thrown at them. She smiled and said cheerfully, "Good morning, my dear. Coffee?"

Preston looked at her for a few seconds, then said sternly, "You're two minutes late."

She laughed and smiled. "Sorry, Master. I had to get Michael out of bed." She poured both of them a cup of coffee. She handed the steaming cup to him, then sipped her own as she looked out the window.

She saw Steve and Vicki out in the woods, kissing. It seemed Vicki had made her choice. "Vicki and Steve are out kissing in the woods. I hope this doesn't cause trouble between Steve and John. I think it would be best if we worked them real hard so they'll be too tired to fight over her."

Preston said, "You better have a talk with her. She'll have to be real careful now not to flirt and say anything suggestive to John. This situation could blow up like dynamite in all of our faces if she isn't careful."

She turned to look at him and said, "I already had that talk with her when I explained she had to pick one of them or neither of them. I also told her she had to be considerate of their feelings. I guess I'll talk to her about it again and caution her how explosive this could get."

"Well, we may be able to find a woman for John this spring. I'm sure there must be some single women out there looking for a strong man to care for them and provide food." Before Amy had a chance to comment, Preston looked out of the east side window. "What the hell? There's a tractor coming straight for us. It's an old Ford 8n with, I think, a tilling disk." He grabbed his radio. "Command, we have a lone tractor heading this way."

Joe answered with, "What?"

Preston repeated, "A lone tractor is coming this way with just one guy on it, as far as I can tell."

Joe replied, "I think I know who it is. Stay put. I'll get back to you."

Amy opened up the loop hole and yelled out, "Hey kids, stop making out. We have company coming. Get your gear and get into position now." Vicki and Steve took off running towards the house. Amy and Preston got into position.

Joe stepped out on the porch and looked at the tractor with binoculars. He smiled. It was just as he thought. The old tractors were still working. It was his other neighbor, Don, from down yonder a ways, coming over to see them. He walked up to the gate and waited for him.

Don pulled up in the driveway and turned the engine off. Don said, "Are you going to open the gate so I can plow your fields or stand there looking at me like a little kid?"

Joe grinned. "You made it through winter."

Don smiled. "Of course we made it through winter. You think I'm wet behind the ears or something? We've had worse times than this before and made it through just fine, thank you very much."

Joe laughed. "It's good to see you, Don." They shook hands.

Don said, "Of course, now that money is worthless, what do you got to trade for me plowing your fields?"

"What you looking for?"

Don sighed and said as he reached into his front pocket, "You know Marianne. That woman can raise some Cain when she needs stuff. Here's list of what she's looking for." He handed the list to Joe. Joe read the list. Sewing needles, tooth paste, bath soap, dish soap, laundry soap, shampoo, conditioner, bleach and baking soda. "She told me I would be king of the house if I can find those items."

Joe grinned. "You plow those fields and that list will be covered."

Don thought for a moment. "Oh, one more thing. Do you have an eyeglass repair kit?"

Joe thought for a moment. "I think we do."

Don looked relieved. "Thank God. She lost that little screw for the arm of her reading glasses. You fix those glasses so she can start reading again so I don't have to listen to her anymore and I'll plow whatever fields you want."

Joe smiled and said with a laugh, "I'll set you up good, my friend." Joe unlocked the gate and swung it open. Don climbed up in the tractor and then asked, "Same as last year?"

Joe said, "Yeah, same as last year, plus a new acre." Don said, "You be sure not to forget that repair kit and I'll do the plowing." Don started the tractor up and drove out to the fields.

Joe called Preston down from the loft and Amy took over the rest of his watch. Preston saw he was smiling like he'd just won the lottery. "Thank God a tractor to plow the land is like manna from heaven about now. It will make our life so much easier. We'll still have to plant the seeds by hand, but this is a great thing to have the fields plowed for us." They gladly paid Don one of everything he asked for. Joe gave Jane a hug. "Thank God you bought those ten eyeglass repair kits at the dollar store last year."

Jane smiled at him and said smugly, "I told you they'd be needed."

"Yeah, rub it in." They all shared a laugh. "Well, that is one worry off our minds now."

Preston looked at Joe. "Did you see the new accessories attached to the tractor? Do you think he had some problems over the winter?"

Joe smiled. "It looks like it." On each side of the hood of the tractor was a new holster. One side had a 30 M1 carbine with a twenty round magazine. The other side had a double barrel 12 gauge shotgun and Don was wearing a 1911 Colt .45 in a holster on his side.

The next day, Joe and Preston were out scouting around the property. Preston said, "We have to get The Last Chance ready. We have too many people and no back up plan."

Joe smiled. "Tomorrow you take Amy, John and Steve and get it done in a week."

Preston had been thinking the same thing. "I take it you, Jane, Vicki and Michael will be planting seeds while we do that?"

"Of course. I want that place sealed up tight. Get the wood stove hooked up and the roof draining into the thousand pound water tank we had buried out there. Hook the hand pump up to the kitchen sink. Take the two one hundred pound propane tanks out there and hook them up to the apartment-size stove we bought." They had started this project last year on the back property of a neighbor. They had bought five acres of a wooded lot. They cleared the space for the cabin and leveled it off, then buried a thousand gallon water tank. Joe had made a barrel stove and cut off the top and lowered it about three inches and put a flat piece of steel on top and a water jacket on the side. They needed something set up in case they ever got overrun or there was a disaster or fire at the farm.

The work was hard and the days were long, but no one complained. Preston was pretty happy with what they'd accomplished in one week. It was April fifteenth. It used to be the most dreaded day of the year in America in the old world. They'd need another week here to finish everything up. They still needed to put in the drain for the kitchen sink. They were digging a hole in the ground and putting in a fifty-five gallon drum with holes in it surrounded by six inches of rocks. Not the best, but it should handle what comes from the sink. The bathroom was an outhouse in the summer and a five gallon bucket with a lid in winter. While they were busy getting The Last Chance ready, everyone else was planting wheat, corn, white beans, green beans, peas, squash, onions, beets, carrots, tomatoes, potatoes, lettuce, cucumbers, celery, watermelon, cantaloupe and other vegetables and herbs.

Around April 25th, refugees started passing by. They heard nothing but bad news from them. Then came the most dreadful news of all. A two thousand plus army was marching their way. They called themselves Rainbow Warriors and they were heading south, straight for them. They heard that this so-called army killed everyone who wouldn't convert to worshiping Gaia and to pledge to never harm another animal. They were complete control freaks. They were burning down the houses, which forced everyone to live in their command housing units. Classes were given to brainwash the people into believing and accepting their Nazi control over everything. Everyone was afraid and running for their lives. The stories just kept getting wilder and wilder. It was hard to find out what was true and what was rumor. Preston kept saying that they should have opened up a season on those Eco Nazis years ago. It would have avoided all of this now. It would also have thinned out the number of mentally insane people running around the country causing havoc now.

The Last Chance was finally almost finished. They brought Preston's two bikes and one they had picked up for Michael. They had traded some extra things they had for bike tires and an old bike frame. They had fixed it up and painted it a dark blue and gave it to him on his birthday last month. They also stashed some emergency supplies out there and got it as ready as they could. Joe started drilling everyone on escape routes out to the Last Chance. Everyone hoped the army wouldn't make it this far. Joe said "I'm not leaving. I'm not running. I'm not hiding, either. We have to kill as many as we can. I have a few surprises for those scumbags. The good news is we can shoot them on sight. I'll be generous and share with you, Preston. You can kill half and I'll kill the other half." They shared a laugh They started making a four-tiered defense. They both knew they would never be able to stop an army of two thousand. But they sure as hell were not going to sit on their asses and make it easy for them either. Their plan might have worked, too, if they had only known that the Rainbow Warriors had a few tricks up their sleeves too.

Joe and Preston were overlooking the defenses one evening. Preston said, "You remember Phil. He bought that twenty acres just north of Yellowstone Park? How he bragged that if the end of world happened, it wouldn't matter, because he'd have all the elk he could ever want to eat."

"I remember always wanting to see his place. Beautiful country out there."

"The last time I talked to him, he was madder than a wet hornet. He said those damn wolves had wiped out most of the elk. His neighbor out there was running cattle and was forced out of business because he lost so many animals to the wolves. His other neighbor used to be a big time outfitter. They were forced out of business, too, because of the wolves. Years ago, *Outdoor Life* magazine did a full spread on all the trophy elk his clients always got. Now, there just isn't enough elk left to hunt after the wolves killed most of them."

Joe laughed. "I bet those wolf lovers in Montana and Idaho have been strung up by starving people. Kind of hard to find elk to hunt when the wolves have wiped them all out."

Preston laughed, too. "I bet more than one wolf lover across the land has had their house burned to the ground and were strung up on a tree with a sign saying, 'Wolf lovers, thanks for helping starve my family. Burn in hell."

The moose population in Yellowstone National Park trend count shows a decrease to almost zero. (Source: 2009 Wolf-Ungulate Study Montana Fish, Wildlife & Parks) The Gallatin Canyon elk herd trend count between Bozeman and Big Sky has dropped from around 1,048 to 338 in 2008. (Source: Montana Fish, Wildlife & Parks)

• The Madison Firehole elk herd trend count has dropped from 700 to 108 in 2008. (Source: Montana Fish, Wildlife & Parks)

• The calf survival rate for those same elk herds mentioned above, where wolves (and bears) are present, is extremely low, amounting to as little as 10% or less recruitment or survival rate. Nearly any wildlife professional will tell you this is an unacceptable recruitment or survival rate. Acceptable wildlife science tells us that a 25-40% survival rate is necessary for herd sustainability. Studies show that each wolf kills up to 23 elk from November through April; that equates to up to 40,000 elk killed in six months. Nowhere near the majority of these elk kills are simply the sick and the old dying, as the animal rights groups claim.

By May, a steady stream of refugees started flowing by the farm. They looked like zombies. Some stopped and begged for food. Others just walked on past. It was hard to get any work done. They heard all about the horrors coming their way, but from what everyone was saying these Eco Rainbow Warriors stayed close to the interstate. Maybe they'd get lucky and be spared. At least the rains were coming hard and steady. The plants were sprouting. It was looking like a great crop would come in. Wild flowers were blooming, songbirds were busy building nests and the squirrels were running around everywhere. The refugees thinned down to just a few. Everyone was starting to enjoy life and looked forward to the harvest. There was just something about growing your own food that felt very good and right. They all took pride in their hard work.

Vicki and Steve became a couple. They announced this one night and were disappointed that everyone had known about it already. They thought they'd been sneaking around, keeping it secret. John congratulated them, too. He stepped aside when he saw they were serious about each other. Preston and Joe were greatly relieved. They'd seen a lot of best friends end up at each others throats because a girl played them off against each other, then move on to a new guy, leaving behind a destroyed relationship between the two men. They were thankful that Vicki wasn't that kind of girl.

Preston and Amy were outside sitting on the grass, enjoying a beautiful sunset together. Preston's mind was wandering all over the place. He started thinking about children. He figured that Amy or Vicki would end up pregnant this coming year. It was bound to happen sooner or later. The world may have fallen apart, but couples were still getting together. Life moves forward no matter what. It really wasn't the end of the world, but a chance at a new beginning and a chance for true freedom. He thought about the town near them and wondered what kind of trade had been set up. They had another hard winter to get through and it was coming a lot faster than he liked. It would take a lot to make it through this next winter. It had been a struggle this past winter even though they had stored plenty for survival. The future was a huge blank, like an empty book waiting to be written. He thought, *I must be getting old.* Thoughts like these had never really bothered him before. But, on the other hand, he'd never lived through the end of the world before, either. Always before when he was in some hellhole, fighting for who really knew what, it was a comfort to know they'd be going home to America again, where everything was pretty normal. Well, here he was in America, and nothing would ever be normal here again.

Amy nudged him with her elbow. "What are you thinking so hard about?"

Preston turned to her and smiled. Amy smiled back. He said, "I was thinking about getting through next winter and wondering about all the things that come next after that."

Amy laughed. "Nothing to it, it's a piece of cake. Just remember, if we live through next winter, then you can rebuild America the year after that. We'll know what we're doing by that time. If not, it won't really matter because we'll be dead. So see, there's nothing to worry about. I have complete faith and trust in you to rebuild America right this time, with no loopholes that politicians can use to gain power to manipulate everyone to their own ends again."

Preston laughed. "Gee, no pressure, huh?"

Amy laughed again. "Stop worrying. This is a beautiful day. Just enjoy it. The future will take care of itself. We just have to stay alive long enough to shape it the way it should be."

Preston reached over and pulled her close and said with a smile and a twinkle in his eyes, "Maybe we can find a preacher man. We need to get us all properly married, you know. What do you think of a fall harvest wedding? Who knows, it could be a dual wedding. Steve and Vicki may want to make their relationship permanent, too ."

Amy's smile grew wider. "That sounds just wonderful."

Chapter 34

Rainbow Warriors

"Now is no time to think of what you do not have. Think of what you can do with what there is."

Ernest Hemingway

Clint and Junior had been going around the community finding people and letting them know what was coming their way and trying to organize a fighting group. Clint had found a place about fifteen miles to the northeast from where he had his camp before meeting Junior and Gayle that had a small survivalists' farm. Several were ex-military. All the people in the community started making plans for the coming Rainbow Warriors. As soon as they found out Clint had been a S.E.R.E. instructor, they started to pay close attention to everything he said. Clint outlined his plan and they agreed to it.

Clint was sitting at the kitchen table, making notes and a few drawings for the men to see so they'd know what he had in mind. He had two teams of two men each at strategic places along the road to keep watch for the Rainbow Warriors and give them time to get into place. He planned on engaging them twenty miles out from here, in the middle of nowhere. He didn't want any homes or people close enough that they could take their anger and revenge out on. He planned to make them jump at every little sound and make them scared of their own shadows. He planned on hitting them and then disappearing, making them think ghosts were after them. As he sat there making notations, he noticed out of the corner of his eye that Katlin was standing in the doorway. He looked up at her, smiling.

She smiled back. "Am I interrupting?"

He laid his pen down. "Nothing too important that I can't stop for awhile and pay attention to my best girl."

She looked sternly at him. "I best be the only girl. If I'm not, things could get real ugly, real fast."

He laughed and raised his hands in mock surrender. "You're absolutely right. I'm shaking in my boots. You wield a mean scalpel and needle."

She said, with a raised eyebrow, staring at him in mock seriousness, "Just keep that in mind if you plan on keeping all your body parts."

He laughed again, then pulled her down on his lap, kissing her. He stared in her eyes. "I like all my body parts just where they are."

She kissed him back. "So do I. Let's keep them that way."

He knew they were talking about more than her just being the only woman in his life. He said seriously, "I plan to. I've waited my whole life for you. Now that I've got you, I have more incentive to make sure everything goes as planned."

She said seriously with a worried look, "See that it does. I don't want to lose you, either."

He smiled. "Yes, ma'am."

It was decided she would be the field surgeon. Clint had explained the fact that they would be dealing with a long line of men spread out along the highway, and that those in front would not know what was happening in the middle or rear of the column. The front and back of the column wouldn't know what was happening in the middle, either. All three areas were vulnerable to attack. Even if they had radios, it wouldn't matter, because mostly the ones affected wouldn't be left to tell the others about what happened. The curves in the road would help hide what happened from both ends, too. This was something to exploit. The curves in the road would be ideal places to have ambushes. No one would see them coming or even know what happened until they got close.

They had a meeting with the volunteers to fight this coming insane army. Clint reminded the men that the column of enemy would be a mile or so long. The most important objectives would be to disable any and all large artillery and to kill all the horses. Doing both would help weaken the enemy in a large way. It would also help disrupt their communications if messengers had to travel on foot between officers to deliver messages. It would slow them down and disrupt their response time. "Any disruption we can cause, is good for us. Any way we can slow them down, is also good for us. Anything that we can destroy or take away will weaken them and strengthen us."

Another area they'd be extremely vulnerable in would be their supplies. H reminded the men that armies can only last as long as their supplies. He explained that they probably hoped to resupply from the farms and homes they ran across. That is one of the reasons Clint wanted to fight them away from places they might be able to retaliate against or to restock from. Another thing to keep in mind was that when those men got hungry, they couldn't just go out and hunt because they don't eat meat. That was a plus. Feeding a thousand strong army would really wipe out a lot of game in this area and take food away from the residents of this community. The men needed to eat to have the energy to march and fight. In the plan Clint outlined, he'd taken those facts and made them work for them in a big way.

Clint told them that if they took out the middle guys of the column, it would cause a psychological effect that no one would want to be in the middle of the column and that would cause tremendous problems for the men in charge when and if they tried to rally the men to fight back. That's the kind of thing that works the most effectively. Clint called it the ghost or phantom effect. The ordinary soldier's reaction would probably be to stay close together in small groups for protection, because there's safety in numbers, right? The men agreed. Clint nodded and told them, "But strategically, that's the wrong thing to do. Bunching up in groups only makes it easier for us to kill more of them at one time." He grinned.

Clint continued on, telling them that most of these men are used to cities. They're totally lost and out of their depth when they get to the woods. That's something else that can be used against them. Most trees and wooded terrain look the same to city dwellers. Also, something else to keep in mind is they're vulnerable when they sleep. "Remember, we know these woods and they don't. There is a lot that can be done under the cover of darkness. Plus, you need to take into consideration that these men were mostly like gang members and not trained, disciplined troops. You also needed to keep in mind that the Rainbow Warriors are fanatical in their beliefs. Fanatical people are already unbalanced in the way they think about things, especially if you add in a religious angle where they think they're answering a calling from a higher power. They aren't able to handle any kind of an organized resistance. In their minds, it should be plain for everyone to see that they're doing the right thing by forcing everyone to believe what they believe. Most people call the higher power God and these people call their God or Goddess, Gaia, Mother Earth. The true believers will expect help from this higher being. It would be easy to literally drive them over the edge of reason and make them jump at every noise they hear, phantom or real, because they are already halfway there. Another way to target them would be to hunt animals and leave them for the army to find. It would mess with their belief system and make them angry. Angry people cannot reason well and will cause them to make mistakes that they ordinarily wouldn't. Killing the horses will also have that effect on them."

A couple of days later, one of the teams saw a couple of guys carrying AK-47s, walking slowly and very arrogantly down the middle of the road. They were talking loudly occasionally, walking around the stalled vehicles side by side. They didn't even bother to look around and see if anyone was around. The two men on the watch team shared an incredible look. They took off running back to the next watch team and reported. One man was sent back to tell Clint. The other three stayed and would report back when they saw the actual army coming. The man got word to Clint that the army was coming and two scouts were out front. Clint and Junior grabbed their packs, along with a few extra bags Katlin had packed with medical supplies and some blankets and things she would need. She grabbed her portable hospital bag and the three of them headed out to the meeting place. Katlin would be staying not too far from the main camp area where all the men would meet occasionally between the scheduled ambushes. This is where she would stay while everyone else, except the two men Clint appointed as her bodyguards, would be out engaging the enemy. Katlin had shared with the men what had happened in Green Bay. None were surprised because they all shared their knowledge of the "Crazy Larry" reports. Clint had explained to everyone that they were going to use ancient battle plans that were very effective. They would mostly be exploiting their enemies' weaknesses. "We will steal, destroy and disrupt. We will be ghosts and phantoms, with deadly accurate fire. We will strike and then disappear into the woods as if we were never there. We will put the fear of our God into them." The men had cheered. Most of the men didn't really believe they would be able to do much against an army a thousand men strong, but knew they had to do something, and Clint's plans were a lot better than doing nothing or facing them straight on.

Clint and Junior left Katlin at the main meeting area and took off to deal with the two scouts. When they got close, Clint asked Junior if he had packed several decks of cards that he had asked him to. Junior told him yes, and wanted to know what they were going to use them for. When they'd been out collecting things for the baby, Clint had picked up every deck of cards he could find. Junior didn't think too much of it at the time. He figured Clint wanted them for trading or something. Clint smiled and told him to take out the ace of spades and the ace of hearts. When Junior had those two in his hand, Clint told him to look closely at the cards. Junior did, and then looked at him questioningly.

Clint said, "They look pretty innocent, don't they?" Junior said that they did. Clint asked him if they looked like they were a deadly weapon that will help win the battle. Junior said no, they don't look like that at all. Clint smiled at him. Junior was thinking Clint would use them to throw at an enemy and kill them. He'd seen something like that in a few movies. Maybe he'd do something even more deadly, like make an explosive out of them. Junior told him his theories. Clint laughed and told him he didn't have to do anything but write a few words on them. Junior was puzzled. How was a few words a deadly weapon? Clint told him to watch and see and remember the "Pen is mightier than the sword." Clint took the ace of spades and pulled a red sharpie marker out of his pocket and wrote on it, 'Turn back and maybe you will live.' Then he took the ace of hearts and put a circle around the heart in the center, then drew a line through it and below it he wrote, 'Pass this point and all of you will die.' Junior was confused. He asked Clint how was this was going to stop a thousand man army? Clint smiled and told him this is called psychological warfare. "Pay attention to how well this will work for us." Junior nodded as they hid in the brush, waiting for the two scouts.

About fifteen minutes later, the two scouts came arrogantly walking down the middle of the road, acting like they were out for a stroll along the beach. They certainly didn't look like they were scouts for an army. They didn't even look around to see if anyone was there or not. They were totally engrossed in their conversation. Junior looked quizzically at Clint and nodded once at the scouts. Clint nodded slightly back in acknowledgment. Junior wondered how these two men had survived this long being so stupid. Clint had told Junior and his small group that this army was used to going up against one and two family farms since they left Green Bay. They were not prepared for what was going to happen. They were bold, arrogant and thought they were the meanest, heavily armed, smartest people around. They were a large army, who could possibly stand before them? Clint had told them it was their job to show them how wrong they were to think and believe that. "We will break their morale and put nothing but doubts into their heads and make them jump at every sound and shadow in fear."

Junior was ready to kill the two scouts. These two were too stupid to live. After hearing the things that Katlin told them, Junior agreed with her that none of them deserved to live. It had been one horror story after another. Last night, Katlin had told them that a doctor friend, his wife and daughter, her parents and two nurses tried to escape together. Somehow they found out about their escape plan. As they made their way out of the city, her mother was shot and killed right in front of her. Robbie didn't see it. He had been looking the other way and it was pretty dark out with no moon. He didn't understand what had happened. Then they shot down the others. Her father gave his life saving her and Robbie by shoving her down under a truck before they shot him. She had rolled away, holding Robbie, and kept on going, knowing it was certain death to stop. She had to protect Robbie. She and Robbie made it out and went to their family cabin on Lake Superior.

Clint and Junior lay along the side of the road and waited until the two scouts were fifty feet away. They both fired at almost the same instant, making the sound mix together into one loud shot. Both scouts fell over dead. They ran up and stripped them of their guns and ammo. The guns were AK-47s with German magazine pouches. They both were carrying four extra thirty round magazines, plus one in the rifle, making that one hundred fifty rounds per rifle. Good to know. Clint grinned as he dragged one dead man about five feet farther up the road and stuck the ace of hearts in his mouth. He quickly went over to the other dead man and put the ace of spades in his mouth. Clint and Junior disappeared back into the woods and ran a mile along the road to another two man team. When they stopped, Clint whispered with an evil grin, "See how arrogant and stupid they are? We're now facing an army of nine hundred ninety-eight."

Jack and Phil waited for Clint and Junior to join them up on the ridge, where they were hidden in the brush. Jack asked Clint how it went. Jack and Phil exchanged a grin at the news. Clint had all the men wearing camo face paint that he had shown them how to properly apply and they wore camo clothing. They blended right into the scenery. The two enemy scouts had been two miles in front of the main army, so they had about a half an hour to wait until the army caught up. They got comfortable and waited in silence to see the effect of killing the two scouts had. Those in charge were in for a huge surprise. Little did they know a nightmare was waiting for them in the middle of nowhere. Clint smiled. This was so his element and he was going to use his knowledge to make them pay for their crimes. What goes around comes around. Clint had explained to the small fifteen man group he had picked to fight against these Rainbow Warriors that he had to observe the column of the army, because it would tell him a lot and he could adjust his plans to be more effective. Where was the leader? His top men? How many horses did they have? Who rode them and who didn't? What kind of artillery did they have? How did they march? How disciplined were they? What kind of weapons and equipment? What was the reaction from finding the dead scouts? These were some of the things he wanted to know.

They could hear the army a long time before they saw them coming around the curve to the straightaway where the two dead scouts were. The first men around the curve stopped when they saw the two bodies lying on the road. Clint had made sure the two bodies were in plain sight and nothing blocked the view.

****

One man in the middle of their little group signaled to each side and the two men on the outside held their hands out in a stopping motion. The same man that signaled conferred with two other men, and then those two men walked cautiously up near the two dead scouts. Some of the men were looking around nervously, pointing their rifles out into the woods along each side of the road. When the two men got closer to the dead scouts, they turned around and nodded at the man that had sent them forward. They looked around nervously and then headed back. They conferred some more and then another man took off running back the way they came. The rest of the men moved cautiously, looking all around, towards where the two bodies lay. The man giving the orders was a lieutenant, according to the insignia on his uniform. He looked the bodies over, noticing the playing cards in their mouths. He could see the writing on the playing cards.

He waited for the General to ride up. He didn't touch anything so the General would see them as they found them. The Lieutenant had a worried look on his face and thought, *the General wasn't going to like this. No he wasn't going to like this at all.* No telling what the General was going to do about it. He hoped he survived the raging fit the General was going to have. He swallowed nervously as he waited. Since they had left Green Bay, the General had been getting worse and worse, bitching and complaining about being out here in the wilderness instead of back in the city. He kept saying no civilized man should be out here. Just savages and uneducated men would even want to be out here in nowheresville. The Lieutenant sighed.

It took the General about five minutes to ride up to the front on his horse. When he saw the two dead scouts lying in the road, he slowed his horse to a walk and came up close to the Lieutenant. He looked at the bodies and said, "What happened to them? What's that in their mouths?"

The Lieutenant said, "This is how we found them. They have playing cards in their mouths with writing on them."

The General said in an outraged voice, "What?" The Lieutenant explained again. The General said fiercely, "Take your handkerchief and hand them to me. I don't want to touch them." The Lieutenant bent down and grabbed the ace of spades with his handkerchief and handed it up to the General. He looked at the card and narrowed his eyes. He handed it back to the Lieutenant. "Destroy this piece of filth and get me the other card." The Lieutenant put the ace of spades into his pocket as he walked over to the other body and grabbed the ace of hearts with his handkerchief. He handed it up to the General and waited for his orders. The General read the card. Then he threw it and the handkerchief down to the ground and said with a raging roar to all the men gathered around, "We're going redneck hunting. Death to all that oppose us!"

The men yelled out, "Yeah!" A lot of men had crept around the curve to see what was happening. The General then screamed out, "Send ten men out front as scouts and they had better pay attention better then these two did. Let's see these rednecks stop that many. Take the two bodies. Tonight we'll burn them in the fire and send them back to the earth just as it should be. Gaia will welcome them with open arms." The men roared with approval. The General turned his horse around and took off back to where he had been.

The General was madder than he'd ever been before. How dare these uncouth, under-educated backwoods people strike down Gaia's warriors on their righteous mission to cleanse the earth of the evil meat-eaters. He hated the woods. He hated the bugs and insects. He hated that there was so much cover around them that could hide an enemy. He wanted to go back to Green Bay and civilization, but first he had to fulfill his orders. *Whoever they were, they were going to pay,* he vowed. *Yes, they were going to pay.* He would find them and let the men torture them to death.

****

Clint, Junior, Jack and Phil watched the whole encounter with mini binoculars that wouldn't reflect any light. Clint smiled and thought, *what an arrogant idiot that General is. He's using brute force and no strategy. He's sending out a ten man scouting party and not even mentioning to the morons to stay off the road. They'll stay on the road, just as the other two stupidly had.* They watched the ten scouts walking down the road. Clint looked at Jack and whispered, "You sure you can hit them? That's a long shot."

Jack smiled and whispered, "I can hit them from here. It's only nine hundred yards."

Clint nodded. "Remember to let another fifty or more pass by first. Then fire five rounds and kill anyone that looks like a leader. Then you two get out of here and back to the canoe. Get upriver and set up the next ambush. We'll meet you there later." Jack and Phil nodded in acknowledgment. Clint looked at Junior. "You ready?" Junior inclined his head once that he was ready.

Phil whispered, "You two be careful back there." Clint and Junior nodded. Clint motioned to Junior and they took off down the other side of the ridge. Now it was really paying off knowing the area and terrain. They raced to the river and got in their canoe and headed downstream about a mile. They carefully went over to the bank and got out, stepping on rocks and grass so as not to leave any footprints. They hid the canoe in a large brush pile off to the side. They followed a deer trail that had been set up at least a century ago. They came up on the bank above the road, then climbed up a steep bank that went straight up for about fifty feet. As they crawled to the top, they could hear the enemy below. They waited for their signal. As soon as they heard firing up front, they would do their part. There was not a chance that they would miss hearing the shots from up here. Clint grinned as they waited. The sound of a 50 cal going off was a very loud and distinctive sound.

What they were after was the crew for the artillery. Clint was guessing that only a few of them understood how to operate the weapon. Clint hoped they'd be able to wound and kill everyone who could operate the 105mm howitzer and kill the horses that pulled it. That howitzer was a thing of beauty, but a nightmare for anyone that had to face it. The military had been using cannons for hundreds of years. They were extremely effective. They was used to take out bunkers, machine guns and snipers. It was hell on any structure. And if they had any anti-personnel canister ammunition, it would be brutal, because they were used for defeating infantry.

Clint and Junior watched the long line of men going down the road. Then they spotted the howitzer being pulled up the hill by laboring horses. Clint nodded at Junior when they heard the firing start at the front and the line of men stopped moving forward. Junior shot two men sitting in the cart in front of the howitzer and Clint shot the two men closest to it. They quickly started to pour lead at the others around the howitzer. They had to duck because fifty rifles answered back to their two. They crawled back down and then ran down fifty feet farther over and crawled back up and opened up once again. Junior aimed for the horses and anyone close to the cart. They quickly ran out of ammo and the breach locked open on the enemies AK-47s. They each inserted a playing card inside and set the rifles down. They took off running for the canoe. Junior had put the ace of diamonds in the opened breach that had written on it in red marker, 'You were warned. Now you will die.' Clint had the ace of clubs and had written on it, 'With your own guns we will kill you.' As they ran for the canoe, fifty guys came over the hill chasing them, firing their rifles all over the place. Clint and Junior ran faster as the bullets landed all around them. They could see some sparks when a bullet would hit the rocks. When they came to the bank of the river, they both jumped down, being careful to make sure their heads were below the ledge so they wouldn't get shot. They looked at each other. Both of them were taking in big gulps of air. They had run at top speed for a long distance. Clint said, "It's too dangerous to try to get into the canoe." He looked all around and then back at Junior. "I don't think we can get away."

Chapter 35

We Are The Resistance

"The tree of liberty must be refreshed from time to time, with the blood of patriots and tyrants."

Thomas Jefferson

Eric sat by the stream and thought about what Bert had said as he watched the bush head for the other side of the valley. He made up his mind and stood up. Whether it was a joke or a delusion, he needed to talk to Mark about it. Mark had the tactical training. He'd been to Front Sight and took sniper classes and was trained in military strategy. He needed to know there was a threat heading straight for them. He untied the horse from the plow and led it over to the stream for a drink. When it was done, he tied it to a tree. He walked over to one of the other men plowing in the next field. When he saw Eric coming, the man stopped and waited. Eric explained that he had to go talk to Mark and would send a replacement to finish his section of plowing. The man nodded and Eric took off to get cleaned up. He was going home to their original cabin. He also wondered who Mark would welcome into the cabin like Bert said. As he contemplated who it could be, a thought struck him. What if by some miracle the Andersons had made it up here after all? Well, if it was them, they were going to owe them a lot of food and other things. That's the only thing that made sense. There wasn't anyone else Mark would welcome into the cabin like that. He went by Lisa, who was planting vegetables in the fields they'd already plowed. She looked up and saw him standing there. She said something to one of the other women and then headed over.

She said, "What's up?" He told her everything that Bert had said. "If Bert said it, then it's true. Bert isn't a joking kind of man."

He said, "I'm going to go back to the cabin and talk to Mark. You stay here. I'll be back tomorrow. Don't tell Abby and the children anything. Make up an excuse for why I went back to the other cabin overnight." She looked him in the eyes and saw how upset he was. She nodded. He kissed her, then took off jogging. She watched him until he was out of sight. She sighed deeply. She had a bad feeling about all of this. She shivered in the hot sun and her arms broke out in goosebumps, making her even more apprehensive about the whole thing. She rubbed her arms to chase away the goosebumps, then went back to planting. There was nothing more she could do. She'd have to be patient and wait for further developments.

When Eric neared the cabin, two of the security team stepped out of the woods. Eric signaled, "Everything okay?" They nodded. Eric walked to the back door and knocked. "Mark, I need to talk to you." Chris looked out, saw it was Eric, and let him inside. Eric heard several people talking in the living room and headed straight there. The first thing Eric noticed was that none of them looked like the Andersons. As he was scanning the people trying to figure out why Mark would welcome them into the cabin, he saw a black woman holding a baby and recognition slammed into him. *Oh my God, it's Channon.* Eric jerked in shock. *How in the hell did Channon get up here?* Eric stood in the kitchen and motioned for Mark to come outside. Mark told Eric about finding Channon on the road and the news they brought of the army coming their way. When he was done, Eric then shared his own news that Bert had shared.

Lonnie joined Mark and Eric outside. Mark said, "Let's take a walk." The three of them walked for awhile in the woods in back of the cabin. Mark stopped. "Lonnie, what else can you tell us about this army?"

Lonnie said, "Well, they don't shoot very well. They're used to taking on small groups and using their superior numbers to overrun them. When they meet any real resistance, they bring up the 105s to change the odds in their favor." Just then the bush they were standing next to stood up, making the men jump in surprise.

Eric said, "Bert, would you stop doing that?"

Bert laughed. "Okay. But it's a lot of fun watching you all jump like that." The three men looked uncomfortably at each other. Bert removed his face mask. "What do you three knuckleheads think you're going to do against an army of that size?"

Mark looked him straight in the eyes. "What do you suggest?"

Bert replied, "I have a friend that lives in Redding. He's a retired Major from the U. S. Marines. His name is Major Gary Beckerton. I met him overseas; he's a great guy. He's studied military operations most of his life. If I can get to him, I know he'll help raise the men we need to fight these evil scum that are coming our way."

Mark said, "Good plan."

"How are you going to get past the security detail up there?" asked Eric.

Bert laughed. "The same way I got past your security here at the cabin." They all thought about what he'd just said for a few moments. "You guys need to move everything useful from this cabin down into the valley. That should take you about a week. I should be back by then." Bert looked at Lonnie. "The other man that traveled with you, do either of you have military training? Do you have any sniper experience?"

Lonnie said, "Yes, Tom and I were in the Army. I fought in Iraq in 2010. He was there in 2011. Jack was a Marine and was over there too. Jack and I have experience with being a sniper."

Bert said, "Good, you and the other sniper will be our scouts. You need to find this Army. I need a report of strength size and how long it takes them to move the weapons. Do they have anything besides the 105s and small arms? We'll meet back here in seven days. Get the women and children down in the valley. Move everything you can from here. Tell Jeff he has to seal the back road too."

They almost had everything moved from the large cabin before it was time for the meeting with Bert. Jeff had already been briefed. When Mark and Eric arrived, men had already been assigned to help move the more important supplies from the cabin. Earlier that morning, Mark had heard several people telling others that they should just hole up in their valley and not worry about the army. Everyone would be safe here. He talked to Jeff about it and agreed to address this issue at the meeting. Mark explained to everyone that if they didn't plan on fighting the army now, they'd just end up fighting them anyway when they came up the back road and discovered the valley. They'd find the valley because they had scouts out in front, looking for people along the roads. If they didn't make some kind of agreement with Bert and Redding, they would end up fighting an army of five thousand with very little ammunition on their own. The enemy also had two 105mm artillery pieces that would make mincemeat of them. He explained about the 105s and what they can do. That got everyone's attention real quick. He went on to explain that if they didn't want to fight the whole army by themselves, which would be an insane idea, they needed Bert and Redding's help. It would be to their benefit to fight as one force against this enemy. This army was killing anyone that didn't agree with them and they were burning all the buildings along the way, so no one had anywhere to live. This was the only way they might stand a chance of succeeding against them.

He sure hoped that Ryan was right about all the stuff Bert had. Those two 105mm scared the hell out of him. He prayed that Bert would know how to take those two 105s out or it was going to be a very short battle. Lonnie, Tom and Jack had filled him in on exactly what happened to Chuck's group. It had been a literal massacre. Bert arrived with a Colonel Albert Harrison, his friend, Major Beckerton, and a First Lieutenant Barry Young in military uniforms from Redding and Bert wasn't happy with everyone else from the Frontier town being there. So they decided to meet at the Cabin. They were all going to have to work together if they hoped to survive the coming army. Mark, Eric, Lonnie and Jack briefed the Colonel on the advancing Army. They pulled out their maps. "When we left two days ago, they were here. They travel twenty to twenty-five miles a day. At the current rate of advancement, that puts them here in three days."

Major Beckerton said, "Three days. I thought we'd have more time."

"Well, we have to make our plans right now,"said the Colonel.

Bert smiled. "That's music to my ears. I have a few toys to add to the party. I have some C-4. We could send a raiding party and blow up the 105s before they get here."

The Major asked, "How much C-4 do you have?"

"Not much. Only about thirty pounds or so."

The Colonel smiled back. "It's enough to cause landslides on the highway and trap them."

" Okay," said the Major. "We trap them on the Highway. Where are the 105s?"

"At the rear," Lonnie said.

The Major said, "I understand you know how this Army fights?" Bert and the military men all perked up when they found out they had survived an encounter with the enemy. All of them had a lot of questions for Lonnie and Jack. It was over two hours later before the meeting broke up. Lonnie and Jack were tired. They had interrogated them pretty thoroughly. They made them remember some things and details that they didn't even realize that they knew.

Colonel Harrison said, "Okay, it's agreed we trap them on the road as they go down the mountain. I would guess about five miles from the back landslide to the front landslide. We cut them off from their supplies. Then we pick them off and starve them out and make sure to kill them."

The Major smiled. "What other toys do you have, Bert?"

"I have two Kalashnikov RPK-74s and several cases of grenades. I found them one day laying on the dock in Russia and thought they needed a good home."

The Major said, "Good, we'll put one on each end. Once they figure out we have them trapped, we'll have to contain them."

"Okay," Bert said, "we told you about our toys. What are you bringing to the party?"

The Colonel said, "We have one thousand men. We'll trap them on the road, then we should be able to safely pick them off from above. We'll position one hundred men on each end. The Lieutenant will be in the rear, in charge of a one hundred men detachment. The Major will take a one hundred men detachment for the front barricade, leaving myself in charge of the eight hundred men on top. The front detachment will have to be hidden from view." Bert picked a spot for them. "A three man team will blow the C-4 as soon as they hear the first explosion. Then one hundred men will take over their supply trucks and 105s. As soon as the supplies are secured, the remaining force will stop the retreat to keep them all pinned down in the trap. Once we hear the first explosion, my men will advance on top and start the turkey shoot. The front force will blow their section, causing the landslide, and hold them in the trap."

Bert held Mark back after they'd moved a lot of his supplies out for the enemy engagement. Lonnie had whistled a couple of times and muttered things like, "Now you're talking, and it's going to be a pleasure," as they moved the boxes around as Bert directed them. Lonnie was rattling off things that didn't mean anything to him, like two Kalashnikov RPK-74s. Lonnie saw that Mark didn't understand what they were. "These are light machine guns with one hundred round drum magazines. These here are hand grenades. They're Russian made. He must have picked them up after the Soviet Union collapsed. These will make a big difference in our coming battle."

Mark nodded his understanding. "Don't tell anyone about these weapons. It is top secret and a need to know situation."

Lonnie nodded. "And I don't need to know."

Mark said, "After you take these where Bert wants them, get ready to move out to scout out the enemy. Stay hidden and don't take any chances. We need you all to return and help us fight." Lonnie nodded.

When they were alone, Bert said, "You're going to split up all the men from the valley into two groups. Pick a leader for the second group and make sure it's someone you trust with your life. You'll be with me. We only share the plan with the leaders of the groups and the top men from Redding. The other men will learn about the plans when necessary. That way it's less likely that any information will get to the enemy if anyone gets captured. The plan has to work as set up or it won't work at all. Do you understand?"

Mark said, "Yes."

"Come with me," said Bert. He turned and went back down into his underground house. Mark finally saw what Ryan had seen. Mark smiled for the first time in days. Ryan hadn't exaggerated at all. In fact, he'd understated what Bert had. All those ammo cans and crates made his heart race with excitement. He started to feel a little more confident that they just might be able to stop this army. He sent a prayer of thanks heavenward for the bounty that had been provided.

Bert walked over to a glass cabinet that held various weapons and pull opened one of the doors. He looked the weapons over and then picked out a couple of knives. He set them aside and then looked under the cabinet at the shelves of ammo and pulled out several cans. "Grab two and let's go." Mark did as he was ordered and started hauling up the cases of ammo. The men would be back to move these to the designated areas. They had to hurry because it was already getting dark. Bert had shown Mark on the map approximately where he wanted the supplies placed. He told Mark to place a few guards with them to keep them safe and hidden. Mark had Eric pick the men for the watch detail to stay with the supplies. After the men returned for the next load, Bert said that would be all they'd do for now; they'd start again in the morning. He told Mark to be here at 6:30 am sharp to get the rest of the supplies moved before the meeting with the Redding men at 9:00 am. Then they'd go over the final battle plan. He told Mark that the men from Redding were bringing a demolition expert with them to figure out the best use of the C-4 and where to place it. A lot of the details would have to wait until the scouts came back and reported, but some of it could be set up ahead of time.

Mark nodded. "We'll be here at 6:30." He turned and helped carry some things to the trees to be transported.

Eric woke up and looked at the clock. It was 2:00 in the morning. He quietly climbed out of bed and went into the living room. He had a disturbing dream about something bad happening to Lisa. The details of the dream faded away and just left him with the impression of doom. He knew he wouldn't be able to go back to sleep for a while. He decided to go for a walk and hopefully the feeling would go away. He didn't want to let everyone know how worried he was about their chances of surviving the coming battle. He stood on the porch and looked around. Everything was quiet and settled down for the night, just as it should be. He sighed and thought, *Our chances of surviving this battle are really low. Even with Bert's supplies.*

The demolition expert arrived right on time. Bert handed over the C-4 and blasting caps. Bert was training Mark and Eric how to use the machine guns. They would be using them in the upcoming battle. Bert said, "After you both master using the machine gun, then we'll train a few more men how to reload and use them, too. If either one of you are hit or killed, the next man behind you has to know how to take over." They had been preparing and practicing for two days. As Bert was demonstrating how to reload, word reached them that four of the scouts were back. They put everything away and went over to the cabin to meet the scouts. Lonnie was already waiting for them. They went inside and Bert said, "Report."

Lonnie said, "My team observed the main army. It took over an hour for the five thousand men to march by. Most of the officers were riding horses. They have the 105s mounted on the back of two five-ton trucks with tarps over them, with trucks close by loaded with ammo for the 105s. They have two semi-trucks following them with their supplies. They also have a five thousand gallon fuel truck with the semis. The soldiers are all carrying rifles and standard battle load in vests. It looks like one of the semis carries extra ammo so they don't have to. I observed them getting food supplies out of one of the semi's also. They seemed to be pretty disciplined troops, too. They followed orders and march like they know what they're doing. They're burning all buildings they see. They should be here tomorrow in the early afternoon." Mark and Eric shared an intense look.

Bert said, "Well, we'd better send word to Redding. The battle starts tomorrow." Bert looked at Eric. "You will take the Lieutenant and his men in the valley I showed you. Remember, you need to kill any scouts you see silently. Don't disable the vehicles, just kill the drivers and guards." That evening, the Lieutenant and one hundred men arrived. The Lieutenant was smiling. "I have a surprise for you. We have a qualified 105 team with us. If we capture their guns, we can give them a taste of their own medicine."

"Good news," Eric said, smiling, "Maybe with the grace of God, we can win. Okay, I'll show you the valley we're spending the night in. No fires, no tents, hidden all the way."

"Of course," said the Lieutenant.

The demolition expert picked the spots, two and a half miles apart. The most important thing was at the rear to cut them off from the big guns and supplies. He would be in charge of blowing this section. Bert would be in charge of the front C-4. A back-up plan was in place in case they were getting overrun. It should take out the 105s. Same in front, just in case they change things around and put their big guns up front. The Colonel was not able to get all his men up on top. The twenty men that did make it were to scout the area and report back. The waiting was putting everyone on edge. The tension was building and everyone was thinking, *we need more time. But the enemy was advancing. The plan was in motion. There was no time to change plans now. We have to make this work.*

The Colonel and the Major had a private meeting. "What do you think our chances are, Major?"

"If everything works, we should be in good shape. If their scouts don't see the one hundred man rear team. If the demolition expert is right. If the rock and landslides close off the road. If our ammo holds outs. If the little training we've done with the troops is enough. If God is on our side, we just might be able to pull this off." The Colonel smiled. "That's one heck of a lot of ifs in that assessment, Major. I don't like ifs. But for what little we have and no support artillery, or helicopters and tanks, we just might have a chance."

The scouts returned. "The mountain pass was rough in the dark. It was too dangerous to move an Army up. We have to wait until first light. There are areas we won't be able to reach, but due to the curve in the road, we should be able to cover ninety percent. Some pretty long shots. Eight hundred yards or better."

"Thank you," replied the Major. The scouts left to eat and get some rest.

The Colonel asked, "What do we have that a long-range sniper could make that shot with?"

"We have about twenty-five men that are qualified snipers that could do it. I'll have to set them up in the morning," the Major replied. That night the tension really built up. Sleep was not restful as the cool night set in. Before daybreak, the men were woken up, fed, and at first light, they were on their way.

Eric saw the scouts coming. The crossbow teams were instructed to time their shots; four crossbow bolts fire at the same time. When the scouts were thirty yards from the ambush site, Eric signaled the men to fire. Both were hit. One died instantly with a head shot. The second scout was only wounded with two bolts sticking out of his chest. He stood there in frozen animation, not sure what happened. He felt the pain, but was more stunned and wondered where they had come from. He tried to grab the sling off his shoulder to bring his AK into the battle. He heard another strange thunk noise, but before he could figure it out another bolt ripped through his throat. He was dead before he hit the ground. Four men raced up, making sure they were dead. Then they grabbed them and pulled them under some downed brush, stripping them of weapons and ammo.

Just then they heard a radio. "Scout team report." There was eerie silence suddenly in the valley. Everyone strained their eyes to find the source. "Scout team report." Lonnie ran over to the bodies and listened. "Scout team report," there was a radio on one of the vests, so he pulled it out. Only one radio for two scouts was not very smart. He handed it to the Lieutenant. *God, he wished he could be in contact with his command.*

He asked, "Lonnie, how do their scout teams work?"

"Normally we saw two on each side of the road, about mile up in front of the main column."

The Lieutenant looked at the sun and judged that it was an hour after daylight. They were moving faster than we thought. The main force will be here in an hour. He said, "Lonnie, take two men and go warn the demo team the guests are coming early."

The colonel was on top and finally got all his men into position. *This would take days to set up properly. No time to worry about that now.* "Spread the men the best you can. Find the dead spots, set up the snipers. Get the guys with the grenades in the right spots. Make it fast, then back off out of sight." The Colonel was studying the terrain. *Who knows the terrain the best will win this fight,* he thought. He sent his youngest, strongest men to the front. They had to cover the two and a half miles and spread out. Eight hundred men sounded like a lot, but spread out over two and half miles was barely adequate. He had barely spread his men across the top of the trap when he looked and saw the army coming. It was only 9:30 am. *Damn, they're early.* A runner had been set up to be at his side with a red rag, to run along to all troops, that meant get back out of sight.

****

"Sir, we lost comms with scout team two for the last hour." His men were laughing as they burned the cabin. "That puts them in this area."

The General was in a good mood. They had marched forward with his massive Rainbow Warriors cleansing the earth of evil meat-eaters. *Soon the planet would be at peace,* he thought. He said out loud, "Send out another team to look for them. I bet they're in a valley and just out of radio range."

"But sir, they have orders to report back if they lose contact for more than an hour."

"Send out a team. We move forward. I want to be out of this pass before too long." *Missing scouts. Nothing to worry about. We will march forward and nothing can stop us. Not even that little militia unit back a ways could slow them down.* He smiled and ordered the men to keep marching. They entered the trap zone.

****

Within an hour, they would be trapped. If all goes according to plan.

The new scouts were getting close to where Eric and his team waited. They could hear the army marching past. They could smell the smoke from the cabin fire. The tension was building. The enemy scouts were on alert, but they were too arrogant. They were walking like cows in the woods. You could hear them coming long before you ever saw them. They stopped at the kill sight.

Seeing the fresh blood, the lead scout bent down and touched the wet grass. "Blood," he said. He stood up, hit the radio button to report, but never got the chance. A crossbow bolt hit him in the head. He felt his partner duck and was hit with only one bolt. The other deflected off a branch. But a critical mistake happened. His partner had the radio. He lay on the ground, twenty feet away from the radio. He had his rifle out. His left arm was bleeding where the bolt ripped clean through. He guessed the ambush came from the brush pile in front of him. He started pouring lead. Eric saw this and fired a single shot from his borrowed AR-15, hitting the man in the head.

****

The army kept marching. They were down in the valley. That must have muffled the noise. The First Lieutenant rode up. The comms guy said to the First Lieutenant, "Sir, we lost comms." He turned to the General. "Sir. Something is wrong. The second scout team is not reporting."

The General said, "Lieutenant, scouts are expendable. They probably found some hippie girls and they're having a good time. Just relax. We've had no resistance in what, four days? Let's get off this mountain, then we can get all the scouts' reports on the bottom, when we know the radios will work for sure."

****

The three men hiding in the drainage culvert were slowly going crazy as the army marched above them. An hour is long time for them to sit still. Slowly the time clicked on by. It was time to set off the first blast to signal everyone else that the battle had begun. The demolition expert crawled out from the culvert. He sat down, planning to watch his masterpiece rock slide take out the rear troops. He smiled. *Let the fun begin*, he thought. Holding the twist plunger in his hand, he peeked up over the top. Perfect. The main body was caught in the trap. He never saw the guard who shot him in the back. He fell down in the ditch, trying to twist the handle to make the explosion go off. The whole plan was based on him setting off the first explosion. His world was becoming dark. He thought, *Why won't my hand turn?* He heard someone running his way and some shouts as his awareness faded out.

Chapter 36

A Hell Of A Way To Start The Morning

"Leaders are visionaries with a poorly developed sense of fear and no concept of the odds against them."

Robert Jarvik

Joe and Jane exchanged an apprehensive look. They quietly got off the bikes they had ridden and leaned them against the side of the barn. They looked all around, scrutinizing every detail. Everything had a rundown, abandoned look to it. Their neighbors, Jim and Marge, should have been out working in the fields, or at least the garden. The garden along the left side of the house looked neglected and overgrown. That wasn't like Marge at all. As Jane looked around, she got a chill along her spine. Something was very wrong here. Jane had her 22-250 on a sling over her shoulder. She pulled it upwards and held it just a little bit tighter to be ready to fire if it became necessary. Joe leaned close to her ear and whispered softly, "I have a bad feeling about this. Let's be real careful-like."

They circled around, using whatever they could for cover on their way to the front porch. When they reached it, they both stayed low and quickly made their way up the stairs to the front door. They exchanged another look. Jane nodded her head once, signaling that she was ready. Joe had his back against the house as he reached over to the side and gently opened up the storm door as quietly as he could. He stayed out of the doorway. He put his foot out to the side to hold the storm door open. As he reached for the door handle, he saw that the door wasn't all the way closed. His bad feeling intensified. He signaled to Jane that he was going inside. She acknowledged the signal and prepared to follow. The scent of death was everywhere. Joe shoved the door open and quickly stepped inside. He turned to the left. Jane was right behind him and she turned to the right after stepping through the door, still crouched down. The room was empty. Joe led the way and they searched the house, staying close to the walls in case someone was inside and armed. Someone had clearly ransacked the place.

Together they reached the last bedroom in the hallway. The dead bodies would be in there, because all the other rooms had been empty of anyone or anything, dead or alive. The smell was strongest here. The only sound that could be heard was the buzz of hundreds of flies in the otherwise silent house. They exchanged a look and Joe signaled he was going in. Jane nodded her head. The bedroom door was already open wide, so all they had to do was rush in and hope they didn't get shot. Joe took a step sideways to line up with the door and then rushed into the room, ready to fire his AR-15. He stopped abruptly after taking two steps inside the bedroom.

Jane ran into his back and almost knocked both of them down when he stopped so abruptly. Jane muttered quietly, "What the hell?" She tried to keep her balance and did some fancy footwork to step over to the side.

When she looked up after regaining her balance her whole body went rigid in shock. Blood was everywhere. It was splattered all over the walls and even the ceiling. There were two adult-sized bodies lying on the blood-soaked bed, decaying with maggots, worms and flies all over them. The buzz of the flies was very loud in the silence. The look and smell was overwhelming, making her gag. She turned and ran out of the room, holding her hand over her nose and mouth. She didn't stop until she was outside and then retched up everything in her stomach and dry heaved for a few minutes. Joe had followed her outside to protect her, in case someone was still around when she would be in the vulnerable position of throwing up. When she was done, Joe handed her a canteen filled with water to rinse her mouth out. She reached for the canteen with a badly shaking hand. She hoarsely whispered, "Thank you." Joe patted her back in comfort. She rinsed her mouth and spit the water out on the ground. "I'm sorry. It was just such a shock seeing them like that."

He said, "I know. No one is ever ready to see something like that." He took the canteen from her and clipped it back on his belt. He handed her a one ounce plastic bottle she'd made up for everyone to carry that had mentholated vapor rub in it. She spread some all around the bottom of her nose and above her lip. It helped to handle the smell of decaying bodies. Unfortunately, it was a fact of life now to run into one from time to time. But this, this was something else entirely. Those two bodies had been horribly butchered. It definitely wasn't something you saw everyday.

When Jane was more composed, she said, "I'm all right now. We have to burn the bodies. It's the least we could do for them."

Joe said, "If you would rather go home, I can get Preston to come back with me. You don't have to stay here and help."

She shook her head. "No, I'll help you. You shouldn't have to do this, either." She sighed and thought about the good times they had with their neighbors, Jim and Marge. They hadn't deserved to die like this. A few other neighbors down the way had mentioned this morning that no one had seen them for over a month. She and Joe decided to see if they were sick or in need of help. As soon as they'd seen the place, they knew something wasn't right. They'd obviously been dead for a few weeks. Who could have done this? That's what she wanted to know. Who would have destroyed the kitchen and thrown flour, corn meal, rice and oatmeal all over the floor? Who would waste food like that? She turned to Joe and said in a hard voice, "They didn't deserve to die like that."

Joe sighed. "No, they didn't deserve that. Well, let's get started. It's going to be a very long day." They turned around and headed back into the house.

It was late in the evening when Jane and Joe returned to their homestead. They both had heavy hearts and had spent the day trying to make sense of the horrible violence of their friend's deaths. The clues left behind by their killers were unmistakable. Both of their heads were still reeling from shock and horror after piecing together the evidence to tell them what had taken place in that farm house five miles down the road. It was a nightmare. They still didn't want to believe what the evidence plainly said. Joe radioed Steve ,who would be on watch up in the loft, that they were a quarter mile from the front gate, driving an old red Ford pickup. Preston and Amy came running out of the house in full battle gear after hearing Joe's tone of voice over the radio. Something was very wrong. Joe didn't sound like himself at all, and he was driving a pickup truck? Amy raced behind the sandbags and covered Preston with her 22-250 as he jogged along the driveway up to the front gate. Joe and Jane had been gone a long time today. Preston, Amy and the rest of them had figured that the neighbors, Jim and Marge, must have needed some help. Now, they weren't sure if their conclusions had been right at all. A few more minutes and the red pickup came into view.

Preston looked to see if someone was following them. Everything around them looked okay. They didn't look like either of them were hurt or anything. Both of them looked pretty done in, though, like it had been a very rough, stressful day. Preston opened the gate and let them inside. As they passed by Amy, she could smell a lot of wood smoke and knew death had probably been involved. She sighed, and hoped their neighbors had been all right, although them driving the pickup was not a good sign that all had been well.

Preston asked, "Joe, are you all right? Did Jim lend you his truck? What's the matter?"

Joe glanced over at Jane, then said, "Not right now.'" He looked over at Amy to include her. "They were dead. We'll tell you about it later. Now, can you two bring this stuff inside?" He didn't wait for them to answer. "I'll park by the back door and we'll join you inside later."

Preston and Amy exchanged a concerned look and then he said, "Sure, no problem, Joe." Jane didn't even look their way. They followed the truck around back and Joe and Jane got out. They walked to the back of the truck and Joe pulled out the bikes. They took them and disappeared into the barn.

Preston said, "It must have been very bad over there."

Amy said, "Well, we'll find out later. Let's get this stuff in the house."

A little while later Jane leaned her hip against the sink with her arms crossed in front of her, still staring down the empty hallway, lost in thought. Whatever she was thinking wasn't good, because she had a very sad, haunted look about her. Amy walked over and gave her a big hug.

Jane pulled back after a few minutes and had tears in her eyes. "Thanks, I needed that."

Amy smiled. "Anytime." Joe and Jane exchanged an uneasy look, showing how uncomfortable they were discussing this. Steve set his radio on the table and pressed the send button, so John up in the barn loft could hear what they were discussing. They did this all the time so that the person on watch would know what was going on and they wouldn't have to waste a lot of time repeating everything to the person on watch. If something happened and John needed to tell them something, he'd signal by pushing the talk button twice, so they'd know to listen and shut up.

Joe sighed. "It is a bit unbelievable. You'll want to deny what we're going to say tonight, but it's the absolute truth." Everyone shared an uneasy look and wondered what could have happened.

Jane said, "When we got over to Marge and Jim's, everything had a rundown, abandoned look. Even the garden had been neglected, with a lot of dead plants and weeds. The grass in front and on the sides of the house was pretty tall from all the rain we had earlier. You could tell no one had been going in and out of the house much in the last few weeks."

Jane hesitated and glanced over at Joe. He took over. "We left the bikes leaning up against the far side of the barn, hidden in the tall brush, and cautiously made our way up to the front door. When we got there, I noticed the inside door wasn't all the way closed. Only the storm door was shut, and it shuts automatically." He stopped and looked at Jane. He took her hand and held it tightly. "We could smell the scent of death from the front door. When we got inside, we searched the house from room to room. Someone had ransacked the place and thrown a lot of stuff around each room. It didn't look like they were looking for anything. It just looked like someone wanted to make a mess and break things." He stopped for a few seconds and took a sip of his coffee, then cleared his throat. "The house was clear until we got to their bedroom. They both died in their bed. They had been dead for a few weeks at least." Everyone waited tensely for him to continue sharing their experience.

Amy was thinking that what had spooked Joe and Jane so much was their friends had probably taken poison together or something, not being able to cope with this new world. It was sad, but it was also a fact of life now. But that didn't explain the mess and broken things in the other rooms, or the reason Joe said it was unbelievable what had happened to them.

Maybe one of them killed the other and then committed suicide? Must be something like that.

Preston was thinking that these deaths had hit them hard because Joe and Jane had known them for a long time and considered them close friends.

Vicki was upset that they lost some friends like she had, and knew how rotten it made you feel when you survived and they didn't.

Steve had only met the neighbors once, and didn't know them very well. He was sorry they were dead, but felt pretty distant from feeling any real grief. In this new world they lived in, you either got over things fast or it would drive you crazy. Death was everywhere.

Amy looked around at everyone; it seemed no one else wanted to broach the subject, so she took a deep breath and asked, "Why is that unbelievable? What else happened that you haven't shared?" Joe and Jane exchanged another look that was hard to interpret.

Joe looked each one of them intently in the eyes. Everyone unconsciously leaned back slightly, away from the look in his eyes and the horror they could feel coming off him in disturbing waves. They had never seen Joe react like this before. Not even when they had faced overwhelming odds and their chance of survival was slim. Whatever he was going to say was going to be bad, very bad. They braced themselves for a new threat that was going turn their world upside down once again. Preston found himself pulling Amy closer, as if to protect and shield her from this new threat. The look in Joe's eyes told him it was something absolutely horrible. Preston's whole body tensed as he prepared himself mentally and emotionally for whatever was coming.

Joe finally broke the silence. "They were asleep in their bed when they were attacked and killed. Both Jim and Marge had a loaded rifle on each side of the bed within reach, and Jim had a 9mm in the bedside table drawer. As far as we can tell, neither one of them had a chance to even reach for them." He paused for a few moments and squeezed his eyes tightly shut, like he was trying to shut out the memory of what he had seen. Everyone winced and waited, holding their breath for what he'd say next. He cleared his throat and said in a tightly controlled, even voice, "There was blood splattered all over the bedroom walls, even the ceiling. Their mattress and sheets were soaked. They bled so much that the blood dripped down through the mattress, onto the carpet underneath into a large puddle. Stab wounds shredded most of their stomachs and major organs. There were so many stab wounds we couldn't count them all." Everyone gasped in shock and didn't know quite what to do. They weren't expecting that.

Preston yelled out a startled, "What?"

Amy looked horrified and looked around at everyone, then said urgently in a pleading voice to Joe, "Please don't tell us we have a serial killer out there."

Jane said softly, nodding her head, "We do. And that isn't the most horrifying thing, either."

Joe and Jane exchanged a hopeless, disturbed look. Jane hung her head down, and stared at something they couldn't even imagine, let alone try to understand. But whatever it was, they were glad they couldn't see it. Everyone waited in horrible agony. Jane took a deep breath and said in an even softer voice, almost whispering, "It was children."

Everyone looked around at each other, blinking in confusion, like they couldn't have heard her right. They leaned forward a little closer so they could hear better. Steve said in a voice filled with disbelief, shaking his head, "I couldn't have heard what I thought you said. Would you please repeat that?"

Jane said very clearly and distinctly, in a louder voice, still staring at the table, "I said, children killed them."

For one second, there was complete silence. Vicki started crying softly. Steve finally noticed this and went over and wrapped his arms around her, offering some comfort to this dreadful news. The new world had struck once again and turned everything they knew upside down. Nothing was the same. Every time they turned around, some new horrible thing was happening. It was amazing how easily humans had turned back into barbaric savages. It was almost like there had never been a modern society at all. Maybe there really hadn't been, and everyone had just fooled themselves.

Amy and Preston started asking questions and Joe and Jane filled them in on the details of what they'd found. Joe said, "There were seven different children-sized bloody footprints and hand prints leading out of the bedroom and all over the house. We also found seven sharp kitchen knives dropped on the floor of the bedroom. The largest footprints looked like they belonged to a ten-year-old, and the youngest looked to be around five or six."

"After seeing the footprints, hand prints and knives," said Jane, "we realized what they meant and the wasted food in the kitchen made more sense. They didn't know how to cook it, so it wasn't really food to them."

Joe said, "We think what happened was that one or two of the children, probably some of the younger ones who looked cute, was sent up to the house, saying they were lost or hungry. Anyone with a heart would have taken them in to feed them and clean them up. Then, in the middle of the night, when the adults were asleep, they'd open the door up and let the rest of the group inside."

Jane said after a minute of silence, "Marge would have been very susceptible to a child in need of anything. She couldn't have children."

Vicki asked horrified, "What could have happened to those children to make them do such an awful thing?"

Amy said, "Who knows? It could be they were abandoned, or their parents died from disease, or were killed, or any number of things could have warped their minds. But what they did shows they no longer trust any adults, no matter how nice or kind they are." Everyone nodded.

No one saw any children over there," said Joe, "or it would have been mentioned in the gossip. That means they did this, took what they wanted, and left quickly before anyone could discover them."

Preston nodded. "That brings up some pretty disturbing questions. It means they've done this before."

Vicki said sadly, "Children who are demented serial killers. One more thing to add to the list of grievances against the people who caused all of this." Everyone nodded in agreement. The discussion broke up a little while later. There really wasn't anything else to say. They prepared for bed with heavy hearts over this disturbing new revelation and waited for sleep to claim them.

This was a brave new world they lived in, and the weak and the young got chewed up and spit out if they didn't have the fortitude to handle it.

Every day there were groups of people along the highway heading south or southwest. Some of the people came down the country road where the farmstead was. Preston and Joe offered clean, safe, filtered rainwater to drink in exchange for information about the army. They all had the same story; a huge army was coming this way and they were running for their lives. None of them had any real information, though. Just rumors that the army was burning everything to the ground and killing anyone that didn't worship their animal god. Some claimed to have seen this army, and then as they moved away, seen huge fires burning in the evenings that could have been small towns. These people had circled out around the army to avoid them. It was rumored that those caught fleeing were shot. They even killed the children. Joe and Preston kept questioning people when they could about eyewitness accounts. So far, none had actually seen it, only been warned by others fleeing the north.

They had many discussions around the kitchen table in the evenings. They had reinforced everything they could and prepared for a battle. Joe said, "Even if there is no army coming, which could be the case, it won't hurt us to be more prepared. It never hurts to prepare for the worst and hope for the best." So, everyone was on alert. Then three days went by. There were only a few people hurrying down the road. They offered clean, filtered water to two men for information, and they said that the army had turned back to the Twin Cities and that nothing was coming this way except some people heading south. That's what they were doing. They hoped to find some place to work for food and shelter where it was warmer. The next day, they didn't see anyone coming down the road.

There were a few minor things left to do at the 'Last Chance' to get it ready as their fall back place. Michael volunteered to go stay out there for a few days and finish it up. He was eleven now and thought he was capable of staying by himself out there. Jane and Amy were reluctant to agree to this. Joe and Preston thought it was a good idea and talked the women into it. The men promised to check on him often to alleviate their fears.

Steve had the 2:00 am to 6:00 am watch tonight. The rainstorm was going full speed ahead and there was no sign it was going to slow down any time soon. It looked like the world had been transported inside a black hole; even the night vision couldn't see very far. The wind was howling so loud a marching band could be going by outside and he wouldn't be able to hear it. The flashes of lightning would blind him for a few moments and make it impossible to see anything with the night vision. All he could see was flashes of trees and leaves being blown around, leaving behind the uneasy impression of a scene out of a low budget horror movie. Sometimes he could swear he saw people and things moving out there, but he also knew it was his eyes playing tricks on him. He had to constantly restrain himself from calling out an alert over the radio. They would forever tease him if he did that and it turned out to just be the storm. He'd never live that one down. This whole night was making him jittery; he jumped at shadows and any little sound after the flashes of lightning and crack of thunder. He wouldn't have been surprised to see Eric, the sheriff from HBO's *True Blood*, hanging outside the window trying to trick him into getting inside. He smiled to himself and shook his head. Wow, he was really losing it. He involuntary glanced at his watch to make sure daybreak was coming soon. He caught himself and chuckled. He must be more tired than he'd thought, to be thinking of nightmarish things like this and being reassured by the sun rising to save him from monsters. As if the world wasn't already a horrible enough place to live in. He poured himself a cup of coffee to help ease his jitters. Lightning flashed and then a few seconds later, thunder boomed really loud; the sound rolled around, echoing through the trees. He looked around with nervous eyes, then jumped suddenly and squealed out a cry of surprise, spilling his coffee, when he saw someone looming in the doorway to the loft.

John was jerked awake by the sound of thunder booming nearby. He glanced up at the clock and saw that it was a little after 4:00 AM. He turned over and tried to go back to sleep, he had the 6:00 am to 10:00 am watch this morning and he was still tired. Every time he was just drifting off to sleep, thunder would boom again, waking him up. After ten minutes, he finally threw back the covers, and with a feeling of irritation and got up. The thunder wasn't going to let him get back to sleep anytime soon, so he might as well be up. He yawned and walked over to the window to look out at the storm. He couldn't see anything, it was pitch black outside. If he couldn't hear the wind driving the rain against the side of the trailer, he wouldn't even had known it was raining outside. Hopefully it would stop soon. He might as well go up to the loft and visit with Steve until his watch shift started. It was boring to just sit around and wait for the time to pass.

Vicki was woken up by the sound of thunder as it boomed outside. She looked at the clock and it said 3:10. She lay in bed for a while, trying to slow her breathing to settle down her heartbeat. She had woken up with her heart pounding and feeling scared. She had always hated thunderstorms. The display of power they showed was truly frightening. She had been terrified of thunderstorms from as far back as she could remember. She finally decided to get up and do something to take her mind off the storm. She got dressed, went into the kitchen, and stirred up the fire in the cook stove.

Vicki stood in the doorway to the loft. "I couldn't sleep, so I came over to be with you." Vicki sat down. She was in no hurry to go back to the house and sit alone until the others got up.

A little while later, Vicki poured them all a fresh cup of coffee. Steve looked out the window on the east side to watch the sky start to lighten. Well, his watch would be over soon. It seemed like this night had lasted a couple of days. He was glad that Vicki and John were here with him. He moved his shoulders around to help loosen his stiff, tensed muscles, then reached for his coffee cup. As he took a sip, he glanced out the west side window. The coffee cup dropped unnoticed out of his hand, splashing hot coffee all over his legs and he grabbed his radio as fast as he could, glancing out the east window as he did. He pressed the talk button and started yelling, "Oh my God, we're surrounded by an army!"

Rainbow Warriors had surrounded the farmstead in the dead of night. They used the storm to cover the noise of the army moving into position. There were thousands of them against one lonely farmstead out in the middle of nowhere. These Eco Nazi, Rainbow Warriors were battle-hardened and had the scars to prove it. They looked ragged and worn. Whatever they had faced on their way here had left its mark. It was evidence that not everyone had joined their animal-worshiping cult. The evidence also showed that those battles had extracted a very high price. The men were dirty, hungry and their uniforms were ragged and torn. Except for the officers. The officers looked like they were in a little better shape. The officers also rode horses and didn't have to walk as the other men did.

Joe started issuing orders as soon as he heard Steve's report of being surrounded. The three of them in the loft hurried over to the shooting holes and got ready for the fight of their lives. Their hearts were pounding hard in their chests, flooding them with adrenaline. Vicki had worn her battle vest and carried her rifle with her up to the loft because they were on alert status. They all got ready for the coming battle by placing magazines and other paraphernalia within easy reach. The three of them watched the sun slowly rise filling the early morning sky with dazzling reds, yellows and orange starkly illuminating the ugly side of humanity right outside their door. Now, they waited for the signal to start shooting. It was a hell of a way to start the morning.

The Rainbow Warriors numbered in the thousands and demanded they surrender the farm and any and all supplies they had. They were to walk outside with their hands on their heads. A primal response arose inside Preston and demanded they fight to the death. "Give up our supplies," he growled deep in his chest, "When hell freezes over." He grabbed the radio pushing the button down as he brought it up to speak. "Everyone listen up, this is going to be down right bloody, nasty and brutal. We have no choice except to fight to the death. We are the Alamo and must kill every single one of them. There are no other options. Shoot them, wound them, stab them with your knife. Hell, use a battle ax for all I care, just kill every single one of them. There isn't time to hesitate or all will be lost. People, we go down fighting to our very last breath." He released the button and turned towards Joe.

"You have anything to add?"

Joe shook his head no.

"So, what's the plan?"

"We kill them all."

Preston grinned. "This is going to be a real pleasure."

"You and Amy go upstairs. Take out the asshole that's yelling for us to surrender."

He and Amy headed upstairs. They shared an intense look in the hallway before going to opposite rooms. There wasn't anything left to say that already hadn't been said. They each went to their shooting holes and got ready for the coming battle.

Joe and Jane went to their shooting holes on the ground level and got everything laid out for quick reloading of their weapons. They waited for Preston to start the battle. That was the signal for the rest of them to start shooting their targets. The first targets were anyone giving orders.

Preston had grabbed the M1 Garand 30-06 and carried it with his AR-15 upstairs. He laid his AR-15 down next to him and picked up the 30-06. He loaded it with 150-grain corelock soft points. He held the barrel inside the room so no one outside would know where the shots were coming from. He steadied his aim. It was time to put the fear of God into these scumbags. The shot rang out ripping through the bullhorn into the leader's face. The man was dead before he hit the ground. He continued to fire with deadly precision in a hail of bullets at the slow reacting enemy. He heard everyone else start firing at these Nazi's too. He was angry beyond belief. Who in the hell did they think they were to come here and tell them what to do? The clip fell out of the gun locking the breach open. He was out of bullets. He tossed that rifle aside and picked up his AR-15 shooting at anyone that dared to show a body part. The Rainbow Warriors opened up firing at the house and barn. They had no where to concentrate their fire power on because they couldn't see where the bullets were coming from so they just starting shooting at the windows, doors of the house and at the barn. All the preparations they had made were paying off. The enemy was directing their fire power where none of them were. He saw the enemy start to pull back. He grabbed his radio. "Show them no mercy. Shoot them in the back as they run and hide."

When there was no one left to shoot at he felt the heat radiating off his barrel. He looked down. There were ten empty magazines on the floor. He kicked them over to the side out of the way. He still had ten full magazines left for their next assault. He picked up the radio. "Anyone hit?"

"No." They all replied.

The house was in shambles. There were hundred's of bullet holes that had ripped through the siding, windows and doors. It looked like the house was in the middle of a war zone. Several minutes passed in silence. Everyone waited patiently for what was going to happen next.

Joe looked out the hole. "Shit." He grabbed the radio. "About fifty are trying a rear assault. Stand by." When they had gotten passed a red ribbon flapping in the wind Joe said into the radio. "They are under the wire. I repeat. They are under the wire." Just as he said this a new assault started in the front at the same time. It was a more coordinated and thought out assault this time. They were using cover fire for advancement.

Steve in the barn had been waiting for that call over the radio. He yanked down hard on a paracord attached to a stick. Twenty-five three quarter inch steel pipes were loaded with three inch triple ought buckshot. Each pipe had fifteen point thirty-three caliber round balls inside. Three hundred seventy five point thirty-three caliber balls fanned out into a deadly wall of lead. It had been well camouflaged in the bed of an old truck that the bad guys had planned to use for cover.

The three quarter inch steel pipes rested against a steel plate with a hole drilled for each shell with a cut down nail that was the firing pin. Behind the cut down nails was a spring holding back another steel plate. Pulling the paracord allowed the back steel plate to slam against the firing pins in a deafening roar as all twenty five pipes fired at the same time. To say it was devastating was an under statement.

The group of about fifty charging from the back was totally surprised by this unseen defense they ran straight into. Over half laid dead on the ground and another ten were seriously wounded. Those that were left turned to run away and were cut down by Joe and John. More bodies fell to the ground and didn't move again.

The group in the front assault were gaining ground but they made a critical mistake trying to take this farmhouse with a straight on frontal assault. When six men in the lead were at the precise spot Preston yelled into the radio. "Now, Amy." She yanked on a paracord and the four inch homemade pipe cannon's poured a ten foot wide deadly wall of grapeshot.

Hell rained down on the bad guys. Needless to say, they were all cut to pieces. A few wounded tried to get away and she cut them down.

On the left side of the farmhouse were most of the enemy were they tried an assault there too. Twenty to thirty men were using the covering fire to get close to the farmhouse. Preston waited until most of them were in the exact spot that would take them out. He yanked the paracord. Another twenty-five three quarter inch steel pipes went off with deadly results.

All three attacks happened and were stopped within a few minutes of each other. As soon as the enemy heard the homemade defenses go off they all started pouring lead again into the farmhouse and barn. This time they didn't concentrate their fire on the windows and doors. Bullets were flying all over the place in the house and barn. John said into the radio with a voice thick with emotion. "My best friend is dead." Before anyone could say anything in response to that sad news, Jane yelled into her radio. "I'm hit." Joe immediately went to her. She had been shot in her upper right arm. Joe looked her arm and shoulder over and picked up the radio. "She took one in the upper arm by her shoulder. I'm taking her to the basement to take care of the wound." The basement had no windows and was safer with the thick rock foundation and walls.

Preston said angrily into the radio. "Amy. Ground floor now. Back side. It's just you and me kid. Make every shot count." Amy and Preston hurried as fast as they could to get down to the ground floor and defend it. It was dangerous going because bullets were still flying all around inside the farmhouse. After a few more minutes the firing on the farmhouse and barn stopped. Now, they all could hear men crying and moaning on the battlefield. Some were praying for someone to come save them. They were eerie, lonely cries of pain and misery. One guy was screaming. Preston said into the radio. "John, put that screaming POS out of his misery." He heard one shot and the screaming stopped. He had been worried that no one would answer his call from the barn. He sighed in relief.

They had retreated back but, who knows what was going on inside their heads? He looked around carefully. Three assaults had been repelled. *Are these guys stupid or what? They lost close to one hundred fifty men in a matter of minutes. Bet they weren't expecting that.*

Preston lifted his radio. "Amy, I need you to check all sides. You're my eyes. I am going down to check on Jane."

"Roger."

Preston ran down the basement stairs as fast as he could. Joe was putting a battle dressing on her shoulder. He looked up at Preston with blood trickling down his face from broken glass.

"The bullet ripped all the way through, but luckily missed the bones." Preston nodded and hurried back upstairs.

Before Preston could get back into position Amy's voice came out of the radio.

"Oh my God, they have a big gun. A really big gun."

John up in the barn pushed down the button on his radio.

"Artillery gun moving into position."

Preston hurried back to the basement stairs and yelled down to Joe. "Time to go buddy."

Joe looked at Jane then back up at Preston.

"Get Amy out of here."

"No. You are coming with us. I'm not leaving you."

John on the radio yelled out. "Their loading it. What do I do?"

Joe raised his radio up and yelled. "Last chance, last chance. Go, go, go."

Preston looked intently into Joe's eyes. Joe said.

"Go. Leave now."

Preston turned away with a heavy heart. He pulled his radio up and yelled.

"Amy, out the back door now. Move it!"

Preston met up with Amy by the back door. Amy looked questioningly at him. He shook his head no.

Amy said panicky. "We can't leave them. No, I won't." He stood rigid with anger in his eyes. He reached out and pushed her roughly out the door.

"You will. Go, now. Or I will drag you." His two best friends stayed behind so he could save her and by God, that was exactly what he was going to do.

They used what cover they could and made their way to the woods dodging bullets. One skimmed along Preston's arm leaving behind a bloody depression and he didn't even notice. An artillery round went off. They just kept going. He was so mad at Joe. Making him leave them behind like that. Joe had known he had to get to Amy and get her out of there. She depended on him. Just as they reached the woods an explosion knocked them off their feet. They looked back and the farmhouse was gone. Before they could stand up again the barn disappeared into a pile of rubble and noise. They put their arms over their heads to protect them from falling debris. After a few moments Preston jumped up and grabbed Amy.

"Go. They will be coming."

They took off running down a deer trail. Two guys stepped out and Preston cut them down and never slowed. On the left a guy appeared and Amy shot him and kept on going. She had tears running down her face and didn't even realize it. They jumped down into the ditch. He pulled Amy close. They both were breathing hard.

"Are you hit"

"No. I got this when the explosion knocked us off our feet." Preston looked down where she was indicating and saw a small branch embedded into her left thigh. He pulled his knife out and cut it down so only a couple inches stuck out of her leg.

They waited for five minutes then had to leave because a group of guys were coming their way. They hadn't seen any sign of anyone else making it out. The ditch was their meet up place. They traveled the ditch down to the deer trail that would take them to the Last Chance. They didn't run into anyone else so far.

A little over an hour later they made it to the Last Chance. It was so well hidden. They built it right into the hill. If you didn't know where to look you would go right by it and not know it. Michael peeked out the door with a anxious look on his face. Preston and Amy looked bloody, dirty, tattered and worn.

"Where is everyone?"

They went into the little cabin. Amy hugged Michael to her and whispered hoarsely.

"We're all that made it." Michael and Amy both had tears running down their faces. Michael asked.

"What do we do now?" Preston angrily answered.

"We survive. Then we build an army of our own and destroy those evil bastards."

Chapter 37

Indian Guardian Spirit

"In this world a man must be either an anvil or hammer."
Henry Wadsworth Longfellow

Clint and Junior shared an intense look after Clint had said, "I don't think we can get away." Junior looked around quickly, evaluating everything in their sight. He smiled and turned to Clint, signaling, 'Follow me.' Clint nodded, then leaned up a little and fired at the men running after them. The men all dived to the ground, trying to dodge the bullets. Clint crawled behind Junior for a little way, and Junior pointed at a small indent under the bank. Junior stashed his rifle there and Clint did the same. Junior moved some brush in front of it to cover the rifles from sight. Junior entered the water and started to swim to a beaver bank den. When he neared it, he dived down and swam under the water, looking for the opening. He found it and swam up inside of the den. He quickly looked around to make sure there weren't any beavers inside. Clint surfaced a few seconds later. Junior sighed in relief. Beavers could be vicious defending their territory. There was barely enough room for both of them to fit inside. Junior was the closest to the riverbank and was almost out of the water. He maneuvered around so Clint could get out of the water a little more. With both of them being big men, the only way this worked was for them to curl up into almost a fetal position.

They could hear the men coming closer and bullets hitting the water all around them. The enemy was out there yelling and screaming, and a few were trying to give some orders, but the men weren't paying any attention. Now that they were safely inside of the den, Junior noticed how cold the water and air was, but their body heat was quickly warming the den up. They could hear the men running up and down the bank, yelling to each other. One man yelled that he had found them and multiple shots were fired in rapid secession. Clint and Junior shared a grin. The shots being fired were farther down the river than they were.

Another man yelled several times to cease-fire. It took awhile for the men to hear him and stop shooting. A man down farther started yelling that they were being stupid, shooting at shadows. Several more minutes passed, then there was more shouting with excited voices saying that they had found something and the sound of men running down farther on the river. Clint and Junior heard several metallic sounds. They exchanged a look. Both of them knew that they'd found the canoe. A man was yelling, "See? They aren't ghosts. They're real men and they're here somewhere; we're going to find them!" They then heard many shots fired and more metallic clinks. Clint and Junior shared another look. Obviously they had just shot up the canoe and rendered it unusable. A man yelled out loudly, making his voice carry for a long distance, "Spread out and find them. They're here somewhere."

Fifteen minutes passed and they could hear the men going up and down the river. Sometimes they could hear a few shots being fired. A few men stopped on the river, close to the beaver den, talking. A man said quietly, "I don't think that canoe was theirs. It wasn't even wet until it got thrown into the river. It had weeds and bushes growing right next to it and around it."

Another man said softly, "If it wasn't theirs, then where are they?"

Another man said in a whisper, "Maybe they have some guardian spirits here or something and that's why we can't find them; they could be supernatural and not human. They don't want anyone here on their land. There aren't even any houses around here. That, Carl said, should be a clue telling us that no one ever settled around here. The spirits wouldn't allow anyone to be here."

A man scoffed at that idea. "Don't be stupid and listen to that nonsense. That's just plain ridiculous. Indians didn't have playing cards."

The man said back to him in a loud, emotional whisper, "Well, if they are human, then where are they? How come we can't find any footprints, huh? Explain that!"

The man said scornfully, "You're just jumping at shadows and coming up with ridiculous reasons trying to find an explanation. Supernatural! Yeah, right."

Another man whispered thoughtfully, "Maybe it's an Indian spirit that used to gamble." Everyone turned and looked at him, considering what he said.

The disbeliever said, "Enough already. Now, you're just being plain idiots." He turned and stomped off.

There was several seconds of silence, then one of the men said, "Did Indians even know how to gamble?" There were a few moments of silence as the men considered this new angle of reasoning.

One of the men spoke up. "Well, it would only stand to reason that they did know how to gamble."

Silence again for a few moments, and then a man asked, "Why do you think they'd know how to gamble?"

The man whispered loudly, "Well, they hung around the military forts."

A few seconds of silence and a man said, "What does that mean? They hung around the forts."

The man whispered, "The forts were filled with military men. Every military man I ever knew played poker with his buddies. If the Indians hung around, being scouts and such, then they would have learned to gamble, don't you think?"

There was silence for a few moments then a man said excitedly, "Are we stupid or what?" He slapped himself loudly in the forehead.

A few of the men said, "What?"

The man said in a rush, hurrying to get the words out fast, "Duh. Have any of you heard of the Indian Casinos? How can they have casinos if they don't know how to gamble?"

Several men gasped out loud, agreeing with this man. Saying things like, "you're right" and "of course." Then there was silence again.

One man whispered urgently, "We better be careful. Those spirits don't like us being here on their land." There were several sounds of agreement.

A man asked, "How do we protect ourselves from Indian guardian spirits?"

The man that had started this whole debate said, "I asked Carl about that, and he said there wasn't any way to do that unless you're an American Indian, and he didn't know of any Indians in our army that could tell us how. But that might not work either, he said. If you're not an Indian, then you are the enemy."

Several men moaned and cussed for a few minutes. One man said disgustedly, "Great. That's just great. Now we have to worry about vengeful Indian guarding spirits on top of everything else."

Another man said, "Well, I wasn't going to say anything, but now that you brought that up, I've been thinking about something along those lines since we started discussing this subject. What if those Indian guardian spirits thinks we're like, the cavalry, because we're carrying rifles and our leaders are riding horses and we have cannons being pulled by horses, too?"

One man moaned, "We're doomed. We are completely and utterly doomed."

Another man said, "We have to promise to watch each others backs." There were several agreements made and they sounded more upbeat. Several men moved on. Clint and Junior heard them walk off down the river. They were having a very hard time keeping from roaring with laughter.

Then they heard a man whisper, "Amigo, how do we protect each others backs from these spirits? Are bullets going to stop them?"

Another voice said, "I don't think so. I wish they'd let us keep our crosses. I think we'll need the virgin mother to protect us from them."

The other voice said, "Shhhh. Don't say that too loud. Don't ever let them hear you say that. You don't want to know what they'll do to you."

The other voice said, "I just want to go home. I want it to be like it used to be. I know the streets. This shit is some very scary stuff. How do you fight something you can't see?"

The other voice said, "Shhh. Not so loud. Calm down. Don't let them know you're upset."

The other one said, "Then shut up right now. We have to wait until we get more to join us before we take over from these loco assholes."

The other one said, "As soon as we do, I'm having the biggest steak I can find and stuff myself so full I won't be able to move."

The other voice said, "If you keep talking like that you'll get killed. You know how they react to things like that. Now shut up."

The other one said, "I know, I know. I just can't help it sometimes. I don't like it out here. It's creepy. Everything is just so open. No place to hide or be sheltered from the rain or the wind. It's, it's, just unnatural."

The other one said, "Come on. We have to start looking around or they'll see us just standing here." They could hear footsteps going off into the distance. Clint and Junior exchanged a speculative look. Both were thinking of how to exploit those fears into downright terror.

****

It had been about forty-five minutes since they'd entered the beaver den. They could still hear them moving around. Every so often they could hear footsteps coming close to the den as the men passed back and forth. Now they could hear several footsteps coming close again. For some reason, this seemed to be the spot where most of them stopped.

****

One man said, "Whoever they are, they're long gone. I'm hungry. When is it going to be lunchtime?"

Another man said, "Whenever they say it is."

Another man said, "Were any of you close enough to see them run off?" A few voices said no, they hadn't seen anything. The same man then asked, "Then why were you shooting?"

The man said, "Because everyone else was."

Then one man said, "I think I saw two of them running for the river, but I'm not real sure. Did you hear what Carl said about Indian guardian spirits?" Several voices said yes.

The one that had spoken before said, "The more I think about it, the more I'm convinced all I saw was some shadows. Everything seems to look alike out here. Half the time I swear I'm seeing someone standing in the trees, and when I look, it isn't anything but trees and bushes, swaying in the wind."

Another voice said, "I could swear I saw someone wearing buckskin clothes standing in the forest back a few miles, watching us pass by. That was before they found the dead scouts, too. Maybe that was a warning or something."

A man asked, "A warning about what?" Several explained Carl's theory of Indian guardian spirits. There was silence for a few moments and then the men took off back the way they came. Clint and Junior exchanged another grin.

Ten minutes later, more footsteps were heard coming closer. The footsteps kept coming closer and closer. Junior looked up at the ceiling of the den, hoping that they didn't think to peek inside and see them through the air hole on top. Junior could see part of a man's boot through the air hole. He exchanged a concerned look with Clint. They both were afraid to breathe too deeply and be heard.

A man's voice said, "No one is around here. They have us chasing after nothing again."

Another voice said, "They're long gone from here. Why can't those officers see that?"

Another voice said, "If there was anyone here to begin with."

Another voice said, "What do you mean?" The voice told him Carl's theory with a lot of other wild details added. Junior especially liked the part of about the Indian guarding spirits thinking it was the cavalry coming again.

Another man said, "Well, there isn't anywhere to hide around here."

A voice said, "What's that?"

Several asked, "What's what?"

The man said, "The thing you have your foot on?"

A voice said, "I think it's a house for animals."

The other voice said, "How big is it on the inside?"

The voice said, "I don't know. But it can't be very big." Several shuffling steps could be heard backing away from the den. Clint and Junior looked at each other in alarm and wondered the same thing. What were they doing out there? Junior barely whispered into Clint's ear, "Let's get ready to move into the water."

Clint started to back away into the water just as they heard several shots being fired at the den. They could clearly hear the bullets embedding into the three-foot thick mud walls and a few hitting the water around them. Then the sound abruptly stopped. They had to blink rapidly to clear their eyes from the fine dirt particles that had fallen on their faces from the impact of the bullets.

****

They heard an angry voice yell out, "Stop. What do you think you're doing?"

A voice said, "They could be hiding inside that thing."

The angry voice said, "That's sacrilegious. Mother Earth, Gaia's creatures live inside there." Next they heard a shot fired and a thud as a body hit the ground. The voice said, "We're here to protect the forest animals. They are Gaia's creatures. You took an oath to never harm one. The penalty is death to disobey and harm one of the enlightened ones. Now, the rest of you get back to your sergeant. We're moving out soon." You could hear several, 'yes, sirs,' then footsteps walking away.

A man said, "Ahh, sir?" The footsteps stopped. The first man went on and asked, "What do we do about him?"

The man said, "Leave him right where he is. He doesn't deserve the fire. He can be food for the enlightened ones that he tried to kill."

****

Then Clint and Junior heard a lot of footsteps moving away. They shared an incredible look. Junior slightly shook his head in disgust about how ignorant they were about animals. This was a beaver den and everyone with as much intelligence as a carrot knew that they ate trees, not meat. They waited for over an hour after they heard the men leave before venturing out for a look. The whole ordeal had lasted two and a half hours. Clint led the way out. Junior appeared beside him in the water after a few seconds. They swam to the shore and stayed close to the den, looking around to see if they left any watchers around to find them. A body lay on the ground with a bullet hole in the forehead. They both looked around carefully, trying to spot if anyone was watching them. So far, no one was shooting at them. Clint thought that was always a plus. They made their way over to the spot where they had stashed the rifles. The brush Junior had pulled over in front of it was almost completely moved aside. Junior shook his head at their stupidity. If anyone had bothered to really look, the rifles were almost in plain sight. Junior led the way to a very old animal trail. He kept up a fast pace to warm them up. They had gotten pretty chilled being wet so long. It was only forty-five degrees out. He had been praying a lot during those few hours they had waited right under the enemy's noses. A few miles down the trail, Junior stopped so they could talk. Junior said, "We have a choice to make right now. This trail splits off going three ways."

Clint said, "What did you have in mind?"

Junior said, "I think we better head to where we stashed our packs and get changed into dry clothes before going on to the next meet site. The temp is going to drop tonight, and we don't want to be in wet clothes when that happens."

Clint thought for a few moments. "I agree. We're already so late, a few more minutes won't matter. Let's go."

Junior nodded. "Gayle was right. We did need a couple of changes of clothes."

Clint smiled. "She won't let us live that one down anytime soon, either."

Junior smiled and took off, heading towards their packs. Gayle had insisted they hide a couple of packs with dry clothes, dry boots, an extra coat, hat and gloves and a few knives and other essentials, so if they needed them, they wouldn't have to come all the way back to the house. They both reached down and opened up the pouch they had in a zipped pocket. They grabbed a few pieces of jerky to eat. They had missed lunch and were hungry. When they arrived at the meet site in the late afternoon in dry, warm clothes, they both felt a lot better. All the men were there except those on duty.

****

The General eyed the devastation around him with total disbelief. He couldn't believe his eyes. He muttered, "These backwoods rednecks have 50 cals." The men didn't even know where the shots had come from. They'd been walking in bunched up groups on the road. He had told the sergeants over and over to order the men not to walk in bunches. Every morning, they started out fine, but as the day wore on, more and more of them would walk in groups close together. Well, now the idiots would understand why they should have listened and obeyed their orders. The first shot from the 50 cal had hit one guy in the neck and almost decapitated him before it went right through into another man standing behind him, and went through that man's chest, and into another man standing behind him through his stomach, and into the foot of the fourth man standing behind him. The second shot took out three men in a similar way. This all happened before his Rainbow Warriors reacted and took cover. His first lieutenant had been standing, issuing orders and had been hit with the third round. The fourth round hit the supply cart driver, who was hiding behind the cart. The fifth shot missed a sergeant hiding in the ditch. He had nine men down with the enemy only firing five shots. His warriors had returned fire wildly into the woods on both sides of the road, aiming at nothing. He started shouting at them to cease fire. He yelled for a whole minute and they wouldn't stop shooting. *This cannot be happening.* And how was he going to deal with the rumors that were floating around about the playing card aces found in the scouts' mouths?

As he stood there debating how to handle this mess, a man came running up to him with a second lieutenant trailing right behind him. He was going to have to promote everyone, too, now. He sighed.

The second lieutenant said, "Sir." The man that had been running was sweaty and out of breath. He looked around, wild-eyed at the devastation.

The General asked, "What now? Can't you see I'm busy?"

The sweaty man croaked out, "Yes, sir." He held out two playing cards to the General.

The General put his gloves on, then took the cards, an ace of diamonds and an ace of clubs, and read them. "What the hell does this mean? Kill us with our own guns?"

The scared, sweaty man swallowed loudly. "Sir, they used our scouts' rifles on us."

The General narrowed his eyes at the sweaty man. "And when did they do this?"

The man gulped. "They hit us at the rear, too, sir."

The General put the two cards in a pocket and then looked at the man intently. "What happened?" The man told him. The General's face turned red. "They used our own guns to kill our horses? How many of them did you kill? How many were there?"

The man gulped again. "Two men. They got away."

The General backhanded the man and knocked him to the ground. He roared, "Get up and tell me that again."

The man stood up. He had a split lip with a little blood on his chin. He faced the General and said, stuttering slightly, "Ssssir, it was two men. They got away."

The General spun around, gesturing with his gloved hands. "Idiots. All of you are idiots." He turned back around to the man and yelled, "Two men. Just two men killed six horses and wounded the other two. Two men killed seven of our warriors and wounded two others at the rear and one of our own idiot warriors fell and broke his leg diving for cover." He threw his hands up in the air. "I am surrounded by idiots." He started pacing back and forth rapidly, thinking hard. No one moved. Most of them were too afraid to breathe deeply, for fear of drawing his attention. The General spun around and walked up to the sweaty man. "Tell no one about these aces."

The man got even paler as he stuttered, "Sssir, everyone in the rear already knows."

The General sighed and muttered, 'Idiots again.' Then he looked at the second lieutenant. "You are now promoted to first lieutenant. Get these bodies and we'll add them to the fire tonight. Let's move on. Leave the artillery here and we'll come back for it later today. We'll make camp in one mile."

The newly appointed first lieutenant said, "Yes, sir." He turned and started issuing orders. The General got on his horse and started back to his place in the column. He was deep in thought about the artillery they had to leave behind. What to do with it now? Haul it to their camp and what? Destroy it? Use the first team of horses to haul it? Make some men haul it? Making these idiot men take turns hauling it sounded the best. This deserved some deep thought and consideration.

****

The men at the meet site had good news for Clint and Junior. They had stopped the army. The army had traveled one mile farther on and then made camp. Jack and Phil were laughing as they described the scene, which made them laugh even harder. Phil said between laughs, "You should have seen them making camp. Their camp is hilly, with a lot of ravines and hardly any flat land. They had some men digging level spots for the officers' tents." He roared with laughter.

Jack said, "That isn't as funny as seeing that group of men trying to haul that artillery cart up the hill and back to their camp." They roared with laughter again. Junior and Clint told them about how their encounter had gone, which made the two men laugh wildly again. Jack said, "They looked so very hard for you. Oh yeah, way to go." Then roared in laughter again.

Cliff said in admiration, "You both must have nerves of steel." A couple of the other men were muttering about vengeful Indian guardian spirits and laughing up a storm. Clint smiled and let them go at it awhile longer. He knew these men had never seen real combat before and they were just relieving the tension by making fun of the enemy. He had talked to Junior about several ideas that had occurred to him about how to exploit the guardian Indian spirit legend. Junior had shared a few ideas, too. They came up with a plan to use tonight to scare the crap out of the enemy that would help cement the legend.

Clint told the men, "Now the enemy has stopped early for the night. That's a bonus. It gives us even more time to set up the next ambush. Let's get it set up first. Then we have a plan to make the Indian guarding spirits visit the enemy. Well, at least one of them will, anyway." He turned to Junior. "I need you and your team to go get those four inch pipes we prepared with the one eighth hole drilled into the ends of the caps."

Junior said, "Okay." He turned to Jim and Keith. "Let's go." They got up and the three of them trotted off to get the pipes.

Clint turned to Larry and Phil and said, "I need you two to bring all those rusty nails, nuts, bolts, washers and gravel to the next ambush site. Don't forget the rags." They nodded and trotted off to do it. He turned to Jack, who had the 50 cal, and asked, "Do you have the reloading powder and the cannon fuses ready?"

Jack said, "Yes, I have them stashed on the way to the next ambush site because I didn't know how much time we were going to have; I thought we could save a little time with the stuff halfway there."

Clint grinned. "Good thinking. Let's go get them now." Jack nodded and stood up.

A man named Brent approached Clint. "I really didn't believe half the stuff you were telling us before how just fifteen of us could take on a thousand man army and actually do any real damage. Well, I have to tell you. I believe you now."

Several of the other men agreed and said, "Yes, he made a believer out of me, too."

Clint smiled. "Let's go to the next ambush site and prepare a few surprises for our invaders for tomorrow while we still have daylight."

Jack shook his head in wonder. "Tomorrow they won't know what hit them. What idiots they are for giving us so much time to prepare a welcome committee." The other men laughed and agreed. Clint took another man aside and gave him a list of things he wanted him to bring to the camp. He also told him where to find most of the items. Several of the ranchers and farmers he'd talked to had volunteered to help in any way they could. He'd seen some things at their places they could use for tonight's surprise performance. They all headed out to gather up the equipment in pairs, going down different animal trails.

They all arrived at the next ambush site with all the supplies to make homemade cannons. First, they poured in one pound of gunpowder into the four inch pipe. Then they inserted a rag and packed it down gently. It needed to be solid, but not too hard. It was kind of a delicate procedure. Then they poured in the rusty nuts, bolts, gravel, etcetera. Then a rag was gently stuffed in to hold it all in place. Clint had four spots picked out where the men would wait for the army tomorrow. On each side of the road, one man would be a scout and give the five minute signal to light the fuse, and then disappear into the woods. Four other men, one at each cannon, would light the five second fuse at the proper time when the scouts told them, duck down and disappear into the woods after the explosion. The key to the whole thing was timing. It had to be timed with military precision to get the devastation that Clint wanted. The spot Clint picked out had a narrowed down curve in the road. Two cannons were aimed at the road at the beginning of the curve and the other two cannons would take care of the road on the other side of the curve. The cannons were offset from each other across the road. These homemade cannons would rain down death for about a hundred yards on the road. They had the cannon lighters dressed in ghillie suits to hide them from sight and blend into the surroundings. They had used the natural brush to hide the homemade cannons in depressions. They wired the cannons to trees to hold them in place. The hardest part would be waiting for the most men to bunch up on the road to cover one hundred yards, so the scouts could give the signal for the five minute countdown. It would be somewhere in the middle of the army. This was to show them that no one was safe, no matter where they traveled in the army. Clint inspected all four sites to make sure they were set up exactly right. When he was satisfied with everything, they headed out to the main camp for supper. It was already getting dark. They had a lot to prepare for tonight's Indian guardian spirit performance and he wanted to take care of the scouts tonight if they were stupid enough not to join the main army too.

When Clint and Junior arrived at the main camp, Clint said, "I have some plans to share. We're going to give them an Indian guardian spirit tonight." He called out to everyone to gather around and filled them in on his plan. Everyone started to laugh and looked at him with admiration in their eyes.

Cliff said, "Remind me to always stay on your good side. I wouldn't want you coming after me." Clint didn't say anything to that, he just smiled.

A little while later, the man he'd sent out to get the special items for tonight appeared with another man, leading a horse carrying some saddle bags. The man was one of the ranchers in the area who had ridden in a rodeo not too long ago. He eyed Clint a little hesitantly and said, "I can't for the life of me figure out what you plan to do with this list of stuff. And also, what in the hell is an Indian guardian spirit?"

Clint laughed and explained everything. The rancher was named Kyle and he loved the whole idea. He was excited now. Two of the men helped unload the horse. They opened up two large burlap sacks and unloaded four compound bows and arrows. Inside one of the large sacks was a bunch of homemade whittled arrows with natural feathers on them with real Indian arrowheads tied on with leather straps. They were tied together with a long thin leather strap about the thickness of a shoelace. They looked like they should be in a museum somewhere.

Junior asked Kyle, "Where did you get the Indian arrows from? I hope they aren't valuable."

Kyle laughed. "No. They aren't valuable. A friend of mine made them. He's a Native American. We used them for a show we put on at the rodeos." The men also took out a sack filled with long turkey feathers and a sack that had four chem light sticks in it. "I brought my rodeo coat with the fringe on the arms to use tonight."

Before Clint could say anything, another man he'd sent to find the scouts walked into camp. He walked up to Clint, nodded, and said, "You were right. Two miles."

Clint nodded. "Okay, we now know that the scouts didn't join up with the main part of the army, so we can pay them a visit tonight, too."

Junior laughed. "Soon no one is going to want to be a scout for that army. It's hazardous to their health." All the men laughed.

Clint looked at Kyle. "I don't know if the chemical will damage your coat or not."

Kyle said, "I really don't care. To use it for this purpose, I can honestly say is a fitting ending for it if that's the way it turns out."

Clint nodded. "Okay, Junior, can you make the warrior spear?" Junior nodded and held up the stick he'd been out looking for. He looked it over one more time. He grabbed the long leather strap, sat down, and brought out an old hunting knife. He used another knife to take the handle off so all he had was the metal part attached to the blade. He tied the steel blade tightly to the stick with an under and over cross stitch, like a big X. He tied a few feathers to small leather straps and put them on the handle of the spear. He held it up to show everyone. Clint smiled and nodded. It looked pretty authentic with the two feathers hanging down on each side by the blade as long as you didn't examine it too closely.

Junior said, "Should we try to make a headdress for an Indian war chief?"

Clint said, "It would take too much time. Our Indian guardian spirit is going to have to be just a brave warrior defending his land."

Junior nodded, smiling, and a few men chuckled. Clint turned to Kyle and told him to get some sleep; they'd wake him up at around 3:00 am when they got back from taking care of the scouts. He planned the appearance of the Indian guardian spirit to be around 4:00 to 5:00 am. That would be when the most of the enemy should be at the scouts' campsite, conducting an investigation into who killed their scouts. Kyle nodded and headed over to a cleared area with his sleeping bag.

Clint, Junior, Jack and Phil took off at 11:00 pm and headed to the scouts' camp. Clint wanted to wait for most of them to be asleep before hitting them. The plan was pretty simple. It was always better to keep any plan simple, then there was less to go wrong. He planned to watch them for a few hours and know exactly where everyone was first. They were right out in the open. Junior looked at Clint and rolled his eyes at the scouts' stupidity. Clint just smiled in return. He signaled where he wanted everyone. They settled down to wait and watch.

The enemy men had some bottles of what looked like whiskey they were passing around. It was hard to tell in the moonlight. The men didn't have a campfire. They were just sitting in the dark, talking quietly. Five men were already asleep in their sleeping bags. The other five men were talking a little about what happened this morning. They didn't act like they knew anything about what happened after that.

****

A couple of men started complaining about not being able to have a fire. If they had a fire they could at least play some poker to pass the time. Mentioning playing cards brought them right back to talking about the messages. After a little while, two men crawled into their sleeping bags. The three remaining men huddled a little closer in the cold night air and started talking about how weird and spooky it was that they hadn't found very many people on this trip. Out here there were very few houses or farms, and that seemed very unusual to them. Where were the people they were supposed to be educating about Gaia? They had walked down many side roads and the few houses they'd found had been deserted and anything of value was long gone. Two men were talking worriedly about food. Where were they going to get their food if there wasn't any people out here? Taking food away from those they killed or converted was how they replenished their supplies. Off in the distance, a wolf howled. The men stopped talking, listening to it. The men looked around uneasily. It was spooky sitting out here in the dark.

One man said, "It's a waste of time to be sitting out here without a fire. There's no one around to see it. I'm getting cold."

Another man said, "We can see better without a fire. You know that's what we're supposed to be looking for. Then in the morning, we'll find them and let the rest of the army know where they are. That's our job."

The other man said, "If there are no people around here, then who killed the two scouts this morning and put playing cards in their mouths?"

The man that wanted a fire said, "I'm beginning to think it must've been someone passing through. We've looked all over the place and found no sign of anyone having been around here in a long time. I'm turning in." He stood up and walked over to a pile of stuff lying on the ground, grabbed a sleeping bag, and walked off a little distance and unrolled it. He crawled inside and was soon snoring.

****

All the men in the sleeping bags were asleep. Clint knew this from their snores. The two left on watch huddled together, still passing the bottle back and forth. They were both facing the same way, with their backs toward Clint and Junior and facing Jack and Phil. About fifteen minutes after the third man had turned in, Junior had silently moved back. One of the men stood up and walked towards Junior's hiding spot in the brush, unzipping his pants. When the man returned to sit next to the other, Junior moved over a little and then got back into position. About a half hour later, Clint signaled that they were at the five minute count down. He got an answering signal from Jack, Phil and Junior. The plan was Junior and he would take out the two on watch, and Jack and Phil would shoot the ones in the sleeping bags. Clint nodded at Junior and Junior nodded back at him. They both let their arrows go at almost the same instant. Two deep thunks were heard, then two more followed them close behind, sinking into other bodies. The two on watch gurgled a little and fell over. All four of them were aiming and releasing arrows as fast as they could.

Phil took a couple of steps forward, grabbed another arrow, aimed, and let go, hitting a man in the chest. He reached for another arrow. Before he could aim and let the arrow loose, the man he'd just shot lifted his right hand up a few inches, unseen by the four men shooting arrows. His arm had been lying beside his body and was hidden in dark shadows. In his hand was a pistol. The man pulled the trigger and a bullet slammed into the center of Phil's chest. Before the man could fire again, Clint hit him with another arrow that went into his chest. A half of a second later, another arrow hit the man in the chest. Jack had released the second arrow, but it was way too late. Phil lay on the ground, not moving. Jack ran over to him. Clint looked around and there were arrows sticking out of every man there. Clint signaled to Junior and they laid their bows down and started exchanging the arrows as fast as they could. They were taking out the modern arrows and replacing them with the Indian arrows. Clint walked up to one of the bodies and pushed the arrow all the way through, then laid it aside. He pushed one of the homemade arrows through the same hole. It made a sickening, squishy sound. When they were done, Clint gathered up all their stuff.

Junior had spread out a fresh bloody cow hide that Lyle had brought and settled the tail and hooves on one side of the hide. In the middle he dumped the large bloody gut pile. Clint grabbed the arrow he had prepared beforehand and stuck it deep into the bloody gut pile. Attached to the arrow was a playing card and a turkey feather tied to a leather cord. Clint and Junior stepped over by Phil and Jack. Phil was lying on the ground staring up at the sky. He was dead. Jack let out a small sob kind of sound and turned away. The smell of fresh blood was very strong all around the small campsite.

Jack looked at Clint with pain-filled eyes and said, "I shouldn't have let him come. He was never as good with a bow as I was."

Clint said, looking him straight in the eyes, "We'll talk about this later. Right now we have to go. Someone will come and investigate that shot. Hurry." He leaned down and picked Phil up in a fireman carry over his shoulder.

Junior had collected all of the weapons and ammo that was in the camp and put them into his pack. He slipped his and Clint's bow over his shoulders and said, "Jack, grab the other bow and let's go." Jack was staring off into the night with a stricken look on his face. Junior reached out and nudged his arm gently, getting his attention. Jack turned and looked at him. Junior said more forcefully, "Jack, pick up the other bow and let's go before someone comes and sees us here." Jack bent down and picked up the bow. Junior motioned for him to go between Clint and him and they all took off. After a several yards, Junior turned back and looked at the scene behind them. It looked like a massacre. The only thing moving was a playing card and feather swaying around gently with the wind. On the card was written, 'I am the spirit of the wolf, defending my people's land. Next comes the spirit of the bear.' Clint had used the joker playing card for this message.

Junior was taking a turn holding Phil's body when they reached the area where they were going to cross the road. Clint signaled for Jack and Junior to wait there. He walked up to a lone car on the road and pulled out another playing card with a feather on it and tied it to the car's radio antenna. That card was the queen of spades along with the message, 'Mama bears protect her cubs.' Clint signaled and they resumed walking. Junior felt really bad about Phil dying. He hadn't known him all that well, but he had seemed like an okay guy. Well, this would mean they were down to just thirteen men now. It was over for Jack now, too. He didn't think that Jack would be able to throw his grief aside and be alert and focused enough to do anything else in the battle. He sighed and realized how tired he was. It would be a long time until he'd be able to get any sleep. They still had to do the Indian guardian spirit performance.

Well, that was going to be interesting. He couldn't wait to see the results. Clint signaled that it was time for him to carry Phil and Junior would carry the bows. They switched and then started out.

It was 3:30 am when they got back to the main camp. Coffee was starting to be a scarce commodity for everyone in the community. Junior's dad had stocked thirty-six large cans of coffee so they'd be good for a long time yet. Clint and Junior had talked about whether they should share coffee with the others and had decided that they wouldn't. They wouldn't let anyone know how well-prepared they were or what they had.

Clint finished wiping the chemical from inside of the glow sticks all around Kyle, the horse and the spear. Everyone stared at Kyle sitting on the horse all aglow. Clint had even put some streaks on his cheeks like he was wearing warpaint. Clint said, "Now walk out about fifty feet and hold up the spear and let's see how well it shows up. Kyle gently nudged the horse in the right side with his knee and the horse turned to the right and trotted off into the brush along an animal trail. He stopped and turned sideways and held up the spear.

They all stared in awe at the apparition that Clint had made. Those Rainbow Warriors were in for a really good scare. Clint said, "Now wave the spear around." Kyle did so. Clint smiled. Yup, this turned out better than he thought it would. When Kyle moved around or shook the spear, the chemical left behind a light trail. That was a person's eyes trying to adjust to the bright light in the darkness. Well, Kyle and the horse looked like a sickly yellow and green ghost. They couldn't miss it. Kyle had reassured Clint that he could make the horse rear up, moving its front legs just like they did in the movies and gallop off into the night. They had chosen for him to show himself up on a ridge that wasn't too close and wasn't too far, either, that looked down over the scouts' bodies. When Kyle galloped off into the night and disappeared over the ridge, it would look like parts of him were disappearing.

Kyle came trotting up to them and said, "I was thinking that we should probably have the Indian guardian spirit make an appearance very once in a while to discourage others from traveling this way. What do you think?"

Clint said, "I think that's a great idea. Most people, whether they admit it or not, are a little superstitious and it can't hurt to play on that. It will probably save a lot of lives that way on both sides in the future. We'll keep the legend of the Indian Guardian Spirit alive." Kyle nodded in agreement. "Are you ready?"

Kyle said, "Yes. This is going to be fun."

Clint said, "Well, I hope you and Morning Star don't get hurt. This is still a dangerous thing to do."

Kyle smiled. "I wouldn't miss this opportunity for anything in the world. Not even coffee." That made everyone laugh.

Clint said, "Be careful. Don't stay too long and don't take any chances. They'll be shooting real bullets at you and Morning Star. Don't forget that fact."

Kyle said, "They'll be so scared and shook up, they won't be able to hit anything. I've seen spooked cowboys that have had years of experience shooting not be able to hit a damn thing if they get a little upset or scared. Don't worry. I plan on having fun. I don't plan on being dead." Kyle pulled out a blanket and put it over his head, adjusting it so he could see out the holes that Clint had cut for him. It didn't hide him very well but at least if he ran across someone, they wouldn't see that it was Kyle who was the Indian guardian spirit. Clint nodded and Kyle gently kneed the horse and they walked off into the woods. Soon all that could be seen was a small flash of light here and there through the trees for a second, then it would be gone. It was almost as if fireflies were flitting around in the woods. Clint, Junior and a few other men took off at a trot to get into position. They didn't want to miss the show. They were climbing trees to be out of the way and to have an uninterrupted view. The hard part was going to be; not to laugh or fall out of the trees and give their presence away.

****

The first lieutenant sent for a second lieutenant and told him to pick twenty men and go find out who had fired off a gunshot. The second lieutenant quickly picked the men and they left to investigate. They searched all over and didn't see anyone in the darkness. The second lieutenant was now heading out in the direction of the scouts to see if they heard the gunshot. He was thinking that it was probably nothing, because it had only been one gunshot. It had better not have been the scouts messing around again or he was going to make them wish he hadn't been woken up. One of the men he'd picked was complaining that he had just gotten to sleep after his watch duty when he was told to come and help investigate. He'd thought it was probably just the stupid scouts being drunk and shooting off their guns. That had happened before. A few men agreed. Another asked, "Why did they need to investigate one lousy gunshot anyways?" A few others were talking about the events of the day and the supposed Indian guarding spirit. A few of the other men were ragging on those that believed Carl and the stupid story he kept telling everyone.

The second lieutenant rolled his eyes. He knew they should be quiet and not talk, but it was better in the long run to just let them have their say and get it over with. The whole army had heard about this Indian guardian spirit. There had only been around fifty guys hunting for whoever it was that had hit them in the rear. But according to every story, all their reliable sources had been there. There was no way that many men could have been there. The second lieutenant harshly gave an order for them to be quiet. The men shut up, but still walked loudly. As they neared the scouts' camp, the second lieutenant motioned for them to stop. They could just make out that the men were all lying down. There should have been at least two men awake on watch. The men in the group eyed each other uneasily. The second lieutenant motioned for them to move forward. They did. Then the smell hit them. Several men looked around uneasily, spooked by what they didn't know. They could barely see the bundles lying on the ground. The second lieutenant motioned for them to move forward again. The men hesitantly moved forward a few steps. That was when they noticed the short sticks by the sleeping men. Several of the men exchanged looks, wondering what the hell was going on. The second lieutenant motioned them forward and they all took a few steps, looking all around for danger. They could feel it in the air. It made the hair on their arms and the back of their necks stick up in a primal warning of danger.

The second lieutenant and a few others stepped close to one of the men lying in a sleeping bag. "Everyone look around. See if you can find any clues to who did this." The men exchanged another uneasy look. Who did what? That's what they wanted to know.

The second lieutenant said, "You three go back to camp and tell the first lieutenant what happened." The three men nodded and took off running. It looked like they couldn't get away fast enough. The men in front spread out, looking for clues, and then the rest of them could see what happened. Someone had killed all the men with arrows. Some of them had more than one arrow sticking out of them. Then they noticed the hide spread out and the bloody gut pile with a playing card and a feather tied to an arrow. Everyone looked around nervously, expecting a ghost or someone to jump out at them.

It looked like a scene out of a horror movie. One of those movies where people go camping and some deranged killer comes along and knocks them off one by one. The men were whispering to each other and moving around in small groups. No one wanted to stand alone for fear of being the next victim. A man asked the second lieutenant, "Sir, what happened here? Who do you think did this?"

The second lieutenant said, "I don't know. The first lieutenant and the General are going to want to know who did this, so all you men get busy and find some clues." The two men that had been on watch just laid on the ground where they had fallen. At least that mystery had been solved. The men milled around, looking at the dead men and the gut pile. They looked everywhere and didn't see a single thing that looked like a clue.

"What did a clue look like, anyway?" one man asked another. No one knew what to look for. There were seventeen men standing around looking at everything and no one found anything that made any sense or gave them a hint of about what happened.

A man walked over and nervously read what was written on the joker playing card. He felt a shock run through his body. He quickly got his friend and had him read the message. They shared a scared look. They moved off a ways. The one that had read the message first said, "I heard a wolf howl tonight. Did you hear it?" The other man answered yes. A few other men joined them and they told them about the message and the wolf howl. They all agreed; they had heard the howl, too. They all looked around nervously. The other men that had joined them left one by one to tell someone else about the message and to give their opinions. Soon only the first two men were left standing there. They looked at each other. The one man whispered to the other, "This vengeful spirit won't stop until it's killed all of us."

The other man agreed with him. "I'm not sticking around here waiting to die." The first man agreed. The man said, "They have finally ran into something that will stop them." The other man nodded. They started inching towards the bushes. When they reached them, they took off walking. Neither man looked back.

On the other side of the campsite, a sergeant that had been looking closely at the bodies said to the second lieutenant, "Sir, those look like arrows I saw in a museum once. They were artifacts of the American Indians. Sir, would it be all right for me to take one of these arrows out and look at it?"

The second lieutenant said, "Take one out of a body that has more than one. What are you looking for?"

"I'm looking to see if these are really homemade Indian arrows or a clever deception to make us think they are." The second lieutenant nodded. The sergeant reached down and pushed an arrow all the way through one of the bodies. He held it up and looked at it closely. He could clearly see it was homemade. He examined the feathers on the end and how they were fixed into the wood of the arrow. He then looked closely at the arrowhead tied on with a thin piece of leather. He stared at the arrow in disbelief.

The second lieutenant said, "What did you find?"

The sergeant swallowed nervously and looked around uneasily. "Sir, from what I can tell, these are real Indian arrows. But I'm not an expert." He handed the arrow to the second lieutenant, who took it and looked at it closely. It did look primitive. The second lieutenant sighed and thought, *I agree with the General. These men are idiots. None of them had even noticed that all the weapons and ammo was missing.* Just then they heard a large group of men coming. All the men turned quickly towards the sound, aiming their guns nervously at whatever was coming towards them.

****

Kyle rode to the ridge. This was the highest spot so everyone would be able to see the Indian guardian spirit clearly. He left Morning Star at the bottom of the ridge. Morning Star would stay where he left him. He didn't need to tie him to anything, he was a very well-trained rodeo horse. He lay down on the far side of the ridge and hid behind a tree. He was watching for the light signal from Clint. Then it would be time for the Indian guardian spirit to appear. He smiled. This was fun. It reminded him of his younger days and some of the pranks he'd been in on. He got comfortable and waited.

****

Clint, Junior and the other men selected trees near the dead scouts and quietly climbed up and got comfortable. They did this right under the noses of the men that had come to investigate. They were making so much noise it would have taken a miracle for any of them to have spotted or heard them climbing the trees. Clint and the other men could hear just about everything they were saying. They saw the two men that deserted. Clint smiled.

****

The second lieutenant barked out, "Lower your weapons. Our men are coming." The three men he'd sent to the General were leading the way. It looked like there was a hundred or so men with him. The fifteen men left backed away so those that had just arrived could see what happened. They had listened to what the sergeant and the second lieutenant had to say about the arrows and were jumpier than ever. A man said, "Hey. Where did Tim and Andy go?" Everyone looked around and couldn't find them.

The second lieutenant was talking with the other second lieutenant that had just arrived, telling him everything they knew of so far. Both men turned around when they heard a man asking where Tim and Andy were. They both told their groups to spread out and find them. *This night just kept getting worse and worse,* the second lieutenant thought. The men spread out. The second lieutenant was just showing the other second lieutenant the Indian arrow when they all heard a loud Indian war whoop. Everyone turned toward the sound.

****

Clint gave the signal. He pulled his glove down a little and showed his glowing skin. He timed it that way, watching the second lieutenants talk about the Indian arrow. He smiled at their reactions. There was dead silence all around them. All of their attention was turned to the war whoop. Now they could hear a galloping horse coming closer. Clint smiled widely.

****

All of a sudden, a glowing figure of an Indian brave on a pony slowly appeared up on the rise, in bits and pieces until they could finally see the whole apparition. The glowing specter stopped and let out another war whoop, shaking his hand over his head, holding a war spear.

You could see the fringe on his arm shaking around with the war spear and feathers. The figure glowed an unearthly color of yellowish-green. The horse reared up. The horse's legs pawed the air and it let out a long, high-pitched neigh and dropped to the ground. The Indian brave galloped off over the rise, still shaking his war spear, and giving out another loud war whoop. The specter was disappearing a piece at a time, just as it had appeared.

A second lieutenant's voice rang out loudly like a rifle crack, "Fire!" All the men started firing their rifles. It sounded like a war was taking place. They could see the sparks, and the smell of gunpowder was strong. The men were firing as fast as they could. Their eyes were wide in terror at seeing the ghostly Indian guardian spirit. Bullets were flying wildly. The second lieutenant yelled out, "Cease fire!" There was dead silence except for the loud, rapid breaths the men were taking.

All of a sudden, over a hundred voices could be heard, excitedly yelling about the Indian guardian spirit. It sounded especially loud after the silence. One man was heard saying, "I had him dead in my sights. I couldn't have missed. No way could I have missed that shot." The men around him believed him completely; he was the best shot in this group. The men had bunched up together. They had stopped looking for the missing men. Many of them said that the Indian guardian spirit had gotten the two missing men. Some were saying things about how they needed to apologize to Carl now after seeing the Indian guardian spirit for themselves. The two second lieutenants just shook their heads, trying to figure out what they'd really seen. They didn't want to admit to seeing a ghost. What was worrying them was who was going to end up telling this to the General? The two second lieutenants shared an unhappy look.

One of the second lieutenants ordered several men to go look for a body by the ridge. They had heard Ken say he had fired at the glowing figure and had it in his sights. Ken didn't miss. The men refused to leave the safety of the group. The two second lieutenants had a private conference. They decided it could wait until daylight, then they'd go look for a body. If it was human, it would be dead, and they would find the body. Then they could prove to the men that it hadn't been a ghost. They gave orders for the dead scouts' bodies to be brought to the main camp and not to disturb the arrows. The General was going to want to see this for himself. They gathered up everything and went to the army campsite to report. One of the second lieutenants thought, *Well, at least they had a lot of witnesses.* He had a feeling they were going to need them. This was not going to be pleasant. He sighed. Both second lieutenants shared a look. No, this was not going to be pleasant at all.

****

Clint and the other men waited for the army to disappear down the road before climbing down from the trees. Clint signaled to stay quiet. Voices carried a long way in the stillness of the predawn air. They made their way quickly back to the main camp, smiling and grinning. It had been a blast watching. Better than anything they'd ever done before. They were proud and happy.

They all saw Kyle long before they got close to the campsite. That made the men laugh. Clint was relieved that he hadn't been shot. The first thing Kyle said to him was, "I told you they wouldn't be able to hit the broad side of a barn." Clint laughed. "Well, how did I do?" The men that witnessed the specter gave him a rave review. They shared everything they'd seen and heard.

Junior asked Kyle, "How did it feel being an Indian guardian spirit?"

Kyle laughed. "Damn good." Everyone petted Morning Star and told him he was the best ghost horse ever.

One of the men said, "Jack left with Phil's body. He left the 50 cal in case he doesn't get back in time. He's going to try to come back. He wants them all to die for killing Phil. He's taking Phil's body over to his mother's house."

Clint nodded. "This isn't over by a long shot yet." The men agreed.

****

Cliff, Larry, Charlie and Katlin were on the move again to the next designated safe house. So far no one had needed her services. She smiled. The scouts Clint had sent a few times a day to tell them news and the location of the enemy had told them about Phil dying. The three older men had known Phil since he was born. They were saddened someone so young had died. But they all agreed it was for a worthy cause. There was no better way to die, they felt, than to fight for freedom. Cliff and Charlie had been in Vietnam, Larry had been in the Navy and had never seen any action. All of them had a good laugh this morning after hearing about the Indian guardian spirit performance. Ray was the scout that had stopped by this morning after witnessing it all from a tree. He had given up a few hours of sleep to come and tell them.

All of them had talked about making a run into the two nearest towns to see what was left and who was still around. Katlin wanted to check out the hospitals and doctors' offices for useful things to set up the clinic. Kyle had sent several of his ranch hands out on foraging runs to find medications and medical supplies for the clinic from abandoned places, but Clint had told them to wait on checking the towns until this battle was over and they would make some plans. He also talked to Kyle and a few other ranchers and farmers about going out to look for solar panels, batteries and all that was needed to set them up for power. Most of the ranches and farms had working vehicles because they were older models and had plenty of gas stored. Mostly they were farm trucks. Clint had mentioned they would all sit down and make some plans to improve conditions in the community. Everyone thought that was a wonderful idea. Windmills and things like that could help produce power in the winter. Clint also mentioned he and Junior were going to need some help this summer putting on an addition to Junior's house. He needed help with labor and building materials. Many people had volunteered. There were a lot of abandoned houses around and they could get the building materials they needed from there. There were so many things that needed to be done before winter came. Clint explained that if they all worked together, they could greatly improve the whole community and their living conditions.

****

After eating a quick breakfast, Clint, Junior and the men got into position by the cannons. It was just a little past dawn. Now they had to wait for the army. He hoped the scouts had practiced enough yesterday to get it right. A lot depended on this being as devastating as possible. It was basically all up to the scouts now. They had to time it somewhere in the middle of the army, where a lot of men were bunched together on the curve in the road. A lot rested on the scouts guessing right on how fast the army was traveling, too. He knew better than to second guess everything now. It was too late to change any plans. He had just always hated waiting for anything. It seemed to him that his whole life had been spent waiting in some God-forsaken place for a few minutes of action. He sighed. He really hoped no one fell asleep and missed lighting the fuse. That would blow the plan all to hell. Idle people could fall asleep very easily, especially when you couldn't move around or talk to keep you awake. The men had been too excited last night to get much sleep, so everyone was going on adrenaline today. The scout signaled to Clint that the five enemy scouts were coming. He got Junior's attention and signaled. Junior nodded. Junior was going to light off the last cannon. They were all concealed in the brush and the cannon lighters were in ghillie suits to blend in so they could get away in the confusion. He, too, was in his ghillie suit. He had two men watching the army; they had reported that they were marching as usual and that the five scouts were two miles ahead again. That meant that the army was thirty minutes behind them and the middle of the army would be an hour after the scouts passed. He signaled this to the scout on his side and he'd signal to the other scout so they could all get ready. Timing was everything.

The first man, Keith, was the lighter of the first cannon on the south side of the road. Jim was the second lighter, he was across and up farther than Keith on the north side of the road. All the cannons were staggered on each side of the road. Then around the other side of the curve, the first man on the south side was Scott. Then down farther on the north was Junior and Clint. The homemade cannons were fifty yards apart on each side of the road, so they covered one hundred yards of the road total. They waited for the enemy scouts to appear. When Keith saw the scouts coming, he had to bite down a little on his tongue to keep himself from laughing out loud. None of them knew how to act in the woods. He would have laughed his ass off at these city clowns in the old world. Clint's men blended into the brush so well that a scout walked by Keith just five feet away and didn't notice him at all. Keith rolled his eyes at how clueless they were. He had been worried all morning about the scouts noticing them in the brush. After seeing them, he realized that a child could sneak by them and they'd never know it. After the scouts disappeared around the curve, Chuck signaled to him they would wait around one hour from now. When they saw a large group of men bunched up on the road around that time, they would start the countdown. Keith acknowledged. They settled down to wait. Keith felt a lot more confident now after seeing how sloppy the scouts were. He looked at his watch; it said 9:00 am. Today would be the first time the men lighting the fuses had seen combat of any kind.

Clint and the men watched the army march past them. They had no clue what was about to happen. The men looked tired and jumpy. Every little noise and they were turning and aiming into the woods. Once it was a squirrel in a tree that started scolding them for being in its territory. Most of them looked too tired to be much good. Clint guessed they didn't get much sleep last night. He couldn't help but share a grin with Junior. It was almost time. Chuck leaned down and whispered into Keith's ear, "Four minutes and fifty seconds, light the fuse. Start now." Keith had his watch out and nodded, watching the hands. Chuck started walking and Steve watched him pace across the road. Steve whispered to Jim, "Four minutes and ten seconds, light the fuse. Start now." Jim had his watch out and timed it and nodded. As soon as Chuck was even with him, they walked on each side of the road around the curve, keeping pace with each other. When Chuck almost reached Scott he said, "Two minutes twenty seconds, light the fuse. Start now." Scott nodded and Chuck kept walking, keeping pace with Steve across the road. They could barely see each other. When Steve reached Clint and Junior he whispered, "One minute fifty seconds, light the fuse. Start now." Junior had his watch out and timed it. He nodded. Steve and Chuck both stepped back and disappeared into the woods. They would wait at the next meet site for the others to show up. They had kept pace, so it should go off like clockwork. They had done their part, now the rest was up to the men lighting the fuses.

Keith had his dad's zippo lighter out and opened up, ready to strike. He kept his eyes on the watch. It was one minute twenty seconds now to light the fuse. He was thinking this lighter was supposed to be wind proof. He sure hoped so. He stood up. Now it was fifteen seconds, twelve seconds, eight seconds, five seconds, he tried to light the lighter. It wouldn't catch. He tried again and it caught. His hand was shaking so hard he almost wasn't able to get the flame over to the fuse. The fuse sputtered and took off, racing toward the homemade cannon. He heard a shout and looked up at the road and someone was pointing at him. He glanced down at the fuse as it raced towards the cannon. He turned to run and hardly had taken a step when several bullets ripped through him. As he fell to the ground, he heard the cannon go off with a deafening roar, raining down destruction on the enemy. He smiled. He'd done it. Just then he heard another cannon roar. He didn't feel anything after that.

Jim raised his head as he heard the rifle shots and looked out to see what was happening. He saw Keith go down in a rain of bullets. Before he could do anything, the fuse he had lit met the end of the cap, igniting the gunpowder, slamming the pipe backwards and caving half his head in. The fuse lighters were supposed to duck and then leave after the cannon went off. Clint had explained to the men several times how important it was to duck down and stay there until the blast was over. Five seconds later, the third cannon roared its fiery destruction. Four seconds after that the fourth and final cannon roared and rained hell down on the enemy standing on the road.

Clint stood up and poured lead at the enemy with his AR-15, giving Junior cover so they could get away. They both took off running. The enemy, after spotting Keith, was alerted to their presence along the road. Clint said, "Keep going. Don't stop." Clint changed magazines as they raced off into the woods. Clint and Junior saw the five scouts passing in front of them. Junior shot the first one he saw as they ran. Clint and Junior looked around and spotted three of them. Where was the fourth man at? The three scouts they saw were spread out in the woods. Clint and Junior raced for the river. Shots rang out around them, making the brush snap and break, sending pieces flying all around them. Clint was firing behind them, making the scouts dive for cover. Junior looked around for a target and didn't spot anyone. They kept on running. Clint yelled, Don't stop!" They made the mile to the river. Junior jumped down the bank. He turned to provide cover for Clint, but there were no more shots. Clint dropped down and leaned up against the bank next to him. Both of them were breathing hard. Clint said, "Are you hit?"

Junior said, "I don't think so."

Clint said, "Good. Quick, get in the canoe and let's get across the river." They climbed in and started paddling.

****

The scouts ran back towards the army. They were going to get more men to help search for the two men they'd seen. The scouts had no idea what had happened to the army with the cannons. Hell on earth had rained down on them. There were mangled and torn bodies lying all over the place. Other men were crying out for help and still others screaming and moaning in pain. Some men were walking around in a daze. It looked like a fourth of the army was down. The scouts stopped on the edge of the woods, looking at the scene before them in horror. Someone spotted some men at the edge of the woods and and cried out, "There they are." Over a hundred guns opened fired, looking for revenge. The scouts were cut down by their own men. They never got to report seeing and chasing the two men in the woods. The medics were understaffed for devastation like this. No one had expected to run into this much hell. The General had barely missed getting hit by the explosion. Another twenty feet and he would have been in the thick of it. Nailed to a tree on the back side, facing away from the road, was an ace of hearts, and written on it in red marker was, 'Now you all die.' The General looked around at the scene before him and wondered, *who in the hell they were fighting? Was this the ghost of Rambo?* The head medic reported they had sixty-one dead and one hundred twenty-three wounded. A quarter of his army was out of commission.

He gave orders for them to make camp so they can take care of their wounded and give the dead a proper send off to meet Mother Gaia.

****

Clint and Junior raced to the next meet spot. The scouts Clint had set up to watch the army came in and reported that the army made camp right there and the General was giving a big speech about how they had proof they were fighting real men and not ghosts.

Clint said, "That General is an idiot. If he doesn't achieve a victory soon, his men will lose faith in him." He then smiled. "Our next attack will be just the thing to help him on his way. We need the sniper detail to get ready now. We have eleven men with scoped rifles. They should be able to hit the enemy at two hundred yards. We need to find a spot where the 50 cal can give us cover. We'll set up a seven man team here and the 50 cal on the ridge, six hundred yards away. We send a four man team down to kill the rest of the horses. It's time to build some blunder busters for tonight."

Several men asked, "What's that?"

Clint said, "It's four pipes, spread out. We stuff the back of them tightly with the same things as the cannons, then rags, then five pounds of shot in each barrel. This will have to be mounted on small logs on the front and back, tied down tightly. We'll use lighter fluid on a rag tied around a stick to light them. The first one can't fire until all the fuses are lit. The first fuse will have to be sixteen seconds, then fourteen, then twelve and then ten. Once the last one is lit, that person's job is done. He beelines to the woods and fades into the darkness."

Junior asked, "What will we use? We used up most of the nuts, bolts and stuff we had for the cannons."

Clint smile and said, "We'll use the broken glass we collected, what we have left from making the cannons, gravel, anything that's small and will fit inside." He turned to Junior. "Send everyone to help retrieve the supplies we stashed and to bring several containers full of gravel. Put all of it in the wheelbarrows to bring it here. We'll eat and rest in shifts after we get done preparing everything for tonight."

Junior said, "Ahh, that's what you wanted all the broken glass for." Clint had sent out several details over the last week to go around and collect all the broken glass they could find. Clint nodded. Junior turned around and motioned everyone to follow him. Clint sat down to rest and to think. He sure hoped the enemy didn't change the way they'd been doing things. He needed them to line up their tents in rows to sleep just as they'd been doing. That way they could kill and wound the most men. Tonight's attack would prove to the enemy there was nowhere to hide and nowhere they would be safe from attack. He sighed and waited for the men to get back so they could get busy making several good ole Betsy's. The enemy was in for a rough time tonight. He smiled as he waited.

****

The General was happy. He walked with a spring in his steps. He'd shown the men two dead bodies of the enemy to prove they weren't fighting ghosts. The idea they were fighting ghosts was totally ridiculous; it showed the men's lack of a proper education. He didn't think half the men could even read or write. They were just cannon fodder anyway. He had no idea how the enemy had pulled off the ghost sighting last night. They'd probably used phosphorescent paint or something. At last, something was going right. He told the men he didn't want to hear anyone even whisper about any ghosts anymore. They were fighting breathing, backwoods, ignorant rednecks. He smiled and whistled a happy tune. If his men weren't idiots, they would have captured those backwoods rednecks right from the beginning. It was their fault nothing was going right and they had so many wounded and dying. As he walked around, the men eyed him warily. It wasn't a good sign to see the General smile and walk around with a happy spring to his steps. It usually meant something bad was going to happen to them. The General had talked with his Colonel and his first lieutenant about sending out more men farther ahead and find where this other army was. Everything that had happened to them was just the enemy trying to slow them down so their army could have more time to prepare for battle. They had to press on as fast as they could to stop this other army. So far they hadn't been able to cover very much ground because of all of the delaying tactics the enemy had used. Well, he had told his officers that wasn't going to happen again. He was sending out several five man teams to scout around the woods beside the army as they camped and traveled, so they could find these men and get rid of them. He'd told them he was going to be in the history books as the first General in Gaia's army to engage a real enemy army. Victory would soon be his. He'd given a speech earlier to all the men and made a big deal about showing them the dead enemy bodies. He was completely confident now that he'd figured out what this enemy army was up to. Victory was within his grasp.

The Colonel and the first lieutenant went off into the woods a little ways, but were still in sight of the camp and the guards. They wanted their conference out where no one could hear them. The first lieutenant said, "It seems the General doesn't understand that we had men die today because we didn't have enough medics to handle the wounded in a timely manner. We even ran out of some of the supplies."

The Colonel said, "I know. I couldn't believe it when he made everyone stop what they were doing and gather around so he could give a speech and show off the two dead enemies. We still had men that needed medical attention. He's getting worse every day. He yelled at a man before his speech because his coffee wasn't hot enough. He didn't even appreciate that the men made sure to make some. They did this while helping set up the camp, attending the wounded, and gathering the dead bodies of their fallen brothers. You and I were even out there helping with everything and lending a hand. He sat on his horse and watched us with his head up in the clouds as if he didn't have a care in the world."

"He has no idea how the men feel about him, either. Did you notice the look on some of their faces when he was telling them about an army out there we'll be facing soon and that victory will be his?"

"Yes, I did notice. I also heard some of the things the men said after his speech. All the General did was completely confuse the men and to make them worry." The Colonel spat onto the ground.

"The men still believe that a ghost spirit is after us," said the first lieutenant. "They also think this ghost spirit is a shapeshifter or able to control the wild animals. Now they're worried because we have an army after us, too."

"I think these men that have been attacking us are a scout recon team of Special Forces that was sent out to wear us down before the army reaches us."

"Yes, I was thinking the same thing. You and I were in the military and know what a real, disciplined army can do." They shared a meaningful look.

The Colonel said, "I can't believe the General thinks we could take on a real army and beat them. We only have one 105mm artillery gun. We don't have enough ammo for any kind of a small battle, so how could we take on a whole army? We won't stand a chance in hell of surviving anything like that."

"Look at what one small recon team of special forces has done to us already. They haven't even used any real artillery yet and they've taken out a fourth of our men. This army will slaughter us completely from miles away. The General doesn't seem to understand that the enemy doesn't have to come close and engage in battle with the men shooting rifles at each other. We probably won't even see the enemy at all except for clean up teams after most of us are dead and dying."

"They haven't had to use any real artillery. The Special Forces recon team are doing just fine on their own decimating us. The General is right about our men. They're all idiots. They think that because they have a rifle and can shoot, that makes them a soldier."

The first lieutenant said, "All the victories they've had up until now have been against civilians. Mostly single houses and farms. None of them, including the General, seem to understand what will happen as we get closer to a real army." They both shared an intense, serious look.

"The sergeants have reported that more men are missing every time they turn around. We still haven't found the two men from last night that went missing."

"Well, can you blame them? They're scared they'll be the next casualty of this ghost spirit. The General isn't doing anything to make anyone feel any safer."

The Colonel said, "Every day he gets worse and worse. Most of his demands are just plain stupid."

"Sometimes I think he's reenacting Custer's last stand."

The Colonel looked at the first lieutenant. "I'm starting to believe that, too." They both saw a man walking towards them. They waited in silence for his approach.

The man walked up to the Colonel. "Sir, the General wants to see you." The colonel nodded and they all walked back to camp.

****

The men returned with the wheelbarrows and the supplies to make the blunder busters. Clint had sent out two men to go look over the enemy camp and report back on their set up. So much would depend on if they kept to the same arrangement. The first thing Clint said was, "The enemy will probably increase their scout patrols now. I don't think they have very many men that are familiar with being in the woods. Scouts have to have a great knowledge of the woods to spot ambushes and traps. They haven't sent any out with experience yet that we've been able to detect. Our attack tonight will be in darkness when they are sleeping and it will add to the confusion they'll experience. We'll have to be a little more careful to avoid the extra patrols that will be wandering around. I doubt they'll go very far into the woods. They'll probably hang around close to camp. Most of them will be experiencing the herd mentality about now. The herd mentality is that there is safety in numbers. Also, they won't want to be very far from the campfires and be in the dark. The darkness breeds irrational fears. Most people have a deep-seated primal fear of the dark. In the woods, it gets really dark with a lot of odd shapes that can look pretty spooky to anyone that isn't familiar with it. We'll use their fear of the woods against them. We've shown them already that there is no real safety, no matter where they are. Tonight our job is to continue the lesson." The men smiled and laughed. They were all tired and were going on very little sleep. Clint had made sure to rotate the men doing the scouting and the ones going to relay news to Katlin so no one got overly tired or used more than the others.

Clint motioned for everyone to bring the wheelbarrows closer. They unloaded them. Junior said, "Are we making these just like the cannons?"

Clint said, "The concept is very similar. We'll be using three pounds of shot and one pound of powder per blunder buster. We're putting four them for each set angled outward slightly to cover a larger area. One of the blunder busters will have a five foot piece of rusted chain in it per set of four. You'll notice that the holes for the fuses were drilled on top near the back and not on the back of the cap. All the pipes are four inches in diameter." He held one up so everyone could see it. "Make sure to put some broken glass in each of them." The men got busy and made up twenty-four. When they were done, he held up a log that was four inches in diameter and four feet long. He said, "These smaller logs will be placed in the front. Notice how the cuts are about half way through and angled outward so the pipe sets down inside of the cut on the log. It will hold the pipe so it doesn't move around. Notice that the two on the left are angled in that direction slightly and the two on the right are angled in that direction." He showed them all what he meant. The men nodded in understanding. He picked up the other size log. "This log is eight inches in diameter. Notice how the notches cut into it only go about half way so the pipe sets into the log half way from the front and the from top. The notches are slightly angled also, and the pipe sets down inside the notch snugly. The back half of the log is the whole eight inch diameter." He showed them what he meant and fitted a pipe down into the cut out space in the log. Clint next held up four fuses that were different lengths. He said, "The longest one is twenty seconds long, the next one is sixteen seconds long, the next one is twelve seconds long and the last one is eight seconds long. You light them from the longest to the shortest and they will fire at almost the same time. You set them up with the longest one on the farthest left and so on to the shortest."

A man said, "How do we light the fuses?"

Clint smiled. "I was getting to that." The men laughed nervously. Clint then picked up a three foot long stick that had a rag tightly wrapped at the end of it. "Before we leave tonight, we'll soak these in lighter fluid and cover them with these plastic bags so it doesn't evaporate too quickly." He held up a large plastic container of starting fluid that people used to for barbeques. Everyone nodded in understanding. "We'll place these sets of four pipes one hundred yards apart." He nodded to Junior. Junior passed everyone a sheet of paper. On the paper was a drawing of the enemy camp. On one side of the camp were three sets of blunder busters facing towards the center. On the other side was the other sets of blunder busters, also aimed at the center. They were staggered one hundred feet apart. The first side was marked one hundred yards, the next one was two hundred yards and the third one was three hundred yards. The other side of the camp had the first set of blunder busters at one hundred fifty yards, the second one was two hundred fifty yards, and the last one was at three hundred fifty yards.

Clint said, "The enemy camp is about a half mile long. The first sets of blunder busters will fire on both sides at approximately the same time. They're the guns you see on the drawings as the first set of blunder busters at one hundred yards and one hundred fifty yards. Twenty seconds later, the set at two hundred yards and two hundred fifty yards will fire. Ten seconds after that, the set at three hundred yards and three hundred fifty yards will fire. Everyone will time this by the signal of flaming arrows firing on the enemy camp. When you see the arrows flying, start your count downs. As soon as you light all the fuses, you'll disappear into the woods and go to our meet site. The men left alive will start firing their weapons wildly all around and will especially be aiming where the blunder busters are. You'll need to hurry so you don't get hit." He paused. "Any questions?" Everyone shook their heads no. "As we draw near the enemy camp to set up tonight, we'll search out the guards and patrols that are close. We'll use .22's with subsonic rounds. One shot to the back of the head. We'll set up our strike to start at 3:10 am. Those on watch will be tired and not very alert. Those asleep will be in a deep, exhausted sleep. They haven't had much sleep the last two nights. They'll also be recovering from the very eventful day they had today." The men smiled and some laughed. "We'll eat and sleep now, in shifts. We want to be very rested and alert tonight." He named off who would be on each shift.

The two scouts that Clint had sent out reported that the enemy camp was just as it had been last night. Clint smiled at how utterly stupid the person was in charge of that army.

Junior laughed. "I guess the person in charge never read or understood *The Art of War* by Sun Tzu." He quoted, "Speed is the essence of war. Take advantage of the enemy's unpreparedness; travel by unexpected routes and strike him where he had no precautions."

Clint smiled. "You have learned well, grasshopper." Junior and the men laughed. Anyone who planned on attacking an enemy should have read and understood this book first.

Everyone gathered everything up at Clint's signal and prepared to leave for their next encounter with the enemy. Clint, Junior and two other men had the .22's; they would go first and kill the guards and anyone else they ran across to clear the way for the blunder busters. Clint and Junior took one side of the enemy camp and the other two men took the other side and they started hunting guards. There had been over twenty guards stationed around the camp. No one ran into any trouble. Clint thought, *so far, so good.* He signaled for the two man teams to set up the blunder busters. They hid the wheelbarrows in the bushes. It took two men to lift them out of the wheelbarrows and carry them to the spots marked on the map. Each set weighed seventy-eight pounds. When they were set up with the person who was going to light the fuse, the other men joined Clint and Junior and got out the compound bows. Clint had dipped the first four inches of the arrows in some tar so they would burn hot and long and not go out too quickly. One man held the burning rag so the others could light their arrows from it. Their job was to set everything they could on fire, including the tents and all the supply wagons. Clint watched the clock. They lit their arrows and let them fly.

The very first set of blunder busters at the one hundred yard mark ran into a man that was a light sleeper. He heard some noise and woke up. He saw two men and called out an alarm. This happened just at the time the arrows started flying. The two men were cut down in a rain of bullets from the nervous men in the camp. Everyone in the camp was jumpy as hell waiting for the next attack. Word spread almost immediately that intruders were seen. Others were awakened by the noise and the shouts. Most of the army had awakened and were standing up, trying to see what was going on. Nineteen seconds later, the first set on the opposite side fired. Most of the men that shot the two men from Clint's group were now lying on the ground in bloody heaps. Those that hadn't been hit stared in shock at the bloody scene. Twenty seconds later, the second sets went off. Nine seconds later, the third set went off. All the men that lit fuses got away safely into the woods except the first two. One died a minute later and the other man was able to make it to the meet site. He was hit in the upper arm on his left side. The whole attack took less than two minutes. Junior had lit the last set off on the west side of the camp. He then went and met up with Clint. The men in the camp were inexperienced. They stood around in shock, staring at the latest attack as the blunder busters had gone off and got struck down by the next set. One hundred forty-seven were dead and two hundred and nineteen were wounded in the attack. Over half the army was either dead or wounded now.

The scene was something out of a nightmare. Men were screaming, moaning and crying. Tents and wagons were burning. Smoke hung over almost everything. Men lay in bloody heaps all over the camp. The rest of the men were firing out into the darkness every which way. Bullets were flying everywhere and some even killed their own men, mistaking them for the enemy. Most of them hadn't had time to put on their coats with the green patch that identified them as Rainbow Warriors. Everyone was shouting conflicting orders and most of the men ignored them anyway, shooting out wildly into the darkness. Then the supply wagon with their gun ammo exploded in a fiery billow of black smoke and sparks. At the other end of the camp, the wagon that carried the 105mm ammo exploded, throwing burning bits of metal all over. Even one of their food wagons exploded from the cooking oil and the fuel stored there. Some of the horses got loose and ran through the camp, wildly kicking and knocking men out of the way, sometimes stepping on wounded men lying on the ground as they made a dash to get away from the fire, smoke and noise. The tents that hadn't been burning burst into flames with the heat and burning embers that rained down on everything. Fires small and large were burning all over the camp. Smoke was billowing out of the large fires, and wispy, thin pieces of smoke floated here and there, like spectral fingers pointing out the devastation. It gave everything a surreal sort of look. The camp looked like something Dante' would have painted as a representation of hell.

The General and Colonel weren't hit and tried to restore some order. A sergeant said to the first lieutenant, "Sir, someone better get control of this army before we have a mutiny on our hands. The first to die will be the officers. You know that."

The first lieutenant said, "What do you mean, Sergeant?"

"Sir, everyone knows the General is an incompetent idiot and will get all of us killed. Sir, you better tell the Colonel to take control right now before it's too late." The first lieutenant and the sergeant stared at each other for a few seconds. The first lieutenant nodded and turned away, and trotting off in the direction of the General and the Colonel.

When the first lieutenant neared them, he slowed to a walk and approached the Colonel. The General was screaming incoherently. The Colonel had murder in his eyes as he looked at the first lieutenant. The first lieutenant whispered in his ear, "It's time."

The Colonel pulled his right arm up quickly and shot the General in the head with his .45 pistol. The men close to them just stopped whatever they were doing and stared at the General lying on the ground dead. The Colonel yelled out, "I'm taking command. We are going back to Green Bay." The men starting cheering. Even some of the wounded men lying on the ground joined in. But the screams for medics, the screams for help, moans and crying could still be heard far out into the darkness.

As soon as Junior met up with Clint, they took off running to the end of the camp where the horses were. Clint had told Junior their last job tonight would be to kill as many horses as they could. The officers that were left were going to be walking just like everyone else. Clint smiled. As they neared the horses, they stopped and looked around. They couldn't see anyone around. They silently crept up close, keeping their eyes out for anyone. Clint had his AR-15 and Junior had his SKS. They finally spotted three bodies lying on the ground over next to some singed trees that were slightly burning.

It looked like they'd been standing too close to the supply wagon when it exploded. Clint and Junior started shooting the horses.

The horses' screams of fear and pain joined in with the cries of the wounded men in the camp. The smoke from the fire was hiding them from view. That wasn't a good thing because they couldn't see anyone coming their way, either. The plan was to shoot until they emptied their clips, reload on the run and then disappear into the darkness. They heard a couple of shouts and feet running towards them. They turned and ran down a ditch and climbed up the other side. They could still hear the running footsteps. Junior's only thought was to get up the side of the ditch and into the safety of the darkness. Bushes, tree branches and leaves all around them had hot burning cinders landing on them like rain. They could hear bullets fly by them. Just as they reached the darkness, Junior felt a hard tug on his left shoulder that almost made him lose his balance and fall down. He tried to straighten out his feet and balance to keep on going. To stop was certain death. He must not have done a good job because he fell to the ground anyway. He thought he heard Clint's AR-15 firing back, but wasn't really sure. They had reloaded on the run to the woods. His thoughts were confused. He slowly crawled over to a tree and leaned against it. His left arm was numb and a little shaky. He could feel something hot and wet running down his back. He thought it was strange that it didn't hurt. He'd always heard getting shot hurt really bad. Either he wasn't as hurt as he first thought, or this isn't as bad as it was supposed to be. He couldn't make up his mind.

Clint ran up to him. "Are you all right? We have to go right now."

Junior looked at him and Clint could see he was in a daze. Junior said, "Help me up." Clint reached down and pulled him up on his feet.

Clint said, "Where you hit?"

"Left shoulder. It's not bad. It doesn't even hurt."

Clint frowned. That wasn't a good sign. That meant Junior was in shock. "Let's get out of here and then I'll patch you up. Put your good arm around my shoulders." Clint led them out farther, keeping up a good pace. Bullets were still flying all around them but none had come close enough to hit them. After a mile, Clint found a low spot and lowered Junior down to the ground. Clint turned on his small blue LED light. He then grabbed two battle dressings and some surgical tape. He looked at Junior's shoulder. "You are lucky. They used full metal jackets and it went right on through. Nothing major was hit. No arteries." Clint taped the dressing to the front of the wound then taped a dressing to the exit hole. He helped Junior get back into his coat. "We have to go. We have to put a lot more distance between us before we can rest. Are you up to it?"

Junior smiled. "No problem. Just slow down a little. You were practically dragging me." Clint nodded and helped Junior to stand up. Junior gasped in pain. It was really starting to hurt and throb now. Clint helped him to put his right arm over his shoulder and they took off at a fast pace. After awhile, Clint stopped to listen for any pursuit. He waited for about three minutes straining his ears to hear every little sound around them.

Nothing. He couldn't hear any pursuit at all. He sat Junior down under some trees and brush. Clint said, "I figure we've gone about two miles. I don't hear any sounds of pursuit." He reached down and helped Junior to take a long drink from his camel back. He reached inside his pack and brought out a power bar and unwrapped it for Junior. He handed it to him. "Eat all of this. You need to keep your strength up." He knew it would help Junior's body to deal with the shock of being injured and with the blood loss. He looked at his watch. It was later than he'd thought. It was just past 5:30 am. It would be daylight soon. They had to move and put more distance between them before risking settling down to rest. Junior was tired and pale; there was a pinched look around his eyes from the pain. He was going to pass out soon. Clint stood up. "Come on. We have to put more distance between us before we can get some rest." Junior looked up at him with tired, pain-filled eyes. Clint helped him to stand. "We'll go another two miles and then we'll find a concealed spot and you can rest some. Okay?"

Junior said tiredly, "Okay." As they walked, the sun started to rise and break up the gloom. Clint looked around. He wasn't very familiar with this area. They had ended up on the wrong side of the road, traveling in a completely different direction and he was taking Junior even farther away from the meet site so they could circle around and not be spotted by any enemy scouts. The men that had shot at them had cut off the direction they were supposed to go to get to the meet site. He knew there was a stream around here somewhere. When they found it he would know approximately where they were.

****

The rest of the men waited for an hour at the meet site for Clint and Junior to show up. They all stared at each other, not wanting to be the first one to say they had to leave. Lenny had wrapped his arm with a handkerchief tightly and the hole that went all the way through in the upper part of his arm had stopped bleeding. It still hurt, though. Dan cleared his throat. "I'm not going to just leave with Clint and Junior missing. That wouldn't be right."

Roger said, "If it wasn't for the two of them, all of us would either be dead or slaves of those Rainbow Warriors." The men all shared another look.

Dean said, "Someone needs to be in charge now to make the decisions." The rest of the men agreed.

Sam asked, "So who's going to be in charge?"

Henry said, "I say we put Dean in charge. He has experience with organizing men." Dean was Kyle's ranch manager and had a lot of experience with running the ranch, doing rodeos, and arranging things. All the other men agreed. "Okay, Dean is in charge now."

Dean took a deep breath. "Okay. Dan, you and Roger go look for Clint and Junior. Stay away from the army. If they're anywhere, they'll be out in the woods. Report back to the next meet site in four hours." Dan and Roger nodded. Dean turned to Sam. "You and Henry keep watch on the army and report back what they're up to. Half of their army is either dead or wounded. If they're smart, they'll leave. We need to know what they're up to before making any other plans. Report back at the next meet site in four hours." Sam and Henry nodded. Dean looked at Lenny. "Lenny, you come with me. We'll move to the next meet site. If Clint and Junior do show up, it'll be at the next meet site because we were supposed to already be gone from here. We'll look around as much as possible on the way to the new site. If they haven't shown up by the time all of you come back and report, we'll have to go tell the doctor." The men exchanged unhappy looks. They all liked the doctor and thought she was a real nice lady. They didn't want to have to tell her Clint was missing. Dean said, "How much dried meat do you all have left?" Everyone told him they had a lot left in their pouches. "All right, everyone eat some dried meat for breakfast on the way to your jobs. Let's move out and get this done." They all took off in pairs.

****

Clint was holding Junior up as best as he could. Junior was stumbling and fading fast. He was exhausted and his body was starting to shut down to conserve energy. They finally reached the stream and Clint got his bearings. They were a long ways from the meet site and on the wrong side of the road. Junior whispered, "Stop." Clint stopped and looked at him. Junior said in a faint voice, "I have to rest."

Clint leaned him up against a tree trunk and looked around, assessing the area. He said, "You make it to the top of that ridge, and then you can rest for awhile, okay?"

Junior looked at him doubtfully, but whispered, "Okay." Clint glanced at his watch. They were almost five hours overdue now. Damn, he needed to know what the army was doing to know which way to go. They should be returning to Green Bay. They'd lost over half of their army by his calculations. He really hoped that was true. He wondered what the rest of the men were going to do now. Would they keep going to the different meet sites for awhile and see if they showed up? He hoped so. If what was left of the army wasn't turning around, they'd need to keep up their terror campaign until they changed their minds. He was practically dragging Junior up the rise to the ridge. He didn't notice they were leaving impressions of their boots in the damp ground behind them. They made it up on the ridge and he helped Junior to lie down under some bushes. He was already out cold. He covered him with his poncho. Clint lay down on his stomach on the ground next to some bushes so he could see over the ridge and keep an eye out for anyone following them. Had they sent out some teams to find them? He suspected that they would. That was why he'd taken Junior out so far. He couldn't chance running across a team with Junior out of it like he was. They were probably looking for wounded men they could torture for information. He looked at his watch to time two hours. Then they were going to have to move on. They had to stay ahead of any teams scouring the woods.

Dean and Lenny waited for the teams to come and report. They had searched all over trying to find any trace or hint of Clint or Junior. They hadn't found any sign at all. They had searched thoroughly and took their time. Both of them had a lot of experience tracking animals in the woods. Especially looking for horses that jumped the fences and sometimes a deer or a coyote or wolf that was causing havoc. They were very disappointed that they hadn't been at the meet site waiting for them. They boiled some water to make a hot cup of tea. They were finally getting used to drinking it instead of coffee. They had both discovered that some of the herbal teas were very tasty. But it didn't matter how good it tasted, it still wasn't coffee. Junior had showed them how to roast dandelion roots and use it as a coffee substitute. It wasn't too bad, but again, it wasn't coffee. They sat in silence while they waited and sipped their tea. They could hear someone coming quietly. They both aimed their rifles.

Sam and Henry stepped out of the brush and walked into the meet site. Dean gestured at the pan of hot water. Both men pulled out their metal cups and made a cup of tea. While it steeped, Sam said, "The army is moving out. They're making stretchers to carry their wounded. The General is dead. We saw his body lying in the ditch where someone had thrown him. I think one of his own men killed him because he only had one bullet hole in the side of his head. If we'd have gotten him, there would have been more damage to his body."

Dean nodded. "Did you see any sign of Clint or Junior?"

Sam said, "No. I looked at all the dead bodies I could with binoculars to make sure they weren't lying out there somewhere, having been caught like Ray and the rest were as they ran out into the woods. They left our dead men right where they fell. I think if they'd been shot, their bodies would still be lying out there somewhere, but we couldn't find them. I think they're too spooked to touch or move our dead men. Or they just don't care one way or the other. They also moved the camp back down the road about a mile; I guess to get away from all the blood, gore, and smoke. They built a large fire and were having some kind of a ceremony and burning their dead."

"They've sent out several patrol teams into the woods," said Henry. "I don't know what they're looking for, but I think they hope to find one of us and make us talk. They're easy to avoid. They sound like a herd of elephants stomping around. And talking. All of them keep talking. I don't know how they except to find anything, making so much noise."

They all sat in silence for awhile. Dean finally said, "Okay. We'll wait one hour more. If they still haven't shown up, we'll have no choice but to tell the doctor." The men nodded and sat in silence, each one praying that Clint and Junior were okay. They had accomplished what they set out to do. The army was leaving with its tail tucked between its legs. They had stopped an army and made them turn back. None of them felt like celebrating that fact. Only six of them were left; Lenny was wounded and the two most important men were missing. Clint had told them that even if they did manage to stop the army, it wasn't over yet. They'd be back with more men next time and they'd probably be better trained, too. If they had any chance of winning the next time, they needed Clint and Junior to show them what to do or this would all have been for nothing, except to piss the off the enemy. None of them knew what to do to stop an army. They had learned a lot from Clint, but none of them could replace not even one of his fingers with their combined knowledge.

When the hour was up, they all looked to Dean to tell them what to do. Dean sighed. "Roger, I want you to go on to the next meet site. I want you to wait until it is time to go on to the next meet site after that. If they haven't showed up by then, we'll have to face the truth they aren't coming back. They must have been wounded and died out there. We'll find their bodies some time just like we've found others that went missing. When the time is up, Roger, you will join up with us on our way back to Clint and Junior's place. It shouldn't be hard for all of us to meet up because we'll be on our way back with the doctor and the supplies." Roger nodded. Dean turned and looked at the other men. "Dan, you, Sam and Henry go watch the army and spread out; keep them in sight. Make sure they leave. Trail off from them and make sure no one stays behind. You know what to do to any stragglers you find. I'll send three or four more men to take over for you sometime tonight." They nodded in understanding. Dean sighed again. "Lenny, you go with me. We'll have the doctor patch you up. Any questions?" Everyone shook their heads. "Okay, let's get to it."

****

Clint was watching the whole area from the ridge. It is almost time to wake Junior up so they could head out. Out of the corner of his eye, he saw a reflection from something shiny in the sunlight. He turned and scanned the area, looking for movement. He spotted a man out in front with five others following behind him. The man in front was scanning the ground and bent down to look more closely at something. A shot of adrenaline ran through Clint's body as he realized this man was a real tracker. He aimed and fired at the tracker. The man fell over and didn't move. The other men started shouting. He scooted back out of sight and went over to Junior. There wasn't time to wake him. He picked him up and carried him over his shoulder. He was dead weight. Junior didn't even move, but Clint could feel him breathing, so he was still alive. He moved as fast as he could, trying to get down the other side of the ridge. He could hear the men running up the ridge towards them. He stumbled a little and had to steady his balance or they were both going to fall down. He heard some shots and a few bullets flew past him. He turned and shot at the man, one handed. The man was shooting at him at the same time. Clint felt a bullet slam into him. At that same moment, a bullet slammed into the chest of the man at the top of the ridge, and he fell backwards and slid down.

The other men yelled and Clint heard a man say, "The hell with this. I'm getting out of here." He heard the men running away. Clint lost his balance because his knees gave out and they both fell to the ground in a heap. Clint grabbed Junior and tried to drag him over under some brush to hide him when all of a sudden he felt very weak and then darkness claimed him and he fell over next to Junior.

****

It was almost 2:00 in the afternoon when Dean and Lenny reached the abandoned A-frame cabin that Katlin and the men were staying in that day. They were reluctant to go up to the door. All of a sudden, Cliff stepped out from behind a tree and made them jump in surprise. "Why are you just standing there, staring at the cabin?" Dean looked at Cliff. "What's wrong?"

Dean said, "Clint and Junior have been missing since 3:30 am last night."

"Those two are fine. They're probably just holed up somewhere, waiting to get away."

Lenny said, "I don't think so. We've looked everywhere and can't find them."

Cliff said, "Well, if you haven't found their dead bodies, then they're probably still alive somewhere." Dean looked down at the ground and swallowed, shaking his head. "Come inside and we'll talk about this. You can tell us what happened."

Dean and Lenny followed behind him and entered the cabin. Katlin was sitting in a chair, reading a book. She looked up at them. She marked her page, then closed the book and set it down on a table. She said, smiling, "So, how did it go last night?" Dean and Lenny looked at each other then back at her. Katlin frowned and her heart started beating hard in her chest. She said sharply, "What happened?"

Dean said, "Clint and Junior are missing. No one can find them and the last time we saw them was at around 3:30 in the morning as we were all disappearing into the woods."

Katlin didn't say anything for a minute, thinking very fast, considering this idea and that idea of what could be keeping them. She finally said, "I see." She sat down slowly. "Tell me everything." Dean and Lenny shared another look.

Cliff said, "Sit down. You're going to give the doctor a kink in her neck, making her look up at the two of you." They both walked closer to where Katlin was sitting and sat down on a couch, facing her. Dean took a deep breath and told them everything that happened. When he was done, there was complete silence. Katlin didn't react. The men stared at her, waiting for something. They didn't know know what, crying, cussing, something.

Katlin had climbed inside herself and shut off all outside awareness. She felt a pain so deep and sharp she wasn't sure she could breathe. She thought of Gayle. She was all alone now, too. She had been in heaven for such a short time. All of that was now shattered. She was alone once again. She'd started to believe Gayle when she had kept saying Clint was almost invincible, being a S.E.R.E. guy. An insane thought went through her mind, *Now they wouldn't need an addition to the small house.* Robbie, oh God how could she tell Robbie that Clint and Junior wasn't ever going to come home again? She felt darkness coming towards her and then she felt nothing at all. A few seconds later, she turned her head to get away from something that smelled awful. Then she realized she knew what that smell was. She opened her eyes and five men were staring down at her and one was holding a broken capsule in his hand. She quickly knocked his hand away and sat up. Why was she lying on the floor? Then she remembered. She sobbed as tears ran down her face. The men backed away and sighed in relief. She was alive. For a moment there, Dean had thought they'd killed her. He obviously needed some sleep. He wasn't thinking to clearly. Larry handed her a handkerchief and she took it. She wiped her eyes and said, "Thank you." She sniffed a couple of times and then started to get up and the men jumped to help her stand. "Thank you, again." She stuffed the handkerchief into a front pocket of her jeans. She took a couple of deep breaths and turned to Lenny. "Lenny, let's have a look at that gunshot wound." The men exchanged puzzled looks. "No, I haven't lost my mind. I'm a doctor. Now get over here and let me see how bad it is." Lenny shrugged and walked over to the small dining room table where she had her bag set up and sat down in a chair.

After she'd finished stitching him up and bandaging his arm she said, "Now that wasn't too bad, was it?"

Lenny said, "No, it wasn't too bad." What he was really thinking was, as compared to what? An amputation, a heart transplant or something much worse? His wound had settled down to a dull ache and now it was throbbing and painful after she poked around inside it. It was also burning from the stuff she poured inside. Women always seemed to make the cuts and sores hurt worse. He sighed. "Thank you, Katlin." She nodded and gathered everything up. They had gotten everything ready to leave as soon as she was done patching up Lenny. She made a real effort not to think about Clint, Junior, Gayle, or Robbie right now. She didn't want to think about anything at all. She put her coat on and they walked outside. She just kept walking. Placing one foot in front of the other. At some point, Roger joined them. She really didn't pay any attention. She did see him shake his head at Dean. She didn't want to know what that shake meant. She looked around a little and noticed that it was going to be dark soon.

She recognized the path that led to the house. She stopped walking. She really didn't want to go inside and have to tell Gayle and Robbie. She wasn't sure she could. Cliff said, "Are you okay?" She shook her head no. She had to fight the tears back that wanted to spill over and run down her cheeks. She was going to have to be strong for Robbie and Gayle. Gayle needed her to be alert and focused. This could be a real dangerous time for her. She took a deep breath and started walking forward. The men followed.

Cliff knocked on the door and they heard the lookout hole open up and Robbie looked out at them and yelled, "Mom!" Then he said, "They're back." They heard Robbie slam it shut. They could hear the door being unlocked. Gayle was standing there with a smile as Robbie raised the door up so they could come inside. As they walked in she said, "Where's Junior and Clint?"

Katlin said, "Gayle, sit down." Gayle looked at her and then started to cry great, wracking sobs that shook her whole body. Katlin helped her to sit down on the couch. The men just sort of shuffled around in the candlelight. That was one thing Clint had told Gayle and Robbie; if anyone dropped by, use candles for light. She'd shut off the light and lit a candle when she heard them. After a few minutes, Katlin looked up at Cliff and said, "You all go on home to your families. They need to see that you're all right."

Cliff said, "We aren't leaving until we make sure you both are all right. Do you have anything we can do? Bring in some firewood or anything?"

Katlin shook her head. "Thank you for protecting me. You all just go on home now." The men didn't want to leave them alone, but didn't know what else to do.

Dean said, "We'll be by tomorrow to check on you and see if you need anything." Katlin nodded. Robbie came over and stood next to her, and Gayle and said in a low sad voice, "They aren't coming back, are they?" Katlin's tears ran down her cheeks as she shook her head no. The men turned to leave and Dean opened up the door and tied the rope off to a metal piece on the beam. They walked outside."

Chapter 38

The Heat of Battle - Missing &
Wounded

"All warfare is based on deception."

Sun Tzu, *The Art Of War*

They had been spotted. The second and third man in the culvert were returning fire. They were to protect the man whose job was to set off the C-4 charge for the rock slide. The second man looked over and saw that he was badly wounded or dead. He was lying still on the ground. The device was still in his hands. They had all been instructed on how to work the device in case of casualties. He made his way over to the downed man and reached for the device. He quickly looked around. At any moment they were going to be overrun by the enemy. It seemed like every second, more guns were returning fire. As he reached for the device, his body jerked and he felt a burning sensation in his back and shoulder. He was trying to make his fingers grab the device, but became aware that he couldn't feel his arm or hand at all.

He dropped his rifle and reached out with his other hand and grabbed it. He then realized that he couldn't hold it with his other hand to push the lever down and turn it. He wedged it under his knee to hold it in place, then pushed the lever down. He tried to twist it. He didn't have a very good hold on the device and it slipped away from under his knee. He thought, *I have to hurry or it will be too late.* He grabbed the device again and held it tight against his leg, trying to twist it into place. He finally had it almost in the right position. He heard the third man with him cry out. He ignored everything and concentrated on what he was doing. *There,* he thought. He heard a large boom and felt the ground shake. He fell over onto his side and smiled. He'd done it. Just then, the enemy was at the culvert and his body jerked several times; everything started fading and turned black.

****

Two field hospitals had been set up; one on the Redding side of the mountain and one near where the large log cabin had been. All that was left of the cabin was a burned out mess of charred rubble that sent out tendrils of smoke here and there. Each hospital had two doctors and ten nurses. They had a tent for the wounded and a tent set up for surgery. Redding had shared a little of its medicine with Dr. Anderson from the frontier town. Abby and Dr. Anderson had made up several antibiotic ointments with herbs for wounds. They were saving the antibiotics that Redding had provided for gunshot wounds and injuries that needed surgery. They had very little saline and glucose solutions for IVs. Dr. Anderson wouldn't let Abby help at the hospital because she was too close to delivery. He didn't want her going into labor from stress or exhaustion. That upset Abby greatly. She wanted to help. But all her friends agreed it would be for the best. Mark told her she was to stay in the frontier town and that was his final decision. Her and the baby's health came first.

All of the men from the frontier town were anxious to fight against the enemy. The ones that weren't picked to be on the front lines were staying to guard the town and the back road. There had been several arguments over who was staying and who was going. All the men wanted to fight on the front lines and be heroes. Bert left it up to Mark to decide who did what. Jeff and Mark had a meeting about how to handle the situation. It got to be such a problem, Jeff told all the men Mark was in charge of security and they were to do as he said or they were free to leave the frontier town. That settled everyone down. Mark divided up the fighting men between his group and Eric's group; they would be at the front and back of the trap for the army. Redding had three thousand fighting men. They were sending one thousand men to help fight. The other men were to stay and protect Redding. Bert wanted one hundred men at the front and two hundred men at the back. The rest were in two groups and would be up on the mountain overlooking the pass.

The plan was to set up the C-4 two and a half miles apart and trap the enemy in the pass between the two rock slides. They would hopefully take out the 105s in the rock slides, and they'd go over the side of the mountain. That was the plan. The enemy had two semi-trucks and a five thousand gallon fuel truck three to four miles behind them that carried all their supplies. The two 105s were on the back of diesel pickup trucks and another diesel truck each for the ammo. One was in the front and the other one was closer to the back. Bert's plan was to cut them off from their supply trucks. Then the men from Redding would shoot and drop grenades on them. Bert's two groups would have to hold the enemy in the pass. On each end, they were setting up the Kalashnikov RPK-74s. Bert and Mark's one hundred man group was in the front, closer to Redding, and the back group, with one hundred men, had Major Gary Beckerton, Eric and Lonnie. Colonel Albert Harrison was in charge of eight hundred men on top of the mountain. It all depended on taking out those two 105s. They didn't have any weapons that could match them in firepower.

It was hard to hide one hundred hundred men in the forest and to stay still and silent so the army could pass by without noticing them. Every one of the men in the woods knew their lives depended on it. Eric, Lonnie, Major Beckerton, and the other men were in the woods, hiding as the army marched past. Major Beckerton gave the signal to be relayed to the three-man team in the culvert to blow the C-4 charge after the army had marched past. They waited for the boom of the explosion, then they would separate. Half of them would hold the line in the pass and the other half would take the two semis and the fuel truck. They waited for the explosion. After several minutes, they heard rifles firing instead of the blast. Eric and Lonnie exchanged a worried look. Without hearing that explosion, Mark wouldn't know to set off his explosion in the front. The two explosions had to go off pretty close to each other or the plan would fail. Eric looked at Major Beckerton and he motioned for them to wait a few more minutes. Eric had to keep wiping his sweaty hands on his pant legs as they waited. What would they do if the three men in the culvert didn't set off the explosion?

Eric's body was coiled so tight he felt sure something was going to snap soon if they didn't move. Then they heard the blast. Eric and all the men jumped up and ran toward their positions. Before they had gone ten feet, they heard the other explosion. They quickly set up the Kalashnikov RPK-74 on top of a ten foot high rubble of rocks in a huge dust cloud. Hundreds of tons of rock had been blown down the mountain. The rocks were unstable, and many of the men fell down as they tried to climb to the top of the rock barricade. Eric was shooting the machine gun. He started shooting short bursts to drive the enemy to the middle as fast as he could. He was part of a three-man machine gun team. The other two loaded ammo for the machine gun, and were ready to take over if he was taken out. He was firing before the dust had started to settle. The dust cloud had covered their advance onto the pile of blasted rock. The enemy didn't have a chance of seeing them. The others opened up, firing at the enemy along the top of the blasted barricade. There were screams, men shouting, horses screaming in agony and men moaning. They were all a bit deaf from the roar of the rock slide, but could still hear the chaos. The first thing Eric noticed was the 105 was gone from the back as the cloud of dust started to settle. He didn't have time to feel happy that the plan had worked. The army was panicking. It was much too late for them to do anything to stop what was happening. But they would try.

The other half of Eric's group ran up the gully alongside the road towards the semi-trucks. The first truck driver saw a lot of men coming straight at them. These men were not wearing the Rainbow Warrior patch and uniform, and they were aiming rifles at them. He called out a warning, but there really wasn't anything they could do. They only had twenty men to guard the supply trucks. All three trucks came to a stop. They were surrounded. Lonnie ordered all the men in the trucks to get out. One man riding in the passenger seat in the middle truck pulled his rifle up, but before he could aim, he had twenty or more gunshots embedded into him. He fell sideways against the passenger door. There was broken glass all over the inside and some on the road outside of the truck too. The driver had been killed in the crossfire and slumped over the steering wheel. The other men in the trucks got out and surrendered.

Lonnie yelled, "Drop all your weapons. Put your hands on top of your head." When they had done so, Lonnie motioned and Tom, along with several other men, made sure they had no concealed weapons.

Lonnie motioned all the prisoners over to the side of the road near the cliff. While they were doing that, nine men got into the trucks. Each truck had one driver and two riding shotgun. They had planned this out ahead of time. They'd take the semis by the lane provided for trucks having trouble with their brakes. They would easily be able to turn the trucks around and take them back down the mountain and up into the valley by the back road. They had twenty-four men ready to unload some of the ammo and rifles from the supply trucks. They would be distributing rifles and ammo to the various groups. Bert had told all of them to take every rifle they could get from the enemy and use it against them. That should take care of their rifle and ammo shortages. They had no other choice. Bert didn't have an unlimited amount of ammo and Redding wasn't sharing very much, either. They had plenty of rifles, but very little ammo, definitely not enough for any kind of real battle. The men liked the idea of using the enemies' weapons and ammo against them. Poetic justice at it's finest.

Lonnie and the men waited until the trucks were leaving to deliver their precious cargo before dealing with their prisoners. The eighteen prisoners were scared and nervous. None of them had ever heard of any Rainbow Warriors being taken prisoner before. They didn't know what to do or what was going to happen. None of them had ever run into any kind of trouble like this. Twenty-five men were guarding the prisoners. The rest had already left with the guns and ammo they had collected to join in the battle. Lonnie motioned for six of his men to leave the group guarding the prisoners. They wouldn't be needed. Lonnie yelled out, "Aim!" The prisoners started shouting and begging for mercy, claiming they had already surrendered as they watched in terror as the men brought their rifles up to their shoulders, looking down their gun sights at them. Lonnie looked them over with haunted eyes, remembering friends falling to the ground, wounded or dead all around him, and said in a very strong voice, "We'll give you as much mercy as you gave my friends. Fire!" Eighteen rifles fired in quick succession. One shot into the middle of their chests. After the last one had been thrown off the cliff, Lonnie said, "Let's go." They jogged back to join in the fight for their freedom.

The enemy army was spread out over two and a half miles. After the explosions, there was a lot of confusion. Most of the enemy didn't even realize they were boxed in. Only those in the front and the back knew what was going on, but they didn't figure it out soon enough, or they would have fought harder to get over the rock barricade. Bert, Mark and his group set up the machine gun as quickly as they could. Mark started firing, using a one hundred round drum before the dust had even started to settle. The rest of the men quickly got up on the rocks and started firing. The front and back groups were forcing the enemy to move closer to the middle. The men on top of the mountain couldn't see through the dust cloud and had to wait for it to clear before they could begin shooting. They didn't have the ammo to waste and couldn't just randomly start shooting. They had to try to make as many bullets count as possible.

The whole army was in a complete panic. As soon as it cleared enough to see targets, the men on top of the pass opened up, raining hell down on them. Every so often a man would throw a grenade down when the enemy formed groups. It had been agreed that none of the enemy would be allowed to surrender. None would be spared. This disease, this cancer, would be stopped right here, right now. None of them deserved any kind of mercy. They would be treated as they had treated all those people they had slaughtered for having a different belief. The plan was for Bert and Redding's men to have no losses. They would hold the pass for five days, then go in and take care of anyone left alive. They would split the booty of whatever was recovered with Redding. Deep down, they knew they'd take losses. It was inevitable. There were always losses and wounded when combat was involved.

In the rear where Eric was, the enemy's top officer was pretty sharp. He figured out they were being cut off from their supplies and that they had to get over that barricade at all costs. He ordered one thousand men to assault the barricade. Eric was lying down on the rocks with just his head poking above, with the machine gun sweeping back and forth, raining death out on the enemy. By the time the dust had settled, all the men in his group were firing over the barricade at a thousand screaming men trying to charge over the barricade and escape. As they killed each man coming at them, two more would run up to take his place. The enemy officer was screaming out orders to get over the barricade and protect the trucks. The officer knew without those supply trucks, they were dead. One of the snipers on the barricade got the officer in his sights and dropped him.

Mark told the men to take out anyone who was giving orders as a priority. Eric yelled, "Magazine!" His loader handed him a fresh one hundred round drum. Eric tossed the empty drum behind him to the third man to reload. He racked the bolt back and couldn't believe the men just kept coming. He opened up again, firing short bursts, remembering that Bert had told him only to fire short bursts or the barrel would melt. The enemy was coming too fast, pushing from behind. They had to stop this charge or they would be overrun in no time flat. He barely had time to wonder when Lonnie and the rest of their group would get there to help hold the enemy. When were the guys on top going to start firing? He called for another magazine, yelling back, "Keep reloading. Don't let me run dry or we're done for." The heat from the barrel was very intense, making him sweat. Bullets were ricocheting all around him. There was a concentrated number of bullets being directed his way, trying to stop the machine gun fire. All of a sudden, Eric felt a burning sensation along his left cheek and his ear started stinging. He saw several men aiming for him and swept the machine gun towards them, firing a short burst. Then he felt something hit his shoulder and was flying backwards. He rolled all the way down the rocks and stopped after hitting his head on a large boulder. Then he knew nothing.

Just as Lonnie and the rest of the men arrived, they saw Eric flung backwards off the rocks and roll down to a stop. They saw several of their men lying still in unnatural poses. The men quickly climbed the rocks and started firing. Eric's loader took over firing the machine gun. The bodies were piling up. The first wave from the enemy climbed over the bodies of their comrades in their fight to get over the barricade. Bert had planned a counter move to stop them from getting out of the trap. Twenty-five men had twelve gauge shotguns loaded with buckshot. Just as they almost reached the top of the barricade, the shotguns opened up. One enemy, almost to the top, shot the gunner of the machine gun before going down under a blast from a shotgun. The machine gun was now silent. The third man on the machine gun team crawled up and moved the body of his friend out of the way and took over. The men on top of the pass could now see enough and started their assault from above and broke the enemies' charge. The men holding the barricade cheered. Another few minutes like that and the plan would have failed. There was total chaos now on the enemy side. They were all trying to find somewhere to hide. There was a lot of pushing and shoving going on, causing men to lose their footing and fall. Those that fell got trampled on. Some men were pushed or shoved and slid over the side of the road, falling hundreds of feet down the mountain. Men were screaming, shouting, crying and moaning. The men holding the back barricade would never forget the sounds, smells, or the terror they felt during this fight as they dealt out death to the enemy.

Lonnie was by Eric as soon as they had the enemy on the run, calling for a medic. His call for a medic was one of many. He reached down and checked Eric's pulse. It was weak, but it was there. Eric looked a pale, sickly, gray color. Lonnie couldn't tell if it was from the rock dust or from being wounded. He had a deep bloody groove along his left cheek from a bullet that had torn off most of the bottom of his earlobe. His shoulder was bleeding and the blood was being absorbed by his coat, so it looked like he had a very large wound under his coat. Two men came running up with a stretcher and loaded Eric onto it. They took off at a trot. Lonnie looked over at Major Beckerton; he was directing some men to reinforce a couple of spots on the barricade that looked weak.

Major Beckerton motioned to Lonnie and he trotted over. Major Beckerton said, "Thirty-eight are dead and seventeen are wounded." Lonnie nodded and watched the men taking away the bodies of their fallen comrades. He climbed back up to his spot on the barricade. He looked at all the dead bodies of the enemy. There were hundreds lying all over the place. He watched the enemy running away towards the middle of the pass, just as they wanted. The ones that made it found some cover. The men on top of the pass were shooting anything that showed enough to hit. He felt a measure of satisfaction. It wouldn't bring back his friends, that was true, but these murderers wouldn't go on to kill other innocent people. He looked around at the men around him. This wasn't like a normal war where each side had unique weapons and uniforms. This was a real civilian militia with every kind of rifle from a .223, to a .243, to a .270, a .308, some 30-06's, a .338, a 45-70, a few .444 Marlins and hell, even an old 50-110 buffalo gun, and they wore hunting clothes. One critical thing the enemy didn't know was how very low on ammo they were. Some guys only had fifty rounds for their rifles and shotguns, others had seventy to eighty rounds and a few had two hundred or more rounds. Lonnie was waiting for the all clear signal. Then teams would be sent over the barricade to collect all the rifles and ammo while the men on top kept the enemy busy hiding and dodging bullets. He could hear some of the men saying they were out of ammo now. Lonnie sent a prayer of thanks heavenward that they hadn't run out of ammo during the charge to get over the barricade. He only had three-thirty rounds left himself. If they had gotten over the barricade, all would have been lost.

Teams were collecting the rifles and ammo now. Any enemy left alive was being shot in the head with .22 pistols. Most of the rifles and ammo would be hauled up to the men on top of the pass. They had the job of killing the thousands of enemies left in the pass. Major Beckerton was saying to the men getting ready to haul the rifles and ammo up the mountain, "Bring back fifty men to reinforce our defense down here."

Bert and Mark at the front had a much easier time. After the blast that caused the rock slide and created a barricade, Mark opened up with the machine gun, firing short bursts. The enemy troops broke off and ran back the way they came. They had no idea they were trapped. The rest of the men with Bert and Mark aimed and shot as many retreating as they could. When the dust cleared enough to see better, the men on top of the pass opened up and really caused the enemy to scatter and run. During all this confusion on the enemy's side, both the back and front men at the barricades were moving rocks to create a second barricade, one hundred yards apart. Bert had explained that fifty men would be behind the first barricade and the rest would be behind the second one. They would light bonfires in between the two barricades so the enemy couldn't sneak up on them at night. The first fifty men would hold the main line there, but if there was a large charge, they were to retreat to the second barricade and that one hundred yard separation would be the kill zone. Bert also used the last of his C-4 buried in the mountain as a last resort; if they were getting overrun, he would blow it. The C-4 was his insurance to make sure the enemy didn't escape out of the trap. He had less men than they had in the back barricade. The extra men from the frontier town were with Gary and Eric. He needed that last resort just in case the enemy tried to overrun them with their overwhelming numbers in the front.

When they started, it was five to one odds against them. They could do this and win, but they had to fight smart because they didn't have enough men to fight with brute strength alone to go one on one.

At the end of the first day's fighting, the enemy had sustained heavy losses. The men on top of the pass had used up most of the grenades. There was over seventeen hundred dead or wounded. They had lost both 105s. They still had one truck full of ammo for the 105 that was useless to them now. It was buried underneath a pile of boulders. This was a very dangerous time. The enemy knew they were trapped in the pass. They were still outnumbered three to one. Being separated from the supply trucks had broken the enemy's morale. They had no water, food or medical supplies. The only ammo or medical supplies available was what they carried with them. It wouldn't be long until they would get desperate for food and water and try to push their way out of the trap. These charges would happen at night under the cover of darkness.

Everyone on Bert and Mark's team that had empty weapons were sent back to Redding. The rest would be resupplied, either some time late tonight or early tomorrow morning, from what they got from the enemy's supply trucks. In the meantime, they collected as many rifles and magazines as they safely could from the dead bodies of the enemy. They couldn't count on being resupplied anytime soon. It took time for a small group of people to distribute rifles and ammo from the valley to the other side of the mountain. Doing it with horses in darkness was very dangerous. They'd do it as fast as they safely could. But the men on top of the pass were the highest priority. They had planned on making the trip to resupply all the men once a day until this was over. Bert had estimated that after about five days, the enemy in the pass would be weakened enough that they could go in and eliminate any left alive.

****

Lisa was holding Hope and keeping her eye on Amanda at the same time. They were in the backyard of their cabin in the valley. Amanda and two other little girls were playing with dolls and a dollhouse and they were bickering and whining. The younger children were upset and were reacting to the tension they were feeling all around them. They knew something was very wrong, but lacked the needed skills to pick up hints in the conversations going on around them. Even baby Hope was fussing. She had taken Hope to give Channon a break. She was pacing back and forth on the back deck. Maria and Channon were doing laundry. Abby was lying down because her back was hurting. Cheryl and Ryan were out irrigating the gardens with others. Chris was out setting up #110 conibear traps for the small critters that were digging up and stealing some of the growing vegetables.

Everyone was trying to keep busy. Being idle allowed fear and concern to take over your thoughts. Everyone was worried sick and wondering who would live and who would die today in battle. Lisa had been praying on and off ever since the men had left. She had a large knot of fear in her chest since the battle started, and it made taking a deep breath almost impossible. She just knew something was horribly wrong. She heard a pickup truck stop in front of the cabin and raced inside to find out what was wrong. Maria let Karen and another woman into the cabin. By the sympathetic look on their faces when they turned to her, she knew that Eric had to be dead or dying. She shook her head no. This couldn't really be happening. Her eyes blurred and she realized that she was crying. Channon took Hope out of her arms and patted her arm in a comforting way. Maria grabbed her other arm and they held each other tight.

Karen said, "Eric has been wounded. He's in surgery. We don't know how bad he is. Jeff said to bring you to the main cave to await news there."

"I have to go to him," Lisa said.

Karen said, "You'll just be in the way. They don't have the space for anyone at the hospital. When he gets out of surgery, after the doctors say it is all right, he'll be brought here. They have more wounded than they counted on and they're running out of space to put them. The ones they can patch up are sent back out to fight again. Where's Abby? We need her."

Abby stepped into the living room. "I'm right here." She was rubbing her back with her hands.

They heard another truck pull up outside. Chris and Ryan came running fearfully into the house. When they saw Lisa crying and holding on to Maria. Chris said, "What happened?"

Karen explained again all that she knew. Chris and Ryan both looked like someone had ended the world all over again. Abby reached out and hugged them to her. "Let's go. We may learn more after we get to the cave." She turned to Karen and Jennifer. "Have the other women bring all the sheets and bandages we washed and prepared. We have to set up before they start bringing the wounded to us. Have the women bring the back up herbs and ointments I put in the apothecary in case they were needed." She sighed. Dr. Anderson had really hoped that she wouldn't have to be in charge of caring for any wounded. He also hoped they'd be able to care for all the wounded at the hospital they set up out in the woods. Well, things rarely worked out the way anyone hoped. Cheryl came inside and said she'd watch Amanda and for them to go on and do what they needed to do. They all piled into the trucks and took off for the main cave. Cheryl started calling the other women and let them know that they would be needed in the main cave to care for the wounded men. She and a woman named Deanna would watch everyone's children.

It took them an hour, but they got everything set up to care for the wounded. Even Chris and Ryan scrubbed up and helped move things around. They made up the beds with clean linens in the small cabins in the cave for the wounded men. That way they could keep them somewhere where they could rest and not be affected by the hustle and bustle in the main part of the cave. Chris and Ryan were in charge of filling containers with water and putting them and a cup with a straw by the beds. Abby was in the middle of explaining to Chris how she wanted them to handle burning the used bandages in the large wood furnace when four injured men were brought in. Abby directed where they were to go. An R.N. had accompanied them and explained the doctors' orders for each man's care from the charts they'd made up for each man. Eric was one of the men. Lisa was immediately by his side. The nurse and the men that brought the wounded left to go back to the hospital.

Abby was shocked at how badly Eric was injured. His collarbone had been broken by the impact of the bullet entering his shoulder at an angle. It also had left behind a lot of torn muscles and a very large exit hole in his back. His gunshot shoulder had been dislocated during his fall down the rocks, which in turn tore more muscles and ligaments in his shoulder. If he survived, he would need more surgery at a later date to fix it all. He had lost a large amount of blood. He had an IV with saline. Hopefully, it would help speed up his body's production of blood to replace what was lost. But the worst was a large lump on the side of his head by his temple. He had been knocked unconscious on the rocks and after two hours in recovery, he still hadn't regained consciousness. The doctors feared he was in a coma. But at least his pupils did react to light, so there was hope that he might wake up. They didn't have an x-ray machine to know if his skull was cracked. His left cheek was bandaged from his mouth past his ear to his neck. A bullet had left a deep groove a few centimeters in his cheek and had torn off the bottom part of his left earlobe. That was just cosmetic damage. They had to remove the jagged bits of torn flesh from his ear and stitch it closed. Reverend Blackstone brought Lisa a chair and helped her to sit down by Eric's bedside. Lisa shared in a prayer with Reverend Blackstone, Chris and Ryan.

The other three men were injured just as badly as Eric. Abby was taking their blood pressure and pulse and recording it, along with their temperatures, every half hour. She closely watched all their IVs. They had brought her a case of saline solution IV bags. All four of them had lost a lot of blood. A nurse was due to check on the men in an hour. Abby was glad, because two of the men's temperatures were rising. Eric was one of them.

It was 11:00 pm and the nurse would be here in a half hour. Abby got up and paced the floor. Her back hurt so very bad. There was no comfortable position she could find any more to relieve the pain. Ryan had fallen asleep a little while ago, sitting in the chair at the bottom of Eric's bed. Maria and Jennifer had gotten him into a sleeping bag. Chris took up the vigil at the bottom of Eric's bed. Lisa just sat next to Eric, holding his hand and talking to him softly, trying not to cry. She knew it wasn't good that his temperature was rising. It was time for Abby to make her rounds, so she went and washed up. She grabbed the box of disposable gloves and moved to the first cabin and checked on the three men.

She had just come out of the small cabin and threw her gloves in the trash when she felt something warm running down between her legs. She looked down in surprise at the puddle on the floor beneath her feet. Shock ran through her body. How could she have peed her pants and not known it?

Jennifer and Maria saw the shocked look on Abby's face and ran over to her. Maria urgently said, "What's the matter?"

Before Abby could say anything Jennifer said, "Abby, come with me and we'll get you cleaned up."

Maria looked fearfully at Jennifer and said, "What is it? What's happened?"

Jennifer tried to smile and said in a strained voice, "Abby's water just broke. Her baby will be born soon." Maria looked like she was going to pass out. All Maria could think was *not now*. Oh God, how could they deliver a baby now in the middle of a battle? Abby wasn't due yet for another month. This couldn't be good.

Abby went with Jennifer and Maria turned to Eric's cabin. She went in and walked over to Eric's bed and stood next to Lisa's chair. She reached out and patted Eric's arm and said, "You'd better wake up, Eric. Abby is in labor. You're going to be an uncle in a few hours." Lisa gasped out loud and looked up at Maria with a stunned, terrified look on her face.

Bert and Mark were back behind the second barricade. Mark was pacing. Bert looked at his watch and said, "It's almost 2:00 am. Why don't you get some sleep? I'll wake you up in a few hours if nothing happens."

Mark looked at him. "Maybe later. It doesn't make any sense. Why haven't they tried to attack us?"

Bert said, "Maybe they aren't desperate enough yet."

Mark just looked at him. "I have a bad feeling. They have to be up to something. I wish we could see what they're doing."

Bert said, "Even if we could see them, we probably wouldn't know what they're up to. If anything, what we really need is to hear them. Then we'd know what they're up to." Mark just kept pacing, his mind whirling with uneasy thoughts. He was very worried about Eric; he just had this feeling ever since they blew the C-4 that Eric needed him. He shook off the feeling, telling himself he was just being paranoid. Eric could take care of himself. Mark looked over at the first barricade. Everything was peaceful. How could they be in the middle of a battle and everything be peaceful? He started pacing again. Something just wasn't right.

A little while later, multiple gunshots erupted out of the silent night. Men were crawling over the first barricade, firing. Twenty of the men manning the barricade fell over, either dead or wounded. The officer in charge of the enemy had sent one hundred of his elite fighting force to clear the way for their escape. They had crept up in the shadows and the men guarding the barricade hadn't seen them until they appeared over the barricade. Battle cries echoed all around them. Mark raced over to the machine gun at the top of the second barricade. After the fighting started, the rest of the troops surged forward. A thousand men screaming for blood charged forward.

Bert yelled out, "Hold the line!" The one hundred yard kill zone was filling up fast. Thirty of the running men were their own men, trying to get to the safety of the second barricade ahead of the enemy. It sounded like the hounds of hell were right on their heels. Bert yelled out, "Aim for the top of the first barricade and give them hell." The line of men on the second barricade opened up with a deafening roar. Their men caught between the barricades were on their own until they could figure out who was who.

The first one made it over the second barricade in a complete panic, screaming, "We lost the line! They're coming! Run! We can't stop them!"

Bert yelled out, "Hold the line! Fire!"

Only twelve of their men made it over the top of the second barricade. The one hundred man elite fighting force was knocked down to eighty-five and were still coming full speed ahead. Bert yelled to Mark, "Shoot everyone in the kill zone! Let no one get past!" The night was filled with flashes from gunfire, ricocheting bullets and battle cries of an unseen force racing straight for them. Each man holding the line of the second barricade felt like they were alone, fighting for their survival. The smell of cordite filled the air. Men were screaming in pain and crying. The echoes from the wounded competed with the sound of gunshots. Bert called Mark over and had a man on his reloading team take over the machine gun. This was getting bad, real bad. The thundering sound of one thousand troops pouring over the first barricade sounded like a stampeding herd. The enemy had some troops scale up the mountain just high enough to rain bullets down behind the second barricade. The enemy was tossing in everything they had to break the line at the barricade. It was do or die for all of them on each side of the battle. The men standing in back of the fighters on the second barricade who had shotguns were ordered to kill anything that came over the top. Their job was to not allow even one man over the second barricade.

The one thousand backup troops were making it over the first barricade. No matter how many they killed more just kept coming. When four hundred or so were in the kill zone, Bert knew they could no longer stop them. He had no choice. He set off the second charge of C-4. The blast silenced the night for a few seconds, then the rumbling of rocks, gravel and sand raced down the mountain like a avalanche of roaring thunder, shaking and pushing or burying everything in its way. This same sound had been heard once already in this same spot much earlier in the day. When it hit the bottom of the mountain, it shoved four hundred or so men right off the road and over the side of the cliff. The real unlucky ones were buried in the rubble, making them look like some broken, discarded toys. The man that had taken over the machine gun had been crushed by a forty pound rock. The price of battle was high, for the price of freedom must always be paid in blood. Bert and Mark were the last ones trying to make sure all of their men got away, and they couldn't see or hear the mini rock slide racing straight towards them in the dark. One man heard a yell and turned around just in time to see Bert and Mark swept off the road and over the cliff with several large rocks and boulders following them. In a blink of an eye, they both were gone from sight.

Everyone up on top of the pass heard the gun battle going on. It was very loud and the sounds carried over long distances in the quiet night. They couldn't fire down for fear of hitting their own men. They stood around anxiously, wanting to help their men down there under attack. Then came the blast of the second C-4 explosion. Several men on top were almost thrown down the mountain to the pass below. They had no way to tell if the trap was still holding the enemy or not. They also didn't know if anyone from their side was left alive. Every man on top prayed that the now very large barricade would still hold the enemy in the trap. It was a long wait until it was light enough to see what happened. The men waited impatiently. Anyone that had been tired or had been dozing off had a very rude awakening. Most of the men had shaky hands for a few minutes from the adrenaline dump they experienced when the battle started below. Everyone was wide-awake and very alert. Colonel Harrison had sent one hundred men to the rear after dark to bring rifles and ammo from the enemy's supply truck. They should be back before daylight. They were really low on ammo. Almost desperately low. They had to resupply before daylight so they could make sure to keep the enemy pinned down in the trap and to eliminate as many as they could. They also had a lot of stun grenades they'd brought from the various police departments to keep the enemy from taking refuge in any overhangs that might hide them from sight, and also to discourage the enemy from bunching up in large groups.

When it was finally light enough to see, they couldn't believe the devastation that the second explosion had caused. But the important thing was they could see that there were still about fifty men manning the second barricade. Colonel Harrison picked fifty men to send down to reinforce the men at the front of the trap. He also sent down rifles and ammo to resupply them. The men that were left after the night battle were battle shocked, bloodied and had the thousand-mile stare. They were ready for revenge. They were no longer just desperate men trying to survive. Now they were battle-hardened men on a mission to spill blood in payment from these murdering Eco Nazis. Holding friends and family members in one's arms as they gasped their final dying breath changes a man.

The Colonel had sent down five men with some food to prepare breakfast for the men at the front. Both groups on the top were going to shoot until they were almost out of ammo again. Plus, every now and again they were going to roll large rocks down on the enemy below and start some small avalanches of falling rocks. Word reached Colonel Harrison that Bert and Mark had went over the side in the second explosion. He sent word to Major Beckerton to give them hell and shoot any body part that showed their way. They would all hold them in the pass for four days more, then when the enemy was weakened, they would send in teams to clean up anyone who was left alive. They had no food or water. He also sent word of what happened to Bert and Mark. The Colonel had the front line, the back line and the men on top set up snipers all along the pass to take out anyone who tried to clear a path through the rubble to get out and to stop anyone from trying to climb up or down the mountain. The flies were getting thick and crawling all around the dead and wounded. Everywhere the men looked there were dead bodies.

Lisa bathed Eric's body with cold water, trying to bring his temperature down. His fever had spiked in the middle of the night. Dr. Anderson had come to check on the patients after the R.N. had reported the fevers. He brought broad-spectrum antibiotics to add to the patients' IVs to help fight off the infections. He also checked on Abby's progress. It was her first baby and it was going to be hours yet before it was born. She was doing fine. The baby seemed fine, too. He was concerned about her and the baby because she had gone into labor almost a month early.

He was really worried about Eric, also. The next forty-eight hours would determine if he lived or died. Eric still hadn't woken up. Dr. Anderson was still there when word reached them that Bert and Mark had gone over the cliff in a rock slide. Maria had been a tower of strength for everyone and keeping everything as organized as possible during the whole day and night. This broke her down. Dr. Anderson brought Lisa outside of the small cabin and told her about Bert and Mark. Maria was crying and rocking back and forth when Lisa found her. They both broke out crying and tried to comfort each other as best they could. Chris and Ryan came over and wanted to know what was going on. Lisa told them. Chris and Ryan both had tears in their eyes. Maria hugged Ryan and Lisa grabbed Chris and held on to him tightly.

Amanda had demanded to be brought to her mommy earlier in the evening. Amanda woke up and came to them, rubbing her eyes with her hands, and wanted to know what was wrong. She'd been sleeping in one of the beds in the small cabin Eric was in. Lisa tried to tell her, but couldn't get the words out. Chris explained what happened. Amanda looked at them like they were crazy. She climbed up on Lisa's lap and hugged her tight and said, "Don't cry, Mommy. Daddy Mark and Mr. Gunner are okay. He and Mr. Gunner will be back soon." She paused, then leaned back and patted both of Lisa's cheeks with her small hands, looking into her eyes. "Don't worry, Mommy. Daddy Eric is going to wake up. He just needs to sleep so he can get all better. He's sick." Lisa and Maria didn't know what to say. She obviously didn't understand what they meant or else she wasn't able to face the thought of losing both her daddies.

Channon had come up to them so quietly that they hadn't noticed. She reached out and hugged Maria. When she stepped back, she looked at Amanda and reached out and rubbed her back. She said softly, "Sweetheart, how do you know this?" Amanda turned her head and looked at her, smiling, making her whole face light up. Her eyes were sparkling with love and happiness. She said, "God told me."

She gave everyone her look of happiness and then promptly yawned real loudly and laid her head on Lisa's shoulder and fell asleep. Lisa, Maria, Channon, Chris and Ryan didn't move a muscle. They were frozen in place, not even blinking, trying to process what Amanda said.

Maria finally said in a shaky emotional filled voice, "She must mean that's what she thinks is going on. Reverend Blackstone has been praying with everyone and saying that what happens is up to God. She wants her daddies to be all right, so she thinks that's what God has said."

Everyone nodded except Channon. She shook her head and body as if she was coming out of a daze or a trance and looked around at everyone not saying anything. She took a couple of deep breaths and said, "Abby is close to delivering. She's asking for you both to be with her."

Lisa turned to Maria. "Are you up to this?"

Maria hesitated, looking down for a few moments. She finally looked at Lisa and said, "There's time to mourn Mark later. I will mourn him for the rest of my life." She reached out and grabbed Lisa's hand, holding it tightly. "Let's not tell Abby about Mark just yet. There's plenty of time to tell her later. This is a joyous occasion. Her child is about to be born."

Tears filled her eyes and she said in a husky voice, "Mark was looking forward to this baby being born. He was so excited about seeing and holding the Little Warrior. He said we'd all train him or her just right. With all of us helping to raise this child, it would make him or her turn out to be the best human being that could ever be." The three women had tears in their eyes and large lumps in their throats. Maria stood up, clearing her throat and wiping her eyes. "Give me a minute. Then we put on smiles and go help Abby bring the Little Warrior into the world. Abby needs us to be strong right now and help her get through this. Everything else can just the hell wait until later." The women were a bit shocked. Maria rarely cussed or swore. They tried to pull themselves together because Abby needed them to be strong. Maria also needed them to be strong and to do this for Abby.

Throughout the day, the men on top of the pass killed about three hundred of the enemy soldiers. They fired on any exposed body part they could find. The murdering Eco

Nazi animal worshipers were dying of thirst and hunger. The thirst was the worst to endure. The daytime was very warm and the sun beat down on them until sunset, making them sweat out what little moisture remained in their bodies. Every hour the enemy was growing weaker. First Lieutenant Young came up with an idea of how to taunt and torture the enemy trapped in the pass and make them weaker and nervous at the same time.

First Lieutenant Young went over and asked for a meeting with the Colonel to explain his idea. Colonel Harrison asked him out of curiosity, "Give me some reasons why we should waste our time doing this?"

Lieutenant Young was ready to answer. "Sir, this will have a large, demoralizing effect on the enemy. It will also keep the thought of drinking and eating foremost in their minds at all times. If they are thinking constantly of food and drink, they won't have time to make serious plans of escape. It will also make them unstable psychologically and more prone to being irritable with each other. This will, in turn, make them more apt to come out of hiding, then our snipers can take more of them out. It also may have a direct effect to stay separate from each other, because they would be afraid that the other men might look at them and think of killing them to drink their blood and eat their flesh. It will mess with their minds even more because they don't believe in eating flesh. Some of the enemies down there just might get desperate enough to do it. This will further demoralize the enemy and make our job easier, because then they'd start killing each other. We'll remind them what happened to the Donner party."

Colonel Harrison smiled. Gary had really thought this out. He liked this idea. It would give their men something to do also. Just watching and waiting for an opportunity to shoot someone could get really boring and the mind had a tendency to wander to other thoughts. This would keep their men focused on the enemy at all times. He asked, "How would this help our men?" He was curious how Gary would answer.

First Lieutenant Young answered, "Sir, it will give them something to occupy them. Most of our men are sitting around doing nothing but eating and sleeping. The most exciting thing going on right now is the hunt for large rocks and boulders to roll down on the enemy. This will keep the men focused and it will be a morale booster at the same time. It will also give the men something to look forward to when they get off watch or sniper duty. We'll limit the amount of messages thrown down to the enemy, so they will have the best emotional impact. We can make it a competition between our men to come up with the best torture messages."

Colonel Harrison said, "I like it. Tell your ideas to Sergeant Crawford so he can get his side doing the same thing." First Lieutenant Young said, "Yes, sir." He saluted and then turned around and went to look for the Sergeant. This was going to be fun.

****

The officer in charge of the enemy knew they had to break free soon or they would all die or worse. The horrible barbaric men that had trapped them here all day long kept throwing down rocks with little notes attached to them in between the times they rolled large rocks and boulders down on them. The notes would say things like, 'Are you thirsty? Wouldn't a cold beer taste really good about now?' And 'Are you thirsty? Too bad you don't have any water.' Some would have a picture cut out from a magazine of lakes, streams, rivers, people drinking water or just a picture of a glass of cold water or a picture of a bottle, or a can or a stein filled with foaming beer. Other notes said 'we're drinking all of your water. Ha, ha, ha, ha, ha.' But the worst pictures were the ones that showed people in them with suggestions written on them that would say 'the human body is seventy-five to eighty percent water.' Some pictures would show people eating with suggestions that a dead body could be eaten as meat. Some notes would taunt them with saying that they had all the water and food they needed to survive right there inside of each other. Other ones said, 'Remember the Donner party and how they survived.' He had to do something to stop this. The men were getting upset and arguing. A few fights had broken out, which caused the fighting men to break cover and get shot. He ordered the men not to read the notes, but they did it anyway. It was the only communication with the outside world they had. Their world had shifted and shrunk to this pass. He had to come up with a way to get out of here. He tried to think, but the thoughts from the messages kept interfering. He shook his head to clear his mind so he could think.

The officer in charge of the enemy thought of all the ways to get out of this trap. The weakest link seemed to be the rear barricade. The front was filled with too much rubble and boulders to even try to get across after the second explosion. This was going to have to be a do or die situation. They had no other choice. He sent word along the men that they either fought their way out or they would all starve or die of thirst. He wanted his men to understand that this had to work or else. There wasn't anything else they could do. They had very little ammo left. They were down to 2,731 men. The people that attacked them had killed almost half of his army already. It really pissed him off that they were using their own guns and ammo to do it with, too. They were also eating all their food and drinking their water. The officer sent word again along to each man that could still fight that a few hours after dark, they would make a break for it over the barricade in the back. There was nothing else they could do.

What the enemy didn't know was that Major Beckerton and his men had been very busy. He had heard what happened to everyone in the front. Major Beckerton had his men dig foxholes and surround each shooting position with sand bags. They were covered on the top and both sides. They all had enemy AK-47s and over ten thousand rounds of ammo. They were ready for when the enemy tried the same thing back here that they tried in the front. There really wasn't anything else they could do except try to overrun them with sheer numbers and brute strength. They had no other options. Major Beckerton told the men to kill them all. No survivors. He made sure the men ate at meals times and that they had plenty of water to drink. He had the men sleep in shifts so everyone would be rested and alert come nighttime. When it was dark, they would try to break out under the cover of darkness.

****

The enemies were like zombies. They were so thirsty it was hard to talk. All the men could think of was drinking as much cool water as they could hold. The attack started at midnight. The battle was fierce. Only people who have been that desperate could fully understand what those men went through and were experiencing. In front of the foxholes, the bodies stacked up higher and higher like cord wood, but they just kept coming. The men defending the back barricade's rifle barrels were glowing red from firing so often. The smell of blood, cordite and sweat thickened the air. The enemy was crawling up over the stacked bodies, trying to get out. The bodies stacked up so high they could no longer see over them. It was after 2:00 am before they stopped coming. Smoke was as thick as fog floating over the battle site, rippling in the gentle breeze. There was a medieval surreal feeling in the air. The bonfires, screams, moans and smell of blood from the dead and wounded gave the scene a nightmarish quality to it. No man should ever have to see this kind of hell on earth.

****

The enemy officer sat between two large boulders looking out, squinting in the bright sunlight. He had come to the conclusion that the only thing they could do would be to formally surrender. He had lost 1,342 men last night. He was badly shaken. Just a few days ago, he had a marching army that trailed two miles long. No one dared oppose them. Now he had one fourth of his fighting force left and some of them were wounded. All of them were dying of thirst and hunger. He still had 1,389 men. Almost 1400 men was still a sizable fighting force. But these dumb rednecks had proven that fighting them was not possible. These men must be a large army of Special Forces from the military or something. It was the only thing that made any sense. He sighed. His men were depending on him to provide them with water and food and a chance to come back and fight another day. Well, whoever these men were, they would be honor bound to allow them to walk away from this trap. Then they could return to their main base and rearm themselves with more artillery and men and change their attack plans. *We will come back here and kill every single one of them and make an example out of them for the whole country to see what happens when you oppose Gaia's will.* These men would be crippled by their honor and sense of fair play. It was to his advantage to take them up on it. They would be stupid. He would never let an enemy leave and freely walk away. He smiled for the first time since this all started. He called out to the men to look for a long stick. He told one of them to give him their t-shirt. He then explained his plan to the men.

****

The men on watch on top of the pass saw the enemy wave a while cloth down below. This made the men laugh. They sent one of the men to tell Colonel Harrison that the enemy was waving a while flag. They were surrendering. The Colonel called for a meeting with Major Beckerton and First Lieutenant Young. The meeting lasted an hour. Orders were given for everyone to get over to the road behind the back barricade and to be ready if there was any kind of trouble. They were to line up on the mountain side of the road. The enemy was surrendering.

Colonel Harrison wrote out a message for whoever was in charge of the enemy to meet him alone at the back barricade to discuss terms of surrender. This message was delivered down the mountain by way of being tied to a rock. The men laughed so hard. All the men gathered on the road and lined up on both sides. There was still the one hundred men at the front barricade in case it was a trick. Lonnie was not happy when he found out that they were going to let them surrender and walk away. Major Beckerton took him aside and told him to be patient. There was no way they were really surrendering. That was the conclusion they had come to. The enemy would wait for an opportune time and then attack to get water and food. If they really were surrendering, it was going to be too bad for them. Colonel Harrison was not going to have all the enemy men searched. Some would keep a weapon. We'll have some of our men eating bread and drinking water right in front of them. They'll not be able to help themselves. This would even make them weaker. The Colonel said he had no intention of setting these killers loose in the countryside to prey on anyone they came across for food and water on their trek back home. So, stay alert and be ready. Lonnie nodded and smiled.

It was almost dinnertime when the Colonel got to the back barricade. Bread and fresh water was being passed along the men. This was to hold them until later when they'd eat a real meal. Every fourth man was asked to wait to eat and drink the water until the surrendered men were walking past. The Colonel was now getting ready to talk to the enemy and accept his surrender. There were several snipers set up, keeping their eyes on the enemy and making sure they behaved. Lonnie watched the Colonel grab a hot cup of coffee to take with him. He couldn't help himself and broke out in laughter. The Colonel was retired from the Marines. Man, he sure had balls, that was for sure, and was his kind of guy.

The Colonel walked slowly up toward the barricade, where a man in his thirties was standing in a torn and dirty uniform that had the Rainbow Warrior patch on it. The man had a few bloody, crusted wounds that didn't look so good. He stopped a good distance from the barricade to make this man walk up to him. He took a sip of coffee and said loudly, "What rank are you?"

The pompous man straightened up and almost fell on the loose rocks several times. The man gave the Colonel a glare and said in a croaky dry voice, "General."

The Colonel said, "Well General, here are the terms for your surrender. You will march your men in single file. You will put your rifles, handguns and any other weapons you have in a neat pile as you walk past. Hold your hats in your hand with your shirts and coats off. My army will be lined along the road. The other half will be in sniper spots with you in their sights. Go back to wherever the hell you came from and never return."

The Colonel turned to go, and the General said, all full of himself, "You only won this battle because you cut us off. If we'd been in the open, this would have a different ending."

The Colonel turned back towards the General. He took another slow sip of coffee and said, smiling, "Yes, it would have had a much different ending. We would've killed you quicker if we hadn't had to draw you out from under the rocks you were hiding under." The General gave him a look so filled with hatred the Colonel wondered how he didn't choke to death on all that hate. The Colonel barked out sternly in his best military commanding voice, "Do you agree to the terms?" He paused, taking another sip of coffee. "Just so we're clear, General. You killed a lot of good men here. All their friends and family are lined up on the road out there. Many are looking for revenge and others are just looking to even the score. If anything looks wrong to them, if any little thing is the slightest bit off, I can guarantee you that all hell will break loose and none of you will walk away from here. Now, I've had enough of killing. Haven't you?" The General had no choice but to agree with him and said, "Yes." The Colonel turned and walked away.

****

The General turned around and walked back to his men, thinking how stupid that man was. They weren't even going to pat them down for weapons and make sure they were unarmed.

****

The Colonel was thinking that his forces had been reduced to 623 men. Over one hundred of them were wounded. It wasn't the show of force he wished he could show this supposed General. Wounded men sitting down holding a rifle does not send fear into the hearts of the enemy. No, it's seen as a sign of weakness. He had sent word to Redding, requesting a thousand more fresh troops, but had not heard back from them. He had no choice but to bluff his way out, saying what they were seeing was just half his force. The enemy didn't need to know how low on men he really was. They were still out numbered, two to one.

****

The General told his men that every other man was to hide a pistol on them. If this were a double cross, they would need a way to defend themselves. He told them the terms of surrender and that they would be able to get some water and food as soon as they got out of sight. The men lined up, eager to leave this death trap.

****

Six of the Colonel's men lined up by the second barricade to oversee the enemy putting their weapons into a pile. The enemy's line was almost a mile long. About twenty minutes later, someone yelled that a surrendered man had a gun and the Colonel's men opened up on the enemy. It was over in minutes. All but ten were dead or critically wounded. The Colonel told the ten men to leave with this message, "Don't ever come back here. Spread the word that hell lives up north. Don't ever bring up your Eco Nazi animal crap again. If we see or hear of an army forming again, we will come down and wipe you out." The ten men were tripping over themselves in their haste to get away from these crazy people up north.

The Colonel had the men start bonfires to burn some of the dead bodies. The rest they rolled over the cliff. It took them all night. As the sun rose, the Colonel told the men to get a few hours' rest, then they would go home. He thanked the men from the frontier town and sent them home. He told them he and a few other men would come over and they could divide everything up later. He was going to use the semis to get his men and equipment home.

Abby was resting when the men got back and told everyone the battle was over and they had won. There were a lot of cheers and congratulations. The women were waiting for the men. They were making up a feast in celebration. Everyone went home to the valley. Dr. Anderson had moved the patients to the small hospital he had in the back of his office last night after Abby delivered a son. They brought a few more men in for Dr. Anderson to watch over and more medications for them. Lisa was asleep in the chair next to Eric's bed, holding his hot hand. He still hadn't woken up and his fever had started to rise again. The antibiotics had stopped working. It was starting to look like Eric wasn't going to make it. She had spent all night telling Eric to fight to live. They needed him now more than ever with Mark dead. Channon had taken the children home and put them to bed last night. Maria had been back and forth all night between Abby and Eric's rooms.

Maria was holding Abby's new son and thinking of Mark. She felt like her heart had been ripped out with a dull knife. She couldn't go back to their cabin in the valley. She just couldn't. There was way too many memories waiting there for her. How was she going to get through each day without Mark? The future seemed agonizingly long and black, stretched out to infinity, without Mark there to share it with her.

Afterwords

First of all, I want to thank everyone who had the faith to stay with us on this long journey to complete this book. It was a rough, hard journey, and a few differences of opinions along the way, but we finally hammered it out.

We want a say a special thanks to our editor. We would not have gotten this far without you. Thanks for putting up with us.

We will provide a quick couple of pages with a few hints for the three survival groups in our next book to let everyone know where the characters are going for the beginning chapters of book 2, *Perceptions Of Reality* of the *Grid Down* book series.

A project of this size and length takes a lot of research. The Romans we brought into Mark and Eric's group was from research. There are actual groups and clubs that re-enact different Roman eras that meet monthly and dress up in period attire and re-enact battles and lifestyles. We thought it was pretty amazing.

People at the beginning of strange events or disasters in their lives will do some very strange things. When they realize there are no longer any societal norms to guide them, they may indeed switch into some fantasy life. We brought this in more for a strange event that happened (EMPs) that brought forth strange encounters and behaviors. Just another way of saying to be ready for the unexpected. Life, most of the time, is stranger than fiction.

Again, the tree people clubs in the book actually do exist. There are several types of groups that do this sort of thing. Research into Frontier or Old Time Towns and you'll quickly learn that such things are happening all across the country.

One thing that one astute reader pointed out that was a mistake on my part was existing solar systems would be fried during an EMP attack and might actually cause a fire. You see, when the EMP pulse hits, the high energy has to go somewhere, even huge electrical lines could possibly catch on fire during an event of this magnitude. The solar panel themselves? Unsure if they would be usable to work again. One thing you need to understand about solar panels is they have diodes in them. This prevents the battery from back feeding during the night, wasting your battery power. Spare diodes would be a good thing to have on hand and understand how to properly wire them in. You see a diode is like a check valve. It allows electricity to flow only in one direction. If you wire them in wrong, you will never charge your batteries.

We have a great bunch of people that have followed this story from the beginning. They have given us many tips and advice along the way. We thank you all for your contributions to making this book better. You know who you are. Give yourself a large pat on the back. You've earned it.

When we started this project I said it was going to be a really good book and that people are going to die in it. Just like in real life, there are no guarantees. Something I didn't understand was how people would take this reality. When there are no rules, no one knows the outcome. That's the point we wanted everyone to understand.

Everything we wrote is possible to do by a prepared person who has supplies and knowledge. That's our opinion. Who is going to survive? Don't just buy tons of stuff and store it. Practice with it and become proficient with it. Everything you do has a learning curve. That learning curve can cost you your life if you wait until an EMP or some other disaster hits before you take out your supplies and use them.

George Sr. was killed off early to show everyone that even the best supplied plans have flaws and weak spots that can't always be anticipated. But also, the real reason was for your children. Your knowledge is a precious thing. Think about it seriously for one minute. You die in the first days of a major event or disaster. Do your children know how to do everything for your cabin or compound or whatever? A well-written manual for them to follow would sure help them even the chances of surviving, wouldn't it? In a manual or journal, you can write down everything your children will need to know. How the water pump works, spare parts and where they are located, solar system, spare parts for other things, on and on. A list of what was stored and an estimate of how long each thing should last will be a wealth of information for your children. The in depth knowledge of the wildlife, fish, and plants would be a Godsend for your children so they know where in your area they can get fresh food.

A few links for the good people.

http://www.lulu.com/product/paperback/the-essential-wild-food-survival-guide/1349 103productTrackingContext=search_results/search_shelf/center/

One of the best wild plant books on the market. http://www.takeapartdome.com/

An easily erected temporary building that can be used for a multitude of uses: sugar shack, garden produce sales, hunting blind, fishing shack, camping, green house, sauna and many other things that I haven't even thought of yet. Let your imagination soar! First, I have seen the dome. But anyone can see the usefulness of this. I believe a well-rounded person should know the basics of electricity, welding, carpentry work. Remember, knowledge is power. How to take junk and turn it into something useful is also a good idea. This book is not the end the journey, but just the first step in a long series of books.

http://www.globalsecurity.org/wmd/library/congress/2004_r/04-07-22emp.pdf

Report of the Commission to Assess the Threat to the United States from Electromagnetic Pulse (EMP) Attack

Several potential adversaries have or can acquire the capability to attack the United States with a high- altitude nuclear weapon-generated electromagnetic pulse (EMP). A determined adversary can achieve an EMP attack capability without having a high level of sophistication. An EMP is one of a small number of threats that can hold our society at risk of catastrophic consequences. An EMP will cover the wide geographic region within line of sight to the nuclear weapon. It has the capability to produce significant damage to critical infrastructures and thus to the very fabric of U.S. society, as well as to the ability of the United States and Western nations to project influence and military power.

The common element that can produce such an impact from an EMP is primarily electronics, so pervasive in all aspects of our society and military, coupled through critical infrastructures. Our vulnerability is increasing daily as our use of and dependence on electronics continues to grow. The impact of an EMP is asymmetric in relation to potential protagonists who are not as dependent on modern electronics.

The current vulnerability of our critical infrastructures can both invite and reward attack if not corrected.

Correction is feasible and well within the Nation's means and resources to accomplish.

Thanks for reading our book,

Bruce 'Buckshot' Hemming & Sara Freeman

Grid Down Volume 2 – Perceptions Of Reality

Chapter 1 Excerpt 'Lost & Forgotten'

Jane slowly became aware of her surroundings. It was hot and she was covered in perspiration. That's what woke her up. She was very thirsty and her ears were ringing. She opened her eyes a little and saw that she was in a place that was very dark. She didn't recognize where she was. She cautiously moved her arms and legs, taking stock if she was injured anywhere besides the throbbing ache in her shoulder. Moving her arm made her shoulder ache more like a bad tooth. She stopped moving and tried to concentrate on remembering what had happened. She was very confused and tried to sort out all the thoughts running through her mind. Where was she? Why was her shoulder aching so badly? In the next instant total recall slammed into her mind and she remembered everything. She sat up so fast that her awareness started to fade and she felt the blackness coming for her once again. She lowered her head and kept saying over and over in her mind, 'I will not faint.' As soon as she knew that the dizziness had passed and she wouldn't pass out, she started yelling in panic, "Joe! Oh my God, Joe! Where are you?"

She must be in the tornado shelter. Reaching with her hand out, she felt the post of a 2 x 4 frame. Yep, she was in the tornado shelter. She slowly scooted over to the table and turned on the battery powered 300-lumen lantern. Her vision was still blurry, but she finally saw Joe lying on the floor, a few feet on her left. She scooted over to him as fast as she could, ignoring the pain in her shoulder. She reached out hurriedly and ran her hand down his sweaty cheek to his neck and found a pulse. She relaxed a little and let out the breath she had been holding. Hot tears ran down her cheeks in relief. He was alive and that was the only thing that truly mattered at this moment. She continued to run her hand over his body, trying to check for injuries. Doing it one-handed was hard, and she was afraid she might miss something important.

She glanced up at his face after determining that he didn't have any serious injuries as far she could tell. Joe had his eyes open and was watching her run her hand over his body. When she was finished he said, "Am I going to live, Doc?"

Jane smacked him playfully on the top of his head and said, "Maybe, I haven't decided yet."

He smiled and laughed. "Uppity woman."

She smiled at him and said in mock severity, "And don't you forget it, Mister." Jane looked around at the small steel reinforced room in the basement that Joe had built for tornado protection. She hadn't been down here since he finished the project a few years ago. She'd forgotten all about this room even being down here in the basement.

She gave him an intense look and said, "If I ever bitch about your stupid ideas and wasting money again, just tell me to shut up."

"I will remember and hold you to that promise."

"What happened? I'm a little fuzzy on the details after I got shot."

Joe looked around the room and was very glad that he'd taken the time and money to build it. He had used a quarter inch steel on the ceiling with steel support beams and posts.

This room had saved their lives. He built it for protection from tornadoes. The room had everything they would need, even a two-burner cook stove. He looked at Jane. "Tim yelled on the radio that they were bringing the artillery cannons up closer. I grabbed you and dived into this room. I barely got the door shut before they shelled the house. I hit my head on the door, and that's all I remember until you woke me up just a little while ago. We'll wait a few hours after we don't hear any noise from outside, then get out of here."

Jane nodded. "All right, do we have any water in here? I'm really thirsty."

Joe got stiffly up and walked over to a shelf in the room. He opened a box and pulled out two water bottles.

Every now and again Joe would sniff the air to check for fires outside their room. That was their worst danger. He knew fires would be burning whatever was left from the artillery round, which would complete the destruction of the farmhouse. He prayed that the others got out in time. He had yelled for everybody to retreat as he dived for the door down here and the safety that the room would provide. He looked forlornly at the pieces of his radio he picked up that had been scattered around the room. He must have smashed it when he hit the ground as he dived in the room. There was no way to fix it. Jane's radio was still in her L.B.E. vest that he'd taken off to bandage her shoulder, and it was probably lying under who knew how much rubble. He could kick himself for not storing extra radios down here. Now there was no way to contact anyone in their group and find out who made it and who didn't.

He was pretty sure that Preston had enough time to get Amy and himself far enough away to have survived the destruction of the farmhouse and barn. He had a sick feeling in the pit of his stomach about the rest of the group that had been in the barn loft. There wouldn't have been time for them to get out if the enemy had fired both artillery cannons at almost the same time.

He got up and checked on Jane. She had instructed him on how to debris her shoulder properly and he had stitched up the entry and exit holes the bullet had made. She started a fourteen-day dose of antibiotics and took some pain medication from the medical supplies he had made sure to store down here and was now resting on one of the cots in the room. He would let her rest until it was time to leave. Who knew what they might face or have to do to survive when they finally got out of here?

A few hours later, Joe woke Jane up. He helped her sit up and handed her a cup of hot coffee. He sat on a five-gallon bucket across from her and drank his own cup of coffee. He looked her over, evaluating her condition. "You don't look too bad. How does the shoulder feel?"

She eyed him like he had asked a very stupid question. "I feel like I got run over by a Mack truck and then someone decided to dig a hole in my shoulder. When the pain medication wears off, I'll let you know how I really feel."

He smiled at her. "That good, huh?"

She returned his smile a little. "Are we getting out of here anytime soon?"

Joe turned around and reached behind him for two paper plates. Each plate had an M.R.E. on it. He turned back around facing her. "We'll eat first. Then we'll get out of here."

When they got done eating, Joe grabbed the plates and the discarded package wrappers and put them into a trash bag. He then stood up. "I'm going to go outside and look around and make sure its safe. You stay here and rest. Lock the door after I'm out. I'll give you the signal when I come back so you'll know its me." Jane stood up and looked at the metal bar that pivoted up and down that was the lock for the door with a worried look on her face. Joe grabbed his AR-15 and patted down his vest, making sure he had put all the magazines back after filling them up from one of the ammo cans he had down here. He had already checked his rifle over to make sure it was in top working condition. He leaned down and kissed Jane and said confidently, "It will be all right. We will make it through this."

He reached out for the metal bar and pulled it up to unlock the door. He had to struggle to get the bar all the way up so he would be able to get the door open. When the shell had hit the house, it must have done a little damage to the door frame, making the bar a tighter fit than it was meant to be. This wasn't a good sign. His heart started jumping around in his chest, flooding his body with adrenaline. He reached down and gripped the door handle tightly and turned his hand to open the door. The door handle wouldn't turn or move at all. He took a hasty breath, bracing himself, and gave the door handle a hard twist to the right. A popping sound was all that happened. He twisted the door handle again and it turned easily in his hand right and left. The door handle had popped out of the mechanism and was freely turning, not connected to anything. He sighed and turned to look at Jane.

She said, "What? What's wrong?"

"The door handle broke and isn't connected to the mechanism that opens and closes the door."

Jane looked startled and said breathlessly, "You can fix it right? Tell me you will be able to open this damn door."

If Joe could have seen outside the door, he would understand how big of a mess they were in. The main twelve by eight inch oak support beam for the house had fallen across the door at a ninety-degree angle with one end still supported by the steel floor joist. When this happened, it literally moved the wall that the door was on inwards a little bit, further jamming the steel door tighter into the frame. Debris and rubble were jammed tight all around the door and wall, holding it securely in place.

Joe looked at Jane. "Something must be jammed into the door frame and it's holding the door closed."

Jane said with an edge of panic in her voice, "Preston does know to come look for us down here, right? You did tell him about this hidden room?" Joe looked away from the burning intensity of her accusing eyes. After being married for so many years, she knew what the answers to her questions were. Joe couldn't look her in the eyes. In full panic mode now, she cried out in a shrill voice that kept climbing higher and higher, "What the hell were you thinking, not telling Preston about the room down here? You stupid bonehead, he's the only one that would even think to look for us down here." The room they were in was behind the house furnace, and completely hidden from sight. Joe had stacked old boxes along the wall to further make it look like there was nothing else back here and now no one would even know to look for them.

They probably thought that both of them were dead and buried under the rubble of the house. Tears ran rapidly down Jane's face, dripping off her chin. She was silent for a minute, absorbing this awful news and started sobbing loudly. Her body was shaking in time with her deep sobs. She finally was able to say haltingly, "Great job, genius. Now, this room will be our tomb." Her body just sort of collapsed and she lay down on the floor, almost in slow motion.

Her sobs were the only sound that could be heard. This was the last straw for Jane. All they had faced and gone through today and since the world had ended paled in comparison to this latest disaster. Her shoulder throbbed and burned like fire, making her sob harder. It was all just way too much to handle right now. In her misery, she had realized that even if Preston had known about this room, there was no guarantee that he had survived the army they had faced. Maybe none of them had survived, and she and Joe were entombed down here, just dying a lot slower than they had. But, they were dead now, too. There was no one that would come looking for them, let alone help dig them out. Maybe they were already dead and this was hell and they would be entombed down here together for all eternity, trying to get out of this room.

Chapter 2 Excerpt 'Hope Springs Eternal'

Maria sat on the porch swing, looking up at the black velvet sky sprinkled with blurry twinkling glitter. That's how Amanda always described the stars in the night sky. She said her mother told her that God had sprinkled the dark in the heavens with glitter so we would always have His divine light to guide us. He gave us the sun for the daytime and the moon and twinkling stars at night. Even thoughts of Amanda and the cute things she came up with couldn't make her stop crying. She had been crying for two days now and couldn't seem to stop, no matter what she did or thought. It was like her tear ducts didn't take orders from her mind or body anymore and they had an independent mind of their own. She felt numb to everything except for the burning pain in her chest where her heart used to be.

Mark was so much a part of her that it felt like some demon her grandmother used to tell her about had ripped her soul out of her body along with her heart. The future stretched out before her as a long barren road to be walked alone. She still had trouble believing this could have happened. She thought she had already survived the worst that the world had to offer. She was wrong about that, so very wrong. This was complete hell. Nothing that had happened to her before this even came close to what she felt right now.

She prayed that Mark was knocked out or already dead from a rock before he went over the cliff in the rock slide. She couldn't stand the thought of him being in pain or suffering as he tumbled down to the ground, or the sheer terror of being buried alive in the tons of rocks that followed them over the cliff. She squeezed her eyes tightly closed and shivered at the thought. She wasn't sure if she was going to be able to make it through this. What was the use of staying alive just to have this burning hole in her chest and to be alone? The future looked very dark and cold without him. Why go on? That was the question that kept going through her mind. Did she even want to try to go on without him?

She felt a feather of a touch on her arm, almost like you would imagine what bird feathers would feel like as they brushed across your arm, which made her jump in surprise. Amanda was standing there with her hand on her arm. "Don't cry, Mommy. You don't need to worry. Mark and Mr. Gunner will be home tomorrow. I'll stay with you so you won't be lonely." Amanda climbed up on her lap, putting her arms around her neck, laying her head on Maria's shoulder and promptly fell asleep. Maria sat in stunned silence for several minutes, trying to absorb what just happened. She would have thought she was dreaming except for a few facts. The first one was that she was not asleep. The second one was that she was holding a flesh and blood Amanda and not some dream Amanda. The really weird thing about all of this was that Amanda had a soft glow about her, kind of like she was lit up from the inside. The kind of glow that her grandmother used to tell her angels had. Another thought just occurred to her. She was no longer crying. Was she losing her mind now, too, seeing otherworldly things that weren't there? She took a deep breath and then stood up, adjusting Amanda for a firmer grip so she wouldn't drop her, and walked inside the cabin. She took Amanda back to her room and laid her gently down on the bed and pulled the blanket over her again. She kissed her cheek and smoothed her hair down away from her face. Amanda wasn't glowing now. She stood there in the dark, just watching her sleep for a long time.

Maria made her way quickly over to the clinic. The place was dimly lit when she walked inside. She continued walking quietly down the hallway, passing a nurse writing something at the desk. She signaled that she was going through to the patients' rooms and the nurse nodded that she understood. Someone had told her the nurse's name but she couldn't remember what it was. She really hadn't been paying much attention at the time. She peeked into Abby's room and they were all asleep. Abby was holding the baby in her arms, with the rail to the bed up on the side where the baby was. Alan was asleep in the chair. The baby was making little sucking sounds in its sleep. She stepped back and continued walking down to Eric's room. She knew Lisa would be there. Lisa hadn't left Eric's side since he'd been brought in. Channon and Hope were staying the night at Lisa and Eric's cabin to take care of the kids. Maria had not been in any shape to care for them by herself.

She walked into Eric's room. Lisa was holding Eric's hand, sitting in a chair right by the bed. She turned and looked at Maria when she walked in. Maria motioned for her to come outside the room. Lisa kissed Eric's hand, then placed it under the covers and stood up and followed Maria out into the hall. Lisa noticed right away that Maria wasn't crying. She wasn't sure what was up, but Maria had a weird expression on her face. Maria said, "How is he?"

Lisa said tiredly, "His fever keeps spiking up into the danger zone and we have to cool his body down. But Dr. Anderson said he's starting to fight the fever. The biggest problem is the lump on his head. He still hasn't woken up. I wish he would just wake up." She paused. "How are you holding up?"

Maria didn't answer her question and said instead, "I think I'm finally losing it."

Lisa looked at her intensely and said, "What do you mean?"

Maria took a deep breath and let it out in a loud huff. "I was sitting in the swing on your front porch because I just... I just can't go into my cabin just yet." Lisa nodded her understanding. "I was just sitting there crying and wondering if I wanted to go on without Mark."

Lisa grabbed her and hugged her tightly and said fiercely, "Don't you ever say that again, Maria, or I will kick your butt. Do you hear me?" Maria didn't say anything, and Lisa backed up a step and held her at arms length. "I mean it, too. I know we're not Mark, but we can't live without you. Especially now that Eric is injured. Please tell me that you aren't going to do anything like that. I couldn't stand it." Tears blurred her vision and then rolled down her cheeks. Lisa whispered, stricken with fear, "Please tell me you aren't going to leave me, too."

Maria said, "I don't know how I'm going to be able to go on without him."

Lisa pulled her close again and hugged her, saying more softly, "We're here for you. We love you. We'll do it together."

Maria just held her tightly and then whispered, "That isn't what I wanted to talk about."

Lisa let go of her, then wiped the tears off her cheeks. "Okay, what did you want to talk about?"

Maria hesitated a few moments then related all that happened when Amanda had come out to the porch.

Lisa said, "It is just the way her young mind is coping with all this."

Maria didn't say anything. A few moments later she said, "But Amanda said last night that God told her not to worry, that they were all right, too. Do you think God could be talking to her?"

Lisa sighed and then rubbed her face with both hands, giving her time to decide how to answer that question. Maria had so much pain in her eyes with just a hint of hope thrown in. Lisa thought, *How do I answer that? Oh God, should I give her hope or tell her she needs to accept Mark's death and go on?* She took the easy route of answering the question. She said, "Well, maybe. I guess. We'll know for sure one way or the other tomorrow." Maria studied her friends face. She didn't really believe it, but was just being a good supportive friend with her answer.

****

Pain was the first sensation that faintly registered. Mark felt like someone had kicked the shit out of him. Maybe someone beat him up with a baseball bat. Or maybe he got run over by a truck. Each second that ticked by, the clearer the sensation of pain was. The pain was especially strong in his right leg. He tried to ignore it and go back to sleep. It wasn't working. Now he became aware that he was very thirsty. He tried to ignore that, too. He wondered, *What the hell happened?* He decided to move his right leg a little to see if he could lessen the pain; he screamed when he tried. He almost passed out and broke out in a cold sweat. It took a few minutes of resting and not moving to get the pain a little under control. He finally realized that he was lying on the ground in the sunshine and his whole body was now wet with sweat. He cracked his eyes open a little and was blinded by the sun. This was going to take awhile. After several minutes, he was able to get his eyes all the way open to look around. He was lying on his back on a ledge and he could see straight up for about twenty feet. That must have been where he'd fallen from. He looked around the ledge he was on and noticed someone was lying about ten feet away from him among the rocks and dirt. The body was lying completely still and covered in gray dust and had pebbles and rocks on the persons back. He thought, *Where the hell am I? What happened?*

Chapter 3 Excerpt 'The Long Way Home'

Junior became aware that he was cold and shivering. His left shoulder ached like nothing he'd ever felt before. He could feel a soft, chilly breeze caressing his face like fingers of ice. He must be outside. He automatically reached out with his good arm for the sleeping bag that he must be sleeping on to pull it up closer so he could block the wind and warm up. He had slept outdoors so much that it seemed perfectly natural for him to be sleeping on the ground like this. His hand groped around, trying to find the top to the sleeping bag.

He next became aware that he was lying on the ground with his backpack still on and something inside of it was digging painfully into his lower back and a few other places as well. Maybe that was why his shoulder was aching so much. Was something inside of the backpack sticking him in the shoulder? Did he fall down somehow or trip over something? He slowly opened his eyes and saw it was pitch black, wherever he was. There was no moon or stars in the sky. It must be a very cloudy night then. He tried to remember what he was doing outside as he shifted his body a little to ease the pain in his shoulder. Red-hot pain shot through him, radiating out from his left shoulder, making him stop all movement abruptly. It hurt so much he could only take slow shallow panting breaths as the darkness came for him again.

Junior became aware again slowly. He was still lying on the ground. He was acutely aware of the pain in his left shoulder. He was shivering and each movement caused an unbelievable amount of pain to shoot out from his shoulder. He felt hot and cold at the same time. He licked his dry, cracked lips and could taste the blood that welled up in some of the cracks on his lips. He was very thirsty. His throat was completely dry. He tried to swallow to wash the taste of blood off his tongue, but it stuck in his throat, causing him to cough a little. That sent more pain radiating out from his shoulder, making him moan loudly in his misery. He was afraid that he would pass out again. He opened his eyes and remembered waking up like this before. It was still pitch black. He looked around, trying to make sense of the inky shadows of darkness. He tried to remember what had happened. Why was his shoulder hurting so much? Where was Clint?

He slowly remembered bits and pieces of the battle, trying to make sense out of those strange nightmarish scenes running through his mind. In the next instant, he remembered everything. He had been shot. That was why his shoulder hurt so much. He cautiously probed his left shoulder with his right hand, trying to see if he could feel how bad the wound was. He had a thick battle dressing on. He thought he could feel a bandage on his back, too. That would be a good thing. Hopefully the bullet passed completely through. He slowly moved an inch at a time and tried to sit up. Moving made his head very dizzy, and he really hoped he didn't pass out again. It took him several minutes, but he was able to get into a half sitting position. He scooted over to lean his good side against a tree trunk so he could rest and relax for a minute and clear his head. He panted hard, like he had just run twenty miles and tried to get the pain in his shoulder under control. He kept saying over and over again like a nineteen sixty's hippie mantra, 'Mind over matter.' When the pain had eased a little, he groped around with his good hand and found the nipple for his camel back water container and sucked down a long drink. God, that tasted so good. His head was clearing up a little and he could think more clearly.

When he had his breathing under control and wasn't panting like a dog anymore, he slowly reached into his pocket and pulled out a small blue LED light. He couldn't see far with it, but maybe he could get an idea where he was. He didn't recognize anything. The best thing he could to do was to wait for daybreak. Maybe Clint would be back then. He leaned his head back and closed his eyes.

Daybreak came slowly. Clint still hadn't returned. That meant that Clint had to be dead or injured. He slowly ate a power bar and drank a lot of water. There were creeks and streams all around here in the woods. He just had to find one and follow it north and it would lead him towards the house. He used the tree to help him stand up. Scanning the area, he spotted Clint's rifle sticking out over by a log. The foremost thought in his mind was that Clint needed him to do this and he was determined to not let him down. He crawled over to the log and peered over. Clint was lying in an awkward heap on the ground. He slowly turned Clint over and checked if he was still breathing. He let out the breath he had been holding in a relieved whoosh of sound. There was hope. Now he had to find help.

He looked around for a branch to help him walk and saw one up ahead a few feet that just might work. He grabbed the branch and tested it out. As soon as he could, he started walking. He concentrated on putting one foot in front of the other.

****

Katlin was walking aimlessly in the woods not far from the road. She had taken to doing this daily to just get away for a short while to feel her own pain and grief without anyone else around. She was armed with her 9mm carbine and a nice sharp hunting knife in case any of the enemy was still around. They had better not run into her. The way she felt right now was not very merciful or caring. They had taken the second man she had loved just as the first man had been taken from her. Was she cursed to live her life alone? It sure felt that way right now. Did she bring this on by being here because of her curse?

She couldn't stand to think that she had caused Clint any harm. She loved him deeply and fiercely, almost from the very first time she had seen him. It had hit her very fast and hard, like an arrow straight to her heart. It had felt like it was meant to be. Like she had been waiting for him or something corny like that. She sighed and tears welled up in her eyes again, blurring her vision. She had already cried so many tears and probably would cry over this lost love for the rest of her life. Robbie had taken all of this in a very strange way and a lot harder than she thought. Just this morning he had yelled at her to stop saying they were dead and to go out and look for them. They probably needed her help and she was just staying here and letting them die for real. She had lost it when he said that and had grabbed her coat and rifle and run outside, trying to get away from those hateful, accusing words.

What would make him say something like that to her? She didn't understand his determination that they were out there somewhere, needing her help. Oh, she understood the psychology of his reaction but Robbie had always been such an intelligent caring child and now for him to blame her totally confused and bewildered her. How do you deal with that kind of thing? How do I make him understand that I'm not to blame for them dying? She wiped the tears off her cheeks and took a deep breath and let it out slowly trying to get some sort of control on her emotions so she could figure out a way to help Robbie. Crying wasn't going to give her the answers she needed. She prayed for guidance and strength so she could help her troubled grief filled son.

She had been walking and thinking for a long time now. She stopped and looked all around. Where was she? She had lost sight of the road. She had never come this way or this far before. She looked up at the sun and got her bearings. She turned around to go back before she went farther and got lost. She hadn't gone far when a feeling overcame her that she had to turn around and go farther yet, that she hadn't found what she was here looking for. She shook her head trying to get control of her emotions. What on earth had put that kind of a thought in her mind? Was Robbie's obsession rubbing off on her, too? She had to get control of herself right now. Was this what it was like to lose your mind?

No matter what she told herself, she couldn't quite convince herself to go on back to the house yet. Well, even if she was losing her mind, what would it hurt to go a little further? Then she would know for sure and hopefully find out why she had this feeling and those fanciful thoughts. She sighed and realized she was probably delusional from grief. Oh, what the hell. She would go on a little further and prove to herself that she was just chasing rainbows or whatever. This was totally not like her at all. She had always prided herself on being reasonable and practical. But this feeling would not go away.

She squared her shoulders and stood ramrod straight and walked on further, confident that it was just a waste of time. Not that she had any important appointments that she would be missing or anything of that nature. It was just some time that would be wasted and she had plenty of that. She scrutinized the area around her as she walked on. After about ten minutes, she saw something lying on the ground over by some brush up ahead. Could that be a person's legs over there? She cautiously crept up on the brush and slowly separated them to get a look at what was lying there. It was a man. She couldn't tell if he was alive or dead. She kicked his foot with her boot. He moved like a rag doll that had been jarred or moved. He never changed expression as far as she could tell. She pulled out her knife and leaned her rifle against a tree trunk and bent down a few feet back away from him to be as far out of reach as possible in case this was some kind of trick. She turned him over as much as she could. This man was filthy. It looked like he had rolled around in the mud and had leaves and debris stuck to his face and hair. She turned him a little more to get a good look at him and her heart almost jumped out of her chest when she recognized him. A breath caught in her throat almost choking her. *Oh my, God, it's Junior,* she thought in total amazement.

She felt for a pulse and found it. It was weak but steady. She looked all around, trying to see if Clint was with him. She pulled the backpack off him and examined him closely. His shoulder had been bandaged and he had a bandage on his back, too, when she looked. He had obviously been shot. She dragged him back into the brush and laid him down gently. She looked through his backpack and found his poncho and covered him up. She quickly pulled off her coat then her outer shirt and took off her t-shirt she had on under everything. She quickly got dressed again and used her knife to cut her t-shirt into strips so she could mark the trail and be able to find him again quickly. She grabbed her rifle and took off running, stopping every few hundred yards and marking the trail back to him. She had to find someone to help her bring him home and she needed a few people to look for Clint. *Oh my God,* she thought in amazement, *Clint could be alive out here somewhere too.*

RESOURCES:
http://www.directive21.com/
LPC Survival Ltd.
3225 Mcleod drive
Las Vegas, Nevada 89121
Contact: The Berkey Guy
Phone: 1-877-886-3653
Email:erkeylight@directive21.com

Chapter 1

Dr. Pianka's Final Solution   http://austringer.net/wp/index.php/2006/04/02/now-in-the-do-as-we-say-not-as-we-do-dept

Homeland Security on guard for 'right-wing extremists.   http://www.wnd.com/index.php?fa=PAGE.view&pageId=94803

Chapter 3

Food Crisis   (http://www.washingtonpost.com/wp-dyn/content/article/2009/11/16/AR2009111601598.html?wpisrc=newsletter)

Electromagnetic Pulse (EMP) http://en.wikipedia.org/wiki/Electromagnetic_pulse

Known Unknowns: Unconventional 'Strategic Shocks' in Defense Strategy Development" of crash-induced unrest   http://www.policypointers. org/Page/View/8519 [click on Policypointers' pdf link to see the report] http:// www.truthdig.com/report/item/20090216_bad_news_from_americas_top_spy/

Emergency Snare Kit   http://www.snare-trap- survive.com

Chapter 8

Emergency Snare Kit, Buckshot, Buckshot's Survival Snaring DVD, Buckshot's Wilderness Survival DVD Volume 3   http://www.snare-trap-survive.com

Chapter 9

Hunting, snaring, trapping http://www.snare-trap-survive.com

Tubeless, airless tires (www.airfreetires.com)

Chapter 10

Number 1 Long Spring Traps and Number 110 Conibear Traps   www.snare-trap-survive.com

Buckshot's Water Trapping DVD   www.snare-trap-survive.com

.300 Weatherby Magnum Rifle with a Leupold Mark 4 Extended Range Tactical M1 Rifle Scope Price $2,049.00. Factory-tuned, fully adjustable trigger* hand-laminated, raised comb, Monte Carlo composite stock with matte gel coat finish and spider web accents. Button-rifled, heavy contour, free-floated stainless steel barrel with target crown (.705 muzzle diameter) CNC-machined 6061 T-6 aluminum bedding plate Pachmayr® Decelerator® pad * Sear engagement factory set at .008 to .014, with let-off weight set at approximately 3.5 pounds. Additional sear engagements must be performed by a Weatherby Service Center or qualified gunsmith.

The Scope on the Weatherby.   http://www.midwayusa.com/viewproduct/productnumber=243146&utm_source=froogle&utm_medium=free&utm_campaign=657 Leupold Mark 4 Extended Range Tactical M1 Rifle Scope 30mm Tube 8.5-25x 50mm Side Focus First Focal TMR Reticle Matte Our Price: $1,899.99 ® Mark 4® Long Range/Tactical riflescopes are arguably some of the most dependable, highest performing riflescopes you'll find anywhere. It's no surprise that a Leupold® Mark 4® Long Range/Tactical riflescope was chosen as the primary day optic for the US Army's M-24 rifle system. Just the riflescope, mounts, sling and ammo come to well over $4000.00. http://www.weatherby.com/product/rifles/markv/accumark

Ruger M77 Hawkeye Bolt Action Rifle 7164, 270 Winchester, 22", Real tree Hardwood HD Stock, Stainless Finish, 4 Rds with a Leupold VX-II Rifle Scope Price: $643.12 http://www.ableammo.com/catalog/product_info.php?products_id=100800 The Scope on the Ruger M77 Hawkeye Bolt Action Rifle. http://www.midwayusa.com/viewproduct/?productnumber=212924 Leupold VX-II Rifle Scope 3-9x 40mm Duplex Reticle Gloss Price: $299.99.

1 Remington SPS Tactical 308 Black Hogue Stock 20" Heavy Barrel Price $638.99. Model 700 Special Purpose Synthetic Tactical Model 700 SPS tactical rifle with Hogue over mold soft touch stock, dual point piller bedding for solid foundation to bed action. All black oxide blasted finish with 20" heavy contour tactical style barrel. The Scope for the Remington Model 700 SPS tactical rifle. (http://www.precisionscopes.com/product/Leupold-66310 http://www.precisionscopes.com/files/491938/uploaded/VX3_4_5-14x50_black.jpg) Leupold 66310 - Boone & Crockett - Matte - 1" - 4.5-14x50mm Price $739.95 http://www.impactguns.com/store/047700842073.htm

The Leupold VX-3 4.5-14x50 Scope Boone & Crockett 66310 will be at home on your favorite rifle, whether you are hunting whitetail from a tree stand, or stalking sheep in rugged terrain. The VX-3 4.5-14x50 Scope Boone & Crockett 66310 is loaded with optical technology: Xtended Twilight Lens System, Diamond Coat 2 lens coating, blackened lens edges, second generation waterproofing, twin bias spring erector system, and cryogenically treated adjustments.

Chapter 11

Study on plants' neurosystems (feeling pain) http://ds9.botanik.uni-bonn.de/zellbio/AG-Baluska-Volkmann/plantneuro/neuroview.php

Chapter 12

Buckshot's lessons on trapping and snaring www.snare-trap-survive.com
To Learn To Break The Hide, Watch Buckshot's Wilderness Survival Volume 3 DVD www.snare-trap-survive.com

Chapter 15

Buckshot's Complete Survival Trapping Guide www. snare-trap-survive.com)
Camlock snares for deer www.snare-trap-survive.com
Buckshot's Preparing Wild Game For the Table www.snare-trap-survive.com

Chapter 18

Buckshot's Preparing Wild Game for the Table DVD www.snare-trap-survive.com

Chapter 19

Camlock snares www.snare-trap-survive.com
Professional grade snares made from aircraft cable www.snare-trap-survive.com

Chapter 21

Medium sized snares www.snare-trap-survive.com
Buckshot's Animal Skinning DVD www.snare-trap-survive.com
Mora Survival Knife www.snare-trap-survive.com
That Buckshot guy's website www.snare-trap-survive.com
Buckshot's Skinning DVD www.snare-trap-survive.com

Chapter 22

Buckshot's Survival Trapping Guide www.snare-trap-survive.com
Seven foot long camlock www.snare-trap-survive.com

Chapter 25

Buckshot's Skinning DVD www.snare-trap-survive.com
Buckshot Trapping Books www.snare-trap-survive.com
Camlock snares www.snare-trap-survive.com
Camlock repair kits www.snare-trap-survive.com
Sewing Awl www.snare-trap-survive.com

Chapter 27

Lee two cavity .38 caliber mold and had collected lead wheel weights.   http://www. natchezss. com/product.cfmcontentID=productDetail&brand=LE&prodID=LEE90423&pr odTit=LEE%20D/C%20MOLD%20BALL%20.380

Exploding targets   http://www.theexplodingtargets. com/

Glow in the dark paint   http://www.glopaint.com/24orders.htm

William Bradford, *See, I Told You So*   http://www.myfreedompost.com/2009/11/pilgrims-failed- experiment-with.html

Chapter 31

Buckshot Wilderness Survival DVDs   www.snare-trap-survive.com

Buckshot's Wilderness Survival DVD Volume 2   www.snare-trap- survive

Buckshot's Beaver Blaster Lure   www.snare-trap-survive.com

http://www.hipointfirearms.com/carbines/carbines_9mm.html

Chapter 34

http://www.globalsecurity.org/military/systems/munitions/105.htm

http://en.wikipedia.org/wiki/M3_howitzer

http://www.directive21.com/

 LPC Survival Ltd.

3225 Mcleod drive

Las Vegas, Nevada 89121

Contact: The Berkey Guy

Phone: 1-877-886-3653

Email:Berkeylight@directive21.com

16943319R00302

Made in the USA
Lexington, KY
19 August 2012